Planet of the Orange-red Sun

Series Volume 7

Rebellions

Planet of the Orange-red Sun Series

Volume 7
Rebellions

Vic Broquard

http://www.Broquard-ebooks.com
Broquard eBooks
103 Timberlane
East Peoria, IL 61611
author@Broquard-eBooks.com

Artwork by Crooked Willow Studios.

For Morgan and L. Ron Hubbard

Table of Contents

Part I In the Beginning

Part II The Imperial Senate and War Efforts

Part I In the Beginning

Chapter 1 Unexpected Beginning

"What the devil are we supposed to do? Throw these damned potatoes at them?" shrieked the cook. Josh stopped peeling the spuds and looked out of the galley portal. They had just dropped out of hyper-drive above Rimon-F only to land in the middle of a space battle. Like fireflies on a summer's night, Rimon's star fighters blinked, brilliant flashes of light marking their destruction from the streaking fires from the cannons of the three massive Imperium battle cruisers.

Potatoes. Involuntarily, parting memories filled Josh's mind. It was his eighteenth birthday and his dad ordered, "Josh, it's time now for you to take more responsibility for our potato farm. Starting tomorrow, you're in charge of the south 160 acres."

Josh grimaced. He hated potato farming and farming in general. Indeed, his last three years had been nothing but one continuous stream of bickering with his father over this very topic. "The hell I am. I've told you a thousand times, I don't want to be a potato farmer. I hate farming and everything with it!"

"Don't give me any more lip, son! You'll do it or else — or else I'll take away your cell phone and Internet access," his burly father yelled back, veins thickening at his temples. In fact, he had done just that — several times now. Josh grimaced. The one thing he hated even more was to be denied his fancy cell phone. With it, he had total electronic access to the entire world and parts of the galaxy for that matter. Everyone had one, just as soon as they were old enough to read and write.

Seeing that immovable look on his father's face, he covertly replied, "All right, tomorrow then. I'm going into Boise this afternoon. Got to say farewell to some of my friends who're leaving Idaho."

Believing he'd won the argument, his father's temper subsided somewhat. "All right then. Just make damn sure that you're back here by supper. You've got a whole lot of work to handle tomorrow morning — first thing." Josh nodded and flew from the kitchen, making straight for his room.

Once there, he shut his door and slumped on his bed. This is it! Time I make my move. I will be a spacer one way or another. Ever since he first saw the sparkling stars against the black Idaho skies, Josh knew he was destined to be out there flying among the stars. Hastily, he stuffed a few things into a backpack and snuck out of the house. A minute later, his old motorcycle sputtered to life, and he was off to Boise. As he pulled out of the farm's mile long dirt lane for the last time, he had no thoughts of his parents or their stupid potato farm. He hated it — hated them for forcing him into a life he detested. No way was he going to be a stupid farmer. He was going to be a spacer!

Josh's mind returned to the present, some four years later. He was twenty-two now and had worked his way up to the lowly position of Federation Transport Courier Second Class assigned to the transport ship, the Silver Streak. They'd received an urgent order to go to the capital city of Feliz on Rimon-F and transport Princess Meg Dillon to safety. Many had been expecting an attack from the Federation's enemy, the Imperium. As Federation fighters vanished in brilliant but soundless flashes, Josh knew the war had arrived.

Further he knew Cookie was expressing everyone's sudden frustration. They were wholly unarmed, a mere transport ship with four crewmembers. Well, he thought, that's not entirely true. Captain Hons and Navigator Jans each have a d-gun. Disintegrator guns were the latest Federation weapons, based upon captured Imperium guns.

Josh stopped peeling potatoes and headed off to his post in the ship's entrance bay, where he was supposed to welcome their passengers. Over the intercom, Captain Hons called out, "We're arriving in a battle zone. I trust they'll honor our ship's markings as a civilian transport ship. If not, been nice knowing you all. We're still supposed to meet a surface shuttle carrying our passenger. Josh, are you ready to receive them?"

He pressed the intercom button and replied, "Aye Captain. Ready." Ready? Josh was anything but ready for a war. His position in the Federation Spacer's Guild was darn near the lowest possible, Transport Courier Second Class. He was bad with math and terrible with physics. His body was tall and thin, wholly unacceptable for the heavy fighters, who wore battle armor to protect them, though at the moment, Josh was thankful he had been unable to make the grade as a fighter pilot. Armor or not, he didn't think the men were surviving the brilliant flashes of light that came from the destruction of their fancy fighter ships.

Still he was always polite and a diligent worker, far more determined to fly among the stars than any of the many candidates in Spacer School. In the end, that had gotten him this position and his lifelong dream. A year after his posting to the Silver Streak, he was still studying in his spare time, hoping to improve his lot, perhaps one day piloting one of these transport ships. At this moment, high above the planet where the air was so thin that the sounds of the massive explosions were not heard, Josh began to wonder if that was going to be a short-lived dream. Any moment he expected to be disintegrated along with the ship.

Wonder if I'll feel anything when they shoot us? Will I even know it if it happens? He continued to watch the ongoing battle from the portal of the entrance bay. *Will they even dare send up their shuttle?* Outside the sky above the orange planet seemed a complete chaos to him. Fighter ships darted all around, flashing bits of silver sunlight into his eyes. The huge, lumbering battle cruisers continued to swat them as though they were mere flies. For the first time since he'd entered the Spacer's Guild, Josh felt as utterly helpless as he had back on his father's potato farm in Idaho. Do I even have a future, he asked himself, but didn't answer.

"Prepare for shuttle docking," Captain Hons' voice barked over the intercom, bringing Josh alert. Hastily, he pressed the proper sequence of buttons activating the automatic docking guidance systems and noted the unseen shuttle had now locked onto the signal. Shortly he heard and felt the dull thud of the two ships joining. Mechanically, he activated several more systems securing the shuttle and forcing air into the short docking tunnel. Then he opened the door on his side, standing at attention awaiting the arrival of the passengers.

Presently, a grey-uniformed man marched into the chamber, leading a young woman. "Princess Meg Dillon. Your orders, sir," he exchanged salutes with Josh, handing him the grey envelop with the Federation seal on it. He turned and left, returning to his shuttle, leaving the young woman behind.

Josh looked at the princess. Her round face displayed clearly her deep fear and concern for her world's safety. Yet she bit her red lips, putting on a brave face. She wore a silvery, long satin gown, accented by her wavy, shoulder length black hair and eyes. Josh found her rather attractive. "This way, Princess Meg. I'll show you to your quarters and deliver these orders to our captain."

"Thank you. Are we going to be blasted out of the skies like our brave fighters are?" she asked, her voice trembling a little. She'd seen the holocaust of destruction on her precarious flight up to the transport ship and found it difficult to mask her growing fears.

"Princess, I sure hope not. We are an unarmed transport ship. This way." He led her to an adjacent but small cabin.

Just as he was about to dash off to deliver the orders to Captain Hons, his voice came over the intercom once more. "Josh, it looks like an Imperium ship is heading our way. I've been ordered to stand still. We're in trouble. I hope they take prisoners."

"Damn!" Josh exclaimed.

"Will I be safe? I would rather die than be captured!" Meg gushed, her withheld fears coming to the fore. She grabbed Josh's arm tightly.

Josh had one attribute that had never failed him: he could think rapidly when he needed to. "I have an idea, Meg. Come with me to my quarters." He pulled her to the next compartment, his room. "Here, get out of your clothes and put on these of mine. Fast. Hide your clothes at the bottom of my footlocker there. Be quick about it. As soon as you've changed, open the door. Hurry, we don't have much time." He stepped out of the door, allowing her some privacy. "Keep us posted, captain," he replied through the hallway's intercom.

"They'll be arriving in about three minutes," the captain's strained voice barked back. Josh sensed Hons was also extremely worried. Well, he has a d-gun at least, Josh thought.

"Hurry up, Meg. Less than three minutes," he yelled through the door.

A bit later, she opened it, having changed her clothes faster than she'd ever done in her life. Josh looked her over and tucked some of her hair up and into the cap. "Okay, that'll do. Come on, to the docking room. You stand behind me and say nothing. We're going to pretend you are my junior officer."

Captain Hons' voice called out, "They're demanding we activate the automatic docking system. Do it, Josh!"

"Aye, aye sir," he replied mechanically and began pushing the series of buttons, as he had just done minutes before. Then he pressed the intercom button and reported, "Done, sir." Cleverly, he added, "That other shuttle did not have our passenger on it, merely some orders for you about where we are to take her when she does arrive."

"Damn, she wasn't onboard their shuttle? Damn. Not much chance of us getting away now. Pray they take prisoners, everyone," Hons replied, his voice also trembling slightly. He was just as fearful as Meg was. As he stood there waiting the Imperial ship to dock, Josh wondered why he was not terrified. What little anxiety he'd first felt was now gone.

Once more he felt the dull thud as the two ships gently touched each other and the docking clamps made the connection secure. He pressed another series of buttons and heard the air hissing as it filled the short tube connecting the two ships. Josh positioned himself in front of Meg and held the still unopened orders out in front of his body, clearly visible. He stood at attention as always.

Shortly, the door opened and several Imperium troopers marched into the small transport room. They wore heavy battle armor, red and silver colored, and carried drawn d-guns. A uniformed man, again in the red and silver of the Imperium, stepped in behind the three men. "Transport Courier Second Class Josh Hamilton, sir," he barked in proper spacer fashion.

"Where is Princess Meg Dillon?" the officer barked without introducing himself.

"She has not yet arrived, sir. The shuttle just here has brought us these orders that are supposed to tell us where to take her," Josh replied briskly. He felt cocky, but had no idea why. This was obviously a life and death situation, but to him it seemed an exciting game.

"I'll take those. You two stay here," the officer ordered. Pointing to one man, he added, "You watch them. The rest of you, search this transport thoroughly." He and the other two men marched out of the transport meeting room, their heavy footsteps echoing on the metallic floor of the hallway. Josh stood motionless, but heard doors being slammed open or closed, he could not tell for sure which. He waited patiently and observed what he could see of the well-armored guards. Josh could see why he was rejected. If he was wearing all that body armor, he probably couldn't even stand up let alone move. He wondered if it really did protect them all that much but dared not ask.

Sometime later, the officer returned along with his two soldiers. "Okay Transport Courier Second Class Josh Hamilton, can you fly this transport?"

Josh thought fast. Why was he asking such a question? Captain Hons and his navigator were in charge. "No sir. I am only trained to handle the docking equipment." He lied, well a little. Perhaps he could fly the transport, having spent hundreds of hours in the simulators training to do so. Yet he had not actually flown one though. If he ever got his next promotion, he would be able to fly one, if and when the cook was out of commission along with the captain and navigator.

"Well, that's just saved your life. You wait here. Soon other transports will be docking with you. Operate the docking controls and find quarters for the passengers that will be arriving. Do that and we won't kill you just yet. Understand me?" the officer barked.

"Aye, aye sir," Josh saluted, knowing now he'd answered the question in the right way. The four turned and left, returning to their own transport ship. Mechanically, Josh reset the controls after they left.

"Whew, that was close," he finally said. "They didn't kill us, Princess Meg." He switched on the intercom and barked, "Captain, they have left. How is everything up front? We are supposed to be getting more passengers from the Imperium folks. Captain? Captain?" He heard nothing. Behind him, Meg's legs gave out and she slumped to the floor.

Josh tried the navigator and then Cookie. Nothing but an ominous silence came in reply to his increasingly frantic messages. At last, he realized something was wrong. "Come on, princess, we best go see what's happened to the captain and the others. Stay behind me."

"Meg, best just call me Meg. My legs are shaking. I thought for sure they would kill us or worse," she whispered. "Why aren't they answering you?"

Josh began to worry. This was out of character for Hons and the others. Combined with the question the officer had just asked him, he began to fear what he would find when he reached the other three men. They entered the small galley where less than an hour ago he'd been peeling potatoes for Cookie. "Oh my god!" he exclaimed. Meg stifled a shriek. Cookie was dead, a perfectly round blaster hole through his head. He'd been shot right between his eyes, execution style. Hastily, Josh dashed on up to the front of the ship. He stopped abruptly, Meg's body bumping into his.

"What's happening?" she whispered. Looking over his shoulder, she saw that both men had been executed in a similar manner as had the cook. Josh slumped hard against the metal doorframe.

For a moment, neither spoke. Then, Meg said, "Thank you Josh for your quick thinking. You saved us both from being executed as well. I can navigate a transport, if you could somehow manage to fly it. Then, we can maybe escape the Imperial forces."

"Huh? Oh, well, I probably can fly it. I've spent hundreds of hours in the simulators. I can't believe they executed them. Why? They weren't any threat to them. Cookie is just a cook, for god's sake." Anger began to seep into Josh's mind. "The bastards!"

"Come on. We'll have to move their bodies out of here, if we are going to try to fly this thing," Meg ordered. Her will had steeled now, having seen the world had just gone black and white — alive or dead. Two choices, no middle ground, she wanted to live.

"Huh? Yeh, right. Help me drag them back to the air lock. We'll give them a Spacer's Burial," Josh answered. It took their combined strength to get the burly captain and heavyset navigator out of their seats and back to the air lock where shuttles docked. The cook was easier since he was lying on the floor. A half hour later, Josh had the three bodies in the air lock.

"Spacers one and all. I hereby commit your bodies to the space you loved," Josh said solemnly. He then looked at her and whispered, "Meg, I can't think of anything else to say."

She spoke up and said formally, "You three died bravely and your sacrifices for the good of the Federation will not be forgotten." Meg asked him for their names and he recited them mechanically. Then she pressed the Open button. The air flew out of the chamber, taking the bodies with it, floating off into the space, joining the debris from the many others who had died and were still dying as they tried to defend Rimon-F.

"You've done this before?" Josh blurted out, somewhat surprised at how well her words sounded and how efficient she was being. He'd never seen death before; the shock was only now settling on him.

"Not really, but I've been trained to be a leader of my people. Guess that's not going to happen now. Okay, Josh, hold it together. We have to get out of here, if we can," she replied stoically.

Just as they started to make their way back to the front of the transport, a voice came over the intercom via the ship's radio. Josh made a mental note that the Imperium officer must have left the radio on, as well as the intercom. "Prepare for docking. We have a dozen passengers for you. More coming shortly."

Hastily, Josh and Meg ran back to the controls. "Meg, you stay back and out of the way. Maybe show the new passengers to some quarters. Doesn't matter which ones." She nodded and he headed to his control panel. Soon a dull thud announced the Imperium ship had docked with his transport. Shortly, the door opened and, to Josh's surprise, various young women were forced into the exchange room.

Sobbing and soft crying greeted him, as one by one young women were forced through the connection into the transport receiving room. Torn dresses and red marks on legs, arms, and heads suggested they had not come willingly. As they entered, Josh motioned towards the hallway. Like sheep, they stumbled on down the narrow hall, eyes downcast. Towards the end, one woman was leaning heavily upon another. Soon, Josh saw why. The poor woman had been shot with a d-gun. Her right hand was missing, she cradled her bloody stump against what remained of her satin dress.

Josh's basic training flashed through his mind, echoing the lecturing words of his drill instructor. "D-guns have two key benefits. First, because of the high heat energy contained in their beams, they cauterize the wounds inflicted, often allowing for the capture of the target. Second, d-gun beams have a built-in feedback circuit that senses when the beam strikes a surface. The circuit then prevents the beam from traveling on through that surface. Thus, you can shoot a man in the head and not have the beam pass on through to cut a hole in the bulkhead behind him or cut into the machinery he may be in front of, preventing collateral damage, such as cutting a hole in the side of the ship. Remember that; one day it may save your life." Well, Josh thought, the woman is alive and not bleeding to death.

She was the last woman and now the same smirking officer appeared. "Get them prepared for travel. One more smaller batch and we'll be off. Half hour more or less." He smirked, turned sharply, and left. A moment later, he heard their door shut and the grappling locks disengage. Mechanically, he reset his controls and headed down the hallway.

"My god, Missy, what happened to you?" Meg's frantic and piercing voice rose above the grief-stricken women, bringing Josh sharply alert. Quickly he moved up to the women.

The woman supporting the badly injured Missy replied, "Princess! They stormed the Royal Palace and killed your parents and brother. Missy tried to stop them from killing Henry, but they shot her as well. I heard they also have destroyed the Parliament. It's horrible. They have been rounding up some of us. We are to be taken onto their battle cruisers to be raped or worse by their soldiers, once they have secured our world. How could this have happened? Where are the Federation ships?"

Meg nearly collapsed with the awful news. Only her wounded assistant kept her from succumbing. Seeing Josh at hand, she cried, "Josh, they've wounded my Personal Secretary, Missy, and killed her husband, my brother, Prince Henry, and my parents. This is mom's Personal Secretary, Noel. We have to do something now; the bastards are going to take all of these women and torture them. Missy needs medical help immediately. We have to do something fast! Can you blow up this transport? We don't want to suffer rape and torture and humiliations."

Again, Josh faced an emergency but as always, he seemed somewhat detached from it all. "We have a small medical room, that way, Number Six. Take her there and see what can be done for her. I've no medical training. I'll see what I can do. They will be back in less than a half hour, Meg." He squeezed past the three women and made his way to the pilot's seat at the very front of the transport.

"Well, the controls look like those in the simulator. Here goes nothing," he said to himself. Quickly he began the startup sequence, bringing the transport to life once more. Talking to the controls, he said, "The second the Silver Streak begins to move, they will see us — be on us in a flash. One shot from their cannons and we're gone. What an interesting situation. I need to move to get us out of here, but as soon as I do so, we'll become a target for all those cannons. Must move — can't move. Interesting."

"What's interesting?" A very worried Meg said. She'd just come up front from the medical room. "I got a temporary bandage on Missy. Can you fly us out of here?"

"Maybe. The engines are online, but the second we

move, the Imperial battle cruisers will likely open fire on us. We can't take a single hit without being disintegrated, Meg," Josh replied, still slightly detached from the whole situation.

"So what can we do?" Meg asked, growing fearful once again. "I'd rather die trying something than face what those bastards have planned for us."

"If we can get into hyper-drive, they can't find us," he offered, glancing at the navigation panel in front of Meg, who had taken the Navigator's Seat."

"I can program it to take us someplace," she replied, glancing out of the window at the ongoing carnage all around them. She spotted the Imperial transport ship heading their way. "Crap! Here they come again. We have only a minute before they'll want to dock again. Do something, Josh!"

No destination was entered into the hyper-drive navigation system. Acting on a hunch, Josh fired up the engines and punched the hyper-drive button. At once, a message in red began flashing. No destination entered. He hit the button again, as he looked up at the incoming ships. He and Meg saw the nearest battle cruiser responding to them. He saw its cannon erupt as he continued to punch the button. Just as the disintegrating beam arrived at the unarmed Silver Streak, the ship vanished. Josh and Meg stared out of the window at the total blackness of hyperspace. Gone were the Imperial battle cruisers; also gone was the orange planet of Rimon-F. Both stared at the nothingness for a moment.

"You did it! Where are we?" Meg finally spoke, her voice a mixture of surprise and awe. "I don't think we are being followed." She hastily examined the instrument panel for signs of other ships in their vicinity. The panel was completely blank.

"Well now that is interesting. We are in hyperspace — somewhere. I've no idea where. This isn't supposed to happen," Josh replied, rather surprised he was still alive. A split second longer and he and the ship would have been mere space debris.

"What do you mean this isn't supposed to happen?" Meg asked, growing curious. She and her companions were safe for the moment at least. She too had seen just how narrow their escape had been.

"Well, mind you, I am not really trained in all this stuff, but a destination is supposed to be entered into the nav system before you engage hyper-drive. I got it engaged with no destination entered. I've no idea where we are, except we are stationary in hyperspace. Again, that isn't supposed to be possible, but the instruments say our velocity is zero. How very strange. Still we are alive. I wonder what else no one has bothered to tell me about flying the transport?"

"Brilliant thinking, Josh. There simply wasn't time for me to enter any destination. So should I enter the destination now? I know where dad was sending me," Meg volunteered. "We can get medical help for Missy there."

"Best not, Meg. We ought to think this through. I gave those destination orders to that Imperium officer, so they know where we were supposed to be taking you. I am sure they'll go there looking for you," Josh advised.

Her face fell. "You're right. That's the first place they'd look for me. Damn. Now what do we do? Missy needs medical care soon."

Although the Federation of Planets was quite large, at the moment, Josh could not think of a good planet to take them to. Instead, he blurted out, "How about taking you back to our base on Satellite Base Nine? I'm sure they have good medical care there. I bet they would know the best place for you and the women to go to from there. Okay?"

"Okay. Can you enter the coordinates? I can but I don't know what they are," Meg replied. She was at a loss now. While she wanted to return to her home world and somehow help in the fight against the invaders, she knew she didn't know where it would be safe for them to land or where those fighting back were now located. She lacked key data and perhaps at this base some general might know. At least she could report on the Imperium invasion of her world and beg for Federation counterattacks. Meg resolved to play the role of diplomat for the time being at least.

Josh flushed, "Er, not really. I will look around and see if I can find them. They must be here somewhere."

Meg gave him a dirty look, but Noel interrupted their

conversation. "Princess Meg, come quick. It's Missy's arm; it's bleeding again, and I can't stop it."

"Okay, you find the coordinates and get us there, I'll go see if there is anything I can do for Missy, Josh," Meg replied, rising and following a very worried Noel back to the medical room, barely large enough for the three of them. Missy was lying down on the single bed, her right arm lying horizontal on the bed's side extension where wounds were treated. Her temporary bandage was blood soaked. She changed the bandage and tied a tourniquet just above the stump, but didn't know what else she could do. Missy needed immediate proper medical care. Her lifelong friend and Personal Secretary was unconscious now, which Meg thought was a blessing as she finished up and looked down at her.

"Are we safe? Where are we? Where are we going, Princess Meg?" Noel asked as Meg rose.

"Safe enough. We're somewhere in hyperspace, thanks to Josh's brilliant thinking. Another second and we'd not be alive. However, where we're at is unknown, but he is trying to get us to his home base. I best get back to him and lend him a hand. He isn't even a pilot or a navigator."

"Really? But he is flying us?" Noel asked rather confused.

"He's had simulator training, nothing more as I understand him. He's a strange young man. Not the brightest fellow, but he is extremely cool in tense situations. He thinks fast on his feet. He's saved me twice now with his quick thinking. Strange fellow. I just hope he can find the coordinates of this space station of his," Meg replied.

She found Josh looking through a large display of coordinates on the nav display. "Hi Meg. I finally found a listing of coordinates. Here is our base. Can you enter them? I've never done it before and I don't want to screw it up and wind us up inside some sun somewhere," Josh admitted a little sheepishly.

"Sure thing. Scoot over," Meg replied. As she sat down at the nav controls, she felt she ought to be honest with him. "I haven't entered them before myself, but I have watched others do it many times. I think I can safely do it, Josh. Here goes," she flashed him a brief smile and then began to enter the long series of 3D spatial coordinates. After double-checking the values, she said, "Okay, now what?"

Josh had no idea. He laughed sheepishly. "Er, I haven't the faintest idea. I've always been told the coordinates are entered first before it is engaged. Now that it is active, I don't have a clue what we are supposed to do." Suddenly the transport lurched forward, pinning both to the backs of their seats for a moment. The ship lunged forward in a terrific acceleration. Once it subsided, he added sheepishly, "I guess we do nothing."

Meg chuckled and looked at the nav readouts. "Yes, we are on course to those coordinates now. It indicates a two-hour travel time. I best go check on the others. Can you take a look at Missy for me and see if there is anything else that can be done for her before we get there?" Meg asked.

"Sure, but you probably know far more about it than I do," Josh admitted.

As the two moved down the hallway, the other women stuck their heads out of their quarters. "Are we okay?" "Where are we going?" "Are we safe now?" "What was that?" Questions came fast from the shaken, worried young women.

Princess Meg answered, "Calm down everyone. We are safe. Josh got us safely into hyperspace and that lurch was just the transport getting up to speed. We are on our way the safety of his spaceport. Be there in two hours. If some of you can cook, why don't you see if you can fix us all something from the galley?" Give them something to do — something normal, she thought to herself.

"Cookie was making some stew before all this happened," Josh suddenly recalled peeling potatoes for the stew pot. Can't I ever get away from those darn potatoes, he wondered?

"I'll see to it, princess," Noel said, relieved to have something she really could do. "May we clean ourselves up? I can help you, princess, since Missy is hurt."

Meg sighed, "Well, I suppose I should look regal when we arrive at the station. Okay, Noel, let's get going. I stuffed my clothes in Josh's footlocker. I'll show you where."

"I'll go help with the stew," Josh suggested, unable to think of anything more useful to do. The ship was on automatic pilot and would not need his attention until they approached home base. In the small galley just large enough for the cook and himself, he found the stew was still simmering on the stove. Each burner had tall metal sides preventing anything from sliding off during bumps and sharp turns or accelerations. Only if they tipped the ship nearly over would the stove spill whatever was on it. He tasted it and again admired Cookie's culinary skills. "I'll miss you, Cookie, but at least I don't have to peel potatoes right now." He set about making coffee and boiled some water for tea as well. Josh hated coffee, but had a passion for imported, expensive teas.

Before long, a young woman joined him. "Hello. I am Rae. Princess Meg said to see about something to eat?" Josh guessed she was in her late teens, rather cute with blue eyes and curly blonde hair that touched her shoulders. Her dress was a little dirty and her knees had turned black and blue. He presumed that she'd taken a bad fall while being captured. "We can't eat in here, though. It's way too small."

"Right. We come in one by one and get served. We take it back to our quarters to eat. I think Cookie's stew is done. I'm making coffee and heating water for tea. Why don't you see about serving everyone? I'm sure I don't know what you women prefer. I hope our crude transport food will be acceptable," Josh apologized in advance. He figured these women were probably used to very fine dining, since they were from the royal court of Rimon-F.

"I'm sure it will be, Josh. Thank you for saving all of us. We were going to be raped and then killed — that officer told us so. We owe you our lives," Rae explained, flirting with him slightly.

"Oh it was nothing. Just doing my job," Josh attempted to squeeze out of the role of hero into which she was putting him.

"Why was Princess Meg wearing one of your spacer uniforms? Lots of us were wondering about that," Rae asked, beginning to get the plates, cups, and silverware out of the cupboards.

"A disguise. When I heard we were going to be boarded right after she arrived, I thought if she looked like a crewmember, then I could pretend we only received orders — that she hadn't arrived yet. The Imperium officer actually believed me. It was close. He and his thugs then killed Cookie, our captain, and navigator."

"But you can fly the transport, right?" Rae asked.

"Actually, Rae, this is my first time flying it. I've had lots of hours in the practice simulator. So far, so good," he admitted.

"Wow," she said rather worriedly.

"It's on automatic pilot now, so there isn't much risk of anything going wrong. Besides, if I can't handle it, once we get to the spaceport, they could send someone out to us to help dock the transport," he defused her fears.

Just then, other women began arriving. Hastily Josh helped himself and took his plate and tea with him, heading back to the pilot's seat. On his way, he met Princess Meg and Noel in the hallway. Once more, she looked like a regal princess, and she flashed him a smile as they passed each other.

A little later Meg joined him, taking the navigator's seat. While eating, she asked, "So Josh, how long have you been a spacer?"

"Four years now. My folks were potato farmers in Idaho. I hated it, ran off, and joined the Spacing Guild when I turned eighteen. I'm not very good, actually. My body is too small and weak to wear the heavy body armor. Anyway, all I really wanted to do was to fly among the stars. Unfortunately, I am not so good at math. Physics and I don't get along so well. They made me a Transport Courier Second Class. Really, that's a glorified gopher, but I've been studying to become a transport pilot one day. Then I can truly fly among the stars and not just be a passenger, which is all that I am right now. I'm sorry the Imperium troopers murdered your family. What will you do now? Are you next in line to rule Rimon-F?"

"Thanks, it was quite a shock to hear about their deaths. I don't think it has really sunk in yet — what with our narrow brush with death and all that. Well, yes, I suppose I'm now the ruler. Parliament makes the laws and the king carries them out planet-wide. Do you think the Imperium has killed everyone on Rimon-F?"

"Dunno, princess. We heard rumors around the station that the Imperium forces were in Federation space, but beyond that, I'm afraid no one told me anything. I'm just a gopher really. Why would the Imperium want to attack Rimon-F anyway?"

"I am not sure, Josh. Maybe because we are rich in silicates used in computer chips or maybe because we also refine a lot of fuel used in Federation ships. I just don't know. Anyway, Josh, your quick, brilliant thinking saved us all. Never doubt yourself. You are smarter than you let on, you know," she flashed him a big smile.

"Don't know about that. Still I did get us out of that pickle, even if it was unorthodox."

"If you had followed the protocols and entered the coordinates first, we would have been disintegrated long before you could have gotten us into hyperspace. Go with your hunches, Josh. So far, you've been dead on with them. Pretty amazing, if you ask me." Josh flushed, unused to such compliments. While he was on the space station proper, many others never failed to toss at him jokes about his being a dummy. He could only endure the jests.

Both the pilot's console and the navigator's displays began flashing a red warning message. They were about to drop out of hyper-drive, having reached their destination, Satellite Base Nine. Josh took control of the transport's control stick. I hope I don't screw this up too badly, he thought to himself, as they dropped out into normal space some distance from the orbiting station. He saw the blue-green world far below them. Down there somewhere, his father was probably hoeing potatoes, he thought, but quickly put his attention on flying the ship.

Over the communications network, he reported in, "This is transport Silver Streak. We are in trouble here. Standing by for instructions."

A controller's voice came back. "Silver Streak, what kind of trouble are you in? Where's Captain Hons?"

"Dead sir. So are Navigator and Cookie. We arrived at Rimon-F just as three Imperium battle cruisers were launching an all-out attack on them. We got boarded by the Imperium soldiers, who killed all three. I've Princess Meg Dillon with me and eleven other young women who we've rescued as well. One woman took a blaster shot to her right arm and is in a bad way. She needs medical attention as soon as possible. Oh, this is Josh Hamilton, sir."

"Copy Silver Streak. Who is piloting the transport?"

"I am sir."

There was a long delay before the controller continued. "Okay son. Our records show you have logged many hours in the simulator. Think you can bring her in? If not, hold your position and we'll send out someone who can dock her."

"I'll try. Gosh, there are an awful lot of ships around here," Josh replied, unwilling to relinquish control of the transport just yet. He might not ever get another chance to fly it. From their windows, he and Meg saw hundreds of fighter ships, transports, and even three battle cruisers hovering some distance from the huge orbiting station. Many others were docked.

"Okay son. Slow and easy. Port 112. Turn the nav system to channel 44. Follow the nav signal on in to the docking bay. Slow and easy son," the controller's voice ordered. Meg switched the nav system over to channel 44. Suddenly Josh found a flight path being displayed before him. Piece of cake, he told himself, as he pulled back a little on the stick. Slowly the transport began moving once more.

A few minutes later, he sat back. "Well that was easy, actually. We made it. Come on; let's get everyone off, and get Missy to the medical station."

"Well done, Josh. Thanks again," Meg complimented him. Secretly, she'd kept her fingers crossed. She rose and followed him to the rear. Soon the door opened, and a rather large number of people met them. Josh recognized those from the medical unit; they wore white gowns, but he was very surprised to see General Hank Thompson, Commander of the entire space station, there as well.

"Princess Meg Dillon, I presume," the tall military man

said formally.

"Yes. My Personal Assistant, Missy, is in dire need of medical attention. Forces from the Imperium have invaded our world, Rimon-F. They've murdered my parents and brother. I am now our official ruler," she said just as formally.

"My condolences, Princess Meg. We have already received confirmation of the surprise attack upon Rimon-F. If you will follow me, we have much to discuss. These medical personnel will tend to your wounded. The quartermaster will escort the other women to temporary housing. We are nearly at full occupancy at the moment. War with the Imperium has finally come and our station here has become a temporary staging area."

"Lead on, general."

"Oh, Transport Courier Second Class Josh Hamilton, report to Major Howard right away," he added. Josh saluted, but stayed a bit to help the other women off his transport. When he reported to Major Howard who was in charge of the entire fleet of transport ships, he was asked to give a full accounting of what had happened with particular attention to the deaths of his three crewmembers. He was then dismissed and sent to his quarters to clean up.

Meanwhile, Princess Meg met with General Hank and several other field generals. She was asked to give a full accounting of what she had seen and what had happened to her. They asked many questions about the strength of the Imperium forces and the three battle cruisers in particular. Meg also explained how only the quick thinking on Josh's part had saved them all. After all, she thought, he needs to validation for what he did. A few hours later, she went to the medical wing where she found Noel sitting beside Missy's bed.

Her longtime companion and assistant was now awake, recovering from her surgery. Though weak, she held up her heavily bandaged right arm. It now looked very conical, barely an inch across where her wrist had been. "They've managed to save my arm and have me fitted for a mechanical hand," she whispered.

Noel added, "She's going to make it. The doctor said that in a few months, she'd be fitted with the best prosthetic

20

hand they have. Isn't that good news?" She tried to show a brave, positive face for Missy's sake.

"It won't be the same, but I am alive. I guess that's something, but Henry is dead. Whatever will I do without him? I miss him already," Missy whispered, trying hard not to begin crying again. Just now, her losses were too raw for her mind to bear.

"I know, Missy. I miss all three of them too. We'll get by somehow, Missy. I swear I will do all that I can to punish those who killed them. I swear it," Meg promised, squeezing her left hand in hers. That brought a flicker of a smile to Missy's rather drawn face.

"But how will we?" Noel asked.

"General Hank has promised to send a strong force to Rimon-F to try to take back our world or what's left of it," Meg replied. "But that's got to wait until they get mobilized — whatever that means. Meantime we are his guests here. I am supposed to dine with him later tonight."

"Oh. That's a good first step," she replied.

The next day, Major Howard summoned Josh to his office. After exchanging proper salutes, Major Howard said formally, "Josh Hamilton, you are hereby promoted to Transport Pilot First Class."

Expecting some sort of reprimand for his unorthodox used of the transport, Josh nearly fainted. "What?"

"You've proven you can fly her and you can think in a crisis. We are now at war with the Imperium. We need all the transport pilots we can get. I'm assigning Navigator Billy West to you, along with Tim Smith and Leonard Jones. Tim will serve as your cook. See the quartermaster for a new uniform, son, and report to the Silver Streak to meet you new crewmembers. I've an assignment for your ship at 09:00 hours; be ready by then. Congratulations Transport Pilot First Class Josh Hamilton," he replied, saluting him. Josh barely remembered to salute in response.

As he skipped along towards the quartermaster, Josh felt light as a feather. His long-time goal of flying among the stars was now a reality! After picking up two new uniforms, he headed back to his quarters to change. A half hour later, he proudly walked the corridors to where the Silver Streak was docked. There he saw three young men, barely eighteen he thought, awaiting him. As he approached, all three snapped to attention and saluted him. He'd momentarily forgotten he was now officially a captain.

"At ease. I'm Josh Hamilton, your pilot," he introduced himself. One by one, the three introduced themselves, beginning with his new navigator Billy West.

"So you really did enter hyperspace with zero velocity and no coordinates set?" Billy gushed once the formal presentations were finished. "It's going around the navigator circles. That isn't supposed to happen."

"Well, it did. Another split second and we would have been space debris. There wasn't any time to either get up to speed or enter any coordinates. The Imperium battle cruiser fired a salvo directly at us," Josh answered, noticing the awe in the three young teens faces.

"Wow! A real Imperium battle cruiser! What did it look like?" Tim asked.

"Let's get onboard. I need some tea and I'll tell you all about it. Actually, it was surreal, seeing all those Rimon-F fighters disintegrating right and left. All you could see were the brilliant light flashes," he explained as they followed him into the Silver Streak.

"I bet the noise was something else," Tim said eagerly.

"Totally silent, Tim. We were above the atmosphere. No sound, just the light flashes," Josh explained. "Oh, I nearly forgot, at 09:00 we are supposed to get an assignment."

At the appointed time, they received their orders to transport a dozen combat ready soldiers to the Federation battle cruiser Wasp. When they returned, all four were issued their own d-guns and sent to the practice range to learn how to use them. This rather pleased all four, especially Leonard, who now held Josh's old position. Under peacetime conditions, he would not have been issued one. While they were there, Princess Meg and Noel joined them.

"Glad to see you got promoted, Captain Josh," Meg complimented him.

"Thanks. We are here to learn how to fire these d-guns,"

he replied.

"So are we," Meg explained, "Noel and I intend to fight back to help free our world."

"Yes, but we have to figure out how to use these without shooting ourselves," Noel teased. Josh noticed the pride that was very visible on her face. Just then, their training instructor arrived and the six began their lengthy introduction to proper d-gun operation.

Chapter 2 The Rebellion Begins on Rimon-F

Gone was the swarm of fighters. Only one lumbering Imperium battle cruiser was in high orbit around the orange planet below the Silver Streak. Along with six others, the transport ship appeared out of hyperspace at the precise coordinates the general had given them. A month had passed since the opening salvo of the galactic war. Word had reached the general that the Imperium had more or less left the planetary system. Now the scattered remnants of the Rimon-F army units were attempting to retake the fuel refineries from the occupying Imperium forces.

Josh and the other six transports brought fresh ground troops and supplies to the rebels. Princess Meg insisted on coming along, declaring her mere presence would inspire the rebels, showing them they still had an official leader in charge. Besides, she desperately needed to know firsthand what the situation was like on her home world.

The coordinates for their arrival point put their position far beyond the range of the Imperium cruiser's cannons. While they obviously were detected upon arrival, they met with no resistance. Josh quickly began the descent to the planet's surface. Billy West entered the landing site's coordinates. Josh only had to follow the guiding line on his display. Shortly, he sat the transport down on a small grassy field surrounded by tree-lined hills. One by one, the other six transports sat down beside his. From his window, he saw uniformed men rushing out of the trees heading towards them. He gave the all clear message to Leonard. From his instrument panel, he noted Leonard had opened the door. Josh imagined the men rushing in to begin unloading the supply of heavy blasters they were bringing. Bored, he rose and headed to the rear to watch.

"Hi Meg," he greeted the princess, who now wore a battlefield uniform, though he could not tell her rank from it. Rimon-F uniforms differed from those of the spacers.

24

"Hey Josh. Wish me luck. I'm off to help our resistance fighters," she replied rather demurely he thought.

"Good luck. I am supposed to wait here for your return. Don't get yourself killed," he added lamely. She was going off to battle, he presumed. He would be just sitting here doing nothing. Well, that was not entirely true. His job was to get the supplies and men safely here. A small role, but a vital one, he told himself. Waiting was boring beyond belief. In his imagination, Josh began to see the rebels going into action, storming the fuel refinery, and attacking the defending Imperium garrison forces. However, after imaging all the death and destruction, he decided being a bored transport captain was the proper position for himself.

Four hours later, Princess Meg and her two body guards returned. All three were filthy, covered in mud and other debris. Smiles told Josh all he really wanted to know — they had been successful.

Meg, on the other hand, just had to tell him all about their sortie. Standing behind him as he and Billy lifted off the planet, she outlined their sneak attack. She ended with, "Josh, we got them all! The refinery is back in Federation hands now. One small step. Now we have to get the other refineries back from the Imperium forces and then the chip manufacturing plants are next. They may have won the initial battle, but we are retaking our world!"

"Yes, well done," Josh replied lamely. He could not think of anything better to say. "How many of your people were hurt?" he asked what he really wanted to know. To him, death — that was all that came from attacks and rebellions.

"Well we lost ten brave men and five are wounded, but we've retaken the refinery, Josh. That's important. Plus, I got word that my younger brother Ralph managed to escape the initial attack and is leading part of the rebellion on the other side of Rimon-F," she added with some pride.

"That's good to hear. So your whole family wasn't wiped out. Say, does that mean that you are still the leader of Rimon-F or is Ralph?" he asked, wondering what her official position would now become.

"I sent word to him. We are going to plan a meeting

soon, but I have to report back to the general first," she deflected his question adroitly. Josh didn't press the issue.

During the next month, Josh ferried Princess Meg, supplies, and armored men to various other locations on Rimon-F. Raid after raid proved successful. Yes, he had taken the general and Meg to meet with King Ralph the following week. The two men outlined strategies for the eventual retaking of the planet. Princess Meg's role would remain as their go-between, arranging for men and supplies to be sent when needed, as well as leading the occasional raid herself when the target was beyond the range of Ralph.

Josh did notice that Princess Meg's attitude slowly transformed during these weeks into a battle-hardened fighter. Although he had no way of knowing, Meg also excelled at recruiting others to assist their struggle on Rimon-F, gaining valuable resources for their continuing fight. This was in spite of the daily news of warfare elsewhere within the huge Federation of Planets.

Three months after the initial surprise attack, King Ralph had finally driven the last of the Imperium ground troops off Rimon-F. Still, they kept their massive battle cruiser in high orbit, deterring anything but transports from coming or going. In order to get the fuel and computer chips from Rimon-F refineries and factories off-world, a fleet of transports were pressed into service hauling the supplies to the star base, from where they were then reloaded and sent to where they were needed. It was a crude system, but effective. The Federation could not afford to send its battle cruisers to knock out the Imperium cruiser. They were desperately needed elsewhere in the Federation. Josh was grateful the terrible battles were being fought elsewhere than where he was. He didn't complain about the daily transport runs to Rimon-F, though his own crew did. They longed to see a "real" space battle. Josh hoped he never saw one again.

Six months from the initial attack, life had become a routine of daily flights between the refinery and the space platform. However, that now changed. "Josh, we are not making a run planet-side today," Princess Meg told him early in the morning. "I've been summoned to a special meeting with the general. You are too, though you've not yet gotten your orders."

"Okay. What meeting?" Josh asked, surprised by the sudden change. He was quite used to these daily flights now. Meg refused to say, primarily because she didn't know herself. A half hour later, Josh received his orders to join the planning meeting with Meg. She sure knows what's going on around here, he mused, escorting her to the meeting room. Walking along the long metal corridors of the space station, their boots made unison clicking noises.

General Hank Thompson welcomed them into the spacious planning room. On one wall was a giant flat screen showing the entire Federation space and the "known" Imperium space. Various colored dots indicated the fleets and the current battle zones, Josh presumed. A dozen high level officers were also present, including his superior, Major Howard. The two took the last remaining seats.

"Okay, everyone is present," the commanding figure of General Hank took charge. "As you know, the Imperium has been systematically attempting to knock out our major fuel production planets. Thus far, they have only met with marginal successes, most notably on Rimon-F. However, thanks to Major Howard's transport fleet and Princess Meg's ground support, what could have been a disaster has become mostly a minor inconvenience." Several men nodded to Meg and to Hank, who could not help but smile and return the nods of appreciation. Josh sure didn't think it had been a minor inconvenience!

"Now then, it is time to give the Imperium a taste of their own medicine," the general continued. "Several years ago, our allies, the Goringi, made an unsuccessful raid on one of their remote but most productive fuel refineries. It is located on a remote planet near the rim of the galaxy in a largely unexplored sector. More precisely, it is on the pale blue moon Palidez of that planet. They very nearly succeeded, but were defeated by the presence of two Imperium battle cruisers. The Goringi reported they destroyed one cruiser, but that has never been verified."

"Our intelligence indicates they have now heavily re-enforced their presence in that sector. Thus, it would be impossible for us to launch a raid on their refinery in the same way they attacked ours. Simply put, gentlemen and princess, to do so would require pulling half of our entire fleet of cruisers out of their critical positions. That we cannot afford to do. The Federation Planning Committee has come up with another idea to strike their critical refinery on that moon."

Everyone now sat up in their seats, listening closely to the general's words. This was extremely interesting to everyone present, except perhaps Josh. "From our intelligence, the Planning Committee has worked out that the Imperium is expecting us to launch a major assault on their refineries. However, they have devised a very clever scheme that subverts the Imperium's counter-plans." Now everyone paid close attention, even Josh who had no idea why he was here.

"It seems the Imperium has made a fundamental miscalculation. They are set up to repel any invading fighters or battle cruisers, like those that the Goringi sent. Those would not stand the slightest chance of getting anywhere near that moon, let alone the refineries there. However, the Planning Committee has worked out that a single transport could sneak through their net, land, and execute a commando raid, blowing up their refineries on the moon! A single transport ship — that's the flaw in the Imperium thinking. Ignore the little guys. Hah. Therefore, I have received orders to send a single transport to this moon. If the raid succeeds, we will cripple their fuel production. I don't have to tell you how strategic that is or how vital this mission will be! We have a golden opportunity to strike a crippling blow to the enemy!"

Josh gulped. Transport? He looked around the table. He was the only transport pilot here, along with his commanding officer. He knew he had been chosen to pilot the transport. Why else was he here? He gulped again. The war had once again become really real to him. He couldn't ignore it any longer.

A giant chart appeared on the wall. All heads turned in unison to look at the general's diagram. "The transport will drop out of hyperspace here, as shown with the small image.

28

With luck, it will be on the opposite side of the pale blue moon from the battle cruiser. True, once the transport does drop out of hyperspace, the cruiser will instantly know of its arrival. The transport will immediately head down to the surface of the moon and the refinery base as shown. Against such a tiny, fast moving target and allowing for reaction times, the transport ought to be on the moon's surface long before the cruiser realizes what is happening. Once close to the surface, they dare not fire their cannons at it. Now, the commandos exit, place their satchel charges, and return to the transport. As it lifts off, they detonate the charges. In the confusion of the explosions, they jump safely into hyperspace."

Major Howard exclaimed, "General! This might just work!"

Amid other murmurs, General Hank added, "Yes, but there is a great risk that it could also fail. If the transport drops out of hyperspace too close to the battle cruiser, it can be blown up long before it can land. When the ground explosions occur and the transport lifts off, the transport will be exceedingly vulnerable. The cruiser could wipe them out before they can get safely into hyperspace. Timing is everything. That's why we've chosen our fastest-reacting transport pilot for this mission, Josh Hamilton. He has proven he can get into hyperspace faster than any other pilot ever has. The Planning Committee feels with Josh, the mission stands a fifty-fifty chance of successfully returning."

He went on, "Princess Meg will be part of the commando team and act as Josh's navigator. Since her world was demolished and because of her tireless efforts at retaking the refineries of her world, they felt it only right that she leads the commando raid on their refineries. The biggest hurdle to overcome is the extreme distance. From the overall view," he explained, as the original monster-sized projection of the galaxy reappeared on the wall, "the distance to this remote planet is three times the maximum range of a normal transport ship. The Planning Committee has worked out that if they refuel here at the very edge of Federation space, they will just barely have enough to get to the planet, but not enough to return." Sighs and moans echoed.

"So they have worked out an alternative. The transport will refuel here, deep within Imperium space. They will send a cruiser with fuel here. Timing is everything. The cruiser and the transport must drop out of hyperspace at very precise coordinates and at identical times. The refueling will take thirty minutes — tops. Once the transport refuels and slips back into hyperspace, the cruiser will do so as well. On the return trip, when the transport drops out of hyperspace at that location, they will send a coded message and slip back into hyperspace. At the prearranged time, they will drop back out and find the cruiser there. They will be grappled and taken onboard the cruiser, which then slips back into hyperspace, bringing the victors home to us."

"Still, fuel is going to be critical. Hence, besides Josh and the needed satchel charges, there will only be room for four more, including Princess Meg. Weight is the issue and there is not enough weight tolerance for a man to replace her. So Meg goes. They estimate the four commandos ought to be able to lay the charges and get out in an hour."

Princess Meg smiled. "Thank you. I will not fail. Do we have any idea of the layout of the refineries? Where do we land? Where are the charges to be placed for maximum damage? Details?"

"Alas, Princess Meg, we know next to nothing about this moon base. I am afraid you and your three men will have to work out those details once you are there," the general answered her.

She smiled. "Ah, so we are going into an unknown zone at tremendous risk to blow up an unknown facility and we have what? An hour at most to do it? Ignoring the fact they will likely have the place heavily guarded?"

"Er, right, Princess Meg. Still, their fuel is highly volatile. The Planning Committee feels that you have an eighty percent chance of causing significant destruction, given that hour window of operation." He sighed. "I know that this sounds more like a suicide mission, but look. If we can put a significant dent in their fuel production capacities, that will give us an enormous advantage, which we desperately need at this point in the war."

"Okay, count me in! I will avenge my parents, my brother, and all those valiant men and women who lost their lives defending Rimon-F! Give me my choice of men and plenty of charges and I'll blow that refinery to kingdom come!" Princess Meg declared with a great deal of enthusiasm.

Josh, however, groaned. This had the makings of a suicide mission beyond all suicide missions. They could be destroyed refueling long before they ever got going. They could be blasted into oblivion upon arrival. They could be shot or captured once they landed. They could be blown up in the explosion. They could be disintegrated the instant they lifted off. Josh only saw his own imminent demise in this trip. Yet Meg was enthusiastically behind it. Did she have a penchant for martyrdom, he wondered. Her words rang in his mind, "So how soon can we get this mission underway?" Meg asked.

With a broad smile, General Hank replied, "One week. That will give you time to pick your men, get all four trained, and allow us to get the cruiser into position. I can't begin to tell you, Princess, how vital this mission is for our war effort. If you are successful, you will be giving the entire Federation the best chance ever."

Major Howard spoke up, "Okay then. Captain Josh, you come with me. Let's get you indoctrinated on your role. Memorize the coordinates. We'll need to strip your transport down to bare metal. Eliminate all the excess weight we can. Temporarily, your crew will be reassigned and told only that you and the transport are going on a special mission. Let's get snapping. We've a lot of work to do, captain." The meeting broke up.

As Meg walked out, she whispered to Josh, "Thank you for flying us there and back. I know you are the very best transport pilot in the fleet. If anyone can get us there and back safely, it's you. Thanks." She smiled her disarming smile, and Josh found himself smiling back, in spite of his vast trepidations.

The week passed quickly for Josh. First, his crew gathered up their things. It was all he could do to keep from answering their many questions about this "secret mission" he was about to undertake. "I wish we were coming along!" Billy exclaimed, highly envious of Josh if not downright jealous of him. "How come you get to see all the action?"

"I think it's a suicide mission, but I can't say more, fellows. If I survive, I'll tell you all about it. Promise."

"Promise. We'll hold you to that one, captain," Billy retorted, still unhappy he could not accompany him.

Next, everything in the transport that was unnecessary was removed. He hated to see the galley stripped. No tea. They would be eating field rations on this trip, which was to last at most three days. Well, Josh decided, he could eat anything for three days. Besides, we probably won't make it anyway, he thought, growing more morose with each day. After the removal of all unnecessary items, the ship was carefully weighted. Apparently, the powers that be thought that was sufficient. Now they began loading satchel charges into the transport entry room. Here they would remain, ready for a fast retrieval once they landed, when timing was everything.

Welders came and worked their magic, turning what had been the galley and two other rooms into fuel tanks. After that, the tanks were tested and the ship completely fueled. The ground crew again weighted the ship and reported an accurate estimate of the distance the transport could travel, assuming it was fully loaded. This data was then given to the navigator staff, who worked out the rendezvous coordinates where the transport would be refueled by the cruiser. Two additional fuel intake ports now cut the refueling time by a third. This, Josh liked.

At last the day came. Josh stood at the entrance door, as three extremely heavily armed, robust commandos tromped into the transport. These men were as rugged as they looked. All three insisted in thoroughly inspecting all the satchel charges before allowing the transport to lift off. Princess Meg entered last, wearing combat fatigues and carrying a sniper d-gun, as well as several other d-guns strapped to her waist. She looked like a commando, Josh thought.

She spoke up, "Men, this is our pilot, Captain Josh Hamilton, the best transport pilot in the Federation. Trust him. He will get us there and back again safe and sound. To victory!" The three men thrust their fists into the air, mimicking hers. Josh grinned, at least they have confidence, he thought.

She handed Josh a small pouch, about a foot tall and wide, six inches thick. "Your food, Josh, three days' worth. Just remember to drink lots of water. They are quite compact. Don't worry. I'll show you how to fix them. Are we all set?"

"Not yet, we need to verify these charges are properly setup. There won't be time when we land," one man spoke up. A half hour later, the three commandos were satisfied, and Josh slowly backed the transport out of the spaceport. Already Meg had entered the coordinates of their refueling rendezvous into the nav system.

As Josh watched the port slowly moving away from him — actually he was moving away from it — he wondered if he would ever see the spaceport again. *Silly, think of the trip. You are going to fly among the stars — big time, this time. Into Imperium space no less. You have your wish to fly among the stars. I hope I can see this port again.* To say he had serious misgivings about this mission would be an understatement.

Hours later, he moaned, "No tea? Not for three days?" Meg had just shown him how to eat the field rations. The contents of each meal packet was dehydrated, and one needed to drink significant quantities of water with each meal. His eyes fell onto the contents of the one he was eating. *Potatoes! God! Can I ever escape those things?* He wondered to himself.

Meg chatted, "I figured you were a meat and potatoes kind of guy, so your rations are a bit heavy on those kinds of meals. I prefer more fish and broccoli myself. Just remember to drink lots of water or you will get a serious belly ache."

Twenty-four hours later, Josh began to worry. Dropping out of hyperspace, their fuel gauge read empty. "Damn, I wonder if I can even maneuver this ship!" Meg was looking out of the windows for their promised cruiser, though its presence would automatically appear on the display screens before them.

"There is it! Right on schedule!" Meg called out and opened a secure channel to the giant ship, which totally dwarfed their tiny transport.

"I'm maneuvering on vapors!" Josh called out. "Tell

them that!" At last, he was in position and heard the three banging noises as the fuel nozzles connected. He flipped the controls, starting the automatic refueling process.

"Major Domo here. Refueling should be done in thirty minutes. We will alert you to any hostile ships that might appear. I must say how much we are all counting on your mission! From the entire crew of the Battle Cruiser Dominator, we all wish you the best of luck and look forward to picking you up in two days!"

"Thanks, Major Domo," Meg replied. "We will blow their fuel refinery to kingdom come!"

"Your revenge will be sweet, Princess Meg. We've all heard that they did to Rimon-F and your ruling family. Go get them, Princess!" he replied. The two chatted, but Josh tuned them out. He had no heart for such talk of death and destruction. Why can't people just get along with others, he wondered? Life could be so wonderful if they did or at least he thought so.

A half hour later, both ships accelerated and jumped into hyperspace again. Now they were on their own with so many things that could go so very wrong. The first of which, Josh continued to worry about. What if those coordinates Meg had fed into their nav system were wrong? They could end up in nowhere without enough fuel to get back. Of course, they could also appear right beside a defending Imperium battle cruiser and the game would be over before it started. Josh fretted nervously as the hours passed. The needed eleven hours passed slowly for him, though he ate three meals in the meantime and slept a little.

An hour before their scheduled drop out of hyperspace, the four met for a discussion. Meg explained to Josh, "Okay, when we drop out, head for the moon's surface as fast as safely possible. First, we are going to have to locate the refinery. That means you will probably have to circle the moon at least once. The four of us will be watching the surface from four different vantage points, so one circle should tell us all. Once we have located the biggest plant, we need you to head there. We'll have to estimate how the plant is garrisoned and we'll tell you where we think it best to land. We'll likely have to wear space suits — no air. Once we land, expect all hell to break out. Bill and Fred will cover Tom and me, as we try to lay the satchel charges. If there is no resistance, Bill and Fred will also lay the charges."

"Once we have them in place, we'll fight our way back to the transport, Josh. Once we are onboard, I'll trigger the charges. That will be your signal to get us the hell out of here and into hyperspace as fast as you can. Got it?"

"Yes, got it," Josh replied, as if she was his superior officer.

"One more thing, Josh, we might not make it back. If we get some satchel charges laid and we get killed or if we cannot get back here, one of us will give you this sign," she waved her arms in the air as if trying to draw his attention. "If you see any one of us doing that, then we are lost. It'll be up to you to press this button here. That will trigger the charges and give you the best chance to escape yourself. Promise me, Josh, if you see one of us waving, do it! Don't let us die in vain. Promise me, Josh."

He looked at her stern, resolute face, and then the three commandos, echoing her look. "I promise. God, I hope it doesn't come to that. I am responsible for getting you here and back safely."

"It probably won't come to that, Josh. We know what we are doing. Still, if it does, blow this refinery to kingdom come and get yourself out of here," she added. He promised again and satisfied her.

Presently, the five-minute warning light flashed, and the five took their assigned places. As Josh watched the countdown, he took a deep breath, reminding himself this would be a simple flight. There was nothing fancy in his part, simple flight.

Right on schedule, the Silver Streak slipped out of hyperspace. From his window, Josh saw a dull red-orange sun in the distance, a dull looking planet below him. Ahead, the moon loomed large. His eyes spotted the giant Imperium battle cruiser about a hundred twenty degrees around the moon from his location. At once, he moved his control stick forward and increased his speed, diving for the moon's surface. He leveled off at what he thought was a safe distance, the rocky surface of the moon streaking beneath him. He focused on flying the ship, leaving the others to look for the refinery. Circle the moon, circle the moon went through his head.

He heard the others shouting over the open intercom, but paid them no attention. Actually at this speed, flying required his full attention. At last, Meg ordered him to turn right and slow down. They had spotted four refineries, but this one seemed larger. As he neared it, he saw plumes of dust drifting up into space from the giant machines. Humongous pipes seemed to run in a patchwork forming a cloth of metal weave — at least that is how it appeared to his brief glance.

"There, there, set us down there," Meg ordered and raced for the rear to don her helmet, joining her three companions. "Testing." The four quickly added their words, and Josh verified that all five were hearing each other. At least he could hear what was going on, unless or until their comm sets were damaged.

He heard the air lock open and knew they were exiting the ship. He now joined them, helping Bill to load the air lock with satchels, then closing it and allowing the air to escape. Outside, Meg and Fred quickly removed the satchels and re-closed the door. Tom stood guard. Five minutes later, the last of the satchels were gone as were Bill and Tom. The four loaded themselves with the many satchels, which weighted drastically less due to the slight gravity of this moon. Josh went back to his pilot's seat to await the future. He did notice, however, that a whole lot of that dust had gotten into the ship's air. He blew his nose several times, getting the bluish dust out of it.

Watching from his window and listening to the four's barking voices, Josh again was most thankful he was a mere pilot. Before long, Imperium troops in their spacesuits swarmed out of their barracks. A firefight began. While Fred and Meg began laying the charges along the many interconnecting pipes, Tom and Bill laid down covering fire. The firefight soon turned one-sided. The Imperium soldiers were wearing full battle armor over their spacesuits. Hence, when a d-gun blast struck one of them, it only damaged their armor before the beam ended. It would take a second, precisely aimed shot through the hole in the armor to kill the Imperium soldier.

Tom went down. A sickening, sucking sound announced his death. He took a d-gun blast to his chest. It opened up a hole in his spacesuit. The almost non-existent atmosphere sucked his air and soft tissues out of the gaping hole. Josh was very thankful that from his position he could not see Tom's death. Fred then took up his position, leaving Meg darting about, as if she were some kind of graceful ballet dancer in the low gravity, planting more charges when her body returned to the surface. It was all surreal to Josh. Then Bill took a direct hit. Finally, Josh heard Fred dying. One by one, the Imperium soldiers were wiping them out. Had they even killed one enemy soldier, Josh wondered?

"Charges set!" Meg yelled and began dodging blasts, while bouncing back towards the transport ship. "Get ready! Remember, if I go down, blow it up!" He watched her giant, bouncing steps and the near misses from the rapid d-gun blasts. At least two dozen soldiers were trying to kill her. Then, he lost sight of her from his window. He had one hand on the button and one hand on his control stick, ready to carry out his part. Then he heard her shriek; Meg had been hit. He waited. Later asked why he hesitated, he could only say he didn't hear that sucking sound which had accompanied the deaths of the three commandos. He waited. Meg has been shot. He knew he ought to press the detonate button and get the hell off the moon, but he hesitated and waited.

After a minute, he heard the sound of the air lock. Was an Imperium soldier boarding his Silver Streak? Again, he hesitated. If so, he'd have one chance to blow the refinery before having his own brains blown out. Then he heard the voice of Meg, "Blow it! Blow it! I'm onboard; blow it! I'm wounded and can't! Blow it, Josh!"

He pressed the button and pulled back on his stick. Simultaneously, two things happened. A giant explosion occurred followed by numerous secondary ones. All Josh could see were brilliant flashes of light, but he felt slight concussion waves through the ship. The thin atmosphere only transmitted a tiny amount of sound. The Silver Streak rose off the ground and jerked violently as it flew through the concussion waves of the explosions just below the ship.

As he gained altitude, he prepared to press the hyperspace button. Boom. The Silver Streak lurched violently to one side. A dozen alarm buttons began signaling various warnings. He banked hard to the right, staring down at the strange looking planet far below him. Boom. The ship took a second hit. Both had been grazing hits. He was not disintegrated yet. He furiously pounded on the hyper-drive button. Nothing happened; he continued to head downward towards the planet below. At last, he focused and saw the lights indicated a damaged hyper-drive. They could not slip into hyperspace. Now he began to weave right and left, hoping to present a more difficult target for the battle cruiser's cannons. He saw a few energy streaks flying off to the port and starboard sides and knew this was the right action to take.

Down he dove, speed increasing rapidly. What he could not see were the huge flames following the ship. The fuel tanks ruptured and shot flames into space instead of exploding. The Silver Streak was now a "flaming comet." All that he knew was the transport was not responding to his control stick very well at all. As the planet loomed closer, he began to slow the ship down. Unfortunately, the ship no longer responded as it should!

"What's happening?" Meg screamed in panic over the intercom.

"We're hit. Hyper-drive is out. Damage everywhere. We're going down. Trying to get us to the planet below. You okay?"

"I'm still alive. Can we land?" Meg yelled in spite of the throbbing pain in her left arm. She'd gotten her helmet off and was struggling with her right hand to get herself out of the space suit, quite a challenge. She had to in order to get to her wound, but the wild movements to the left and right made that most difficult. Worse, she was coughing from all the strange dust that had gotten into the transport's air.

"Don't know. It's not responding. Hang on." Josh saw

the world appearing before him. Water covered most of the surface. At last, he saw land ahead. Somewhat relieved, he began trying everything he could to slow the ship down and get it leveled off. He had no idea that the fuel fire had exhausted itself and that now the plunging Silver Streak was emitting an enormous smoke trail. He had almost no control of the ship. Nothing in his hours in the flight simulator prepared him for this.

Pretend I am riding my scooter and the brakes have gone out. What do I do? He thought to himself. *Force it to slow down. Go up hill.* With all his strength, he pulled back on the sluggish controls. It began to work, slowly. Now he was over the land mass. It was daytime perhaps, a ruddy red light. Green swept beneath him. Grass he thought. Ahead, he saw rugged mountains and ceased trying to pull up. The ship zoomed over the peaks, but only just barely. Now he pulled back hard and the ship began slowing down.

"We're going to crash. Brace yourself!" he yelled into the intercom, hoping that Meg could somehow keep from being thrown about. Josh continued to play with the controls doing a bit of this and that, trying everything imaginable to slow the transport down. Gradually the airspeed dropped. Ahead he saw long, rolling grassland and no forests. Now or never, he thought and allowed the ship to touch down.

His angle of approach was ideal, given the shape of the transport. It skidded along the ground, tearing out an ever-deeper path in the soft earth, though the ride was bumpy. All the windows shattered, covering him in tiny shards. Finally, all motion stopped. He was alive. They had somehow managed a safe landing. He struggled to his feet. Dusting off the glass, he raced to the rear to check on Meg.

She had gotten out of her space suit, but her left arm was bleeding significantly. She'd taken a blaster shot and her left hand was missing. She looked pale and bruised from the landing. Hastily, he tied a tourniquet around her lower arm and helped her to her feet. Together, they pushed their way out of the destroyed air lock, stepping on to the soft grasslands. The air was breathable, but chilly. The illumination from the orange-red sun was dim and very spooky to the two. Neither had ever seen anything like this.

"Look. Here comes someone," Josh pointed out. In the distance, they saw mounted men riding hard towards them. As they watched, the figures grew in size.

"My god! They're barbarian warriors!" Meg exclaimed. They saw whirling blades out in front of the leader, a burly, gruff looking man. Neither had the slightest doubt of the intentions of these men. Both Josh and Meg drew their blasters. The leader galloped towards them, yelling wildly, his twin scything blades cutting the air out before him. Behind him, hundreds more came galloping. The two reacted and fired.

Chapter 3 The Evolution of the Conquistatore Mortale

The planet of the orange-red sun known in the Imperium as Ashford-5, but called Tierra by its inhabitants, had entered a new period of hard-won peace. Tierra had one known continent — bat-shaped, some six thousand miles east-west and four thousand north-south at its middle, shrinking to three thousand along its wings. The tall and forbidding Goza Mountains divided the Westerlings from the Midlands, while the rugged Buku Hills separated the Midlands from the Easterlings. While there is a distinctive physical separation between these thirds of the continent, their customs are rather similar throughout, though their languages vary somewhat. At this time, the major trading routes between the three areas paralleled the southern coastline.

The large concentrations of psi power or the *mentales* gifts as they were commonly called, still resided in the towers, the *Círculo de la Torres*. Each tower had one or more circles called *Círculo de mentes* often consisting of nine members plus a Regulator who monitored the physical bodies of the others, while they were working as a unified whole. Here in 1270, there were eleven of these powerful towers, and they controlled and ruled the lands around them. Only a few towers still occupied their original locations, having been forced to move during the wars and upheavals of the past centuries. The relatively recent Renegade Tower was new and controversial. They controlled the Coastal City-States Alliance, meaning all the coastal cities of Tierra, thanks to Calder's Grand Plan.

In the Westerlings, the once almighty Valen Tower had lost much of its lands. The old two northern kingdoms of Abvera and Zamora were now called Malaca, ruled from that inland city. Malaca covered one-third of the Westerlings, though much was in the frozen north. Lord Gervasi Quito Malaca had just built a new tower there, solidifying his control of the northern lands of the Westerlings. The other thirds, the old kingdoms of Trujillo and Almendia were divided, under the control of Valen Tower and the Renegade Tower in Villa del Rey. The Renegade tower controlled all the coastal lands, while Valen, located close to the Goza Mountains, controlled the vast inland areas. Disputes were commonplace beyond about two hundred miles inland from the lengthy coastline.

In the Midlands, which had seen enormous upheavals, only three towers remained in their original locations. In the vast farmlands of the south, Rusden Tower controlled most of the breadbasket country between the desert of old Bashir to the south and Salt Creek to the north. Running through the Midlands, the mighty Wyndl River formed its eastern boundary. In the far north, Brom Tower controlled the northern lands as it always had, including Hilliard Heights and Chester. Wyth Tower some five hundred miles south of Brom controlled what had been the Kingdom of Bettingham, shaped like an isosceles triangle. Although destroyed, the areas of the other two original towers and cities in the south of the kingdom were still uninhabitable due to radiation, namely Bettingham and Bedwurth.

Bettingham Tower now resided in the northeastern city of Walsham. South of them at the major fork in Wyndl River, where the Wal River joined it, lay Wye and the relocated tower. They controlled all the lands to the west of the Wyndl River to the Goza Mountains, including the large cities of Wycombe and Wye. Across the river from them lay Northend where Haverhills Tower had relocated. South of Northend lay the long disputed Kingdom of Matruk, an Easterlings country, although it was west of the division line of the Buku Hills. Its largest town was Southend and was a major part of the Easterlings breadbasket.

East of Matruk lay the Easterlings land of Alba and the lone Easterlings Tower of Adelmira. Unfortunately on the southern coast, its largest city, Turda, now belonged to the Renegade Tower and their City-States alliance. North and east of Alba lay the vast sandy desert of the Arad, whose capital city on the coast was Tecuci. Over a thousand miles further on up the coast lay the port town of Po. Above the Arad lay the cold steppes of Domei with its capital city of Teraspoli, again on the seacoast. The two sultans who controlled Domei and the Arad declared independence of Adelmira Tower. They also claimed control over the two countries. Hence, they were an anomaly within the City-States Alliance, controlling whole kingdoms, not just a coastal city and surrounding lands.

There were very few with the *mentales* gifts in the Easterlings. Why? Only a very few people on Tierra knew the true source of such powerful mental gifts, the dust from crushed psi-crystals. The aliens from the Imperium, who had landed here almost three centuries ago to refine the psi-crystals into the fuel used to power their entire space fleet, had their refinery destroyed in a humongous blast, which had altered the pole of the entire planet, for the worst. The dust from the explosion covered portions of the Westerlings near the Goza Mountains and Plateau Grado, where the aliens had made their spaceport and refinery, and over much of the Midlands. As a result, those with the *mentales* gifts were found widely in these regions.

The aliens still maintained their spaceport on the plateau, but now mined their precious fuel from one of Tierra's two moons, the pale blue Palidez. Adjacent to the southeastern corner of their base lay Exchange City, where the two cultures shared a city and where the yearly lease payments of iron ore and a bit of gold were made in early July. Much trading of other goods was also done in this city, an open city to everyone.

The old tower in Exchange city, where the Emperor and Empress once held court, was now the meeting place for the tower members and rulers of Tierra. Meetings were held in the spring and fall, on the average, though some came at the time of the lease payment in July.

Also important was Tierra's penta-pantheon of gods and goddesses. In this century, the actual existence of these five spiritual beings was known to only a handful of people. Wystan was the God of Battles and Warriors. For eons, he had been actively fomenting great wars and battles, for which he lusted. He cared not for the fates of women. His opposite, Lysandra, the Goddess of Life and of Death, took the side of the women of Tierra. However, she usually demanded a huge sacrifice for her direct intervention, when a woman prayed for her help. Calder was the God of the Sea and he hated Wystan. Some twenty years ago, he had concocted a brilliant plan to wrestle control of Tierra's men from Wystan and he very nearly succeeded. At this point in time, both Wystan and Calder had fallen from grace. No longer were they gods, but were now being "human beings." Little is known of the activities of the other two. Neutral Alleric is at the top of the pentagram, all-powerful, but seldom mixing in human affairs. He seems to care more for the planet than its people. Ariana, the Goddess of Fertility, has been active for quite some time, but almost nothing is known of her direct involvement.

The ancient god known as Wystan was a god no more. Now he was securely attached to the head of a robust human teen known throughout his village of Viterbo, Domei, as Damiano Donatello. True, he occasionally had notions that he was a god, invincible in battle, but at nineteen, he had long forgotten his days as Wystan. He had more important things upon which to dwell. Strength, prowess, cunning, and fighting skills — these increasingly demanded his full attention.

Viterbo was a small village on the rolling, desolate steppes of the frozen northern lands of Domei. It lay almost two thousand miles west of the capital and port city of Teraspoli, where Sultan Gino Gianpiero ruled ruthlessly. It lay some nine hundred miles east of the Buku Hills and a hundred miles north of the Fiume Senza Acqua, the river without water that stretched from the Buku Hills to the far distant ocean, forming the southern border between Domei and the desert kingdom of the Arad. About the only time water was present in the shallow, wide river was after the spring snow melt. The weather in Domei was nearly always cold, bitterly so five hundred miles further north, where no man lived any longer, not for centuries since the polar shift occurred. Here in Viterbo, the summer was what other lands called either spring or autumn.

However, these steppes did produce small, hairy horses in great abundance. Hardy and swift, these mounts were the lifeblood of those who lived so far beyond the thriving coastal cities and towns. They served in many ways, none the least as mounts for the hunters and warriors. Their hides provided warm clothing and even huts, when the village hunting party went on a Great Hunt, bringing back food for the long winters. However, Viterbo had something else that most other nearby villages did not: an iron ore mine. Tierra lacked most all heavier elements and iron ore was rare. Much was imported from the aliens as part of their land lease payments. However, very little of that ore ever found its way to this remote portion of Tierra. Hence, miners, smelter-smiths, blacksmiths, and weapons makers were highly prized occupations in and around Viterbo.

Yet, these occupations did not interest Damiano, beyond having access to good weapons. Rather, he was interested in one thing: conquering the world. When he was twelve, he'd covertly slain his younger brother, Julio, who in his eyes was a weakling, caring nothing for swordplay and battles or even hunting. In those early years, he was often viewed as the village bully, taking nothing from anyone, not even the adults. By nineteen none of the two thousand inhabitants ever dared to cross him, for such was a certain death sentence. He had killed a dozen people already.

He had two younger sisters, though. They and his parents were, as most all of Viterbo, firmly rooted in the ancient tradition of binding. During the daytime, all women and girls wore a waistband to which their upper arms were chained just above their elbows, allowing some motion with their lower arms and hands. They wore very tight hobble skirts that allowed them to take only the tiniest of steps. At night, the skirts and chains were undone but then their arms were crossed behind their upper backs, and inserted into horsehide tubes and secured. Thus, traditionally, it was the husband's duty to assist his wife at all times. Indeed, the Easterlings women claimed their men spent at least a quarter of each day with them, quite unlike the physically unbound women of the Westerlings and Midlands.

When he was twelve, his father insisted he take over these duties for his two younger sisters. Damiano saw this as a horrible waste of his time. He flatly refused to do so. "Look, if they want to be bound, then let them bind and care for themselves. I have work to do. I can't be bothered by such trivial things!" Try as they might, his parents could not convince him otherwise, though he did occasionally help his sisters when they did need help with something heavy. This attitude of his would play a pivotal role later on.

It was June 1270, tax collecting time once again. Each year in June, Sultan Gino Gianpiero sent his tax collectors across the vast steppes collecting his tribute. "Why the hell should we give up a tenth of our hard earned profits to some fat sultan two thousand miles away? Tell me that?" Damiano asked. A large crowd of villagers had gathered around the central plaza and water well, where the tax collectors would meet with each household, extracting payments. "I tell you that is utter foolishness! What does the sultan ever do for us? Has anyone here ever seen the fat man? I say from now on, Viterbo shall never pay a single coin, horse, or pot to the sultan."

"But he will send an army to force us," someone called out.

"Then, I will kill all of them! Trust me, we are far more powerful than the sultan's weaklings he calls soldiers," Damiano countered. "We are the strongest, best fighters in all Domei! None can touch us."

"But he has magicians, tower-trained men who will incinerate us," another worried elder protested.

"Tower-trained? Hah! Have you ever seen them outside their cold, damp, miserable towers? I say not. Magic cannot defeat our strength, not ever. They are rare, nay exceedingly rare. We are many. To the many belongs the spoils of this earth, not to the few," Damiano shouted back.

His last line brought quite a few cheers. Here in the desolate steppes, the mere idea of great spoils indicated riches beyond imagination. Only one elder had ever been to Teraspoli and seen the grandness of the sultan's palace. He was forever telling others about the wondrous splendors he'd seen. Someone called out, "Tax collectors are coming!"

Damiano yelled above the stirring crowd, "Viterbo! This day I shall single handedly throw off the centuries of burdens the sultan had laid upon us all, for I am the mightiest fighter the world has ever seen! If I fail, then you may continue to be sheep before the almighty sultan. If I win, then follow me to greatness!" Damiano drew his scimitar, waving it in the air. He dashed off to saddle his sturdy horse. Minutes later, he cantered through the village plaza, scimitar waving to the throng who, instead of scattering, decided to watch and see what would happen. Several elders complained bitterly that Damiano was about to bring the wrath of the sultan down upon them all. Many listened to them, but not Damiano, who reached the edge of the village and halted as the caravan of tax collectors and sultan's soldiers slowly rode up to the village.

When they were within hearing distance, he stood up in his saddle and yelled, "Viterbo no longer pays any taxes to the fat sultan. Turn around and find some other weaklings to prey upon. Enter Viterbo and I will slay you all, for I am Damiano Donatello, Conquistatore Mortale!"

Hastily, a dozen soldiers drew their scimitars and moved ahead of the dozen tax collectors and their wagons, already laden with the spoils of other villages. "So be it. You will all die today by my hand!" Damiano yelled, kicked his horse into an all-out gallop, charging into the midst of the dozen soldiers. Yelling wildly, his scimitar flashed this way and that as he passed through the surprised soldiers. With each pass, more and more of the men fell wounded or dead onto the hard ground. Five minutes later, the dozen soldiers were finished, and he went for the terrified tax collectors.

After outright killing three of them, the remaining nine began crying, "Mercy! Mercy!" Others cried, "Have pity on us. We just carry out the sultan's orders."

Damiano's reply was unmistakable. "There is no place in this world for weaklings. A man must stand for his rights or he is not a man. Thee are not men, but worms." Promptly, he killed the remaining nine, dismounted and beheaded the dozen soldiers, whether they were dead already or not. Finished, he waved his arms in victory. The shocked village men began swarming to the grizzly scene. "Elders, I, Damiano Donatello, the Conquistatore Mortale, doth present you with the first of many just rewards. I give you the first of many riches you rightly deserve. Dole them out equitably to everyone in the village!"

Considering it was too late to do otherwise, the elders did just that, while Damiano rode back to his small circle of friends. "Well done, Damiano, well done indeed," twenty year old Fausto slapped him on his back. "It was as easy as I told you it would be." Fausto was the wisest of his friends and had ventured the farthest from Viterbo during his many hunts. Ettore, twenty-one, and Luigi, nineteen, were superb horsemen and fighters. The four had formed a tight bond these last three years.

"Well, it has begun," Ettore said. "Give them time to absorb their riches and we can begin."

"Right, Ettore! They have a taste of riches. Next week, we'll form up our first cadre of fighters and begin conquering the entire world!" Damiano declared, utterly confident and totally certain he spoke the truth.

"Hey, one thing I've not figured out yet, Damiano. Let's say we get a hundred of the fighters of Viterbo to go with us, how can a hundred defeat the thousands of the sultan's soldiers? How are we going to get more able fighters?" asked the young Luigi.

Damiano slapped the muscular youth on his shoulders, "You missed the last planning session, my friend. We are going to attack the next village and make them an offer that they can't resist. Join with us and have a portion of the spoils returned to their village or die. Simple. By the time we reach the ocean and Teraspoli, we will have an army with us. Simple."

Luigi laughed. "I see. That will teach me to be away on a hunt while you three are a'planning." All four laughed.

As planned, a week later, Damiano held another meeting in the village plaza. Many men attended, though some out of mere curiosity. Every family had received a king's ransom from the tax collector's wagons. That alone swayed many of the younger men.

"The time has come for us, the most powerful men on Tierra, to take back our world from the pathetic weaklings, the cowards, and the unworthy who have forsaken us while lining their own pockets with the riches and wealth of the world. It is time for we, the righteous and the powerful, to take our rightful place as the true rulers of Tierra. This is a harsh world, and only the strong survive. We are survivors and long denied our rightful, well-deserved place as the true rulers of our lands. No longer shall we suffer the oppression forced upon us by the pathetic weaklings in the magic towers. No longer shall we suffer at the whims of fat sultans thousands of miles from our homes. No longer shall we be denied the fruits of the wide world out there. Join with Fausto, Ettore, Luigi, and me and together, we shall reclaim what is rightfully ours. We will conquer the world. We will show the world we are the mightiest fighters Tierra has ever seen. Only the fit shall rule. Only the fit shall live. Saddle your horse, pack provisions on a spare, sharpen your blades, for tomorrow we begin our conquest of the world. As always, a portion of the riches we reclaim shall be sent back to your families, but none to those pathetic families who choose not to send forth one of their best fighters." His three friends began wildly cheering and more than a few in the crowd joined in.

Afterwards sipping honey ale at the local tavern, Damiano asked, "So how many do you think will join with us tomorrow?"

Belching, Fausto replied, "Many my friend, many. I counted at least fifty good men nodding."

"Yes, nodding is one thing, but will they actually come with us?" asked Luigi.

"We should leave the door open to others who might want to join up with us later on," Ettore suggested. "Some might have hunting obligations for their families to honor first."

"Aye, point taken, Ettore. Spread the word tomorrow. Others are welcome to join up, but only if they had previous obligations. I want none who are taking a wait and see attitude. That's symptomatic of the weak. I'll slay all such men. They'll route at the first hardship. We only want true men at the start. Perhaps later on, we can accept a few of the weaker men into our ranks. We'll see," Damiano both agreed and suggested.

The next day, Damiano's faith in Fausto was renewed.

Precisely fifty strong fighters showed up with their packhorses in tow. Ettore reported that ten others truly wanted to come, but needed to handle matters of honor first. "I let it be known that other men than those would not be welcome. Jumping onto the winning horse is not an option with us. I think the message was clear, but we'll see."

As the gallant fighters rode proudly out of Viterbo that morning, Damiano asked, "Okay, Fausto, where do we strike next?" He relied on the wisdom of his close friend.

"We go after the tax collectors. It is a sure way to ensure spoils are returned to each village in short order. Good for morale and for building up our army," he replied. "By my reckoning, they ought to be in Varese about now."

"Varese it is! Lead on, oh great wise one," he replied and his friends chuckled.

The next morning, they arrived at the village of Varese. As expected, the tax collectors were there, confiscating one tenth from all the families. A dozen soldiers stood idly by, bored with their duties, as nothing ever happened, save continual bickering. The fifty-four men rode into the center of the town.

Once there, Damiano called out, "I am Damiano Donatello, Conquistatore Mortale. I have come to free Varese from the evil tax collectors of the fat sultan and set Varese free once more! Kill them all!" The blood bath lasted barely three minutes before the dozen soldiers and tax collectors were slain. At this point, word spread and villagers came running to the central plaza to see for themselves what was going on.

Damiano had his men begin dividing the wagon's contents into halves. Part would be sent back to Viterbo, part would be given to those in Varese. Still on horseback, he yelled loudly, "I am Damiano Donatello, Conquistatore Mortale. I have freed Varese from the heavy yoke of the far distant and uncaring fat sultan. The time has come for us, the most powerful men on Tierra, to take back our world from the pathetic weaklings, the cowards, and the unworthy who have forsaken us while lining their own pockets with the riches and wealth of the world. It is time for we, the righteous and the powerful, to take our rightful place as the true rulers of

Tierra." For nearly five minutes, he continued his explanation and made his request to have the best fighters of Varese join him. In return, a portion of the riches would be sent back to their families.

"From now on, you can count on Damiano Donatello, Conquistatore Mortale, to defend your village. If trouble comes, send someone for me. My retribution against those who would harm you will be severe and without mercy! I so swear to you! I am returning half of the riches the tax collectors have taken from your village and the others they've visited so far. Freedom must be hard fought and is a most lofty, honorable goal. Send only your best fighters to join us. Rewards beyond your wildest dreams shall be yours." Again, aided by the cheers of his own men, quite a few villagers shouted their wholehearted agreement.

Just under a hundred men rode out of Varese the next morning. For two months, Fausto guided them unerringly. Village after village fell, most with tax collectors at hand. By the middle of August, his army had swelled to nearly one thousand men. The Conquistatore Mortale now controlled almost all the habitable regions of Domei. Only a long narrow strip some hundred miles from the seacoast remained securely under the control of Sultan Gino Gianpiero. Of course, this was the wealthiest portion of the country. Soon winter would come to the steppes.

As they were debating where to winter over, an outrider rode into the large encampment at a small oasis. He rode straight to Conquistatore Mortale's command tent. "My Lord, the sultan has sent out an army to find and attack us. They are a thousand strong."

"Ah, good. Let them come! We will defeat them before the winter comes!" Damiano replied.

Fausto intervened, "Where are they now? Where are they headed? How many on horseback? How many foot soldiers? Speak up, report the critical information, son."

The young lad flushed and began again. "A hundred are mounted I think. Most are on foot. They have a group of archers with them as well. A large number of supply wagons follow along behind them." He went on to outline where he'd last seen them.

"The map, Fausto, bring out the map!" Damiano ordered, growing excited. "Now we can finally have a *real* battle. No more of these pathetic skirmishes with tax collectors! A *real* battle is at hand!"

Fausto retrieved his map and together, they studied the position of the sultan's army and where their own forces were located. A new facet of Damiano's now appeared, one that would soon be highly respected by not only his own men but also all of their enemies. "Ah ha. We will take them on here at Figi's Pass. They will have to march down the narrow gully. Our forces can hit them from both the front and rear, crushing them utterly with no escape possible! Ettore, round up half of our forces and circle around them. You have their rear. I'll lead the other half to their front. However, first, we will have to get them to follow us into the trap. I'll handle that one. Give me a hundred of our fastest riders. I will goad them into following us into the pass. Luigi, you take charge of my half until I join you. Keep them out of sight. No fighting until they are halfway through the pass. Ettore, when their rear supply wagons are about to enter the pass, you are to strike. That will be your sign. Tell the men to show no mercy whatsoever. They are all to die. If they have some women with them, then the men may have them. To victory, men!"

Later that day, Damiano led a hundred men off to find the army of the sultan. Two days later, they found them. He played cat and mouse with them. They would charge at the front ranks, but staying out of archery range. Once the mounted soldiers began charging towards them, they retreated, heading always towards the steep gorge known as Figi's Pass. Three days later, they retreated into the pass proper with the sultan's entire army doggedly trailing after them. The pass was three hundred feet across, but its sides were rocky and steep, though not particularly tall, barely a hundred feet above the uneven floor. Still, it would make a perfect trap. Mile by mile, Damiano and his men continued to retreat, just out of range, maddening the enemy officers who pressed on with their pursuit of him.

Late that afternoon, Damiano and his hundred men

joined up with four hundred others, who were hiding, waiting for his signal. "Brave warriors, today your mettle shall be tested and found worthy to be the rulers of all Tierra. We face at long last the sultan's pathetically weak army. They have taken the bait and lay before us, trapped. Even now, Ettore is leading our other half up the pass from their rear. There can be no escape for them, trapped between the hammer and the anvil. Remember: show no mercy, for they will show you none. We are the most powerful fighting force on Tierra. Let's show the world what we are made of! To glorious battle, my men!"

Damiano led the charge back down the pass himself, far out in front of the rest of his galloping men! His motto was: lead by example. He passed through the startled front lines of the sultan's cavalry like wind through a wheat field, his scimitar flashing wildly, driven by his powerful muscles and aided by his forward momentum. Now into the foot soldiers he went. His horse trampled some, while his blade sliced others. Right behind him, five hundred followed in a tidal wave of death. Ahead, he saw the soldiers' morale breaking. Many began to retreat only to find those behind them trying to retreat into them from Ettore's five hundred fighters cutting through them from their rear. Arrows flew wildly. One actually hit Damiano in his chest; he ignored the pain and pulled it out without breaking his gallop.

Only after he and his men had passed through Ettore's men did he rein in and scramble to reverse direction. "Damn it! Now I am at the rear of my army!"

A soldier near him laughed. "Hey, give us a chance at some fighting will you?" Damiano laughed heartily and followed at the rear of his five hundred men. A half hour later, it was over. One thousand six of the sultan's soldiers were dead. His men then went from body to body executing any that still lived and searching them. A few of his men were wounded, including himself. These he ordered back to the wagons to be patched up.

"Damiano, you're wounded, too." Fausto pointed out.

"Nothing but an arrow."

"Still, let me look at it, please," Fausto insisted. Begrudgingly, Damiano slipped off his horsehide shirt. Blood oozed from the wound. "Best let me wash it and bandage it," he advised. A number of his other men watched this scene unfolding.

"Oh hell. Body: heal!" Damiano spoke in a very commanding tone. To the utter amazement of Fausto and the others who were watching, the wound began to heal as if by magic. Fausto still washed it off, but already the bleeding had stopped.

Seeing this with their own eyes, several men began shouting, "Immortale Conquistatore Mortale! Immortale Conquistatore Mortale!" Others cried out, "See, he cannot be hurt!" It was from this incident that Damiano Donatello became known far and wide across Tierra as the Immortale Conquistatore Mortale and thus greatly feared by his enemies.

Later back at the supply wagons, all the male drivers had been slain, leaving some two dozen bound women, the wives and fiancés of the dead soldiers. These, he gave to his men to do with as they chose. Now they had a goodly supply of excellent food to add to their own, plenty to ride out the winter, thanks to the accommodating sultan, to say nothing of many more weapons.

Around the many campfires that night, word spread about their Immortale Conquistatore Mortale. If any of his thousand fighters had any doubts about the skill and leadership of Damiano, they were dispelled completely with this decisive battle. He'd proven he was a master strategist as well as tactician. Now they would follow him without question.

He met with Fausto, Ettore, and Luigi that night. "So what now, oh wise Fausto?" he asked.

"Snow will be coming soon. We don't want to fight in the winter. There isn't enough time to take on Teraspoli this season. It is warmer the further south we go," Fausto pointed out.

"Right. It will take more than a thousand men to take Teraspoli. What about heading south through the oasis of Campo and hitting Po on the seacoast? Po is rather large and we can winter over there, adding to our army before we drive up the coast to Teraspoli next summer," Damiano asked.

"I think that is a wise move indeed. Po has a population

of some ten thousand, I think. We ought to be able to start conscripting into our fodder army now. When we go after the large heavily fortified cities, we are going to need pawns," Fausto replied. "Already we have lost too many men that we've left watching over captured villages. It will be good to renew our numbers. Once Teraspoli falls, we can conscript vast numbers there before heading south."

"Conscription it is then. They will fight or die. Their choice. Besides, today's battle has shown me my own weakness. When charging into the fray, this single scimitar is far too small. I have an idea that I want to work on during the winter. When we get to Po, find me their best weapons maker, Fausto. I want to be able to mow the enemy down with my charges. Plus, I want a longer reach." He refused to elaborate further.

Ten days later, they crossed the dry riverbed of the Fiume Senza Acqua and entered the warmer sandy desert of the Arad, where water was a scarce commodity indeed. Great sand dunes forced them to take circuitous routes instead of their usual straight-line approach used in the steppes of Domei. However, they did not intend to remain in the high desert for long. It took only two days to reach the small oasis of Campo, where a well-worn track led eastward towards the port town of Po, their winter destination, though it was now just the 1st of September.

Although Wystan or rather Damiano Donatello didn't know it, he had just set in motion two events. First, he was soon to become world famous. Second, he paved the way to his own personal torture.

Chapter 4 When Unknowing Gods Meet

The ancient god of the sea, Calder, antagonist of Wystan, was now a victim of his own creations. In an effort to outdo Wystan, he created his batch of some five hundred "mermaids," so called because of their excellent swimming skills. More technically, they were called Priestess Daughters of the Seas, and he gave them immense psi powers. Of course, they needed such powers just to survive. They could heal the sick and injured. Their blessing of a ship and its crew guaranteed a safe, productive sea journey. His goal of establishing a Tierra-wide coastal network of trade to counter the formal towers of Tierra actually came about.

He gave his mermaids additional powers; he had to, because of his massive alterations to their physical bodies. These poor women now had no arms at all, overly large breasts, and strange legs. Their upper legs were bowed out slightly, joining at a single knee. They had one lower leg with an overly large foot. Forced to hop in order to move about, these women were very nearly helpless without Calder's gift of telekinesis and teleportation. Their leg could only move in one plane, though they were extremely mobile in that plane. That is, their toes of their foot could touch the center of their forehead and their heel could go all the way backwards to touch the back of their head. Yet, they had almost no lateral motion in their leg. They could not touch their ears, for example. However, with their immense powers for a time, they lacked nothing.

When Calder abandoned them, these highly valued priestesses suddenly lost all of their special powers, becoming almost completely helpless. While the Goddess Lysandra and Benjamina were able to have others on Tierra rescue most of the mermaids, a few were beyond their reach. One of them, she refused to aid at all, and that one was the young mermaid body which was now Calder. Like Wystan, Calder had been electronically zapped and was mostly unconscious when he landed back on Tierra and was sucked into this newborn mermaid body. Unable to get out, he soon forgot his past and became Elena Venuto, the daughter of Beppe and Elda, who was also a mermaid. While she was a priestess of Calder, Beppe had been Elda's guardian and they were married. When the chaos erupted at the time of the loss of their powers, he fought those who were trying to snatch up Elda. While he was able to escape with his wife, he lost his arm in that battle.

They returned to his home oasis of Campo in the Arad. There, disabled as he was, he began a small business making adobe bricks for those in the oasis. Here, Elda had her first daughter, Elena. Two years later, she had Felisa, and two years after that, Adalina. All three were mermaids, much to the disappointment of both Beppe and Elda, whose life now was one of abject misery. Without her powers, she was virtually helpless, only able to hop about on her single foot. While they were disappointed, they still nevertheless doted on and deeply loved their three daughters, Beppe's Angels as he always called them.

By the time that Adalina was born, both had given up all hope of Elda's powers ever returning. They continued to try to have a little boy. When Elena was ten, Elda died in childbirth, leaving Beppe to raise his trio of angels.

As a little girl, Elena hopped about the small oasis playing with the other children her age. Their favorite game was kick ball, and she was able to play well. Of course, if she lost her balance and fell, getting back up on her foot was quite a challenge. While the other children thought that she was a little strange, like little children, they accepted her deformity.

Later on, when she began to grow into womanhood, the twelve-year old boys and girls began to ostracize her. They teased her and her sisters, sometimes knocking them over just to watch their awkward motions in regaining their foot. Life as a teen became increasingly difficult for Elena, Felisa, and Adalina. They did get a slight bit of relief. When their onetime girlfriends reached their tenth birthday, they became bound women just as their mothers were. Now wearing the hobble skirts, they could not keep up with the mermaids and their fast hopping. With their arms held tight against their sides, they found that they had to learn completely new ways to do nearly everything.

In the Easterlings, cutting one's hair was a taboo. Men wore their long hair in a single braid, while the women wore theirs in two braids. With his single arm, Beppe was unable to braid his own or his angels' hair, so theirs simply fell as it may. By their late teens, the mermaids' hair nearly reached their ankles, as it did with most men and women of the Easterlings.

Beppe and his family were the poorest in the oasis. Occasionally, other women would come by and help wash Elda's hair and that of her three daughters. Mostly, it was up to Beppe and the trio to handle ordinary things. He made them each a special hairbrush with a leather loop so that they could hold in their foot. While one teen sat on a wicker chair, the other two would sit on the floor and try to brush out her hair for her.

The three mermaids slept in one bed. Once Elda passed away, Beppe put the three girls in their larger bed, taking their smaller one for himself. Every night without fail, he helped get them into bed, tucked in, and gave each one a kiss on her forehead, telling her that he loved her dearly. Yes, there was a lot of love in the Venuto family long after Elda had died.

When Elena turned eighteen, many others with whom she had grown up were now getting married or had boyfriends. She often saw them at secluded areas around the sprawling oasis passionately kissing. Naturally, she asked Beppe about such matters. Poor Beppe did his best to explain, but he had no answer to her question, "When will some fellow ask me to marry him? When will I get to kiss like the others are doing?"

As the days passed by and Elena turned nineteen, Beppe, now forty-one, began to worry seriously about what was going to happen to his three angels when he died. They simply could not survive on their own. He had to cook their meals, help them eat, dress them, on and on. There was so very little that they could actually do for themselves or by themselves. Until now, he held out hope that some young men in the oasis would fall in love with them, just as he had with Elda, seeing her inner beauty, not her malformed body. That had not happened yet, and he could see no signs of it ever happening here at Campo. Who would care for them when he passed away? When he was alone late at night, this thought occupied his thoughts. Long ago, they had sold all the valuable jewelry that Elda had been given when she became a mermaid. He could not pay anyone to care for them, and yet his heart wanted to give them only the very best.

At least the three teens were able to help him make adobe bricks. He fashioned a yoke with two buckets on either side. They made many trips to the oasis to bring back the water he used to mix with the mud as well as for washing and cooking. This they could do as long as they kept the loads balanced. Additionally, they were able to hop about and help mix the straw, mud, and water as well. So yes, they did help him earn his meager wages, and he was always very proud that they did so.

Would better dresses help, he wondered? They all wore white cotton sack dresses, crudely made and easy for him to handle, since he had to dress and undress them each day, using his one hand. By September 1270, Beppe was growing quite depressed over all this, which seemingly had no solution.

Around ten that morning, the trio was about to carry a load of water from the oasis pool to their adobe home at the edge of Campo, when they stopped to see the wall of horsemen riding towards their oasis. One by one, others came outside to look or stopped what they were doing to see. Never had any seen so many horsemen.

Damiano rode at the head of his army straight into Campo, heading for the large open area around the central, life-giving pool. Palm trees, dates, and figs lined the area in a seemingly random pattern. He reined in and stared at the three mermaids. All were very attractive women, that is, from their necks up, taking after their mother. Damiano stared at Elena and she, him. He had the strangest notion that somehow he knew this incredibly strange looking teen, no older than himself. Likewise, Elena looked at him; something felt familiar about him, but she had no idea what, only that she didn't like him at all.

As he dismounted, Fausto came up beside him. "Well, I'll be! Three mermaids! Incredible."

"Mermaids? So far from the ocean?" Damiano asked.

"What is your name, mermaid? How come you are here?"

"Elena Venuto, sir. We were born here. We have lived our whole lives here. Who are you?" she replied, knowing quite well that she ought not ask questions of strange men. That was considered far too outgoing for traditional Easterlings women.

"Spunky too, I see. Everyone, I am Damiano Donatello, the Immortale Conquistatore Mortale! I am reclaiming all of Tierra from the sultans and towers. Power to us, the people. I claim ownership of your oasis now. Tomorrow, all suitable men are hereby conscripted into my army. We will move on down to Po and capture it next. We will send back tribute proportional to the number of your men who are with us. Do not challenge me. I show no mercy and will kill anyone who stands in my way."

An elderly woman cried out, "But we can't eat gold and gems. We need food. Send us food for our men."

Fausto whispered, "She has a point."

"Agreed," Damiano called out, "but only what extra food my army doesn't need. You can always buy food with the tribute we send back. My men will go door to door and pick out suitable men to join our mighty army. Please return to your homes now, while we water our horses."

The trio began hopping down the street before the still-mounted Damiano. He stared after the trio, both enamored and fascinated at their long, straight hair and large breasts bobbing seductively up and down. "They are hot, boss. Strange, but hot. Stay alert, I don't trust these Arad men; they might try to harm you to avoid being conscripted," Fausto whispered.

"I am alert. It is a good thing we've been confiscating all the enemy weapons from each battle. Now we have enough to arm another thousand men or more. But yes, they are hot, though indeed very strange. Perhaps they are the way women *should* be. I bet they cannot cause any trouble. They would not be able to stab me while I am sleeping or poison me or anything else." Both men chuckled and began to water their horses. Nevertheless, Damiano watched to see what house the trio entered.

Later as his men began drafting the younger men fit for

his army, he personally visited their home. He was unable to keep his attention off the three mermaids. As he entered the poorly made adobe home, he saw the three now sitting on wicker chairs and an older man with one arm. Beppe spoke up, "If you are here to conscript, I am afraid I am no longer useful as a soldier. I lost my arm in a fight many years ago. Now I struggle to support my three angels here."

"I see. I take it you were successful in your battle?" Damiano asked, curious about the women and this older man.

"Yes, I was able to rescue my wife from the enemy, sir."

"Well done. Bear your burden with pride. Good warriors are hard to find. Fear not, we do not need your services. Your daughters are very pretty and interesting. I bid you good day." Damiano replied and left. Somehow, he felt he ought to know that older teen, but he'd never seen a mermaid before. Perhaps it is just their very strange bodies, he thought. Still, they would make ideal women. Although Damiano could not say why, he distrusted women.

Around a thousand called Campo home; half were women. Of the five hundred men, half were either too old or too young to be conscripted. However, when they left the next day, they did take two hundred fifty men with them, having left three others dead. The first three men they conscripted had protested, and Damiano simply executed them. That snuffed all other resistance.

Amid wailing of women, they rode out of Campo, but left one of his men to rule and control the oasis, a young fighter named Arturo. Shortly afterwards, the oasis elders met to figure out what they could do. With all able-bodied men now gone, Campo was in dire straits. Eventually, the women ceased all binding and removed their hobble skirts. They had no other viable choice but to break with their centuries-old traditions. There was no one to help them, a particularly dismal situation for the younger women. Elena saw many of her former girlfriends now sobbing; they'd lost their new husbands. "They will be back," she tried to console some, but few believed her. Village by village, the Easterlings women had little choice but to break with their long standing binding traditions, once the Immortale Conquistatore Mortale had passed through the village or town.

On the other hand, Beppe was now even more depressed. As a former soldier, he doubted very much the conscripted men would ever be allowed to return to Campo. Finding prospective husbands would be next to impossible, especially if these barbarians raided the other oases in the area and conquered Po, the largest town within a thousand miles of Campo. Can I possibly have other women taking on the extra burdens of my angels when I am gone, he wondered? Sadly, he shook his head no.

As Damiano rode at the front of his ever-growing army, he could not get the visions of the three mermaids out of his mind. Why am I so intrigued by them? Somehow, I feel I should know the answer to that, but it eludes me totally. Well, women cannot be trusted, not even bound women. Let them give us babies, but stay apart from real warriors, he thought. Try as he might, he could not figure out why he was so against women, only he did not trust them in the slightest. That Wystan and the Goddess Lysandra had been at odds with each other for centuries was the reason, but those memories were no longer available to his recall. Only the memories of this current lifetime were present. He did not even know the others memories were still there, but inaccessible, let alone why they were inaccessible to him now.

Fausto alone knew just how vehement Damiano was towards women and having them close to himself. He also knew his leader was not a lover of men or boys, much to his own relief. He believed he understood why Damiano felt so strongly. The temptation to poison him, to stab him while he slept, to remove his manhood — all of these things and many more, any bound woman was capable of executing, perhaps in some misguided attempt at revenge for something Damiano had done or perhaps failed to do. Yet surely, Fausto thought, somewhere there are ideal women, who could never pose the slightest threat to his leader. Now that he'd seen the three mermaids, he was convinced that there were such women. Secretly he vowed to pursue such avenues. It would be good for the men to see their leader partook of women, just as they did with every chance Damiano gave them. Otherwise, rumors might begin, nasty rumors that could threaten to impede or halt their conquest of the world.

Meanwhile, the twenty year old Arturo had to find a place to stay in Campo. At first, he decided he would stay in the oasis leader's home. After one night, he found the hostility against him unbearable. He also didn't trust them not to try to poison him, holding him somehow responsible for the deaths of their three young men at Damiano's hands. The next day, he ran into Beppe near the central pool.

"Morning, Arturo is it? Beppe Venuto. I was a fighter just like yourself once, protecting the Daughters of the Seas. How's it going for you? Kind of rough I expect."

Arturo gave a funny sort of laugh. "Not so good. Many hold me responsible for the killings. I am here to protect the oasis. Can't they understand that? If the sultan sends soldiers here, I will bring the wrath of the Immortale Conquistatore Mortale down on them. But no, they act as if I am the murderer."

"Suppose so. That is the lot of us fighters. Look at me. I lost my arm in the service, and what respect do I get? Hardly any, though a few older women have helped my angels and me some over the years. You could stay at our house. It is the poorest in the oasis, but the safest, I expect. We don't have much food to eat though," Beppe offered. Maybe he will fall in love with my mermaids, he thought. That is why he made the offer.

"Say, you are right. It would be the safest place. We soldiers have to stick together, Beppe. I'll commandeer better food for us," Arturo volunteered. Beppe smiled, thinking this was probably his last chance to find a husband for one or more of his angels. Certainly, the trio enjoyed having Arturo staying with them. Soon a friendship was struck between them, much to the consternation of the others in the oasis. Then, they soon forgot about it; after all, Beppe had always been strange, having brought a mermaid here.

Warlord Luca Marco used to rule over Tetrano Oasis, located twenty-five miles inland from the coast, at the edge of the semi-arable strip of land along the coast, where some crops could be grown. He was a ruthless warlord, but at sixty-four and in failing health, he had given control over to his older son Armo. Now in his thirties, Armo was just as ruthless as his father. He had long ago arranged for the assassination of his only rival, his younger brother. He had two wives, Nicola and Nerina, who abided by the traditional bindings. With them, he had two sons and two daughters, the oldest of which was just twelve.

Tetrano Oasis was thriving. The sea trade via Po had propelled their population to double, to nearly two thousand. Armo had a small army of a hundred soldiers, who controlled the people with an iron fist, ensuring production of their crops. His coffers were rich in silver and gems, and he paid his soldiers well, ensuring their loyalty. Yet Armo was worried. All summer rumors reached Tetrano Oasis from visiting caravans. A warlord had gone berserk up in the steppes of Domei, calling himself the Immortale Conquistatore Mortale. Word had just reached him that these marauders had entered the Arad just north of the oasis. He could only conclude that Po was their intended destination. That meant they would be coming through this oasis, as it was the only reasonable route to Po from the northern areas of the Arad.

His thoughts now turned to how to protect his oasis. He ordered every available man to begin forming up an adobe wall around the perimeter of the oasis. He armed every man he could until he ran out of weapons. Iron was scarce and thus weapons were extremely valuable. Just now, Warlord Armo wished he'd spent some of his vast treasury buying more scimitars. He had twenty archers though, and decided to make good use of them as well, positioning them just behind the low adobe walls. With luck, this marauder would see he was defending his oasis and would just bypass it, continuing down onto the fertile coastal plains and Po.

He sent out a few patrols to look for the raiders. Finally, they returned with the news they were coming, barely a few miles away. That there were thousands of them Armo just could not believe. Surely, his scouts must be exaggerating. Yelling orders right and left, he got his men to the adobe wall lines and archers in position. Additionally, he had unarmed men standing behind, with orders to run up to the front lines and pick up the wounded or fallen soldier's weapons. None dare disobey him. All knew he would not hesitate to kill them. They were facing death from their lord or from the marauders. Morale, they had not, particularly when the waves of the mounted, screaming soldiers, led by Damiano himself swarmed down and around their oasis.

"Charge!" yelled Damiano. "Show no mercy!" He galloped towards the low adobe wall amid a volley of some twenty arrows. A few hit either rider or horseman; fewer still were stopped by them, as the heat and lust of battle was once more upon them, adrenaline flowing. Up and over the wall went Damiano, his scimitar flashing right and left. Almost parallel to him, waves of his men followed suit. Warlord Armo's hundred fighters and make-shift hundred more lasted only until the third wave galloped over the wall. Damiano reined in before a screaming Warlord Armo, still trying to muster his forces and to get the unarmed reserves to grab any weapon and fight for their oasis and lives.

Quickly surrounded, Warlord Armo finally threw down his scimitar. "Okay, you win. What will it take to get you out of here? I have a big treasury. I can pay you to just go away." Damiano spat on him and had his men tie him up. As soon as the commotion died down, that is, as soon as his men had cut the throats of all the soldiers who had fallen, making sure none survived, he made his usual speech, including the fact he was conscripting all still alive able-bodied men.

"I shall set an example for everyone. Your warlord is nothing but a lousy coward. Here is how I treat cowards," he yelled. By now, as many of the oasis inhabitants as could came out to see what was happening. Damiano sent two men off to find a hot blacksmith shop. When they returned with several hot irons, he had his men tie Warlord Armo's arms outward, stretched between two horses.

"What are you doing to me?" Armo screamed in terror.

"Giving a coward what he deserves," Damiano yelled back and brought his hand down sharply. At once, two of his men galloped up and swung their scimitars sharply downward, severing each of Armo's arms around his elbows. At once, the others used the hot iron bars to staunch the profusely bleeding stumps, though Armo had already passed out. Once the bleeding more or less stopped, a couple of men bound his stumps, and Damiano sent for the man's wives.

Nicola and Nerina made their careful, slow way from the walled complex out onto the street, fearful of their own lives. "Ah, there you are. I give you back the coward that you married. Pick him up and take him out of the oasis and care for him, if you so desire." At least his men took pity on the bound women and lifted their husband up for them, draping an arm over each of their shoulders. That roused him somewhat. Taking their two-inch steps, the two terrified women began to walk their staggering husband out of the oasis, heading south towards Po. Later that night, an elderly cousin of his snuck out with a wagon and met the three, who had only been able to walk less than a mile from the oasis during the long day. By the next morning, everyone in Po knew what was soon heading their way.

Meanwhile, his men sacked the oasis, confiscating all weapons for their own use. After raiding Warlord Armo's treasury, as usual, Damiano had it divided up into proportions and sent back to villages in the steppes, keeping his promises. His men raided the stores of the warlord and sent a goodly portion back with the treasure as well. He also ordered the execution of all the warlord's children and his father as well, in spite of the fact Luca was almost incapacitated by arthritis. As usual, he then installed one of his men as the new overseer of Tetrano Oasis, the most prosperous village they had yet encountered. He could now taste the vast riches of the fertile coastal regions.

The next day, he and his leaders made plans for the assault on Po. This would be their first major attack since defeating the thousand-man army from Teraspoli.

Chapter 5 The Sacking of Po

"Yes, look what the beast did to our husband, Lord Armo," wailed Nicola. "They murdered all of our children too. You must do something to help us," she pleaded. She, Nerina, and their brave old cousin brought the wounded man to Po and to the sultan's palace. Already, thirty year old Sultan Dario Trantino had Armo taken to the infirmary where Nerina was with him. His two wives, Milana and Paolina, both twenty-five, gasped hearing of the wanton slaying of children, fearing for their own young son and two daughters.

The Trantino family was on the forefront in changing from the ancient binding traditions to the modern styles made popular by their past empresses. While the position of empress was long gone, the compromising fashions remained, due in no small part to their local Elegant Fashions Inc. That is, they wore the new arm-fetter-gowns, five inch in diameter lip plates, long earrings that rested above their breasts, narrow waist pipe corsets, and toe shoes. Yes, their speech was hard to understand; they were short of breath and did not exert themselves, and they walked with extreme difficulty, both slowly and carefully.

"Yes, I will do what I can. For now, you should attend your husband. I am sure that he needs you, and I have much swift planning to do. Thank you for coming at once to me with this — the most atrocious news ever." Nicola felt somewhat relieved, sensing Sultan Dario Trantino would take action against the barbarians, who so mutilated her husband and murdered their children. A palace guard escorted her out of the audience chamber to the infirmary.

Meanwhile, Sultan Dario Trantino sent his wives back to their gardens and summoned all of his advisors and generals. Po was a wealthy port town, part of the worldwide City-States Alliance and backed by the Renegade Tower. The first action he took was to alert the tower's representative, who notified the tower, located thousands of miles away in Villa del Rey, about the impending attack on one of their towns. He didn't count on any real support from the *mentales* tower personnel anytime soon though.

Po was home to almost twenty thousand people, having grown swiftly with the surge of commerce. Joining the alliance was the catalyst for tremendous growth during the past twenty years. Between his city guards and his small army, he had around a thousand fighters. He could not trust the women's estimates of thousands in this barbarian's horde. Still, many rumors had been flowing steadily into Po these past weeks. According to many, their leader was invincible; he could not be killed. Dario discarded that notion. All men die, was his reply.

"We must organize fast. We have perhaps a day at most before they come charging out of the desert," Sultan Dario ordered. "Have the entire army mobilized and in battle ranks just outside the city. Mobilize all the younger men that we can; arm them from the armory where possible. When the scimitars run out, put them on the fire brigades. I don't want these barbarians burning down our town. Send all ships to sea, loaded or empty. Get my private yacht ready to sail. I want my wives and children at sea when they attack."

"What about the crippled warlord Armo?" an aide asked.

"Forget about him. He doesn't matter one iota."

"Do you suppose we should attempt some negotiations with them first?" another aide asked.

"Yes, I will attempt to do so. Have my horse and gear ready along with a white flag. I will try being civilized first. If that fails, generals, you are to defend Po to the last man. You hear me?" They saluted and promised to do so, but Sultan Dario did not seriously believe they would. Armies were known to route and retreat. His army was wholly untested, well-armed, but untried. There had been no battles, not for years. Skirmishes occasionally, yes, but nothing like what was supposedly coming their way.

That done, he wrote out letters and sent them off by courier, one to the sultan in Teraspoli and one to his own leader, Sultan Fausto Ferro of Tecuci. While he begged Fausto to send immediate aid, he begged Gino to rein in his wayward barbarian. Sultan Dario was a practical man. He knew the letters would arrive long after the confrontation was finished, but still, his protests and requests would be heard. After all, those two rulers were supposed to be running the two countries, Arad and Domei. No, if the two armies were about balanced, he might consider slugging it out, hoping to stall and delay this barbarian until help could arrive. On the other hand, if outclassed, Sultan Dario knew he would do what he could to avoid open warfare. Let the barbarians run rampant through the city, stealing what they desired. That would give the two leaders time to mobilize large armies and put an end to this barbarian horde.

Later that evening, the Renegade Tower responded. Rafael Valen and Fidela Valen, both *mentales* gifted members of the tower, arrived via a Circle teleport. At once, they were taken to the sultan. "My Lord, we came as soon as we got word of the impending attack. Rafael Valen, my cousin, Fidela Valen. Can you fill us in on the details? We've heard a few rumors of trouble brewing up in Domei, but not here in the Arad."

Sultan Dario breathed a sigh of relief. At least their tower was taking this seriously. Now no matter what happened, the world would fully know of the threat of this barbarian and his horde. He filled them in and then took the two to see Warlord Armo, who was recovering in the infirmary. Naturally, he was very eager to tell them every gory detail of the slaughter and the utter viciousness of their leader, this Damiano Donatello, the Immortale Conquistatore Mortale.

Later from his palace rooftop observation platform, the two and Sultan Dario surveyed his preparations. Campfires dotted the outskirts of the sprawling town. Roughly semicircular, Po's outer circumference was at least eight miles. Fifteen hundred men were now deployed, but that was pathetic, one man every thirty feet! Instead, they opted to form larger units spaced uniformly around the lengthy perimeter. "I will attempt to talk to them before committing to a pitched battle. Will you two accompany me?"

"Absolutely. All the Renegade Tower members will be

watching and hearing what is said, via Fidela, My Lord Sultan. No matter what happens, the world will know fully the measure of this barbarian and his horde. While we might not be able to stop him here at Po, rest assured he will be stopped at some point, even if we have to march an army overland or by sea from the Midlands and the Westerlings!" Rafael declared vehemently. This was the first real test of the Renegade Tower and their relatively new City-State Alliance. Much depended upon the defeat of this barbarian. He didn't say the defeat would occur here at Po, though. He and his cousin seriously doubted that. The two forces were likely well matched, but the barbarians had the advantage of being mounted, and the sultan's forces had the disadvantage of being forced to spread out to protect the city — a double whammy, he thought.

Around noon the next day, Damiano halted his advance guard on a hill overlooking the sprawling port town of Po. Obviously, he was expected. Smoke curls from many campfires dotted the perimeter of the town. He waited for Fausto join him before making any concrete plans. "They are expecting us," his friend commented, pulling his small horse up beside Damiano's.

"Aye, that's for sure. Wise of them. We can take them, right? They are forced to spread themselves thin to protect the whole town," he suggested.

"Yes, but we are mounted and can strike here and there, cutting them down bit by bit."

"True, Fausto, but the real question is how many archers do they have and are there any of those blasted magicians down there waiting for us? That's what I would like to know before I commit myself. Ettore, Luigi, spread our foot soldiers out in a hemisphere, matching theirs. Keep our mounted men ahead of them, but out of archery range. I sense they have a fair number of those, perhaps not many."

"Right. Archers are supposedly outlawed in war, but desperate men don't follow the rules," Ettore replied. He moved off, issuing the orders, while Damiano continued to study the layout, looking for their weaknesses. As his army began to move, he and Fausto kicked their horses once more, leading the way.

They halted outside of the range of the hunter's arrows, but they were close enough to see the enemy soldiers they were about to face in combat. "Looks like trained men, Fausto, most anyway. This will be a hard-fought battle. Here's how we can best take them. We flank them with our thousand horsemen, and then hit them hard, riding through their arcing lines around the town. After we pass through them, have the foot soldiers move in and finish the remnants off," Damiano outlined the attack, taking advantage of the field and position of the opposition.

"Hey what's this? White flag? Parley?" Fausto asked a little confused. Sure enough, three riders were slowly riding out from the lines. One held a white flag.

"Hum, well, I really am curious about what they have to say. Probably just more weakling pleadings. Still, I am curious. Come on; find me a flag and ride with me, Fausto."

"Hey, we are coming too," Ettore put in. Luigi nodded.

"Okay, let's go see what they have to say," Damiano replied. Slowly the four headed off towards the three riders, who halted halfway between the two opposing lines, waiting for them.

When the four halted, the man in the middle spoke up. "I am Sultan Dario Trantino, ruler of Po, which is a part of the City-States Alliance of the Renegade Tower. With me are Rafael and Fidela Valen, *mentales* gifted from the Renegade Tower. To whom am I speaking?" he asked, looking from man to man.

"I am Damiano Donatello, the Immortale Conquistatore Mortale."

Now focusing his attention fully on Damiano, he continued, "As far as I know, I have no quarrel with you, sir. What is the meaning of this confrontation? Po is a peaceful coastal town."

"I have freed many villages from the heavy yoke of far distant and uncaring fat sultans. The time has come for us, the most powerful men on Tierra, to take back our world from you pathetic weaklings, you cowards, and the unworthy who have forsaken us while lining their own pockets with the riches and wealth of the world. It is time for us, the righteous and the powerful, to take our rightful place as the true rulers of Tierra." For nearly five minutes, he continued his explanation.

"After we take Po, we will winter over here and conscript your able-bodied men into our ever growing army. Come spring, we will continue our march of conquest, until we control all of Tierra! From now on, you can count on Damiano Donatello, Immortale Conquistatore Mortale, to defend your town. If trouble comes, send someone for me. My retribution against those who would harm you will be severe and without mercy! I so swear to you!"

"So you would slaughter all these soldiers and destroy our town? Rape our women and force those who are left to join your army? Have I got it straight?" Sultan Dario asked. At first, he thought Damiano might be made to see reason, but now he was convinced that he was a sociopath.

"You could surrender now and I'll take your soldiers there into my army along with other able-bodied men in Po. I have no intention of burning down your town. Who gives a crap about the women anyway? They exist only to make more warriors," Damiano replied.

"I had expected you to be an honorable man, but now I see that honor is a foreign concept to you," Sultan Dario said gruffly. "My honor will not permit me to allow you to take my well-paid soldiers and force them into your army along with many other young men of Po, to say nothing of the dishonor you do to our women. Know this, Damiano Donatello, the whole world will know of your actions here in Po today. I had intended to suggest you and I fight it out with each other and leave our armies out of it. The winner takes all, but now I see your true colors. You do not have the faintest notion of honor and would never honor any such agreement. I hope to meet you on the battlefield then. At least if I am slain, I will have preserved my honor and my own personal integrity. I love Po and will gladly die to protect her from dishonorable scum such as yourself. This parley is over, dishonorable barbarian!" He spat on the ground, neck reined his horse and cantered back towards his lines, followed by the two Valens.

Damiano nearly burst with a rising anger. "How dare

that man call me dishonorable!" he screamed. Without thinking clearly, he kicked his horse into a gallop and drew his scimitar, fully intent upon attacking Sultan Dario on the spot! Fausto gave a frantic signal to the other leaders to launch the attack as planned, and then tried to follow him, along with Ettore and Luigi. In the three's eyes, Damiano was acting rashly.

Rafael heard the riders closing and carefully focused his psi energies. The crystal around his neck activated in a strong blue light, just as they reached their own lines. The four galloping horses behind them suddenly tripped, spilling their riders onto the hard ground, breaking their forelegs. Dario dismounted, ordered his own attack, and then moved to face the dismounted barbarian personally. Rafael and Fidela hastily continued on back into town.

Damiano felt his horse stumbling and executed a flying dismount, rolling forward. By the time he regained his feet and scimitar, any chance of attacking the sultan from behind was gone. His three companions struggled to their feet, somewhat stunned. He drew his dagger. With his two weapons, he prepared to fight this nasty sultan. Likewise, Sultan Dario drew his two weapons. Typically, the Easterlings fighting style was with two weapons, a scimitar and a dagger. Many of his men rushed up to engage the other three men, even as the horsemen began charging the eight mile long line of defenders, and as the foot soldiers ran towards their four leaders.

Damiano and Dario were well-matched, trading parries and thrusts, dodging and striking steel upon steel. Determination glared from both men's eyes. After three minutes, both had delivered significant cuts to each other — they were that well-matched. Dario, being older and not in as good a shape as the nineteen year old Damiano, began to weaken. The end came two minutes later when Damiano's speed won out. His dagger thrust pierced Sultan Dario's heart; the honorable man gasped, dropped his weapons, and fell. Damiano let out a loud yell of victory.

Soon, the waves of his cavalry swept past the four, ending the resistance close to them. The remaining foot soldiers finished off any stragglers around their four leaders.

The cost was high, however. All four were wounded; Ettore the worst. Damiano had six open cuts on his arms and chest. Again, he commanded with full intention, "Body: heal!" As before, his wounds began to do just that, much to the awe and amazement of those around him. Unfortunately, his three companions would take the winter to fully heal.

Once the four were attended to and bandaged, Fausto finally said, "Damiano, that was fool hardy. You almost got us all killed!"

"No, *that* was a real battle! He was a *true* warrior, so hard to find these days. We must honor him with a proper burial," Damiano replied, ignoring Fausto's complaint. "Glorious battle. We've won the day! Po is ours! Come on;, let's get a party together and take control of Po before those inside get any wild ideas."

From atop the palace observation deck, the two Valens saw the entire battle. No one saw them suddenly vanish when their Circle teleported them back to Villa del Rey. Within days, all the towers knew of Damiano Donatello, the Immortale Conquistatore Mortale. Many minds began devising ways to stop him.

Po was theirs. However, not a single ship returned to Po. All trade ended and would not resume until Po had been retaken and these barbarians driven out. The cost was great for Damiano's forces. Five hundred men were either dead or maimed. The maimed or those who had lost a limb or limbs had to be sent home, once they had healed sufficiently. True, they sacked the town, sending many riches back to the many villages from which their fighters had come.

By spring, they had conscripted another thousand men and armed them. However, Damiano knew they would never fight for him with their hearts in it. Rather, they had to be watched night and day for desertions. They had to kill nearly a hundred before conscription finally worked.

They took up residence for the winter in the Royal Palace. Food and drink were plentiful, and his warriors enjoyed their six months of rest and relaxation. Many needed the months to heal their battle wounds.

When Fausto had recovered enough and the city was

secured, he went in search of the best blacksmith and weapons maker in Po, at least among those still living. He remembered what Damiano had asked of him, though he still had no idea why he wanted them. "Ah, well done, Fausto. Look and listen. I need a new, better weapon. This last battle has shown me that I must be far more offensive. Gentlemen, I will pay you royally for building this for me." He produced a sketch of a new weapon that he called the cutting scythe. Essentially, it consisted of two very sharp blades attached to either end of a fifteen-foot long chain. "With this, I can swing the blades in a fast, circular path, cutting off arms and heads from a distance as I approach them, long before they can reach me. Plus, if need be, I can extend my reach with one of the blades out to perhaps fifteen feet before me!"

Fausto was impressed. Two weeks later when the first one was delivered, he became even more impressed. "It takes some learning, like any weapon," Damiano explained, as he practiced with them, slicing and dicing pumpkins sitting on wooden posts. Before spring came, his three friends, along with twenty other warriors, had their own cutting scythes. The benefits of this new weapon would be enormous. All looked forward to putting them to the decisive test against the soldiers of Sultan Gino up in Teraspoli.

By late October, Damiano had finished purging the city of the many advisors to the late sultan and his predecessor, Dario's father. He had them all drawn and quartered. Eliminate those who might attempt to overthrow his rule once he marched his army out of Po come spring — that was his stated objective. His soldiers carried out those orders ruthlessly, showing no mercy.

Late November, Fausto also made another startling discovery for his boss, which dovetailed nicely with the noblewomen, who still resided in and near the royal palace. These women of fashion emulated the sultan's wives. That is, they wore the arm-fetter-gowns, lip plates, long earrings, pipe corsets, and toe shoes. Even Damiano was impressed with how elegant and attractive these rich noblewomen looked and just how constrained they were, especially their difficulty in walking and bending. While attracted to them, Damiano still refused their advances, shuttling them over to some of his men. Why? They could still drive a dagger into his chest while he slept or even poison his food. To succumb to their charms was an open invitation to an assassination attempt, especially after the huge purge. He and his trio of friends knew this and spoke of it often. That's why Fausto was so impressed with what he uncovered while nosing around the seedier sections of Po.

Crispino Torina was physician in Po, specializing in battle wounds. That is, he removed arms and legs with great skill. When the priestesses, the Daughters of the Seas, were active some twenty years ago, he was enamored of their unique body forms. When they lost their powers, he went to their temple and watched as various men absconded with some of the mermaids. Those women, he was not after, but rather he was seeking the means by which they were made. In the building, he discovered one of the alien medical machines, used in part of the process. After much trial and error, he discovered how to use the machine in his line of work, removing limbs.

One of his close friends, Durante Metrio, ran an escort service for the very wealthy of Po. Metrio's Escorts were some of the finest looking women in Po. Their nightly services were very expensive, catering to those with somewhat exotic tastes, and fueled in part by the changes in women's fashions that were being promoted by the empress, Elegant Fashions Inc, and the mermaids themselves. Many of his escorts wore the arm-fetter-gowns, lip plates, long earrings, pipe corsets, and toe shoes found so commonly among the wealthy noblewomen of Po.

Over some expensive ale one evening, Durante complained he was unable to acquire any of the mermaids when they lost their powers. A competing escort service had and he was unable to compete with them. That somehow this man managed to have them stolen away from him later on had not mattered to Durante or Crispino. "I need something exclusive, Crispino, a form of woman that no one else has," he lamented, downing the last of his mug's ale and pouring it full once more, topping off Crispino's mug as well.

"You know, old buddy, I just might be able to satisfy that need of yours," he suggested and then belched. "The mermaids caused quite a stir, didn't they? But what I want to know is what aspect of their form so enchanted your customers or rather those of his?" Thus, the two began a lengthy discussion.

A couple of mugs later, Crispino said, "Okay then, you provide the bodies and I'll manipulate them into the desired forms. Deal." They toasted each other, sealing their conspiracy and bargain.

Before they actually got started on their mutual project, Crispino stumbled upon an interesting phenomenon, one that at first startled him and for which he had no ready explanation. One of the sultan's soldiers had taken a very deep sword wound to his right arm. Crispino had no choice but to remove what was left of it. During the operation and while the soldier was unconscious, Crispino had a stomachache. All during the procedure, he kept saying, "My stomach sure hurts. I hope I don't have to vomit before I get this done."

When the man recovered, Crispino began asking him how he felt. He'd done this type of surgery for years. Almost without fail, those who lost a limb were grief stricken, depressed, worried, and sometimes even praying to die, knowing they would be crippled for the rest of their lives. However, this man began saying, "Doc, my stomach hurts. I think I am going to vomit, but I hope I don't have to vomit before I get done."

"Done with what?" a very startled Crispino asked.

The man looked dazed. After a moment, he added, "Don't know doc. Just my stomach hurts and I hope I don't have to vomit before whatever." Crispino checked his patient over but saw nothing wrong. There was no infection; the surgery had saved the man's life. In time, he would recover, though the prospects of a one-armed man were not good — everyone knew that.

Each day, the story was the same. No matter what prescription he gave to help ease his stomachache, it remained there, though he never actually vomited. Curious now,

Crispino began to make experiments along these same lines. Whenever he had an unconscious patient, he began talking in very specific ways, making rather unique statements around the person. Later when they woke up, he paid close attention to their behavior and to what they were saying and feeling.

Two weeks later when he and Durante next met to begin their great experiments, he related what he'd found, though he was rather drunk at the time. "It's very strange, old friend. Do ya know that what I say 'round an unconscious person is later acted out by the patient. Came across it two weeks ago now. Had to do emergency surgery on a soldier's arm. I had a stomachache and kept talking about it, while I performed the operation." He went on to describe the man's behavior during the two weeks afterwards. "Yes, Durante, yes. He still complains of a stomachache. I've tried saying other unique things. The silliest one is: I sound like a bird when I am talking. Yes, I really did say that. Low and behold, when the woman woke up from the surgery, she began complaining that now she sounded like a bird. She is convinced that is so. Isn't this fascinating?"

"Down right fascinating, Crispino. I've been thinking about our project and specifically how I am going to handle the women, when they wake up minus some appendages. Well, you know what I mean about that. Women can be awfully hysterical over such things," Durante stated, downing more of his ale.

"That I do. That I do. It's very severe with soldiers who lose a limb or two." He belched. "Their depression, their grief, their feelings of hopelessness — it's sometimes far worse than their injuries," Crispino replied. "You know, all this has me thinking, Durante. What if when I work my magic on them, I tell them the 'right things' — you know, like maybe 'you are now very sexy.' Afterwards, they should display that new attitude, kind of like brainwashing them or something or perhaps hypnotizing them. What da'ja think?"

"Brilliant, Crispino, positively brilliant. Have them wake up from the table and feel and behave just as we want them to — now that would be more than ideal. It'da be groundbreaking!"

Crispino puffed up at the compliments. He then suggested, "Ah, but you are going to have to help me out on this. What ought I say to 'em? What kind of behavior patterns do ya need 'em to display? That is your side of the business, you see," he finished off his mug and refilled it.

Durante began making suggestions, brain-storming ideas. Whenever he came up with a good one, Crispino jotted it down on an ale-stained paper. Two more mugs later, he looked at the list. It was a lengthy one, but if even half of these "suggestions" took, the women would be nearly ideal for his friend's escort service.

Twenty-five year old Annetta was his most attractive and most in demand woman. Durante was hesitant to experiment with her first. If it failed to work, if his "clientele" did not accepted the modifications, he would lose too much money. Instead, he chose the twenty-one year old Celia, who was his number four woman. If it failed, his business would not suffer significantly.

A month after their first meeting, he had convinced Celia that obtaining further body modifications would be to her best interests, that is, allow her to make far more money. He promised she would always be well-cared for, no matter how it turned out. He carefully didn't say precisely what the modifications would be, though. Already Celia always wore fancy satin arm-fetter-gowns, six-inch lip plates, long earrings that rested on her upper chest, a pipe corset that gave her a fourteen inch waist line that highly accentuated her hips and bosom, and, of course, the toe shoes. She had had a pair of ribs removed at Elegant Fashions Inc to allow the corset to close fully. There, her feet had also been modified, and now she could only wear the toe shoes, forcing her to walk on the tips of her toes like the other fashionable noblewomen and wives of the sultan.

Durante brought her to Doctor Crispino's office, supporting her as she took her tiny, carefully measured steps. Like all those who wore the toe shoes or toe boots, having someone supporting her was almost a necessity to help keep her balance, since her upper arms were held tightly against the sides of her satin gown. He assisted her onto the operation table and then watched as Crispino put her under for the operation. Of course, the operation could have been done with the alien machine's local anesthetic, but they wanted her unconscious for the experiment.

While Crispino went about the surgery, he began reciting the carefully worded lines that he and Durante had agreed to try. "Your arms are now absolutely gorgeous. You have the arms that others envy. You are now the sexiest woman in Po. All men will do most anything just to take you out on a date. Your body is now super sensitive to the touch. You need pleasuring often. All men will find you are the most attractive woman in the room. You will be able to pleasure men easily. You will not be handicapped, but you will need pleasuring frequently." He read off a dozen more that were similar in nature. The two men figured that, if even half of these would take, her behavior would be exemplary, and she would have no adverse reactions to the surgery and her new lifestyle.

Celia awoke an hour later. As she came too, she looked at her arms, rather what was left of them. Crispino had used the alien machine to remove her lower arms at her elbows. The machine had also filed some of the upper arm bones down and shaped the muscles before fully healing them. Her upper arms were quite conical in shape, the tips being barely an inch across. Neither man knew why the machine shaped them this way; for they knew nothing of the alien prosthetics for which the machine was preparing her arms. They only knew that they looked — well quite unusual.

Celia raised her stumps and said, "Oh my! Look at my absolutely gorgeous arms! Oh, I feel so sexy now, Durante!" She rubbed them against her breasts and satin gown. "Oh, this is so sensitive, so utterly sexy, Durante! Oh, I need pleasuring, please, Durante. I need it now. Don't be a bore. Please do me now or let me do you? Oh, how about you, Doctor Crispino? Is it okay if he pleasures me some, Durante? I forgot to ask you."

"Celia, you look stupendous now! You are now the sexiest woman in all Po! Come, let me help you up. Let's get you back to our place and your satin sheets. You will enjoy it even more there. Can you wait that long?" Durante re-enforced the laid in behavior patterns.

"I will? Okay then, I will try to wait, but I am the sexist woman now. I will really be able to make so much more money now, won't I?"

"I am certain that you will, Celia, and you'll enjoy every minute of it," he replied, most impressed with the results. Crispino beamed, his work was most successful. He promised to check on her recovery in a few days.

When the two met for ale three days later, Durante said, "Crispino, you are a genius! Celia is working out just fine. She is behaving just as we wanted her to behave. Plus, she's already attracting men's attention everywhere she goes. Now I have another problem."

"That is good to hear, but what problem has arisen? I thought that you said she is working out just fine," asked a slightly worried Crispino.

"Oh it is my top woman, Annetta. She's complaining that Celia is now taking away all her business and she wants to be modified like her. Can we do her soon? I hate complaining women. I have six other women, who have agreed to tend to their needs, in the hope that one day they too can be similarly modified," Durante explained.

"Sure thing. Same procedure?"

"Well, nearly. Annetta wants to look more like the mermaids. Let's completely remove her arms. I told her that I didn't know if that was possible, but that I would check with the doctor. She's heard some of the men that take her out talking about having taken out the mermaids in the past. I think she's rather miffed about it."

"No problem. It's as easily done as Celia's arms. When should we do it?" he asked.

Thus began a twenty-year close association between the two men, to the utter dismay and envy of all the other high-end escort services in Po. Certain men traveled hundreds of miles just to "date" one of Durante's lovely women, each of whom by 1270 was quite wealthy. As they grew older, many of his original women chose to retire, but as always, Durante continued to "recruit" new, attractive young women, promising them great wealth, which now he could easily prove.

So it was that Fausto stumbled upon Metrio's Escorts. As soon as he entered the establishment, he knew it serviced only the very wealthy. The entrance room was plush. Thick red carpet, exotic tapestries, golden light fixtures, and the smell of polish on the chairs and couches — all suggested fine elegance. An older man in a very fancy grey suit stepped out to greet him. "Welcome to my humble escort service. I am Durante Metrio. How may I serve your exotic tastes in fine, luxurious, young women?" Durante saw what appeared to be a well-armed soldier. What with the barbarian's army throng swarming over the town, he knew eventually they would visit his establishment. Still, he held out hopes they would not ransack the place and violate his well-cared for women. Be pleasant to this fellow, he cautioned himself; don't provoke trouble, and it may not find you.

"Hello. Curious. I am the right arm of Lord Damiano Donatello, the Immortale Conquistatore Mortale, your new ruler. I would like to see what it is you offer for escorts, if I may," Fausto replied. He decided to use his best manners, for it seemed appropriate here. Sometimes he hated the rough, heavy-handed approach his friend often used with others.

"Ah, yes. I have only the very best in all of Po, indeed the best within a thousand miles. Each woman has been carefully selected and prepared to suit the needs and tastes of those who appreciate such exotic beauties. If you will step into the preview room, I will have the women present themselves for your inspection. I have five major categories of exotic women, from those who appear as the noblewomen of Po and all other coastal cities to the most exotic. All are most elegantly dressed and are trained to fully satisfy. This way."

He led Fausto into a much larger side room, where they took seats against a back wall. Open doorways were at the two side walls, forming a walkway for the women, who began to enter from the right of the men, walking over to the left doorway. As each smiling woman entered, she gave Fausto a flirting eye contact and a coy smile, before taking her place along the wall opposite the two men. Note, their smiles were invisible because of their golden lip plates. The first two women looked like the many elegantly dressed noblewomen

Fausto had seen around Po. All wore their very long hair nicely brushed out, draped down their backs, not tied up in a pair of braids. They wore fancy satin arm-fetter-gowns in colors matching their personal tastes, six inch, golden lip plates, long earrings resting on their upper chests, a pipe corset that gave them a strikingly tiny, fourteen inch waist line that highly accentuated their hips and bosoms, and of course black patent toe shoes. Fausto nodded to each; he'd seen women dressed like this before, but they were pretty, he admitted.

The next pair looked much the same as the first two women, but Fausto immediately took note. They were missing their lower arms and hands! Their upper arms were rather conical in shape, tiny at their ends. *Now this is most hopeful indeed!* He thought to himself, *just what Damiano could use!* After these two flirted with him and took their position next to the first pair, another pair moved slowly and carefully into the lineup, again making eye contact with Fausto and giving him a loving smile. They, however, had no arms at all!

Next, two similarly dressed mermaids came hopping in, smiling at Fausto as well. However, they did not wear the toe shoes that the others wore. Instead, their overly large foot wore a shiny black patent leather flat that allowed them to hop. Fausto smiled back, most impressed.

However, two more women entered and they totally shocked Fausto. While they wore shortened satin gowns, similar six inch, golden lip plates, long earrings that rested on their upper chests, and a pipe corset, they too had only their conical shaped upper arms. What so shocked Fausto was that their lower legs and feet were missing. Both women wore heavily padded leather cylinder-looking boots. They rather waddled across the floor on their two shortened legs, their never-cut hair dragging along the floor behind them. Their short arms wiggled about, helping them keep their precarious balance on their upper legs while walking. Both also smiled invisibly at Fausto and flirted with him with their eyes. Fausto swallowed hard. Here was the answer that he was seeking: a way for Damiano to have women and yet be totally certain they could never harm him!

Durante was watching Fausto's reaction to his exotic

women very carefully. I have him now, he thought, as he detected the look on his face as the last two women waddled in and took their place in the selection lineup. "I take it you are most pleased with my selections?" he said coyly, knowing Fausto definitely was.

"Yes, very much so. Lord Damiano Donatello, the Immortale Conquistatore Mortale, would greatly desire some of them, perhaps even to wed them. How is it that such lovely women have suffered such tragic accidents? Losing an arm is common for great warriors, but losing all four limbs? Such a tragedy they must have had."

"Oh no, no, none of my women have ever had an accident. Come with me into my office and I will explain over some of Po's finest ale," Durante suggested, motioning with his arm for the women to exit and return to their chambers. Fausto rose and followed him. Ale was just what he needed now.

Sipping ale, Durante explained, "You see, none of these women have ever felt any pain when getting their modifications. All desired them so they can make more money. I must admit they are all most wealthy women right now. I allow them to retire when they choose to do so. They have earned sufficient funds to support themselves. Of course, most have to have constant assistance with the needs of living. Here behind the scenes, I have two women who look after their needs, always."

"But how is this possible? They seem very happy and content, wholly unlike soldiers who lose and arm or leg in battle. My god, man — those men have horrible times adjusting to their new lives. I've seen many just give up and die. Yet these women, especially the last two, seem so content, so happy. How can this be?" Fausto asked, still somewhat dumbstruck with what he'd seen.

"Ah yes, we very carefully prepare them to feel this way. I agree with you, it is a delicate matter, especially so for the last two women. They are programmed to desire to be pleasured often and to give pleasure as well. Some of their clientele believe they are extremely sexy, and the women certainly *do* believe that of themselves. However, their behavior is a *delicate* matter. If they are put into positions where they are very helpless or feel that they are, all of this behavior modification begins to break down. In the past, I have had to ban a couple of men for life. They mistreated the women, causing them to feel they were helpless in some way. It took us many months to recover them and get them out of the depressions that you mentioned. So these women must be properly cared for at all times."

"Amazing. But how is it possible they felt no pain? Surely, the operations were very nasty and painful. Our wounded men take many months to heal from the loss of a limb in battle, if indeed they actually do recover and heal. Some die of infections," Fausto asked, growing more curious about the process.

"Ah, I guarantee you they felt no pain and were healed within just a few minutes. You see, you have the aliens on Plateau Grado to thank for that. We have one of their medical machines that we use. It took us a very long time to figure out how it works, but so far, we've only scratched the surface of what it can do. I'm told there are at least a hundred other things it can do, only we have no idea what those things are. Unfortunately, there are no aliens around here to teach us how to use their machines. Perhaps if your leader can conquer the world, he can force the aliens to teach us about their machines and how to use them. Now that would be something useful, wouldn't it?" Durante replied and asked, coyly planting the idea in Fausto's mind. Perhaps nothing would come of it, but on the off chance that these men did conquer the world, maybe they could get the aliens to educate his friend.

"Ah, the aliens again. I will mention this to my lord. However, I would like to bring Damiano here to see the women himself. If he is most pleased, I am sure that he would like to begin his own harem with some of them. Could that be arranged?" Fausto asked.

"Oh dear me," Durante replied. All along, he feared that something like this would happen to his business, when Po was overrun with the barbarians. Now it was happening. He chose his words carefully. "I would be most honored to supply our new lord with women for him to marry. As you may suspect, each woman has cost me a rather hefty sum to prepare her as she is now. While My Lord Damiano could just steal them from me, it would be more honorable of him to recompense me for them — say an amount he feels worthy of such elegant women. In addition, these women have their own savings. I would like his word he will allow them to keep their hard-earned savings. If at such time as he no longer desires them, I would request he do the honorable thing and allow them to depart. With their savings, they can continue to live well on their own. If My Lord would agree to these small matters, then I would be most gracious and speak most highly of his greatness and honor. Only make sure he understands he must never make the women feel completely helpless, as that may well break down their carefully prepared, loving behavior patterns. Here, I use other women to assist them, but it does not matter as long as the caretakers are kind, considerate, and are always there for the women when they need something."

Fausto smiled. He knew Damiano cared nothing for what wealth they might have. He would allow them to keep such. If and when he no longer desired them, they would likely be far from here, and no one would really know what happened to them, so that part really was totally moot. Caretakers would be the only obstacle. "I am sure My Lord will be most agreeable with your honorable requests. I will bring him to see the women shortly. About their caretakers, can you tell me a bit more what is required of them?"

Durante outlined the basic things that had to be done for the women, from brushing their hair to dressing and undressing them, to feeding them, to bathing them, and to even helping some use the bathrooms. After finishing the ale, Fausto thanked him and left to find Damiano. Meanwhile, Durante began preparing the women for the golden opportunity to become married to the man who was conquering the world.

An hour later, having told Damiano about the women, they were discussing the sole problem of their constant care givers. "We could hire an older woman to look after them," Fausto suggested. "We could make her sleep elsewhere than our huts at night."

"Yes, I like that better than having a eunuch around or an effeminate man," Damiano decided. "Keep her away from us, though. So are you also tempted by these women?"

"Indeed I am. I too fear being stabbed or poisoned while I am sleeping. Guards cannot protect us while we are sleeping with our women. Those I saw would be wholly incapable of harming us in any way whatsoever. Besides, it will play well with our soldiers to see us partaking of women as they do. Already there has been much talk about our abstinence from the plunders of the villages that we take," Fausto replied.

"Good, then it is settled. We will begin our harem today. Find us an appropriate transport for the women, regal I suppose, and find us that caretaker. When you are ready, I would like to see these delicacies for myself," he replied. He knew this had to be done, if only to keep up the morale of his men. It would not do for them to believe he was not a lover of women.

Fausto commandeered the sultan's large, ornate carriage with four horses to be the women's transport vehicle. He found a suitable older woman to care for them, Calvina, who was forty-five and widowed. She had been making a meager living as a dressmaker and was very pleased to be chosen to care for the elegant noblewomen of the conquering lord. That she was also not very bright was a benefit. Fausto sensed she would not have the brains to plot against them. Once these details were handled, the two men rode in the spacious carriage to Durante's store.

After introducing Damiano to Durante, the two men were given the formal lineup, just as Fausto had had some hours before. To say that Damiano was pleased with what he saw would be entirely too succinct. "Ah, absolutely *perfect* women, my good Durante! You are to be highly commended indeed!" he replied as his eyes gazed upon the full lineup. Each woman was highly attractive in her own way, not a homely face in the lot.

Out of politeness to the women, Durante led them into another room, pouring out more of his most expensive ale. "So which ones meet your criteria, My Lord? Or if you prefer, I could make some humble suggestions?"

"The armless women — are they able to perform well?" Fausto asked what he presumed was on Damiano's mind.

"They all do their very best to pleasure you, but just between us, those with their short arms actually do much better and are far less frustrated than the armless women," he answered from years of experience. "One has to be far more careful with the armless women so as not to upset them or allow them to feel frustrated they cannot perform well enough to suit you. Also they are better at keeping their balance with their short arms."

"I see. That makes sense. Could you allow My Lord and me a private moment to discuss our choices?" Fausto asked diplomatically. Damiano smiled; his friend always seemed to know just what he wanted without his having to vocalize it. Durante bowed and excused himself.

"So what do you think?" Fausto leered over his ale mug at his friend. "I'm game for one of the short armed women and perhaps one of the short legged women."

Damiano laughed, "We think alike. Same here, but I would also like the two mermaids as well. They are very rare, and it would be seemly for the world's conqueror to boast such unique women in his harem, don't you think?" Fausto agreed, and they chatted a bit before he went to the door to fetch Durante.

"Oh my, six of them!" Durante exclaimed, hearing their choices.

"Yes, I hope you will find this ample reward," Damiano said calmly, handing him a large pouch filled with gemstones pilfered from the sultan's palace. That he overpaid Durante tenfold for the women, he neither knew nor cared. He was obtaining women he could bed in complete safety. They could not harm him.

"Ah, most generous, My Lord! They are all very excited about becoming wedded to the men who are conquering the world. Shall I arrange for the marriage ceremony now? Also, you should be clear about their order. They will insist on knowing who is the Number One wife, who is Number Two, and so on. As you probably know, the Number One wife takes precedence over the other wives — the traditional pecking order among wives, you see."

Damiano chuckled. "Let's get this over with quickly. I am anxious to bed them." Durante grinned and left to summon a magistrate to perform the brief ceremony. He had already alerted the man to this possibility. Meanwhile the chosen women were brought before their prospective husbands and introduced to them.

Damiano was quite pleased to announce to his four women: "Ah, lovely Antonia, you will be my Number One wife." She bowed her head, extremely pleased to be his chosen one. She had both short arms and short legs. "Celia, you will be my Number Two wife." She too was pleased, she had short arms, and she giggled a little. Antonia was twenty-one and Celia, twenty-two, both quite beautiful women. "Ah my sisters. Elnora, you will be Number Three and your sister Gianna, Number Four, since Elnora is older." Both were mermaids and twenty-three and twenty-one, respectively. Both were also quite happy with having been chosen to be real wives and no long mere escorts for leering men.

Nearby, Fausto explained, "My dear Daniela, you will be my Number One wife and you, Gabriella will be Number Two." Both were quite pleased. Twenty year old Daniela had both short arms and legs, while twenty-one year old Gabriella had only short arms and walked carefully in her toe shoes.

After the brief ceremony, Durante sent some helpers to fetch the women's clothing and few personal things. Meanwhile, Damiano took him aside. "I know that we have just taken away a good deal of your escorts. Perhaps I can help you recover some. I know where you can find three young mermaids to replace Elnora and Gianna." Suddenly Durante was all ears and listened to him as he described the three sisters up in Campo. He thanked Damiano profusely.

Finally, with their arms around Antonia and Daniela, they began walking their new brides out to the waiting carriage. The two Number One wives beamed with pleasure. Fausto caught the four who were not chosen to be wedded watching. He overhead them saying, "Now we get our chance to be modified like them!" He wondered why women would so desire to have this done to themselves and concluded that he just did not understand women at all, but perhaps his two wives would soon educate him.

While they were occupied escorting the women out to the carriage, Durante chatted with their new caretaker, Calvina, and gave her a duty list of the usual things the women needed done, along with a daily schedule. The older woman was most appreciative of this, as she knew she had her work laid out for her with these elegant women. All were so very pretty, she thought, and such helpless, poor things.

A week later, Durante pulled his carriage to a halt near the oasis at Campo. He was directed to Beppe and his three angels. "I have a most wonderful offer to make," he began, outlining the elegance and great care that he was offering the trio, along with the promise that within a few years they would be wealthy enough to support themselves if they ever chose to live on their own. Beppe sighed, seeing this as the only way he could ensure his three angels had a worthwhile future, but he would miss them dearly.

Chapter 6 The Sacking of Teraspoli

March of 1271, Damiano gallantly led his revitalized army northward out of Po, heading up the coast towards his target of Teraspoli. He and two dozen of his men were now skilled with the new scything blades, though they had yet to be field tested in battle. He left fifty men in charge of Po. His army now numbered around fifteen hundred mounted men and about fifteen hundred foot soldiers, all armed. However, a good two thousand were conscripts, who wished they were elsewhere.

Over fifty had tried various ways to escape, but they had all been captured and executed before the entire army. Brutally so, Damiano had them drawn and quartered between four horses, showing the screaming men no mercy whatsoever. At this point in time, the conscripts were more afraid of Damiano's wrath than they were of going into battle.

Behind the mighty army, a host of supply wagons lumbered, along with an armed escort protecting the fancy carriage bearing the six wives and their caretaker. He left Po a ruined town, most stores and merchants had been ransacked. Anything of significant value was long ago confiscated and much sent off to towns and villages in Domei as payment for the services of their fighters. Only a few escaped the sacking, Durante had been one such person. Morale of his steppes men was quite high indeed, aided as well by their pleasure at seeing their leaders marrying and forming up a small harem of quite exotic young women. That minor worry had vanished from the two men's minds. Both found the women were extremely docile and most pleasureful. They looked forward to the evenings in their tents with them.

About a thousand miles of coastline, dotted with villages and towns, lay between them and Teraspoli, rich and ripe for the taking. Nearly every day brought them a minor skirmish with a small village or town. The scything blades proved highly effective on the battlefield. More often than not, the rapidly whirling blades severed the arms of their opponents long before they could reach those wielding them. As a result slowly, fear began to spread far in advance of the lumbering army.

A month later, they discovered the wealthier inhabitants of the towns and villages had fled their homes by sea. However, they didn't know whether they had relocated to Teraspoli or elsewhere. In Damiano's mind, it didn't matter in the slightest. Sooner or later, he would be arriving at whatever place they chose to resettle and take them out then. For now, his focus was on the objective: Teraspoli, home to twenty-five thousand, the largest city in his homeland of Domei and the home of Sultan Gino Gianpiero.

He sent a band of twenty-five scouts out ahead of him. Their objective: scout out the layout of Teraspoli and return with the data he needed to plan the assault effectively.

Sultan Gino knew he was in for major problems come spring. With the total destruction of most of his army and the critical loss of all of their weapons, while he still could call upon some five thousand able-bodied men, he could not arm them. True, he still had his five hundred strong palace guards, all well-armed. In the armory were enough weapons to arm perhaps a thousand, if they each only received a single blade. Going up against these proven fighters with only a dagger seemed foolish to the sultan. Worse, all of his experienced generals were gone now. Who would lead these fresh recruits?

Fortunately, the Renegade Circle kept in constant contact with him. "I need weapons to arm my recruits, I beg you, send weapons soon," he told Rafael.

"I will see if the sultan in Tecuci can send some up by sea," Rafael promised. "Plus, I will see if other cities in the south can spare some as well. Somehow, we'll get scimitars here. You get the men ready for combat." Instant communication across Tierra via the Renegade Tower and telepathy was the one aspect that Damiano could not defeat nor did he even take that into account in his planning.

Sultan Fausto Ferro of Tecuci was fifty-seven, but still fit. He kept his fingernails short, and he was a superb fighter and a master of strategy. Over twenty years ago, he and his ever-growing force of fighters had finally gained total control over the port city. He had a small harem of wives. Sonia was the eldest at forty-nine. Then came Susana, thirty-eight, and Rosetta, thirty-seven. Each wore the latest fashions, emulating their distant empress from many years past. That is, they wore the new arm-fetter-gowns, lip plates, long earrings, pipe corsets, and toe shoes. Sultan Fausto explained to his wives over dinner, "Sultan Gino is weak; he cannot even control his own lands and this upstart of a barbarian. This Damiano has gone too far, invading the Arad. I will have to retake Po from him, come spring."

"Surely you can stop the madman. I heard he cuts off men's arms using horses. How can this be? What kind of sadist is he?" asked Sonia, trying hard to speak as clearly as she could. Her lip plates made being understood rather difficult for her. Sounds made primarily by lips, such as "b" and "p" were indistinguishable.

"How does he do this?" he repeated what he thought she'd asked. She nodded. "I believe these barbarians tie ropes around each hand and leg and then tie the other ends to four horses. After stretching the victim out spread-eagle, they slap the horses' rears, and they try to gallop away, ripping arms and legs off. Most gruesome to watch. Barbaric," he answered.

"How awful. You must stop him, dear!" Sonia replied.

"Stop him?" he asked, she nodded. "Absolutely. But what of this Renegade Tower request that I send Gino weapons? Do I dare weaken our position by doing so? Ah, that is the fundamental question I must answer and soon, I fear."

"Would Gino come to our aid?" Sonia asked, saying it twice.

"Would he help us?" he asked, she nodded. "He has never helped us in anyway. However, Teraspoli is a member of our City-State Alliance. So I have an obligation to send him something. Politics again."

"Send him poor ones," Sonia suggested.

"Send him poor weapons?" he asked and she nodded. "Ah, brilliant Number One. Yes, I can send him those and be seen as coming to his aid. Perfect. Tomorrow I will order the armory searched, and all weapons not in good shape shall be sent by boat to Teraspoli. Thank you my love." She would have smiled, but with her lip plates, it wasn't visible any longer.

"But if he has taken Po, will he not come south after us?" Sonia asked, her mind thinking ahead of other possibilities.

"Come after us?" he asked and she nodded. "Hum, good point. He has taken Po, our second largest town. Twelve hundred miles to us and about a thousand to Teraspoli. Which way will he go? Sonia, you never cease to amaze me. You have a brilliant mind as well as a perfect body." Again, she smiled invisibly and his other two wives frowned, annoyed she was getting all of his attention and praise.

Not wanting to be left out entirely, Susana spoke up. "Even if this barbarian goes after Teraspoli in the spring, won't he come after us next?"

"Come after us next, Susana?" he asked. She nodded. "Why yes, if Sultan Gino fails to stop him and the barbarian captures Teraspoli, I should think we are next on his agenda, my dear. My, my, such wives that I have, both beautiful and wise." Now Susana smiled invisibly, having scored at least one point this evening. "Yes, I must also plan for that eventuality as well, but first, I must see to the retaking of Po."

A week later, via Rafael and the Renegade Circle, Sultan Fausto Ferro sent word to Sultan Gino in Teraspoli that he was sending along five hundred fifty scimitars. He also sent word he would see to the retaking of Po. Rafael thanked him for his response, though he also knew the scimitars were of poor quality. He sent word to his Circle members that he felt that Sultan Gino had no chance to save Teraspoli and that their best chance to stop this barbarian lay with Sultan Fausto of Tecuci, Arad. They should focus on getting him more support. This, neither sultan knew.

Yet even more subterfuge was at work. Up in Po, the Sisterhood had two guild houses and had some fifty women members. All had some fighter training, but only a few were equal to the soldiers. Hated or despised by both men and women of Po, they quietly stayed out of the battle for the town. However, during the ransacking of the town, in which the conquering soldiers looted most merchants who had anything of real value, they ran into trouble. At the first of their guild houses, a band of six soldiers came by pounding on the door.

The doorkeeper answered. "We are here to loot your building. Stand aside or be slain," the half-drunken man cried out. She slammed the door in his face and sounded the alarm.

"Men are not allowed in this guild house. This is a Sisterhood home, barbarian," the Guild Mother yelled out at the fuming men. "Go away. There is nothing for you to steal in here."

"Aye, we want to bed your women, if nothing else. To the victor goes the spoils," one yelled back at her. "Come on. Let's break the door down." They began smashing the wooden door of the adobe and wood building.

Inside, the twenty women gathered up their few belongings and their weapons, primarily short swords and daggers. Two women headed out the back to saddle up their few horses, while the better fighters took defensive positions in the entrance room, where visitors were sometimes met. Meanwhile, the other women fled out the back, heading swiftly through the streets for their second guild house.

The door soon splintered and the drunken men rushed inside, preparing to rape a whole bunch of women. The fighters reacted swiftly, downing three of the men before they realized they were in a fight. After another fell, the remaining two turned and fled, calling out for help. At once, the four uninjured fighters headed for the back door, making sure no woman was left behind. A half hour later, all had gathered at their second guild house, planning what to do next.

"Sooner or later these beasts are going to raid this house too," Gianna complained. She was the best fighter in the Po Sisterhood. "Are we going to make a stand or not?" Her face showed the steeled look of determination.

"But that will just get us all killed," Fina complained. She was one of their better cooks.

"Hey, I heard some of them talking about wintering over here in Po. They aren't going anywhere for at least six months," Gisella spoke up. She was another of their better fighters.

At last, one of their Guild Mothers, Clara, spoke up. "Sisters, please. This is a decision for your Guild Mothers. We have decided we are going to pack up and stay with our fellow Sisters in Tecuci. Let's get packing. Gisella, Gianna, you get our fighters prepared. We might have to fight our way out of Po." While several fighters grumbled about cow towing to these beasts, they obeyed her, but suggested they slip out after dark, if possible.

Thus, in mid-November, the Po Sisters joined up with the much larger Sisterhood in Tecuci. Not long after that, Sultan Fausto requested one of their members join his planning group, where the plans for retaking Po and defeating the barbarians were being discussed. Gianna from Po and Celia from Tecuci, the reputed two best fighters, became their representatives to the critical meeting. As the two women wearing men's apparel walked into the assemblage of advisors, generals, and other staff, all eyes drilled them. However, Sultan Fausto took the edge off immediately, "Welcome Sisters. Please have a seat and join us. I am most pleased that you and your fellow Sisters are willing to help in this critical situation. After the meeting, I would like a private word with you both, if I may. Now then, let's get down to business."

"Prime concern must be to give our people a chance to flee if we do not succeed," he began. Seeing many protesting what must seem to them a pessimistic attitude, he raised his hands to silence them. "I fully intend to win over these barbarians. However, I have my people to consider as well. If things go wrong, I want to give those who desire to flee a chance. Thus, we will not hold our army here in Tecuci and wait for the barbarians to surround our city. No, I will take the battle to them and on ground of my choosing. I propose to meet them, should they attempt to invade the Arad further, up near Po. If we win, we will drive them back into the steppes. If by some unthinkable chance we lose the battle, then they will be at least a thousand miles from here — give those that want to flee the opportunity to do so or to prepare and hide their valuables." That calmed the protests.

"According to the Sisterhood, right now, they are wintering over in Po — ransacking the town. Come spring, my guess is they will go after Teraspoli. Sultan Gino has already entirely lost the vast majority of his army to these barbarians.

That makes his city a relatively easy target. That's why I expect this Damiano fellow to go after them next. If he does, either he will leave a substantial force in Po or he will leave only a token. We will send out some spies to watch and see what develops there and take appropriate action."

"Also, generals, send out your best scouts. Find us the ideal battlefield on which to meet these barbarians. Give us the field advantage. Now then, if they leave a token force in Po, my guess is they will barracks up in the palace there. It's the most defensible structure in Po. Let us discuss the easiest ways to remove them." He turned their attention to this smaller matter.

Gianna of Po spoke up. "My Lord, if there are only a few left and if they are indeed holding up in the palace, then we can easily get them at night. We know the palace layout well."

"My Lord, you can't let these women retake Po. That is unseemly at best!" barked one of his generals. Gianna glared at him, as if her eyes could burn his flesh.

Sultan Fausto raised his hands again. "General, she has a point. She is from Po and knows the palace. We do not. Let's hear her out." Although fuming still, he ceased openly protesting. The discussions continued for several hours.

As the men filed out, Sultan Fausto motioned again for the two Sisterhood fighters to remain. When only the three remained, he closed the door. "Sisters, I am going to give your Sisterhood what may well be my last request. If by some chance of fate we lose the battle with these barbarians, I am hereby charging your Sisterhood to evacuate Tecuci and take my wives and younger children to safety along with a goodly portion of my personal treasury. Lead them overland through the desert on down to Adelmira Tower. There you are to hold up and see what progresses. If Tecuci falls, then my best guess is they will continue their southerly sweep on down to Turda, Alba. If they go that route and if Turda also falls, then I charge you to take them northwest to Northend and from there if things continue ill, all the way to Brom, if necessary. I will send along sufficient funds to cover your expenses and a handsome profit. Mind you, I will be sending my older sons and the main Arad treasury south by sailing ships in hopes they can raise an army to retake and free Tecuci. Will you speak with your Guild Mothers and let me know if the Sisterhood will accept this royal assignment?"

"Aye, My Lord, though we would greatly desire to help fight these barbarians. This is our homeland too, though many think ill of us. We live here too, but we will do as you ask and present your assignment to the Guild Mothers," Gianna replied. He thanked them and they left, grumbling about not having much of a chance to fight.

The Renegade Circle members kept in daily touch with their spies in Po. Thus, the two sultans knew the very day Damiano and his army marched out of Po, heading north towards Teraspoli. While Sultan Gino fumed and swore, he knew his forces were terribly weak and would likely not withstand this large an assault from the barbarians. Wisely, he shipped his wives, children, and their families, along with most of his treasury out of Teraspoli, sending them down to Tecuci for safekeeping.

In Tecuci, word came Damiano had left only fifty or so to guard Po. "Now we have them!" Sultan Fausto exclaimed and issued his many prepared orders. The Sisterhood fighters, some twenty strong, led a group of another fifty soldiers northwards towards Po. Their objective: retake Po by making a night attack on the palace where Damiano's guards now stayed. Much to the men's distaste and distrust, in unequivocal terms, their sultan placed Gianna in charge of the band. Riding hard, they reached Po three weeks later, far ahead of the main army, following slowly behind them.

Gianna halted them on the outskirts of Po, hidden behind a rise. "We wait here for dark — then slip into town. Eat up — might not get the chance til morning," she ordered. As always, the Sisters fixed their own food and kept apart from the men who distrusted or despised them. Thus far, Gianna had kept arguments between them at bay. If the men would just act civilized a bit longer, we can do this, she thought.

Twice before nightfall, she had to intervene, stopping a potential deadly fight. "But he started it," Melania complained bitterly. "You know I don't take that kind of insult from men!"

"Cool it, Melania. Remember, he's a man and hasn't a brain. I need you tonight when we go over the walls. Okay?" Gianna tried to cool her fighter down. She grumbled, but agreed, sheathing her short sword. Turning to the man, she added, "And you ought to know better. Save your blade for the barbarians in the palace." The man glared at her, but sheathed his scimitar and dagger.

No one was more relieved than Gianna when darkness fell. Though it was getting chilly, the air was moist from the sea off to their right. She divided the group into quarters. Each small group would enter the town from a different zone, meeting at the palace. If they encountered any of the barbarians on guard duty, they were at liberty to dispatch them. Gianna anticipated they would all be holding up in the defensible palace. This proved correct as the smaller groups merged a block from the palace, located in the center of Po, some distance from the docks.

A half hour of careful observation indicated only four men were watching the outer walls, one on each side, pacing slowly up and down its length. She ordered each group to take a side. Using grappling hooks, they climbed the eight-foot adobe walls, while the guard was further down that side. Within minutes, those four were dispatched. Stealthily, the Sisterhood fighters led their groups into prearranged sections of the palace. Within fifteen minutes, they had retaken the palace and with no casualties. Most of the men were asleep. Though the sounds of battle roused them, they were not dressed and had little chance against the determined fighters.

When they finished their work, a man slipped out of the shadows and reported to Gianna. It was Amo Rafael. "Excellent work, Gianna. I will report you have secured the palace and Po. Well done."

"Tell the sultan there were no casualties and that we will head back tomorrow," she replied. She hated to have only this small taste of the coming battles, but the Guild Mothers had accepted Sultan Fausto's assignment. Now it was up to her and several others to make darn sure no harm came to his wives and younger children. Regretfully, the next day she led her band of Sisterhood fighters back towards Tecuci, leaving the men in charge of Po. In a way, she was glad not to have to stay in Po. The town was ransacked; people were in desperate straits. At least Rafael was able to send word to the sultan that Po was desperate for food supplies. Only months later were Gianna and her fighters thankful for their current mission. They were still alive.

The first of June came. Damiano's army reached the outskirts of Teraspoli, the capital and port city of Domei. Many of the wiser noblemen had already fled, taking their families and wealth with them, much to the disgruntlement of Sultan Gino. He could hardly blame them; his reconstituted army was little more than a rag-tag bunch of fearful men, poorly armed for the most part. He too had sent his family off to Tecuci via the royal yacht, along with a good deal of his own personal wealth. He refused to allow his children to stay and fight, insisting they flee and use the funds to try to raise an army to retake Teraspoli, should he fail in holding it.

He looked out on his forces. They were arrayed as best he could devise. Surrounded by his five hundred palace guards, Sultan Gino rode out to the battlefield, prepared to defend his city at all costs. It would be at all costs. They passed by the last line of defensive men, armed with pitchforks and axes. He doubted very much if they would make much of a difference, still he would not deny them a chance at defending their homes, businesses, and families. Everyone knew of the total sacking of Po. Surely, the barbarians would do the same to Teraspoli.

Using the same tactics as before, Damiano led the first wave of his horsemen, five hundred in a long line. Ettore led the second wave of an equal number some fifty feet behind the first wave. The many foot soldiers were spread out encompassing the entire length of the enemy positions. They would rush forward after the horsemen and finish off the destroyed line, and then smash into the final line of men holding pitchforks and axes. That was the plan.

As Damiano led the charge, his twin scything blades whirling before him, controlling his horse with his legs. A dozen to either side also were using their scything blades as well. He spotted the strongest group, the mounted palace guards and Sultan Gino. He headed directly towards them.

"What new devilry is this?" Sultan Gino exclaimed, seeing the whirling blades coming at him and his men. "Damn them to hell, charge!" he ordered, kicking his horse into a canter.

Against the scything blades, he had no chance. They extended Damiano's reach by some eight feet before his lathered horse's head, far out of reach of the extended scimitar of Sultan Gino. The sultan felt a searing pain and watched in utter dismay as his right arm fell to the ground, severed just below his elbow. He never saw the other blade as it very nearly decapitated him, nor did he feel his body hit the ground, bones breaking and blood flowing.

To say this was a major battle would be an exaggeration. Against the superior forces of Damiano, the defenders had no chance. The first wave wiped out nearly half of the palace guards, while the second wave finished them as a fighting unit. After slamming into the wall of pitchforks and axes, Damiano pulled his cavalrymen back. Too many had received nasty puncture wounds. Instead, he watched while his larger force of foot soldiers slammed into them. An hour later, his men were going from body to body, either killing the wounded men or making sure the body was dead. Weapons were confiscated and his own wounded tended to. He too had a few puncture wounds and some cuts, but as before, he commanded his body to heal.

Later he joined his three friends as they were bandaging each other from their relatively minor wounds. All four chatted about just how effective the scything blades had been, laughing at how funny the sultan had looked when his arm was severed as Damiano attacked him. On the other hand, many of his conscripted solders were not laughing. Some had been killed and others severely wounded. Those that were given little chance of healing were simply "put out of their pain and misery," often by Damiano personally.

Later in the afternoon, Damiano gave the orders to sack the city. Again, his men eventually proportioned out the spoils, sending wagonloads back to their own villages. His conscription efforts in Teraspoli yielded only another hundred men, but even these were pushing it. Most of these were beyond their prime; plus he had to slay another five to convince them they had to become part of his army if they wanted to live.

After basking in the luxury of Gino's palace for two weeks, while his men finished sacking the city and having their fun with the women that they found, Damiano decided to leave a hundred fighters here to ensure law and order. However, to his surprise, another band of a hundred plus fighters from many different villages of the steppes arrived, seeking an audience with him. Because of his losses, Damiano consented and met with their spokesman.

"Oh Great Lord, permit us to join the fight to free our people. We have seen under your great leadership, it is indeed possible. Forgive us for ever doubting you," he began, pouring it on rather heavily. He well knew Damiano had threatened to kill those who tried to join up later on. To his great luck, Damiano agreed, but only because he needed replacements of some quality.

"Take your men and report to Lord Ettore. Soon we march on Tecuci. If you prove your mettle in that battle, you will then get your share of the riches of the Arad," he pronounced. The man backed out, bowing profusely and thanking him repeatedly. "We will see," Damiano muttered to himself.

Middle June, Damiano marched his army out of Teraspoli heading southwards, back towards Po and the mostly untouched Arad. Wisely for now, he ordered his men to ignore the many inland oasis scattered among the great sand dunes that comprised the vast majority of the Arad. "We make for Tecuci, down the coast, where the villages are many and riches await us," he explained. "Any word from our men in Po?"

Fausto answered, "None. Peculiar. They were under orders to keep up posted on a weekly basis. I've heard nothing since we left. Should I send a patrol out ahead of us to find out what those slouches are up to?"

"Aye, do it. I'll have their hides if they have been sitting around getting drunk," Damiano growled.

Seven weeks later, they arrived back at Po, recapturing the town without a fight. The patrol reported assassins had eliminated the entire garrison force not long after they had left for Teraspoli. However, his scouts reported Sultan Fausto had brought up an army from Tecuci and was preparing to meet them in battle.

While resting up in Po, Damiano sent out numerous scouting parties. Their goal was to locate the enemy army, their numbers, their deployment, and the terrain. As the news began returning, he and Fausto studied the few maps they'd found in Po.

Chapter 7 The Sacking of Tecuci

Some hundred miles south of Po, Sultan Fausto found just the right terrain for his coming battle. Here, steep cliffs made the beaches below them inaccessible. A group of low rolling hills to the west of the fertile valley would hide his cavalry, while his foot soldiers formed up battle lines across the valley. Once the barbarian committed his cavalry, charging his lines, he would lead his own cavalry down from behind the hills, striking the enemy from its rear, cutting through its foot soldiers before engaging the enemy cavalry. As long as the enemy didn't spot his cavalry, the plan was sound.

The second week of August, the enemy approached. As soon as his scouts reported sighting the army leaving Po, four members of the Renegade Circle joined Sultan Fausto. Rafael, his cousin, and two others remained close to the ruler, checking over his plans and working out what they could do to help stop this barbarian.

When Damiano and Fausto got the latest reports in from their advanced scouts, again, they went back to their sketchy maps. "I don't like this, Fausto. The sultan has his foot soldiers in ranks blocking us. We can't go around them on the coastal side, cliffs. What bothers me more is where is his cavalry? Surely, he has mounted men. He can't possibly think stationary lines will stop us. Is he that stupid?"

"Maybe so. There are not many horses in the Arad, I'm told," Fausto replied. He was only now beginning to feel his own lack of detailed information. He'd never been this far south in the Arad.

"He's a sultan, for crap's sake. He can't be this dumb, Fausto. He must have his cavalry hidden from us. Now where would I put them if I were him?" Damiano asked. He studied the map and then declared, "Ah ha. Fausto, I'd put them here in the western hills and out of sight. Allow us to swarm down the valley into his stationary lines, commit ourselves. Then, he comes charging down from the hills into our flank and rear and we are caught between the hammer and anvil this time.

Oh, this sultan is good, Fausto! But I am better!"

He studied the map once more. "Here's what we will do. Take half of our cavalry and go twenty miles inland or whatever the dunes dictate. Bring them around here to the back sides of the hills. I'll have our foot soldiers march towards his lines and follow them with the other half, but spread out in a long line perpendicular to the enemy's ranks ahead of us. Then, when the sultan comes charging out of the hills, we will merely turn and have a line of cavalry to face them. Meanwhile, you bring the other half up from behind. Then he will be caught in our trap instead. Once we've handled the cavalry, we can then circle around their lines and hit them from behind, providing some needed relief for our foot soldiers."

"What if there is no cavalry at all?" Fausto asked.

"Then you bring your cavalry around behind their lines while I reposition my half. Once we are both ready, we charge their lines from both directions. Again, we will have them between the hammer and anvil. Either way, Fausto, the field will be ours — another glorious victory!"

Lines of foot soldiers faced each other. The sultan's forces were dug in and ready. Some even had gone so far as to make long spears or pikes in an attempt to protect themselves from the charging horses. The long lines of Damiano's marched steadily towards the obviously prepared defensive lines. Only their terror of Damiano's wrath kept them moving forward towards their own deaths. Perhaps by some magic of Lord Damiano's they might be spared; so many had seen this happen before. "Not today" echoed through many minds, for their cavalry was not going to charge the lines like before. No, they were going to clash into them themselves. Many wondered why? Why wasn't he using his magical blades, hewing the lines down, breaking their morale so they would only have to mop up? Had Lord Damiano sensed their fear, their desire to flee and was now punishing them? Many such thoughts flooded the minds of the conscripts, forced against their will to fight.

Closer. Now they could see the steeled faces of their enemy ranks. More than one conscript looked about for any way to escape, but there was none. A steep cliff lay to their left and the long line of the cavalry lay to their right, almost as if Lord Damiano was doing this just to force them into the battle, giving them no choice but to fight and die. One conscript panicked, dropped his weapon, and fled back towards Po. Damiano signaled. One of his cavalrymen cantered after him and brought his scimitar down upon the young man's neck. He wheeled around and cantered back into the formation. Many saw this and decided to take their chances. Fleeing was certain death.

Just as they were almost within striking distance, the thunderous noise of galloping horses pulled all eyes to the right and the hills. Hundreds of the sultan's cavalrymen came charging downhill. At once, Damiano gave the signal and his long line turned ninety degrees, kicking their horses into a canter. For a minute, the advancing line of foot soldiers halted to see the action on their right. From atop the hill, three reined in, as if watching.

Damiano spotted Sultan Fausto leading the charge and moved to intercept him. As he approached, his scything blades whirling, controlling his galloping horse with his knees, the three on the hilltop acted. A giant ball of flames engulfed Damiano and several near him. Those around him screamed in terror and intense pain. Men and horses burned. Damiano cried out, "Body: heal!" Nevertheless, his horse went down and he hit the ground and rolled. Almost as if by some practiced move, he rolled up onto his feet. He shook off the fall and got his scything blades going just as Sultan Fausto neared, ready to strike a killing blow with his scimitar.

Now the long reach of his new weapon was tested. He let part of the chain go, the blade spun out further, connected with Sultan Fausto, slicing to the bone of his sword arm. His weapon fell from his hand. "What devilry is this?" he screamed. The next swirl of the scything blade severed his neck and he fell to the ground, dead before his body landed.

Steel upon steel echoed in Damiano's ears; defensively he continued to whirl his blade around him, forcing all to stay at least ten feet from him. "Just a bit longer," he said to the air. Then he heard the welcoming sound of more hooves. Fausto and the remainder of his cavalry came charging down from the hilltop from behind the enemy cavalry. He looked for the three horsemen who had used their magical fires upon him, but saw only three empty saddles. He presumed that Fausto had eliminated them. Only later did he learn that as Fausto came charging up from behind them, the three simply vanished from their horses.

Fausto made for the charred Damiano, bringing up a horse from a fallen cavalryman. Still in great pain, Damiano forced his aching body to mount. Just then Ettore took charge and ordered half of the cavalry on into the front lines of the sultan's defensive lines. Quickly, his foot soldiers raced after them, doing the cleanup work of the shattered lines. At Fausto's insistence, Damiano stood and watched his army doing its work.

An hour later, the blood bath was over. Casualties were high and this time, Damiano gave the surrendering soldiers one chance to join him or die. Hundreds chose to live, but of course, Damiano would never trust them. Nevertheless, he needed more soldiers of any kind. As his supply wagons rolled up, the wounded returned to them to get medical attention, including Damiano.

"My god man, how is it that you are not dead?" Fausto finally asked what he most wanted to know. He'd seen the *mentales* gifted on the hilltop casting their magic, but was unable to reach them in time to stop them. He'd seen a dozen cavalrymen around Damiano burned to death. Damiano was at the center of the fiery blast and yet Damiano still lived — burned and with his clothes charred. The other wounded now got a close look at their leader and their cries went up, "Immortale Conquistatore Mortale! Immortale Conquistatore Mortale! Immortale Conquistatore Mortale!" In response, Damiano punched his hand high in the air, causing even more cheering.

As the yelling subsided, he finally answered his friend, "Mere magic cannot kill me, Fausto. You should know that by now."

Several hours later, the three hundred of his wounded men were more or less patched up. Meanwhile, the others followed his usual protocol, going from body to body ensuring they were dead, and confiscating all weapons. As always, they just left the dead on the battlefield for the carrion birds. At Po and later at Teraspoli, women and older men, though sometimes children, came out onto the field looking for their men and carting bodies away for a proper burial. Here as at the valley pass, the carrion birds would provide cleanup in time.

Camp was made a mile further down the coast, where they found the supply wagons of the late sultan. Around the campfires, Fausto, Ettore, and a very wounded Luigi sat with Damiano, who had taken off his charred clothing and was mostly naked, allowing his flesh to heal. "So we are still eleven hundred miles from Tecuci. What now?" Ettore asked.

"With Sultan Fausto and his army gone, there is nothing standing in our way. Perfect. I want you, Ettore to take half our uninjured cavalry and a couple hundred foot soldiers and some supply wagons. Sweep through the Arad and liberate all the oases you can find. Conscript the able-bodied men as we have been doing. Meet up with us south of Tecuci close to the border with Alba. We will move forward slowly, giving the victorious men time to heal their wounds and time to sack the coastal villages along the way. We will sack Tecuci and bring many needed supplies with us to the rendezvous. We will take four months or so to get there, by my guess. Plan to meet mid-December. The new year will bring us yet another new country under our conquest. Oh yes — don't go near Adelmira Tower. Stay well away from those magicians, Ettore. Yes, we will eventually deal with them, but only after we control all the Easterlings. Then, we will simply starve them into submission. We can use them to help us counter the other towers when we get to them. Yes, by next year, we will be sweeping through the Midlands!"

A footnote to history: With the deaths and loss of so many able-bodied men, the Easterlings women had little choice but to give up their centuries old practice of bindings. Now their very survival depended in a large part on themselves. Damiano had inadvertently set the bound Easterlings women free, whereas to this point in time, only the wealthy had adopted some of their long dead empress's compromises. The full impact of this sudden change would not become apparent for some time yet.

However, in the fragile economy of the desert of Arad, this drastic change began to appear as Ettore swept through oasis after oasis, stealing supplies, horses, and younger men. Oasi Basso, a small village of a hundred adobe huts surrounding the life-giving pool, lay some hundred fifty miles west and a little north of Tecuci. Ettore and his small band struck here on the first of September. He divided his forces into ten smaller raiding parties, sending each of them up and into the heart of the Arad from ten different entry points down the length of the long coastline. Six of these had headed into the Arad north of his point, while three had ridden further south before heading into the heart of the desert kingdom.

His fifty men rode into Oasi Basso in the late afternoon, following a crude map that he'd forced a man in the previous oasis to draw up for him. The heat was still oppressive; dust covered the men's sweaty bodies. "How the hell can anyone live in this land?" he cursed angrily to his companions at least a dozen times this day. He noted the deeper they went into the Arad, the more oppressive the heat became.

Ettore was being successful, though. Already, he had conscripted thirty new men for his Lord's army, but only ten were able to ride. Horses were in short supply. Thus, he force-marched the other forty, making them keep pace with those on horseback. His guards mercilessly whipped any that slowed down. Once, his lone supply wagon bringing up the very rear rolled over and killed two men who had dropped from heat exhaustion. What did he care? These peasants would only serve as fodder in the next great battle at Turda in all likelihood. That could not come soon enough for Ettore, who was used to the frigid steppes, not this sweltering heat and endless sands.

Entering Oasi Basso, he made his usual speech, but only after taking a long drink of water from the cool, blue pool. As always, he heard bitter complaints and protests. "But you can't take all of our horses. Without them, I cannot bring in our monthly food supplies," their merchant Abramo complained.

"You are dooming the whole village to starvation." He ended that protest by slicing the man's head nearly off his head. He had to kill two other young men, before resistance to his conscription orders were obeyed. When he left the next morning taking three dozen of the young men of the village — that is all the able-bodied men, a goodly portion of their food, and all of their horses — many women shuffled outside their homes and began wailing.

Grief over the loss of their younger men and husbands, grief over the deaths of their sole merchant and the other men, grief over the loss of their precious food stores, grief over the loss of the horses which were their only way beyond the oasis, and grief over the obvious doom echoed loudly throughout the oasis. Andreina, the forty year old wife of the sole merchant, finally stopped crying. "What are we going to do now? We are all doomed. Do we lie down and wait for death to take us — wait as we all starve to death? We depended upon our men and horses. Now we are helpless."

Another woman, Allegra, spoke up, "In these skirts, we cannot even walk to Vento Oasis. Even if we could, the barbarians came from there, and Vento is likely as doomed as we are. I for one am going to throw off my bondage, tradition or no tradition. I can't live without my Alfredo to help me." Right there, she undid the chains holding her arms to her sides, tossing them onto the sands. "Women have had enough at the hands of these invaders. If our sultan has fallen, then there is no help coming either. I say we take back our oasis. There are only two guards left and they have two horses we must have for the supply wagon. Who is with me?"

Slowly, but surely, the other women followed suit, tossing their chains symbolically into the growing pile. Later, having slit their hobble skirts so they could walk far better, Andreina caught Allegra's attention. Whispering, she said, "Do you really want to get rid of those two guards and get their horses for us?"

"Absolutely. Without the horses, we don't have a chance. My food won't last a week. My children are going to starve to death. I will do what I have to do for my babes," she replied vehemently, spitting on the ground.

"I was hoping so. Come by my place near suppertime. I will let you take some supper to our two guards. Get them to eat it and we'll have our wish," Andreina whispered sinisterly. "I've been saving a little something back. Now is the time for its use."

Allegra frowned and then caught her meaning. Her frown changed to a coy smile, she agreed. That afternoon, Andreina whipped up a tasty stew and then added the black, flaky powder that she had hidden in a small pouch on the top shelf of her many cupboards. The dried scorpion venom mixed with dried viper venom might succeed, she thought. She'd gotten this small pouch from her mother, and her, from her mother. The story she'd been told was that it had been made by a true witch in ancient times. Now she intended to put it to good use.

Her late husband always took a trip into Tecuci each month, bringing back food and other supplies for the oasis. She stored them in her cupboards, doling them out to the villagers during the week. At least the soldiers had not found their secret stash of coins. With the guard's two horses, perhaps she could make that long trip to get supplies, if there were any to be had in Tecuci. Therein lay their last hope.

Right on time, Allegra arrived. "Here is the pot. Do *not* let anyone else eat from it. I am not sure how much they will need to eat, we'll just have to see, Allegra. Good luck."

"I'll flirt with the bastards if I have to — they'll eat it or else," she swore angrily. "How fast will it act? Do I need to get away quickly?"

"I've no idea. It is just something my great-great-grandmother prepared years and years ago. We'll see." She handed the pot to the twenty-three year old Allegra, who had a two-year old girl and a nine-month old little boy. Carefully, Allegra took the pot and left.

She found the two guards trying to bully their supper from another frantic woman who had barely enough to feed her three children. "Hey, here you guys go. Leave her alone. Can't you see that she cannot even feed her children? Are you all inhuman beasts? Here, stew from someone who has a bit to spare."

"Well, give it here. Does it taste good?" one replied gruffly.

"I don't know. I didn't taste it. If I did, I'd probably eat it all myself. As it is, I've barely enough to feed my own kids. Here," she handed him the pot. The two headed off to their small camp near the pool beneath the only shade in the oasis. She walked back to her own home, but paused to watch. Both had not eaten since breakfast, and they greedily cleaned the whole pot, tossing it aside. Allegra smiled and entered her own meager adobe to care for her two children, forgoing anything for herself for now. She'd tighten her own belt; her two children were all that mattered now.

She'd just finished feeding her two when she heard a commotion outside. She stuck her head out to see Andreina and several other women dragging the two dead guards out of the village. Another woman walked beside them carrying a shovel. Allegra smiled. "Beasts!"

Later, Andreina stopped by, saying, "Well done Allegra. They ate the whole pot. No more guards. I have their two horses now and their weapons. Tomorrow I will go in search of food supplies, but I will need some to help me. If I can get others to look after your two here, will you come with me and help protect our precious foods? I've gotten Bianca to agree to come along as well."

"Sure, I will do anything to help us survive now. When do we leave?" Allegra asked. "I can't believe that we did this! It is high time we women take control over life. Men have forsaken us and I won't stand for that — not any longer!" she declared vehemently. Her voice was resolute.

Meanwhile, news of the destruction of the Arad army and the death of Sultan Fausto was greeted with despair — none worse than in the sultan's large family. "Mom, we must follow his orders," Sonia's eldest son, twenty-nine year old Angelo commanded. "I would have given anything to have ridden at his side, but he would not have it. In us — we — Batrolo, Claudio and Basillio — we must do as he wanted — set sail for the southern lands and recruit an army to retake our beloved Arad. Mom, you and Suzana, Rosetta, and the younger ones have to go overland to near Adelmira. Stay out of the reach of this barbarian. We'll send word to you later — once we have an army ready to retake Arad. And no, Corrado, you are only thirteen. You go with your mom and protect your sisters too."

Corrado, who had been begging to go with his four older brothers, now pouted. Having to go with all the women seemed to him to be a fate worse than death.

Their second youngest sister, Arabella spoke up, "Angelo, we all know dad's orders. But think of Corrado will you? He will be the only male among us and the hundred Sisterhood fighters. He'll be humiliated. Besides, he's nearly fourteen and of age anyway. Don't do this to him, please, big brother." She stuck up for Corrado.

Eighteen year old Basilio added, "Angelo, she's right. You can't do this to him. Even though dad wanted him to be safe, surely he will be safe with the four of us." Hearing them all coming to his side at long last, Corrado looked at his tall brother, his fingers crossed.

Angelo conceded, "Okay, okay. Corrado, you can come with us. You are right sis; it would be unseemly for him to be the only male among the host of women. Still, I wish Corrado would go with them. Lord knows when they might just need a man around."

Corrado let out a huge sigh of relief. "Thanks. I won't be in the way. You'll see. I'll be packed in a minute."

An hour later, Angelo, Bartolo, Claudio, and their wives said farewell to their mothers. Their older sister Bettina chose to stay in Tecuci with her husband. Seventeen year old Claudio and then Basilio and Corrado hugged their mothers. The large group left the palace and got onto the royal yacht, setting sail with the high tide for the southern lands. They also brought along most all the Tecuci treasury. Sonia would be taking the substantial Ferro family treasure with her.

To go overland in the heat of the summer was not something to be taken lightly. Indeed, Guild Mother Clara came by to discuss this very thing, once she heard the others had finally set sail. "Look, I know you are all noblewomen, but there is no place for you in the desert — not dressed like you are. You will melt the first day out. Do you really want us to have to carry you into and out of the wagons? Those skirts will have to go."

Sonia sighed, "We figured as much, Clara." She spoke slowly and as clearly as she could, knowing that with her large lip plates, others simply could not understand her well. "We will try removing our corsets, but our backs are very weak."

"Okay, I will get you all proper desert dresses, white cotton, loose fitting, but please, no binding while we are on our journey. Frankly, most of we Sisters are sick and tired of such nonsense. Still, if you insist upon it, a few of us still hold to the old traditions. It will help if you can somehow strengthen you backs in the meantime. What about your shoes?"

Sonia sighed again. "We can't wear anything else."

"You can't wear regular sandals?" the top Sisterhood fighter, Celia, asked, though she knew darn well these noblewomen couldn't. They'd had their feet altered with the alien machines at the Elegant Fashions Inc store. Only twelve year old Elena had not yet undergone the transformations. Although she had begged more than once to have them done, her mother, Rosetta, kept telling her she had to wait until she turned fourteen, just like all of her older sisters had had to wait.

Elena spoke up, knowing how hard it was for others to understand her mothers. "Their feet will not go flat on the ground anymore. They have to wear the toe shoes or crawl on their knees. Maybe they can walk if someone will help support them. I will help Arabella walk." She looked enviously at her fifteen year old sister, who had had all the ornamentations and body modifications done last year. She also knew the misery Arabella felt for nearly a half year, until she got comfortable with her new look. On the other hand, she also saw all the young men who congregated around Arabella at the various celebrations and was envious of her older sister.

"Well, that much we can do. As long as you are not bound, not wearing tight corsets, and wear cool dresses, you should be all right. I will see to the dresses," Clara consented, knowing she'd gotten all the compromises she could hope to get from these noblewomen. In fact, it had gone better than she had hoped. Sonia and the others had been quite reasonable, she thought as she left them.

Still with all the packing and acquisitions, they were unable physically to depart for two more weeks. One wagon carried their treasury. One wagon carried all of their fancy gowns they would not put on until they arrived in civilization at the end of their long journey. The five women rode in a third wagon especially built for passengers. It had four vertical posts in the corners, which held up a thin, white covering to protect them from the sun's direct rays. In addition, coverings could be lowered down each side for further shade, if necessary.

The Sisterhood numbered a hundred women. Thus, they brought along four more supply wagons, including two water wagons. While they anticipated camping at oases along the way, in the Arad, one must never count upon that. Water was precious and life-giving here. The cooks and their helpers drove those wagons. The rest rode horses. Their first day of travel took them through the rather fertile lowlands here near the coast. The next day, they entered the high desert.

Months later, the mighty army of Damiano finally entered the capital city of Tecuci. By now, they'd sacked all the coastal villages between Po and Tecuci, sending back a good deal of riches to villages in the steppes of Domei. With a great enthusiasm, his swarm descended upon the helpless Tecuci, pillaging, raping, robbing, and even killing any who resisted. For two weeks, the capital was ravaged before Damiano led his forces on southwards down the coast towards the proposed meeting at the border of the Arad and Alba. His men conscripted nearly another thousand younger men, but were able to add only a few horses.

By mid-December, he and his army arrived at the meeting place. Here they camped, awaiting the arrival of Ettore and his raiding Arad forces. Damiano anticipated adding another thousand cavalry and foot soldiers to his already massive army. However, after waiting for two weeks without any word from Ettore, Damiano decided to press on southward. He left a small garrison of fifty men to await Ettore's arrival.

Just before they began marching southwestward, Damiano gave a short speech to his main leaders. "We can't wait any longer on Ettore. He will just have to catchup with us. He can eat our dirt for a change. We march on Turda next. Fausto and I expect we will arrive there around the first of March. From there mighty warriors, we will push into the lush, plush heartland of the Midlands! By this time next year, we will control all the Midlands as well! To victory!" They all cheered. Thus far, nothing had stood in the way of their mighty, invincible leader.

Chapter 8 Women's Rebellion

Gianna and her band of twenty fighters from Po took turns riding point with Celia and her band of twenty from Tecuci. After their first day of travel through the rather fertile lowlands near the coast, they learned bands of the barbarians had already passed through here. For unknown reasons, they had not stopped nor sacked these small coastal villages. The next day, the wives and daughters of the late sultan, along with around a hundred Sisterhood women, finally entered the sand dune covered desert of the High Arad and met the intense heat and dryness of the Arad.

By nightfall, they had reached the first, small oasis. Here they discovered just what the barbarians were doing. Sonia was appalled at what she heard. All the precious horses of the oasis were confiscated, along with much of their food supplies. That they also conscripted nearly every able-bodied man in the oasis so appalled her that she begged the Sisterhood to wipe out the two barbarian men left to guard the oasis. Gianna and Celia didn't have to be asked twice!

Though Sonia had to repeat it twice before the village elder fully understood her, she didn't back down. "The barbarians have not yet reached Tecuci. Take the two guards' horses, go to Tecuci, and purchase all the food that you need. As your Sultaness, I give you the funds and so order it." When the old man finally understood her properly, he thanked her profusely, promising to see that it was done as she asked.

"Is sultaness even a word?" asked Guild Mother Clara, very much impressed with Sonia's response to the brutality they'd just seen.

"I don't know, but I feel a responsibility for our people. Fausto is dead and our sons are away to the south trying to hire an army to retake our Arad," Sonia replied, several times until Clara grasped what she was saying.

The next evening, they pulled into a very confused Oasi Basso. Andreina, Allegra, and Bianca had intended to take the wagon to Tecuci to get precious food supplies, but they ran into a major problem. The wagon had broken down barely a mile from the oasis. It had taken all the boys and older men most of the day to get it fixed and back into operation. "Okay, we are delayed one day. Surely we can tighten our belts and hold out," Andreina explained to the whole village who had gathered to watch the old men fix the wagon. They all knew their lives now depended on this lone, old wagon. Just then, the large Sisterhood group rode slowly into their oasis, causing many to panic before they saw who this new group actually was.

"Hello. The Sisterhood requests to spend the night at your oasis," Gianna explained as she rode up and dismounted before the rapidly dispersing throng.

"Water is about all that we have. Can you spare some food?" Andreina spoke up before the elder men could.

"What's happened here?" Gianna asked, unwilling to commit their food reserves without asking the Guild Mothers first. She heard the same story as she'd heard from the survivors of the previous oasis. By then, the entire caravan had pulled into and around the central pool. With a Sisterhood woman on either side, the four women walked precariously up to the group of villagers. Several older men recognized Sultan Fausto's wives. Quickly word of their presence spread among the villages, accompanied by many whispers.

"Is it true the barbarians have killed our Sultan and destroyed the army?" someone called out from the crowd.

Sonia wanted to explain, but decided against it. Few would be able to understand her. "Gianna, please tell them about it," she asked twice until Gianna got what she was trying to say.

While the Sisterhood cooks began preparing their dinner and others tended the horses, the two fighters, Gianna and Celia, outlined in detail what all had been happening this past month. After hearing all this, Andreina, now the unofficial spokeswoman for Oasi Basso, told them again what happened here and what they had done to get these two horses back. "We are going to fight back somehow," she declared and many women, Allegra and Bianca among them, shouted their support. However, the older men merely shook their heads, resigned to their doom. What could mere women do against the barbarians? Nothing, they presumed.

Later around their wagons while eating their supper, Sonia reached a decision. "Look, honorable Guild Mothers, there has to be a total change of plans here."

"Mom, why don't I translate for you? That way you don't have to say things two or three times," Elena volunteered, seeing a way that she could be helpful too. Sonia grinned, but it was, of course, invisible. She nodded and Elena quickly repeated what she'd just said. All four Guild Mothers looked up startled.

Via Elena, Sonia continued, "We cannot simply pass on through our lands here and ignore the horrific plight of all of our remaining people. We simply cannot. I know Fausto would not do so either. I know we women have not real power, but under the circumstance, it is high time we did! Change of plans is in order. From what we've seen, the barbarians are systematically going through the Arad taking over and nearly destroying every oasis. We are perhaps a few days behind them. If we do nothing, everyone in every oasis is doomed! I will not stand by while our people starve to death! I can't live with myself if I did that. So a change of plans is needed."

"We need to do three things right away. First, send out scouts to see just how wide spread the destruction of the invaders has been. Second, send many back into Tecuci before the arrival of the barbarian army. I will give you the funds to purchase many wagons and all the supplies you can find. Bring them here into the desert to be divided up among the oases that have been ransacked. Third, teach us to fight. I want to retake all the desert oases back from these beastly men. While we might not be able to drive them from our coastal lands, here in the desert, we have the advantage — that is you do. You know the desert and how to survive here, the barbarians do not." Sonia finished up but felt the need to add, "I know I am breaking all of our women's traditions, but our men have failed us. It is up to us women to take back our land."

"But Your Highness," Clara used her formal title, "Sultan Fausto expressly ordered us to take you to a palace of safety." She could not believe what she was hearing from this noblewoman. It was totally out of place — totally the opposite of any anticipated reaction. Her reaction and requests were more like those that she would have made if she were in charge. Were these exotic beauties more like her and her Sisterhood women than she had ever suspected?

"He didn't know what we would find out here in our lands. We must be flexible and change when the situation demands it," Sonia replied. Suzana and Rosetta began clapping and soon the whole throng of Sisterhood women joined in, followed by the women of the oasis as well.

"You are more like us than I ever imagined, Sonia. So be it then. We change our plans. However, I must insist on keeping you royalty safe from harm. You cannot fight if you cannot stand on your own feet without help," Guild Mother Clara declared, after seeing the nods from her other three Guild Mothers.

"Teach us to fight too," Allegra spoke up as well. "I know our arms don't work quite right, but we want to help as well." Clara was fully aware of just what Allegra meant by this. A woman's shoulders froze up the longer she was bound. After some twenty or so years of constant binding, most women's shoulders had calcified, and they simply could not move their upper arms at their shoulders much at all, at least at their shoulders. Further, their upper arms were incredibly weak from virtually no exercise at all. Allegra was still rather young, so there was perhaps some hope for her.

"We will do as we can, but we Sisters fight with short swords or daggers. We do not have the strength to wield the men's scimitars. We have scant weapons to spare, Allegra, but we will see what can be done," Clara countered. She then said, "Okay, Gianna, Gisella, Celia, Melania, gather up your best trackers and scouts. We should hold a planning session now so we can get started early in the morning." All four grinned.

Now this is more like it, Gianna thought, signaling her key Sisters. Interesting that the older men have been totally silent, she mused, just like men.

The next day, Gianna accompanied by her expert guide, Melania, led twenty fighters off to begin visiting some of the other nearby oases of the Arad. Celia led another group of twenty accompanied by Andreina, back to Tecuci. In their saddlebags, they carried around ten thousand worth of coins and gems with which to purchase all the food supplies, wagons, and horses they could find, but before the barbarian army arrived to sack Tecuci. Gisella and the remaining sixty began to train the volunteer women. At best, she hoped to be able to teach them to dodge the blows of the men.

Elena volunteered at once. "Look, my arms move perfectly still." Though she was only thirteen, Gisella accepted her, while Arabella sat back watching her younger sister. Tears streaked her face, and in her toe shoes, she couldn't stand on this rough, soft ground without someone holding on to her, ignoring the difficulties her lip plates and long earrings also presented.

At once, Gisella saw the problem the women's shoulders created. Hastily, she began separating out those whose arms were still fairly normal. Elena's group then had some twenty younger women in it. The second group still had some motion available to them, at least partially. The third group, that is, the vast majority of the older women, could barely more their arms at their shoulders, if at all. She knew that this third group simply could not fight, but had not the heart to tell them directly so.

Gisella divided her fellow Sisters into two groups, putting the third group off for now. She took charge of the young group, knowing they could be trained, given enough time and the weapons. Thus began a day of awkward falls and bruises for many women, as they began to learn to defend themselves, at least a little bit. As the older women watched, they quickly realized that although they wanted to fight back too, their bodies would not be able to do so, not like this. Of course, Sonia, Susana, and Rosetta were also in this third group, if they could somehow manage even to walk on their own.

Late in the day, Sonia saw all the crestfallen looks on these women and suggested, "Some of us will just have to help fight back in other ways. I can't move my arms much either." After repeating it a couple of times, they caught her meaning.

"So what are we to do to help?" one older woman asked,

very much disappointed.

"We help as we can. Someone can fix their meals for them, tend to their children's needs, and freeing them to be able to fight. That's a start at least," Sonia answered several times until they grasped what she was saying.

"True. Allegra does have two young ones that will need constant attending. I see what you mean. We help them so they are able to fight," the woman began seeing a path by which she too could help.

At the end of the day, Rosetta was quite proud of her youngest. Elena took her knocks and continued to try her best to learn to defend herself. As the sultan's youngest wife, Rosetta was always Number Three, but now the shy, quiet woman found her daughter to be all that she could not and secretly vowed never to allow her to undergo the body modifications she had. Rosetta felt rather helpless. Sonia had the brains. All she had was her good looks. Suzana was in a similar position; Sultan Fausto had married her for her beauty and youth. Now, that was all that she had to offer.

Meanwhile, Sonia put her lower arm around Arabella, who could not hide her grief at being left out of the action. She whispered, "Your time will come, my beautiful Arabella. Just remember how badly you wanted to look like me last year. Now we have to live with our decisions. I know it's so hard for you just now." Arabella desperately wanted lay her head in her mother's lap and cry, but her lip plates prevented it, and besides, it would look girlish, for she was a young woman now.

Just after dinner, Gisella found the royal family gathered around their wagon. "Elena, you were good today. I hope your body isn't hurting too badly." Elena smiled and said it wasn't that bad. Gisella then hesitated a bit.

"Something on your mind?" Sonia probed, but Elena quickly interpreted for Gisella's benefit.

Gisella flushed a little, "Well, I know it's none of my business, but I have heard up in Brom, they can somehow repair your lips so you don't have to wear those gold plates and they can partially repair your feet. Some say they still have to wear high heels though. Perhaps you might think about this."

"Thank you, Gisella. Do you suppose that it is true?"

Sonia asked with Elena translating. Arabella looked up and paid close attention.

"That is what I have heard. Of course, I can't say positively one way or another, but I can try to find out more if we get to civilization one day," Gisella volunteered. Sonia thanked her and asked her to try, knowing that would give Arabella and the others some choices which they currently didn't have.

The next day, Gianna's riders began returning with news. The next nearest oases had been raided and were in the same dire straits as Oasi Basso, most disheartening. Nevertheless, Sonia had expected this report. Each rider also reported, one way or another, they had dispatched the two guards Ettore had left behind to keep the oasis secured. Embolden by what they were doing here, Sonia wrote out a dispatch, outlining that she and the women of the oases and the Sisterhood were now reclaiming the desert lands. Further, she promised them food supplies as soon as they could get them. She also suggested to survive, the women must cast off their ancient traditions of binding. Further, those who wished to learn to defend themselves and fight back should find a way to get to Oasi Basso. She then had the returning riders take her message back and deliver it to each of the desperate oasis villages. I have to give them news and some hope, she explained to the Guild Mothers, who seemed very pleased with her.

The two moons rose over the star-filled skies, casting a pale blue glow mixed with a pale orange hue over the still waters. Allegra came up to the royal women, bearing a crude tray, cups, and spoons. "I brought you some hot herbal tea, My Ladies. It might help you to sleep. I brought spoons." She sat the tray down before them.

"Thank you," Sonia said slowly and as clearly as possible. "Join us?"

"Thank you. My babies are sleeping now. Okay." Allegra sat down beside them. "You know, you three and Andreina are very brave women. You've both just lost your husbands. I'll probably never see mine again. I don't know how you can bear it. I'm so lost without mine."

Speaking slowly, Sonia replied with a sigh, "Yes, our grief is very raw, Allegra. Yet, we have been fortunate to have been spared seeing Fausto killed on the battlefield. That is good, I think."

"Yes," Allegra agreed, "Poor Andreina is not so lucky. She watched her husband of thirty years murdered before her own eyes. You know, I've been thinking. When they took my husband away from me, I just wanted to kill them all. You know — *think* them dead somehow. I just knew if I could think the right thought, then I could kill them all. Silly of me isn't it? It was more than just wishing they were dead. I've done that sometimes when I get mad. But this was different. I had the notion I could will them dead."

"Not silly, Allegra. Yes, we miss our Fausto very much, just as Andreina must be missing her husband too," Sonia replied still going slowly so Allegra could make out her words, she hoped so anyway. Elena had already fallen asleep; she was worn out from all the fighting practice.

"Do you think some of the magicians in Adelmira Tower can do that? I mean kill a man just by thinking him dead?" Allegra asked.

Sonia smiled, but it was invisible. "If I had that ability, I am afraid too many men would die." After Allegra grasped what she said, she laughed along with the other three wives.

"But I don't see what is so funny," Arabella interrupted. "If I could think a man dead, I could help retake our Arad back." She was quite serious.

Sonia smiled again, but Arabella could not see it. "Dear, if we could do that, why, we would be a goddess or something. I don't think I would want such a power unless I could also wish a man back alive if I made a mistake. Think about it, dear. Suppose in your anger, you wished a man dead only to find out later he was a kind, loving father, a kind man who never harmed anyone. All of us at some time or other gets mad and does something we later regret having done. That isolated action does not deserve death. No, I could not live with myself if I made such a mistake. I think it best we do not have goddess powers, dear. I know I sometimes make mistakes."

Allegra whispered, "You are most wise, My Lady, I had

not thought of that. What if I made a mistake and wished the wrong man dead? Still, when they were taking my husband away, I really did wish I could kill them all just by thinking it so. Now I am no longer bound, maybe I can learn to fight well enough to try, but maybe not, since my arms can't move as well as Elena's can. I'm in the second group. We have been exercising our arms, but my shoulders really do hurt when I move my upper arms too much. Still, I can move much more than poor Andreina can. She can't move them much at all. I do see your point, My Lady. You are the wisest woman I have ever known."

Sonia smiled again, but only she knew she was doing so. "You are too kind, dear Allegra. You too are wise. Was it not you who first threw off your yoke of bondage?"

"Well yes, but I was thinking of my babes and how we could possibly survive with him gone now," Allegra admitted.

"So are we all, Allegra," Sonia replied. "You know, it is we women who carry the new life within our bellies, we who endure bringing forth the new life. We do our best to raise our children into adulthood, teaching them the best that we can. We truly nurture life. Yet we, too, are prone to making mistakes or errors in judgment. For my own part, perhaps I ought to have insisted Arabella wait another two years before she got all of her body modifications to be like we three."

"It must be awful to be as bound as you are," Allegra suggested.

"Not really, Allegra," Sonia admitted. "Fausto and we three had nearly thirty years of great pleasure and enjoyment from each other. While now it is most debilitating, I would not have changed it. We have such fond, loving memories. However, Arabella does not. She was most happy and pleased to look like we noblewomen of Tecuci, but she only has such a short memory of the good times. Like all of us now, she has no prospects for a kind, loving husband."

At the mention of boyfriends, Arabella roused. "Yes mom, I did too. Drago Mondo. But he is fleeing with his family."

Sonia explained, "Well, yes, Drago is her age, fifteen, and the younger son of Lord Mondo, a wealthy nobleman in

Tecuci. He made his fortune as a merchant — one of those far-seeing men who leapt at the opportunities the Renegade Tower and their City-States Alliance offered to Tecuci, when they brought in those strange priestesses, the mermaids. I am sure her young boyfriend is now safely at sea. If not, he will be conscripted into the barbarian's army and probably be killed."

Arabella fought back tears. Drago was cute, handsome in fact, something of a musician. Like his father, he had the knack of seeing what might become valuable in time. Real wheat from the breadbasket lands of the Midlands was one such commodity. Before the alliance came, such was almost unknown in the Easterlings. Now wheat was in great demand, and the Mondo clan had made a fortune in its trade. Drago's knack was for music and dance tunes. Several songs he either composed or brought here from the Westerlings had already begun to catch on — especially something called a Fandango Dance from some place called Malaca. Alone in the desert, Arabella greatly longed for his cheerful face and the sound of his guitars and lutes. Staring at the star-filled sky, she wondered where he was now. Perhaps looking at the same sky from the deck of some ship at sea, she thought. If only he stayed safe — she wished with all her heart.

As the small group sat there and the bonfire's red coals flickered, a pale yellow light appeared, catching their attention. Slowly it grew in brightness and the form of a young woman appeared within it. Thin, gauze-like robes appeared over her shapely form. Lysandra, the Goddess of Life and of Death, appeared once more to some human females of her beloved Tierra. Sonia, Suzana, Rosetta, Arabella, and Allegra blinked and rubbed their eyes, hardly daring to believe what they were seeing. Had there been something awful in that herbal tea?

Many other Sisters saw the yellow glow enveloping the small group, but all they could do was watch in awe. Lysandra appeared to be speaking, but in fact, her words were heard only in the minds of the five women.

"I am Lysandra, Goddess of Life and Death. Hard times have come for all women of the Easterlings and perhaps even the Midlands. Men have once again lost control of themselves and are threatening to destroy all the Easterlings and perhaps even more. Sonia — " (Each woman heard her own name here.) "You are on a good path. Continue walking it. Though it may be a difficult one, you will have my blessing. Tonight, I have heard your discussion and come with an offer for you."

"I will bestow upon you the power to think a man dead and have it so. You merely say 'I wish this man dead.' If you are able to see that man, it will be so. However, there is one man upon whom this will not work and that is the leader of the barbarians, Damiano Donatello, who calls himself the Immortale Conquistatore Mortale. He cannot be slain by anyone of Tierra. With my gift, you can use it to retake your lands." She paused to allow the magnitude of her offer to sink into their minds.

"Of course, for my invaluable assistance, there is a price you must pay. If I give you this god-like power, I will take your hands in trade. Sonia, will you accept my gift, my trade?" Again, each woman heard her name spoken, as if Lysandra was speaking solely to her.

Sonia did not hesitate. "No, your price is too steep. I am a mere mortal, a human. I know I have made mistakes, errors of judgment. I could not accept such power unless you tempered it by giving me the power to bring the dead back to life. I can error. If I will a man to death wrongly, I must be able to bring him back to life. Can you also give me that? No, I thought not," Sonia declared. "I do appreciate your blessings. I will continue on the path before me, freeing women from their bondage. Perhaps it is time for Easterlings women to rule and not our men who have failed us."

"Wise is Sonia Ferro. Continue on your path with my blessings," Lysandra replied.

Suzana Ferro replied, "Alas, I would have taken your offer, Goddess Lysandra, except the only man I would wish dead is the only exception, this leader of the barbarians, this Damiano fellow. Strike off the head of the viper and the snake dies. Chop off its tail and it still can strike you. No thank you, my goddess."

"Wise is Suzana Ferro. Continue with my blessings," Lysandra replied.

Rosetta Ferro replied, "Your offer is most tempting, my goddess. Thus far, I have not seen any men I would truly wish dead. I am too weak to face this the Immortale Conquistatore Mortale fellow who is destroying our world. My fear of his wrath is too great. And you have said your gift would not work on him, so I can see no point in accepting your gift. I am not a fighter; I do not seek conflict with men. I am but a mere woman who has spent her life pleasing her husband, and bearing and raising our children. I will put my faith in our sons to bring back order to the Arad. I know little of ruling and of such decisions of life and death, nor do I wish to learn such things, my goddess. I am a woman and wish for nothing more. Well, I do wish I may be fortunate enough to find another man as kind, as loving, as gentle as our Fausto Ferro," she admitted.

"Wise woman is Rosetta Ferro. Continue walking your path with my blessings," Lysandra replied.

Arabella was visibly torn. "Are you saying, if I would think to myself, 'I wish that man dead,' and if I was actually seeing him, then he would die right there? He would be stopped in his tracks, before he could do even more killing and harm?"

"Yes, my lovely Arabella. Once you complete the full thought, the man would be instantly dead."

"Goddess Lysandra, I truly do want to do my part to help our women, our people, but I have been foolish and gotten all of these attractive body modifications. Now I can't learn to fight, like my little sister. I feel so utterly left out of everything, so helpless to do anything useful. I want to help them, everyone, but I can't."

"Yes, but did you not want to look like your mothers, like the other noblewomen of Tecuci?"

Arabella sighed, "Well, yes I did. I know, I begged and begged mom to let me get these ornaments. That is true, but now they are preventing me from doing anything useful to help. I am not wise like mom is. Everyone respects her opinions on everything. I so wanted to be like mom, but now I know she is wise and I am not. Would you really remove my hands if I accept your gift?"

"Yes, that is the price you must pay for this god-like power, this precious gift which would enable you to do your part in freeing your people," she replied.

"Would it hurt? The body modifications didn't really hurt. They were very hard to get used to afterwards, but I didn't feel any pain," she asked timidly.

"No, you would feel no pain, not even a tingle," Lysandra answered her.

"But I need so much help now. Could I even be able to live without my hands? Wouldn't I be even more helpless without them?" she asked, trying hard to think it through. "Mom did say we could make a mistake and wish the wrong man dead. Is that so? I would feel awful if I did that."

"Yes, that is so. If you act hastily and without observing directly yourself, you could make a mistake and wish the wrong man dead. You must learn to be wise and keep your own council. Others may lie to you, seeking their own ends. That is true. In part, that is why you must be able to see the man you wish to be dead. Yes, this is an awesome power, not to be taken lightly or flippantly. Children often get into minor scrapes and wish their opponent was dead only to consider them their best friends the next day. So yes, Arabella, you must be wise, observe, listen, gather all the evidence firsthand, and then make your decision about his life."

"So some could be rehabilitated if given a chance?" she asked.

"Certainly so. The poor conscripted men, who have been forced to go along with it, will gladly run away, given the first opportunity to do so. The barbarian knows this and keeps them under tight control. This means you must be wise in your decisions, Arabella."

"Okay, it makes sense. Oh, could I even be able to live without my hands? Wouldn't I be even more helpless without them?" she asked again.

"Of course you would be able to live without them. Hands are not necessary to keep a body alive, as you know. Yet, you would be more physically handicapped without them; there is no question of that. With such power must come physical restraints, you see. You have to temper your awesome power with restraints. That is what is so horribly wrong with Damiano Donatello, the Immortale Conquistatore Mortale. He has awesome powers, but he lacks any physical restraints upon their use. He does what he wants and feels no consequences of his actions. In this world, there are always consequences for one's actions. He has yet to learn this."

"Will he? I mean will he ever learn it?" Arabella asked, growing curious.

"Such is my goal, Arabella. Now how about my offer? Will you accept my gift so you may aid the others?"

"Okay, I will accept your offer. I want to help, and, as I am now, I can see no way to be anything but a burden," Arabella replied.

"You are wise, Arabella. Use your gift wisely and you will not regret your choice. Use it wrongly and you will rue this night," Lysandra replied.

At the same time, Allegra replied, "Me? You are offering this to me? I am a nobody, a simple mother of two young babes here in this remote oasis. Surely you are teasing me, goddess."

"I am offering you a chance to make a difference in your world, Allegra. I know how badly you want to fight back against these barbarians, who have so horribly affected your life and those of everyone here in the Arad desert. I am offering you a way to fight back, to help save other's lives, and to protect your babies from future harm. We both know your arms will never truly return to what they were when you were a little girl. Perhaps in the past, the continual bondage of the Easterlings women was a good thing. Now however, it is going to be your undoing, unless somehow you women can fight back. I am offering you a way to do just that."

"But, without my hands, how will I be able to care for my babies? I would be so helpless," Allegra protested. While the power would be more than she imagined she would ever be able to wield, the physical restraint to everyday life seemed huge.

"Ah, the women you call mermaids have managed and so have many other afflicted women. It can be done, but yes, it will be hard on you. With such immense power, there must be some physical restraints upon its use," Lysandra countered.

"Yes, I can see that. But what if I make a mistake? My Lady Sonia just warned me about that."

"That is why you must see your victim. Observe, my Allegra, see for yourself whether this man deserves to get another chance at life or deserves to die and try again. Be your own council, do not let others influence you in your decisions," Lysandra counseled her.

"Yes, that makes sense. See for myself. Hey, what do you mean by try again?" she asked, suddenly duplicating her meaning.

Lysandra did not answer her directly. Instead, Allegra suddenly saw some distant memories of a man apparently being burned at the stake along with several others. Although his clothes burned away, he was not harmed, and he walked away, joining a group of other men, who left the town and headed to the north. Memories jumped. She saw him arriving in some tall mountains and there watched, as the men built what could only be described as some kind of monastery or religious building. When the memories faded, Lysandra said, "When this is finished, seek those in Brom for more answers. Will you accept my gift?"

"Was that me? Okay, I will accept your gift. We must fight to take back our world from these evil men before all is lost forever. I want very much to do my part, but with my arms as they are, I cannot. With your gift, I can help everyone retake our villages. I hope that I am making the right choice, Lysandra."

"You are wise, Allegra. Use my gift wisely to make the Arad safe for women to raise their children once more," Lysandra replied.

The observers saw a bright flash of yellow light and then it faded away. Slowly the pale dual moonlight returned, along with the star-filled sky and the twinkling of the red embers of their cooking fire. "My god! We've been visited by the Goddess Lysandra!" Sonia finally found her voice and looked quickly at the others sitting around her. Nearby, the many Sisterhood women, who had also witnessed this appearance of Lysandra, the Goddess of Life and of Death, roused from their stunned awe and looked at each other and the five before whom the goddess had appeared.

"My god! Arabella! You didn't, did you?" Sonia exclaimed as her eyes saw Arabella's empty arms. Her hands had completely vanished, as had Allegra's.

"Allegra too!" Suzana exclaimed, very much surprised and shocked.

"I want to fight and do my part too, mom. Now I can. Oh, Allegra, you did too," Arabella said defiantly, then noticing Allegra.

"She has given me the power to strike back and help too," Allegra whispered, somewhat in shock over what she'd just done. "I can kill a man just by wishing he were dead. Now I can help free us from these barbarians. Only I am going to have to see the men to do this."

"Me too, mom. Just by thinking it, I can end the life of evil, wicked men, but not their awful leader. I don't know why that is though, but now I can help too," Arabella added.

Sonia was speechless. Guild Mother Clara whispered, "Sonia, that was the Goddess Lysandra, was it not? What has happened to Arabella and Allegra? What do they mean they can kill the barbarians? Now they cannot even hold a weapon and are totally helpless women. I don't understand. None of us do."

Sonia sighed. "Allegro, perhaps you can explain this. It is so hard for them to understand me," she said slowly and carefully.

"You want me to tell them?" Allegro repeated, making sure that she understood her. Sonia nodded, and Allegro began reciting what the goddess had told her.

When Allegro finished, Clara exclaimed, "The Goddess Lysandra is on our side! Now we cannot fail. Allegro, Arabella, I will see that someone is assigned to be your personal assistants and someone to help you with your two children, Allegro. Now we do not have always to risk the lives of our brave fighters. This is truly a miracle! Truly!" Many echoed her sentiments, and the word quickly spread throughout the village. Many, who were already sleeping, woke up and came out just to look at the two women to see for themselves.

Sonia, still upset over Arabella's choice, spoke up. "Arabella, Allegra, please, please, be extremely careful with your gifts. Do not act in haste. When you kill someone, if you have made a mistake, they cannot be brought back to life. I have made many mistakes in my forty-nine years. Please promise me you will be extremely careful."

"Sure mom. We have to see the man in order to wish him dead. Observe, that's what she said," Arabella explained.

"And *not* listen to what others say. Look for ourselves," Allegro added. "Thanks, Guild Mother Clara. I will need lots of help with my two babies, but now I can truly help make a difference!"

Everyone was just too excited to head to bed. The large group sat chatting for another hour before turning in. As promised, two Sisterhood women helped Allegra and Arabella. In the morning, Clara promised better arrangements for these two blessed women. She and Sonia sat up even longer discussing how they could best make use of their "gifts."

By the time the breakfast was done, both women were beginning to wonder if they had made the right choice. Their lives were now drastically altered, especially for the young mother of two, who now needed help with everything from diapers to feeding her two year old. Clara assigned six women to care for them, each taking an eight-hour shift. Someone would be sleeping with them, just in case they needed something during the night. Clara was taking no chances with them.

Sonia was still bothered by their ill choices. As far as she was concerned, both had made the wrong choice. At breakfast, she said, "Look, I know that you want to help stop these men, but is outright death the answer? Neither of you have ever taken a life. Do be careful and make certain that is what is best for everyone. I am very worried for you."

"We'll be okay, mom. You have to trust us now. We won't let you or anyone down," Arabella tried to appease her mother. Even so, she still wondered if she'd made the right choice.

Clara dismissed Sonia's concerns. "We have talked this over, and we feel one of you two ought to be here at Oasi Basso in case the evil men should return. One should go out with Gianna's party. Perhaps the smartest thing is to take turns at it."

Arabella countered, "You have a lot of fighters here already. We know the barbarians have left several at each oasis. Gianna needs us both. Let us both go out this first time, and we can see how it is going to work out for us. Perhaps after that, one of us can stay here and take turns going out. We don't want anything to happen to Gianna or her group, not when we could prevent it so easily." In the end, Clara agreed with her. Later that day, she sent the two back with the latest messenger, along with four women to help them with life things.

As they were mounting up to leave, Sonia overheard Arabella whispering to Allegra, "We have to try and be as independent as we can. May be we can mount by holding on with our bent arms like this." She cradled her arm around the saddle and was able to mount.

Allegra emulated her, whispering back. "Right. We must, but your toe shoes make you much taller than me." Both giggled. Arabella had finally found some benefit in her shoes. Then, the band was off, though Sonia watched them until they were out of sight behind a tall sand dune.

They were gone for five days, during which Sonia continued to fret and worry about her youngest daughter. Elena, on the other hand, was quite happy learning defend herself and to handle a dagger, pleasing Rosetta, her mother. Clara and her three fellow Guild Mothers insisted on having Sonia help her work out long-range plans for the desert region and the many oases.

"Once the barbarians finish sacking the coastal zone, they will move on into Alba, unless they should chose to winter over in Tecuci," Sonia speculated. "My bet is they will continue marching south. Unlike their homeland in the frozen steppes of Domei, here it is warm in the winters — especially so along the coastal regions."

"Then if so, we can try to retake Tecuci or at least try to get in some supplies. If Tecuci has fallen, will your City-States Alliance bring in shipments of food or will they stay away?"

Clara asked what was uppermost in her mind.

Sonia reflected on the many negotiations she'd sat in on with her husband, who always valued her opinion, though it was given afterwards. "If the key noblemen, the key merchants, have indeed fled for their lives, then I would say no they would not. If they are still there and are able somehow to pay for the goods, then I think the alliance will make the shipments. Why? Oh, food is going to be in short supply, even if your women are successful on their emergency trip to Tecuci."

"Precisely so. I am thinking months ahead now. Have to. If the ports are useless, then we have to bring in food overland via Adelmira Tower. The magicians there ought to be able to safeguard our shipments as long as we stay close to their tower and the Buku Hills, but it is a fifteen hundred mile trip just to get to Adelmira from here," Clara explained.

"More like two thousand miles, Clara," Guild Mother Imelda pointed out. "They have to follow paths around the dunes which adds much to the journey. That makes it a month and a half journey, one way, assuming that all the supplies are there in Adelmira, which they are not likely to be."

"Say, may I make a suggestion?" the usually quiet Suzana spoke up. "I am not doing anything useful here. Why don't I take part of our funds and go to this Adelmira town. I can stay there and negotiate with the tower magicians to send a message to the Renegade Tower asking for help. I can be the go-between person. Plus, if our other children manage to send a message for us, I will be there to get it and to let them know what we are doing here."

"I like that, My Lady," Clara replied. "I can give you a lengthy message to our Sisterhood there. We could use more Sisters, if they are willing to get involved in our struggle here. I will arrange the trip today, if Sonia agrees."

Sonia agreed, but added, "Be very cautious. The barbarians will be ahead of you. They might turn around and return, intending to join back up with their leader along the coast." The Sisterhood acknowledged this distinct possibility and swore to be alert for such an action. Plans were made. A group of twenty fighters, a cook, and Suzana left the next morning, taking one supply wagon loaded with water and some funds with them.

Late afternoon of the fifth day since the two Lysandra-blessed women left, they returned, accompanied by two fighter-messengers and their four helpers. The whole village and the many Sisters gathered around them, eager to hear the news. Both Allegra and Arabella were extremely pleased and quite excited. Because of her speech difficulties, Arabella let Allegra tell their stories to the enthusiastic throng. Even the older men listened intently to the young woman.

"We did it! We came into Oasis Bona and found two of the barbarians in the process of raping two young women. It worked just as Lysandra said it would. Arabella and I each wished one of the barbarians dead and so it was. A flash of yellow light and the men just died. Of course, the women were hysterical for a while, but Gianna got them calmed down." She gaily explained how they'd done the same at the next oasis.

After accepting the praises of the crowd, the Sisterhood messengers met with the Guild Mothers. One explained, "Gianna requests you keep sending them out to the front lines. She says that they will help keep her fighters from being wounded or killed. Five have already taken minor wounds." The six discussed the events further. The Guild Mothers wanted the two Sisters to reiterate and back up what Allegra had said which they did. Allegra had not exaggerated at all, pleasing the four Guild Mothers. However, they were still hesitant about sending both women out at the same time.

As the supper fires crackled around the oasis and in many adobe homes, another caravan of wagons and riders rolled slowly into the oasis. Andreina and Bianca proudly led the group into the oasis, joining the many Sisterhood wagons. Most everyone stopped their activities to stare at the arrivals, many coming out of their adobe homes to watch and listen. Little children swarmed around the wagons and the dismounting Sisters.

"We have food!" Andreina called out. Cheers and clapping spontaneously broke out in response. When she could get another word heard, she added, "We have many more wagons coming in the next few days." More applause drowned her out again, and several Sisters helped her down from her wagon, when her villagers swarmed and pummeled her with questions.

Meanwhile, a lone young man rode up to the throng. He'd been bringing up their rear. As soon as Arabella spotted him, she let out a squeal and began trying to make her careful, slow way towards him. Her two helpers jumped up and put their arms around her, steadying her. She called out, "Drago! Drago! Over here!" It was her sixteen year old boyfriend. He nudged his horse around the edge of the large gathering and found a place to dismount very cautiously. "Oh my!" Arabella exclaimed when she finally got a good view of him. He was now almost as ornamented as she!

Like many of the noblemen of the City-States Alliance, he had gotten his own body modified similarly to hers. He sported the distinctive five-inch, golden lip plates and the exotic toe boots. While only apparent from his stiff posture, he also had a pair of ribs removed and wore the rigid corset that gave him a fourteen-inch waistline as well. He didn't have the long, dangling earrings that she did, however. When the two were finally closer, she called out, "You did it, Drago! You look spectacular too."

He grinned widely, but it was invisible of course. "Yes, now I am worthy of you. This is not how I wanted you first to see me. I wanted you to see me in the fancy white linen suit with the tiny waist. Had to take those off; too hot here in the desert. Oh! My god, Arabella! Your hands! Did the barbarians get to you already? I'll kill them!"

"No, no, Drago. It was the Goddess Lysandra! She's blessed me. I am very powerful now. I can kill a man just by thinking it so. I saved a young girl who was being raped by a barbarian three days ago." By now, they were close and she threw her arms around him, and he, her. Carefully, they touched the tips of their lips to each other. "I do love you so, Drago."

"I know, I love you too, Arabella. I just couldn't leave on the boats with everyone else and leave you behind. I ran off, went to the Elegant Fashions Inc, and got the modifications done. I was just about to ride off into the desert alone, when all these Sisters showed up. Well, I met with them, found out you were here, and begged them to let me follow them here. I don't think they were very happy about that though. Here I am, Arabella. I won't leave your side again, not ever!" the young Drago exclaimed. "Now we can be together, always."

By now, Sonia had made her precarious way to her daughter's side. "Drago! What have you done to yourself?" she asked.

He replied defiantly, "Now no one can say I am not good enough for Arabella. We love each other, and I swear I will be by her side forever, My Lady."

Sonia laughed. "Okay, Drago, okay. Arabella now does need your help. I so allow it. Next, I suppose you two want to get married."

"Really mom? You will allow us to marry? Really?" Arabella asked incredulously. In the past, they had faced rebuff after rebuff from her father and mother. In part, this was one of the driving forces that had convinced Drago to become ornamented as many of the high noblemen of Tecuci had. Neither Drago nor Arabella had accepted the real reason her parents were rebuffing them — that they were both too young.

"Of course, dear. I can see not even a war will keep you two apart," Sonia replied with an invisible grin. The two hugged even tighter. "Now bring your Drago over to our campsite. Supper is nearly ready. There is so much news to hear."

Via different people, slowly the news was relayed. Most of the wealthier merchants and nobles had fled the city. The Sisterhood and Andreina had managed to purchase twenty wagons and had them brimming with food supplies. The main group of wagons was about two days behind Andreina, who had insisted on getting some supplies back as soon as possible. Drago added the city was mostly in a state of panic and chaos. Then again, that was pretty much what Sonia had expected to hear, sad as it was.

The next day, the village elder married Drago and Arabella. He then took over for the two Sisters, who had been her constant companions the past week. Meanwhile, Andreina handed out supplies to all the villagers. By late afternoon, they headed off along with Allegra to rejoin the two bands of Sisterhood fighters. The remainder of the wagons left with them, intent upon dispensing the life-giving supplies to other nearby oases that were in equally dire circumstances.

When Arabella and Drago finally met up with Gianna's party, Gianna really detested having the young man with them and refused to "protect him." "Don't worry about me. I am here to protect my Arabella," Drago replied humbly. Later around the campfires at night, her opinion of Drago began melting. He brought along his lute and guitar. Each evening he played and sang for Arabella and the other women. Within a week, he was accepted into their tightknit fighter group.

Allegra joined up with Celia's band of fighters. Together, they pressed further west. Celia attempted to follow the band of barbarians. Her idea was to catch up with them and wipe them out. With Allegra's massive blessing, she felt confident they could indeed kill this barbarian group.

They were now heading into the hottest, driest area of the Arad — that is, a zone extending from the Buku Hills eastwards for about two hundred miles. Here, oases were few and far between. One simply had to carry water with one. Either that or die. Further, for days now, the trail of the barbarians was filled with the bodies of dead conscripts. While Celia did not know the root cause, Allegra began to suspect what was happening, based on her last sight of her husband when the barbarians left her oasis.

Ettore, unused to desert conditions and wholly ignorant of the land, continued to force-march the new conscripts. Using whips, his riders made the men jog to keep pace with the horse riders. Without water and salt, the men weakened and slowly succumbed to heat exhaustion and heat strokes. Hence, bit by bit, their passage through the high Arad became littered with the dead conscripts. Ettore chalked this up to the fact the Arad men were basically weaklings. Still, a precious few were able to gain a mount, when the barbarians confiscated horses from the oases they conquered, as few as the mounts were.

Allegra's husband, Bastiano, was desert wise and cunning. Although back in his oasis, he was a mere mat weaver, nevertheless, he knew the desert well. He made frequent excursions into the desert regions looking for the plants from which he obtained the fibers to construct his mats. Nearly everyone in his oasis had one or more of Bastiano's mats. When the barbarians came to the oasis, he had his small pouch of salt on his person. Thus, he was one of the very few conscripts who were actually prepared for such a desert journey. After the first day of forced-marching, he realized if he even was going to survive this nightmare, then he would need every grain of his meager salt supply. He knew he just had to keep his wits about him.

As they moved further west and into the worst part of the Arad, already half of the conscripts had died. Now Bastiano saw his chance. The leaders, Ettore in particular, were growing concerned. In fact, they were lost. The rough maps they had made from the conscripts no longer seemed accurate enough. Bastiano knew this was so. Why? Early this morning, Ettore had led them in the wrong direction, having gone left around a dune instead of right. That meant the next oasis would be missed. These idiot barbarians carried little water with them. Always, they expected to arrive at an oasis by nightfall or certainly by the second nightfall. Bastiano had once been out here on the high Arad. Once had been entirely sufficient!

His eyes roamed over the collected group of his fellow conscripts. Their physical condition was terrible. Lips had turned black, cracked, and bloody. Even with their desert apparel, he knew they would not survive. Even if Ettore could be convinced to return to the last oasis, if he could even find it, the conscripts on foot would never survive the trip. Sadly, he knew, just as they did that their death would come the next day, if not during the chill of night. More than anything now, Bastiano wanted revenge. He wanted these barbarians dead. At last, he took a gamble.

"My Lord, the oasis is that way," he pointed further west towards the Buku Hills.

Ettore grumbled and said that he was tricking them.

Instead, the next morning, Ettore led the party to the right of the great sand dune. Bastiano smiled. He knew soon they would be forced to go west anyway. During the long day, he watched with an ever-growing sadness as the conscripts on foot dropped to the ground, dying. At this point, the riders no longer bothered to execute the fallen. They did not have the energy to do so. Intense sweating and lack of salt were steadily taking their toll on both horse and rider. By noon, the searing sun took the last of the conscripts walking on foot, as well as one who was riding. Finally, Bastiano was allowed to mount the well-lathered horse.

Even so, Bastiano knew the horse would also not last until nightfall, not without water and salt. Still, it was better than walking. Before he too perished in the unforgiving desert, he swore to see these evil, wicked barbarians die. If he could just witness that, he could die in peace. Loping along at the very rear of the riders, he finally licked the very last grains of his salt. He knew he needed much more salt. There were some plants that could provide it, as well as some liquid, but he also knew, if he stopped and found them, the barbarians would also consume them, prolonging their lives. Hence, he did not do so.

As the day progressed, the barbarians began removing their heavy, sweat-soaked leather armor. Many just dropped them onto the sands beside them as they ambled ever westward. Bastiano smiled. He still wore his loose fitting, white cotton robe, protecting his skin from the sun. Wholly unused to such high heat, the barbarians began to bake. Skin turned crimson. By nightfall, half of the barbarian riders had fallen by the wayside. Some had heat strokes; some of their horses succumbed, leaving them on foot where heat stroke soon took them as well.

When they finally halted for the night, Ettore was mostly in a daze. Bastiano kept his body motions to the bare minimum, conserving his depleted body. When most had drifted into an ill sleep, he finally stirred and crawled to a small patch of desert plants. Greedily, he uprooted them and sucked in the salty moisture from the plants. While it was not enough to quench his thirst, it was sufficient to keep him going a little longer. "Gods, please let me live another day that I might see these vicious barbarians die before me," he whispered to the star-filled sky.

At dawn, Ettore rose, somewhat recovered. He and his men ate the last of their salted meat, sharing a small portion with Bastiano. "So which way is the oasis? Speak up or die," Ettore commanded of Bastiano. He pointed due west. "You better be right! Mount up. Water is just ahead," he called out. His voice sounded very strange, he thought. Bastiano avoided grinning. To do so would only crack the scabs on his parched lips. Once more, the long, thin line of the barbarians moved out across the barren sands between two huge dunes.

"Take point," Ettore ordered. Slowly Bastiano's horse moved out in front of the fifty remaining men. Ettore pulled in behind him. On they rode as the merciless sun rose, orange-red, in the sky. Soon, its heat warmed the chilly night from the men. Before long, though, all were again sweating profusely.

As the day wore on, Bastiano occasionally glanced behind him. With each glance, he saw fewer and fewer riders. Inwardly, he smiled. Not much longer now, he thought. By noon, only ten followed him. By two, there were but five behind him. At last, there was none!

Bastiano's horse collapsed. He was only barely able to get off in time avoiding getting pinned beneath it. Staggering, he walked back and stood over the dead body of Ettore, the barbarian from the steppes of Domei. "Goodbye and good riddance, barbarian," Bastiano whispered, barely able to even speak himself. He looked about for any life-giving plants. Here, the land was nearly barren of all life. Yet there was one small plant, pushing its weedy shafts upwards above the searing gravel and sand.

A bit later, he sucked in the last of its meager fluids. He lay down, covering his head with part of his robe, awaiting certain death. He was at peace. He'd led the barbarians to their deaths, ridding the Arad of this scourge. Now Allegra and his children might have some chance for a life.

All day, Celia and her band continued to follow the body-littered trail of the barbarians. "They are going into the high Arad," Allegra pointed out. "I think they are lost. The last oasis must lie that way," she pointed off to their right.

"Good. We must be gaining on them, the fools. Come on; perhaps we can catch them yet today and put them out of their misery!" Celia barked, growing more and more enthused with each dead man alongside the path.

Before long, Allegra began to suspect someone was purposely leading them astray. This she pointed out to Celia, who agreed. "You are right. Anyone with any brains knows you never enter the High Arad without bringing your own water and plenty of it. There are no oases out here. Someone is deliberately leading them west and not veering south to safety. The carrion birds are having a royal feast!"

"I feel sorry for the poor horses," Allegra muttered.

"We have to be getting really close to them now," Celia pointed out. They had stopped to water their horses and themselves, along with dishing out plenty of salt. "This carcass is fresh. Come on; let's pick up the pace a little. We can catch them before dark! I can't wait to drive my blade through the barbarian leader!"

Around two that afternoon, they came upon the last of the dead horses and men. Carrion birds were already picking at many. Celia rode around them to the front. Soon, she called out, "This is the last of them. There are no traces of horse or feet going beyond this last one here!"

Allegra dismounted and walked up to the last man. She noticed that the carrion birds were still circling this one. Moreover, she recognized the white cotton robes. Could this be her husband? "Bastiano?" she whispered to herself. She bent down and used her stumps to pull back the hood.

"Bastiano! Help! He's alive! Help me, please help me!" she cried out. At once, several Sisters hopped off their horses and came running up, carrying water. Allegra felt utterly helpless to assist her dying husband! Yet the women did and hastily forced some water into his mouth and began soaking his head, cooling it off. Then they even wetted his robe, doing what they could to get his temperature down. Meanwhile two others hastily erected a temporary thin sheet over him, holding it between two horses, shielding him from the searing sun. Poor Allegra could only hover over him. At last, she was able to rub a water soaked cloth gently over his parched face, holding it between her stumps.

An hour later, Bastiano showed signs of recovering. At once, they got more water into him and some salt. Slowly, he regained consciousness and saw the terrified face of his wife looking down at him. "Allegra?" he whispered hoarsely.

"I'm here. We have lots of water. You just have to live! Please, Bastiano, I need you," she bawled.

By now, their supply wagon finally joined them. Hastily, the women lifted Bastiano into the shelter of the wagon. Allegra climbed in and sat by his side, along with her helper, who continued to get water into him and dabbed his blistered face before applying a healing salve. Only then did he regain enough consciousness to notice Allegra's missing hands. Hastily, she had to explain her precious gift from Lysandra.

When they finally camped for the night, Bastiano had recovered enough to answer Celia's many questions. He confirmed what she'd deduced. He had led the barbarians to their deaths. Her opinion of the man grew. Five days later, they arrived back at their oasis, where Celia reported to her Guild Mothers.

In the days that followed, similar stories began coming back. In the end, Ettore led five hundred of the best Domei cavalry into the Arad, but none ever returned. Sultaness Sonia continued to supply all the oases with life-giving food and supplies. In return, they backed her completely, accepting her as their ruler.

February came and the Sisterhood band and Sonia retook Tecuci. The battle was very lopsided. The hundred Sisterhood fighters surrounded the Royal Palace, where the fifty men who were defending the Royal Palace had taken refuge. One by one, Allegra and Arabella pointed their arms at a man, who promptly died. Soon the barbarians began begging not to be killed. The two women showed them the same mercy that they had shown so many others.

After all fifty were slain, Sonia was pronounced Sultaness Sonia Ferro, sole ruler of the Kingdom of the Arad. This marked the first time in the history of Tierra that a woman was the sole ruler of an entire kingdom. Further, from this point on, women controlled the power in the Arad and for many years to come. An entire generation of men had been wiped out.

Chapter 9 Chaos in Turda, Alba

Several years ago, Lord Turda had turned control of the city-state of Turda over to his eldest son, the now thirty-five year old Bartolomeo Turda. Between the two, they had carefully maneuvered these past twenty years and totally altered the economic base of Turda. In the distant past, it had been a trade city, which dealt primarily with local crops, shipping much northward. Now, Turda was seen as the gateway to the entire Easterlings. Vast quantities of Westerlings and Midlands goods and crops flowed into and out of Turda.

Their fleet of ships numbered fifty of the newer caravels. With such extensive trading, Turda was thriving beyond anyone's imagination — all thanks to Lord Turda and his son. They had halted their population decline. Today, Turda boasted over thirty thousand in just the city alone. Far more dwelt in the surrounding towns and villages, mostly along the coastline where they too could get a smaller piece of the immense trade.

The new Lord Turda, Bartolomeo, was thin and wiry, but always dressed in the finest suits that Elegant Fashions Inc could provide. He had two wives in his small harem. Dona was thirty-four and had born him a son, Bernardo, who was now a precocious fourteen year old. Later, she had Edda. Although only twelve, Edda acted much older, often pretending she was fourteen too. Many said she would become as beautiful as her mother. Three years ago, he'd married Eula, who was now twenty-five, and pregnant, much to the pleasure of all three. Dona enjoyed not having to bear him another child. Of course, the wives were fully ornamented, just as many of the other noblewomen of Turda were.

In this, Edda felt very much left out, constantly begging both her mother and Bartolomeo to allow her to be ornamented now. The standard age was fourteen. This Edda knew well, but that was obviously meant for others, not her, the Lord's daughter! Edda was also very clever. She always managed somehow to be in the same room as Lord Turda, when he was conducting an important meeting, especially business discussions. Residing quietly in some corner, Edda paid close attention to what was said and how her father manipulated others to get what he desired.

Today was no exception. Edda had seen the *mentales* gifted Amo Rafael arriving at the Royal Palace. His presence could only mean something vitally important was about to happen. She knew Rafael was a very important man in the Renegade Tower. However, to her, the tower people signified magic. Ever since she once saw him simply vanish from the room, she knew it had to be magic. Lord Bartolomeo tried to tell her it was nothing more than *mentales* teleportation, but she knew better. Rafael possessed powerful magic. Cleverly, she meandered into her father's meeting room, found a pile of books stacked on the floor and hid behind them. She adjusted the stack some and then picked up one at random, just in case she was spotted. She would have an excuse: I am reading. Before long, Lord Bartolomeo, Rafael, and four of her dad's advisors entered the room and shut the door.

"Bad news, My Lord. Teraspoli has fallen," Rafael began.

"Well, we all expected that. The fool sent his entire army out into the steppes and lost them all. Idiot. He should have been protecting his city," Bartolomeo replied. "So, it's up to Sultan Ferro to stop these marauders — these barbarians?"

"Quite right. We are doing all we can to assist him. He is going to take a different approach," Rafael continued. "As you know, Po fell last fall. Hence, Sultan Ferro is going to take his entire army north, some thousand miles from Tecuci and try to stop the barbarians, long before they can get to Tecuci. That way, if he fails, those in Tecuci will have plenty of time to evacuate the city and avoid being sacked or worse."

Lord Turda commented, "Hum, he has a good point. If he fails, his harem, family, and the country's treasury can be evacuated to safety. Deny these bastards their treasure. Good move. I should adopt that here as well, should it come to that. So, Amo Rafael, do you think Sultan Ferro will be able to stop these barbarians? What's with the title Immortale Conquistatore Mortale anyway? Is he really un-killable? Isn't he just another man? Or is he one of your kind — a magician, a *mentales* run amok?"

Rafael chose his words carefully. "He is a man, just like us. I've seen him. And yet, he possesses some ability to heal his own wounds, but never any other man's wounds that I've seen. Beyond that, he appears to be a superb horseman with superior fighting skills, a talent for devastating tactics on the battlefield, and full of charisma. Men follow him unto their deaths without question. I did not sense he is *mentales* gifted at all. Still, who can say what the measure of the man really is. He certainly is antisocial in the extreme — a real sociopath. Like all men, he can and will one day die."

"I see. If he does get by Sultan Ferro, then obviously Turda is next on his list. It would be prudent, don't you think, for your Renegade Tower to prepare for such an event? Turda is the prize of prizes here in the Easterlings. The largest city — the wealthiest — the richest. Take my request back to your Venerado Valen. If battle comes to Turda, I will expect the Renegade Tower to back me with a sizeable force."

"I will do so. While I cannot speak for Venerado Valen, I would not be surprised if he sent a substantial force to assist Sultan Ferro. I know that I, for one, will fight at the sultan's side. I aim to incinerate this barbarian," Rafael declared. He'd seen more than enough of the sheer savageness of Damiano and wanted the man stopped any way possible.

"Good. Well, I best be making some plans."

"Same here. I will return to Villa del Rey and convey your message to Venerado Valen now. I will stay in touch, My Lord," Rafael replied politely. Momentarily, he vanished from the room. After a bit of chat, his aides also left.

Edda grinned and rose from her hiding place, revealing to her father the subtle point that she had overhead the whole discussion. "Ah, eavesdropping again, my little Edda," he grinned, picking her up and giving her a little hug.

"Yes, papa," she replied demurely. "If Sultan Ferro cannot stop the barbarians, I am sure they will come here next. We are quite wealthy."

"Yes, but don't you breathe a word of what you heard here today, my little angel. It would only upset your mother," he attempted to bargain with her.

"Oh I won't papa. But papa, if they do come here, then I won't get a chance to get all of my fancy ornaments like mom has. I will be just ugly me forever. No real man will ever come to court me then."

"Sure they will. You are going to be a very beautiful young woman," he replied.

"No they won't. You didn't marry Elma because she was not ornamented. You married Eula because she is. If the barbarians come, I ought to be ornamented so when you send me to safety, noblemen will court me there. You don't want to doom me to becoming a mere merchant's wife, do you?" She tried to think of the lowest status person she could, but her words came out faster than she could think.

"But there will always be time for you to get your ornaments, my dear."

"Not if the barbarians come. You will be out fighting them. If you lose, then we will be forced into exile and I will remain ugly forever, forced to become some fat merchant's wife," she countered.

"Hum, you do have a point. If things go ill for Sultan Ferro, then I will be preoccupied with very serious matters."

"See, I am right. You will be very busy, and no one will have time to help me become beautifully ornamented. Then, I will be doomed," she played on his concession perfectly.

"True, everyone will be terribly busy if that happens. It might not, though, remember that, Edda."

"But it might, papa. If it does, you don't want me to have no chance at all of marrying a fine nobleman, do you? Mama certainly doesn't want that either."

Just then, Dona made her slow, careful way into the room. "Mama doesn't want what?" she asked speaking slowly and carefully so they could understand her better. She wore a beautiful red satin arm-fetter-gown. She'd let her hair down and had it brushed out seductively.

Bartolomeo came to her and gave her a loving hug and a gentle kiss on her front lips. "It's Edda. We ought to allow her to get her fancy ornaments now, dearest. I know she isn't quite fourteen yet. But the way that events are going, it might be wise of us to get it done now so she can get used to them — just in case."

"So you think the battle will come here to Turda?" she asked worriedly.

"Probably not, but if it does, Edda ought to be comfortable with her ornaments. Don't you think?"

"Yes, it is very difficult to get used to them. Okay, Edda, I will grant your wish," Dona agreed. "Tomorrow we will visit Elegant Fashions Inc. Now leave your father and me alone." Edda thanked them both and skipped gaily out of the room. She had scored a major victory. She turned her head at the door, saw Dona kissing him, and smiled. Tomorrow would be her big day; she just knew it.

The next morning, she got her wish. Dona took her to the store. She was asked to walk around and look at all the fashions, while Dona and the store manager discussed the situation. Edda pretended to do as asked, but kept an ear open on what they were saying. The manager was complaining about her age, that it was not healthy for someone so young to undergo the body modifications. However, she could not go against the wishes of the sultan. At last, Edda heard the words she most wanted to hear. The manager sighed, "Okay then. I will set it up. However, as you know, what modifications are done to her are up to her. You have no say; it is just what Edda wants. She gets to pick and choose what she desires in the way of the modifications and the outfits. Agreed?"

"Yes, I have some other errands to run," Dona admitted.

"Perfect. We should have her finished in about three hours. Come back then to pick her up. Again, thank you for choosing Elegant Fashions Inc. We do our best to please your tastes in luxury," the manager replied.

Once her mother left, the manager had Edda sit before her desk. Together, they began outlining just what ornamentations Edda desired. She also carefully measured Edda. "My, if you want the pipe corset, I am afraid your waist will be even smaller than your mothers, about twelve inches. Of course, as your body fills out, you can increase it to the usual fourteen inches."

"Oh no, I want it to stay twelve inches. I'd have the smallest waist around!" Edda exclaimed. The manager's eyebrows rose.

"Alright then, let's talk about your lip plates. Yours would have to be a little smaller since your mouth is a bit smaller than normal," she explained.

Edda looked crestfallen. "Isn't there anything you can do to make them bigger? I don't want to look very different from everyone else. They must be big too, maybe even bigger than mom's. Please, you must find a way," Edda begged. "You and mom, you look so utterly beautiful with yours. You can't condemn me to looking less than the best." Eventually, the manager gave in and said she would see what could be done.

"Now about your earrings: we have many styles and sizes." She produced a small catalogue. Edda wondered how such a thing could have been made. She'd never seen anything like this colored book, and began to suspect it was an alien product. Once more, Edda made her choice, choosing the biggest set in the brochure. She suspected hers would be longer and thicker than her mother's — at least she hoped so.

The rest of the discussion went rapidly. She accepted the dozen pairs of black nylons that the manager suggested, along with the undergarments. Edda picked out six elegant gowns and accepted the suggestion to have some of the fancy arm-fetter-gowns, as well as some that were merely fetter-gowns. Why? Edda was not quite yet convinced she wanted her arms so immobile as her mothers. Not just yet, though she could try those out and see. If she didn't like them, she could wear the others. She picked out four pairs of toe shoes, following the manager's suggestion of having two pairs of the black patent type and two that matched a pair of her gowns.

"There, that's everything, Edda. Now then, I need you to sign here. You see, none of these body modifications can be undone. Once you have them done, you can't change your mind. Your signature says you fully understand these modifications are permanent."

Edda quickly signed. "Now I too will be a most beautiful woman! I've wanted this for years," she added, quite pleased she'd made it happen. After that, she rose and followed the slow, carefully walking manager to the backroom. This time, Edda noticed how she was walking in her toe shoes. She could scarcely contain her exultation, her excitement. I'm going to be really beautiful now, she thought, as she sat down on the operation table.

Sometime later, she awoke. Edda tried, but could not remember what had happened to her. Something about breathing deeply and now she was awake. She felt funny. No, different, I feel different, she thought, slowly regaining consciousness. Her lips felt — well, stretched seemed to come to mind. She was still lying down, but something was pulling her ears off her head. She raised her arms to feel what, but they seemed attached to her sides. She came too and saw her mother's face looking down at her.

"Well, you do look gorgeous, Edda. Here, let me help you sit up. There's a mirror over there," Dona said warmly.

Edda felt very stiff and realized that must be the pipe corset. Once sitting up, she gazed into the mirror and looked at her new self. Her lip plates were six inches in diameter, larger than anyone she knew. Her huge, long earrings draped down to her bosom, pulling hard on her ears. Breathing was very hard; her waist was extremely tiny, twelve inches as promised. She saw she was wearing a pair of the black stockings and the red arm-fetter-gown, done in cherry satin. Her shiny toe shoes and hose contrasted well with her gown.

"Wow! Mom, I am truly beautiful! Oh, I can't breathe!"

"Take short, shallow breaths, dear. In time, you will get used to it. Also, you now have to learn to *talk* much slower and very carefully or no one is going to understand you," Dona advised. "Walking is going to be quite a challenge. At least it was for me and for Eula. Come on; let's get you up." The manager stepped into the room. With one woman on each side of her, Edda got precariously onto her feet. "It takes time, dear," Dona advised again.

After walking around the room a little, the manager said they could leave. Dona already had someone carry Edda's many packages out into their carriage. With her lower arm around her daughter's tiny waist, Dona helped Edda keep her balance as they walked through the store to the carriage.

There, her driver had to lift each woman up and into the carriage. Edda, gasping for breath, felt elated. Now she was being assisted just like her mother. She felt very grown up, even though her discomfort was growing by leaps and bounds.

Back at the palace, her father complimented her new looks and gave her a warm, loving hug. He now had solved one of his longstanding minor problems: how to keep Edda from sneaking in on his many meetings. She would be moving as slowly as his wives. Gone was her childish mobility. Moreover, as constrained as she was now, she would not be able to "hide" in his office any longer. Problem solved, he mused as he praised her new look.

For the next month, Edda had to focus all of her energies on learning to adapt to all of her physical changes. Eavesdropping on her dad's meetings didn't even enter her mind. Rather how to walk without falling was. How to keep from fainting from lack of air was. She didn't mind too much, for she felt like a real woman now. More importantly, she began to anxiously await the winter celebration that brought in the new year.

Every year, Lord Turda held a huge banquet and dance. Everyone of importance in Turda was invited and usually five hundred attended the ball. This time, she would make her grand entrance as a real noblewoman! Everyone would notice her and how exquisite she looked. This alone kept her working diligently at learning to walk elegantly and control her breathing. Until now, she had not really paid any attention to the younger boys who occasionally attended the formal affair with their parents. This year, she certainly would, she promised herself. Nothing else mattered, much to the relief of Lord Turda, who enjoyed not having her constantly hiding during his many meetings.

For the past two months, the meetings had been many and frightening. Rafael brought him the worst possible news. Lord Ferro had been killed and the battle lost. He didn't need the *mentales* gifted man to tell him Turda was next in line for the barbarians! Rather, he and his aides began to work out just how to defend Turda. For many reasons, Lord Turda was very pleased he no longer had constantly to watch out for Edda being in his meeting rooms, hiding somewhere.

At one meeting in December, he explained to the group of generals, Rafael, and his advisors. "Look, we have perhaps seventy-five hundred able-bodied men here in Turda proper. However, even if I wanted to, I could not field an army of that size. There simply aren't enough weapons. What do we have, Drago? Twenty-five hundred?" His aide nodded.

"How about asking normal citizens, who possess one or more weapons, to either donate them to the army or to join the army and help defend Turda?" Rafael asked.

Lord Turda agreed. "Now then, we need to pick the battlefield. We need to meet these barbarians far from Turda. If we fail, my people must have time to evacuate the city."

"My Lord, our scouts are reporting they are marching down the coast of the Arad even as we sit here. We have coastal skiffs monitoring their progress. It's not hard to do, look for the mass of men or the flames from the villages they burn along the way," one general reported.

"How close?" Lord Turda asked solemnly.

"Our best guess is if we do nothing, they will arrive here by the first of March. We've about two and a half months to prepare, maximum, My Lord," he replied.

Another general spoke up, "My Lord, if I might make a suggestion?" Lord Turda nodded. "My Lord, in my opinion, the best place to take a stand would be at Grande Curvatura, the southernmost shores of Alba, where the coast bends northwestwards, towards us. There is a small patch of forest lands there where we could hide some of our forces and have them attack from their rear." The generals discussed this notion for some time before agreeing that this would be the best location to attempt to stop the invading horde.

"My Lord, if we are to meet the enemy there, we will need to begin marching by the first of February at the very latest. Perhaps a week sooner would be prudent," an aide suggested.

"All right. At the Year End Ball, I will make the announcement," Lord Turda agreed. "Until then, make all the preparations needed, but keep our plans to march a secret until I announce it." Several hours later, the generals left and

Lord Turda met with his aides.

"We ought to make contingency plans to move Turda's treasury out of Turda, in the event that we fail to stop the barbarians," he announced.

Rafael jumped on that point. "My Lord, Venerado Valen will send a fleet of caravels to assist you. He will personally guarantee the safeguarding of all Turda's funds placed into his ships."

"Now that is most useful indeed. I am afraid most of our huge fleet will be needed to transport the nobles and their goods safely away. Of course, I will send my family away on my yacht. Still, may I request some of my personal funds be safeguarded by Venerado Valen?"

"Absolutely," Rafael replied. "He will also be sending a dozen *mentales* gifted to help you defeat these barbarians. I myself will be leading them. We will be at your side, My Lord. Our skills shall be yours."

"Excellent, Amo Rafael, excellent. I've asked Adelmira Tower to send aid, but thus far I, have heard nothing. Didn't really expect to either," he added. "Do you really think we can stop them? Be honest with me, Amo Rafael."

"My Lord, you put me on the spot. However, I will be honest with you. All the towers on Tierra are now fully informed of this barbarian's actions. Those in the Midlands are especially worried about his next move, if we don't stop him here. Venerado Valen has asked for help from the Midlands rulers and towers. However, they are hedging their bets. Will the barbarians strike inland into the heart of the Midlands after here or will they continue down the coast? That is the question that seems to be uppermost in their minds. Many are refusing to aid us, believing they need to marshal their own forces for a Midlands invasion. In some ways, they are retaliating for the Renegade Tower's having formed the City-States Alliance. I would not look for any real aid from the Midlands. If Turda falls and they continue down the coast, Venerado Valen has gotten serious commitments from all the other major City-States to join their armies together and make a coordinated stand. My guess that would take place somewhere along the extreme southern coast of old Bashir, but that's just my own hunch."

Rafael continued, "But I haven't really answered your direct question. Can we stop them here? I just don't know. I pray we do, but I've seen this Damiano take the full force of one of my powerful balls of fire. Men died all around him, but he suffered only minor burns from his flaming clothes. I wish I knew more about him and the nature or source of his powers, but I don't. If I were you, I would make sure you have your successor named and your family's evacuation well planned. Better to be safe than sorry, My Lord."

"Amo Rafael, never have I had such honest, wise council. You are a treasure among men. Whether we are successful or not, I want you to know I have no regrets. The Renegade Tower has more than lived up to all of its initial promises. I could have no greater honor than to have you and your companions fighting at my side in this, the greatest battle ever fought in Alba's long history," Lord Turda praised Rafael, who nodded humbly.

An aide entered. "My Lord, the sons of Sultan Ferro are begging to have an audience with you. Shall I send them away again or let them enter?"

"Well, I have been putting them off for some weeks. Best send them in," he sighed. He suspected all along what the five men wanted. It was something he could not give. The five walked in and he motioned them to take a seat.

Angelo spoke for the brothers. "My Lord, you have heard of the death of our father and the sacking of our country?" Lord Turda nodded. "Sultan Ferro has sent Arad's treasury with us in hopes we can purchase an army with which to retake our country and free our people from the tyranny of this barbarian Damiano."

"Yes, yes, I expected such. Lord Angelo, as much as I would like to oblige you, at this time, as you well know, those very barbarians are heading here to sack Turda. I must protect my own country first and foremost. However, I give you my word that, if you five will fight with us to defend Turda and if we are victorious, then I will send my army on into the Arad, freeing your towns and cities from the remnants of this barbarian horde. No charge. Consider it payment for your fighting skills here. Save your funds to help rebuild the Arad."

"Allow us time to consider your generous offer, My Lord," Angelo replied. This was not what he had hoped to hear, but he knew he could not get a better deal here. Later when the five were alone, they discussed the offer. Their only other option was to head further west and try to recruit an army in Madya or perhaps at inland Southbend. Those cities were over a thousand miles further away. In the end, Angelo sent word to Lord Turda that four of them would accept his kind offer. Corrado was only thirteen and not yet skillful enough to fight. Instead, they gave him strict orders, if Turda fell, he was to depart in their caravels and make for Villa del Rey, there to plead their case directly to the Renegade Tower.

As the date for the ball drew closer, Dona began giving Edda dancing lessons. While Edda already knew how to dance, that was before her many body modifications. Now she could only barely walk. Knowing just how much Edda was looking forward to the dance, Dona insisted on showing her how dancing was now possible for the women who wore toe shoes and pipe corsets. "Mom, this is hardly dancing. We're just barely able to move an inch," Edda protested.

"How did you think we could dance, Edda? It's almost impossible for us to step backwards and we are standing on our toes. The man will be holding you and supporting you, but still, we just barely move our feet when we dance," she explained and began the lessons.

Edda sighed, gone were all of her fancy dance floor moves she had always done since she was little. Further, after one short dance, Edda was out of breath. "Always remember, dear, only dance one dance and then sit the next one out. If not, you might actually faint. If you have ever noticed, I only dance every third one with your father. Even so, it's all I can do to catch my breath. Now come on, dear. You have to look elegant and graceful, even though it is most difficult for us to do so. Also, remember to talk very slowly and clearly to the boys who dance with you. You will be very hard for the boys to understand, unless they have been around a mother or sister who wears lip plates as we do. Oh, and do be careful not to drool on your dates. I know it is hard to keep from drooling;

our lips do not touch any longer. It helps to keep your head raised, even though you need to see where you are placing your toes with each step. If you keep on looking downward, you can't help but drool, dear." One by one, Edda's beautiful illusions of the glamor of her fancy ornamentations began to shatter.

However, she still looked forward to the ball. Together, the two and the pregnant Eula got ready for the evening's royal ball. Edda wore her best new arm-fetter-gown, the cherry red one that exposed a little of her black nylons along with her highly polished toe shoes. For this formal affair, the women un-braided their long hair, brushing it out and draping it across their backs. "How do I look mom?" Edda asked, looking at her impressive figure in their mirror.

"Stunning, dear, positively stunning. You will catch the eyes of every young lad at the ball. Just remember to go slowly and gracefully. Dance one in three dances at most. Talk as clearly as you can and slowly. Some boys might not be able to understand you well," Dona advised her. "Remember, your arms are bound now."

Edda giggled, "How can I possibly forget that, mom?" She wiggled her lower arms some, but her upper arms were held securely at her sides by the gown, whose design had been popularized many years ago by their Easterlings empresses. Already, Edda had begun to allow her nails to grow, as befitting an elegant woman. She was no longer a little girl, but a woman and wanted her nails to be at least as long as Dona's five-inch talons. Well, that will take time, she concluded. "I'm nervous mom," she admitted as the three women held hands and began to make their careful way from their room to their living room where Bartolomeo would be waiting to escort them on down the long halls to the ballroom.

Edda also knew that her brother, Bernardo, would be escorting her. Bartolomeo always led Dona and Eula into the ball, their arrival announced by a fanfare. As the three entered, both Bartolomeo and Bernardo rose. At least Bernardo was wearing a fine suit, Edda thought. It would be terribly embarrassing to be escorted into the ball by a slob. "Ah, you are ready at last, my three elegant women. You all look most lovely this evening, especially you, my dear Edda. You are so grown up. Why, I remember when you were just this high!" her father said.

"Papa," she chided him. "I am a young woman now." She raised her lower hand a little and Bernardo awkwardly took it.

"Like this, son. This is the proper way to escort an elegant woman," Bartolomeo demonstrated. He placed his arm securely around Dona's waist, but beneath her flowing hair. "Remember, she will be depending upon you to help her keep her balance." His son groaned, but emulated his father.

Edda and Bernardo fell in line behind their parents. Edda whispered, "Dad seems to be paying far more attention to us this year, doesn't he?"

"What? Do talk slower, Edda. You are so hard to understand now that you are like mom," he grumbled. She repeated her words only slower this time.

"Yeh, sis, really he is. He insisted I dress up like this. You know me. I never wear suits to the ball, and I've never escorted you either. Why is he making me do this? Can't you walk in there yourself?" he whispered back.

"Dad is acting very strange tonight. Something must be up," she whispered back twice before he understood. Just then, the music drowned them out followed by the usual trumpet fanfare announcing Lord Turda's entry into the crowded Royal Hall. After he led his two wives into the room amid applause, the trumpet fanfare began again. That was the cue for Edda's grand entrance. Although she thought her knees were shaking from nerves, she held her head high, depending utterly on her brother for support. She felt a rush from the applause that greeted her, but her beaming smile was invisible.

As they made their way into the room, many noblewomen and men stopped them to compliment her and acknowledge her new appearance. Many were as ornamented as she was, but Edda noted few had lip plates as large as hers and none had as tiny a waistline. For a time, she felt like she was floating. The world was beautiful. Young boys soon began hovering around her, and Bernardo took this as a sign to let go of her and head for the ale table. Bereft of his steadying arm, she felt terribly vulnerable. Soon, she caught herself looking downward and, of course, began to drool slightly, embarrassing her further. At last, she allowed a boy who she did not know to slip his arm around her. At least he offered to dance with her.

As anticipated, after even one dance, she was nearly gasping for air. This was so unlike all of her earlier experiences at these balls. Gone were her days of wild dancing and darting about the room. Now each movement had to be carefully thought out well in advance. Before very long, her feet began aching some. This was not turning out to be the way that she had imagined it would be.

Things only got worse. Before long, Lord Turda signaled the musicians, who stopped playing. He stepped upon a raised platform. "Ladies, gentlemen. I must have a vitally important word with all of you. As many of you know, the barbarian horde has sacked all of Domei and the Arad. Already, they are plundering the coastal towns near our border with the Arad. Yes, they are on their way here to sack Turda!"

The gasps and cries of dismay echoed so loudly that he had to pause. Suddenly, Edda felt sick at her stomach. She'd been so concerned about herself these past weeks that she'd forgotten to listen in on her father's meetings. She'd obviously missed much. At last, he was able to continue.

"I have called out our entire army, equipped them with every last blade in our armory. Additionally, five hundred of our citizens have volunteered to help defend Turda as well. The Renegade Tower is sending an entire Circle to help us battle our foes." Again, much applause and cheers drowned him out. When it died down, he continued, "I am going to lead our army and meet these barbarians far, far from Turda." Again, a loud round of cheering caused him to pause.

"However, on the off chance we are defeated, the battle will be far away. This means you will have a few weeks to abandon Turda before the barbarians can enter our magnificent city and sack it. I urge you all to make such preparations as you deem appropriate. I will be sending my own family to safety, before I lead the army out of Turda a few weeks from now. In addition, I will be sending our treasury to a place of safety. We have the guarantee of the Renegade Tower that they will protect our money so we can rebuild once the fiends depart. I urge those of you who can to do the same. If I should perish, my son, Bernardo, is of age and will become your next Lord Turda in my place. Should something happen to him, then the throne falls to my most elegant daughter, Edda. However, Eula is expecting. If she has my son, then Edda may rule until he becomes of age. I so swear before you all. Now then, let us all enjoy this ball, for none of us can know what the future may hold for us all."

Edda's mind was a whirlwind of conflicting ideas and thoughts. She stood stunned, unable to move. Part of her recognized just what he had done. He had made the succession of the ruling throne of Turda official. Bernardo would take his place if he died. Well, she knew would always be the case. What shocked her was her father naming her as secondary heir, should Bernardo perish too! She never, ever expected this. Women were never the rulers; she knew that well. She now knew she had missed everything that had been vitally important these past many weeks, and she silently cursed herself for having doted on her own vanity. Contrasting with these lofty thoughts were those that told her she had made a horrible mistake in getting all of these body modifications! She could barely walk, barely make herself understood, and barely breathe. If ever she needed her freedom of movement, it was now! Unable to control her mind and body, Edda fainted, but the boy holding her managed to arrest her fall. Later on, she learned many of the other elegant women also fainted, including her mother.

Hours later that night, the Turda family sat in their living room. At least the men could undo their tight suits and relax. Edda struggled just to keep breathing, but so did Dona. Bernardo, defiant and angry, said, "Look, dad. I want to fight too. How is it going to seem to everyone else here in Turda if I stay behind and flee if you are killed? I will not have the respect of anyone. If I am to rule, then I must be *seen* to fight against our enemies too. Can't you see that? You can't send me away with the women — not if you want me to be able to rule later on. You just can't."

"Son, if I perish, I need you to take my shoes," Lord Turda tried to get his son to see reason. However, he knew well Bernardo spoke the truth. No one would follow the rule of a coward. "I can say I am sending you away with our treasury to guard it with your life." He tried another approach.

"You ruined any chance of that when you told everyone the tower would do that for us, dad. You know that as well as I do," he retorted.

"True, but I could say I am ordering you to escort the women to a place of safety," Lord Turda tried the last notion he could think of to prevent his son fighting alongside of himself.

"Oh sure, dad. I am to protect them from sea monsters. That won't fly either. Once they are onboard the caravel, they will be safe, especially if they go to Villa del Rey."

"Okay, okay. You win, Bernardo. I think you are making a terrible mistake, but I see your point," Lord Turda gave in. All along, he suspected this might happen. Edda suddenly realized why he had officially announced she would rule if Bernardo also perished! How much she had missed by not being present at these many meetings! Again, she cursed herself for having gotten all the body modifications.

Dona sighed. She knew if Bartolomeo perished, then surely Bernardo would as well. She began crying softly. Her well-ordered world was collapsing on her. "But dear, we don't speak the Westerlings language. We'll be lost there."

"My lovelies, where else can I send you where you will be safe? If Turda falls, only Matruk remains, and they will be the next to be attacked. The nearer cities of old Bashir offer no one a real life. The only place I can get you to where you can be safe is the Westerlings. Villa del Rey is where the Renegade Tower is. There, you have the best chance of survival. Besides, they will be in charge of our country's treasury, though I will send along our own personal fortune with you, my dear."

"But," she sobbed.

"I will see someone comes tomorrow to teach you all the Westerlings tongue. Take heart. I might not be killed. I have high hopes we will win the battle and kill this hideous barbarian," he attempted to cheer her up. At last, he turned his attention onto Edda.

"Dear Edda, I know all this is hard for you, but after seeing you tonight, I can rest in peace knowing my little girl is all grown up and has become a gorgeous, elegant flower! Pick your beau wisely, as I know you will. I have never been so proud of you, my little Edda, as I was tonight. You are truly a beautiful young woman, just as your mother is. I know you will do all you can to help Eula with her baby when it comes in April." He cleverly gave her an order to look after Eula and her child when it came. Edda also picked this up.

"I will papa. So many boys were courting me tonight. They've never paid so much attention to me as they did tonight," she replied, indicating subtly she would care for Eula when the time came.

"Of course they did, Edda. You are absolutely stunning. Why, if I were only twenty years younger," he winked and teased her. She grinned, but it was invisible. Dona also smiled. "Now then, we still have a few weeks left before I have to lead our army forth. Let's make the most of it, shall we? I love you all very much." One by one, the women rose carefully to their toes, and he hugged each in turn. Begrudgingly, Bernardo slipped his hand around Edda's tiny waist, helping her to her room. All he could think of was the mighty battle to come and how he would be victorious on the battlefield, making his father proud of him.

Edda had quite other thoughts. It dawned on her that although she was not officially of age, that is, fourteen, her father had made no mention of someone acting as regent for her until she turned fourteen. Of course, he had for Eula's unborn baby, but not her. In a flash, Edda realized this was another reason her father had consented to her getting all of her adult ornaments. Everyone knew you had to be fourteen to get them. Seeing her with them at the ball, everyone would believe that she was of age. *Papa, you are so clever,* she thought. *I will be next year.*

During the next few weeks, many men came to meet with Lord Turda. Edda grew more and more frustrated with her severe physical limitations. She was used to spotting the arriving men and making a dash for the meeting room, where she would cleverly find a place to hide before her father and the visitors entered the room. In her arm-fetter-gown and toe shoes, Edda barely crossed the room from the window before they had entered and closed the meeting room door! Her own desire to be elegant had cost her dearly, she knew that now, but there was no going back. She knew what she'd had done to her body was permanent.

Hence, Edda began to spend her days trying to make the best of her now impossible situation. At first, she began wearing only the fetter-gowns for every day. This gave her back compete freedom of her arms. However, her mother did insist she change into her formal arm-fetter-gown for dinners. "Dear, you must learn to get by in them. At all formal occasions, you will be wearing them, and you must be able to eat and carry out normal actions. They do take a great deal of getting used to. Remember how you were at the ball. You didn't have anything to eat or drink like everyone else did. It is unseemly to ask a man to feed you." Edda flushed beet red. Embarrassed, she dutifully changed each evening for suppers, only to find that eating without drooling and making a mess of herself was extremely challenging.

Next, Edda returned to Elegant Fashions Inc. This time, she bought several plain gowns. They were still very fancy and made of pod-silk or satin. However, these obstructed neither her arms nor her legs. At once, she discovered she could now walk far better. Still, she was not fast enough to respond to visitors, but at least she was able to get to the meeting door as the men entered. Now her father merely shook his head "no" at her as he ducked inside. Even so, he never failed to give her a warm smile.

She'd barely made these adjustments when the whole household was turned upside down. Packing for their potential evacuation began. Many servants began crating up their household valuables. Edda found her mothers needed her to help direct the servants' actions. In the middle of all this, her father finally did ask her to come into his meeting room.

"Edda, my dear. I am sorry you could not sit in on these meetings of late. It has been for your own good. I'm afraid if you heard what was being discussed you would be terribly upset and distressed. You have had more than enough stress dealing with your new look. Be that as it may, come here and have a look at these papers. As my heir-second, I want you to know precisely the financial state of Turda and of our family. This one here details Turda's treasury, which is being picked up by a caravel from Venerado Valen for us. This one outlines our family's funds. I will send it along with you and my wives. These are your copies. Guard them well."

"Edda, I've never told you this, but now I must. If I had my choice, I would wish you to be my heir. You have shown you are both clever and wise. I know that you know how I run Turda. You know nearly every business decision I've made for the last eight years and just why I made them. You've a shrewd business head on your shoulders. Bernardo, I'm afraid, is wholly ignorant of all such things, but I have no choice but to make him my first heir. Customs and traditions dictate that such falls to the first born son."

Edda interrupted, "So is that why you allowed him to join you in the battle?" She didn't add so he could also get killed. She didn't need to.

His face grimaced a little. "Yes, but *never* tell him that. He sees himself a mighty warrior and that is as it should be. He is a man and men often pride themselves on their fighting prowess. I certainly did when I was his age. If something should happen to me in the battle, he is likely to be affected as well. If the rulership of Turda falls to you, remember all that I've taught you, and do your very best, my little Edda, who is no longer little, except in the memories of an old man."

"Papa, you are not an old man," she chided him. Thirty-five was middle age, not old.

He grinned, "I know, but just now I see my little girl all grown up." He wiped a tear from his eye. After a moment to recover, he continued. "If I am gone, remember to marry wisely, for a man will try to usurp your rulership, if he can. Many will wish to marry you to gain rulership of Turda. Be most careful of such two-faced men. That is the best advice I can give you."

"Papa, you sound like you know you are not coming

back," Edda protested. Tears trickled down her cheeks; she was unable to hold back her emotions.

He wiped her cheeks with his silk handkerchief. "There, there. I am just being practical as you know I always am. I must lead the army forth to war tomorrow. This may be my last opportunity to tell you these things. Remember to be as practical as I have and Turda will thrive."

"I will papa." She couldn't think of anything to say.

"Now go and get changed for dinner. You know your mother wants you to become skilled in those fancy gowns. Oh, by the way, I do love seeing you wearing these types of gowns. You can walk far better in them, and I get to see a teasing bit more of your legs. Men will like that." She flushed and grinned, filing his compliment and subtle advice in her mind for future reference. He had noticed her slight change and approved of it. That meant the world to Edda at this moment.

The next day, she, along with her mothers, watched the great fanfare that accompanied Lord Turda and Bernardo, as they ceremoniously led the army out of Turda — at least as far as they could see them here before the Royal Palace. Edda had a sinking feeling this would be the last that she would see of them. Perhaps Dona and Eula felt the same, but neither said so, focusing on their continued packing.

Chapter 10 The Fall of Turda

The Sisterhood in Turda had grown some during the last twenty years. They numbered thirty-five women, not quite double in size. Many had grown old and some had died. Among the latter was their late Guild Mother Luciana Vitalia. Perhaps far more important was the fact that twenty years ago, the Goddess Lysandra had visited their guild and asked them to help rescue a number of Calder's abandoned and helpless mermaids here in the Easterlings. Eight Sisters had volunteered and at great peril to themselves had done the deed.

While Lysandra had not specifically rewarded the eight for their valiant deeds, she did so indirectly. These eight were privy to the workings and location of the Tierra Underground! They took the rescued and utterly helpless mermaids to the Underground up in Brom. There, they were shown the buried spaceship with its artificial world of bots, Madiera, where these mermaids had the physical assistance they needed just to be able to live independently. Furthermore, the Underground leader, Benjamina, had given them the *mentales* gifts and the training needed to use it properly, including the all-powerful crystals they always wore around their necks. If this was not enough, Benjamina saw they all received her newly developed mental therapy, which had erased all the hideous trauma they had endured at the hands of men in their lives, which in some cases had been very brutal indeed. The eight returned to Turda full of life, vitality, and with goodly *mentales* powers.

Angelica Freda e Alessandra, the free mate of Bianca Alessandra e Freda, was now their Guild Mother. She was sixty and her mate, fifty-nine. The only Sisterhood member, who had once been a noblewoman and originally *mentales* gifted with the ability to teleport, Donatella Alba e Falda, was forty-eight. Her free mate, Marcella Falda e Alba, was forty. Marcella was a superb fighter, always protecting her mate. Their best scout, Felisa Sandro e Vanetta, was fifty and had married their group's precocious thief, Gina Vanetta e Sandro, who was two years younger and could also teleport now. These two made quite a pair. Savina Vana, their fifty-nine year old cook was still the undisputed chef of their guild house. The eighth original woman, Milana, who was a master of horses, had married a man and was no longer present.

Still, the overall number of women who took refuge here had continued to grow, but far more slowly than in other areas. Lord Turda and the prosperity he'd brought to Turda these past twenty years played a strong role in ending the widespread abuse of women in this single city. While many of the younger Sisters considered the seven were "old," they were held in the highest respect and esteem. They were legends within the broader Sisterhood of Tierra, and they had strong *mentales* gifts, rarely found here in the Easterlings. Yet, these were not the only reasons. While they were mostly approaching their fifties and sixties, all were still vibrant and agile. Few could beat Angelica, Bianca, and Marcella in their practice fighting sessions, much to the dismay of the younger women.

So it was the seven were not surprised when the Goddess Lysandra again appeared in their guild house one evening in mid-January. The group of thirty-five women were dining, telling jokes, and gobbling down Savina's especially tasty stew, when a yellow glow began forming in their midst. Hush fell at once. Only Gina's voice broke the sudden silence, "Oh no. Here we go again." Beside her, Felisa grinned and poked her free mate in the ribs. Gina was never reverent about anything, save thieving and Felisa.

Slowly the form of a woman in robes appeared to all eyes. She was standing on their long table. Guild Mother Angelica swallowed hard and spoke up, "Welcome Goddess Lysandra to our humble home. How may we serve you this time?" Many younger women gasped. Angelica actually addressed the goddess!

Lysandra spoke to all of them. "You have heard the rumors. War is coming to Turda. It is true, the barbarians from Domei have destroyed both Domei and the Arad, and will soon try to do the same to Turda. In a few days, Lord Turda will march forth an army to stop them. Do not join with him. Do not go thither to that battle, for it cannot be won."

"Yes, we have heard all manner of wild rumors, goddess. Indeed, we have only today received a formal request from Lord Turda to send our fighters to help him defeat the barbarians. I have as yet not answered him. I shall therefore decline his request," Angelica replied.

Lysandra continued. "Such men need a reason, Angelica. Tell him you have been charged by me to protect something of immense value to him. But tell him no more." Angelica nodded and the goddess went on, "I have given my blessings to several women in the Arad. They are slowly taking back their country from the barbarians. However, I fear for their safety. I wish you to send a good deal of your Sisters to your guild house in Adelmira. Have them prevent any barbarians from attempting to sneak into the Arad from the high desert back doors. Have them also keep a watchful, protective eye on one of the late sultan's wives, Suzana Ferro. She is there now."

"It will be done, goddess," Angelica replied.

"Now then, I have a special mission for the seven of you, one which even I cannot yet predict. There is a young woman who you must protect with your lives, unless she gets safely onto a caravel with her mother. If she does go to sea, then you are free to join the others at Adelmira."

"All right! A real mission! Count on us!" Gina spoke up, highly enthusiastically, shocking the other Sisters. Felisa again poked her in her ribs. Angelica smiled and agreed. Lysandra then gave the seven more details. Once she vanished, the entire guild house talked at once. All knew that they were incredibly blessed! The *real* goddess had come to them!

Early February 1272, Lord Turda and his forces arrived at the great bend where the coastline changed direction. This rounded point marked the southernmost portion of the entire Easterlings. His army consisted of two thousand five hundred foot soldiers and some five hundred mounted men. Most all were well equipped, but a few carried only a single weapon — either a scimitar or a dagger. Great tents were setup at the rear, where a host of cooks prepared their meals. Also, here Lord Turda made his camp among the many supply wagons. A dozen powerful "magicians" from the Renegade Tower joined him, but stayed in their own tent beside his and his son's. Amo Rafael was their leader.

Lord Turda spread his army out in a single three-tiered line. Each soldier stood about five feet from his companions on either side. The line stretched nearly a mile long! Should those in the front line fall, there were two more directly behind him to fill in the gap. It was a strong defense. However, their left flank touched the dense patch of forest in which he had concealed his five hundred mounted men. When battle was joined, they were to angle around and come at the enemy from their rear, smashing them. Even Rafael agreed the lord's plan was sound and well-conceived. Soon, they received reports of enemy scouts arriving, surveying the army. They stayed well back, however, giving Lord Turda's forces no opportunity to capture them.

"They are arranged in a line from the forest to the shores," Fausto began, sketching out the reported layout of Lord Turda's forces, as relayed to him from their advance scouts. "It is at least a mile long."

"Where is his cavalry?" Damiano asked, while still kissing and fondling his Number One wife. He hated to be distracted from her, but the notion of yet another great battle finally drew his full attention. He motioned for her to leave them. She struggled to her short legs and began her awkward waddling walk, her short arms waving about as she tried to keep her balance. Once she was gone, he put his full attention onto the map sketch that Fausto was still making.

"By all reports, he has none," Fausto answered.

Damiano pulled on his chin. "That's highly unlikely, Fausto. No, he has them hidden. There can only be one place they are hiding — here in this forest." He put his finger down hard on that part of the map. "See, he wants us to smash into his line, and then he'll hit us from behind. That is certainly what I would do if I were in his shoes." Fausto smiled, once more amazed at his leader's insight. He knew he would have fallen into that trap, had he been leading the men.

"What we need to do is make our foot soldiers rather immune to such a counter-attack and yet allow them to slice their defensive line. I have an idea that will do just that. Look here, Fausto. Suppose we form up our foot soldiers into triangular wedges with the point of the triangle pointing to their front lines. We can punch a hole easily through all three rows — say here and here. Once their line is penetrated, the wedge flows left and right, heading down their lines on either side, their flanks, crushing them utterly. Now their cavalry will come riding up from our rear like so, but they will slam into the long, solid backside of the triangle and be completely stopped. That's when we bring our cavalry up from way back here, slamming into their confused cavalry. Now not only will their line be destroyed, but their cavalry will be boxed in with nowhere to go. Deadly. The field shall be ours, my good Fausto! Yes, Lord Turda had a good plan, but mine is vastly superior to his!"

An amazed Fausto replied, "I will issue the orders. Perhaps Ettore and his new forces will join us. If so, he can mop up," he chuckled.

On the third of February, battle was joined. Lord Turda watched as two enormous, triangular wedges of foot soldiers led by Damiano himself marched slowly towards his three-tiered line. "How the hell do we stop that?" he cried out.

"My Lord, we *mentales* will do our best with them. They are boxed in close so that our spells can do maximum damage," Rafael replied. In his mind, this was the first break they'd had fighting these barbarians. Before, they had always been spread out. Now their spells could affect many men at one time.

Trumpets blared on both sides, sounding the battle charges. Damiano with his constantly swirling scything blades led point of the first triangular wedge. Some distance to his left, another general, who also swung the scything blades, led the second wedge. Screaming loudly, Damiano began to run and the two wedges joined in. Their noise was deadening as they headed towards the three-tiered defensive line. Just then, the dozen tower "magicians" began to activate their crystals. Great balls of fire descended upon the wedges. Men dropped

171

to the ground, while others screamed in hideous pain.

For a moment, it looked like the advance was stopped, but then Damiano and his scything blades came out of the rising smoke clouds and hit the front lines. Nothing could stand in his way. Men fell right and left. Then the remainder of the wedge finally joined him enlarging the hole in their lines. Not long after that, the second wedge broke through. Another volley of the balls of flame descended upon the wedges, along with many other deadly spells. Bodies dropped right and left. Before long, the sounds of galloping cavalry were heard. Rafael had sent a telepathic message to those generals, and now they came charging towards the rear lines of the two wedges. Again, hope sprang in Lord Turda's mind, but the fighting approached his position, and he and Bernardo prepared themselves for the battle at hand.

Just as his cavalrymen smashed into the rear of the two wedges, Fausto arrived with Damiano's cavalry, boxing in Lord Turda's mounted men. The rear of the wedges turned to face them, while the enemy cavalry were at their backs. Again, the tide of battle shifted, this time to Damiano's favor.

Damiano ignored the searing pain from his many burns, commanding his body to heal, while he continued to fight. He spotted Lord Turda and slowly fought his way towards him. Finally and with numerous dead and maimed soldiers behind him, Damiano reached Lord Turda and his son. Neither stood a chance against the twin scything blades. They were both cut down long before their own scimitars could even reach Damiano. Only now did Damiano finally pause in his charge. He stopped to gaze on the glorious battlefield.

From his rear position, Rafael and his eleven companions saw the lord and his son fall. The defensive line was shattered; the men dying in handfuls with no place to flee. Most of the cavalry were down. Reluctantly, Rafael sent a message to the other Circle back in Villa del Rey. One by one, the dozen tower men and women simply vanished from the battlefield. Once more, the battle was lost. This time, casualties were drastically higher than ever before and on both sides. That was the only good news Rafael could report. He also sent word to Turda that their lord and his son had been killed and the battle, lost. The news put Turda into a maddening chaos, far worse than before.

Several hours later, cries of Immortale Conquistatore Mortale were chanted wildly for some time. Men saw the nasty burn wounds of Damiano healing right before their eyes! When the chanting subsided, Damiano yelled loudly, "Glorious victory! Heal your wounds, for Turda is ours! Wealth and riches are there for your taking! Well done, valorous warriors!" More cheering followed.

However, the cost of the battle was steep on both sides. Damiano lost over half of his foot soldiers, but they mattered little to him. They were mere fodder, conscripts. He could get more in Turda. Another hundred of his powerful cavalry perished or were maimed and had to be sent home. Fewer than five hundred of Turda's defense force remained alive; half of these were wounded and thus executed. The remaining two hundred plus were conscripted into his victorious army. Again, he was counting upon conscripting thousands more when he entered Turda. Still, over half of the deceased's weapons were nothing but scrap metal. Weeks later, many scavengers gathered up the broken metal bits. They could be melted down and forged into new weapons. Iron was that scarce here in the Easterlings.

Once more, Damiano merely left the dead where they fell, making no attempts whatsoever to bury the dead. The scavengers had a feast.

The news and shock of the death of Lord Turda and the entire army put the city into complete chaos. The very few city guards who remained were unable to maintain the remotest sense of order. Thirty thousand men, women, and children were in an utter panic.

The nobles, who, at the very instant they heard the news, fled to the docks and their waiting caravels, made it safely there and were able to depart Turda. Those who delayed even an hour met the chaos head on. Everywhere, people were frantically trying to flee the city. The streets were mobbed with people, so crowded that, for a time, it seemed no one was making any progress at all!

Worse, seeing some nobles fleeing with their wealth, many began attacking them, stealing what they could before they too would flee the city. Almost at once, widespread looting broke out as the have-nots began to take what they could before abandoning the city. Mass pandemonium covered nearly every city block! Many were knifed and left to bleed to death; their possessions stolen.

In the Royal Palace, already all the treasury had been loaded onto caravels. The one carrying the country's funds had already set sail. Dona, Eula, and Edda were stunned when they heard the news directly from Rafael. He urged them to get to their caravel as soon as possible before he vanished, teleported back to Villa del Rey.

"Pack the last of your things, Edda. Put them into your backpack. We should leave as soon as we can," the sobbing Dona ordered. However, speed was impossible for these ornamented women. Two hours later, Edda had her pack stuffed with several complete changes of clothing and her precious listings of the two treasuries. She took the time to tie her two long braids into a bun, securing it to her head. That made carrying the stuffed, but light, backpack easier to manage.

As she waited for Dona and Eula to be ready to go, she looked out on the scene in the streets by the Royal Palace. She could not believe what she was seeing. Never had she seen the street so packed with people. All were in a wild hysteria, caring not for what they were doing to others. She watched as a small boy tripped and fell. Many adults simply trampled him to death, despite the wailing of his nearby mother. She finally got to him, bent down to help him, and was trampled herself. The scene was ghastly; something out of a nightmare!

Then she spotted a dozen palace guards fighting their way into the palace. It was all so surreal to her. Some of the guards entered and one guard entered the room. "My Lady, we are here to escort you to your ship. You stay here; we'll fetch your mothers." His shirt was covered in blood. Edda merely nodded, too much in shock to say anything at all.

Another guard took up a position by the door of this sitting room, where she so often sat watching for men coming to meet with her father. The thought of her father caused her grief to swell up again. She sobbed. Splintering noises broke her grief spell. It could only be their front doors, she analytically thought. She heard the sounds of a mob rushing into the entrance hall. A wave of fear swept over her, and she rose to her toes, catching her balance.

She heard the cries of her mother and the sounds of fighting. The guard at her door drew his sword again. "My Lady, stay put. They are fighting their way here, bringing your mothers to you. We will get you all to safety." A terrified Edda did as asked, what else could she do she wondered.

Out in the hallway, looters were piling inside, hoping to steal something of value before they too fled the city. Something — anything they could sell to buy food and shelter — anything. Although mobbed, the palace guards fought valiantly. However, more continued to push their way inside, diving them back. Now they were at the door to the study, where the lone guard stood.

Above the din, she heard one palace guard call out, "We can't get to Edda! We have to back out the rear. Save the wives at least!" Now she did panic! The mob swarmed the lone guard, who swung his scimitar right and left. Still others took up the push, driving the guard backwards.

Then it happened. Someone stuck a knife in the belly of the guard. As he reacted, others pummeled him and he went down. Now nothing stood between Edda and the insane mob of men. Several stared at her. "Take them gold earrings and disks! They're valuable," some man called out and they rushed towards her. Edda tried to back up, but in toe shoes, that was most difficult. She stumbled and fell, but managed to keep from hitting her face and lip plates on the floor.

Just as a grubby man reached for her right earring intent on pulling it off of her ear, from out of nowhere, a short sword flashed. His hand fell onto the floor. A foot pushed hard into his chest, and he fell over backwards, knocking several others over as well. She then saw a man appear connected to the short sword. No! It was a woman wearing men's clothing. Vaguely her mind registered Sisterhood woman.

When the news of the fall the army came, the seven Sisterhood women were still in their guild house. All the other women had already been evacuated two weeks ago to the safety of their guild house up in Adelmira. Savina constantly grumbled these past twelve days, "Lordy, I ain't got no one to cook for no more!"

"Hey, I'm here. I eat like a horse," Gina teased her, bringing a smile to the old cook's face.

"Sure you ain't pregnant, dear child?" Savina retorted with a laugh.

"She's in big, big trouble if she is," her free mate Felisa added to their mirth. Gina laughed heartily.

"Oh cool it, will you? We are trying to play some cards here," Bianca called out.

"No, Bianca is trying to take away all of our money," Marcella protested. "Stop looking into our minds to see what cards we have. Angelica, control your mate, will you?" Several others laughed.

Savina joked, "You all will be flat broke long before anything happens here." Everyone laughed again. It was terribly boring. With everyone gone and the army off to war, the guild house seemed empty of all activity.

Days passed before they heard the town criers disseminating the news of the deaths of Lord Turda and his son and the loss of the battle. "Crap! It's finally happened," Gina exclaimed.

"Guess Lysandra knows what she's doing," Angelica added. "Come on everyone. Pack up. We best follow her orders."

"I'm on it," Bianca replied. She focused and her germanium crystal activated. She now saw through Edda's eyes, though Edda didn't know it. Angelica packed for her mate and herself, though Donatella stood beside the silent Bianca, ready to go into action if needed.

"Oh good lordy!" the portly Savina came rushing into their common room. "They are rioting in the streets now! Come see," she added. Several rushed to their front windows, including Angelica.

"Crap, they are clogging the streets! Don't those idiots

know no one is going anywhere if they pack the streets so?" Gina cursed them. "Damn fools! What's gotten into them? The barbarians are weeks away from here. Stupid men anyway!"

"Bastards, men are such bastards," Felisa, her free mate added antagonistically. "Once again, we bear witness to the ill of men. I swear the world would be better off if men didn't exist!"

Angelica cautioned her, "If so, how would we ever be able to bear children, Felisa? We would not exist either." Felisa growled, but knew she was right. She was just reacting.

A couple hours later, they had everything ready to go, horses packed. Now it was all up to Bianca, who was monitoring Edda. If she got safely onto the royal yacht, then they could mount up and join the others up in Adelmira. Bianca felt the gentle touch of Donatella joining her and then the familiar and loving presence of Angelica, her free mate. Such mental rapports were vastly superior to sexual sensations. Then, the three saw the mob breaking into the palace. Before long, they saw the lone guard knifed and Donatella acted. She focused and her crystal energized. She appeared on the floor near the fallen Edda. Just as the man reached down to rip off her valuable earrings, she swung her short sword, severing the man's hand. Almost simultaneously, she pushed her foot solidly into his chest, knocking him over. She moved in front of Edda.

Gina followed her, bringing four other Sisters with her. She then vanished and returned a moment later with the rest of their small band. The seven fanned out and began fighting the mostly unarmed mob back. None of the seven paid the slightest attention to the fact that most of these men were unarmed. They left a dozen of them dead before the mob backed off, yielding this one room to the crazy Sisterhood fighters.

Meanwhile, Savina helped Edda to her feet. "The Goddess Lysandra sent us to protect you, child," the portly, good-natured woman explained to the shocked teen. "Looks like she was right. You need protect'n, that's for sure."

"But, but she doesn't exist. She's just a myth," Edda tried to make sense of what was happening, failing badly. "He was going to rip my earring off. What's happening? Why is everyone acting so strange?"

"Panic, child, panic. Everyone is fleeing Turda and trying to take anything of value with them," Savina answered.

Gina put in, "Idiots. They are all idiots. The barbarians won't be here for weeks, yet they act as if they will be here any minute. Fools all of them."

Angelica called out, "We've secured the room. Felisa, do your thing. What's the situation outside? Can we get her to her boat?"

Felisa's crystal activated and Edda watched, both stunned and fascinated at the same time. Gina explained, "She can fly up in the sky like a bird and look down on the city. Pretty darn cool, if you ask me. I can teleport, you know. That's even cooler!" She was quite proud of her skill.

A few minutes later, Felisa opened her eyes, her crystal dimmed. Edda noted it, wondering what these crystals actually did. "Boss, streets are impassable. Hell, they are packed, and no one is making any progress anywhere. I spotted the palace guards. They are about the only ones making any progress. Heading to the docks, but their boat is being attacked by the mob. Lord knows if the crew can keep them off before the women get there. Not wise to take Edda to the yacht right now."

"Okay, then back to the guild house. We can make a stand there," Angelica decided. "Divide up as usual." Edda didn't know what that meant. Donatella held out her hand and Edda mechanically took it. Three others latched on, either to her other hand or to Donatella's other hand.

"Whatever you do, don't let go," Donatella said to the frightened teen. She focused her thoughts. Her crystal activated, casting a bluish light. The next thing Edda knew she stumbled onto the floor in some strange building. Those holding her hand kept her on her toes, though. Shortly, Gina appeared with the others in tow.

"Welcome to our Sisterhood guild house, Edda. I am the Guild Mother, Angelic Freda e Alessandra. My free mate, Bianca Alessandra e Freda," she explained. One by one, she introduced the others.

"I've never met Sisters before. What is a free mate? What does the 'e' mean? Are you married? How can that be? You are both women," Edda asked both confused and interested at the same time.

"Bianca, Gina, go keep watch," Angelica ordered. "When two people want to marry but outside your formal weddings, we become free mates. We women do not want to give up our lineage, like your kind do. We are proud of our parents. Hence, we retain our last name and add an 'e' and then the last name of our partner. And yes, we love each other as much or more than your father and mother, Edda. Most that join the Sisterhood have been badly brutalized by men, one way or another. Here in this house, they find safety, kindness, affection, and sometimes love."

She then changed the topic. "Lysandra charged us with protecting you. Don't ask us why. We have no idea why Lysandra believes you are so important. You are what? Thirteen? How did you get ornamented so young? I thought they enforced the rule that you had to be an adult to get them."

Sheepishly, Edda answered. "Thirteen. I wanted to look like mom, like all the noblewomen. I wanted to look beautiful. I talked dad into it. I think he made them do it. I know. I was very foolish. If I knew then what I know now, I would not have. Why does Lysandra want me? Oh, is it because I am now the ruler of Turda?"

"Hum, maybe so, Edda. We heard that Lord Turda officially named you his heir after your brother. Now that both are dead — sorry for your loss — that does make you the ruler of Turda. I don't think now is the time to try to take charge — not unless you can pull an army out of your back pocket. Oh, you don't have any pockets." Several women laughed, Edda's face crimsoned. "That's a joke, dear." Angelica added.

"The question now is what do we do with you? We are to keep you safe. That much is clear. We had planned to ride out of here to Adelmira, but right now, that is out of the question. No one is going anywhere in those streets. We had hoped to deposit you on your caravel and let you sail away, but that seems out too. We need some place that's safe to wait this thing out. Either that or teleport somewhere," she spoke what she was thinking. "All our gear is on our horses right now."

"I know a place that would be safe," Edda tried to be helpful. Angelica nodded and she volunteered. "In the palace, we have a secret set of rooms in the basement. Hardly anyone knows of it. We could be quite safe there."

Just then, Bianca called out, "Gang, we have to do something now! The mob is heading our way. Make that they are on our doorstep." They heard a small explosion. "That will keep them back a short while! I fire balled them."

"Okay, Edda, I want you to picture this safe area in your mind so that I and Gina can see what you are seeing. Everyone, here to us. Teleport time," Angelica called out.

"But I want to fight the bastards," Bianca complained, though she ran through the house to join them.

"Me too," Marcella added.

"Time enough for that later. We need to get her to a safe place," Angelica ordered, ending their protests. Again, they joined hands, and Edda did sense that they were somehow in her mind. It was the strangest sensation she had ever felt, but somehow it felt so utterly intimate. The next thing she knew, she was stepping onto the hard stone floor of their underground rooms. It was pitch black.

Marcella called out, "Light." Suddenly a glow surrounded her and they could see. There were a number of lanterns on the walls and quickly the women fanned out, lighting them. They were in a large underground room that had a musty odor about it. A crude table and benches rested near one wall.

"There are two more rooms that way. Bedrooms," Edda pointed out. Gina headed off to inspect them and light the lanterns there.

"Hey nice beds. What say we bring our gear from the horses here, boss? Nice place to hold up in," Gina announced. Angelica knew if a place met with Gina's approval, it was rather elegant, if not plush.

"Okay. Gina, Donatella, go fetch our many packs, but be damned careful. We can't afford to lose either of you," Angelica replied.

"On it boss. Savina, there's a sort of stove over there.

See if it works. Found a lot of chamber pots in the bedrooms," Gina advised, before she and Donatella simply vanished from sight.

"How do they do that?" Edda asked.

She followed Savina over to the side wall where the stove and water faucet were located. "*Mentales* gifts, deary. We's all got them. Gifts for us rescuing the mermaids some twenty years ago. These crystals magnify our mental powers. So how does this work? Where's the water come from? Is it any good?"

"Rainwater catcher on the roof. Feeds into a set of barrels. Some pipes bring it down here. For emergencies. But we've never had one until now," Edda replied.

Savina tasted it. "Good. Okay, we got's water. Now this stove. No firewood or charcoal. Just as good though. If we burned much down here, we'd use up all the air. Never you mind, honey, Savina is here. She don't need no firewood or charcoal to cook. Now if my Gina brings me my pots and pans and food supplies, we'll be in business." Edda didn't understand half of what she meant.

She made her slow way over to the table and sat down on a bench. She removed her backpack. At least she had more clothes, she thought. "I guess we'll be safe here for some time," she said, as Angelica walked over to sit down too.

"What's that?" Angelica said. Edda sensed she was thinking something else. "Sorry, we've dropped our light mental contact with your mind. It takes too much of our energies to keep it going for long times. You have to speak more slowly and as clearly as you can or we can't understand you. Lip plates interfere."

Edda flushed again. "Sorry. I said we'll be safe here for some time. No one knows about this place. Sorry."

"That's all right, dear. You've undergone quite a traumatic day. Still, you need to remember others find your speech very hard to follow, but I suppose you already know that."

Edda flushed again, but didn't reply. *How foolish I have been,* she thought. Suddenly Gina appeared loaded with saddlebags and packs. "I'm a bloody horse," she called out and vanished again. Savina laughed heartily. Donatella appeared leaving more packs. Edda watched the action for the next several minutes, absolutely fascinated by these women. Further, they all knew just what to do. Without saying anything, the women set about sorting out the packs and establishing some sense of a domicile once more.

Gina brought the last of their things. "Damn men. They stole the horse right out from under me. Boss, can I go back and kill a few of them? Need to teach them some lessons in manners."

"Not now, Gina. Remember Lysandra's orders," Angelica replied. Gina grimaced and headed over to chat with Savina. Edda watched and saw the stove suddenly turn red hot. "She can heat metal and objects. That's part of her gift," Angelica explained, sensing Edda's intense curiosity.

"Felisa, keep watch over the city, please. Let me know if anything useful develops," Angelica then ordered.

Later, Savina had a large pot of tea steaming. Gina poured everyone a cup. "Spoon please?" Edda said slowly as Gina sat a cup before her.

"Coming up," the still agile thief replied. "Mind if I sit beside you and watch? I've always wondered how you women manage to drink your tea."

Edda giggled. "It is really hard. Have to use a spoon and keep from drooling. It doesn't help all that much to take the plates out. No lips," she explained.

Gina watched her fascinated. "Why would you want such things?" she finally asked.

"We look beautiful like this," Edda replied. Now she wondered if that was even so. Perhaps it was solely to look like all of her social peers. "I don't want to look different than the other noblewomen," she finally admitted.

"Thought so. It's okay by me. A woman ought to have the right to do what she wants with her own body and her own life. Men don't think so, but I do," Gina added.

Edda relaxed and felt somewhat relieved. At least she wasn't being chided for having been so foolish. "I know I was terribly foolish to have all this done, but at the time, I really did want it, more than anything in the world. Of course, then I didn't know all this was coming — that I would lose my dad." A tear formed and she fought to keep it back.

"Hey, you are being honest, Edda," Gina pointed out. "That's really the measure of a woman. I like you." Edda grinned, but it was invisible as always now.

Gina changed the topic, "So boss, what's the plan? When do we get to fight?"

"The plan? Keep her safe for now. If worst comes to worst, we'll teleport to the others in Adelmira. Maybe Lysandra will appear and tell us what she wants done next. Hell, Gina, I don't know any more than you do," Angelica answered, slightly annoyed. She didn't like not knowing any more than Gina or the others did.

Sometime later, Felisa ended her observations, returning to take her tea. "Utter chaos out there, boss. I swear the townsfolk are doing a better job of sacking Turda than the barbarians will do. Hell, when they finally get here, the place will already be looted. Serves them right to get no plunder here." She laughed sarcastically.

Just then, Angelica seemed distant and remote. Everyone quieted down and watched her. Edda whispered to Gina, "What's happening to her?"

"Someone is contacting her — telepathy, you know. Probably some message for us or something," Gina whispered back. After a few minutes, she added, "Boy, this must be a dilly of a message. She's hardly ever tied up this long! Wonder what's going on? Can't be good. Never is. Men, you know. Always causing trouble of one kind or another." Edda began to wonder just what awful things had happened to Gina at or by the hands of men. Surely they were not all evil, her father wasn't.

Finally, Angelica opened her eyes. "Well, that was some news! Gather around. You all want to hear this! That was a relay message via Adelmira Tower. It seems that Sultaness Sonia Ferro, the Number One wife of the late sultan, has now become the ruler of the Arad. She and our Sisterhood there have been re-conquering all the oases from the barbarians and now have control of Tecuci once more. Further, Lysandra has her hands in it. She's given immense powers to two women there. I'm told they can kill a man just by thinking it so! This is a first for Tierra! A woman running an entire kingdom with us Sisters at her side? Incredible. Who would ever have thought such was possible. This Sonia must be one powerful woman. I thought she was just another decorated sultan's wife. Least that's what I've always heard on the rumor line."

After some chatter died down, she continued, "Sultaness Sonia has asked for more Sisterhood aid. I relayed her request on to our main headquarters in Hilliard Heights. There are only a couple of Sisters in Adelmira now; they've all gone off to help Sultaness Sonia, and so our members are holding the fort for them, so to speak. She also wants us to find out if any of their sons have survived. Apparently, they came to Turda to raise an army to retake the Arad."

She continued, "Then, Rafael wanted to know what is happening here. Apparently, he was able to get Dona and Eula onto your caravel, but only with some doing. However, some bad news, Eula has lost her baby. These events caused her to too much stress, he thinks. Right now, their healer, Anita Valen is on the ship trying to save her. His advice for us is to stay put for now. The Renegade Tower knows where we all are at and can send help on a moment's notice if we need it. He is requesting we monitor what the barbarians actually do here when they come. He claims he is rather busy at the moment to come here and watch firsthand. There, that about covers it. Questions?"

"Is sultaness even a word?" Gina spoke up. "Incredible. She's an ornamented woman even. Freeing her country from the barbarians? Their new ruler? A woman? This world is changing at an unreal rate!"

"Well, now we have the plan," Felisa broke in. "We stay put and observe what the barbarians do. I can handle that, I suppose."

"I hope they can save poor Eula," Marcella added. "What we women must bear and then to have men do this to us. Sorry about her, Edda, but you can see a little why we are so bitter towards men and their actions. Wait — that does mean that you are the sole remaining heir to your father's throne!"

Donatella, born a noblewoman, knew the political impact of this better than any of her sisters. "Yes that is officially correct. If Edda doesn't assume power in Turda, then by rights it will fall to Lord Turda's brothers and their first-born sons. If so, you can expect significant fighting among them for the throne, adding more misery to this god-awful mess that we're in."

"How many uncles do you have, Edda? How bad could it be? They've all fled, right?" asked Bianca, growing more curious. What would Edda do?

"Five. One is too old. I really don't like the other four though," Edda replied, remembering to speak slowly and as clearly as she could. "I am not going to run from my new obligations to Turda. I know how dad conducted our business affairs and that we all prospered. I always sat in on his meetings. I can see now he was actually allowing me to sit in on them. Before, I always thought I was being clever and sneaky doing it. Now I can see he wanted me to be there, but hidden because the visitors would not have wanted me there. Papa, why didn't you tell me this before?" Tears came once more.

Felisa quietly changed the topic. "So Sultaness Sonia wants us to find out about her sons?"

Edda quickly said, "They went off to fight with our army."

"Crap! There's not much hope for them," Felisa concluded. "They are either dead or conscripted into the barbarian's army. How are we supposed to find out about their fates? We don't even know them."

Angelica mused, "Well, Edda here could identify them, though I don't know if it would be a good idea to visit the battlefield. The horrors there would give us nightmare for years. Besides, there are likely thousands of dead bodies there. Needle in a haymow. No, we ought to keep our eyes open. If they are alive, they will probably make their way here to Turda."

Savina called out, "Supper is ready." That ended the official discussion, though many continued to chat about the parts that interested them as they ate.

The next day, Edda led them to the secret door that led into the main palace. Felisa used her gift and pronounced it free of the mob. Carefully, the small group opened the door and entered the palace proper. Edda led them from one room to the next. There were a few dead bodies still lying where they fell, but the place was ransacked. However, as Edda explained, all the truly valuable things had been crated up and shipped weeks ago. The robbers only made off with worn tapestries and brass lanterns, things like that. Cautiously, they went to the rooftop observation deck. From here, they could look down into the city. Dead lay everywhere, but for the most part, the living was gone. Only a few roamed the streets. Fear of the chaos from the previous day's mob vanished.

Two slow weeks passed by. Some semblance of normalcy returned to Turda. They spotted a few old men attempting to cart the dead from the streets. However, as Edda put it, the number of visible people on the streets was a hundredth of normal. All began to suspect most of the population had found some means of fleeing before the barbarians arrived.

At last, Felisa alerted them. "Columns of riders are approaching Turda from the east!" Again, the group headed into the safety of their underground hideout. Felisa used her *mentales* gift to keep them apprised of what the barbarians were doing.

"Say, Edda ought to get a look at the riders and see if any of those four sons of Sultaness Sonia are among them," Angelica suggested. "Edda, are you willing to do such a thing?"

"Yes, but they will see me," she replied, not grasping what Angelica actually meant.

She chuckled and then replied, "Dear, Felisa will join your mind with hers and allow you to see what she is seeing. No one can see either her or you. Your body will be right here with us, as Felisa's is now."

"But I don't know how to do that?" she protested, again feeling rather inferior to these women, the most powerful women she had ever known. In fact, she never had known any woman remotely as powerful as these were. She wondered why her father had never mentioned them or the Sisterhood to her before.

Oh! This is so intimate! Edda thought, as she found herself touched with Felisa's mind. Now she seemed to be hovering above her city, like some giant hawk.

Yes, it is a thousand times better than sex, but then you probably haven't slept with a man yet. Sorry, Felisa sent her, realizing again she was really dealing with a thirteen year old girl, not an adult woman. One by one, Felisa focused in on the riders, hundreds of them. None were remotely similar to the four Arad men that Edda had seen. Off in the far distance, she then spotted long lines of foot soldiers, dragging their way towards the city. To Edda's amazement, she seemed to be flying towards them, but she continued to look over the men, as Felisa zoomed along their four-abreast lines. When they reached the end, Edda still had not seen the four men. Felisa then canceled her power, returning their awareness back to the present and their bodies sitting on the crude bench.

"She didn't find them. Foot soldiers are on their way too. Searched them too. We can presume that the four are dead, if you want to relay that," Felisa reported to Angelica.

"What's happened here?" Fausto asked as he entered their prized city, Turda. "Has someone already ransacked it first?"

"Make for the palace, the tallest building. We ought to find treasure there," Damiano ordered.

As his cavalry rode through the littered streets nearly empty of people, he issued orders to start conscripting able-bodied men. By the time they reached the tallest building in Turda, the palace, several had already reported back about the mass exodus of the city. "No matter, we will simply rob them as we move on into Alba or get them at the next town. They can run like the scared rabbits they are, but they cannot hide from me," Damiano declared, putting everyone at ease.

They spent only a brief time in the palace. Obviously, it had already been thoroughly looted. As the foot soldiers swarmed into the town, disappointed at finding nothing much to plunder, they took their frustrations out on those few who remained. Often women and young girls were raped and beaten. Many older men were simply executed for the sport of it. However, his men were able to confiscate a good deal of fresh food supplies those who fled were unable to take with them.

Damiano called Fausto and Luigi together for a conference. "Well, we've only been able to conscript a hundred men and those are pathetic," Damiano announced. "We've lost too many men to continue on down the coast. A change of tactics is needed. We should press on inland, attacking the outlying towns and villages. There, we should be able to conscript many who have fled from Turda as well. We will gradually build up our army as we move inland. Strike the heartland of the Midlands!"

"We should see about finding some maps of Matruk and these nearer Midland countries," Fausto added.

"Aye, that will be most useful. Tell the men we march on the lush farm country tomorrow. Further, tell them until further notice, they get to keep possession of all the spoils that we capture. That ought to get their minds off of having gotten nothing here in Turda," Damiano ordered.

Luigi pointed out, "We ought to be able to pick up many new horses as we dive into these farmlands."

"Good point, Luigi. I am putting you in charge of horse acquisitions. Anything else?" There wasn't and Damiano headed for his tent to take pleasure from and with his four wives. They provided a nice distraction for him and could not possibly pose the slightest threat to him.

Chapter 11 Repercussions

"Well, that is good. The barbarians didn't stay here long," Bianca stated dryly, watching the last of the foot soldiers marching northwestwards out of Turda.

"Well, now I am the ruler, but how am I going to run everything? There probably isn't even one horse in the city," Edda began, speaking slowly. "Food will soon be a problem. They took so many wagons. I need to have the Renegade Tower get at least one caravel of grain here as soon as possible. Yet, I don't have any way to get word to them."

"Hey, you have us," Gina spoke up. "Are you really planning on being the sole ruler of Turda now?"

"Yes, of course. Papa appointed me. Besides, I think I would like to do it. I have seen too much tragedy at the hands of men. But I don't have anyone to help me do this," Edda answered her. Then, she took a gamble, based in part on what she heard was happening in the Arad. "Angelica, can the Sisterhood help me rebuild Turda? If so, I can pay you or better, see that you are given positions of power in Turda. I need help. I know much of how to run our city, but that was when everything was normal. Now I have nothing to work with at all."

Donatella sent, *Angelica. She has a point. You and I should talk this over.*

Angelica said, "Edda, give us a minute to reflect on your offer, please." She and Donatella headed into the next room so as not to be overheard.

Donatella whispered, "This may be a golden opportunity for the entire Sisterhood to gain acceptance and the power we long have lacked. Edda doesn't stand a chance without our help."

"But we've always been on the outside of society — everywhere on Tierra. As soon as the people return to their city, they'll turn hostile again, don't you think?" Angelica countered.

"Not if we make a good go of it. If Edda is as good as she

thinks she is — you know — like her father — she could well bring prosperity back to Turda. Think of the possibilities, Angelica. The Sisterhood in Arad is helping Sonia; we should help Edda here. You know as well as I do that right now we can make a difference," Donatella countered her counter.

"Do you really think we could pull this off? We are only seven," the Guild Mother argued.

"True, but we could call in for immediate assistance from Hilliard Heights — get in some other Sisters from the Midlands and maybe even the Westerlings too. If we are strong enough here, as the population slowly returns to find the city doing well, we might be accepted," Donatella again countered. "Don't you think it is worth a try? Could not this be part of what Lysandra wanted us to do? Protect Edda as she reforms Turda into a woman-run City-State?"

"Hum, you do have a point. Will the nobles accept us? You know how I despise them," Angelica asked.

"If anything, they will be more against Edda than us. If Edda comes through as she believes she can, then as far as the nobles are concerned, money is everything. If they make at least as much money as before, they will go along with Edda. Nobles think first about their money pouches." Both women laughed.

"All right. We'll give it a go. Perhaps you are right. This may be what Lysandra wants — the wider acceptance of women rulers on Tierra. I will ask for power, though, not money," Angelica finally agreed.

A bit later, they returned to Edda. "We accept your offer, Edda. The Turda Sisterhood is at your disposal. We don't want money, beyond what is fair for the work we do. We like your idea of power. Just be forewarned, returning men will not take kindly to we Sisters being in positions of power."

Edda smiled broadly and let out a sigh. "Thank you, thank you. I will never forget what you all have done for me and for Turda."

"Okay then, I will contact Rafael and see to it a caravel of grain gets here as soon as possible. What will by your title? How is all this going to work?" Angelica asked.

"Title? Oh. Well, I don't want to be called sultaness.

That's hardly a word, I don't think. Dad was just Lord Turda, so I will be just Lady Turda. I think the way to proceed is to make you my ministers. You know, have a Minister of Defense, a Minister of Trade, and so on. You would be my top advisors."

"Hey, I'd just rather be your cook," Savina called out.

Everyone laughed as Gina added, "Minister of Cooking."

"We are going to need many more Sisters. I am recalling the other members of our guild who are up in Adelmira and sending out word to the other guild houses. Perhaps other Sisters will be willing to come here and lend a hand," Angelica added.

Gina broke in, "Hey, does this mean we all get to wear crowns or something?" Again, the women laughed.

Edda didn't. "Right now, there isn't any gold left or any crowns. They've all been sent away. When we get all our stuff back, Gina, I think it would be proper for us all to wear a crown, a small one though, so everyone can see you are officially whatever you are. Less trouble that way."

"I get to be the Minister of Thievery," Gina jested and again they roared, relieving the tensions of the past weeks. However, Angelica had to explain the jest to Edda, who didn't know Gina's background.

Later that day as they got a bit more organized, Rafael appeared. "Edda, I have come on behalf of Venerado Valen to inform you that you are officially accepted as the sole ruler of the City-State of Turda. You will be formally introduced to all the other leaders later this year, when we hold our annual meeting in July at Exchange City. In addition, the Renegade Tower also recognizes the Sisterhood members are your lawful ministers. Your word and personnel assignments are your own business. Your choices will be supported by the tower. Further, the tower is already informing all the other leaders of your ascension to your late father's throne. Oh yes, expect your emergency grain shipment in two days. A load of horses will follow within a few weeks. Hang in there a little longer for them."

"Wow! That's fast action. We do need the grain. The barbarians left us with almost nothing," Edda replied, remembering to speak slowly. "I am sorry I can't do the things that everyone else can — you know, this magic stuff — telepathy and all that. So I have made Angelica my Minister of Communications. She will be contacting you and the others on my behalf, if that is okay with you. I am sorry I don't know more about these magic things and the tower and your protocols. I will learn — about the protocols, if only someone can teach me."

"Excellent. I will see everyone knows of her appointment. Angelica, you will have permission to directly contact the Renegade Tower's communications network anytime you need its services." He bowed slightly to Angelica, taking her completely by surprise. Donatella realized what was going on and smiled.

After he left, she whispered to Angelica, "You are slowly being accepted as nobility, by virtue of your new position as minister and because of your *mentales* gifts."

"But I am hardly nobility. You are by birth," she countered.

Donatella grinned, "By birth, yes. But birth does not always nobility make." Both women chuckled at that.

"Next you are going to tell me I have to start wearing dresses again," Angelica teased her.

"It would help in more formal settings, Angelica. Or are you too old to wear a dress?" Donatella teased her back.

"All I wanted to do was to retire in a few years," she half-jested.

By the first of March 1272, all the other City-States in the alliance knew of Lady Edda Turda's rise to the throne and the heavy role the Sisterhood was playing there. Now two of the larger cities of the alliance were under the sole control of women leaders with a strong Sisterhood presence. Until this point in time, such was never dreamed possible by anyone on Tierra, much less the Sisterhood women.

The makeup of the Renegade Tower personnel had changed during the last twenty years. The original founders had retired or passed away. Power passed down to their many children. Pino Valen was now their venerado, replacing Fons

Valen. Why? Fons' son, Andres had effectively disappeared at the same time as his daughter, Gracia, who had become one of the first of Calder's mermaids and who had been their high priestess. His only remaining daughter, Hermina was married to Raul de Portales, whose father was one of the top advisors of Fons. Fons was determined that a Valen remain as their venerado.

They expanded their operation to include two full *Círculo de mentes*. Roberto Valen, now fifty-three was still the capo of the First Circle, the original one, while Ruperto de Portes, thirty-six, was the capo of their Second Circle. In addition, they had nearly fifty other *mentales* gifted around the greater Villa del Rey area, upon which they could call when the need arose.

Of course, most of this close-knit group was still somewhat handicapped. Years ago, they had gone along with the ill-working plan to take over control of all the towers on Tierra. Namely, they had been fully body modified. All wore the pipe corsets, toe shoes or toe boots, and five-inch lip plates. The women also wore the heavy, long earrings. While these could be managed somewhat, they had also had their hands removed, pretending to have contracted a virulent disease. A great many of the other towers' personnel bought into the charade and had similar body modifications. Yet, the plan ultimately failed. Now most of the Renegade Tower members struggled with daily life, using the alien prosthetic hands, poor substitutes for their own hands. All were thankful for their unknown benefactors in Brom, who had given them far better hands than Lord Valen had procured for everyone during his grand plan for world domination. For these reasons, the actual tower personnel seldom were seen in public.

About the only time they went out was to the High Council Meetings. Three of the founder's children had not been modified at all. They had been children during that time period. Rafael and Fidelia were both thirty-three and were often acting as the tower's official representatives on daily business actions. Also Anita, their thirty-four year old healer, often traveled extensively, working her miracles of healing.

Both Anita and Fidelia had married into the Villa del Rey ruling families, namely Leandro del Rey and Gilberto Rosa, respectively. Thus, the tower maintained a close relationship to the rulers of Villa del Rey.

Now the tower faced its worst crisis ever — the barbarian Damiano Donatello. When Po fell, Venerado Pino Valen contacted the other towers on Tierra alerting them to this potentially severe problem. In response, uniformly the other venerados suggested this was entirely an Easterlings and City-States Alliance matter. That view didn't change when Teraspoli fell, nor did it change when Tecuci fell. However, he did get the first concession from several towers, who suggested they would be closely monitoring this barbarian in the future.

When Damiano marched on down into Alba, Venerado Pino had no choice but to dispatch an entire circle there. However, considering how constrained the circle members were, he called in favors from their many "auxiliary" members. It was these men who had accompanied Rafael, Anita, and Fidelia to help Lord Turda fight the barbarians. When they returned with the terrible news of the total destruction of Lord Turda's army, finally the other towers took notice.

Early March 1272, when Damiano led his army northwest into the heart of Matruk and directly towards the heartlands of the Midlands, all the towers began to pay very close attention. Again, remember that at this time in history, the towers were independent of the rulers of the lands in which they were located. There was a separation of rulers and the *mentales* gifted. Lord Amos Wye, via his tower in Wye (the former Bedwurth Tower), and Lord Frank North of Northend, via his tower in Northend (the former Haverhills Tower) insisted on a Spring Council of the Lords. Both their kingdom were next in line, after Matruk. Lord Matruk of Southbend agreed, but he was not too worried, since the barbarians were not heading towards his thriving city. He could afford the loss of farming villages in the north of Matruk.

Based upon Rafael's estimates and the distance across Matruk, the barbarians would not reach Northend until late May or Wye until late June. The rulers still had time to prepare for the onslaught. Yet, they were wise. Both Sultan

Gino and Sultan Ferro had armies and failed to stop them. Lord Turda had an army and the support of an entire circle and still lost the battle. This then caused the other lords considerable worry. Apparently, no single army could stop this renegade barbarian. Worse, by all accounts, he seemed indestructible. Rafael was quite clear about the results of the various *mentales* effects upon him, including the many balls of fire that apparently didn't harm him much at all. Many feared they were facing some new and unknown *mentales* gift.

Making matters worse, it was late winter in the south Midlands and the dead of winter further north in areas such as Brom. Armies would be difficult to raise in the winter. Also these kingdoms were distant from each other. Even if Lord Walsham in the far north left immediately with an army marching south to come to the aid of Lord Northend, he would get there at least a month after the barbarian had finished his work. Many others were far more distant. If Brom sent an army, almost a half a year would be needed to march them down to Matruk, ignoring wholly the massive supply problems. Hence, the three lords demanded a High Council meeting. Reluctantly, all the others agreed, and the date was set for the first of April at the Imperial Castle in Exchange City.

Per the usual rules of the High Council of the Lords, each lord was allowed to bring along two advisors and their tower's venerado or venerada. In some cases, the tower leader was also allowed to bring along a helper. On the other hand, at the July meetings, these restrictions were relaxed, and most of the City-States Alliance leaders came. Of course, all spouses were invited as well.

Because of the weather conditions, most would be teleporting to the early spring, special meeting. The caretakers of the Imperial Tower dutifully lowered all such barriers to teleportation. Exchange City still was covered in snow on the first of April. It was high in the Goza Mountains. This time, Lord Gilberto Rosa of Villa del Rey attended, representing the City-States Alliance. Ama Fidelia, his wife and tower member, came with him as his spouse. Leandro del Rey came as his advisor, bringing along his wife Ama Anita, who was also a tower member. Venerado Roberto Valen attended as Lord

Gilberto's tower representative. He brought his spouse, Natalia, also a tower member. In the past, they received many complaints from the other lords, who claimed that Lord Gilberto was bringing too many tower members, but the rules won. Finally, Rafael Valen was specifically requested to attend, since it was he who had the most direct observations of this barbarian and his army.

On note, Valen Tower, the instigators of massive treachery in the past, had been outlawed from the High Council of Lords. However, after a recent coop there, Lord Alano Valen became the new lord of the kingdom. Their new venerado was his brother, Arturo Valen. After several years, the High Council of Lords permitted the Valens to return to the meetings, though their voting privileges were still reduced. Many still held intense hatred for the many crimes Valen Tower had committed on the Midlands and elsewhere.

Changes in leadership and rulership had been the keynote during the past twenty years of peace and relative prosperity throughout the Westerlings and Midlands. Still, the sharp separation of towers and rulership of kingdoms was maintained. No ruler wanted to give their towers the absolute powers that the towers once had held over their kingdoms. Still, the rulers of the many kingdoms took this utter calm as a sign or omen. With the main exception of the newly formed Renegade Tower, the older rulers took this opportunity to train and establish their new, more youthful replacements. Of course, this usually meant passing the torch to members of their own families.

Critically important were the many changes that were made in Brom and in Brom Tower. The throne of Brom was now in the able hands of young Lord Emilio Bolivar, twenty-five. He had married Anita Brom-Bolivar, one of the rare katalyein *mentales* gifted women and who was a year younger. They had a son, Enrique, who was now five. Emilio doted on his highly respected wife, but he also had a keen mind for politics, which was why he'd been rewarded with the position. He continued to maintain the *Mentales* Squad, which his predecessor had established during the previous shakeup of the rulership of Brom. Amo Domingo Bolivar-Brom now led this group, whose purpose was to provide protection to the royal leaders. He was also twenty-five and had married Sally Riding. Yes, he'd followed the newer practice of marrying outside of the highly inbred group of *mentales* gifted in the Brom area. Already, they had a daughter, Beth, who was four.

Thanks to the Underground and Venerada Marisol, inbreeding was now widely recognized as one of the reasons for the loss of *mentales* gifted among their children. Many who had the gift now married more distant gifted men and women. Sally Riding had come from Hilliard Heights. Already, they had Beth tested for the gift, and it seemed highly likely that she would carry on the gifts that Domingo and Sally possessed. Amo Domingo was rather conservative in his approach to life. Take no chances was his motto, and he was a voice in the royal court for conservatism in all things. During these years of peace, his attitude had paid off and Brom continued to prosper and thrive, in spite of the exceedingly harsh winters.

Venerada Marisol Wycombe-Brom had finally married Phil Brom, who she had been seeing for nearly five years. She was also a katalyein and anything but conservative. She had received quite a lot of the new mental therapy, and at fifty, she was vibrant and enthusiastic. Her husband was a master of eagle training. He and Eric Humberhills of the Underground had formed a business, raising and training eagles. However, tower-trained, he was always on call to lend a hand with one of their three circles. They had two children.

Their daughter, Maricela Wait, was a katalyein like her mother — a gorgeous young woman of twenty. She'd recently married Theo Wait, who was a year older than she and who was just now joining Phil and Eric's eagle training company. He too came from Hilliard Heights. She had received much of the new mental therapy and was extremely alive and vibrant. At this time, 1272, she was being trained by Marisol to become Brom Tower's next venerada. Marisol greatly wanted to retire and devote her remaining years to the mental research therapy being developed by the Underground.

Their son, Ben Wycombe-Brom, was nineteen. A tall, thin lad, he had a sharp mind, but as yet didn't know precisely what he wanted to do. He had received tower training and could join one of the Circles, but chose not to do so just yet. No, he had far too many unanswered questions, many of which centered on the Underground and the "true" history of the past few centuries. Too many "events" had not made any sense to him. His mother and the many others seemed to be keeping many secrets from him and everyone else. On top of that, there were just too darn many "strange" things happening in and around Brom.

These strange happenings were caused by the Underground, directly or indirectly. This small organization was known only to a very few people, the top leaders in Brom. Its purpose was to spy on the aliens, subverting any plots the aliens might foist off on Tierra. Additionally, they spied on all the other towers and lords to prevent wars, conflicts, and especially treasonous actions perpetrated on the world, such as the one that Lord Valen had tried with his "virus." The Underground had been extremely successful during the last fifty years. Remember, Tierra was a closed world, meaning that no alien technology or aid could be given to them. The Underground, however, had so much sophisticated alien technology that even the alien Governor would have been awed. Most of it dealt with electronics, medical, and teleportation devices. Originally founded by Amy and Jan, two of their children had been running it for many years, Benjamina Blackwater and Tim Bellweather.

These two had been instrumental in helping the women refugees in the alien spaceship run by two robots, Alpha and Beta, to settle quietly among the population of Brom. These unique women possessed elemental powers, somewhat similar to those of the *mentales* gifted. The two leaders had married a pair of these women, Elana and Petrona. Elana's skills were earth-based, while Tim's wife, Petrona, had fire-based powers. Later on, the Underground had been successful in rescuing nearly all of Calder's mermaids, after they lost all of their powers and became utterly helpless women. During that time, Benjamina had discovered that people were immortal spiritual beings and had developed the first mental therapy that actually erased the mental and physical trauma a person had experienced in his or her life.

This new technology of the mind was applied to the mermaids, allowing them to mentally recover from their hideous trauma. The Underground also discovered just how a person got the precious *mentales* gifts in the first place: psi crystal dust! Benjamina used this newfound knowledge to give these helpless mermaids back their ability to use telekinesis and thus be able to survive. The mermaids now resided in Madiera, the artificial town within the spaceship that Alpha and Beta ran. The ship was buried in a gully just outside Brom. The Goddess Lysandra had formed a unique set of underground tunnels through the bedrock connecting the spaceship, Brom Tower, and the Underground itself, which occupied many caverns beneath Benjamina and Tim's small stone home in Brom.

In addition, Benjamina trained these mermaids in how to deliver her newly invented mental therapy technology. These women, who once had great pride in their immense healing powers, became quite adept in delivering therapy sessions. During the past twenty years, Benjamina had quietly been arranging therapy sessions for all the Brom Tower personnel and the rulers of Brom. The mermaids would hop from their artificial homes with the many bots that allowed them to live independently, through the tunnels and into the basement of Brom Tower. Here the "patients" would come to receive their therapy sessions. While the patients obviously now knew of the strange mermaids who gave them back their lives, they had no idea where they lived or their numbers. Only a very few knew the details.

The Underground had also undergone many changes these past twenty plus years. Both Tim and Benjamina were sixty-six, and their health was failing, in spite of all the therapy they'd received. Tim was bedridden and not expected to live much longer. Benjamina was still active, working on her therapy research. Rafaela, who had been her right arm in the research all these years, was forty-nine. She and her husband, Andres Bolivar, now carried the bulk of the day-to-day operations for Benjamina.

Annie Wells-Hays and Sam Hays, now in their late forties, had taken over much of the Underground monitoring operations. Similarly, Eric and Sally (Redford) Humberhills were still active, though Eric now had a side business training eagles. Both were thirty-eight. So yes, the Underground definitely needed to pass the torch to a younger generation.

These original members had a dozen children over the years. Because of their highly secluded and secretive nature, the children intermarried when they became adults. This kept the knowledge of the Underground "in house" so to speak. What is remarkable about these twelve is their education. All received an education that a member of the Imperium would have been proud to receive! Further, they all received all the therapy that they ever needed. All were fully trained on the operation and uses of all the alien machines. All knew the true history of what had been happening on Tierra in so far as Benjamina and Tim knew it. Just as their mothers had done for them, Benjamina and Tim did for all the dozen children, grooming them to one day take over for themselves. Additionally, Benjamina made sure that all twelve had powerful *mentales* gifts, using her discovery of the psi powders.

Gradually, the kids began taking over operations of the Underground. At this point in time, Ken and Crystal Blackwater were the official leaders, bowing to Benjamina on the rare occasion. Bart and Anita excelled at running the communications and teleportation devices and took over for Tim. Jake and Misty were highly adept at using the medical machines. They'd even begun to uncover further uses of the machines, having begun deciphering the complex menus. On the other hand, Jamie and Luisa along with Henry and Sally were far more interested in helping further Benjamina's mental therapy. These four now handled most of the daily session scheduling. Finally, Thomas and Janice did a little of this and that; specialized in nothing, they knew a lot about all the operations. They assisted Ken and Crystal or Bart and Anita, whoever needed the help.

Bart and Anita first alerted everyone to a potential hot spot. Their monitoring of all the tower's communications networks had intercepted Rafael's reports on Damiano's capture and subsequent sacking of Po, Arad. "Do we interfere?

Bart asked.

Ken frowned. "Not yet. This is an Easterlings matter at the moment. Surely, Sultan Gino will bring his wayward warlord under control. Keep a watchful eye on it."

"Aye, aye, boss," Bart teased. He and Anita did so, later reporting on the sacking of Teraspoli.

"Well, according to this Rafael fellow, Lord Gino lost his army last year trying to stop this Damiano fellow. So I am not surprised to hear the city fell," Ken stated. "I wonder what is going on with this warlord? We need to find out all we can about him, Bart. Anita, please search all the tower records to see if anyone has any information on this Damiano Donatello. Tom, see if you and Janice can zero in on just why he is given the title of Immortale Conquistatore Mortale. The conqueror part is obvious, but what about the rest."

Data was not forthcoming in any timely fashion. Anita found no trace of his existence in any tower's records. In and of itself, that was not unexpected. Towers only kept records of its own members and sometimes children. When Tecuci fell, more data became available via communications to and from the Renegade Tower.

"How the devil can a man survive being hit with half a dozen *mentales* balls of fire?" asked Bart. "Crap, one could kill me."

"Well, it wouldn't hurt Petrona; she's a fire elemental," Crystal pointed out. "She is mostly immune to fire-based effects. Do you suppose this Damiano has a Madiera fire elemental mother? That might account for his seeming immunity."

Anita replied, "I will look into that. Best check with Petrona. Back in a while, gang." She left to consult with Petrona. True, many of the Madiera women immigrants had married local men, but had any somehow moved to the Easterlings? That possibility seemed remote.

"According to Rafael, Damiano can heal himself. How?" asked Crystal.

Jake answered this one. "He could have the *mentales* healing gift, but usually that implies healing others. I can't imagine a person having that skill and not using it on his own men, especially his top leaders or friends. Rafael has not indicated that Damiano has ever healed anyone but himself."

Ken rubbed his forehead. "This is making less and less sense, gang!"

Bart broke in, "Hey, there is a whole lot of communications going on now. The Renegade Tower is trying to acquire support and aid from all the other towers. Lord Brom is going to be advised soon, I'll wager. Looks like you and Crystal are going to have to get involved."

"Damn!" Ken sighed. "Well, it's happening again, just like mom said it would. Crystal, we need to be as well informed as possible when Lord Bolivar summons us or Venerada Marisol does. Crap. I was enjoying life. Now I guess we have to earn our pay."

"What pay, dear?" Crystal teased him. Everyone laughed. The Underground didn't need money. Jan and Amy had left them a fortune, to say nothing of Tim's contribution that he'd taken from Elegant Fashions Inc after Nita Valen cut off so many hands and nearly destroyed all the *mentales* gifted of the Midlands. Plus, with their clever software, they could hack into any Imperium bank and siphon off what funds they needed.

"Hey gang, listen to this tidbit!" Anita called out. "Sonia Ferro of Arad, the sultan's Number One wife, has just declared herself the ruler of Arad. Is sultaness a word? She's calling herself that. Moreover, she is using the Sisterhood to help her run the Arad. Isn't that something? A woman ruler? See, guys, we can do it too." She teased the others. Several laughed.

"Well, this is a first," Ken admitted.

A day later, Ken and Crystal received a summons from Lord Emilio Bolivar and Venerada Marisol. "I hate these meetings. I have to wear this darn suit," Ken complained as he and his wife began dressing formally.

"You should have to wear what I do. Then, you'd not complain, dear. Just try to get into this corset. Just try to walk in these heels one day," Crystal countered. Indeed, formal gowns and heels were required apparel for any formal meeting with the two rulers. She had the long, thick black hair indicative of her Westerlings ancestry, plus her mother's good looks. In her red satin gown, black hose, and six-inch black heels, she looked ravishing. Ken stole a passionate minute with her before they left. He took her arm, and they walked down the long tunnel that connected their busy chambers with the basement of the tower.

The meeting was held in the tower's first floor reception room. They were the last to arrive. Lord Emilio with his trademark black moustache rose to greet the pair, as did Amo Domingo and Venerada Marisol and her apprentice Ama Maricela. Lord Emilio did not have any *mentales* gifts, as was the situation with almost all the rulers of the kingdoms at this point in time. Still, he cut a striking figure, known for his good looks and his keen swordsmanship. Amo Domingo's *mentales* gifts were primarily fire-based and quite powerful. He allowed his hair to fall to his shoulders, quite unlike the close-cropped leader.

The two armless katalyein women rose as well. Ken and Crystal knew well that neither really liked to get dressed up as they were required to do so. It severely limited their abilities to use their feet as their hands. Both women wore blue satin gowns, the requisite black nylons, and six-inch heels. "Welcome Ken, Crystal. Thank you for coming on such short notice," Venerado Marisol spoke first. "Please be seated everyone." The mother and daughter looked remarkably similar. Both also had the Westerlings style hair, long, straight, thick, and black. Both of their faces were rather round with dark eyebrows and thick lips, attractive in their own right.

"I'll come right to the point. Have you heard about this barbarian fellow who calls himself Damiano Donatello, the Immortale Conquistatore Mortale?" Ken nodded. "Ah good. Venerada?" he turned the meeting over to her.

"We've received a request from the Renegade Tower to help them stop the rampages of this barbarian. Thus far, it seems to be an Easterlings problem, one that Adelmira Tower ought to be addressing, not Brom," she explained.

"Aye, what has the Arad to do with Brom, I say?" Lord Emilio took over. "Nothing. This should be handled by the Easterlings, not us. Yet, I would like to know more about this man and his ultimate objectives. Do you have any knowledge, any information on this barbarian? How is it that he is immune to balls of fire? Is he one of you? A renegade perhaps? I didn't think there are any *mentales* gifted in that part of the world."

Ken smiled. His group was right; he was being pumped for information, as always. "We know he is not a registered *mentales* gifted person. Furthermore, we do not suspect he has any *mentales* gifts. According to this Amo Rafael, he is a barbarian warrior. He's never cast any kind of *mentales* spell that we know of. Yet, he apparently can heal his own wounds."

Anita added, "Right. But that is not characteristic of any known *mentales* gift, unless he flatly refuses to heal anyone else, not even his own closest associates. He would have to be the most selfish man ever. We suspected he might somehow have some Madiera fire elemental blood in him, but we've found no records of any Madiera women moving to the Easterlings, let alone into the frigid steppes of Domei. It seems he was born out there in the middle of nowhere. So any Madiera influence can likely also be discounted. In short, we do not know anything about the true nature of his powers."

Ken took over. "According to Rafael, the man withstood direct hits from balls of fire. Men on either side of him died, but he kept on going, though his clothes were flaming. Also, he has invented some kind of new weapon. Rafael described them as a pair of whirling scything blades attached to a long chain. They allow him to attack his opponents long before they can reach him with their own weapons. Yet, this weapon does not violate the Brom Compact."

"Is he a real threat?" asked Lord Emilio.

Anita chose her words wisely. "Yes and no. Lord Gino sent his entire army after him last year. However, his generals were foolish and fell into a trap Damiano laid for them. It is no wonder that Teraspoli fell so easily. There was no one left to defend the city. As for the Arad, they never possessed a powerful army on horseback. Damiano is making exceptional use of cavalry in his assaults. I believe that is giving him the edge. However, there is no discounting he is proving to be a master at tactics and strategies. That is what I consider to be the most important factor."

"I see. Yes, it would seem so," Amo Domingo replied, in his conservative manner. "We should dwell on his tactics and strategies rather than speculating on his miraculous ability to heal his own wounds."

"Good. Then Venerada Marisol, please send word to the Renegade Tower that we will keep a close eye on developments, but that this is really a matter for the Easterlings lords and their tower at Adelmira, not here in the far north at Brom. Make it sound like we care, but that it is their problem at the present time."

"As you request, My Lord," Venerada Marisol replied. "I would like to make an announcement since you are all here. I am getting too old for this job. As you all know, I have been training my daughter here, Maricela. I am officially turning over the day-to-day operations of venerada to her as of today. I will remain in the background, offering advice and aid, as she needs it. I will send your message, My Lord, along with the change in status of Maricela. I am sure you will find her most competent to lead Brom Tower."

"Congratulations, Venerada Maricela!" Ken said cheerfully. Crystal followed suit. Amo Domingo and Lord Emilio also congratulated her, but with less enthusiasm. They cared little for tower matters, as long as it did not affect themselves. The two men rose and left. Ken and Crystal sensed that Marisol wanted them to stay.

"Thanks for staying a bit longer. I have fully briefed Maricela on the Underground, but she ought to be given a complete tour though. I am going to spend my time helping Benjamina with her research project. I think our future lies in her groundbreaking work. Frankly, this whole Damiano affair has me worried. I don't think it is going to go away so easily, and I want out before it comes to a head. I've seen enough bloodshed and strife in my years as venerada," she admitted.

"You've been the best, Marisol. We will miss you at all the meetings, but I guess we'll be seeing more of you now that you will be with mom," Ken replied. "I know she could use the help. She gets so tired these days. Tim isn't doing so well. Getting old is a bitch."

"Thanks. When is a good time for Maricela to visit?"

"How about now?" Crystal replied.

"Can I change first? Walking in these heels is a bit much," Maricela asked, a little timidly.

"I wholly agree. Let's change first. What say I come back and pick you up in say an hour? We are never formal in the Underground. Wear what is comfortable, Maricela," Crystal replied.

"Great. I know I need to get used to dressing like this all day. I am going to have to go to the High Council meetings and wear nothing but formal apparel for days on end. Still, perhaps I can delay a little longer," she teased. "An hour is fine with me. I am dying to see everything. Mom has told me lots, but seeing is even better!"

A couple of hours later, Crystal led Maricela into their giant communications room, where Bart and Anita were busily transcribing something that they were receiving over the tower comm system. Bart exclaimed, "Hey, stick around! This is hot news!"

"Can you really eaves drop on all tower communications?" Maricela asked.

Crystal replied, allowing the two to continue their rapid writings. "Yes, thanks to Empress Jan's creation here, we are always tapped into every tower's comm system. No communication ever sent is missed by us. We monitor it constantly, taking shifts of course. Mostly it's just routine stuff that we ignore. However, in this case, it looks like something is up."

Maricela laughed. "I had better be careful what I send out then." Crystal grinned.

A bit later, Anita gushed, "Wow. More news on this Damiano fellow. He's really a weird man! Adelmira Tower has cleverly sent out a spy into his camp to try to find out more about him. He and one of his top men have recently gotten married!"

"So how is this news?" asked a confused Maricela.

"It is the women that he's married! As you might expect in the Easterlings, all six are fully ornamented women." Maricela groaned, she knew what that meant: lip plates, long, heavy earrings, impossibly tight corsets, and the debilitating toe shoes. Anita continued, "But what is really, really strange are the women. Two are young mermaids! Now wherever did he find them? I thought that Benjamina rescued all of them, but some must have been missed."

"Well, they must be children of the original mermaids, Anita," Venerada Maricela explained. "It's been years."

"Oh, right. But there's more. The two mermaids are married to Damiano, but he has two more wives, as does his friend. Each has a woman, who has had half of her arms cut off somehow! Even weirder, each has a woman, who not only has half of her arms cut off, but also half of her legs, too!"

"Oh dear god! Those poor women! He is one sick fellow," Venerada Maricela exclaimed.

"The spy reports the women believe they are very sexy and un-handicapped, if you can believe such a report. They are being transported in a wagon behind the army. The spy says the half-legged women actually sort of walk on their stumps — some kind of leather boots," Anita finished up.

"Isn't that just like Adelmira Tower? They send out a spy, and the spy reports on the weird sexual propensities of the barbarian, instead of something useful," Venerada Maricela replied.

"More like how come the men there think they have to have a harem?" Anita added.

"Hey dear, you are more than enough for me," Bart teased her.

She grinned. "I'd better be!" Everyone laughed.

"Seriously, gang. If we get involved, we ought to see about rescuing those six women," Bart spoke up. "Let Ken know, Crystal."

Crystal replied, "Right. But is everyone missing the key point in all this? How the devil did those poor women lose their arms and legs? I smell something rotten here. I am going to put Tom on this one, if you don't need him." They didn't and the two continued with their tour.

That evening around the supper table, the talk was all about the strange wives the two leaders took. Tom already was given his assignment to find out more. "Well, I can see one reason right away," Ken mused. "Look, if you were a conquering warrior, you need to keep up appearances and have a wife or harem as they do in the Easterlings. After all, your men are raping the women in the towns they take. Yet, if you took one of those as your wife, if I were her, I'd stab you while you slept. Revenge is a powerful motivator."

"Yes, but what has this to do with it?" asked Crystal. "Why do men have to rape anyway?"

"Without their arms or lower arms, these wives could not possible stab them while they slept," Ken answered her first question and wisely chose not to answer the second one. "Quite why the other two should be minus their lower legs is frankly not explainable. Tom, see what you can find out. Where did these women come from? How did they get the way that they are? Perhaps they merely suffered some tragic accident. That's the likely cause."

"Aye boss. I am glad finally to get something exciting to do! Dad's been hounding me to take an interest in his birds' business. Now I have a good excuse not to. I'll get on it in the morning," Tom replied, very pleased to have a reason to avoid the eagles. He didn't share his father's love of the feathered species.

With a backpack of food and his short sword, Tom prepared for his explorations. Like all the dozen children whose inborn *mentales* gifts had been greatly enhanced by Benjamina and her psi-dust, he could teleport. They had a rough idea where the barbarians were located. They had sacked Tecuci and were somewhere down the coast heading towards Turda. While that meant he had thousands of miles to cover, he decided to backtrack some. His was an investigation, not an attack.

Chapter 12 Rescue

Tom focused and arrived in Teraspoli, amid the chaos of the ruined city. He began to make inquiries of anyone he met on the street. Two days later, he heard what he needed. Indeed, the barbarian had a wagon carrying his harem here in Teraspoli when he entered the city. He also knew that the Arad city of Po had been attacked before Teraspoli, and according to the locals here, he must have wintered down in Po. It made sense, as the streets were quite deep in snow here in Teraspoli, just as they were back in Brom. He ducked into an alley and teleported again.

Po was now a recovering city. The Sisterhood had been here and the barbarian guards killed. Slowly, the port city was recovering, though most nobles were still absent. At least one caravel of food supplies was in dock, thanks to Sultaness Sonia. Everywhere he went, the locals were praising their new leader, who was ensuring their survival with desperately needed food. Once more, he began making inquiries.

Yes, many remembered seeing a fancy wagon carrying his wives leaving Po. Confusingly, some did not recall them entering Po. Then, he got a breakthrough. One old man pointed out that their wagon was not a wagon, but the dead Lord's Great Carriage! Well, Tom thought, that would make sense. Take only the best transportation available. He made more inquiries.

Several unfruitful days later, Tom was about to give it up, when he changed what he was asking for. That is, instead of asking about the barbarian's harem, he asked about the strange women. In one pub, he finally got a break. An older man who was half-drunk, said, "Yah, we've seen them elegant ladies about town now and then. Always in the company of the richest nobles, they are. They be whores, me thinks. No, escorts someone told me. Yeh, escorts. Funny name for whores, though." He didn't know where such escort services were located though.

That didn't matter. Now Tom had something concrete

to follow. A day later, he had the names of four escort services in Po. The first two were gone, destroyed by the barbarians when they sacked the town. The third one just had the ordinary ornamented women found so often in the cities and towns along the Easterlings coast in this day and age. He wasn't allowed in, though. He did not look like a wealthy nobleman, the doorman told him. Tom didn't press the issue.

He knew he appeared to be nothing more than a poor visitor, probably from the Midlands. His hair was far too short and his clothes looked strange, to say nothing of his week-old stubble. Finally, he decided to case the fourth location, Metrio's Escorts. After finding the place, he noticed it was in a better location in the town, but that few were on the street. This far south, the temperature was warm enough that only a light jacket was needed at night. The ocean moderated the temperatures significantly here. Well, I am in the Arad, he mused. After watching the place during the early evening hours, he saw no one entering or leaving. Conclusion: business must be down, he thought.

He headed for an inn and took a room. The next day, he visited a tailor shop and purchased a fine suit. The man continued to apologize for its poor quality. "They stole all of my finer cloth," he explained.

"Ah, this will do nicely," Tom countered. Now properly attired, he headed for Metrio's Escorts. Upon entering, an older man appeared. His eyes quickly appraised him — that much Tom knew without using his mental gifts. "I hear you have some very fine exotic women here."

"Ah, yes. Stranger to Po, I see. Yes, Durante Metrio. I have the finest, most elegant and exotic women in all of Po and for a thousand miles in all directions," the well-dressed man replied. The entrance was quite plush, Tom noted. "May I be of service?"

"I certainly hope so. Yes, I am from the Midlands, a very wealthy merchant — here checking out how I may best serve Po's current needs and make a tidy profit as well. I have heard rumors that you do indeed have the most exotic women in all Po."

"Why, you have heard correctly. Indeed, six of my

women have been married to the mighty conqueror himself, Damiano Donatello," he pointed out with great pride. Correspondingly, Tom raised his eyebrows, as if very much impressed. "Would you care to see my current selection?"

"Yes, of course, I certainly would! Thank you," Tom replied. Durante led him into the viewing room, and he noticed a pair of open doors on either side and a red carpet leading from one to the other.

"I am afraid that my selections are a little low at this time, what with having married six of my women off to the lord. In time, I assure you that I will have more. Have a seat and my women will present themselves to you. I have something for every man's tastes, but all are most elegant and beautiful. All are programmed to give you much pleasure." He clapped his hands and the procession began. All the women were fully ornamented, as far as their bodies would allow.

"My newest young maiden, the lovely Felicita," Durante announced the entrance of the fourteen year old young woman. Obviously, she was new to all the modifications. She carefully took each step in her toe shoes, which because of her arm-fetter-gown was barely a few inches at a time. She did manage to meet Tom's eyes twice though. Tom noticed that Durante was watching his reactions carefully.

"Next, are the exotic beauties, Annetta and Bianca." These two women entered next, but were comfortable in their walks. Both had no trace of arms, much like the katalyein with which Tom was quite familiar. Then, three mermaids hopped into the room. "Three lovely sisters, Elena, Felisa, and Adalina. Most lovely indeed." Again, their unusual bodies caused no real reaction in Tom. There were nearly five hundred of them in the Madiera artificial town beneath Brom. Some had even given him therapy sessions.

"And finally, my most exotic women of all, the very best in all of Po, the highly sought after, Diamante and Domenica." Tom's eyes reacted. These women had only upper arms whose ends were conical. Tom new that only one of the alien medical machines could have done this to the women. Their upper arms were prepared for the attachment of a lower arm and hand prosthesis. In addition, they were missing their feet and lower legs! The lower parts of their upper legs were in some kind of heavily padded leather tubes that served as shoes. They had to wiggle their arms to help keep their balance to make walking possible. Their long, uncut brown hair trailed across the red carpet behind them. Again, their wild motions and their eyes told him that they were newly made, unused to their amputations. Yet they did their best to make eye contact with him several times.

From his reactions, he knew Durante also knew that he was impressed with these last two women. "I see that you too prefer the most exotic of all women. Shall we adjourn to my office for some ale and discuss your desires?" Tom nodded and watched as the women made their slow way out of the left hand door. He followed Durante into another plush room. He took a seat and Durante poured him a cup of ale. One sip and Tom knew this was an excellent brew.

"So how may I be of service for such a great merchant?" Durante asked.

Tom lightly touched Durante's mind, just enough to pick up his surface thoughts. "Well, as a matter of fact, Durante, I am interested in them all. What a magnificent collection you have. As I understand, the conquering Damiano purchased a fair number of them for his harem. Is this really true? If so, perhaps you and I could also reach a similar arrangement. Money is no object."

Durante reacted well. Tom sensed a great deal of relief, which rather surprised him. "Yes, oh yes we most definitely could reach such an arrangement." Durante attempted to conceal his rush of excitement.

"Excellent, my good man, excellent. They are all so incredibly beautiful. I believe that I would like them all. How can one choose from such a fantastic selection of really elegant women? So exotic, so rare, so beautiful. Tell me, are there more to choose from? How on Tierra did you ever find such beauties? I've never seen anything as wondrous as Diamante and Domenica. In my travels, I have seen mermaids before. Charming and wonderful in their own way."

"Ah, let me assure you they have been all programmed to believe they are the most beautiful women in the world, that they are truly sexy. Plus, they are programmed to experience pleasure and to give you more pleasure than you can imagine possible," Durante explained. *I need this sale,* he thought.

"Now that is truly exceptional! Just what I desire in a woman. Yet, they must have experienced some absolutely terrible accidents; such tragedies they must have suffered! Such pain, and yet somehow they showed none of that to me."

"Oh no, no, you misunderstand. None have and the slightest traumas, no pain, no accidents. You see, I have a friend who can not only perform these operations, but also who programs them to believe all that they do. However, I must caution you, you must never, ever allow them to be in a situation where they feel helpless. That may well break their programming. I have had to permanently ban several noblemen, who did that to some of my women. It took considerable work on our part to reprogram them. You must have caretakers with them at all times to assist them with their many needs, you see."

"Oh, I can see that must be so. Of course, they will need help with most everything. I could not help noticing none are particularly old," Tom probed a bit.

"Yes, that is so. You see, these women are in great demand. They get to keep a portion of the fees they earn. Usually when they are thirty, they have amassed more than enough money to afford to live on their own. Annetta and Bianca anticipate within a few more years, they will be able to retire too, purchasing a small home and a live-in caretaker. I always help them get setup when they retire, you see. Plus, they always get the best medical care in all of Po. I have a doctor always on call, should they take ill or get an infection."

"Now that is very generous of you! I wonder something, Durante, since the sacking of Po, how has your business been? I have been in the city for over a week now and everything seems in shambles. Most noble houses appear empty to my eyes," Tom asked. Already he picked up this idea from Durante's surface thoughts.

Durante sighed, "Well, yes, yes. I must admit that this is quite true. I had hoped otherwise, but alas, we have gone days between visitors. If I be truly honest with you, Tom, I would really like to retire myself. Perhaps we could make some kind of deal for them all."

"I certainly believe that we could do just that. They would make a fine harem start. You say that they have their own funds?" Tom asked, an idea germinating.

"Oh yes, yes indeed. Of course, some have been with me longer and have substantially larger personal funds than the others have. Felicita has only been with me for a month and her account has only just begun and is quite small. Actually, the three sister mermaids are in similar situations, having only recently come to work for me. On the other hand, the other four are reasonably wealthy, just not enough to retire and pay for a constant caretaker."

"I see," Tom replied. "If you don't mind my asking, how much does one of your exotic women believe they need to have saved up so that they could retire? I am curious. You don't have to answer if you would prefer not to reveal such matters." He already knew what Durante would say; he'd seen the number flash in his mind when he asked the question. This was a trick that the mermaids had often used in their therapy. They called it a flash or snap answer.

"Oh I don't mind at all. Most prefer to have ten thousand saved up."

"Such a small amount. Well, I can see that their needs are not that great, just a caretaker and a place to live. That should do them all rather well, as far as I know from all my days as a merchant," Tom replied. "You mentioned this doctor?"

"Ah yes. A very close friend of mine. He looks in on them whenever they have need. They love him."

"If I should acquire all of these lovely women, I would like to retain this doctor for them as well. If they like him this much, I'd hate to force them to go to a stranger. You know how women are with strangers examining their privates," Tom said quietly.

"I am sure that can easily be arranged."

"Excellent, excellent. One more thing, you mentioned these women were somehow made and programmed. What if I should desire some additional exotic women to add to my growing harem? How can I 'acquire' more, especially those like Diamante and Domenica? They are so exotic."

"Ah, the same doctor friend. If we can reach an agreement so that I may retire, I will place him at your complete disposal," Durante offered.

"Perfect, Durante, perfect. Then, shall we discuss terms? I would like to have them all, but with one small requirement."

"Most generous of you. Let us talk indeed. More ale? Pray tell, the requirement?" Durante replied, greatly relieved. He refilled Tom's golden mug.

"You know women and marriages. Sometimes they just don't work out. While I am a great lover of women, some might not prefer to stay with me. I would like the women to have sufficient personal funds so that, if they did not like me, they could, as you say, retire and be able to live on their own. Shall we say each woman comes with a dowry of ten thousand of her own money that I cannot under any circumstances touch? That way, I would be most fair to these magnificent women. Of course, I cannot expect you to make up all of their own current shortfalls. Good grief, four of them would need ten thousand each. Yet, I do not want to be seen as their benefactor, giving them the funds. That would cause them emotional upsets, if they didn't like me and wanted to retire. As you pointed out, I must not give them any reason to feel helpless or their programming would be ruined."

"Ah, most brilliant, most! Yes, I do see your point. If they saw the funds coming from you, then later, if they wanted to retire, they would be torn between two notions. Allow me to work up their funds and how much extra is needed between us. About their purchase price? Would ten thousand each be asking too much of you?" Durante asked. Tom already knew he had lowered his price in half and that he was desperate to get out of the escort business. It had been almost non-existent since the barbarian had come to Po. He was in effect cutting his losses.

"Why not at all, Durante. Not at all. That would only be eighty thousand, plus what extra is needed to make their dowries sufficient," Tom replied.

"Then, we have ourselves a deal! Shall we shake on it?" Durante extended his hand and Tom shook it, sealing the deal. "Give me a day to work out how much extra is needed for their retirement funding. Shall I arrange for a wedding ceremony? If so, you should be careful to identify which woman will be Number One and so on. Easterlings women in a harem must know the numerical order of the wives, you see."

"No, I will take them with me and get to know each one intimately and then decide which one shall be Number One. That is, if that's acceptable to you and to the women," Tom added. Here he was on thin ground. He didn't know the full customs of Easterlings harems.

"Yes, that would be most acceptable. In fact, I will make you an even better offer," Durante said. "If you can get me the funds today, the eighty thousand, then I will make up all of their dowries. All shall come with ten thousand, and I will give you my establishment here. Obviously, the women are quite used to living here. All their things are here, and the transfer of ownership will be far easier on them. What say you?"

"Durante, that is absolutely perfect! I will go fetch the funds. Are gems acceptable?"

"Absolutely. Absolutely!"

"Good. Then I will leave now and return in a few hours with the funds. Tonight, I shall have more pleasure than I ever dreamed possible," Tom replied.

"Oh, of *that* I am most certain! You will find no other women who can give you pleasures like these can!" Durante boasted cheerfully. "While you are gone, I will prepare the women. Shall I retain their two care givers for now?"

"Certainly. That would be most wise. I certainly want them to only have the very best care they have been receiving, Durante. Why, you think of everything!" Tom piled it on a bit thick. He still needed to find the doctor, who was behind this nightmare, and find out just how these women were "programmed."

After finishing his ale, Tom left and ducked into the nearest alley. A moment later, he vanished, reappearing in his room in the Underground at Brom. He rushed out to give the others a full report and to obtain the needed gems. As he was preparing to return a couple of hours later, his wife, Janice volunteered, "Tom, you have my permission to bed some of the women if they need it. This programming has us all worried. If they are not allowed to 'pleasure' you, that might break their programming and cause immense problems for you, especially with the quad amputees. They have to be so utterly helpless. Please don't do anything to upset them in particular or the mermaids either. We will be preparing to receive them tomorrow and get them into therapy sessions right away."

He kissed her. "Thanks love. I hadn't thought of that. You are right, as always. If I should refuse their advances, that might break their programming. I wonder what the devil this doctor fellow did to them? Still, I can't break cover until I meet this doctor. We have to recover that medical machine of his. That's top priority. The aliens are right about one thing. Their technology ought *never* to fall into our hands." She laughed and agreed.

Tom teleported back to the alley and then walked the short block to the fancy escort service office complex. When he entered, he found numerous bags sitting beside the entrance door. The sign out front was also there. He smiled, Durante wasn't kidding, he wanted out of this business immediately. His bags were packed. "Come in, come in. All has been prepared," Durante exclaimed.

They went into his office and Tom handed him the bag of gems. After casually verifying them, Durante opened a drawer that held eight bags. Each one was labeled with the woman's name. "Ten thousand in each bag. I have not yet shown them to the women. I leave that up to you. I have prepared them. They believe that you have purchased them all and this building as well. I suggested you were planning to form a harem of your own. All are most excited to meet you. I have my things all packed and will depart after I introduce you to each of them and the caretakers. Tomorrow, I will drop by, say at ten, and take you to meet Doctor Crispino Torina. I have sent word to him about this transaction and your desires for future women. I will chat with him later tonight. Now, shall I introduce you to your most elegant women?"

"I look forward to your visit at ten tomorrow. Yes, I am most eager to meet these eight women! Thank you ever so much, Durante!" He followed him into a back living room. Here the eight women were sitting on couches or very low chairs in the case of Diamante and Domenica. Each had their hair brushed and draped over their left shoulders, falling across their laps and to the floor. They were still wearing the same satin gowns that he'd seen earlier.

"Ladies, may I present Lord Tom Bell, a most wealthy merchant from the Midlands?" All eyes gazed upon Tom. One by one, he introduced Tom to each of the women. Then he said goodbye to the women and left.

Once Durante had left, Diamante said seductively, "Please, Tom, come and sit by us so that we may pleasure you some. Domenica and I are the most sexiest of all women. We are the most beautiful and exotic of women. We are always the most in demand." Tom flushed, but did as asked, sitting on a pillow placed between the two. At once, they began to rub their lip plates against his cheeks, while rubbing him with their short arms.

"Don't forget the rest of us, we also give great pleasure. We are all very good, too," Annetta called out. Tom gave each of the two women a hug and a gentle kiss upon the front of their lips. He rose and sat between Annette and Bianca. Both leaned into him, pressing their lips and plates gently against the sides of his lips. Without arms and as constrained as their bodies were, in reality, they could do little more. Yet, even doing this much seemed to satisfy their immediate needs. He sensed the urgency of the others and moved over to the couch where the three mermaids sat erect, waiting their turn. Again, lacking arms and so constrained, they gently pressed their lips and plates to his as had the other two. After returning the loving kisses of the three sisters, he sat down beside the fourteen year old Felicita, whose arms were still held tightly at her sides by her arm-fetter-gown. At least she could use her lower arms and gave him a bit of a hug along with her gentle kiss.

Diplomatically, Tom said, "Ladies, you are all magnificently beautiful. How can I possibly choose between you? So I took you all." They all smiled, but such was invisible. Tom, however, sensed their smiles. Their eyes shone brightly.

"Since all of you are here, there are some things that I want to tell you. First, I have seen to it that each of you now has ten thousand in your savings bag. That means that you can retire anytime that you desire."

"Oh! We can retire on ten thousand!" Diamante exclaimed, very much surprised.

"Please, can we actually see these bags?" Annetta asked.

"Yes, I only had fifty in my bag. I have only been here a month and there has been almost no customers," Felicita added.

"We really have ten thousand?" asked Elena. "Really?"

"Yes, you all do. Okay, I can show you your bags. Each has your name on it. How should we do this? They are in a drawer in the office," Tom answered, not expecting such an outburst.

"We can walk, silly," Domenica replied. "Come on; show us." She gave a strange forward lurch and got to her stumps. Wobbling her arms and wiggling, she began to take small, forward steps, dragging her gorgeous hair behind her on the floor. Diamante was right behind her, but far enough back to not step on her hair. The mermaids eagerly lurched to their foot as well, but waited patiently on the other two. Tom moved ahead and led the way into the office. Looking over his shoulder, he saw a long line of very excited women following him.

The first two very short women could just barely see into the drawer. Tom lifted their bags out and opened them, showing them all the precious gems within. Both women were intensely pleased. Then, they very carefully turned around and headed back to their low couches. The three mermaids bent over and gazed upon their gems, absolutely elated. "Now we can return to papa!" Elena exclaimed. Tom began to wonder what was going on with them.

Having seen their bags, the three mermaids hopped out of the way of Annetta and Bianca, who were just as eager to see theirs. Finally, Felicita saw hers but she had tears in her eyes, which Tom kindly wiped before she turned to return to the couch in the other room. "Thank you. I don't want the others to see that I've been crying," she whispered. She too turned and took her tiny steps back into the room, wobbling some in her new toe shoes. Tom's heart went out to these eight women.

After following Felicita back to the living room, he quickly began helping them arrange their long hair, especially Annetta and Bianca. The three mermaids were very used to tossing their hair back, having done it all their lives. Felicita asked, "Can we really retire if we want to? Or are you going to marry us?"

"Well, why don't we all talk about this and your futures," Tom began as diplomatically as he could. He rather wished that Luisa or Jamie were here. They knew far more about therapy, mental reactions, and behavior than he did. "Let's begin with you, Felicita. How come you came to work for Durante?"

"Money. My parents were robbed of everything. There was no food left. He offered me this chance to become rich and I took it. With all this money, I can go home and help my folks recover. Oh, unless I need to pleasure you instead or marry you. Forgive me, sir, I just got too excited about the money. Durante said it would take me ten years or more to earn this much, unless I wanted to become far more exotic like Diamante or Domenica, who can make that much in half the time or less."

"I see. No, you do not need to pleasure me or marry me. In a few days, I will arrange for you to be taken safely back to your parents. That is quite a lot of money to be carrying around in these times. I want to make sure that you and your precious funds get home," Tom replied.

"Oh thank you, thank you," she replied, talking too fast to be clearly understood. She was just learning to deal with the effects of her lip plates, but he was able to pick up her intentions. Besides, he had been around many men and women who wore them and could understand their unusual speech for the most part.

Emboldened by this news, Elena spoke up next. "Lord Tom, my sisters and I would like to return to our home and papa, if we may. Oh, unless you wish us to pleasure you or marry us. We will always give you the best. But papa needs us. He only has one arm and we help him make bricks."

"No, none of you are obligated to pleasure me or marry me, Elena. But I would like to take you to a place where you could live a far better life." He decided against mentioning therapy, for that might break their programming. They all thought highly of themselves as they were.

"But we are supposed to give you pleasure, Lord Tom. We are extremely elegant women and give the best of satisfaction," Elena replied. Then she shifted again, "But papa does really need us. With so much money, papa and we can live very well forever. We can even help the other women in our village. They lost their husbands to the bad man who came riding in one day. Now they are helpless too."

"Okay. Give me a few days to work this out, Elena. I promise you to get you and your sisters back to your father along with your money bags," Tom said kindly. He sensed the immense pride coming from all three sisters. Perhaps Ken might be able to figure out a better handling for the three later on.

"But Lord Tom, we four don't have anyone to go home to," Bianca spoke up.

"And we are the best, most elegant women ever, aren't we, Diamante," Domenica added. "But only a little better than Annetta and Bianca. We four are the very best women. We give only the very best pleasure. Some of our friends, who were like us, got married to the other lord who came here. Antonia and Daniela were like us, the very best. Both were their Number One wives. We want to be your Number One wives. Oh, we both can't be one, but one of us could be two. Annetta and Bianca won't mind being three and four, because they know we are sexier and prettier than they are. They were going to have Durante make them like us one day. Perhaps you can have the doctor do it for them now. Then, they would be like us, and you can marry all four of us. We will always give you only the very best pleasure."

"Yes, we can show you tonight," Diamante gushed. "We will show you, won't we, Domenica? Bianca, Annetta, you come too and show him how good you both are too. Then, he will want to marry you too."

Tom was boxed into a corner and he knew it. "We'll see. I live in the Midlands, so if I married you, you would have to come there with me." He thought that this might cool them off a bit on the marriage angle.

"We don't know their language, but you understand ours fine. We will be your wives, so that doesn't matter," Annetta replied. "A good wife goes where her husband goes. Is that not so?"

"That's usually true, Annetta," he replied. He was out of ideas. "Well, if you four come with me to my home, there you can get a lot of help with things."

Domenica frowned, "But Lord Tom, we don't need any help with things. We are the sexiest women in the world. No one gives pleasure better than we do, right Diamante?"

"She's right. Bianca, Annetta, and we are the very best. Tonight, we will show you," Diamante countered. "We will go to where you live and give you pleasure there."

"Okay, that's fine. I will be very happy to take you home to where I live," he conceded the point.

Just then, the caretakers walked quietly into the room. One said softly, "It is time we prepare them for bed."

"Oh, please put Diamante, Annetta, Bianca and me into the large bed. Lord Tom will be sleeping with us tonight," Domenica ordered.

"Of course, My Lady. It will be so," the older woman said without the slightest trace of surprise. Tom sensed this was a very usual occurrence. Further, with his light touch on the four's minds, he knew they fully expected him to sleep with them. If not, they would feel very much betrayed. "I will call you when they are prepared for you, My Lord." She added. One by one, the eight women followed her out of the room, Diamante and Domenica bringing up the rear.

Tom took this opportunity to focus and make contact with Ken. He relayed all that had happened and what at least four wanted — namely to return to their homes. *I almost broke the mermaid's programming just by hinting that they could return with me. They are really focused on returning to help their father and their village oasis.*

Okay, I will send Henry to you tomorrow. I think someone ought to watch over the others while you take the mermaids home, Ken replied. *I will get Jake and Misty working on the arrangements for the other four. I'll keep you posted. Once you locate this doctor, find out all you can about him and where that infernal machine is at. I'll come snatch it during the night myself.* They chatted a bit longer, and then Ken dropped the connection.

Tom helped himself to a mug of ale that Durante had left behind. An hour later, a caretaker returned. "I have the four others in bed now. The other four are in the master suite awaiting you. If anything is needed during the night, please ring the bell rope. Our room is at the very end of the long hall. Good night, Lord Tom." She bowed and ambled down the hall. He noticed neither of the two women was bound. Evidently, they had discarded that tradition or perhaps found caring for the eight women impossible to do while bound. He sighed and headed for the large bedroom.

All four were already in the giant bed. Their lip plates had been removed and were sitting on a side table. They still wore their pipe corsets. Tom knew that they probably only took those off when bathing. A dim oil lantern provided the only illumination. "Hurry up, silly," Domenica whispered. "We need pleasuring now. We have a great urge to pleasure you too. Please hurry up; we can't stand this long wait." Tom soon had quite an experience.

He awoke and found himself entangled in four sets of long brown hair and four women draped or leaning on him. As carefully as he could, he extricated himself and hastily dressed. Just in time too, for the older caretakers walked in on him. "We will get them dressed and fed, My Lord. Your breakfast awaits you. No need to wait on the women. I am sure you have many things to handle."

"Yes, in fact I do. However, I do not want to leave these beautiful women here alone. I will be sending a friend of mine to guard them and yourselves while I am away. Will that be all right?"

"Why yes, My Lord. Durante always did the same thing — protecting the women," she replied politely.

"Say, how long have you both been caring for these women?" he asked curiously. Have they even been paid much for all their work?

"I've been here ten years and she's been her nearly twenty now. Why?"

"Well, if and when I leave with the women, I want to see that you both are well paid. I will have a money pouch for each of you when I return this afternoon. Thank you for being so kind and considerate to these precious women." Both bowed respectfully, and he noticed they looked extremely pleased. Tom knew money would be quite valuable here in Po as the slow recovery began.

He quickly ate his breakfast and observed they were better cooks than his wife. Then, he quickly notified Ken to send along two more money pouches with five thousand in them for the caretakers. That done, he headed for the front waiting room, hoping and praying that Durante would keep his word. If not, he would have to spend days locating this doctor. At least he knew the man's name, which would definitely help him locate the man. Shortly after that, Henry appeared, smiled, and teasingly said, "Old man, you get all the fun." Tom grinned sheepishly.

Durante arrived right on time. "Well, how did you like your women?" he asked with a wry grin. Tom could not help but grin broadly. No sense in pretending otherwise.

"They are all that you said and then some! Amazing women, simply amazing! I must meet the man responsible," Tom replied.

"Good, good. He would like to meet you as well. Did you sleep with Diamante or Domenica? They are the best, you know."

"Both and with Annetta and Bianca," Tom answered truthfully.

Durante chuckled. "A man with good taste. And you want more, eh?"

Tom took this as a proposition that would get him to the doctor. "Certainly. I don't believe one could ever have too many like those four. Do you?"

"This way. I brought my carriage. I have to admit, Lord

Tom, Diamante and Domenica and the others like them, who came before them, have always been my top moneymakers. Always. The women, who were second in the money earnings, had their arms like those two, but retained their legs. Annetta, Bianca, and the mermaids were always third in line. Honestly, you should consider having Felicita modified to suit your tastes. Normal ornamented women like her are a dime a dozen and rarely make themselves and me much money. Sooner or later, they always realize that and then beg me to be further altered. Now the doctor does charge a lot for the procedures, but he does superb work, does he not?" Durante made pleasant conversation as they rolled along.

"Aye, that he does, simply perfection. No scars and what an attitude. I must ask him how he manages that one," Tom replied. He was not faking it. He wanted to know just what this doctor did to program them. To him, the whole thing was unreal. Before long, they halted before a well-kept adobe home. A simple sign over the front door read: doctor.

Doctor Crispino Torina was around fifty-five, Tom estimated as Durante introduced him. They were in his sitting room, where he met with patients. The man was completely non-descript and unpretentious. "I must admit, old friend, your announcement of your retirement last night took me quite by surprise. Yet, I can see why business is terrible. I envy you. Me? Why there is just too much sickness going around now. I don't dare retire. Too many people need me yet. So this is Lord Tom, merchant from the Midlands?"

"Yes, I have purchased Durante's marvelous women. He had told me that you created those incredible women and somehow programmed them. I am most interested in that," Tom said politely. It wouldn't do to let his detest show through.

Durante hastily spoke up. "Yes, and my or rather his newest young woman, Felicita, may well be most interested in obtaining further modifications, Crispino. She has already seen just how in demand the lovely Diamante and Domenica are. Lord Tom may well wish to pay for her further changes."

"Indeed, she did talk of that last night," Tom added. "Yet, such drastic surgery! It must be terribly painful for them to endure and weeks upon weeks of healing. That alone makes me most hesitant to even permit her to endure that." Tom knew quite well none of this was true, *if* the doctor really did have one of the alien medical machines and knew how to use it.

"Oh, no, no, no! Lord Tom!" Crispino became very animated. A hurt look filled his face. "I am a physician, a doctor. I heal people and cure them. I assure you none of them ever felt the slightest pain. All were healed within minutes and with no scaring whatsoever. I admit that used to be the case, when I first began my long career years ago. Oh my, yes indeed. But then, you see, I was able to obtain one of those alien machines that the Daughters of the Seas were using to make their body modifications. From the men who looked after the mermaids, as we call them, I learned that the lip slitting, the removal of ribs, and the crushing of feet were totally painless and healed within minutes. This I could not believe — as a doctor, you see."

"I paid them a visit and was shown the fancy alien machine that did these things. Well, I was envious of them. Such a machine could revolutionize surgery — and it has mine. But I get ahead of myself. When the mermaids lost their powers, I went to their building to see if they needed medical help. I found men stealing them away and ransacking their quarters. I found their medical machine and took it myself."

"It had only a few options, which I was able to figure out. Those were the usual procedures for body ornamentations. In my spare time, I fiddled with it and suddenly discovered hundreds more options. After years of study in my spare time, I figured out what a few of them did. Limb removal, primarily. Well, I was very excited and used it on a soldier, whose arm had to be amputated. To my amazement, it worked to perfection. Since then, I have been using it when similar situations arise."

"In the case of my dear friend Durante here, he and his women greatly wanted elective surgery to enhance their beauty and to allow them to make more money. Indeed, I believe twelve women have done this, made a fortune, and have retired."

226

"Sixteen, old Crispino. Sixteen have earned a fortune and have retired. Impressive, eh?" Durante corrected him and winked at Tom, who smiled.

"I see. Impressive indeed. But Durante said you somehow program them? The men I've seen who have lost a limb in combat are anything by cheerful about their lives," Tom broached what he needed to find out.

"Oh that. Well, yes, I discovered that quite by accident," Crispino said with a smile. He related the long story of somehow programming a patient by accident. He elaborated on what he'd done with the women. "So you see, it is just a matter of reciting the desired behavior while they are unconscious. When they wake up, they follow that behavior. Here, I have the list of things to say that Durante and I made up. Look them over. If you wish additional things said or if you wish some alternate behavior patterns installed, just jot them down."

He then added, "Don't get me wrong, Lord Tom. If I didn't have this marvelous machine that performed the surgery completely painlessly and healed them in minutes, why, I would never do such a thing. Only because this machine can do these without harming the women and because they then are not helpless but can make enough money to retire within ten years do I do it. How many men can make enough money to retire in just ten years, eh? Not even I, the best surgeon in Po. Wars don't help. Good lord no. That barbarian fellow killed everyone that was wounded. I didn't get even one patient, though thousands perished. Such a waste. Anyway, I digress. I want you to know that I am here if you need my services. But the hour is getting late. I have ten patients to visit yet this morning. I am usually here at night, Lord Tom, unless an emergency calls me. It has been very nice meeting you. Durante, I look forward to spending more time with you, now that you have all the time in the world."

Durante chuckled. Tom rose and shook the doctor's hand. During the carriage ride back, Durante chatted about his friend, but added little new information. He dropped Tom off, but not before he showed Tom where he could rent the only remaining wagon in Po. Horses were at a premium as well as wagons. Tom then quietly teleported back and rented the wagon for a few hours.

When he returned, Henry was chatting with the women, who were sitting on their couches waiting for him. "Okay, Felicita, it is time to return you to your parents," Tom announced. She let out a squeal of joy. The two caretakers helped her pack her many gowns, shoes, and other items into two bags. While he was depositing them in the wagon and fetching her money pouch, Felicita said her goodbyes and wished them all the very best. Tom put his arm around her, steadying her as she made her long, slow walk out of the building. He had to lift her up into the wagon though.

As they rode through the sparsely populated streets, Tom pointed out, "Well, Felicita, you are now a noblewoman, and you do look fabulous."

She giggled. "Yes, I truly am. It is so hard, but now I can make something of myself. Thank you so much for helping us all. It is a miracle! We need some of them here, after what the barbarians have done. Dad says half of the town is gone now." She chatted away. Her parents were both surprised to see her, amazed at her new appearance, and utterly aghast at the fortune that she proudly displayed in her money pouch. As Tom dropped the wagon off, he knew at least three lives would be better now.

How to get the three mermaids back to their oasis was the next hurdle. The scarcity of transportation was significant as well as the distance. It would take several days to drive there, ignoring the potential dangers. Hence, Tom opted for teleportation. He and Henry pretended that Henry's wife, Sally, had come with him, but had stopped to do some shopping before arriving. That explanation was accepted readily.

The three slung the pair of bags that each mermaid had over their backs, held onto that woman's money pouch, and put an arm securely around their mermaid's waist. Then, the three teleported them to Campo Oasis. They were appalled at what they found there. All the younger men were simply gone. The women were no longer bound and had slit their skirts so that they could walk easily, unfettered, as they did the work that their menfolk had done.

At first, Beppe was shocked to see his three daughters returning, but Elena quickly explained they were fabulously rich now. Tom quietly explained some details and showed him the gems in Elena's pouch. "You see, your three angels have returned with quite a large fortune," Tom said. "Not to mention they are now noblewomen, as you can see."

"Yes, yes, they do so look like their mother, my dearest Elda," Beppe said, tears flowing down his cheeks. He was so overcome with emotion, that he simply hugged his three daughters tightly. At last, he managed to say, "Thank you, thank you, Lord Tom, for bringing my angels back to me. I believed I would never see them again."

"You are most welcome. Elena, Felisa, Adalina, I will drop by every now and then to make sure you three are all right and doing well," Tom suggested. He wanted to leave a door open in case later on he could convince them to come to Brom, get therapy, and perhaps even the *mentales* gift of telekinesis, if Benjamina would consent to doing it. As the three headed back to Po, even Sally had to wipe a wet spot off her cheek. That reunion had been very emotional for all.

As they walked into the former escort service building, Sally whispered, "Now comes the really hard part."

"We are ready to go too, Lord Tom," Diamante gushed, the second she saw Tom and the others entering their living room. "All packed." She and the others were very pleased and happy, eager to please him. Sally picked up their surface thoughts. All were intent upon fully satisfying him so that he would marry them. She spotted their memories of six other women similar to themselves being married to two men, the barbarian conquerors.

After Tom gave the two caretakers their money pouches and thanked them for their years of service to the women, he explained, "Okay, ladies. It is time that we return to our place." Each of them slung the women's bags over their shoulders and fastened the women's money pouches securely to their belts. Henry and Sally put an arm around the waist of Annetta and Bianca, while Tom took hold of the short arms of Diamante and Domenica. "Okay, here we go," he said, mostly as a signal for Henry and Sally. The three teleported to the Underground. Of course, none of the four women had ever teleported and had no idea what was happening, let alone where they were when the world suddenly reappeared. This only reinforced their opinion that Lord Tom was a most powerful and worthy man, steeling their determination to make him most happy with themselves.

Ken and the others had not been idle. They converted an underground room in to a master bedroom suite and living quarters for the four arriving women. It was somewhat isolated from the rest of their working spaces, but it connected to a number of smaller rooms where therapy sessions had been given in the past, as well as to the long tunnel that eventually led to the buried spaceship and the Madiera world where the hundreds of mermaids lived.

All the Underground members spoke the three languages found on Tierra. Some traced their ancestry back to the Westerlings, though most were from the Midlands. Why? These men and women dealt with all the peoples of Tierra and thus had to be able to speak all three languages. Some spoke the Easterlings language better than others did. Jamie, Luisa, Henry, and Sally were most fluent in that tongue because of their close association with the Easterlings mermaids and their therapy sessions. In addition, they all spoke the dying dialect variation of the Madiera women, who were by now fairly well absorbed into the world around Brom and the Midlands tongue, which was so uncannily similar to that of the Madiera women's language.

The four women were taken by surprise by the teleport and suddenly seeing so many strangers around them when they appeared. Tom introduced all of his friends, one by one. Luisa then explained that for now, this would be their temporary suite. Tom had made one small goof. He had not considered the physical limitations of Diamante and Domenica, who needed their special low chairs and beds. He promised to make another trip and bring them back, hastily alloying their rising concerns. Almost at once, the actual needs of the women became apparent as well as just how sensitive the four were to any remote suggestion that they were helpless or needed help. Luisa and Sally saw how tenuous the mental health of the four women actually was. Within a few minutes that was more than apparent and the two began to "educate" the others on the best way to handle the four.

"Let me adjust your hair for you, Domenica," Luisa said, as she sat her on the couch.

"Oh, please do. I must look perfect for Lord Tom," she replied, accepting the assistance.

On the other hand, Diamante protested a little when Misty said, "Let me help you with your hair." Quickly, the dozen saw just how very sensitive the four women were about "help."

Before long, it was lunchtime. Luisa carefully avoided saying, "Let us help you eat or let us feed you." Rather, she said, "It's lunch time. Are you as hungry as we are?"

"Oh yes, quite," Annetta replied. "What do Midlands's people eat?"

"Well, today, it is just stew and tea. I hope that will be all right with you," Luisa answered politely.

"Yes, I will take some, please," Annetta replied, just as politely. She did not indicate that Luisa was to feed her, though that is just what Luisa proceeded to do. Crystal, Misty, and Sally followed her lead. Quickly, they saw they had to be very diplomatic in the handling of the four's physical needs.

After lunch, Luisa had therapy sessions arranged for the four. Four older mermaid women from the Easterlings would be delivering them. Luisa realized the four had lived with mermaids for years and thus there would be no cultural or language barriers interfering with the sessions. Tom explained, "Okay my gorgeous women. I have some Easterlings mermaids who wish to visit with you, and they will be asking you many questions. I know they will be interested in what has been going on in their homelands. They've been here for twenty years or so and have not had any chance to visit since then. I trust you will answer their questions as best you can."

"Oh yes. Mermaids here? Oh that is really very good indeed. They are so like us, beautiful women," Bianca replied enthusiastically. From his light touch on her mind, he realized the four equated mermaids with other exotic women like themselves. Well, he thought, that is to be expected.

All four insisted on walking to meet these mermaids. Tom escorted both Diamante and Domenica, holding their short arms in his hands, as they waddled proudly down the hall. Luisa and Sally quietly slipped and arm around the waists of Annetta and Bianca, steadying them as they took their tiny steps in their toe shoes, fettered by their tight-fitting gowns.

Once introduced, the four quietly stepped out, hoping and praying that the mermaids could begin to unravel the awful mess of the women's mental state. Henry and Tom made a quick trip back to Po, returning with the low-to-the-ground couches, chairs, and beds of the two.

The sessions ended at suppertime. However, all four were now sobbing, grief-stricken. "We are so utterly helpless," wailed Domenica. The other three were in equally bad emotional states. They had been so polite and refined at lunch, but now they felt completely helpless and horribly distraught over their physical plight.

When Zita and her three mermaid friends joined them for supper, she explained, "We have begun to erase the programming the doctor laid in over the unconscious pain of their surgeries. This is going to be a *very* long haul. They should get as much rest as possible tonight. We will continue in the morning after breakfast. Tom, it would be wise of you to sleep with the four again tonight, if you don't mind."

After supper, Luisa and three others got the four ready for bed, sitting their lip plates on the side table that Tom had brought back. This along with their low chairs and beds added some much needed continuity to the four, though Luisa arranged them in the one large bed, leaving a space in the middle for Tom. He then joined them, prepared for their massive grief outflowing.

"Oh Tom, we are so helpless. We are not even proper women any longer. How can you ever love us when we are so crippled?" wailed Domenica. The others rapidly bombarded him with similar thoughts and unanswerable questions. Tom slipped into bed between Diamante and Domenica, sliding his arms beneath them and then pulled Annetta and Bianca in close as well, physically comforting them.

"You are all beautiful women. You are not your bodies, which are so helpless. You are all immortal spiritual beings of great beauty. One day you will see this for yourselves, if only you will continue to answer the questions of the mermaids. I promise you that you will feel so much better. It just takes time. I find each of you very beautiful," Tom said soft and lovingly, calming the terrified, frantic women down. Soon they began to relax and fell asleep. For the first time in years, they went to sleep without their urgent need and drive for sexual stimulation first. That part of their "programming" had been broken already.

Around midnight, Tom teleported himself across the room. This was the only way that he could safely extricate his body from the tangle of the snuggling women and the pile of long hair that draped them and him. He hastily dressed and quietly joined Ken in their main communications room.

"Are they sleeping okay?" Ken asked.

"It was a bit wild, but yes, I got them calmed down, and they are sleeping soundly. Let's go get that damnable medical machine," Tom replied somewhat antagonistically.

The two soon arrived outside the doctor's home and office. Another short teleport and they stood in the patient meeting room. Each used a bit of their psi powers to conjure a faint light. They split up and began searching for the machine. Before long, Ken found it in the doctor's operating room. Telepathically, he let Tom know and shortly Tom crept into the room with him. Both put their hands on the machine and teleported it and themselves back to the communications room.

"Now let's see what he has gotten his hands on," Ken pronounced. A quick examination showed it was just a standard medical machine like the many they had themselves. "We are just in time. Look, the reservoir is nearly out of the stem cell solution. A few more operations and the machine would fail."

"I am going to pay the doctor a visit in a couple of days. I want to cast any suggestion off of us that we stole his machine," Tom suggested.

"That would be prudent. Go for it," Ken advised.

Two days later, Tom paid a call on the forlorn doctor. "Good morning, doctor. I've made some decisions and am ready to have some more work done. I say, is something wrong?"

Almost in tears, Doctor Crispino explained, "I've been robbed! Someone stole my precious medical machine!"

"Oh no! How awful!"

"Yes, it's terrible, just terrible. Now my patients will have to suffer terribly, when I have no choice but to remove a limb," he replied.

"Well, that changes everything."

"Indeed. I am afraid that, if you wish more work done, it will be most painful and her recovery time will be many, many weeks. I suppose her programming will not be affected though," he added.

"Oh, I would not dream of putting these elegant, beautiful women through that! That would be inhumane, doctor. I guess I will just have to be content with what I do have now," Tom said with a resolved sigh.

"Ah, yes. I do appreciate your taking that point of view. I could hardly perform the surgery on the women now — not with all the pain and suffering they would have to endure. The aliens certainly are so far more advanced in their medical procedures than I am. Woe unto us. If only the great lords would trade for medical machines instead of gold and iron ore. The world needs such humane marvels as those machines, not more swords and useless gold," the doctor replied.

Tom chatted with him a little longer before taking his leave. He was convinced the doctor would not be performing such surgeries any longer, not unless he ever got his hands on another alien medical machine.

For several more weeks, Tom had to sleep with the four women at night. They desperately needed the moral support only he could give them. By late January, they had gone far enough in their therapy sessions that the four were full of life, often cheerful, and for sure quite vibrant. Vitality had returned to the four.

As they lay in bed, Domenica asked, "Tom, what will

happen to us now? We are really alive, but we are also completely dependent on others for nearly everything."

"That's a good question, Domenica. Here in Brom, quite a few women are like Annetta and Bianca. They have learned to use their feet as their hands. I will see if some can come here, spend time with you two, and see what can be done. It would help all four of you, if your lips were healed, and you didn't have to wear the lip plates. You could use your teeth to help out."

"But would we not then be seen as most beautiful?" asked Annetta.

"True, some of the noblewomen in Brom do wear the lip plates, dear. You need to weigh the ability to do more things for yourselves against merely looking pretty," he replied. "Further, while some noblewomen wear the toe shoes like you, only a few wear the highly restrictive gowns that you both wear. While we cannot undo all that was done to your feet, we can undo some. You would have to wear heels, but walking would be vastly easier for you both. Again, weigh the notion of looking beautiful against being able to do far more for yourselves, Annetta, Bianca."

"We will think about that," Annetta replied.

"But what about us, the half-women?" Domenica asked. "Nothing can be done for us."

"Well, if you got rid of your lip plates, you could use your teeth to help some. At least, you are able to walk a little. That's something. I will ask the others for ideas, Domenica," Tom replied.

The next day, Misty worked the medical machine, undoing the four sets of lip plates and partially repairing Annetta and Bianca's feet. She then got them new heels and dresses. Within a day, they began responding to the vast increase in their own mobility. Next, the four also abandoned their pipe corsets. That done, Venerada Maricela sent over two young katalyein to begin to teach Annetta and Bianca how to use their feet as hands. While those two were definitely on the road to rehabilitation, no one had many real ideas of how to help the other two, not just yet. Misty suggested that they wait until they had finished all of their therapy sessions before trying to solve this one.

Chapter 13 Stakes Rise

"Turda has fallen!" Bart yelled loudly. He'd just intercepted communications from the Renegade Tower. "My god, can nothing stop this barbarian horde?" The others came running into the communications room where he worked.

"Crap. Lord Emilio and Venerada Maricela will be summoning me soon," Ken growled. "Okay, get me all the details as they come in. Damn, where are they going to strike next?"

"Hey, that's just what's flying about the comm network," Bart replied.

Two hours later, Venerada Maricela touched Ken's mind. *Emergency meeting in one hour. Usual place. I presume you have heard Turda has fallen?* Ken replied that he had and would come as prepared as he could.

This time when he and Crystal entered her meeting room, she was not dressed formally, though Lord Emilio and Amo Domingo were. "Good of you to come, Ken, Crystal. Nasty business, this is," growled Emilio, rubbing his large moustache, which he often did when he was annoyed.

"Indeed. I do have some facts for you. None good though. Once again, Damiano has proven to be the smarter tactician and strategist. He out-foxed Lord Turda. He used a new army formation — we're calling it a wedge. Pack your soldiers into an enormous equilateral triangle. Head its point top towards the enemy lines. It punctures the line, and the body of the triangle fans out destroying the line from its sides. Nasty and effective," Ken reported.

"However, the loss of life on both sides was horrific. The only positive aspect is Damiano has lost a sizeable force in this battle. Again, he has proven to be indestructible. This time, a dozen tower men and women from the Renegade Tower were at the Lord's side. Apparently, they hit Damiano with a dozen balls of fire and numerous other attacks, and he emerged relatively unscathed. At least we know he is able to heal himself rapidly."

"As far as we know now, Lord Turda attempted to place the battle far from Turda, just as Sultan Ferro did. Unfortunately, the folks in Turda panicked and sacked their own town as they fled the city the next day. It's mostly a ghost city right now. The real question that is being carefully studied is just where Damiano will head next. Most believe there are three choices. One, head on down the coast towards the old Bashir port city of Madya. Two, head due west to Southbend. Three, angle northwest into the heartland of Matruk and on into the Midlands. It is too soon to tell for sure. Signs are pointing away from his continuing down the coast to Madya."

"Damn, damn, damn!" Emilio cursed angrily. "Look, either way, the Midlands must be his target. If he goes after Southbend, all he has to do is continue going west straight into the Rusden breadbasket. Lord help us all if the breadbasket of the Midlands falls! Of course, if he goes diagonally, then the towers at Wye and Northend are in dire jeopardy. Worse, it is the middle of the winter here. No one can field an army in all this snow. By spring melt, the barbarian can be at the doors of Wye!"

"Get to the point, Lord Emilio," Domingo advised.

"Yes, yes. All in good time. I've received word that Venerado Valen is demanding an emergency meeting of the High Council of Lords in Exchange City. It's scheduled for the 1st of April. I'm allowed an advisor. Ken, Crystal, I would like to have you come with the venerada here and Domingo. I fear I am going to need sound advice. Will you come?"

"You know how I hate to be out and about in the world, but this time, I will make an exception. Somehow this barbarian must be stopped soon," Ken replied. He made it apparent he was doing Emilio a big favor. He never attended such meetings for two reasons. One, he did not want to call attention to himself and the Underground. His parents had made that mistake and it had cost them dearly. Second, with their sound equipment, he could listen in on the meeting from their comm center and thus had no real need to be there.

Emilio picked up on Ken's words. "Thank you, Ken, Crystal. I owe you a really big favor. Do not hesitate to ask for it when you need it." I hope that satisfies him, he thought. I'm going to need him to help me convince the other lords to avoid sending a huge army down there, bankrupting us in the process.

Venerada Maricela spoke up. "As usual, meet here and one of our circles will teleport us to the meeting. Be here at say just after supper the night before. Let's not be the last to arrive on the 1st." Ken smiled; he knew she was one of those people who always arrived early. Well, he thought, she might need the extra time because of her lack of arms. Maricela picked up his thought, flushed, but said nothing.

"Good. I will keep you both posted on further developments," Ken stated dryly and the meeting broke up. Back home, Bart groaned when Ken told everyone he and Crystal had been asked to attend the meeting. He didn't have to say anything more. All knew from the experiences of their parents just how dangerous it was for the Underground to be visible to the world at large, even if no one knew that they were part of the mysterious Underground. An assassin had very nearly uncovered their parents' location.

Days later, further news did come, again via their monitoring of the comm networks and relays in all the towers. Lord Truda's daughter, Edda, who some suggested was not even of age yet, had proclaimed herself the sole and rightful ruler of Turda. More importantly, she had placed the Sisterhood in a position of power there. Sisters had been appointed her official ministers! Not long after that, the comm networks were flooded with messages to be relayed to local Guild Mothers, asking them to send all available and willing Sisters to Turda to help restore order there and to help rebuild the city.

Within a day, Venerada Maricela received a request from the Sisterhood homeland in Hilliard Heights. They wanted to send some fifty women and horses down to Turda. For the first time in over two decades, all three full circles at Brom Tower were called into action simultaneously. Fifty-three women, sixty horses, and ten wagons were teleported down to Turda. It was one of the largest teleportations in Brom history. Lady Edda was beginning to get the support that she needed.

Not long after that, Bart intercepted further messages. The Renegade Tower would be sending several caravels of horses, grains, fodder, and wagons to Turda, but they would not be arriving until early March. After these messages were sent, Adelmira Tower finally took a token action, sending a permanent representative to Edda's court. She would act as a relay point. However, Edda continued to use her new Minister of Communication, Angelica, much to the annoyance of the Adelmira woman. That tower had not sent any aid to Turda until now. Edda was well aware of that, chalking this move up to politics.

Further, word now came on the direction that Damiano was taking. The Renegade Tower told all the other towers and, via them, the ruling lords the barbarians were unequivocally heading northwest through Matruk, heading straight for the heartland of the Midlands and Wye with its tower (Bedwurth). This caused quite a stir and guaranteed that all the rulers would be attending the April meeting.

Emerald green overwhelmed Ken's senses as he got his firsthand look at the former Emperor's Court at the old Emperor's Fortress just outside Exchange City. Technically, it occupied the extreme southeastern corner of Plateau Grado, the land leased by the Imperium for five hundred years. Long ago, this small corner had been given back to Tierra so that they could build the tower and fortress there to house first a ruler from Valen, and later the emperor, empress, and their circle. Now it was an anachronism. Ken's grandmothers had renovated it, installing themselves as the Emperor and Empress, in hopes of securing a lasting peace. Over the years, the ruling lords found ways around that. Today, while it still housed a small circle, the complex was used to host various meetings, particularly the High Council of Lords. Just after supper, one of Brom's circles teleported the eight there.

Lord Emilio Bolivar and his Squad Leader Amo Domingo Bolivar-Brom were the official Brom representatives. Venerada Maricela Wait was his tower representative. Each brought their spouse. Emilio's wife, Anita, was also a katalyein. Maricela rather hated these meetings. She was forced to dress like a noblewoman. That is, she had to wear fancy nylons, a rather tight fitting satin gown, and the six-inch heels, the minimum acceptable height for such high status women. This severely limited her ability to be independent, and she had to depend heavily on her husband, even for eating. On the other hand, Anita loved to dress up and visit with all the other wives of the rulers. She didn't mind giving up her shaky independence for a near total dependence on others. The other wives were quite pleased to assist her.

While Ken rather disliked having to dress up in his fancy suit, Crystal rather enjoyed dressing up. She looked forward to these relatively few times that she could "see the wide world." Both were impressed with the grandeur of the emperor's court rebuilt by their grandmothers.

One of the tower's members led the eight down the corridor from the teleport arrival station to this main court room, where the meeting would be held tomorrow, and then on to their quarters. The women's heels clicked noisily on the stone floor, though in the morning, they would be dwarfed by the sounds of many other heels. As in many royal manors, each ruler and his party were given a suite of rooms. Already, one of the tower members had started a fire in the common room of the suite. It was cozy, homey, but rather small. Five side rooms angled off this suite, one being the communal bath. The other four were bedrooms with large wardrobes where they could store their change of clothes.

Emilio and Domingo headed for their usual rooms, pointing out the bedroom that Ken and Crystal could have. "Holler if you need anything, Anita, Maricela," Crystal called out as she and Ken ducked into their small bedroom. It was quaint, a little dated on its fixtures. Certainly, the bedding was dated. While Ken unpacked their bags, Crystal looked the room over. They had two soft chairs and a small writing table. A faded tapestry hung on one wall and several oil lanterns provided the only light. Further, the room was chilly. It was April. Outside, the heavy snows had yet to melt completely.

By the time the men had unpacked, a servant arrived with a steaming teapot and some biscuits. The four men settled down in the common room, discussing what options might be put forward by other rulers in the morning. Meanwhile, the women gathered in Anita's room, with Crystal and Sally helping Maricela and Anita with their tea and biscuits. Crystal didn't need her *mentales* gifts to know that Maricela was very annoyed at having to have her hold Maricela's biscuit up for her to eat and hold her tea cup to her lips for her, but that Anita didn't mind the inconvenience in the slightest. In fact, Anita rather enjoyed Sally's help.

"I do so love these meeting. We get to see all the new dress styles and heels. I get to dress up, though I do know that I am so limited in what styles I can wear," Anita gabbed. "I suppose we won't be seeing any new styles this time. It's way early in the year. Still, it's my time to chat with the other ruler's wives and find out all manner of 'secrets.' Don't you just love it, Maricela?"

"Not really. I value my freedom of action more, Anita. You know that, but I know what you mean about being limited in styles. More and more of the wives are opting for those toe shoes again. What was once old has become new again," she replied.

Anita giggled, "Emilio says that women wearing them are really sexy-looking. He won't let me get them though."

Crystal spoke up, "Rightly so, Anita. You would lose so much of your independence if you did."

"Yes, of course I would. Still, as the wife of the ruler of Brom, I ought to not look totally old fashioned. I should not embarrass him before all of his peers. Besides, I could easily have a personal assistant with me at all times. So honestly, if more of the wives take up the toe shoes, I may well do so myself." The women continued to chat about the changes in dresses over the years, and Maricela wished she were sitting with the men instead of here. Listening to Anita chatting away, Maricela saw that even though Anita was also a katalyein *mentales* gifted as herself, each woman was unique and had their own personalities, likes, desires, and viewpoints of life and what was important to themselves. Am I isolating myself from life, Maricela wondered?

The next morning, after dining on a light breakfast brought to their suite, they headed off to the meeting. The wives, naturally, assembled in a waiting room next to the throne room, taking tea and chatting among themselves. The few male spouses stood at the back of the throne room watching the spectacle unfolding before them. The rulers, their advisors, their security leaders, and their venerados or veneradas met formally.

This time, Lord Gilberto Rosa, ruler of the City-States Alliance, sat on the old emperor's throne, conducting this special meeting. Venerado Pino Valen sat on the old empress' throne beside him, while his advisor, Leandro del Rey, stood to his left. "Thank you all for coming in these, the darkest of times," Gilberto began. He quickly outlined the history that had brought them to this point in time, filling in many details that had more recently become known.

After that, he was bombarded with questions. "Are you really going to allow Sultaness Sonia Ferro to rule the Arad?" "Are you really going to allow Lady Edda Turda to run Turda? She isn't of age, I'm told." Even more vehemently, someone asked, "Surely you are not going to allow the Sisterhood to gain such widespread control in the Arad and in Turda."

He replied politely, "Who we allow to control our cities and our states is a matter for the City-States Alliance. I have not seen any of you coming to their aid. The Sisterhood has." That quieted the protests for a time.

"We need to focus on just how we are to respond. Obviously, this barbarian Damiano is a freakish anomaly, far, far beyond the control of any one tower. Does anyone know any man or woman who could take a dozen balls of fire cast upon them and yet walk out of that literally unharmed? Yet, that is precisely what happened during the battle east of Turda. Our dozen tower members blasted him with every spell they could and to what avail? They destroyed his clothes. Nothing more! I say we are facing a freak, but an insane freak! He has left all of Domei, all the Arad, and now all of Turda with almost no able-bodied men between sixteen and forty-five! An entire generation of young men is gone and he is only beginning! Today, we must put our minds together and find a way to stop him!"

Ken was lost in thought. He did know someone who

could take a dozen balls of fire and walk away unharmed — Tim's wife, Petrona. Actually, anyone of nearly a hundred fire-elemental Madiera women could for that matter. However, beyond the Underground and a handful of Brom Tower members, no one knew of them. Ken was called back to reality. Someone asked just where the barbarian's army was today.

"As far as we know, he is a thousand miles southeast of Wye, heading for Wye," Venerado Pino answered with authority. This caused quite a stir among the lords, but not Lord Wye, he already knew this and was in the process of mobilizing an army.

"Good god! My Lords, you have to help us now," Lord Wye yelled loudly. "If not, my god, who is next? Rusden? Northend? Wycombe? Hell, he could well be at Brom's gates by winter!" He was exaggerating about Brom or so Emilio whispered to Ken, Domingo, and Maricela.

Lord Emilio spoke up, "With all due respect, Lord Wye, Brom is still snowbound, as you well know. By the time I raise an army for your defense and get them down there, Wye will be long sacked. Surely you should be asking Lord Rusden and Lord Northend for armies. They are closest to your city."

Of course, this raised numerous other objections, primarily from the Westerlings lords, who were many thousands of miles distant. Surprisingly, Lord Gervasi Quito Malaca spoke up. "Malaca stands ready to send an army to your aid. But Lord Bolivar has a valid point. If I bring my army to your aid, it would take two years to march them to Wye. Still, we are open to how Malaca might help you. I just don't see how Malaca's army can be of any use to you." The conversation for the next hour centered on the physical difficulties that most of the lords would have getting an army to Wye, completely ignoring the time needed to raise and equip said army.

Lord Rusden succinctly stated the counter arguments of Lord Northend and himself. "Look, if I send my entire army to your defense and if we lose that battle, I have left my entire kingdom open to these invaders to ransack as they will. Who will come to defend Rusden if my army is gone? Bashir has no army. Will Arabella and the other City-States come to my rescue with an army?" If Wye fell, Northend's nearest possible ally was two thousand miles to the north, Walsham. Wyth was even further to the northwest. Someone else asked where was the Matruk army? Their lord quietly said nothing in response. He was marshaling his forces around Southbend, giving up all the central farmlands of Matruk to Damiano without a fight, save the local town's militias.

They broke for lunch with nothing decided. The impossibilities of sending armies were on everyone's minds. Often ideas sprouted during the casual conversations among the lords during meals and evenings. Today was no exception.

When the meeting resumed, Lord Wye said, "During lunch, someone mentioned something that I believe warrants being discussed. Historically, the towers are supposed to protect the kingdoms they serve. Is that not right?" This was a rhetorical question. No one answered. "So while none of you can get an army to our defense in time, what about sending tower circles?"

The sheer amount of muttering among the group made it impossible for him to continue. He waved his hands and finally regained control. Someone shouted out, "But Damiano survived a dozen balls of fire. What use will a dozen circles be?" Ken knew the answer but grimaced. Beside him, so did Maricela, who thought as he did.

"Look, plenty. Instead of wasting your immense powers on this immune madman, use them to destroy his army! Wipe them all out. Soldiers can be easily killed. We've seen you do that many times. Wipe his army out and then perhaps he will see reason or perhaps we can find a way to subdue him. He cannot single handedly kill a whole army! My god, if necessary we can trample him beneath our feet!"

His idea took hold. At last, the lords saw a way of answering Lord Wye's pleas for help. More importantly, it didn't involve them directly, only their towers. It would be cheap, ludicrously so. No army, no weapons. And if it failed, nothing lost. They would still have their own army nearby. The many venerados and veneradas had no real choice in the matter. Protection of their kingdoms was one of their founding purposes that they had to live up to. There was no wiggle room in this one.

Someone lamented that all the massively powerful ancient weapons were no more. Some cursed the original Emperor Amy and Empress Jan for removing and destroying all those great weapons, anyone of which would be most useful right now. Ken, Crystal, and Maricela cringed.

They broke for an hour to allow the lords to confer with their tower leaders. When they resumed, this plan was adopted. All the towers would send a full circle to Wye's defense, as long as they were not on the front lines. However, they also agreed not to send them until the enemy army actually drew close to Wye's army, which Lord Wye would be positioning just south of Wye on the eastern bank of the Wyndl River. Exactly how to wipe out Damiano was left to Lord Wye and the circles, once they had destroyed his army, man by man.

That decided, Lord Gilberto dismissed the meeting. Everyone now gathered in the Great Hall for the celebratory evening meal and smaller discussions. Lord Gervasi Malaca was a close friend of those in Brom. His wife, Rosita, was also a mermaid, but she was now used to all the stares that she received at these meetings. The two of them dined with the Brom party, partly because they wanted to congratulate Maricela on becoming the new venerada. Unlike Anita and Maricela who had to have their husbands feed them, Rosita had the gift of telekinesis and could feed herself.

Rosita said, "I don't like the idea of outright killing all of those soldiers. Gervasi tells me that a great many of them are conscripted men, forced into his army or be killed. I wish there was some other way."

"So do we all," Maricela replied. "But we've yet to come up with any other workable solution. Still I fear that many of the tower folk will be killed as well. An army is huge and our spells, while deadly, affect only a small area, compared to the army. Surely during the battle, some will break through and slay our precious tower members."

"I hadn't thought of that," Rosita replied. "What kind of freak is this Damiano fellow? They say that he looks like a man."

"We just don't know. From all we've heard, he was born like every other man. He's obviously grown up like a man. And yet, he is somehow immune to death," Maricela answered.

"Could he be a freak like I am or was?" Rosita asked what was really bothering her about all this.

Maricela laughed. "Hardly, Rosita. You were a force for healing and blessing ships, not for the destruction of civilization." The middle-aged mermaid looked quite relieved to hear this and relaxed.

Rosita changed the topic. "We've brought a new fandango with us. Gervasi is going to see if the musicians will play it after supper. I can't wait to dance to it. I can only dance to a fandango, though. I hate being so physically limited, but Gervasi is so understanding."

"What's a fandango?" Ken asked.

"A jumping dance. I can hop well, you see. Gervasi and I will show you and Crystal how it's done, if you like. I warn you, you'll get quite a bit of exercise, but I don't know if you can do it in such high heels," Rosita admitted.

After dinner, the musicians did play it. They gave everyone fair warning though. Crystal kicked off her heels, as did Maricela. "Put your hands around her waist, like Gervasi is doing," Rosita proudly began explaining how it was done. Soon the musicians began playing the very lively dance. Before long, several other women took off their heels and joined in this jumping dance.

When it ended, the dancers were laughing and quite out of breath. Even Rosita's face was flushed, but smiling. "That was fun, thanks," Ken told her. Then others thanked the two as well.

"It's one of the very few things I actually can do without having to use my *mentales* powers to do," she admitted. The evening continued with other slower dance tunes and passed quickly.

Before long, the group disbanded and by seven, Maricela's Circle teleported them all back to Brom. *Stay a while, Ken,* Maricela sent him as they arrived. The others quickly left the teleport area, heading for Brom Manor and didn't notice Ken and Crystal hanging back. Theo took their bags off to their room, leaving the three alone. Almost at once, Marisol joined them, leading them into a side room.

"Maricela has kept me informed of what went on at the meeting," Marisol said solemnly. "Ken, Crystal, I fear that, if we send a circle there, we run a great risk of having them killed. On the surface, it sounds simple, but we both know how wars seldom go as planned. However, like everyone else, I can't see any other way than to eliminate his army to get to him. Do you?"

Sadly Ken shook his head. "Well, think on it and keep Maricela posted, please."

"Will do." They then headed for the tunnels in the basement. As they walked along, Ken said, "There is one way to get to Damiano, but that requires the use of alien weapons, which are outlawed on Tierra."

"I know and I am glad that the Valens didn't bring those up. I suspect that some in Valen Tower may still have such weapons," Crystal replied. "And that would open up a really bad crock of worms. I know, we have some in storage, but still, the aliens on Plateau Grado would immediately know of their use. We need to keep the aliens out of this, if we can."

Ken replied, "Marisol and Maricela have a good point. The towers are all short of *mentales* gifted. If some of their personnel should be killed, the effects would be extremely bad. The silly lords would rather sacrifice their towers than their armies. Yet their real security and protection from the aliens lay with the very people that they are willing to sacrifice! I'm going to talk to mom about this mess. I know, just don't get her upset."

Crystal smiled, that was her thought. The two of them were quite used to just knowing what the other was thinking without actually saying it or using telepathy to find out. Crystal merely said, "Just don't get the aliens involved, please." He grinned. That had to be avoided at all costs.

Chapter 14 Alien Changes

Sector ID Minister Emeryk Donat, originally from Rigel-3, was in total control of this sector of the Imperium and by proxy, the Governor of Ashford-5. However, calamities were happening right and left. The archenemy of the Imperium was the Federation of Planets and there had been some talk of going to war with them for quite some years. However, little came of that talk.

Out here in the largely unexplored rim of the galaxy, fuel was precious — hence, the strategic importance their massive fuel refinery on one of the moons of Ashford-5. Emeryk had received some intelligence that the Goringi, an ally of the Federation, was planning to attack the refinery.

He'd called in two of their battle cruisers and that had saved the day. After a hard-fought battle, which forced one of his cruisers to head off for major repairs, he'd finally driven the Goringi off, giving them a resounding defeat. He'd been gone from Ashford-5 for months. When he arrived back, he discovered that his gorgeous wife had been killed. Unconcerned with such trivial matters, he focused on his job without her distractions. Adalina Valen Donat had actually been kidnaped and turned into a mermaid priestess. Later, she was rescued along with many others and now lived with the mermaids in Madiera, having completely abandoned her husband, who would only now view her as a total freak of nature.

In January 1272, Emeryk received more unsettling news. There was a good chance that war would really break out. While he needed to protect the moon refinery, he also was needed in deep space, coordinating the battle cruisers and gathering intelligence. He spent less and less time planet-side. Finally, he put in a request to his superiors asking a governor to be appointed to Ashford-5. He simply did not have the time for such trivial things. They Okayed it and promised to do so.

Why? If war should break out, the Imperium could best protect their refinery by having a large military presence on the planet's surface. However, that was not in the lease agreement and it could hardly be reopened, not until at least 1500. The Imperium dare not make Ashford-5 an open world for fear their many telepaths would migrate to other worlds, wildly upsetting the balance of power on key worlds. However, if they could get Ashford-5 to send a senator off to the Imperial Senate, then perhaps after learning more about the Imperium, the senator could be persuaded to allow them to expand their land base on Plateau Grado without having to renegotiate the lease agreement.

The top leaders also knew that these natives were notoriously hard to work with. Their relationship had been strained to say the least. They needed someone who could easily gain the trust of these primitives and get them to send a senator off to the Imperial Senate. They needed to find someone who had proven they could get such tricky jobs done. To that end, they took a long hard look at all their other governors throughout the entire Imperium. Such was the importance of Ashford-5 at this point in time.

Konrad Burkhardt was the son of a prominent Imperium Senator from their world of Otto-4 in the Sirius Cluster. Konrad saw himself as one day being the most powerful governor of worlds in the Imperium, looked up to in the history chronicles as the finest governor that ever lived. He absolutely did not want to follow in his father's footsteps and be a political pawn, a senator. No, being a ruling governor of other worlds — that appealed to him.

Konrad was a driven man. During his academy days, he began to map out his future career, ending with his crowning achievement that would forever retain a place in history for him. He saw that he would need to have a wife. All governors had them; such was a vital necessity when dealing with alien cultures over which one had to rule. Not just any wife would do for Konrad. He was not interested in the silliness of love. Nor did he desire to produce offspring. He didn't get along well with children. Perhaps once he was famous, he could somehow manage to deal with having one son, perhaps.

No, his wife would have to be very special indeed. She

would not have to mind in the slightest traveling to all corners of the galaxy, perhaps even sometimes living in primitive conditions. Slowly, he began to work up the specific requirements for his proposed "wife." Then, during one lecture, it struck him hard. Language! All of these strange worlds would require that he speak their native tongues. Okay, he reasoned, the Imperium had language-learning machines. One simply put the earplugs in at night and the computer would play the language into your subconscious. After a number of weeks, why, one could speak the native language. Simple enough, or so he thought.

One day while eating his lunch in the cafeteria, he chanced to overhear an argument between a woman and another man. She said, "Look, Hans. That is not how it works at all. You can have those idiot language learning machines playing words into your head for months, but you simply will still not be able to speak that language like a native. You will sound like a simpleton to the natives. Language is *far* more that uttering the proper sounds."

Her words shattered Konrad's simple plans. If he really did sound like some babbling simpleton to the natives, by god, he would never be able effectively to do his job. Natives would simply not respect him or think much of him. He recalled his off-world baby sitter, whose command of Ottoian was atrocious. Across from him, the man left the woman in a huff.

Konrad stepped forward. "Excuse me, miss. I could not help but overhear what you were saying about the language machines. Frankly, I find this very important. You see, I aim to be a famous governor of primitive worlds. I want to show the entire Imperium how it is done properly. Taking over worlds by force of arms or force of economics is not the best way. So of course, I need to speak their languages fluently and not sound like a babbling simpleton. If the language machines don't work, how then can I learn to speak a native tongue fluently? Oh, I am Konrad Burkhardt, by the way."

"Nadja Meike. Linguistics. You need to supplement those auditory learning files with actual linguistic studies. But I should think that the auditory learning files would be enough to allow a governor to communicate with the local populations well enough."

"Oh no, no, no. To be a truly effective governor, one has to have the complete *respect* of the native people. If you sound to them like a babbling simpleton, they will simply not give you the respect that you absolutely must have to be more than *marginally* effective. That is what is so totally wrong with our system of governors on all these outer worlds. They are only marginally effective at best. I aim to be *totally* effective," Konrad replied.

"Are they run that badly? Anyway, you need a linguist with you in that case. We can study the language, get its proper pronunciations down, its grammar rules worked out, and help you begin to express yourself capably in that tongue, be it Algon-6 or Zoras-2. I am a linguistics major myself. Me personally, I want to travel to all of these so-called primitive worlds and do linguistic research on their languages. All the civilized worlds have had complete and definitive linguistic studies done and published. Yet, there are many primitive worlds out there just waiting to be explored," Nadja said rather gaily.

"Ah, but how do you get to those? That takes a whole lot of credits," Konrad pointed out the obvious. He was rather taken with this young woman. She was shapely and rather pretty, he thought. More importantly, she was planning to become a linguist, which she had just convinced him that he needed.

"Well, credits are not the problem. I come from a very wealthy family, Konrad. No, it is cutting through all that Imperium red tape that is the real barrier to getting to these worlds. Besides, many of them are closed worlds. All the credits in the Imperium aren't going to get me there," she replied rather hostility.

"Ah, you see, you need a governor who can get you to just those worlds," he replied cleverly planting such an idea.

"I can see that. Don't governors spend their whole careers on one world?" she countered.

"Ah, that is the whole darn problem. The current governors have no imagination — cannot truly speak the language which alienates him from the indigenous population

— I can go on and on about their failings. A true governor ought to be able to go to one of these native worlds, rapidly endear himself to the locals, obtain the agreements which the Imperium desires, and then *move on* to the next assignment. Only the incompetent wind up stationed forever on a world, or those who don't actually want to work for a living. I have great plans, Nadja. I am going to overhaul the entire field of governors! Of course, I still have much to learn, like this whole linguistics thing. There are probably more things that I have yet to consider that will play a vital role in making the role of governor a powerful one."

"I see. That does sound quite hopeful. Say, aren't you the senator's son?" she asked, knowing darn well that he was. In fact, she had staged the entire argument in the cafeteria in hopes of attracting his attention. She'd heard from others that Konrad was trying to revolutionize the post of governor, making it into what it was originally designed to do centuries ago: get in, win their trust, obtain whatever the Imperium had wanted to get from that world, and then move on, allowing a normal bureaucrat to take over. If she could hook up with someone like this, why, she would have the keys to these worlds. The linguistic studies that she could perform were mind-blowing. Nadja had to try to net this man.

"Yes, but I don't want that blabbed around campus. He is a silly bureaucrat, a politician. That's the last thing I want to be! So you have independent funds?" he asked. Funds, that was one thing that he lacked somewhat. His father could be hit up for only so many credits before he would tell Konrad to get a real job in the Senate. He knew that his father had wanted him to one day take his senate seat. Funds! She was perfect, he thought. Thus began their close relationship that led to their marriage, when they graduated from the academy on Otto-4.

During their studies, the two worked well together, bouncing ideas off each other. Both knew that she needed to do everything possible to help him win the trust and support of the natives as rapidly as possible. In return, he had to give her carte blanche to study their language in any way that would allow her to do so as rapidly as possible. Further, they worked out all manner of new, guiding principles for how a governor and his wife to operate in the field.

To that end, they analyzed the failures of over a hundred governors, going back two centuries in time. At the top of the list of errors, several continued to be continually repeated. Failure to become fluent in the spoken languages was a big one. Failure to be seen as respecting and adopting the local cultural practices was another. On Aleno-6, it was customary for a visiting dignitary to share wives with the ruler for one night. Failure to do such a thing had kept that governor from succeeding in his mission there for nearly a century and a half. The rulers had no respect for the governor.

"No matter what the culture or practices are," Konrad declared, "you and I are simply going to have to undergo them, to endure them if we must, knowing that we will be vastly more rapidly achieving our objectives."

"You are absolutely right, Konrad. We simply must do that and the faster we adopt their ways and customs the better. This also means dressing in their manner as well. Remember that disaster on Cylone-6 where the governor and his wife refused to wear the local clothing? It took him nearly a hundred years to obtain his original objective. He had to use the rejuvenation machine ten times, before he finally outlived those whom he had greatly offended. We can't afford such delays as that. I estimate that I need at most two years to fully record and study a native language. Then, I will be ready to move on to the next one. That means, we have to get you done that swiftly as well, dear."

"I agree. We should set a target of spending a maximum of two years on one of these native worlds before completely accomplishing my assigned mission," Konrad agreed fully.

"Yes, but if you get it completed, what assurances do you have that the Imperium will reassign you after that?" she asked.

"Key question, dear. I must really demonstrate a complete mastery of the governor's post. Make the Sector ID Ministers aware that they have a powerhouse governor. If we are delayed, I can send word to my father. You know, use a little Senate push," he answered determinedly.

Armed with numerous agreements, plans, procedures,

and specialized linguistic machines, the two embarked on their grand voyage. However, just as they were graduating, Konrad came across something that intrigued him greatly. His father had accidentally leaked this tidbit, and he shared it with Nadja. Many years ago, a new world had been discovered on the outer rim of the galaxy, the fifth planet of a dull orange-red sun called Ashford in the star charts. That the planet was rich in fuel ore wasn't what got their interest. Nor was it the fact that it was a closed world. Rather the tidbit that his father had accidentally revealed was that the natives had a highly telepathic society!

Nadja exclaimed, "Konrad. Somehow, someway, I need to get to that world and study them. No one in history has ever done a linguistic study of a telepathic society!"

"Hey, it is a closed world. Worse, the Sector ID Minister himself is controlling it. I think the original governor made a complete mess of it there. When was the last time you ever heard of the top dog performing governor duties? Never! There must be something extremely valuable, extremely critical on this strange world of Ashford-5. I am setting that as our ultimate goal, dear. Do you concur?"

"Absolutely. Let's get the linguistics sorted out for a number of other worlds and get you widely recognized as the very best governor. Perhaps then, the Sector ID Minister will assign you there. I think we have a whole lot of work cut out for us before then, dear," Nadja replied. From that point on, being assigned to Ashford-5 became both their goals. Workaholics would be a good description of this unlikely couple.

His first assignment offered them a chance to prove all of their theories correct. Assigned to a remote world called Gallim-3, his task was to get the native rulers there to agree to allowing the Imperium to establish a spaceport somewhere on the planet's surface. They needed a refueling stop as the Imperium continued to push outward into the unknown rim of the galaxy. Three exploratory ships had been sent there already, and the last one had recorded samples of the local language. As the two traveled the long voyage there, they listened to those recordings in their earpieces at least a dozen times. Still, Nadja knew that their ability to speak the Gallim language would be marginal at best.

They also stared at the video images the survey ships had taken of the people and the rulers. First contacts were always rough, since the native language was unknown. In her teens, Nadja had once thought she would like to be just such a person to make that initial contact. Later, the study of linguists interested her far more. You could only say "U-ba-ju-ba" so many times before it was boring. Delving into that language wholly, working out its phonemes, its morphemes, its phonics, its grammar rules, its syntax, and even its vocabulary — this was what it was all about. Further, in the back of her mind, she toyed with the idea that perhaps at one time in the far distant past, all peoples spoke the same language. If she studied enough languages, perhaps she would be able to back track. But for now, that was just a wild notion.

As they looked at the people of Gallim-3, both were a little taken aback. The women appeared to have golden eyes. According to the survey ships, this was because the women had some kind of golden spheres covering their actual eyes. Somehow, they could still see. The women all had one inch in diameter disks in their earlobes. From these dangled the longest earrings that either had ever seen, resting often on the woman's breasts. Gold and gem-encrusted read the survey report. However, what shocked the two the most were the faces of the women. All wore some kind of gold mask, close fitting to their faces, conforming to every curve of their face, but with nose holes, eye holes, and a mouth hole. According to the survey reports, these golden masks were screwed permanently onto the woman's head and were never taken off.

In contrast, the men also had golden eye spheres and had a golden shaft inserted through their nose. Otherwise, the men looked normal. Dress styles were simple cotton and probably quite comfortable. "Well, I don't see any way around it, dear. If we are to gain their respect, we are going to have to mold ourselves in their images," Konrad proclaimed.

"Right. I rather like those earrings. Probably worth a fortune. I am game for this. We ought to keep our own medical machine handy so that we can undo some of these things,"

Nadja replied. Before long, she purchased two medical machines and a rejuvenation machine as well.

After landing and meeting firsthand with the Rax or ruler, they quickly arranged to become modified to look like the natives. Rax approved, but was quite surprised. Nadja grit her teeth as a woman tightened the screws that permanently attached the heavy, solid gold, facemask over her face. When the woman put the golden eye spheres in her eyes, she discovered that she could still see somewhat out of the small central openings. Next, Nadja was asked about what she wanted for the gemstones of her earrings.

She had a choice at last. Nadja's people from Otto-4 had a slightly yellowish hue to their skin. Her eyes were sky blue and her hair was rather thick and quite black. She wore it shoulder length. Hence, she opted for red rubies. Further, she discovered the length of the strands was indicative of the woman's position and power, as was the number of strands on each earring. Nadja was clever. She inquired how long and how many the Rax's wife had in hers and had hers equal that woman's set.

"My god, Nadja, your earrings are enormous, but smashingly attractive," Konrad exclaimed when he first saw her new look.

"They are equal to the wife of the Rax. That denotes that I am her equal, just as you are the Rax's equal. Clever, eh?" she proudly replied.

"Brilliant. Can you see? I can only just barely see," he asked.

"Barely see here too. Okay, we are to dine with the Rax and his wife tonight. Let's see if we make the right impression, dear," Nadja suggested.

They did just that, proving Konrad's theory. The Rax enthusiastically received them. When he learned that Nadja wanted to stay with them in their home or with someone the Rax approved of so she could better learn and study their language so that they didn't sound like foreigners, he readily agreed. Very close and warm relations began almost at once. Within a month, Konrad got the agreement the Imperium desired signed, sealed, and delivered.

However, bureaucracies work slowly. It took six months for the agreement to be ratified and preparations made. During this time, Nadja spent all her days with the locals, working on their language. Konrad was very specific in his final report, outlining precisely what they had done to obtain the desired result in that one-month time. He recommended that the next governor and his wife adopt the native customs upon arrival. He even noted that the governor's wife's earrings ought to match those of the wife of the Rax.

After six months, Konrad was utterly bored, but Nadja was not. When their marching orders came, she had collected enough information to publish a proper linguistic study of their language, and she promised the Rax that, in time, others who came to visit would be far better able to speak their language. Contained in their marching orders was a request for Nadja to revise and update the language tapes. This she did while they were en route to their next assignment.

However, the first thing the two did after saying farewell to their new friends on the planet was to remove carefully Nadja's faceplate and both of their eye spheres. It took a bit of healing to repair Konrad's nose and the screw holes in the sides of her face. She decided to continue to wear the exotic earrings for now.

His next assignment was on Strx-4. The previous governor's report began with a heading: Extremely Shapely. "My goodness, look at how their women look!" Nadja exclaimed. Both stared at the multiple images. "Have they got basketballs for boobs?" she added. They compared the written description to the images and found them in general agreement. The women did have perhaps the largest know breasts in the galaxy. However, they also wore a form of tight corset that gave them back support to offset the weight of their breasts, as well as a tiny waistline. Their gowns were very form fitting, accentuating their curves. In addition, the women tended to have straight black hair, but long — very long actually, touching the backs of their ankles. "I do hope that you don't mind monster boobs, dear," Nadja teased him, as they turned to how the men dressed.

They wore their hair in ponytails contrasting with the

women. While their shirts looked like shirts, Konrad gulped. "Oh dear, are they wearing dresses?" he asked confused. The men wore what looked an awful lot like a giant woman's hoop skirt, billowing out some twelve feet and requiring yards of material. The notes indicated that the men often squatted down as opposed to actually sitting on a chair. Both men and women wore sandals. "Well, we gotta do what we gotta do. The previous governor got nowhere. So we are going to change that in a big hurry. I wonder how you can get these changes made? It must take them half a century to get their hair that long," he exaggerated a little.

"I'm off to the medical machines. Get their language tapes ready for us, will you?" she asked. Sometime later, she returned. "I've found a way to enhance my hair growth and yours too so you can have a proper ponytail. As far as the boobs go, dear, that can also be done, but it's pushing the machine some. I believe that I'll need some of their supporting corsets before I alter my breasts. We can use that as a clever introduction to their rulers."

Again, they worked out their plan of attack and subliminally got the basics of the Strx-4 language down before they arrived. Upon moving into the stone home set aside in the central city for them, Konrad requested a meeting with their leader, who considered them ignorant aliens. Konrad ignored the giggles from some of the others who were with him. He explained they knew they were speaking his language poorly, but that Nadja would soon begin a thorough study of it, and they would learn quickly. Next, he asked if he could purchase a man's outfit and if someone could help Nadja with an appropriate corset. The ruler didn't understand why she would need one, her boobs were totally inferior and her hair was too short. However, he did agree to send someone to purchase a man's outfit for Konrad.

After the meeting, Nadja spent several hours in the medical machine before it completed its work. She nearly fell over when she first stood up, sporting her new basketball sized breasts, which were alarmingly heavy. Her hair now fell to her ankles, just as programmed. After seeing her the next day, the ruler and his wives were very much impressed with her.

However, the wives did feel her new breasts before they pronounced them real. Immediately, they all fussed over her. Before long, they had her in one of their supporting corsets. At last, her back ceased feeling as if it was about to break in half. Once they got her in a form-fitting gown, she looked much as they did. They held a royal feast that night in honor of Nadja and Konrad, who found that the only way he could now sit down was to squat. The metal hoops simply didn't bend.

The feast broke the long-standing ice between the two cultures. The ruler readily agreed to allow Nadja to spend long hours with them learning and studying their language. Meanwhile, Konrad and the ruler began working out the desired trading arrangements that the former governor had failed utterly to obtain. Nadja was becoming very adept with picking up the elements of their language, claiming it was similar to one spoken on Tallyford-3. Within three months, Konrad had achieved all twenty agreements the Imperium had wanted from Strx-4. In return, the planet got the medical technology that they greatly desired. Again, it took the bureaucrats six months to seal the deal and send another governor and his wife to take over. They did order the newcomers to follow the lead established by Nadja and Konrad.

Once on board the spaceship, Konrad was only too eager to get out of the native clothes. "Doing anything in that skirt thing is downright impossible! And I hate ponytails," he exclaimed, heading off to get his hair cut. Nadja was enjoying her long, silky hair and decided to keep it. The monster boobs and supporting corset were another matter. However, before she reached any decision, she looked up what was now known about the women's styles on Ashford-5, their ultimate destination. Apparently, women's breasts there were quite large, but the document had neither photos nor any concrete measurements for her to use as a guide. Hence, she opted to be a bit conservative. Over several days, she gradually had the medical machine reduce her monsters. After getting Konrad's input, she opted for really perky breasts that weighted about five pounds each with an H cup size. If later they found the women on Ashford-5 had smaller breasts, she would further reduce them. At least now, she could manage without having also to wear the very uncomfortable support corset and her back appreciated the huge weight loss.

Their next assignment took them to Chauncy-2. By now, his superiors had begun to see a pattern in his work, significantly above the normal governors. Once more, they prepared themselves in advance. Men of Chauncy-2 wore large moustaches, very heavy jewels around their necks. What Konrad moaned about was the men's earrings. All wore six huge golden hoops in each ear. It was easy enough to have all these fabricated on the ship, and this time he would arrive looking much like the native men. Likewise, Nadja was able to get herself properly attired beforehand. The women all wore a head covering so that none of their hair and head was visible. What took the most work was the golden lattice veil that they wore. Essentially, the veils were fastened to each ear, draped across the lower face, and attached to either side of the lower nose. The gold veil dropped to just below her chin. She cringed at their dresses, little more than a sack with holes for the arms. Nevertheless, when they arrived, both were immediately well received.

However, wife swapping was the traditional way that strangers were greeted. The previous governor thought this was barbaric and refused to have anything to do with it. Konrad and Nadja didn't protest in the slightest, surprising the ruler and his wife. They soon discovered that, when they went to bed, the women uncovered their head and allowed their hair to cover their mate. Still kissing through the golden web was a bit awkward, she discovered.

Once more, the duo proved their mettle. In three months, Konrad had finalized what the Imperium desired as well as providing what the rulers of Chauncy-2 wanted in return. They did it in record time. This time, they were relieved after spending only five months on the planet. Again, as soon as they were safely onboard the spaceship, Konrad got rid of his many earrings and healed their holes. Nadja only had to heal the two small holes in the side of her nose. Both knew that they were indeed making significant progress towards both Konrad's goal and her goal with languages. She was now somewhat backlogged on getting her work into a publishable format.

Their next assignment was to a more primitive planet, Alzone-3. Both knew that they were in for a rough one with this planet and their culture. Konrad would have to wear large earrings as well as a tight corset. Posture was big here among males. Further, he was expected to ride a horse well. He'd never seen such a creature in the flesh before. Nadja was right at home with her huge earrings. Later she would discover that hers were much bigger than those the women on Alzone-3 wore, and, after they left, the women began increasing the size of theirs to match what she had worn. However, she faced an even bigger problem. All the women had slit their upper and lower lips and wore golden lip plates. As she studied the advance scouting reports, she noted that the diameter of the plates was a reflection upon the woman's standing with in their society. The report did not indicate the actual dimensions or shape. Hence, she decided to ask upon arrival.

The ruler was called a rajo and his wife, the raja. Their arrival was rather coldly met until Nadja asked about how she could get an appropriate set of lip plates that would match her status. Raja Ahn took her aside, showing Nadja her giant pair and how they worked. Meanwhile, Konrad insisted that he be outfitted as appropriate to a rajo, claiming that in his world, he was considered a great leader as well. Now Rajo Ohmaj began to warm, especially when Konrad admitted that he did not know how to ride a horse and asked him if someone could teach him how.

When they returned to their new home, Konrad was miserable. He now wore a tight corset, sported long, heavy earrings (though only a third the size of hers), and was going to get lessons in horse riding in the morning, which gave him a fright just thinking about them. On the other hand, she returned with local dresses and a set of lip plates. She insisted that she wanted to use their own medical machine to make the needed modifications. Raja Ahn had shown her the knife that was used and Nadja immediately thought better of that.

"Look dear, these really are quite sophisticated and extremely well designed and to be honest, quite clever. The lip plates are quite thin and lightweight. But look at this. See they clip onto these curved mouthpieces. Easy on, easy off with the disks. Apparently, you clip the plates onto the mouthpieces and then pull your lip loops up and over the ridges of the plates. Raja Ahn said that the mouthpieces are critical. Each one has four posts that go into holes drilled into your gums above your teeth. They act as a solid support and the mouthpieces then fit tightly against your gums and don't give at all. She said centuries ago, women had to knock their front teeth out to support the plates. If they didn't, the plates drooped badly. These new mouthpieces ended that practice."

"They look nasty, dear. Will you be able to manage to eat and talk?" he asked, growing a little concerned.

"Well, as we know, the diameter is a measure of social standing. Mine will have to be a foot across, if I am to be the equal of Raja Ahn. I do hope the medical machine can handle this one. They use long silverware to eat and spoon their drinks, according to her. Talking will be most interesting. Now I understand more about their strange language. Remember all those clicking sounds? Well, theirs is what we linguists call a click language. They have no sounds that are made with the lips, quite unlike us and most other languages. Their women can't make such sounds. The many kinds of clicks, which we think are really bizarre and gave us the most trouble on the listening tapes, are in fact their substitutes for some of those sounds, like 'p' and 'b.' More later, I'm off to the medical lab."

Getting the mouthpieces properly fitted and the precision holes lasered in her mouth was the easy part. Nadja then tackled the lips and the slitting process. At once, she saw that merely slitting them as Raja Ahn had would only give her perhaps four to five inch plates. Her host had told her that a woman's lips were slit when she was four. Then during childhood, her loops were continually stretched with ever-increasing plate sizes until she reached the diameter appropriate to her status. Nadja had no time for that. It took her three hours of playing with all the menu options of the medical machine finally to work out a satisfactory program. The machine would use stem cells to enlarge greatly her lip loops once the initial cuts were made. She decided to error on the side of having thicker lips, rather than thinner lip loops, just in case additional modifications had to be done. At least, she discovered that the process could be reversed later on. She relaxed. If she messed it up completely, she could undo it.

When she finished some three hours later, her new thick lip loops dangled before her mouth, looking terribly strange to her. Raja Ahn had said that they always took them out when sleeping and that their husbands loved it when they kissed them this way. She resolved to test that out this very evening. Carefully, she snapped the foot in diameter plates into their clever clips on the front of the mounts. They fit well. Now came the decisive test. Could she stretch the loops enough to cover the plates? Carefully she did so. According to Raja Ahn, they should feel tight, sort of stretched. Well they did, she thought, resolving to ask her tomorrow to check hers out. She knew that she could make some adjustments if needed.

When she returned to Konrad, both discovered her speech in their native language was almost impossible to understand. She launched into a short lecture on how sounds are formed in the mouth, but by writing out her lecture. "We linguists have identified something close to sixty unique sounds that a human voice can make. They are made from different locations in your mouth. The ones that I am now unable to make are the 'p' and 'b' sounds, primarily. Try them, dear. See, you are using your lips to make them. That is the big difference in what you are hearing from me now. I can't make those sounds any longer. We call those sounds made by the lips bilabial sounds."

"Next, my 'm' sound can't be made any longer. You need lips to help form that sound. Then come the 'f' and 'v' sounds. They are made partially with the lips and partially with the tongue touching the tongue touching the teeth. Again, I can't make those sounds properly any longer. They are called labiodental sounds. Come on; try making those sounds, dear. See how your lips are being used?" Reluctantly, he began making the sounds and saw quickly what she meant.

"Now this is why they have all the clicking sounds we were struggling to get the hang of while we were on our way here. They take the place of the sounds that can't be made by half of the population of Alzone-3. See, linguistics to the rescue. We have to work on our clicks. That's why they were having such a hard time understanding what we were saying, dear. Now then, come to bed. I want to try out something that Raja Ahn told me about kissing." She teased him.

Much later, his comment was simply, "Oh my! More!"

When they were alone, she worked on speaking as clearly as she could and discovered that he understood her better if she talked slower than normal. It would take quite some getting used to. Beginning the next day, Nadja discovered many other things that posed more of an immediate problem than mere speech. Her lips no longer held food or liquids within her mouth. Accidental drooling became a big problem for her, until Raja Ahn pointed out that she needed to keep her head up, allowing liquids to settle naturally in the back of her mouth. Nevertheless, this would continue to be problematical for her in the coming weeks and months.

Seeing where she was going was quite annoying. With plates that matched Raja Ahn's, her vision was significantly reduced. When she held her head up, she couldn't remotely see her feet. Well she couldn't see them anyway when her head was level. However, to see her feet over the huge plates, she nearly had to bend her head completely down, the plates almost touching her large breasts, which were more than double those of Raja Ahn's.

But she wasn't the only one having physical problems. Konrad was not adapting to horse riding at all well. Between the heavy earrings, tight corset, and the bouncing of the horse, he was perfectly miserable. Still, after some two months, both had finally adapted to their situation. More importantly, their constant exposure to the language of Alzone-3 had vastly improved their speech, particularly so for Nadja, who had already begun her intensive study of their highly unusual language.

Four months after they arrived, Rajo Ohmaj finally accepted Konrad as one of them. The ice finally broken, finally Konrad was able to begin real negotiations between the two worlds. After six months, he was able to send the signed agreements off to his headquarters. Interestingly enough, one of the last demands the rajo made was for six hundred medical machines and instructors to teach them how to use them, specifically for breast enhancements. Culture and technology, the two observed, went both ways. However, his report also clearly demanded that the next governor and his wife be ready to accept the physical modifications that allowed the two cultures to mix. He also suggested that the governor learn to ride a horse well before he came. Afterwards, he rather wished that he'd not said that. Their replacements didn't come until about a year after they first arrived.

Nadja used the extra time to get all her field notes worked up and into proper published formats. By the time that their replacements did arrive, she was able to send them back with the spaceship. Of course, the two spent several weeks helping the newcomers adapt to this particularly difficult culture and language.

Once they were finally able to leave, Konrad got his own body fixed up, dumping the earrings and tossing the corsets into the disposal. Nadja, however, retained her lip plates. Why? Once in space, she again checked on available knowledge of the people of Ashford-5. During the year, some remarkable photographs had mysteriously appeared, along with some interesting commentary. The article suggested that not only did the women have monster breasts, but also the women in the higher social classes had begun wearing lip plates, which were seen as somewhat unusual adornments. Most of the article had been censured, however.

The photographs were very low quality. Konrad speculated that someone had illegally taken them on the sly. "I best keep my lip plates for now," Nadja decided.

"Fine with me, dear. I love bedtimes now," he teased her.

This time, they were taken to a highly civilized planet, Balon-4. The dispatch had said only that Konrad was wanted there for a high-level meeting. As they finally settled down for the long trip, they speculated what this was all about. Balon-4 was a major planet of the Imperium boasting no less than four senators. They could only conclude that their work and

Konrad's effectiveness had been duly noted.

One small detail of their lives played a key role at this time. Nadja was wealthy, and, as a young woman, she always wore the latest in fashions, quite unlike most of the academy students. Across the vast Imperium, most people wore the same, drab, disposable, unisex uniforms. When they were torn or dirty, one tossed them into the recycle bin and pressed the button in the bathroom for a new one. All had a faint latex odor about them. Like most all the wealthier, she never lowered herself to wear such things. She went so far as to call them non-clothes while at the academy. Instead, she wore expensive nylons, silk and satin dresses, and of course the high quality leather heels. Anyone of import wore those of the six-inch stiletto variety, though some opted for four or five inch heels, particularly older women.

Once she began dating Konrad, she began buying him suits that were appropriate to his eventual high standing. By the time he began his career, several shipping crates were required to hold all of their apparel. She didn't flinch at having to pay the exorbitant extra cargo fee required to bring the crates along with them. Now having done that paid off. They were going to a high-class planet, if only for a meeting. Hence, the two dug out appropriate apparel suitable for their arrival on Balon-4. "Don't worry. I'll go shopping right away and get us some of the latest fashions. You want more in the brown camel hair style?" He nodded; he loved the feel of those jackets.

When they stepped off the spaceship, he wore an elegant, light brown, camel hair suit with a yellow tie and expensive, natural leather, matching, highly polished shoes. Sunlight actually reflected off his and her shoes. She wore a color-matching outfit, a white silk blouse with a wide, single tied scarf, a matching short skirt that revealed her black seamed stockings and six-inch heels, and a jacket similar to his, though with considerable adjustments for her overly large bosom. They were an inseparable pair, though her exotic jewelry caused all to pay attention to her, that is, her huge earrings and lip plates. Under the yellow sunlight, they appeared to "shine" like the sun of Balon-4. That was their intent.

As they walked through the twenty-story glass and concrete Imperium Admin building, they noted hundreds wore the drab unisex uniforms. The two most definitely made an impression long before they reached the meeting room. Both were surprised to be introduced to the Sector ID Minister for this sector of space! Konrad knew that he was making the kind of progress that he had planned.

After introductions, the older man said, "Well, I see why you are becoming the rising star in the world of governors, Konrad!" He too wore one of the cheap unisex uniforms and looked quite out of place sitting across from these two. "I'll get right to the point. Your work has been duly noted, Konrad. I believe that we will soon have a particularly vital mission for you to tackle. Now this is not for public dissemination, but hostilities between the Federation and the almighty Imperium are breaking out. Perhaps war cannot be avoided. This new assignment will be absolutely vital to the Imperium, should that happen. However, the survey ships have not yet done their work, but their initial reports are most suggestive. Expect a year's delay before we are ready to give you that key assignment. In the meantime, I would like to ask a personal favor of you. Here on Balon-4, the governor has died unexpectedly, leaving a temporary hole. I would like you to step up and fill his role here, until I can get an appropriate replacement brought in. If you do take this, then I would like you to look over the support personnel here and make your decisions on who you would like to have come with you on this next, vital, and key assignment. I will assign all those currently stationed here that you wish as your staff to go with you on this next assignment. Is that fair enough?"

"Excellent, sir. I am always ready to help where needed. Pray, how large a staff will be needed for this key assignment?" Konrad asked.

"Of course, you will get the usual base workers, since yours will be the first Imperium contact there. They will have to build the initial complex from scratch. Base your needs upon the establishing of a Class 5 installation." Konrad's eyes rose. This would be a major operation indeed. Whatever this planet was, it would be hosting a very significant and vital Imperium base! His curiosity was roused, but all that he could get out of the Sector ID Minister was that this would be a first-contact situation with strange human primitives on a vitally important, newly discovered planet. He refused to divulge more at this time. He did suggest that Konrad might be here on Balon-4 for at most a year before everything was ready for his arrival on this mystery world. Much groundwork had to be laid before he and his contact group would be fired off to this new world.

He then led Konrad to his new governor's office, introduced him to the existing staff, and then took Nadja to their linguistics office, where she could have an office as well. "Keep up the fine linguistics studies. While I myself seldom make use of the language machines, I'm told that your modifications to the existing tapes are proving invaluable." He paid her the best compliment that he could. He paused a moment as if weighting something, she thought. He turned back to her and added, "Between you and me, you might want to keep those fancy lip ornaments or whatever they are called." He bowed and left. Curious, she thought. I do believe that he has given me another clue to our new world assignment. I wonder if I can find out anything about it?

Within mere days, both became quite bored. The governor had very little to do on Balon-4, which is what he expected of such a world as this. Nadja discovered the major languages here were already well studied, and she decided to spend her time analyzing spoken language and its several dialects versus their standardized written language. She expected to see the spoken languages undergoing constant change, while the written forms changed little. This was quickly proven to be true. With nothing else to do, she got the last of her field notes published.

After that, she spent hours shopping, acquiring them at least another full crate of new clothes and shoes. Finally, bored utterly, she began purchasing and modifying equipment for gathering, recording, and analyzing languages in the field, both spoken and written. Some of these were actually highly specialized computers, all touch activated and the very latest models. Since she was not a techno-geek, she asked Konrad to send her one of his computer experts to help her get the menu systems properly setup for her style of work.

"You sent for me, Mrs. Burkhardt?" the soft, slightly accented, alto voice said at the door of her open office. Nadja had the room piled high with her new gear. She turned to see who was there. She saw a woman perhaps her own age of twenty-five, with shining yellow eyes and long, black hair, straight and lush, but not as long as hers. Nadja instantly liked her. She didn't wear the non-apparel. She had on a white silk blouse and was very well endowed, though nowhere as large as Nadja. She wore a grey tweed skirt, hemmed at her knees, revealing her black seamed nylons and shining, high quality leather heels, almost the same style as hers, namely oxfords. On the other hand, the woman saw a lightly toned woman with enormous lip plates, monster-sized — but dramatic — earrings, a bosom that many would die for, and elegantly dressed. After recovering from the surprise of seeing Nadja's looks, she added hastily, "I am the computer expert. Governor Burkhardt said you needed me?"

"Yes, I must say this is a most pleasant surprise to see someone else who appreciates quality clothing. I am impressed. Please, call me Nadja. I hope you can understand me. I can't make the 'b,' 'p', 'f', and 'v' sounds, primarily anyway."

"I am Isabella Valen. Please just Isabella. I am much impressed with your fancy ornaments, Nadja. Wherever did you get them?" she asked. Nadja was only too eager to tell her all about her work and the planets that they visited.

Finally, she got down to the business at hand. "I've just purchased all of these new recording and analyzing computers. I need help setting up the touch screens so I can operate them super easily. In the field, I can't go asking someone to stop talking while I get the machines going. I need to be able to simply touch the screens and have them activate. Can you assist me?" Nadja asked.

"Not a problem. I've never met a computer I can't handle. This will be fun. I've never met a linguist before. What is it that you do? Make those language tapes?" Isabella asked.

Nadja was very eager to discuss the love of her life, linguistics, and Isabella paid close attention. For some reason, Isabella seemed to naturally grasp the various concepts of linguistics that she talked about. Quickly, the two became friends. While they spent three days getting all the equipment working "at the touch of a finger" as Nadja put it, the two chatted and had a good deal of fun. Nadja invited her to have supper with them.

A week later, Nadja again ran out of things to do. Konrad, likewise. Hence, she decided to surf the Imperium database and see what more she could find out about Ashford-5. Similarly, Konrad was doing much the same thing out of sheer boredom. Several days later, Nadja spotted Isabella dining alone at lunch and joined her. After some pleasant chatting, Isabella said, "I couldn't help noticing that both Mr. Burkhardt and you are trying to find out more about a planet called Ashford-5."

"What? Did Konrad say something to you?" Nadja asked, growing a little alarmed. Why all this secrecy about the planet? Were they violating some unknown law by looking to see what was known about this world?

"I am the top computer person here at the base. It is my job to keep everything running smoothly. You've both been receiving too many error messages saying the data is not available. I am notified when that happens. It's my job to help those people having trouble get it right, you see," Isabella answered.

Nadja didn't see. "So if I can't figure out how to do something and I keep trying and goofing, you get notified and then come help me figure it out?"

"Yes, that's a layman's way of putting it. I take it you both want to know more about that closed world?"

"Yes, we do."

"May I ask why? I know it is none of my business really. I'm not a gossip, but if you'd rather not tell me, that's okay. I am just very curious, that's all," Isabella explained in a soft voice that could not be easily overheard.

"He and I want to someday get assigned to Ashford-5 as its governor. I want to study its languages," Nadja answered, careful not to mention anything about it being a telepathic society.

"Oh, I see. Yes, that makes sense. Here, if you will allow me, try this link," Isabella said, writing out the reference on one of her sticky-notes that she carried in her purse.

Back in her office, Nadja entered the reference and pressed the onscreen Enter button with her finger. Presto. Suddenly, here were tons more information and photographs than all the other links combined. She'd hit the jackpot. She buzzed Konrad and asked him to come down to her office, but didn't say why. A few minutes later, his jaw dropped.

"How in the world did you find this one? You are a genius!" Konrad gushed.

"Wasn't me. You know computers and me. No, it was your computer expert, Isabella. She gave this link to me," Nadja said and described their brief conversation.

"Best watch what I type in around her," he half-teased. "This is really interesting data that a governor ought to know!" Much of the data came from or via an Imperium incorporated company called Elegant Fashions Inc. "Considering the cost of these, we are probably looking at a company that caters to the wealthy and the ruling class," he concluded.

"At least they have a very refined and sophisticated taste in apparel," she added. "The men's suits are remarkably like those you prefer. Look here, some wear lip plates — oh! Men do too, dear," she added, seeing a photo of both sexes with them. "Ah, my style heels. No wait, what are those?" Both stared at men and women wearing toe shoes and toe boots. "Wow, dear, this place must not be as primitive as we have been led to believe." For quite some time, the two studied the apparel catalog of the company, before turning to other written data.

Several hours later and somewhat perplexed, Konrad asked, "What do you make of this? Why would they order many hundreds of pairs of prosthetic hands? Have they had that many nasty battles? Are they a warlike people?"

"Say, if they do not have access to our medical machines, hundreds upon hundreds must have really suffered. Do they have doctors who could amputate the injured hands?" Nadja asked. "What could cause such bad hand injuries that they would have to be amputated?"

"Gosh, I suppose primitive knives and swords. They must be warlike. Look, here is a second batch of hands being delivered. Hundreds more. Are they having an epidemic?" Konrad asked.

"Look at the price differences. That first bunch was the cheapest available. All the rest are only the most expensive. Hey, look at this! That first bunch was grey Rigel-3 hands. All the rest are more flesh colored. Does that mean the natives attacked the Imperium base and cut off the hands of those who worked there? Did they retaliate against the natives in kind? That would explain it," Nadja speculated. "What are we getting into here?"

"Someone must have made humongous blunders on Ashford-5," Konrad concluded.

Just then, Isabella stopped by her office. "Excuse me, Mrs. Burkhardt, but I wanted to check with you and see if you are now able to find what you have been looking for?"

"Oh yes, very much so. But it's most alarming. Look at this, apparently the natives attacked the Rigel-3 base and cut off our employee's hands. Then later on, the governor ordered an attack on the natives and cut off many of their hands," Nadja exclaimed, wide-eyed.

Isabella laughed. "No silly. You haven't read all that's there. It was the natives who removed their own hands, something about stopping some kind of awful virus. Such things can happen on worlds that lack Imperium medical machines. So what do you think of their fashions?"

"Oh, sorry. We jumped to conclusions. That is awful. Poor natives. Again, the governor must have blundered badly by not bringing emergency medical assistance to the population," Konrad replied, somewhat red-faced. He hated having someone else point out his mistakes.

"It is a closed world. I doubt it would be legal for a governor to do that," Isabella replied. "Have you noticed that elegant men and women are wearing the Imperium pipe corsets? How about those strange, form-fitting gowns? Why would they want to be unable to move their upper arms? I've wondered about that one myself."

"Say, you seem to know a lot about this Ashford-5 world," Konrad pointed out, desperate to get off the defensive and perhaps onto the offensive.

"I collect data on things I find unusual or interesting. That's all. Anyway, I see you are being successful now, Mrs. Burkhardt. "Let me know if I can help either of you with anything else. Remember, I am your computer specialist." She nodded and left the two to continue browsing.

"Strange woman," Konrad commented, "but then so are all computer-freaks. Good to have them around, what with all this technology at hand."

"Yes, she seems very competent. She was able to help me get all my new equipment setup in short order. Now with a touch of my finger, I can start a recording and a zillion other things. Life is getting simpler for doing my linguistic researches."

"Yes, unless you object, I am going to add her to the list of personnel to take with us on our next assignment. We are going to need a whole array of specialists for this coming one. I only wish it would hurry up. I am so bored it's not funny," Konrad admitted.

"I was going to suggest bringing her along, in case I run into troubles with my gear. Do make sure she comes," Nadja replied, still looking at the monitor. "Dear, I tried to get access to the linguistic tapes for Ashford-5, but those are classified and unavailable. Any chance you can get us access to them?"

"Not if they are classified. I don't have clearance. Ah well, I guess this is merely wetting our appetites so we do well on our next assignment. One day we will get there and see for ourselves." She smiled, but it wasn't visible.

After that, they settled into a life of boredom for nearly six months. At least once a day, Nadja went out shopping, adding another two crates of the latest fashions to their collection. Whenever she was really bored, she went shopping. Konrad didn't mind, it was her money, and she apparently had plenty of it. For his part, he began playing cards with some of his staff.

Six months into the year, Konrad received word to begin putting together his team. The Sector ID Minister visited

274

him personally. "I am not yet at liberty to tell you the name or the planet's location. Top secret. However, I can tell you that it is a primitive culture with a very hot climate. I am releasing very preliminary language files. Tell Nadja they are very primitive at this point. Oh, you men might consider growing a beard for this one, that is, if you should wish to appear native-ish. Put together your team. Twenty will do. I'll provide the security men and all the construction personnel. If there is someone who you would like on your team that is currently on another planet, let me know, and I'll see what I can do to get them assigned here. Between you and me, I don't know if you will have to wait six more months. This business with the Federation of Planets is getting unsettling." He refused to say more, and Konrad got into operation.

After relaying the news to Nadja and dropping off the tapes, he began making his list of needed personnel. He put Isabella Valen first on the list. A computer technician would be critical. Nearly the entire Imperium ran off computers of one kind or another. Next, he added a competent doctor and made sure the man brought along only the very best in medical equipment. Helm Voit's bio suggested he had some experience in dealing with native diseases. That solidified his choice of doctor. He chose an anthropologist next, a Sou Lin Chow, reputedly an expert in primitive cultures. At least her bio said so. What else would he need, he thought?

Lacking any clues about what their mission to this planet would be or other details, he couldn't plan very well at all. Was mining going to play a role? Planetary geology? Playing it safe, he picked out a man for each of these, based on their bios. He then added a meteorologist to the mix. After that, he had gone as far as he could without more information. Next, he called each in for an interview. Bios can be faked, bios can be exaggerated, bios can be misunderstood. Besides, he would have to be working with these people. He sent for Isabella first. That interview took all of two minutes, during all but the last second he was explaining the mission and his desire to have her come along as his computer technician. She agreed the moment he allowed her to speak.

He went on down the list. Most asked quite a few

questions, but few that he could answer. The doctor seemed keenly interested, mentioning a slew of rare diseases found in tropical climates. These went over his head, but he said nothing. He eagerly accepted.

Within a couple of days, he had his pick finished. The six plus his wife would do until he got more specifics. Meanwhile, when he returned to their quarters for supper, Nadja was quite excited. "Dear, this is another click language! How intriguing. The tapes are pretty poor though, but based on other click languages, I can begin to make some key assumptions about their language. I can't wait to get there!"

Konrad admitted, "You know, I think this might be our big break. If we pull this one off, we might just get sent to our dream planet!"

Konrad sent his selections on up the lines. Within two days, he received confirmation. All were his. He also received orders to relay to the others to begin amassing what equipment they calculated they would be needing. This kept the group busy and began bringing them together on a daily basis.

After two weeks, Nadja had prepared language-learning tapes and sent them to everyone's computers. Now they all began subliminally learning this language while they slept. After a couple of weeks of this, Nadja began holding daily speech practice session. Everyone but her found mastering the click language terribly difficult, in spite of the tapes.

The following week, that is, a month after the action began, a deep space transport was assigned to Konrad. They then moved their precious equipment and crates onboard. Meantime, ground crews were making minor repairs to the ship. A brief chat with the ground crew chief suggested that another month of waiting was in store for them.

Finally, Konrad received the actual orders. Instead of spending a year here, only eight months had passed. The planet was newly discovered and called Karlson-3. It was a hot planet. Daily highs were in the nineties. The continents were all centered on the equator. Water covered most of the world above and below these landmasses. His assignment, get a signed lease agreement for five hundred years allowing them to construct a hundred square mile spaceport. That seemed easy enough, especially since the scouting parties had finally located the largest tribal leader, who controlled that section of the larger continent on which initial reports suggested would be most suitable for the base.

Further, his new orders indicated they would ship out in two days. The day before they were to depart, he finally received detailed photographs, computer jpg files actually, of the natives. His entire new crew gathered around to stare at them, many gasping. The men all wore golden lip plates, wore thick turbans around their heads, and spouted large beards. The men wore sandals. Konrad groaned. Nadja however gasped!

The women had no hands! Even where their wrists would have been, only small, perfectly formed stumps appeared in the photos. Was it the practice to cut off women's hands? Along with nearly identical lip plates, the women also appeared to have enormous necks of golden rings of some sort. It was obvious from the images that the women could not bend their necks at all. Further, they all wore some kind of toe shoes, standing in perfect posture on their toes. Both men and women were bare from the waist up, displaying their brownish colored skin. All wore what appeared to be relatively simple skirts that only fell to their knees.

While they were all staring at the images on the monitor, a messenger came running up. "Hey, Governor Burkhardt, this just arrived — blood samples from men and women."

"I'll take that, son," Doctor Voit spoke up. "I'll be in my lab if you need me. What time is lift-off, boss?"

"Eight," Konrad replied without thinking. He was still staring at the women. *Do I even dare suggest that she have her hands amputated? Good lord!*

One by one, the others ambled off to deal with last minute preparations. Neither noticed that Isabella moved quietly to the back of the room. "This is unexpected, Konrad. No hands? How can they be anything but utterly and completely helpless women? This must be the most barbaric primitives imaginable — to cut off their women's hands!"

"I know. This is going too far. We both know just how vitally important this mission is for the Imperium, but I can't expect you to do that!" Konrad admitted. He had a sinking feeling that even this detail might just cost him dearly in terms of time to consummate the deal.

Nadja sighed, "Well, if we are ever to get them to send us to Ashford-5, I am going to have to look like those women, dear. When we get back, I will have to make use of prosthetic hands, if I can. With all the new touch-based and voice activated computer and recording equipment that I have, lacking hands should not interfere too much with my linguistic studies, I hope. But how the devil do those women even live? Do the men feed them? Look, they have relatively long hair, probably never cut."

"Are you sure that you want to do this? We both know how critical this mission is going to be, but there are limits," Konrad asked.

"Do we really have any choice? We have to do this. Your methods have worked flawlessly thus far. We don't dare drop something out and then have to spend years working around it. I won't jeopardize our chances for getting to Ashford-5," Nadja declared far more resolutely than she felt. Her mind was racing, imagining how she could possibly even live without hands. It seemed impossible.

Isabella quietly spoke up, taking both by surprise. They hadn't realized she was still present. "Nadja, if you do this thing, I promise you I will help you with everything you need. All I ask is if you do get sent to Ashford-5 that you will take me along with you as your computer expert."

"I'm sorry, Isabella; we didn't see you there. Konrad has a foolproof set of methods of making the governor process work both rapidly and well. Part of it involves adopting their customs and ways, to say nothing of becoming expert in their language. If I don't go all the way, it could well jeopardize his speed of success, if not wholly cause it to fail." She looked at Konrad and then added, "If I do this, I will gladly accept your constant help. I'll need it. Unless Konrad objects, if we can get assigned to Ashford-5, we'll take you with us, unless they will not allow you to go. I can't promise you one hundred percent on that, but we will make every effort to bring you along."

"That is all that I can ask. Thank you," Isabella replied, easing the slight tension in the air.

"But why do you want to go to Ashford-5?" Konrad asked.

"Call it curiosity. From what all I have seen, it must be a very interesting world, one that I would dearly like to see one day," Isabella explained, hoping this would suffice. To her great relief, both readily accepted it.

They chatted a while longer, before Nadja pointed out. "Look, we know perhaps a great many of the wealthy on Ashford-5 have prosthetic hands, so perhaps I would fit right in there, unless of course it is the men who have lost their hands." Konrad grimaced at that thought.

By eight the next morning, they were all aboard and ready for lift-off. At the very last minute, the Sector ID Minister arrived and motioned for Konrad to join him. The two stepped outside, where the spaceport noise made it impossible for them to be overheard. "Just got some alarming news. Hostilities have broken out. This is not to go beyond yourself. Our fuel refinery on Ashford-5 was attacked last night! Don't worry; the Sector ID Minister there handled it and no damage was done. Therefore, see if you can get this one wrapped up in short order. We need to get that base built. As soon as you get it done and, if it is quick, I would like to send you to Ashford-5, if you don't mind."

Konrad tried very hard not to react. *Is my voice steady?* "That would be perfect, sir. Could I bring along my small team with us?"

"Of course. Never break up a working team is my philosophy. Just get us the rights to build that base ASAP," he replied.

"You got it, sir," Konrad said enthusiastically. The minister left and he ducked back into the spaceship. He felt as if he were floating, not walking! It was all that he could do to keep from telling Nadja, when he sat down beside her. Fortunately, the captain's voice came over the comm network. They were about to lift-off.

Several hours later, the acceleration died down and the

group settled in for the long trip to Karlson-3. Before Konrad could figure out a way to let Nadja know the news, Doctor Voit came up to him. "Boss, I've some rather startling news. I've done a rush job on those blood samples. My preliminary findings are extremely interesting. It's genes, not mutilations."

"Huh? What are you saying? Remember, I've no medical training," Konrad asked.

"There is a big difference in the genes between men and women on Karlson-3. It's down at the low level. The women carry a mutated gene that prevents the formation of hands. However, the gene the males pass on is the dominant one. So baby boys have normal hands, but baby girls only have the mutant gene and do not develop hands. Now this is incredibly fascinating and extraordinary! I am going to have to conduct extensive research when we get there."

"Can you cure it?" Konrad asked what he thought an important question.

"Don't know, but that will be one of my objectives, once I fully understand this. You sure do know how to pick the right planets! Thanks for having me along, boss," he said with a broad grin. He turned and left the two. For several minutes, they chatted about this unexpected turn. In many ways, both were relieved that their initial assumption that the men of Karlson-3 were deliberately mutilating their women was dead wrong.

"So what did the minister say just before we left?" Nadja asked, when she finally remembered it.

He whispered, "It is a secret, but as soon as we get this one nailed and in the bag, he wants to send us to Ashford-5!" Nadja stifled a squeal. Later when he had the opportunity, he also relayed that to Isabella and that he had permission to bring her with them. He felt he owed it to her to alert her to this, since she was going way out of her way to help Nadja, if indeed Nadja decided to do it. At the time, he didn't notice that Isabella did not seem overly surprised by his news.

Chapter 15 Making It Happen

During their long trip, they studied the latest reports relayed to them. Sou Lin now was able to give them a better picture of what lay ahead of them. "We are dealing with an iron age people. They have invented iron working, which accounts for the women's toe boots, which are an ingenious combination of leather and iron. Perhaps they will also have swords as weapons. They live in wooden long houses. Expect to see many bronze and iron tools and the like."

"Hey, can I interrupt here," Doctor Voit broke in on their discussion. He'd just arrived from his makeshift shipboard lab. "I know why they wear those toe boots. The women don't have any feet. That recessive gene causes women to have neither feet nor hands. With these boots, the women can walk, instead of crawling."

"Ah, that also means," Sou Lin picked up on this, "that these people are intelligent and inventive. Do not think they are stupid primitives. They are likely quite smart and bright."

"I never make that idiotic assumption, Sou Lin," Konrad replied. "Many governors do just that, which is why they fail more often than not. Do continue," he suggested. The chat continued.

Days later, they landed on Karlson-3, during the middle of the night. Of course, everyone wanted to step outside and breathe fresh air, even if it was hot and humid. The stars were exceptionally brilliant overhead. Again, Konrad missed a small detail. As Isabella gazed up at the night sky, she whispered, "This is very familiar!"

The next morning was decision time. Konrad decided his first meeting with the leader of these people ought to go as well as possible. They had made as many advanced preparations as possible. He visited the doctor and had his lips done. Now he too sported similar lip plates as his wife. His were only five inches in diameter, a third of hers, but they matched the images of the natives they were given. With his beard and makeshift turban, he looked the part, if he could acquire the skirt and sandals.

Nadja sighed and joined him. Doctor Voit oversaw her work personally. He suggested that her stumps be properly shaped to accept the standard Imperium prosthetic hands. Further, her stumps would then more or less look like the women of Karlson-3. While she lay there undergoing that operation, he put her thoughts on her feet. "There is no real need to amputate your feet. There is a procedure that can be done so that you can wear Imperium toe boots easily."

"Well, that sounds a whole lot better," she said, somewhat relieved.

"But the procedure is not wholly reversible. It involves reforming the bones in your feet. Later on, they cannot be fully repaired. You would have to wear your high heels after the repair is finished. Your feet won't be able to lie flat on the floor."

"Well, I wear my heels any time that I can, so that isn't a problem. Go ahead and get them done too. I am glad that we brought some of those exotic boots along. It is absolutely vital that Konrad and I make a very, very good first impression with these people," Nadja explained.

Just as he finished up, Isabella joined them. "Your permanent assistant is here, Nadja. I brought your boots," she said cheerfully.

"God, Isabella, I'm really scared this time. I feel really helpless, and I still have to get those neck rings on me. How am I ever going to walk in those?"

"I'll support you," she replied and proceeded to put the new boots on Nadja's now very misshapen feet. While she was lacing the first one, Nadja tried to flex her other foot and found that other than her ankle moving, hardly any other parts of her foot were movable. They had been more or less fused into this position. "There is a whole lot of padding in the toes, so that should help," Isabella continued to chat. Soon, Nadja had to stand and nearly freaked out. She would have, if Isabella had not been holding on to her. Somehow, she felt calm and tranquil when Isabella was close to her. "I think you must practice walking some before we try to meet with the leaders. Come on; let's have at it, boss."

Several hours later, the group finally disembarked the huge ship. It had sat down in a grassy area about a half mile from a village of thirty long houses. Sou Lin explained, "We are probably looking at an extended clan or tribal village. The advance group arranged for us to land at this location. As you can see, the folks have come out to welcome us. How do you want to proceed boss?"

"Can you possibly manage this, Nadja?" Konrad asked.

"I must. I am your language expert. We cannot afford the tiniest mistake at this point," Nadja whispered back. "But you have to hold onto me, please!"

"Okay, here's how the first contact will go. Nadja and I will present ourselves to these people. You are all to remain here by the door. Sou Lin, you can talk to me through my earpiece. The rest of you, keep your ears open," Konrad ordered. Slipping his arm around her waist, he allowed her to set the pace with her precarious wobbling gait. Slowly, they moved out onto the grasslands. He waived to them, estimating around fifty men, an equal number of women, and perhaps twenty children of various ages looking from further back. All the adults had similar lip plates, but the women also wore what appeared to be bronze rings around their necks, giving the illusion of having long necks. It was plainly obvious none of the women or the girls had any hands. In fact, their arms looked much like Nadja's, only thicker at their wrists.

As they drew closer, one well-muscled man stepped forward as did a woman. When they were close, the man spoke. Unfortunately, many of their words began with various clicking sounds. Nadja always used special symbols indicating the click sounds, since there was no existing alphabet that contained symbols for those sounds. Hence, Nadja used the universal phonetic symbols. He said, "I am ^gar. This is ^achk, my wife. Welcome sky people to ^^kan. How is it that you look like us?"

"Welcome ^gar. Welcome ^achk," Nadja replied, she already saw that the language samples were wholly insufficient. Her speaking first was their private signal that something was amiss with their language tapes. "This is our leader and my husband, Konrad." Of course, she used various clicking sounds emulating his. "Forgive us if we have not yet mastered your language. We will work hard to learn it. I am his wife, Nadja. We come in peace. We wish to honor you and your great people by appearing as you do and respecting your way of life as best we can. I would like to get my neck to be as lovely ^achk's. We both need clothing like you wear, if you can arrange that for us."

^gar nodded affirmatively. She could not tell if he was smiling or not. She asked, "Is ^^kan the name of the whole world or your village or this land around us?" She waved her free arm about, adding gestures to her three key ideas.

"^^kan is our village. Here." He pointed to the homes behind him. "^gahk is whole world. ^gar is leader of leaders. Come, come. We welcome you to ^^kan." The two moved on into the village and the inhabitants rather swarmed around the two.

Konrad paid close attention to the clicking sounds that Nadja and the leader had used. He attempted to speak. "Nadja speaks your language better than I. She will learn and teach me to speak your language better, ^gar." Several children giggled, a key sign that they must sound like the total foreigners that they were. He added, "Children laugh at how poorly I speak your language. They are right to laugh. Wait until they try to speak our language, noble ^gar." He chuckled, indicating a jest. ^gar nodded and chuckled too.

"Come, you honor us. We fix you both up. We feast and talk great things," ^gar said. "I talk slow. You get better. I speak like small child for you." They soon entered one of the long houses. Inside, they found it was one giant room, but with individual living areas distinctly marked. Right away, several men came up, removed their pants, and help them into their skirt-like bottoms. ^gar explained these were cooler and more functional for the women. Next, he undid Konrad's crude turban, laughed, and proceeded to wrap his head with one of theirs.

"^rack will take Nadja now. Fix her neck. Okay? You sit. We drink," ^gar explained. Another man carefully led Nadja further into the house, where a central fire burned along with what appeared to be an anvil. Konrad sat beside the man, who presented him with a long handled spoon. He sat a pot of honey mead between them and showed Konrad how to drink by scooping up some. While holding his head up, he inserted it into his mouth. Konrad mimicked him. It was quite good. Soon they were chatting away, though ^gar often corrected his speech.

Nadja found herself lying down with her neck over the anvil. The man inserted rings of bronze beneath her neck and bent them around, fastening them somehow behind her head. The tenth ring pushed them all up very tightly together. She felt pressure on her shoulder blades and against the base of her head. "Done. Now you one of us," the man said. She was certain he was talking baby talk to her, knowing how poorly she spoke their language. He gently lifted her to her feet. Nadja discovered she could not move her head at all and would have to reposition her body to see to the sides, but she had already seen the women did so too. She said, "Thank you honorable ^rack."

Now ^achk came to her and led her to the women's circle. "Give valuable tools to honored guest. You use these like men's hands," she began a very lengthy explanation. All were extremely well made, bronze for the most part, though some were made of a polished iron. Nearly every tool had a bronze loop strap that the women could easily slip on one of their stumps. The tool was at the other end. There was a spoon tool, a fork took, a long stirring spoon tool, an iron knife tool that was very sharp, a hairbrush tool, and even a tooth brush-like tool. In all, Nadja was given fifty different tools that would enable her to be as independent as the women were.

Nadja carefully studied their language as ^achk patiently named and explained how to use each tool. Hours passed, but Nadja found she was truly enjoying herself. She was in a linguistic heaven! Plus, with these tools, she would not be utterly helpless when among these people. Even more valuable, she knew Isabella was recording everything that was being said here as well as in Konrad's group.

After the tools, Nadja asked for the names of the other women around them and then for all the other objects that she could see in the long house, basic vocabulary building. After that, she worked on how they expressed the concepts of tense.

Meanwhile, Konrad, now slightly intoxicated, but loving every minute of it, began asking questions about the village, how many other tribes were nearby, how he got to be the leader of leaders, and other salient points. He had obtained his position because he was the leader of his tribe, and their tribe had won battles over their neighbors some time back. The villages were widely scattered. Behind the village, they had crops growing, but they also had some domesticated animals and sometimes went on hunts. Usually, he pointed out, the men had to stay close to their women. In this society, it was a man's obligation and duty to look after the women in his family. He also asked why the sky people's women had hands and feet. Did they also look after and care for their women?

Konrad chose his reply carefully. "On our worlds, women are born with hands and feet. Our doctor wants to study your people to see why it is that your women are so different than ours." That seemed to satisfy him. Soon, they began chatting about many other things. Before long, ^gar led him on a tour of their fields and their pens of animals. Konrad recognized what had to be variants of corn, beans, rice, barley, and wheat growing in the well-cultivated fields. The animals looked very different from the one's he had seen, but they were similar enough that he could recognize their basic types. Some were birds, probably their version of chickens. Some had thick wooly coats, probably sheep. The large ones had big udders and were likely cows that provided milk. In the distance, he saw numerous beehives. Therefore, honey was in their diet. He then showed him a number of distant trees. From these, the picked various fruits. One looked something like an apple.

Soon, ^achk brought Nadja outside to see everything as well. "You walk wobbly, like young girl. Don't worry. Just need much practice. I help you walk lots." She too kept her sentences short allowing Nadja to follow along more readily.

"Really? If I walk lots, I will be able to walk as easily as you?" Nadja asked.

She laughed. "When little girls learn to take first steps like little boys, they wobbly like you. Walk much, you see. You get better fast. I speak slow enough for you?"

"Yes, I am learning, ^achk."

"You are getting much better with clicks."

"I want to be able to talk well, like anyone of you do. I will work hard at it."

"Come, I show you more. Men have to weave cloth here." She showed them a crude weaving machine. Fascinated by everything, the day passed rapidly. Konrad got ^gar's promise to take him tomorrow to see the sight that Konrad wanted to lease for the spaceport. It lay some ten miles to the west. The initial survey crew had done their work well. ^gar said that no one lived near there, which was music to Konrad's ears.

That evening when the two finally returned to the ship, Nadja spent an hour with their crew, working on their language skills. Then, they began to work out plans for the immediate future. Nadja would join the local women during the day. "Look, they have all these tools that they use in lieu of hands. While I am studying their language, I need to learn how they do it. I will try to make you all better language tapes ASAP. You have to talk far better. Right now, we are using almost baby talk with them. Theirs is a tough language for us to master."

"But will they be insulted if we don't alter ourselves to look like them?" Isabella asked what they all had been discussing all day.

Konrad answered, "No, ^gar is extremely pleased that Nadja and I, the equivalent of their leader of leaders are doing so. He does not expect the rest of you to emulate us. You are sky people and are different from them. Yet, once again, I was right. By our taking the step to look as they do, they are all looking extremely kindly towards us. Let's keep it that way," He added, "They were afraid of the survey people, *but* because Nadja and I took the trouble to look like them, that is, real people from their point of view, that attitude has drastically changed."

Isabella laughed, "I can see why you are breaking all records as a governor." Several others grinned. Konrad realized right there that they had been studying up on him, just as he had reviewed their bios. He joined her laughter.

A week later, Konrad's whole group was totally accepted in the village. Doctor Voit continued studying their genetic recessive genes, but he also gave everyone a physical exam. To his amazement, there was no disease and no health problems among the tribe. After that, he spent all his time working on the gene problem.

Two weeks later, in response to ^gar's runners, ten other tribal leaders came to visit and see the sky people. As expect, by then, Nadja had improved their overall language skills up to that of a teen. No longer were they baby speaking, but carrying on fairly well understood conversations. This too greatly impressed ^gar and soon the other ten leaders. That the sky people's leader and wife looked like one of them also created a strong affinity between them.

What Konrad had stumbled upon was a simple law. In order to communicate with people, first there has to be some affinity, some liking, between the two. Second, there has to be some common reality being shared. In this case, physically appearing as one of them went a very, very long way in doing that. With affinity and reality established very solidly, only then could meaningful communications be exchanged.

For her part, Nadja proved to be a quick learner. By the time the ten other leaders came, she had mastered the use of many of the tools of the local women. She was now feeding herself just as the women and girls did. She brushed her own hair, even though hers was somewhat longer than the natives. However, what concerned her more was her ability to keep her balance and walk well. She didn't know it then, but Doctor Voit had inserted painkillers in her boots. Hence, she didn't feel any pain during those first two weeks. Each day, ^achk took her for longer and longer walks. After two weeks of this, her gait was similar to that of her host and the other women. While the men were going to meet, ^achk suggested she join some of the women and go berry picking. This involved inserting a basket tool on her left stump and a claw like picker tool on her right one. More importantly, she noticed two men armed with swords came with the ten women. One took the lead and one brought up the rear. She relaxed, knowing the men would really be watching out for them. She added dozens more words to her growing vocabulary.

A month passed rapidly. Runners returned and announced no one objected to the sky people making a base for their sky birds on the designated land. Payment and rules then occupied the men's discussions. Most of the other leaders concurred. The sky people's leader and his wife should look like they did. Konrad held that as a given. But what would serve as a valuable means of exchange? That was the key. True, they could just land and build the spaceport. If they ignored the locals, he knew only trouble, arguments, and conflicts would most likely result — especially so in the longer term, as the locals learned more about the sky people. He had studied those effects in their "ancient" history back at the academy.

Konrad wrestled with this problem each day. What would they consider really valuable in return for the spaceport? They certainly had no use for computers. Perhaps an electric plant? But they had not the knowledge to use it. As the days went by, he wracked his brain for the bright idea that would seal the deal.

The fifth week, Doctor Voit walked out of the ship with a huge smile on his face. He found Konrad as usual chatting with ^gar. "Boss, great news. The recessive gene can be cured in the women. The next generation could all be quite normal. He spoke in Imperium Standard so that ^gar could not understand.

"Fantastic. Let me try this with ^gar," he replied. ^gar looked at him quizzically. He changed back to the local language. "^gar, he is my doctor. He has found a cure for you. If you will allow him to work his magic, from now on, all of your girl babies will be born with hands and feet just like boy babies. Is that something that you and your people would like to have?" No sense insisting on it, he might be terribly affronted by such, he thought.

^gar looked very surprised and asked him to go over that again. Once he did, ^gar looked puzzled and promised to discuss this with the tribe this evening.

Back in the spaceship that night, Sou Lin pointed out, "You are right. It could go either way. These people have built up an entire culture around their women and their unique needs. They might not wish to abandon it all. Women might not have a say in it. Then again, the women seem not to mind that they are different from their men. With the tools, they manage well enough. In fact, having hands might not even be conceivable to the women. It could go either way."

Konrad said, "I can see your point. I was going to offer them prosthetic hands for their women, but they might take that as an invalidation of themselves. I'll file that as a last resort offer."

Doctor Voit spoke up. "Boss, that's a really bad idea. The prosthetic hands operate on the nerve signals the person sends to his now missing hands. These women have never had any hands and such nerve signals. The hands would most likely be just inert weights on their stumps."

"Thanks for preventing me from making a huge blunder!" Konrad replied. I hired the right crew, he thought to himself.

The next day, Konrad again met with ^gar. He shook his head sadly. "Women say that ^gahk women do not have hands and feet — do not want to be like men. Sky people women are like sky people men, but they be not ^gahk people. They do not want to be like ^gahk men. They want to be like ^gahk women as they always have been."

Konrad thanked ^gar for having asked them. His hopes sank. He was so close to sealing the deal and yet so far. Just as he was feeling very depressed, a thought appeared. Education. Would they want to learn more and gain knowledge? He had no idea how that thought occurred to him, but it was brilliant!

"^gar, would you and your people like to learn many new things? We sky people know many, many things, like how to work metal, make lights for the night, even fly in the sky. We could set up schools here, places where some of us could teach some of you many things."

While smiles were invisible, the instant glow in ^gar's eyes was. "Oh yes, yes! All ^gahk people eager to learn new things, many new things from sky people! Even ^achk suggested I ask you about such things, but ^gar hesitant. You might say no. Protect your knowledge. That would be most valuable trade for all ^gahk peoples."

Eagerly, Konrad began rapidly working out the details. The sky people would set up a basic school in each of the villages on the continent, though the total number of them was as yet unknown. They would begin with ^gar's village and his ten neighbors. ^gar's only request was that the sky people who came to teach honor them by appearing as they did, once more reminding him that his people greatly respected the sky people because he and Nadja chose to do appear as one of them.

That afternoon, Konrad had the deal signed, though Sou Lin and Doctor Voit signed as witnesses that ^gar approved the deal. They had no written language. Proudly, Konrad sent the agreement off to his Sector ID Minister. The requirements were simple. The new governor, his wife, and the various schoolteachers all had to "go native," just as he and Nadja had. He pointed out the locals would provide each woman with a full set of tools for her to use, just as they had for Nadja. Now all he could do was to wait for the reply. Would such an agreement be authorized? It was, after all, rather an exotic one. Still, if the Imperium was serious about their desperate need for a base on this world, they should agree to it. After all, the overall cost to the Imperium was virtually trivial, except for the personal cost of the teachers and the governor.

Nadja continued to praise him. "Konrad, that was absolutely brilliant thinking. How did you ever come up with this one? It is precisely the right answer for these people. This is basically an iron age group. Education will bring them rapidly through centuries and centuries of normal growth and development in short order. You can bet in a few years they will readily accept Doctor Voit's cure too. Education is the real key to everything. Honey, you are brilliant!" He smiled broadly, but knew that she couldn't see it.

The next day, Nadja decided that as friendly as she had become with ^achk, she would hazard asking her something very personal. Until now, she'd refrained from asking out of fear of being misunderstood. The motivation behind her questions could well be taken as the sky people's total invalidation of their culture or so Sou Lin had cautioned her and Konrad before they even landed. "^achk, can I ask you something very personal?" The woman bent at her waist, effectively nodding the way that these women did. "I have long wondered why your people, both men and women, wear these lip plates?"

^achk laughed. "To be very pretty. Men make beautiful things from golden metals. We all wear them with great pride to be beautiful, just like you. Only yours are so much better than ours are. ^achk is rather jealous of Nadja's lips. Konrad must be very important and proud man to have you."

Beauty, Nadja thought, *well, that is rather obvious, I suppose. Cultures have different ways of expressing beauty. We wear earrings, necklaces, broaches, and pins.* "What about these neck rings? They make life harder for us women," she asked tentatively. For her, this was the worst aspect of the whole thing. While she could somewhat deal with the loss of her hands, the neck rings made this more like eternal torture. Then it struck her, she hadn't really felt any devastating emotional loss with her hands! She'd expected to be crying herself to sleep each night. Nothing of the sort had happened. Why? Her sudden insight was interrupted by ^achk.

"Neck rings help us walk better. Stand up straight. No slouching. Without them, it is too easy to lose balance and fall. You get used to them too, Nadja. Takes time. You not fall either, see?" she explained carefully. Balance. Nadja couldn't imagine how precarious it must be for these women. At least she had the remnants of her feet. She thanked ^achk and made careful notes of this in their report.

Around noon, Konrad received word back from the ID Minister. He played the short video message for his crew. "Stellar, Governor Konrad! Record time. Six weeks. Just phenomenal. Please give your whole crew my heartiest thanks for this vital work. Timely too. You can let the others know now. The Imperium has declared war on the Federation of Planets, so this new base you've established is even more critical! Well done all of you. I rather guessed what part of your request would require. I've already lined up a replacement governor and gotten his and his wife's agreement to have the modifications done. They are a young couple who are keenly interested in more primitive civilizations. She is an anthropologist by training. Please have Nadja work on her language details as her top priority. I am interviewing potential teachers now. Expect the replacement governor to arrive in two weeks. I can only allow you one additional week to get them up to speed, before I ship you off to your next assignment."

The video continued. "You are now free to discuss this assignment with your party. You are being sent to the closed world of Ashford-5 on a Priority Ten assignment. I don't have to tell you how important this new assignment is. Tomorrow, I will send you a wealth of information about this closed world. Until then, thank you for a most impressive piece of work, Governor Burkhardt!"

Konrad looked at the faces of his team. Isabella looked very pleased indeed. The other five didn't. Doctor Voit spoke up, "Konrad, if it's all the same with you, I would like to stick around here and help out. I am convinced that eventually these women will want the cure that I offer. Besides, I want to finish my research and publish my findings. This discovery will make me famous."

"Sure doc, you can stay. I am sure that there are plenty of competent doctors already on Ashford-5," Konrad replied, putting the man at ease.

"Me too," Sou Lin hastily spoke up. "This is an iron age civilization. There is so much we can learn from them about prehistory. I simply must stay, if you don't object."

"Of course not, Sou Lin. Please stay and learn all that you can. I fully understand," Konrad said very diplomatic. His geologist, meteorologist, and mining engineer also wanted to stay for similar reasons. This was a new planet, wholly unexplored with many mysteries waiting to be researched. Also, the mining engineer voiced his concerns about the rumors that once one got to Ashford-5, they were never permitted to leave that backwater world. This came as a surprise to Konrad, and he vowed to research that detail when he had access to more data. For some reason, he didn't pay attention to the obviously singular fact that Isabella alone wanted to go with them to Ashford-5.

Time passed swiftly. With Isabella's constant help,

Nadja rushed her language studies to a semi-completion stage and got the new language-learning recordings made and sent off. Finally, they bid their new friends farewell. That small group watched the transport spaceship slowly lift off. Once airborne, Nadja exclaimed, "Will someone *please* get these awful neck rings off of my neck? I can't live like this!" Now her long suppressed anger over the terribly debilitating rings surfaced with a passion. Several hours later, she announced, "God that is better. I feel human again. I never want to go through that again!"

"I am so proud of the way you handled that nasty situation, dear," Konrad felt the necessity to praise her for what she'd obviously endured. "Shall we three take a closer look at what is going on on Ashford-5 now? I'd like to get rid of these darn lip plates if I can."

The promised data had only slowly been coming into their shipboard computers. At last, the linguistic data arrived. "Hey, three languages are spoken here," Nadja said gaily. "Say, the three are closely related as well, but they are quite similar to others that I know about. Well, I would not have suspected this since it is a primitive world too. Tonight, I'll have the learning computers running so that we can pick up all three, since we don't know which one or ones are going to be the most important language or languages. How about you both trying to find out about how we need to physically look to be taken as acceptable natives? Do we need lip plates? I'm going to try to get used to these new prosthetic hands." She'd been fitted with the top of the line model hands that at least matched her skin coloring. Still, they looked funny to her. Unless she wore long sleeves or a jacket, everyone would see that they were artificial hands.

Several hours later, Nadja angrily called for Isabella. "Can you replace this monitor, please?" she said in a very disgusting manner. Isabella looked at the fancy screen. It had a small hole in it.

"What happened?" she asked, but she already knew.

"Oh these darn hands. I don't have any sense of touch with them — no feeling. I touched the screen too hard. Okay, I poked a finger through it before I realized I was doing it. These supposed hands are pathetic. I was doing better with my stumps," Nadja grumbled but admitted.

"Then, why don't you just use your stumps? You can always put the hands on when you need pseudo-fingers," Isabella said politely, but focused her intention a bit stronger.

Nadja felt her immense frustrations flowing away. "That's a good idea, Isabella. I am crippled now. There is no way around that fact, so why try, eh? Thank god for touch-screens and menus, right?"

"Right. I'll get this monitor replaced right now. Won't take a minute." She watched as Nadja took both hands off and resumed her work on another monitor. Isabella smiled and raced off to fetch and open up a new box, while tossing the broken monitor in the recycle bin.

When they met in the small dining room for lunch, Nadja had her hands back on. "Well, tapes are ready. Don't know why we still call them tapes. They are really compressed computer sound files, right Isabella?"

Isabella chuckled. "Right. I'll make a computer person out of you yet, Nadja." Both laughed.

"As long as I don't have to use a keyboard," Nadja added, feeling a bit playful, but also a rather sad. She quickly changed the topic, hoping her slight feelings of grief would remain buried. "So, any ideas on how we should dress and look?"

"Well dear, it is most confusing," Konrad admitted. "Conflicting data. Lip plates or no lip plates. Some do, some don't. Toe shoes and boots are the same way. One thing is for sure, the upper class dresses elegantly, so I know that you will like that much — nylons, heels, satin — the whole bit. Satin is made from something called pod-silk, whatever that is. Quite unlike what I would expect from a primitive society. Strange."

Isabella added, "The key seems to be this company called Elegant Fashions Inc. It is both an Imperium licensed company as well as a local planetary company. Very strange, they have it both ways. Anyway, they are either dictating, setting, or reflecting the local fashions. We don't know which of the three yet. While they have outlets in nearly every major city, their main headquarters is in Exchange City, right by our base. My suggestion is to visit them as a first action. We can use their insight to adjust our appearance to match the locals." Neither Konrad nor Nadja realized that Isabella was subtly directing them to this store as nearly their first actions upon landing.

Konrad then focused on the legal issues surrounding their new assignment. "This is a closed world. Imperial Directive #5 is in full force. Under no circumstances is our technology to find its way into the native's hands. Even our doctors are not allowed to cure or heal sick or injured natives. I can't imagine why they have such tight restrictions in place here, but I suppose we will soon find out. I hate having incomplete data."

He went on, "One reason this world is closed is that they really do have telepaths here — apparently quite a lot of them. The documents I've received suggest these gifted people also have some rather immense, far-out powers."

Nadja interrupted, "Like what?"

"Only gives hints. Apparently, when we get there, I should take a look at <u>Marisol's List of *Mentales* Gifts</u>. It is a local document secretly obtained, and it lists all of these special powers. Fortunately, any given person only has a few of these. My god, Nadja, these people might well be classified as 'supermen!' We may have to be very careful, if they can read our minds without our even knowing it. Imagine letting someone like that loose on the Imperium worlds — super-spy!"

Neither noticed the blood rushing to Isabella's face. "They would probably have other uses than spying," she said, focusing on controlling her body's reactions.

"Well, let me have a look at that document when you find it," Nadja requested. "This is going to be the assignment of the century! Imagine studying a telepathic society. I wonder how language and linguistics are modified by their use of telepathy? I have wanted to know that since we first found that hint that Ashford-5 had telepaths when we were back at the academy. Anyway, start using the language files tonight, gang. I am going to spend this afternoon doing a linguistic comparison of their three languages with the Imperium language database. Something doesn't feel quite right, but I can't put my finger on it yet."

"Dear, you don't have any fingers," Konrad attempted a tease. Nadja felt her suppressed emotions swelling almost uncontrollably. Then, like a gentle feather, she felt a sudden calmness sweeping over her and she got his jest.

She laughed, "Good one, dear. Good one. Anyway, my interest is pricked. Catch you all later. Isabella, I promise not to poke holes in any more monitors." She rose and left them.

"She is walking lots better now, have you noticed?" Isabella asked Konrad.

"Why yes, I don't know how she can manage walking on her toes like that. Just between you and me, I find them rather sexy," he found himself admitting something very personal to her. Well, she had become rather close to the both of them these past months. He didn't know how Nadja would have managed without all of Isabella's constant help.

Isabella laughed, tossing her long hair back. "In the Imperium, that is their purpose. They are 'bedtime' shoes and boots. You should tell her about how you feel, Konrad." He flushed and said that he would.

Late that afternoon, Nadja exclaimed, "I knew it! I knew it! They are derivatives of the Indo-European Language family spoken on planets within the Federation of Planets!"

"What's that?" Isabella asked from the doorway to the compartment in which she had setup all of Nadja linguistic computers and equipment for her. She had conveniently positioned herself nearby when Nadja uttered her outburst.

"I knew that there was something strange about these three Ashford-5 languages, Isabella. They are closely related to three languages that we classify as Indo-European, spoken on some planets in the far distant Federation of Planets. Of course, we are apparently at war with them now. Still, isn't this just fascinating?" Nadja exclaimed highly excited about her discovery.

"What does it mean?" Isabella asked. She had no idea of the importance or meaning of Nadja's discovery.

"I can only speculate, but it would not surprise me to discover that this closed world of Ashford-5 at one time either belonged to or was founded by people from the Federation of

Planets," Nadja explained.

"But the Federation of Planets is half a galaxy away from here," Isabella struggled to absorb what Nadja was saying. "There are no planets aligned with the Federation anywhere out here in the rim. How can this be? Maybe they just developed their own language, and it just happens to be similar to that one you said."

"The chances of identical languages being developed at two wholly distant locations in the galaxy are incalculably minuscule, Isabella. Just look at the language of the world that we just left — wholly unlike any other in the Imperium. No, there must be more here than is readily apparent. Research, Isabella, research will answer my questions. I wish we were there already."

Isabella laughed. "So do I." She flushed and hastily changed the topic. "So what do you make of the assignment that Governor Konrad has — to get these people to send a senator to the Imperium Senate to represent Ashford-5?"

"Well, the Sector ID Minister said this is a most critical detail that needs to happen soon. I am neither an anthropologist nor a politician. I've no idea why this thing is so darn vital and critical that the minister would send his best governor here to obtain that. Do you?" Nadja asked.

"Probably as a first step toward opening up the world," Isabella replied and quickly bit her lip. She felt that she'd just said too much! "I best get back to my computer work," she added hastily and left. Nadja forgot what Isabella had just said, returning to her own, far more interesting investigations.

Chapter 16 Revelations

When they were a day away from the planet, Sector ID Minister Emeryk Donat, Konrad's new boss, opened up a video link to the transport from his Imperium battle cruiser. "Ah, going native are we?" he said. "Sector ID Minister Emeryk Donat here. You are my new Governor Konrad Burkhardt?"

"Yes sir. We're just flying in from our last assignment. Haven't had time to get the modifications undone yet sir. Busy learning the language and preparing ourselves," Konrad justified.

"Good, good. As you now know, since the time of original governor, this closed world has been run by the Sector ID Ministers. However, we are now at war and my duties lie elsewhere. I am placing the running of Ashford-5 in your capable hands. The moons, however, are in my hands. As you now know, we have an extremely valuable and strategic fuel refinery on one of the moons. I will be protecting that base. You handle the primitive planet below. I have only one demand. Get them to send a senator to the Imperium Senate as soon as possible. We are at war and simply must have some changes in our lease here. I'm told that you are the best, so do your job and get me that senator."

"Yes sir. Will do."

"I am sending various passwords to your computer technician now. Some of the files are highly restricted. Pay attention to the various security codes on them. Don't worry; I am not sending you codes to unlock those that are none of your business."

"That's a relief. I was hoping so. I don't want to see such things."

"Good. Now you will find dealing with these primitives extremely challenging. They are overly prideful and distrusting of aliens. You have your work cut out for you. I will offer you one suggestion I found useful. Ignore the 'closed world' status as you need to, but keep such tinkering and meddling a secret, for god's sake. I married a local noblewoman, related to one of their rulers, and used her to gain valuable inside information. Do what you have to do to get me that senator! One group, the Easterlings, I believe — their men have harems — multiple wives. Do what you have to do but get me that senator," he repeated for emphasis. "Just don't tell me what 'rules' you are violating to get it. What I don't know won't hurt me."

"Got it, sir. I'll get you your senator, but I will need a little time to get a working understanding here. We've been on the planet for almost three centuries now. I'm mostly ignorant of all that has transpired there. However, those with whom I must deal certainly are well aware of it. Give me some time to get familiar with the whole scene, and I will get you that senator." He attempted to outline briefly the huge challenge he was facing here, a vastly different scenario than opening up a newly discovered world.

"Yes, I figured as much. Still, I'd like to see results by August at the latest. Your computer technician now has the data you'll need to open up a secure channel to me in this battle cruiser no matter wherever it's at. Any questions?"

"Not at this time."

"Good. You will be landing tomorrow. The local date there is April 1, 1272. Good luck and keep me informed of your progress." He signed off and the screen displayed a test pattern.

They chatted about the significance of what he's just said. "Do they really have multiple wives here?" Konrad asked.

"He said that the Easterlings do," Isabella spoke up. "The spaceport is in the Goza Mountains, which separate the Westerlings from the Midlands. The Easterlings lay beyond the Midlands. Land wise, the three distinct groups have about the same area. The Imperium deals mostly with the Westerlings and the Midlands, since the base lies on the border between the two groups."

Nadja sighed, "Well, Konrad, if you need to take another wife to pull this off, it is okay with me as long as I somehow get to do my linguistic studies. Say, Isabella, you have picked up all three of these new languages remarkably swiftly — faster than I did, and I am the linguist."

Isabella focused, controlling her sharp emotional rise.

"Fast learner, I suppose." She tried to defuse the situation. She knew she'd just made a major blunder! *Well, I should have been more careful around her, she is a linguist. This is her specialty,* Isabella thought.

To Isabella's relief, Nadja didn't pursue this any further. "Don't be surprised if we both lean on you for language assistance when we meet these people for the first time."

"Always glad to help, Nadja," Isabella replied with relief. "I'd better go make sure those password codes arrived, boss." She hastily left the two, who began to stow their gear in preparation for tomorrow's landing on Ashford-5, their long-time dreams coming true.

As Nadja mostly watched the others packing up her equipment, she mused. *What am I willing to give up for this chance in a lifetime to study the linguistics of a telepathic society? Everything, including my hands and my poor feet. This is going to make all my awful sacrifices more than worth it. Somehow, I have to get my equipment and me out among the natives. I am glad the minister said that Konrad could relax the closed world restrictions on the sly. I hope the loss of my hands isn't going to interfere. God that would be a total disaster!* Again, she felt the grief and panic beginning to surface and fought valiantly to suppress all those thoughts and emotions once again.

They descended towards Plateau Grado around noon, just as the High Council of the Lords was breaking for lunch, having reached no resolution on the barbarian problem. "My god! Is it really noon here? It looks almost like nighttime!" Konrad exclaimed. From their windows, they got their first look at the orange-red sun and the ruddy low illumination that covered the world of Ashford-5. "Look, there is still snow all over the place."

"We are above the Goza Mountains and here it is still winter," Isabella explained.

"Yes, I can see them. Impressive range," Konrad replied. "I can see the port. Ah, that must be Exchange City. Say, what is that ancient castle-like structure there at the corner of our base?"

"I surely don't know," Isabella admitted, growing

nervous. *So many things have changed,* she thought.

The landing was gentle, and soon the tall, thin, grey Rigel-3 service personnel in their unisex uniforms swarmed around the transport. Several of the other administration officials came out to meet their new boss. The three stepped out onto the concrete covered plateau. Isabella breathed deeply. Her senses tingled, long gone memories of the strange odors flooded her mind. For a moment, she was overwhelmed. The air was cold and frosty, but she didn't mind in the slightest.

"It is so dark," Nadja whispered. Konrad kept his arm around her, and they walked slowly to meet the assembled staff. Almost absentmindedly, Isabella trailed behind them, continuing to breathe deeply, absorbing every faint trace of odors long forgotten. After brief introductions and many raised eyebrows at their strange physical appearance, Konrad felt obligated to explain as they turned to get indoors where it was warm.

"We've just come from a really primitive world and haven't had time to get our bodies fixed back up," he hastily explained. That satisfied their curiosity. They led the way into the twenty-story admin building. Nadja noticed it looked precisely like every other admin building she'd ever seen. One model fills all needs. She even predicted where Konrad's office would be — the suite on the top floor. Further, she guessed their living quarters would be on the tenth floor, the top most floor of the attached housing unit. She was right.

As they entered the complex, each had to pass their ID cards through a reader. "We'll be getting new ones made up for you three yet today," his geologist explained. Nadja was very careful to do this small action herself using her hands. While Konrad slipped his through the reader in one swift motion, she dare not. Still, she managed it without calling undo attention to her prosthetic hands. Right now, she didn't want the embarrassment; her suppressed grief and loss only needed a nudge to roar to the fore.

As she stepped forward, Isabella slid hers through the reader. Suddenly, red lights began flashing and a gong sounded. Several security men with blasters came running up.

"What's up?" asked a surprised Konrad.

The geologist looked confused. "Don't know boss. Something set the alarms off."

"Oh here, let me check on it," a computer tech interrupted them, as the security men arrived, looking confused. "Oh, it must be a computer mixup. Miss Isabella Valen's card triggered a long-standing security alert. I am pulling it up on the monitors now. What?"

Everyone read: Security Alert. Missing person's report filed June 12, 1172. Isabella Valen, a Class V telepath. Reported missing from Valen Tower.

The flustered security man declared, "There must be some mistake, Governor Burkhardt. Miss Isabella isn't one hundred years old."

"Hardly," Isabella fought hard to control the panic in her voice. "I am twenty-five, as you can see."

"Must just be the names, sir. The security alert is triggered on matching names. We'll get that fixed up, Miss Valen, right away. Sorry for the interruption. Your many crates and bags are already being unloaded and taken to your quarters. Come on. I will show you to your new quarters and then your offices," the computer tech said, somewhat embarrassed about the mixup. As they entered the rather sterile building, Isabella quietly let out a deep sigh of relief. That had been entirely too close for comfort!

Later after a tour, the two settled into their new and very plush quarters. The Sector ID Minister had made quite a number of upgrades to this penthouse suite, mostly to accommodate his gorgeous wife's wishes and needs. Now Konrad and Nadja reaped the benefits. Isabella had her own quarters on the floor below theirs, as befitting his new computer tech minister.

"Well Konrad, we ought to visit this Elegant Fashions Inc store as soon as we can. Do we or don't we need to continue wearing these awful lip plates?" Nadja asked. "Do I need to continue wearing these toe shoes?"

"They look rather sexy on you, dear," Konrad countered, expressing some feelings for her that he seldom had. "Besides, just like ^anchk said, with practice you are walking very well."

"Okay, okay, I can take a hint, dear. Still, we must emulate our natives." For a moment, Nadja wondered if there might be something more between them than a marriage of convenience. At least they'd achieved their long planned goal. They were here.

"Quite right. I'll arrange for a visit there tomorrow morning. Can you manage for a few minutes while I see to that?" he asked business-like, once more convincing Nadja that there wasn't any romantic notions between them.

Around nine the next morning, the three sat crammed into a heated electric car. Isabella held the sketch the geologist had made last night for Konrad, outlining the quickest route to the store. He had been acting governor during the ID Minister's long absence, and his eyebrows rose at this seemingly strange initial request, but dutifully obeyed and pointed out that Exchange City was an open city and to be careful of the natives. "They use swords and daggers, boss, so do be careful. Dual laws are present so expect both Imperium guards and local primitive guards are there."

Konrad commented as they passed by the imposing structure, "I'll have to ask what that castle-thing is doing on our plateau." The Imperial Castle looked wholly out of place on the edge of the spaceport. As they entered the city proper, curious odors filled the air. He commented, "Smells like food perhaps. Wonder if it is any good?"

"Probably quite tasty," Isabella replied. "Turn right here." Soon they pulled into the basement parking garage of a five story Imperium-style building, quite unlike the quaint stone buildings of the city. A large sign read Elegant Fashions Inc.

"According to what I was told, our admin now only has the first floor. The company has expanded to the other four floors. The main office is on the top floor, naturally. Ladies, shall we?" Konrad said, opening the doors and helping Nadja out and onto her toes. A bored Imperium guard directed them to the elevator, and shortly they stepped out and into the main office of the store.

"Good morning and welcome to Elegant Fashions Inc. I

was told to expect you, Governor Burkhardt; your acting governor called. I do hope my Imperium Standard is somewhat understandable," the forty-one year old owner said. "I am Inez Franks, owner of Elegant Fashions Inc."

Konrad suppressed a giggle. Her speech was more like floundering in Imperial Standard. "Good morning, Ms. Franks. Call me Konrad. What say we try one of your local languages? We need to learn them well. Westerlings, Easterlings, Midlands?"

Inez raised her eyebrows. "My native tongue is Westerlings," she said in that language.

"Good. I believe that we ought to use that. This is my wife, Nadja. She is a linguistics expert, and we rely upon her to help us learn to speak your language perfectly."

"Say, you are not that bad in it, much like a young child. Still it must be better than my Imperium Standard. Don't get much call to use it here; mostly I read it," Inez replied. Her attention then drifted to Isabella, who was standing behind the two. Konrad did observe she didn't pay much attention at all to what he thought were their startling lip plates or even Nadja's toe boots. Her only reaction was a bit of surprise at the sheer size of Nadja's plates.

"Oh yes, this is my computer technician, Isabella Valen," Konrad introduced her.

"Very pleased to meet you, Ms. Franks. You can call me Isabella, please."

"Oh my. You speak Westerlings like a native! Call me Inez, please. You look so familiar, Isabella." Now Konrad and Nadja glanced from one woman to the other. Inez wore a red satin gown, but her massive bosom was quite prominent. She also wore a pipe corset, black seamed hose, and six-inch black patent heels. Nadja knew she'd fit right in with any elegantly dressed woman of the Imperium. This was not a primitive culture after all! Further, the woman had the same yellow eyes with brown speckles and rich, long black hair that fell to her ankles, straight, shiny, and thick. She detected the slight odor of lavender, most likely coming from her hair. Yet, as she turned to look at Isabella, she saw a striking resemblance between the two women, which rather startled her. Isabella had nearly identical hair and eyes. She too wore a red satin gown, hose, and similar heels. Well, before her toe shoes, she wore that style too, Nadja mused. But there was more. Their faces seemed so similar. *What did Inez just say? Speaks like a native?*

Quite curious, Inez asked, "Valen? Are you originally from here? The city or tower of Valen? Related perhaps? Come with me. I'll show you what I mean," motioning for them to follow her. As they followed Inez, Nadja observed Isabella's face was slightly flushed. What was going on here? Gaily, Inez explained, "These are some portraits of some of my ancestors. That's mom, Nita Valen. That's my great-grandmother and the founder of Elegant Fashions Inc, Carmen Valen. You can see why I am so struck with your looks, Isabella." Indeed, the resemblance of the two portraits and the two women was striking. True, their physical appearance was strange. Nita had no hands, lip plates, a set of neck rings much like those that Nadja had worn, a tiny waist, and toe shoes. Still, ignoring that, the facial resemblance was striking.

Isabella's face felt hot. She was unable to regain control of her body. Too much, too fast. Inez then added, "My maiden name was Valen too, Inez Valen. Can you all see the resemblance? Amazing."

"Isabella?" Konrad asked, both confused and accusatively.

Isabella thought rapidly. She sensed Inez had the *mentales* gift. Any second she could easily touch her mind, and she threw up a mental blocking barrier, just in case. If needed, she could send out a mind blast and stun Konrad and Nadja, and then make her escape. Yet, where would she go? It was winter and she didn't even have a coat. She had no local coins. Worse, she had no idea what Tierra was like now.

She decided to take a gamble. "Carmen Valen was my older sister," she said softly.

"Oh my god! Really?" Inez gasped.

Suddenly, all manner of small things that had happened during the last months came into Konrad and Nadja's minds. Little things. No wonder Isabella wanted so desperately to get to Ashford-5! This was her home. "But you would be a hundred years old!" Konrad protested. "Oh, rejuvenation machine!" He answered his own question.

"Yes, had to. I was only fourteen when the Imperium men kidnaped me in the middle of the night and took me to Balon-4. A fat businessman had bought me from the kidnapers and made me work for him. I had to probe the minds of those he was making business deals. He even had me alter their minds sometimes to get them to accept his deals. It was awful, but I was smart enough to get him to understand that if I lost my virginity, then I would lose some of my skills. After that, no one ever bothered me sexually. After many years, he died. In the confusing aftermath, I was forgotten and slipped away. Although I tried to book passage back to Tierra or Ashford-5 as you call this world, I couldn't. It was a closed world."

She continued, since Konrad was not interrupting her. "So I got into computers and became very skilled in their use. By then, I was independently wealthy, thanks to the businessman. I eventually used the rejuvenation machine — four times now. Always, I have been seeking a way to return home. When I met you two, I saw the best chance ever. I am sorry, but I have been carefully manipulating you both to ensure you would be successful on that iron age planet. I had to give you the idea about education. You were at a total loss. I nearly lost control when that alarm went off when we arrived yesterday."

He still hadn't interrupted her, so she admitted, "Yes, I am what the Imperium classifies as a Class V telepath. But I am far more than that. Here, I am on of the *mentales* gifted. Please, I didn't want to deceive you, but I just had to get home before I died. I don't want to have to force you to do anything, but I will, if you try to arrest me or expose me."

Konrad responded, "My god! The Imperium forces here kidnaped you! That's criminal! Don't worry, Isabella. I have no intention of forcing you to do anything. I certainly am not about to arrest you or do anything of the kind. You are my computer whizz. I promise you I'll look into this kidnaping thing. I doubt after a hundred years I'll be able to apprehend those who were behind such a heinous plot."

Isabella visibly relaxed. Even Nadja could see her

muscles easing up. She replied, "Thank you, boss. Inez, it's been nearly a century since I was here. I suppose much has happened. Does the Westerlings control much of what used to be the Midlands? And what is the nature of that strange castle on the edge of the spaceport near here?"

"Inez explained briefly, "Oh, right. Lots have happened. Your own Lord Valen built it, in conjunction with the Rigel-3 alien leader. Then, another couple of women who were kidnaped from Tierra returned and became our Emperor and Empress. They refurbished the castle and tower, calling it the Imperial Castle and Tower, and they stopped Lord Valen from his big conquest, bringing peace for a while. Now the emperor and empress positions no longer exist. Instead, the many lords control things, with the various towers' help, and the castle is mostly used as a meeting hall."

"The towers no longer rule the kingdoms?" Isabella asked, growing more confused. Inez shook her head. "Well, I am truly lost. So much has changed. I don't suppose that anyone has written up our recent history?"

Inez laughed. "Hardly. I do know someone who does know. I'll see about it. Gosh, Inez, this makes you my great-great aunt! Wow." The two chatted a bit about this weird situation.

"Have the lords kept the peace?" Isabella asked.

"Yes and no. Right now, there is a weird Easterlings barbarian, who has already conquered and laid waste much of the Easterlings, and he is now heading into the heart of the Midlands. All the lords were here yesterday up in the castle trying to figure out how to stop the barbarian. Don't know what they are going to do though. I thought it was strange to hear you speak perfect Westerlings. Isn't this just amazing, Isabella?"

"I can see I have an incredible amount to learn and in short order!" Konrad interrupted them. "Isabella, I will see you get proper dual citizenship immediately. That way, you will be free to come and go on this world. Meantime, we ought to get back on track. Inez, the reason for our visit is we want to know what the latest fashions are so we can be properly attired so we will fit right in with the locals. The reports that we have seen are most confusing. Lip plates or not. Toe shoes or heels. We need your help and guidance."

"I don't understand, Konrad," Inez answered. Her face was one of confusion. "Are you saying you wish to have the body modifications and wear the clothing the lords and tower folks do? The elegantly dressed of Tierra? But no governor has ever done this."

"Precisely so, Inez. Precisely so. How else can I ever hope to gain the trust of these rulers? It looks like my predecessors have made a complete mess of things on this world. Well, I aim to correct all that, if I can," Konrad explained. "I want to meet these leaders personally. Looks like I missed my chance."

"Okay then. They will be meeting here in July when the lease payments are due. You can meet them all at one time. The trouble is that fashions are so fickle. What was old, becomes new. What is new becomes old. Plus, they simply can't make up their minds. Partially, it is because of the intense rivalry between lords and kingdoms. The lip plates, pipe corsets, and toe shoes and toe boots are very popular among the elite of the City-States Alliance. Those are all the coastal towns and cities across all of Tierra. Then, in the Easterlings, the arm-fetter-gowns are worn, replacing their older forms of bondage among the women, but even that is changing. In the Midlands, most women wear form-fitting gowns with pipe corsets and heels, though some still opt for the toe shoes. Most men of the Midlands no longer wear toe boots, though those in the City-States still do. In the heart of the Westerlings, fashions are usually like the Midlands, pipe corsets and heels, with form fitting gowns. Men wear elegant suits, but again in the City-States, the men often also wear pipe corsets. However as I said, it is constantly changing. At least those ancient ball gowns with their enormous hoop skirts have yet to reappear."

"I see. Confusing indeed." Konrad replied, unsure what to do next.

Nadja, who had been listening in dual modes, one, intensely curious, two, as a linguist, spoke up. "I can't help noticing you are missing your hands, much as I am. We also noticed that a very large number of Imperium prosthetic hands were sent to Tierra. Is it customary to have hands removed?"

Inez laughed and looked at her hands. "No, it is a long story. Hundreds of the rulers and tower people were taken in by a hoax perpetrated by the then Lord Valen. He invented a fake virus, which was supposed to have no cure and bring certain death, unless the victim cut off his hands, wore the pipe corsets, toe shoes, neck rings, and lip plates. I admit that I too was such a victim. Honestly, that time was the darkest in my life. I was unable even to function. However, we have some really good people who managed to salvage us. They found a way to restore our lips and partially repair our feet. I can only wear these six-inch heels now, but that's a whole lot better. Also, believe it or not, while you think it is completely painless when you undergo these modifications with your fancy medical machines, that is not the case. There is immense pain, but it is hidden. Some of our people have discovered this and can erase that physical trauma. It saved my life back when I was fourteen."

"Anyway, there are still some of us around who lost our hands during that treasonous time. You and I will have to just make do, Nadja," Inez replied.

"What would you suggest we do?" Konrad finally decided to get her opinion, since it was too confusing for him to reach any reasonable solution.

"Well, Konrad, since you are a man, I would recommend the elegant suits. Here, we are far, far from those coastal areas, so unless you intend on focusing all your attention way down there, I'd get rid of your lip plates. I can heal them up for you, if you like. Since in this area as a rule men don't wear the toe boots, I'd not recommend them for you. I guess the real question is whether to undergo the pipe corset process or not. Some men like the shapely form, and others do not. So I guess that's the only real decision you need to make."

"Excellent, Inez. I will go with your suggestions. I will need say three complete outfits, including winter coats. It is darn cold here. Can the men even breathe in those pipe corsets? I had an awful time recently on one world."

Inez laughed. "Sir, this is quiet warm. It is almost spring. Wait until you really experience winters here. Oh sure, it's a matter of getting used to them. However, no more heavy exercise or running. You'd not be able to catch your breath. Still, the noblemen and rulers are not prone to doing either."

"All right then, I will go with the pipe corsets as well," Konrad decided. If nothing else, he would look the part of a nobleman.

She turned her attention to the two women. Isabella, you are a Westerlings woman, so I would say for you, just wear the usual gowns and heels. Your only key decision is whether to wear the pipe corsets or not. Most of the elegantly dressed Westerlings women do."

"Okay then, I will too. Can you fix me up with say six outfits? Will you be able to accept Imperium credits?"

"Certainly. Not a problem. Now as for you, Nadja, your situation is most unique and full of rich potentials. First, your earrings are absolutely smashing. When other women see them, they are going to be demanding I provide them with similar sets. That's a given."

"Really? They are so heavy."

"Really! Second, your lip plates are dynamite! I've never seen any remotely as large as yours. Again, when those women who wear them see yours, they are going to be demanding that I somehow enlarge theirs. No matter what you do, could I possible study their design and construction so that I could emulate them for those women who want them?"

"Well I suppose so. They are very awkward to live with though. I can't imagine why anyone would want them in the first place," Nadja replied.

"To look stunning and beautiful. To be noticed by men. To say nothing of bedtime experiences," she hinted before continuing. "This world lacks almost all heavier elements, I'm told. So I think fashions are about the only way our people have to display their status. Anyway, as far as your toe shoes go, you can continue to wear them as they will fit in anywhere. The best I can do for you if you no longer want to wear them is partially to repair your feet, after which you will be like me and can only wear these high heels. I must say there are both pros and cons on this choice. If you want to do much traveling, it is tough doing that in toe shoes or boots, but then it is nearly as bad in these heels. I guess you could continue as you are for now. I would advise you that if you keep the toe shoes, then don't wear fetter-gowns. In them, you can barely walk at all."

"Anyway moving on, your big decision is to go with the pipe corsets or not. Again, most elegantly dressed women from all three areas wear them, though I am not a fan of those women who try for a twelve-inch waistline. I think that is taking it too far. Most of the finer dress styles come in pipe corset designs. No one wears the neck rings any longer, but what the heck. Perhaps next year they too will return as the fashionable thing to wear. I certainly hope not and will not be promoting them."

"Okay then, pipe corset it is. I do like the earrings, though they are a nuisance. I'm fairly used to the toe shoes. I can always have them undone, if I find them unmanageable here. So the real decision is to get rid of the lip plates or not."

"Yes, but I've never seen any as large as yours. I don't think that I know enough about the medical machines to attempt to undo yours, Nadja. Perhaps your own medical staff could do it for you. If not, just be prepared to have many other women asking you about them. They are quite spectacular for those who like such things. Me, I was very glad to get my lips repaired. Still if you have many dealings with those along the coastline, you will be the envy of many women there."

"Okay, I will see what our medical staff can do. It looks like three pipe corset operations then. How soon can we get this done and get our new outfits?" Nadja asked. She wanted to get going on her linguistic studies as soon as possible. Already she knew that her Westerlings dialect was vastly inferior to that of Isabella and Inez. She also observed there were subtle differences in the way the two women spoke. Isabella was speaking the language as it was spoken a hundred years ago. Time had changed the spoken language some, as it always does in any culture. This she knew well.

"Well, it can be done today, but first, let's get all your new fashions picked out, shall we?" Inez replied. "The only problem I foresee is your enormous bust size, Nadja. Here on Tierra, we women are used to having monsters, but yours make ours seem small!"

"Well, now that I've seen the sizes of your women, I will have mine reduced to match yours. Shouldn't be a problem. We were on a planet where the women's breasts were the size of basketballs, four times larger than they are now."

Inez grimaced. "Okay then, I will assume that yours are the same as ours when we measure you. This way, please." She led them to another long table filled with books of fashion images. "Sorry, I flip pages poorly. The hands," Inez explained. Isabella and Konrad did most of the page flipping, while Inez kept a record of their choices.

"Oh I do so love shopping," Nadja exclaimed. "These are particularly elegant, Inez. Who designed them?"

"I did," she answered with pride. "We use only the finest pod silk in these. I can't really import Imperium satin, but our own version very nearly matches it." Isabella knew what she meant by pod silk, but the other two didn't; both filed that one away for later investigation.

It was near suppertime when they finally returned to the base. Each woman had six complete new outfits, two dozen pairs of stockings, and six new pairs of heels to match. They were very much impressed with the actual quality of the heels. It was on par with the best that was available at an exorbitant cost within the Imperium. Konrad changed his mind and also had six new suits with all the necessary accessories as well as matching shoes.

As he drove them home, he said, "I didn't feel any pain at all. It's just that I can't breathe!"

"Tell me about it!" Nadja added. "I can't either. She did say that we would get used to it — have to eat smaller meals and more frequent meals. I hope I can get my boobs reduced yet tonight. I want to try on my new outfits."

After supper, both Konrad and Nadja went to the medical department. While Konrad has his lips repaired, she had her breasts further reduced. As she underwent that relatively brief process, she reached another decision. She decided to have her lips repaired as well. Later she explained,

"Konrad, I don't want the women whose speech I am studying to want to emulate me and try to have giant lips plates too. They are far too much trouble, and they totally mess up speech." That process took five times longer than her breast reduction. Of note, both once more felt no pain at all due to the marvels of the Imperium medical machines. Incorrectly, both were convinced these medical procedures were both painless and didn't harm them whatsoever.

The next weeks were busy ones for the three. Konrad knew that to understand what was happening now on Tierra and for which he was now responsible, he had to know what had happened in the past. "There are always two sides to a story," Isabella pointed out. Still, the quickest starting point was to examine the voluminous records stored at the admin office.

Isabella proved invaluable in pulling up various records, documents, and personal logs in roughly chronological order. She had a vested interest in this as well. A hundred years had passed her by, giving her a very lost feeling. The records of the initial governor and the destruction of their refinery shocked all three. He summoned his geologist, who verified the records were correct and explained all manner of further anomalies. The largest one was the unexplainable way in which the terrible daily wobbling of the planet had miraculously subsided. There was no known planetary physical force that could explain it. "It's a complete mystery," he said.

Then, there were the well-documented weather anomalies which continued to be observed even as recently as the past winter. These too had been classified as "mysterious weather." Konrad soon saw that the geologists and meteorologists were having a grand time studying Tierra.

He then stumbled upon the secret kidnaping project. "My god. They stole eight children each year from here! Do you realize how many others are out there like yourself, Isabella? This is intolerable." As outraged as he was, he also knew he was powerless to do anything about it. The project was sanctioned by the Sector ID Ministers and even higher up the command ladder, far beyond his own reach.

An examination of the list of *mentales* gifts also shocked him. The document was marked with the highest security codes, meaning he could not reveal these to the geologists and meteorologists. But then, they probably would discount such things. Konrad didn't. Isabella didn't volunteer what things on the lengthy list she could do, and he thought it prudent not to ask.

Then came the discovery of the ID minister's men bringing Nuclears to Tierra and the detonation of one of them. This was in clear violation of the treaty. Blasters had been imported as well. On the positive side, there were no reports within the last fair number of years of any of their technology appearing among the inhabitants of Tierra or evidence of their use. Konrad just could not believe the sheer number of mistakes that had been made by the Imperium rulers over the past three hundred years. "Were they all incompetent lunatics?" he growled.

"No, the lure of telepaths drove them — at least in part," Isabella pointed out. "I know from much experience, there are many in the Imperium who greatly desire to have a telepath working for them. Spying is only the least of their activities. There are so very few true telepaths on other worlds."

"Still, they ought to have known better," he refused to accept this justification. It wasn't right.

He also got a feeling that there was a great tension and distrust between the *mentales* gifted and their towers of power and the rulers of the various kingdoms, and it seemed to continue on here in the present. The records seemed to indicate various shifts in power, first to one side and then the other. Isabella was keenly interested in the current state of affairs. When she left, the towers were all powerful. Now they seemed to be ghosts of their former selves. How had that happened? Was she in danger among normal people because of her gifts? This she could not quite discern from the records.

The trio also learned other details of immediate importance. Women in this culture were not allowed to travel alone, but always had to be accompanied by one or more men. The Sisterhood was the exception. Here, Isabella had more information than had the Imperium, though it was quite dated. Further, alien travel beyond Exchange City was illegal. Again, the closed world status was the reason behind that. The inhabitants had insisted on that rule and rigidly enforced it, at least according to the records the trio could find. This seemed to sink Nadja's hopes of studying the "real" languages here. Already she had observed those in Exchange City were speaking a crude mixture of all four languages, including Imperium Standard. *Well,* she thought, *that makes sense. It is an open city that deals in trade between the four parties.*

After spending two intensive weeks on this project, Konrad was forced to turn his attention onto the daily operations of the facility. Hence, Nadja and Isabella began spending much of their days visiting with Inez in Exchange City. Here at least, Nadja could work on improving her language skills in the three she needed to master. Isabella continued to pick up hints of the current situation across Tierra, with special emphasis on her home city Valen. It bothered her tremendously that for nearly a half century, Valen was shunned by the entire world! Still she could understand why.

The one thing Inez impressed upon the two women was not to go walking around Exchange City on their own. While there were the usual pickpockets about, kidnaping the governor's wife was not out of the question for some who despised the aliens. At least, Inez pointed out, Nadja's skin color and physical form would not immediately give her away as alien, as it always did with the tall, skinny, Rigel-3 people. Still, daggers and swords were commonplace. Isabella felt confident enough that she could protect herself if she had to, but there was Nadja to consider. While she walked fairly well in her toe shoes, she couldn't move quickly or run or fight. Both still had difficulty catching their breaths. Physical exertion was out of the question.

Still, Isabella longed to taste local food again, to smell the leather and horses, so familiar to her as a girl. Inez finally sensed this and arranged for her husband, Henry, to escort them about the city three times each week. Soon, both women really looked forward to these outings.

Of course, the evening of the second of April, Inez

316

reported the trio's surprise visit to the Underground, namely Ken. She wanted advice on how to deal with the new governor, his wife, and Isabella Valen. For many, the mere mention of the name Valen sparked instant animosity. Rightly so, for many. Further, she reported on the many traumas both the governor and his wife had endured, though they had no idea the hidden traumas were even there. Should they get some of Benjamina's therapy, she had asked.

Ken and his Underground group began lengthy discussions. They had a new governor, an unknown. What was the measure of this man. Was he as blind, stupid, and foolish as many of his predecessors had been? According to Inez, he seemed like an okay fellow and certainly could pass as a native, if his speech improved, wholly unlike the Rigel-3 personnel who had always been here. What if he brought in more of his race? They could easily begin to infiltrate the lands beyond their spaceport.

Ken rubbed his hands through his hair. He was preoccupied with the barbarian who threatened to strike soon. Now he had potentially an even worse situation in the new governor, who could not have come at a worse time, as far as he was concerned. History suggested that in time, one or more of the towers would likely attempt to form an alliance with him, most likely Valen Tower, who had done so repeatedly in the past. At last, he decided to speak to his mother about it and ask her advice.

Benjamina listened to her son relaying all of this very interesting news. When he finished, she said, "Change always comes, son. The challenge is rising to meet the change. Perhaps this time we should take a lesson from Valen Tower. Let's assume this governor is kind, like Inez suggests. After all, he responded well to the revelation of Isabella Valen, even though she had been tweaking his mind and decisions to help get them here. Give the three therapy sessions, and let's see how they respond. Since two are aliens and I have no idea if my therapy will work on them, you should use the best that we have. No, that's not right; the mermaids must remain a secret for now. I know, use Andres and Rafaela. She is my right hand these days and knows as much as I do. But, son, you are going to have to fully trust those two to always make the right decisions and to back them up without questioning them. Can you do that?"

"I can. I trust Andres and Rafaela implicitly. You know that, mom," Ken replied. But he began to wonder if she knew something he had missed in all this; it was unnerving.

She yawned. "Getting old is a bitch, son, but it can't be helped. Well, that's not entirely true. I refuse to use the alien rejuvenation machine." Ken smiled, though sometimes, like now, he wished she would do just that and retake charge of the Underground. The situations were rapidly coming to a head, and he didn't feel up to the heavy decisions that lay ahead.

"Thanks mom. I'll talk to them tomorrow." He gave her a goodnight kiss and left.

Late April, Bart activated the fancy teleport machine, sending the forty-nine year old Andres and Rafaela Bolivar to the fifth floor of Elegant Fashions Inc in Exchange City, where Inez was waiting for the pair. Both wore pipe corsets and both wore matching black patent six-inch heels of the oxford variety. Years ago, they had been victimized by Lord Valen and his hoax. Thanks to a combination of the medical machines, the therapy that Rafaela helped develop, and a miracle from the Goddess Lysandra, they were in very good physical shape, considering what they had been through. However, their feet could only be partially restored after they were modified for toe shoes. Plus with weak backs, they needed to wear their corsets as well. Still, they looked every bit the nobility that they were. Andres now sported a black moustache, which looked good with his black suede suit. Rafaela wore a blue satin gown allowing her long curly hair to drape across her back.

"Welcome, Andres, Rafaela. I haven't see you for quite some time. You've grown a moustache," Inez greeted them. She knew both well.

"Ah yes. Dignified I am," he teased. "Are we early?"

"Of course, dear. When have you ever not been early?" Rafaela teased him. "We move slowly in these heels," she added by way of an explanation, but Inez didn't need one. She was in the same pickle as these two and hundreds of others.

"I wish that you two would come by for visits more

often. Henry and I haven't seen you for ages. I know. You are constantly busy," Inez chatted. "Ah, here come the two women now. Good luck with them. I hope you can help my Isabella. I can't imagine what all she's been through. I have rooms 4 and 5 reserved for you. Thanks for doing this. It's the least that I can do for her."

"I'll do my best, Inez," Rafaela replied with compassion in her voice. She gave her friend a little hug. Before long, the elevator opened and they got to see the pair of younger women.

"Men wear heels here?" Nadja asked. She and Isabella were introduced to the older couple, but were rather surprised to see Andres wearing a fine suit, but with the same style heels as Isabella and she wore.

"We were some of those who were victimized by the virus hoax, just like Inez has been," Andres explained, "While toe shoes and boots look sexy, getting around in them while outside these buildings and in the deep snows we have here is next to impossible. Our feet cannot be fully healed, and these are the lowest heels I can wear. Around Tierra, there are still a fair number like us who are still living." He then changed the topic. "Inez has told me that you study languages and are trying to learn all three that are spoken here on Tierra."

"I see. I am sorry about your feet. Yes, studying languages is my passion." Nadja couldn't help chatting away. Then, she paused, "Which language should I be using with you?" She had been using the Westerlings dialect, just as he had, thanks to an advance suggestion by Inez.

Andres smiled. "We three here speak all three fluently, Nadja. Pick whichever one you speak the best. Also, we speak fairly good Imperium Standard, if you would feel more comfortable in that language."

"Impressive, sir. Perhaps we could spend some time together working on my language skills. It is vitally important for my husband, Konrad Burkhardt, the new governor, to be able to speak your languages very well," Nadja jumped at the possibility of having a good mentor to study.

He laughed, "Sure. We'd be glad to assist you. Honestly, no governor has yet to even bother learning our languages, but first, why don't we get your therapy started?" He cleverly nudged her over to the real reason for their extended stay in Exchange City.

Isabella spoke up and countered, "But I don't really need any psych stuff. I've seen tons of psychobabble throughout the Imperium."

Rafaela countered, "This is not the same thing, I assure you, Isabella. Those psychs that you are referring to are just that. What I find fascinating is that their root word, psyche, means soul or spirit. Yet, they don't even believe in such things and swear that man is just so much animated mud. You will be surprised at what some of your kinsfolk have developed here on Tierra while you were gone. Let's give it a try, shall we?"

Isabella was a Westerlings woman. Inez also came from there. From Rafaela's appearance, she presumed she too had a Westerlings background. Black hair, voice, demeanor. "Well, okay then. But I assure you that I don't need this."

Once seated in their private room, Rafaela suggested, "Now close your eyes. Good. I want you to see if you can go back to the recent time when you got your waist reduced so that you could wear your new pipe corset." She began with the most recent trauma, which just had to be there. She'd erased countless women's buried trauma from this procedure. Two ribs were cut out and internal organs relocated somewhat to allow such a drastic waist reduction.

When they stopped for lunch, which Inez cleverly had delivered, Isabella was certain there was truth to this new therapy. She'd uncovered the intense pain of the operation that the medical machine and its fancy anesthetics had buried. Likewise, Nadja was also experiencing it as well. As she struggled to make her prosthetic hands manipulate the silverware, she said, "Andres, I think I must be full of these hidden traumas! I've had so many modifications done to my body, it's not funny."

When they ended for supper, Isabella had returned to the last time that she had used the rejuvenation machine to restore her youth for the fourth time. Then in the next morning's session, suddenly nearly a century of anguish, grief, loss, and failed attempts to find a way to return to her home world came to the surface, completely overwhelming her. Most of the afternoon, she had cried her eyes out as Rafaela had her go over and over these grief-stricken incidents of loss, each time pushing her to find an earlier time she felt the loss. The next day, they picked up where they'd left off and finally reached the first one, when she had been kidnaped back in the eleven hundreds. By the end of the day, Isabella felt the weight of a hundred years of grief lifted from her.

It had been a rough session for her. As the grief released, she was bitterly angry and wanted to murder all the Rigel-3 aliens here on Tierra. If Rafaela had not kept her going and released her, Isabella would have used her *mentales* gifts, which were substantial being a Valen; she would have done just that, begun a vast murdering campaign on the spaceport. Rafaela also suspected if no one had given Isabella therapy sessions, she might have actually risen to anger on her own and done such a thing, for she was a Valen after all, and from that time period in the past when they were particularly dangerous to others. The anger soon gave way to an intense antagonism towards all Rigel-3 people. Boredom followed. As the supper hour approached, she began to laugh as cheerfulness finally came, fully releasing nearly a century of built up emotions now freed. Over dinner, she continually told everyone how fantastically alive she felt.

Nadja was rather the opposite. With her, she'd discovered one buried painful incident after another, thanks to the many medical procedures she'd undergone. Each one had to be confronted, faced fully, and re-experienced in detail until the pain was discharged. Her words at supper were, "I'll never be able to get through all of these!"

The third day of therapy, Rafaela and Isabella finally reached far enough back in time to recover Isabella's actual birth well over a century in the past. Interestingly and as fascinating as it was to Isabella, birth, did not erase. Rafaela kept asking for something earlier that was similar to the massive pressure sensations, which Isabella continued to feel were part of her birth. Then, Isabella found one. Her mother had taken a bad bump in her belly. Isabella had found a prenatal incident and then another. During the rest of the day, those were worked on. Her mother had a propensity for bumping her belly during her pregnancy. Each one knocked Isabella senseless and unconscious.

During their session the next day, Rafaela continued to ask Isabella for something that was even earlier. This long series of prenatal traumas were simply not erasing. At last, she said that she saw something, but that it couldn't be real. When they stopped for lunch, her therapy was over. She was laughing so hard that she was gasping for air and could hardly eat. "I was there — at Portillo Tower! I died fighting against the forces from Valen and Valen Tower. I got crushed. It is so silly, but I decided Valen was more powerful than I was, so I became a Valen. Hell, that didn't work out. I got myself kidnaped instead! Ha. Ha. Ha."

While they were eating, she suddenly gasped. "Oh my god! I have lived before this lifetime! I am a spiritual being. I am not a body!" She then broke into another round of laughter.

Her enthusiasm was very real and rubbed off on Nadja, who about now needed some encouragement. For her, it had been slug, slug, slug. One painful operation led to the precious one, to the previous one.

The next day, Nadja made Konrad come to get his first session. She was determined he also get rid of the painful procedures he'd undergone. Though far fewer than hers, she wanted him handled too and had done a good job convincing him. Isabella's newfound enthusiasm also helped convince him to clear his slate today and give it a try.

"I don't speak your language well yet, so this isn't going to work," Konrad patiently explained to Rafaela when they were alone in the private room.

"I understand. Can you understand my Imperial Standard?" she asked.

"Sure, it's fairly good. Why?"

"Well, I'll use it. You can talk to me in your native language. I'll understand," she explained politely. He didn't know how she was going to do that, unless perhaps she was a linguist and had been to his home world. He doubted that very much. Still he followed her orders and closed his eyes, returning to the recent medical machine operation to get fitted for his pipe corset and his lips healed. Before long, he began to re-experience the massive pain of having two ribs removed. By lunchtime, he'd relieved most of pain from those two incidents. During the afternoon, she had him go earlier. The relatively other minor ones came to light and were handled. Then, he contacted the time his lips were cut and the lip plates inserted. That one was quite painful as well, though the medical machine had buried it all beneath a good anesthetic.

As he dined with his wife and the others, compliments of Inez, he said, "I guess there is something to all this therapy of yours. Our doctors don't know all this pain is still there. We felt none of it while undergoing the machine's surgery. This is fascinating stuff. You folks here on Tierra invented it?"

"Yes, I helped with it," Rafaela explained, "but it was mostly the doing of a dear friend of ours, Benjamina. She's now too old to travel. Otherwise, she would be here working with you instead of me."

The next day, Konrad ran further back in time and discovered his birth trauma he didn't even know was there. As he later said jokingly, "No one can remember back beyond around three years of age, let alone their births. Ha!" During the afternoon, Konrad also ran into several prenatal traumatic incidents where his mother had had several bad bouts of morning sickness. Her wrenching had also knocked him unconscious and delivered massive squashing-like pressures all over his body.

The following day, Konrad ended up discovering a past life that he had led. Rafaela was following back on this all over pressure, which just would not fully erase. He'd been in a spaceship that had been attacked. During the explosion in which he'd been killed, he'd experienced a massive compression pressure, killing his body. When he joined everyone for supper, he was constantly laughing, having reached a true enthusiasm. His therapy was finished.

"I feel so alive it's not funny. Hey, Isabella, I'm a spiritual being too. I've lived before too," Konrad gushed. Later over tea, he suddenly realized all this time in therapy sessions he'd been speaking in his own language. "Hey,

Rafaela, how is it that you know my language? Have you been to my world somehow?"

She laughed, "Hardly. I've never been off Tierra. No, I have the *mentales* gift. When you started speaking in your own tongue, I just lightly touched your mind and picked up your concepts. You see, verbal and written language are just physical means to translate a thought into a form that can be physically communicated from one person to another. With our telepathy, we can pick up that original thought or intention, which isn't language based. Simple, really."

Nadja picked up on this. "Say, that is why I wanted to come here — to study the linguistics of a telepathic society. I will do anything, give anything to have a chance to study you folks — you telepathic people. Please, can we possibly find a way to make this happen?"

"Time enough for that later on. We have to finish your therapy first and then get you up to speed on our three languages," Andres carefully shunted this one aside for now. He and Rafaela knew they eventually would have to deal with this one, for Nadja was a very driven person and would find a way to make it happen, whether or not they approved of it.

The next day, Nadja had her own breakthrough. At long last, Andres had her back into her birth. As expected, it didn't erase either. Soon, Nadja ran into a prenatal incident. "Oh my god! No wonder I am a linguist! My dad is not my dad! Mom had a secret affair with some foreign man. I've been unknowingly trying to find out who my real father is by identifying the language he spoke!" That was sufficient a revelation to force Andres to end the session for a while. For Nadja, this was a eye-opening.

During the next session, Andres asked for something similar that had happened even earlier. Eventually, Nadja found it. In a previous lifetime, someone was speaking a language that she did not understand. She simply couldn't understand him, and he had killed her because she didn't do whatever it was that he wanted her to. Hence, she had a manic drive to understand languages — either that or be killed. Now she was roaring with laughter, as had Isabella and Konrad. She also knew she wasn't a body; she was an immortal spiritual being. More important, she no longer had a manic compulsion to learn languages. Now she could learn them because she wanted to. In fact, her skills as a linguist increased fourfold.

With therapies completed, Andres and Rafaela agreed to spend some time with Nadja and Konrad helping them master the three languages. "I really do want to be able to address all the many lords who rule here in their own language. They will respect me far more if I do that and dress as they do," Konrad explained. Neither could disagree with him.

Chapter 17 The Barbarian and Justice

Late April, constant updates flooded the various tower comm networks. Many towers sent out those of their *mentales* gifted, who could go invisible, to spy on the approaching army of Damiano. True to form, he and his Domei horsemen pushed ever deeper into the heartland of Matruk, raiding the prosperous farming towns. After raping their women, stealing their valuables, and replenishing their food supplies, he conscripted all able-bodied young men, forcing them into his ever-growing foot soldier army. The more competent of these, he allowed to ride the horses they stole.

Still, each town attempted to stop them. Several times, members from Adelmira Tower had attempted to help the town's militia. While these gifted were able to inflict some casualties on his men, that was the extent of the damage done. With each town captured, Damiano lost some men, but subsequently replaced them. Drastically reduced in the battle above Turda, he slowly rebuilt his army into a sizeable force. He and Fausto knew three-quarters of his army could not be trusted. Hence, many of his trusted Domei men had to be kept on guard duty. Anyone caught deserting was publically drawn and quartered.

As his army marched northwest, it left a trail of dead men and victimized women behind, stretching for well over two thousand miles. The only positive aspect was his progress was slower than he had originally estimated it would be. Still as June neared, so too did he near the huge Midlands city of Wye and its *Círculo de la Torres*. Already, Lord Wye had spent the last two months forming up the largest army Wye had ever seen. He conscripted every able-bodied man in the city and surrounding countryside for fifty miles. Still, he knew his army would not be able to stop Damiano himself. He was counting on the many *Círculo de la Torres* to send all of their *mentales* gifted. Surely, they could stop this madman.

Indeed, several *Círculo de la Torres* hatched their own plans. While their venerados had agreed at the High Council of the Lords to send all their tower people to help defend Wye against the attacking barbarians, Venarado Bedwurth hatched his own plot. He, like many other venerados, simply did not believe Damiano was somehow immune, somehow blessed. He was a man and he could be killed. Late April, they executed their rogue plot.

Via the tower's comm networks, all the towers watched as three complete *Círculo de mentes* from Wye, Walsham, and Adelmira Towers launched their surprise attack on the marching columns. Twenty-seven men and women suddenly appeared on the farmlands out in front of their lines. They fired off a tremendous volley of "spells" that included balls of fire and many other deadly attacks. Men and horses fell to the ground dead in their tracks.

To the shock and utter amazement of the twenty-seven, Damiano came galloping out of the inferno, his two scything blades whirling. Five of their numbers were dead before the frantic towers could teleport their members back. The shock of their failure to stop Damiano reverberated throughout every tower on Tierra that day. Venerados and veneradas fired off messages to each other, in a frantic attempt to work out some new strategy to stop this seemingly invincible man. They knew they only had days at most before Damiano would reach the assembled army of Lord Wye, positioned just southeast of Wye.

Poor Bart and Anita were utterly overwhelmed by the hundreds of messages flying back and forth over the many tower comm networks. They called in Jake and Misty to help and soon added Harry and Sally too, with Jamie and Luisa manning the night shifts. Even Eric and some of the other old-timers were pressed into service to help sort out the confused mess of messages. Ken and Crystal did their best to try to stay on top of the key ideas being proposed right and left.

"Ken, we are going to have to do something!" Crystal exclaimed. "Even the towers are in a state of panic now. If Damiano's army wipes out Wye's army, all the Midlands will go into compete chaos! You can see it in all the messages. Some are even planning to evacuate to the Westerlings. Lord Gervasi has invited anyone who wants to come to Malaca to do so. What are we going to do? We have to act."

Ken sighed. "I know, I know. I have an idea, but I am going to ask mom first."

"I'll go with you," Crystal insisted. They found Benjamina and Elana sitting beside Tim's bed comforting both Tim and his wife, Petrona.

"We've been expecting you, son," Benjamina whispered. "You have to make a terrible decision about life and death. We know. We had to make the same decision many years ago. Often killing a person is a bad choice, because as we all know, you haven't really handled that person. They come back in their next lifetime worse off than before. Eventually, you're going to have to deal with that spiritual being. But son, always think of the greater good."

Ken sighed, "I have mom. I can't think of anything else to do. I've come to ask for Elana and her kin's aid once again."

Elana whispered, "I know, Ken. I know. I have been expecting this for over a month now. You will need a dozen of us. I've picked out the dozen; most of us have done this many years ago. When do you want us?"

"Soon, tomorrow. We need to strike before they reach Wye or the slaughter will be of monumental proportions. I hate to do this, but, Elana, I can see no other way to avoid it," Ken replied. "All Tierra thanks you and your kin, though I wish with all my heart we didn't have to do this."

"I know, Ken, we all do. But there comes a time when one has to act to preserve the good and not let evil destroy the good. Perhaps you will be able to handle them in their next lives under better conditions. We will be ready. What time? At the teleport station?" Elana asked.

"Yes, say around ten. Thank you, Elana. Thank you." Ken said, wishing that it had not come to this. "How is Tim?"

Petrona whispered, "Not so good, I'm afraid." They sat in silence a little longer, watching the unconscious Tim's labored breathing.

At ten the next morning, Bart had brought up an image from the alien's geo-sat satellite onto the large monitor. Now Ken, Elana, Crystal, and eleven other older women, Elana's Earth-kindred, studied the layout of Damaino's army. Nearly seven hundred-fifty cavalry were leading the march, all bunched into a tight formation of fifty to a unit. Behind them, five wide lines of foot soldiers marched. Further back, a horde of supply wagons lumbered along. The ornate carriage bringing the six harem wives stuck out like a plum. It was June 1, 1272.

Just as he was about to begin the operation, the inhuman voice of Alpha came over their comm system. "Ken. Warning. Warning. Aliens are attacking the alien fuel refinery. Explosions have occurred up there. Big ones. Warning. Beta has detected an alien transport ship is taking fire from a Rigel-3 battle cruiser. Warning. Beta says that it has been hit by D-cannons. Warning. Beta reports extensive flames are coming from its rear section. Warning. Beta reports the craft is heading towards Tierra."

"Good god! Alpha! What the devil is going on?" Ken called back at once, growing more frustrated by the moment. If he didn't have enough problems with Damiano, now this? Aliens attacking aliens?

"Yes, Ken," the emotionless voice continued. "A non-Imperium transport, not unlike those that we have seen during our extensive travels, has attacked and blown up part of the Imperium fuel refinery up on the moon. That ship is badly damaged and Beta reports that its flight systems are no longer functional. They will be crashing into Tierra. What are your orders?"

Ken thought fast. He had to. "Can Beta help them somehow land?"

After a brief pause, Alpha reported, "Yes, Ken. Beta thinks that he can help stabilize their flight so that it does not end in a deadly crash. Do you want him to interfere?"

"Yes, yes. They can't be all bad if they are attacking the refinery. Where are they going to land?"

"Crash is the operative word, Ken. Even with Beta's intervention with their control systems, they are going to crash, just not as badly. Trajectory computed. Superimposing on your screen now."

Ken, Crystal, Elana, and her eleven older women stared at the giant monitor. "My god! This is all we need! They are going to crash land close to Damiano and his army. Oh hell. Come on; let's get there. Bart. You ready for us?" Ken cried out.

"On it boss. Okay ready. Step onto the teleport pad in two's. As soon as they disappear, two more hop on. Quickly, quickly now," Bart ordered. He and Anita feverously operated their controls, as one pair after the other came up to the pad and vanished. He was placing them at the predetermined locations around the leading edge of the marching army.

Ken and Crystal appeared on the grasslands southeast of Wye first and immediately dropped to the ground. In the distance, they could see the approaching cavalry that defined the leading edge of Damiano's army, just as they'd seen it on the geo-sat images a moment before. "Alpha, alpha. Talk to me. Where is this falling transport ship?" Ken barked into his communicator attached to his earpiece.

"Look up behind you. Fire ball," Alpha spoke. Ken and Crystal looked behind and up. There was a flaming streak coming their way. In pairs, Elana and her kin appeared in a wide arc around Ken and Crystal. They too dropped onto the ground, awaiting the approaching army and Ken's orders. "Flames are gone. Beta has cut the fuel flow. Crash anticipated in sixty-two seconds. Estimated location: two hundred feet in front of your position. Suggest you cover your heads."

Now they could hear it. Sort of a roaring noise — like thunder that didn't stop. They felt a surge of hot air as it passed barely over their heads. Boom! It crashed. Well, it executed a partially controlled crash, thanks to Beta's intervention. Grass and black dirt flew up in wide arcs, falling gracefully to the ground like fireworks. Alpha was correct. It lay smoldering some two hundred feet in front of them. Ken and Crystal got up and raced for the remains of the transport. As they ran, they saw the enemy cavalry were also galloping towards the crash site as well and would get there long before they did.

Ken raced to the right of the ship; Crystal, to the left. As they angled, they saw Damiano and his whirling scything blades approaching the front of the ship. Just behind him, others were galloping up. Several also had whirling scything blades as well. "Oh hell. Now, Elana. Now," Ken yelled into his comm link.

Suddenly, Ken and Crystal heard the unfamiliar sounds of d-gun fire. They saw energy streaks flying from the front of the ship, but could not see who was firing. Whoever was, was firing wildly. Probably shook up from the crash, Ken thought, running as fast as he could. He and Crystal saw men and horses crashing into the ground. Blast holes and amputations were highly visible. They saw Damiano's horse go down and lost sight of what was happening. Their vision was obstructed by the smoldering ruins of the large transport ship. As they came around to its front from either side, they saw a strangely dressed man and woman wildly firing d-guns. Part of the woman's left arm was missing. She was bleeding. Then both passed out. The scything blades were on the ground and Damiano was screaming hideously. At that instant, the ground opened up beneath the charging horses of his cavalry, who were about to reach Damiano. Horses and men simply dropped into the gaping fissures! More fissures opened up, swallowing the more distant riders! Almost as suddenly as the fissures had opened, they closed! Some seven hundred cavalry had vanished in mere seconds!

Meanwhile, Ken and Crystal reached the unconscious pair. "I'll get these two back to base," Crystal yelled. "She's bleeding to death."

"K. I will stay and coordinate," Ken yelled. "Good going, Elana and all. Now for the foot soldiers. Are you ready for round two?"

"Yes, at your command," Elana replied, adding, "All of them?"

Ken paused. He knew what she meant. Were all of these two thousand plus men to die? He made a split second decision. "Get the front lines. Then wait. Maybe the rest will flee. I'll give them one chance, Elana. I am not a butcher if it can be avoided. One chance. Thank you. Go ahead, Elana. Now."

This time, the dozen earth-kindred worked in tandem. They stood up and raised their handless arms. Again, the earth opened up before and underneath the marching columns of men. They simply fell downwards, vanishing from sight. After their heads vanished, the rumbling earth closed over them, raising a small cloud of dirt that settled back onto the green grass. The front third of the army had vanished. Ken paused to see what would happen next. "Run, you fools. Run," he whispered to himself.

Bart heard him and spoke, "Ken, the very rear lines are making a break for it. Give them a bit of time."

"K, keep me posted. Thanks, Bart," Ken spoke, relieved that not all the men, likely conscripts, would have to be killed.

After a few minutes, Bart reported again. "Ken, about half of the soldiers are running away, but the front lines are continuing."

"Okay, Bart. Elana. I guess we have to do it again, please." Once more, the dozen earth-kindred focused their unique elemental powers. Again, the earth trembled as more giant fissures suddenly appeared and then closed. Now Ken could see for himself. No soldiers were marching towards him. He could see the outlines of men running in all directions away from the battlefield. Even the supply wagons had turned around and were retreating. Only the ornate carriage continued to head straight for him. "Leave that carriage alone. It probably has his wives. They are helpless pawns."

"Bart, get Elana and her friends out of here now. Alpha, what do we do about this ship?" Ken asked.

"Computing now, Ken." Pause. "Ken, Beta says leaving it there has a seventy percent chance of causing additional problems with the aliens."

"How can we get rid of it? Use Elana?" Ken asked.

"Computing." Pause. "Ken, Beta says that will have a fifty percent chance of causing additional problems. Recommended solution: blow it up. Beta believes that he can activate a self-destruct mechanism once you are clear of the blast site. Advise."

"Okay. Blow it up. I'll let you know when I am clear. Hello. Who are you?" The carriage arrived, driven by an older Easterlings woman. He heard women's voices calling out from inside the carriage.

"I am Lord Damiano's harem caretaker. I have brought

his and Fausto's wives. They want to know if he is all right. What has happened here? Where have they all gone? We see no enemy army. Have the gods struck?" She was remarkably calm, Ken thought.

Finally, Ken looked around for Damiano. The man was now unconscious. He'd suffered blaster wounds. Ken let out a rush of air. Disbelief. Both of his lower arms were missing as well as his lower legs. The wild d-gun shots had missed his torso and head, failing to kill him. His horse had not been so lucky. A two-inch hole allowed the dim light to shine through the horse's head. "Damiano is alive."

Ken walked to the right side door of the carriage and opened it, shocked by what he saw. Two wives were mermaids. Two had lost their lower arms and lower legs. Two others had lost their lower arms. "Please, sir. Are our husbands all right?" Antonia asked. "I can't see Damiano from in here. We must help him. He is our husband."

"What about Fausto? Is he all right?" asked Daniela, the other woman without hands and feet.

"Fausto is dead. Damiano still lives."

"Please, if he is injured, we will care for him, if only you can lift him into the carriage for us, please sir," Antonia pleaded.

"My Lady, your wish is my command. But you must promise me that you will care for him," Ken replied politely.

"Oh yes, yes we will. We are the most sexy women on Tierra and he loves us dearly and we love him too. Thank you, thank you, kind sir," Antonia replied, greatly relieved.

Ken picked up what was left of Damiano and carried him to the carriage. As expected, the women gasped. He ignored them and carefully set the man onto the seat between Antonia and Daniela. "There you go. Now he comes to you as sexy as you are."

"Oh thank you sir. Yes, now he too is most sexy as well. We will care for him always," Antonia gushed.

Ken returned to the driver. "Turn around and leave this place as fast as you can. Take the women wherever you wish to. They are in your charge now, woman."

"Yes sir. Thank you sir," the old woman replied and

promptly got her team going, veering around the still smoldering ruins of the transport ship. Ken watched them depart rapidly.

"Are they far enough away, Alpha?"

"Yes, Ken."

"Okay, Bart. Get me out of here." The next instant, Ken vanished from the grasslands, and then another explosion destroyed what remained of the transport ship.

Chapter 18 Fallout

"What the hell just happened?" Lord Wye screamed. "What do you mean the army just vanished? What was that explosion?" All around Tierra, venerados and veneradas sent messages right and left. Many had members of their circles monitoring the advancing army. Via them, they had just witnessed something that none had any explanation for — though some began to call it a divine miracle.

Typically, the observers were using the eagle-view *mentales* gift that some possessed. That is, they were observing the army from some distance far above them. For a time, the germanium crystals that formed the tower's comm networks glowed brightly, as messages flew from tower to tower. Venerados and veneradas then relayed them to their confused lords and his staff. Most reports were variations on this. The ground just opened up beneath their feet. Horses and men fell into the holes, which then closed. The earth swallowed up the army, but something did crash from the sky and it exploded. A few foot soldiers did escape, fleeing for their lives. Weird. One carriage did come up to the thing from the sky, but it too raced away before the explosion. A gaping hole in the ground replaced the sky object, but the cavalry and soldiers were just gone.

Thousands of messages later, that was the officially accepted description of what had happened. None had seen the widely spaced Earth-kindred or Ken and Crystal or the two who landed in the transport ship. Everyone believed Damiano too had been swallowed up by the earth god, as some now were convinced had been behind this miracle. In later years, mothers and fathers would tell their children who were misbehaving, "You better watch yourself or the earth god will swallow you up just like it did to the barbarian Damiano Donatello." Only Venerada Maricela and her mother, Marisol, knew what really happened but they did not relay that to anyone, though Ken later told Lord Emilio Bolivar, who kept it to himself.

Jake and Misty came running to the teleport pad, just as Bart materialized the two unconscious people who had landed in the transport ship. "We'll take over from here," Misty declared. "I'll take the injured woman. You get the man. Careful — they could have all manner of injuries. We'll be in our medical room, Bart."

Their crystals around their necks activated, and the two unconscious bodies rose into the air. The two used their telekinesis powers to lift them to avoid further injuries. Then, they gently floated the two down the hall and into their medical room, where they had several of the alien medical machines set up. Gently, they laid the two onto the exam tables.

She's lost half of her lower left arm and hand. I will prepare her stump for a prosthesis, if we can get one that will fit, Misty sent telepathically. Both knew better than to talk aloud around injured, unconscious people. Whatever they said would be recorded along with the pain and unconsciousness of the victims.

I am checking for injuries on him, Jake sent back.

A half hour later, they stepped out of the room, comparing notes. "He had a concussion and massive bruising all over his body. Otherwise, he is okay. How about her?"

"I have her left arm fixed up. She's badly bruised too. Concussion. No internal damage though. Could have been worse. She has an awful lot of dust in her nasal cavities. Probably in her lungs too. I suppose it'll be best if we sit with them until they regain consciousness," Anita suggested. They did so.

"Say, he did too — have an awful lot of dust in his nose and lungs. I suppose they'll just have to cough it up in time. I did take some samples though."

"I did too. If trouble develops, I'll have to analyze them. Now we wait."

When Ken returned, he found Crystal, Elana, and her eleven kinswomen waiting for him. "Elana, ladies, once again, on behalf of all the free peoples of Tierra, thank you. I know how awful this has been for you to do, but your actions have saved the rest of the entire world from entering a new dark age. You have saved thousands of lives and untold suffering. Thank you. Thank you."

"It is such a tragedy. So many lives, but then they all had a choice," Elana replied. "One's own personal integrity is more important in the long run of lifetimes than one's immediate life." Ken knew precisely what she meant. All had received a whole lot of therapy. All knew some details of some of their previous lifetimes. Elana nodded and led her group off through the tunnels. She joined Benjamina and Petrona at Tim's bedside. Already Benjamina knew all had gone well. She and Elana were very, very close.

"So how are our two space people doing?" Ken asked.

"Don't know. Let's go see," Crystal replied.

Bart called out, "Good god! Look at the comm networks! I've never seen them this active ever! Do you think our system might overload? I do. I am going to dampen it out some. Geesh! You sure know how to cause a stir, boss," he teased.

"Do it. We can't afford to have our monitor system blow a crystal right now," Ken ordered.

Ken and Crystal joined Jake and Misty. There had not yet been any change in their condition. They speculated on the significance of their clothes. Both the woman's shirt and pants were grey, green, and brown splattered. They could not tell what the base color was supposed to be. His shirt and pants differed a little from hers, but he also had some funny looking bars on his shirt, the meaning of which eluded the foursome. They waited patiently, knowing the first problem would be language. Ken anticipated the two waking up and frantically trying to communicate. Neither would understand the other. Well, that's not entirely true. The four could pick up their thoughts readily enough, but how to communicate back to them would be the hurdle. Ken assumed he would have to use gestures to start with.

Both began to stir and the four prepared themselves for what promised to be an interesting interview. The man roused, held onto his head, and groaned, causing the woman also to stir. He opened his eyes and, with effort, got to a sitting position. His eyes darted fearfully around the room, pausing for a second at each person. "Princess Meg!" he exclaimed and looked over at her as she roused. "Princess Meg," he said, "wake up, if you can. I think we're prisoners now."

"Huh? Oh my head." She raised both hands to her head, but then looked shocked, obviously recalling the painful loss of her lower arm and hand. "Josh? Are you all right? Those horsemen. . . Where are we?"

No one was more shocked than the four. "My god, I can understand them!" Ken exclaimed. "Well, mostly. They are speaking a strange Midlands dialect. How is that possible?"

Meg sat up and examined her nicely healed arm. She noticed she'd lost about three inches of her lower arm, but that it was now nice and conical in shape and perfectly formed with no scarring. She looked confused.

"Welcome to Tierra. Can you understand me?" Ken spoke slowly and clearly.

"Yes, rather a strange accent. Have we been rescued? I don't see how. We were on our own. Where are we? Who are you? Where are your uniforms? What's happening? Are we Imperium prisoners now?" Josh asked.

"We rescued you. You are safe. We've healed Meg and made sure you don't have any other injuries. You both suffered a concussion and a whole lot of bruising in the crash landing. You are on Tierra. Yes, the Imperium has a spaceport far south of here, but we don't really have any dealings with them. This is a closed world, and they are not allowed up here. So you both are safe. I am Ken Blackwater, my wife, Crystal. My medical experts, Jake and Misty Blackwater. He's my brother. Who are you and where do you come from?" Ken asked.

"Is that the world that we landed on? Tierra?" Josh asked. Ken nodded. "Oh. I am Captain Josh Hamilton, transport pilot. This isn't Idaho is it? She's Princess Meg Dillon of Rimon-F."

"Pleased to meet you, Captain Josh. What's Idaho? Where is Rimon-F? Another world?" Ken asked slightly confused. Perhaps this was due to the slight differences in their Midlands dialect, he thought.

"Earth. Rimon-F and Earth are two planets in the Federation of Planets. You've heard of us?" he replied and asked hopefully.

"Er, not exactly. To be honest with you, I don't know of any other planets than this one. Sorry. I take it you're fighting against the Imperium. We know you must have played a role in damaging their fuel refinery on the moon," Ken answered.

"My doing," Princess Meg spoke up. "Thank you for saving us. Yes, the Imperium attacked and killed my parents and brother a few months ago. They destroyed half of my people and devastated part of my planet. We refine fuel for the Federation. I think that's why they attacked us. I've been leading the resistance fighters, trying to take back our world. Now I've tried to put a dent in their fuel production on that moon. I lost three of my men, but I think we did some damage to it. I got hit with a blaster shot trying to get back into our transport. Oh, it crashed. Where is it? Where are we? We have to get off this world and back to ours."

"It blew up. Sorry. You are stuck here for now, but you are safe." Both looked crestfallen hearing that they were marooned.

"Well, I picked the right transport pilot. Thank you for saving us, Josh," Princess Meg added. "Wait! How come you can speak Josh's language? English?"

"We have no idea how come you both are speaking our Midlands language. You do have a really strange accent though," Crystal answered.

"But you are far, far beyond Federation space. You are deep in Imperium space, far out on the rim of the galaxy," Princess Meg replied confused.

"Hey, as far as where Tierra is in relation to anything else in the galaxy, we have no idea whatsoever," Ken stated.

"No space travel?" she asked, her face sinking as she absorbed the ill news.

"Nope. Up here in the cold northern lands, we live in stone houses and burn wood for heat. Not much farming though. Too cold. Our farmlands are further south where you crash landed," Ken explained.

"But you have guns and electricity and computers and radios, right? Maybe we can send a message back to our base," Meg suggested hopefully. Ken sensed that she was still trying to work out what this planet had.

"I am sorry, but as far as the planet goes, we have none of those. When men fight, they usually use swords. In the past, we've outlawed projectile weapons. If a man wants to harm another man, they have to face each other, and each has to have an equal chance of killing the other, ignoring the skill factor," Ken explained the various "ultimatums" that were in effect for years now.

"But you have cars and trucks then?" she fumbled for ideas. Ken sensed her thought: *What have we fallen into here?*

"Sorry, we don't know what those are. We get around on foot or on horseback or perhaps in a horse-drawn wagon or carriage. I think in your terms we are a primitive culture," Ken hazarded an evaluation based on what she was thinking.

"Oh god, Josh, we really are marooned here," she sighed.

Ken wasn't about to reveal here in the Underground they had solar panels, battery power, radios, and a vast array of electronic gear, much less the entire spaceship that lay buried in the gully north of Brom with the two robots, Alpha and Beta. Only a handful of key people knew this. "However, you both are safe, and we'll prevent the Imperium from discovering you. You are currently in a secret underground safe house in the far north of the Midlands in a town called Brom. That's about twenty-five hundred miles from where you crash-landed. Actually, you landed right in front of an invading barbarian army. We owe you big time for stopping the barbarian leader with your d-guns. Our people had not been able to stop that madman's rampage. So on behalf of the free people of Tierra, I thank you for that. We arrived at the crash site just as the barbarian was charging you. We got you safely rescued before your ship blew up."

"Oh. Is that who the crazy man on the horse with the swinging blades was? He was about to kill us. We were just protecting ourselves. Say, what happened to our d-guns?" Meg asked.

"Gone in the explosion," Ken replied factually. He'd made sure of that detail.

"Wait. How long have we been unconscious? Must have

been weeks," Josh rubbed his head. "Meg's arm is all healed. Must have been, since you only have horses."

"Actually, you have been unconscious for about four hours," Misty answered. "We got you back here so we could heal Meg just as fast as we could."

Josh rubbed his head. "Now wait just a darn second. If we were almost three thousand miles from here, how could you get us here that fast without a spaceship? What are you doing to us? Oh, maybe a mile here is what we call a few feet. Our foot is this big." Josh placed his hands about a foot apart.

Ken looked frustrated. This isn't going well at all, he thought. "No, that is our foot too. Amazing coincidence. We have the same units of distance. Anyway, there is a logical answer to your question about the distance and time. We actually teleported you here."

"Now just a darn minute!" Meg frowned antagonistically. "You just said that you didn't have electricity or anything modern. So how could you have a teleport machine? It needs electricity to run. What are you trying to pull on us? We aren't stupid, you know."

"No, I don't mean to imply you are anything of the kind. Some on our world used their *mentales* gifts, one of which is the ability to teleport. It's a mental power. Telepathy is quite common here, along with other things," Ken tried to explain.

"Now I know they are putting us on, Josh. Don't believe a thing they are saying," Meg said, gritting her teeth. "They must be trying to interrogate us or something."

Hardly, Meg. We do have telepathy. Each of us has many other things we can do with our mental powers, Ken placed into her mind and his as well. *Not everyone on Tierra has this gift, but quite a few do. That is why this is a closed world, as far as the Imperium is concerned.*

"But, but. You can read my thoughts too?" Meg exclaimed very shocked.

"Yes, forgive me for that parlor trick. I couldn't think of any other way to convince you. While we can read minds, such is never done without the consent of the other person. It is rude and very bad manners, to say the least. No one will pry, so don't worry," Ken calmed her down.

"But we have to find a way to get home," Meg countered.

"Right now, that is impossible, Princess Meg. You are our guests. We will keep the Imperium forces from finding you, but only as long as you always do as we ask. Otherwise, I suspect they will be illegally hunting all over Tierra for you. I think you two probably have really pissed them off," Ken replied.

"Okay. Thanks for that. We really don't have any choice, do we? Here I am all crippled up. Don't suppose you have any prosthesis lying around?" Meg asked sarcastically.

Misty spoke up, "Well, yes, as a matter of fact we do have some of the Imperium prosthetic hands, but you lost a good deal of your lower arm. While I can fit you with their best hand, it's going to look weird — terribly short. I have the right measurements from the medical machine, and we will get a proper one ordered tomorrow. Will that be all right?"

"Now wait a minute. How can you have Imperium hands if this is a closed world? Medical machines? Hey, those are highly specialized and terribly expensive machines, and they use electricity, which you said you don't have!" Meg declared flatly. Ken sensed her mind. *Now I've caught them in some really big lies!*

"Meg, what I was telling you applies to the world at large on which you both crash landed. There is no electricity. What I haven't said yet is we here and our friends are what is known around here as the Underground. We have all of those things you mentioned, and we certainly know how to use them. In fact, this room is deep underground in the bedrock. The Imperium does not know we even exist and neither does nearly every other person on this world, save a very select few. Our job is to protect our world from the Imperium, as well as our own people's madness of wars and such."

"Oh. Then you could send a message off-world? Let our people know that we are alive?" Meg asked.

"We could, I suppose. However, such communications would likely be intercepted by the Imperium. I don't know how anyone could get here to rescue you. After your sabotage on their refinery, they'll have Imperium battle cruisers patrolling everywhere. I would suggest you relax and let some time pass," Ken answered calmly. "For the time being, you are alive, well, and quite safe."

"Okay then. We'll behave. Don't suppose you have anything we could eat?" Meg asked, still a little sarcastically.

"Sure as soon as you are up to it," Misty answered cheerily. "We'd best get you into some local clothes though. You don't want to go around announcing 'here I am' to the Imperium forces."

"I suppose you're right. We aren't going to have to wear bear skins are we?" she retorted, annoyed with her fate.

"Sorry, we don't have any of those. You can dress similar to us or you can get all dolled up. Really, we can look very elegant at special events," Misty suggested. "Are you a real princess?"

"Well, yes, but now I am sharing the rulership of our planet with my younger brother," she admitted. "Let's see what you mean by dressed up." Misty smiled and had her follow her, while Jake took Josh with him.

Later, both reported the two had to blow their noses quite a lot and coughed up a lot of phlegm. Given a choice between a cotton shirt and leather pants and a suede suit and pants, Josh decided on the suede outfit. Leather pants looked too primitive to him. "This suit looks much like the ones we have, especially the shoes," he commented. He didn't say he would feel out of place wearing what appeared to be crude leather pants.

"Holy margarita, Princess Meg, you look stunning," Josh exclaimed. She had also taken one look at what she thought was "primitive" clothing and opted for the formal blue satin gown, and black nylons. The extreme height of the six-inch heels put her off for a bit, but she decided to wear them anyway. It was better than the "primitive looking" lined boots.

She did let Misty know the resemblance. Twirling around in her tight gown, she had said, "You know, this outfit is rather similar to ours, except your heels are terribly high. How do you all manage in them?"

"Thanks. They are the height of fashion across our world among all the noblewomen," Misty had replied.

Seeing Josh's rather dumbfounded expression pleased Meg. "Thanks Josh. I do look good in this gown. Heels are tough though."

"Allow me, princess," Josh suggested, offering his arm. Unused to such heel height, she accepted it willingly. Misty led them into their large dining area. Electric lights illuminated the chamber, though there were oil lanterns on the walls.

"Electric lights tonight in your honor, Meg, Josh," Ken announced. "Normally, we save on the electricity. Have a seat and I'll introduce everyone." He went around the table pointing out each one in turn. "I do hope you like fish, potatoes, and mixed vegetables. We've some fruit or early berry pie for desert, I'm told."

"Oh no, potatoes. They look like potatoes too," Josh complained. Surprised looks greeted him. Before Ken could apologize, he said quickly, "I'm joking. My folks have a potato farm in rural Idaho. I had to help them with the farm, and dad always wanted me to take over the farm. I hated potato farming, so I ran away and joined the spacers. So it's kind of a joke with me. I can't seem to escape them wherever I go. Don't get me wrong, I like to eat them, just not grow them." Ken smiled.

The dinner went well for the newcomers. Over tea afterwards, Ken said, "Get some sleep tonight. Tomorrow, I want you both to get some of our therapy we've developed to erase the aftereffects of trauma. Trust me, you will feel tons better afterwards. Once that's handled, what say I take you topside so you can see our world?"

"I'd like that — to see where we really are at," Meg replied. "Will everyone be staring at my arm? I can't even dress myself now."

"We'll figure something out, don't worry Meg," Crystal suggested, sending her a calming energy flow. She knew Meg would need therapy very soon before the magnitude of her loss hit her hard. The woman was still running on adrenaline for the most part.

After getting them settled for the night, the dozen met to discuss how to proceed. Jamie and Luisa volunteered to start delivering their therapy sessions in the morning. "Look, while the mermaids are the best therapy givers, we don't want these outsiders knowing about them," Jamie stated. "Besides, their physical forms would probably freak out those two. Luisa and I will just have to handle them as best we can. Rafaela and Andres are still with Inez, interfacing with Isabella and the governor and his wife. We don't dare pull them back here now. Sally and Annie have their hands full with Diamante, Domenica, Annetta, and Bianca. We are running out of options. Ken, you and Bart deal with the governor. He's sure to be in a pickle over the refinery attack." Ken agreed.

Crystal then asked what many were wondering, "What about Damiano and those six women in his harem? Are we just going to let them run off? While I don't care about him, those poor six women don't deserve what is very likely going to happen to them."

"Well, there wasn't any time to deal with them," Ken justified. He sighed, "I know dear. I promise you when the dust settles down, I'll see what can be done for them. Say, you don't think this Damiano fellow can regrow lost limbs do you?" That was a sobering thought.

Sobering thoughts were just what was plaguing Governor Konrad Burkhardt. For over a month now, he had been more or less watching the slow advance of the small army. His geologist had pointed them out on some of his geo-sat images. Konrad had asked Inez, Andres, and Rafaela about these men and their significance. Andres had been the most forthcoming. He had said they were a rogue band of Easterlings men, bent on a pillaging spree and they would be handled by some of the Midlands rulers in the late spring. Nothing to worry about.

Still, he did worry. What if this was a full-fledged rebellion happening on his watch? Ought he do something about it? Yet, his hands were tied by the closed world status. He'd mentioned to Andres, "If this wasn't a closed world, I could send in my troops and end this barbarian's pillaging spree in minutes." He was somewhat frustrated.

His frustration crescendoed when he received an emergency message from his boss, Sector ID Minister Emeryk.

"Burkhardt! The Federation has just executed a commando raid on our moon's fuel refinery!"

"Oh god! That's terrible! How bad is it?" Konrad relied, adrenaline began spurting through is body, as if he could do anything about the moon.

"We've limited the damage to one section. Killed three of the commandos, wounded another," Emeryk continued. Konrad wanted to say, "How could you let this happen? You were supposed to be protecting them." He thought better of it. Emeryk continued, "They came in a small transport style ship. My battle cruiser has shot it down in flames. It has crashed out in the middle of what is called the Midlands. Konrad, I am ordering you to send out a search party. Recover that ship and capture any who might have survive the crash. I want to interrogate them," he said snidely. "I don't care about protocols. You retrieve that ship and any survivors. Immediately." He also realized that such a daylight operation would be in violation of their lease agreement. His voice softened a little. "Look at it this way, governor, we cannot allow alien technology to fall into these primitive's hands. Let that be your justification. Get to that site immediately. As far as we can tell here, the area is largely uninhabited."

"Yes sir. I'm on it. Your coordinates are coming in now. I'll get back to you soon," Konrad replied. His geologist was already bringing up the coordinates on his geo-sat imaging machine.

"Boss, it is right in the middle of where that primitive army we're following is at. No, wait! Where the devil has the army gone? I do see smoke curls."

"Go back and check all the images, say for the last twenty-four hours. I'm off to arrange troops to go there immediately," Konrad ordered and left.

An hour later, Konrad led a force of twenty of his security men, all wearing their battle armor and fully armed. Three transports slowly settled down on the grasslands not far from the explosion site. Over the comm channel, the geologist reported, "Boss. It crashed just in front of that army we were watching. On this image, I can see what looks like the men on horseback riding up to the transport ship. At least it looks like that. Then it gets all weird."

"We've got a large crater here and fragments of the ship. What do you mean weird?" Konrad asked.

"Well, you will have to see it for yourself, sir. The ground opened up into some giant fissures. I think the army fell into them. Then the ship exploded, but I can see a carriage, I think, going southeast just out of range of the explosion. Weird. I don't think you will find any survivors."

"Okay, have those images ready for me to look at when I get back," Konrad ordered. "Captain, fan out. Look for ground fissures as well as survivors, but I don't think we're going to find anyone alive, unless they escaped in a carriage. Send a transport ship off to the southeast. Find me that carriage and bring it and everyone onboard back to our base for questioning. They were fairly close to the transport ship just before it blew up. There might be a chance survivors commandeered that primitive carriage to make their escape in; do it now. The rest of you, collect any and all debris."

Some twenty men fanned out and began collecting up bits here and there around the fifty-foot crater. "Melted d-gun, boss," one called out, picking up what remained of a Federation gun. Konrad relaxed; at least he would have something to show Emeryk. An hour later, the two transports lifted off, heading back to their base on Plateau Grado.

Once there, Konrad headed straight for his office. "Okay, show me those images," he barked. His geologist ran the sequence he'd prepared, knowing these would soon be sent to his old boss, Emeryk. The images had his name on them. He was counting upon earning a bit more goodwill from Emeryk as a result. Konrad watched the sequence of still images ten times in a row before commenting.

"How is this possible? Did the crashing of the transport ship unsettle the ground there? Do we know of any ground fissures in that area?"

"No geological features there boss; it is all rich sedimentary soil. Good farmland for this world. I've no explanation," he replied. He had seen something similar to this, but that had been many, many years ago, but just now he thought better of telling Konrad about that strange event.

Where had he filed all those images, he wondered. Ought I say something to Burkhardt about that? Not until I find them, he decided.

"Transport Three is landing now. Captain Rolf reports he has your missing carriage, but no aliens are on board. They are being taken to the infirmary now." Konrad acknowledged him and headed down to the infirmary.

He received the shock of his life upon entering the sterile medical lab. Likewise, his staff there was in quite a shock themselves. He saw six mutilated women. All had five-inch lip plates, enormously long earrings, pipe corsets, and fancy gowns. Two who were minus their lower arms also wore toe shoes. Two were mermaids, whose unique bodies he had never seen before. Two had no lower arms and no lower legs! He was shocked. One poorly dressed old woman hovered over the six women. The resident doctor, who he had yet to remember his name, was busy with a similarly mutilated man, working four simultaneously operating medical machines, one on each of his limbs.

A nurse explained, "The man has suffered four or more d-gun hits. Lost parts of each limb. These six seem healthy. Their injuries must have occurred a long time ago. We cannot understand them and have sent for a ULAT box so we can question them."

Konrad decided to try his hand. He needed answers fast. He said hello to one of the armless women, trying the Midlands dialect first, then Westerlings. When he used his crude Easterlings dialect, she responded. "Oh. Yes, I understand you now. Please, save him. He is our husband. She is Antonia, his Number One wife. I am his Number Two wife. They are Three and Four, but those two lost their husband, so they will be Number Five and Six. Please, save him, please. Now he will be as sexy as we all are."

Konrad shook his head in disbelief. "Okay, don't worry, he will live and be just fine. Who is she?" he pointed to the old woman, hovering over the others like a mother hen.

"She is Agata, our caretaker. I am Celia."

Konrad decided to try talking to her. She was obviously the carriage driver and had seen what had happened. "Agata is it? You were driving the carriage. Tell me what happened? What did you see when you came up to that metal thing on the ground?" He didn't dare call it a spaceship. The poor woman probably had never seen one before.

"Fire in the sky. Boom. Came down. The earth opened up and swallowed everyone and then closed. I took the wives to where their husbands had been — up by the sky thing. Lord Damiano was still there — on the ground — as he is now — wounded. A man walked up and carried him into the carriage. He told me to get away as fast as I could. I turned the carriage around and did so. Huge explosion. I looked back and saw no one there anymore. Kind man gone. Sky thing gone too."

Konrad visibly relaxed. Obviously, the survivors were disintegrated in the blast. Certainly, they were not onboard the carriage. "So how is he doing, doctor?"

"I've just finished up. See for yourself. I've taken the liberty of shaping what remains of his upper arms for prosthetics — a nice conical shape — not that we can give him any though. Closed world and all that. His legs were in bad shape. I had to amputate more of them. Took them both off around his knees. I am going to keep him sedated overnight. Tomorrow, we'll see. What the devil are we going to do with these mutilated women, boss?"

"I don't know. Put them up in some quarters for the night. Assign some women to help them. I'll try to work this out now." Konrad pivoted and headed for his office, mentally outlining he report to the ID Minister.

A few minutes later, he called in. "Okay. Mission accomplished. No survivors. Sending you a series of geo-sat images that my geologist prepared. You can see for yourself what happened on the ground. Our best guess is that the ship crashed in front of a small army. The impact of the crash opened up some ground fissures that swallowed up a couple thousand army men, though it looks like those in the rear managed to escape. A horse drawn carriage you'll be able to see clearly in the images, came on up to the crash site. It carried the harem wives of the leaders of that band. According to the old woman who was driving them, a man came out of the rubble, carrying the badly wounded body of these women's husband. After putting him in the carriage, he told the old woman to leave as fast as she could. That was wise of him. The carriage barely got away before the remains of the transport exploded. The woman turned around and saw the kind man had vanished. We have recovered all the bits of the ship that remains. I am having them crated up and will send them up to you on a shuttle later on. I have the carriage and its passengers in the medical lab. The doctor has performed surgery on the wounded man. They are all from the Easterlings. I am sorry there are no survivors."

"Damn. I was so hoping to interrogate them. Okay, I will review the images. Well done, Burkhardt," Emeryk said halfway kindly.

"So what do I do with the Easterlings?" Konrad asked.

"Whatever you want to do with them. That's all. I will get back to you if I need anything else. Good job. Good thinking on retrieving that carriage." Emeryk broke the connection.

It was evening. Konrad looked out of his window and saw the two moons rising, the bright and white Echador and the pale blue Palidez. Somewhere up there on Palidez, men were working overtime, he mused. Then, his thoughts returned to the shocking condition of the six women and the man. He decided to discuss this with Andres in the morning. As he joined Nadja in their quarters, he related the excitement of the day. She was impressed with the way he handled it and was highly interested in meeting these women for herself. Real Easterlings, she thought.

His breakfast was interrupted by an emergency call from the medical lab. "Boss, you had better come quickly. We've a mess on our hands. Bring Nadja; she can speak to these grief-stricken women too."

Konrad and Nadja headed down to the medical lab on the second floor. Nothing could have prepared them for the grief-filled chaos of the lab and its side rooms in which the six women and man had been housed for the night. Neither could explain the total change in the women's behavior from the day before. Gone was their polite, calm demeanor. No longer did they believe they were the sexiest women in the world. In fact, they no longer even believed Damiano and Fausto had been their husbands!

Rather, they were shrieking, wailing, sobbing, and crying. "I am totally helpless! I can't do anything at all! Why did they do this to me? I wish I were dead!" screamed Antonia as loudly as she could, since that was about all she thought she could now do. In the next room, Daniela was shrieking nearly as loudly, pausing only to sob uncontrollably for a brief moment before launching into another shrieking fit. Nearby, Celia and Gabriella were screaming nearly as wildly. The two mermaids merely sat and cried and cried.

In his room, Damiano was screaming as well, begging anyone who entered his room to kill him. "I can't live like this!" All were yelling, crying, screaming, and waving what little appendages they still had around wildly. None of the nurses could do anything to calm them down, let alone inject them with a strong sedative.

In contrast, the old woman was ranting and raving about having broken their programming, whatever that was. Konrad involuntarily put his hands over his ears, trying to dampen the noise. "Do something!" Nadja yelled. "These poor women!"

The doctor looked at Konrad, satisfied his boss was aware of the situation. He then went from patient to patient, firing a tranquilizer gun into each. The darts contained a powerful sedative. Before long, the chaotic scene quieted down, but not before Konrad heard the man screaming for someone to kill him right now.

"There. Now boss, what do you want us to do with them?" the doctor asked. "Such reactions are commonplace with people who lose limbs, especially this many of them. Too bad our policies do not permit us to intervene on their behalf." Konrad sensed the doctor was subtlety testing him.

"Quite true. I will make some arrangements now. If you will excuse me," he said. "Nadja, come with me." Once into the elevators, he said, "We're going to find Andres and ask him what he thinks we should do with them. They are natives of Tierra and as such; we dare not intervene, even though my heart goes out to those poor women. What kind of a mad beast would do this to such pretty women?"

"A sadist perhaps. Yes, maybe we can ask Andres if his therapy would be of some benefit for them," she replied, still shocked by what she'd just seen.

An hour later, Konrad and Nadja met with Andres, Rafaela, and Inez in the fifth floor office of Elegant Fashions Inc. "It is just horrible, Andres. You cannot imagine how these women are. I've never seen anything like it. Beyond all belief how these women have been chopped up. Two don't even have any arms or legs!" he exclaimed.

Nadja added her exclamations to the mix, "Dear that's not entirely true. They still have their upper arms and upper legs. But my god, two of them don't have any arms at all and two also have only one very strange leg. It's the worst sight that I have ever seen!" Already, Andres had lightly touched their minds and seen the images of the six women and Damiano.

Konrad calmed down a little. "It began yesterday. You know we were watching that small army of yours when it happened." He outlined the Federation's commando attack on their moon base, though he didn't mention the fuel refinery there. Konrad related all he had seen and done, including retrieving their carriage in hopes of finding the surviving commandos. "Andres, while our hearts go out to these pitiful women, the closed world status has my hands tied. Other than the emergency surgery on the man, there is nothing more I can do for them. I have to release them, but in all humanity, I just can't turn them loose. Andres, they are your people, well Easterlings anyway, Tierra's people. Is there any chance at all I could hand them over to you? I can slip you some funds on the side to help defray getting these women back to their homes, wherever they are," he offered sympathetically.

"Certainly, governor. As you say, they are our people. Bring them here to Elegant Fashions Inc, and we will see they are well cared for," Andres replied solemnly.

"Thank you, thank you. I owe you a very big favor, Andres. I won't ever forget your generosity and kindness. If you need something, don't hesitate to ask Nadja or me. We can never repay all of your incredible hospitality and kindness you three have shown us. Certainly, this world is anything but a primitive one. In some ways, you display more humanity than many Imperium worlds with all their vast technology," Konrad admitted. He knew it sounded strange to say this, but at the moment, he knew it to be quite true.

"Thanks, Konrad. We will do our best. Probably it is wise to bring them here while they are sedated," he suggested.

"I'll come with them. I can help you with the six women. Lord knows they are so helpless," Nadja volunteered. "There's nothing in the policies that prohibit me from helping them, is there, Konrad?"

"Not at all. We can always help. I will leave you then and see to the arrangements for their transport here," he replied and left.

"We'd best make some rooms ready," Inez suggested. She, Nadja, and Isabella headed off to fix up some temporary beds. Andres focused and made mental contact with Ken, filling him in on the latest developments and asking him what he should do with them, especially Damiano.

Ken sent, *What you don't handle today always comes back to haunt you tomorrow. Okay, Andres. After you get them stabilized, we'll bring the women here. As far as Damiano goes, give that old woman some funds and the carriage. Let her take care of Damiano there in Exchange City. I know, get her some small home where she can care for him. He needs to experience what he has done to thousands of men.*

An hour later, several Rigel-3 men carried the dozing women and Damiano into the store and up to the fifth floor. Nadja and Inez directed them to the makeshift beds. Another man escorted the old woman, who looked totally confused. She was completely silent though. One man stated their carriage was in the underground parking deck. After they left, Andres and Isabella headed down there to see what they were carrying. Both were surprised to discover the six women's significant dowries along with some gold and gems that Damiano had kept for his own use. The six pouches looked like those Durante had prepared for the women that Tom had rescued months ago.

"She'll get robbed of this carriage in no time here in Exchange City," Andres pointed out. "I know, we will sell it and get her a simple wagon. Why don't you carry their pouches and many bags of clothing up to their rooms while I see to the other details?" Andres suggested.

Later on, he and Inez headed off to find a suitable, small home. When they returned, the women had wakened and were gradually becoming too much to handle. Andres, Isabella, Inez, and Rafaela used their *mentales* gifts and sent the six calming emotions, which kept them from at least screaming wildly once more.

"Ladies," Andres began, "in a few minutes, we will be taking you to a place of safety where you can get the help that you need. Just relax. Things will get better for all of you soon." One by one, Bart teleported them from their beds to the Underground platform, where many kind hands were waiting them. He teleported their many things last.

With the women gone, he turned his attention to the old woman. "Agata, for your kind dedication to these women, I have bought you a home here in this town and a wagon for your needs. Here is a money pouch that will keep you in good shape for quite some time. All I ask of you in return is to care for your lord. Under no circumstances is he to be permitted to die like he wants to. Will you do this?"

"Money? A home of my own? I've never had that. Yes, yes, I will look after him. His wives have disowned him now. He has no one and I have no one. So I will do this thing. Men often lose limbs in battle. He must learn to cope with it as did my late husband. He lost his legs, you know." She opened up and chatted away for some time, before Andres suggested they go see her new home. Damiano was still unconscious, so he carried him down to the new wagon. Inez followed with the old woman's money pouch. An hour later, they had her settled in, food supplies in stock, and Damiano resting in a bed in a side room. Agata still had not stopped chatting and continued to talk to herself when the two left her.

"Poetic justice," Inez commented as she and Andres walked slowly back to her store.

"Right. One day, I will drop by and see how he is doing.

Maybe he will learn something. Then again, maybe not. At least the days of his rampaging destruction of Tierra are over," Andres replied.

Meanwhile, Konrad again got a video link to his boss, the Sector ID Minister. "Governor, I had my technicians go over those images you sent us and enhance them, as well as enlarge sections. What they've found is quite disturbing. You should have them now; put them up on your screen." Konrad did as asked. "Okay. Here is a shot taken just after the Federation transport ship crashed. Look behind it. There. Can you see it? There is a man there for sure, possibly two men. Then, here is the next shot. See, that same man is now in front of the ship. There is the second man, plus there are three distinct bodies lying around him. Now in the next shot, look closely. See, one of the two who came up to the ship and two of the bodies are definitely missing. The other man and the wounded man are still there. Here's the carriage arriving. Here's that man putting your injured local into the carriage. Now look closely. The man is gone, but the ship is still there. Now in this one, the ship is definitely exploding."

"What? Are you saying that two other people came up to the ship and took away the two dead bodies and then vanished themselves? How is this possible?" Konrad asked, baffled by what he was seeing.

"It could well be one of their towers has interfered. Have you had time to study that listing of their *mentales* gifts? Teleportation is one of them. I want you to go to the Imperial Tower at the southeast corner of the base and have them send a message to all the towers. Find out if they teleported the two commandos and if so, order them to turn them over to us. Of course, these images are not conclusive. The bodies could well be dead. It is possible the local two men dragged the dead bodies clear of the wreckage, but were caught in the explosion. That would also explain it. Nevertheless, I want you to check on it immediately."

"Yes, sir, I'll see to it at once," Konrad replied. "I've given that wounded local Easterlings man over to the locals here in Exchange City, as well as the women with him. They knew nothing about the commandos. The old woman didn't see the second man or the two bodies, but then she isn't the brightest of observers."

After the connection was broken, Konrad headed down to grab his electric car again. A few minutes later, he pulled into the Imperial Castle. A guard came out to meet him. "I need to send a message to all of your towers," Konrad spoke as clearly as he could in the Midlands dialect. He was led to the circle's leader, Capo Leonard. Konrad carefully worded his request. The tall, thin man nodded and agreed to send it. With the man's assurances he would report the results back to him later today, Konrad returned to his building and office. His mind was mulling over the possibilities.

Could some of these gifted people have actually rescued the two commandos? If so, then why? How could they possibly have reacted as fast as they apparently had? Even he had not known of the crash landing until hours after it happened. If they had reacted this quickly, then they were leagues ahead of his own people! How could a feudal-like culture possibly be ahead of his own highly technological society? It didn't make any sense at all. Perhaps the two men just happened to be at the right spot at the right time. Serendipity would be a far better explanation and he settled on that.

Bart called out, "Hey Ken. Troubles. They are on to what you did yesterday." Ken came running up.

"Crap. How did they figure this out?" Ken grumbled. "I've got so darn many things going on at one time, it's making me dizzy."

"Probably they enhanced the geo-sat images. I intercepted some coming from a battle cruiser to the spaceport about an hour ago. They are on that monitor over there. You and Crystal are visible in a few frames. Now the Imperial Circle is relaying the governor's message to all the towers," Bart replied.

"What is he saying to them?" Ken asked.

"He wants to know if they know anything about two men who teleported two others away from the ship that crash landed in front of Damiano's army. Of course none do. Still, the Imperium is definitely after our two guests," Bart answered. Ken left to discuss this with the others, warning them. Venerada Maricela contacted Ken, relaying the message from the governor. As always, she covered for him.

An hour later, a dispatch written in Imperium Standard was delivered to Konrad. It was from Capo Leonard. It read: All towers contacted. None has any idea of what you are talking about. They know nothing of a crashed spaceship. They are asking if that crash caused the destruction of the invading barbarian army. If so, advise me.

Konrad mulled over the message. In his mind, this made perfect sense. How could these people, no matter their strange powers, know about a crashing spaceship and get there within mere minutes to rescue the two commandos? Their reply satisfied him completely. He relayed it to his boss. Emeryk didn't like the response though.

"I tell you these people cannot be trusted. They know more than they are saying. Raise your base security level to the highest level. Expect commando raids on your base," Emeryk ordered. Konrad had no choice but to follow that order, as unlikely as it seemed to him.

Ken sent telepathic messages to both Harry and Sally who were giving therapy sessions to Josh and Meg. He wanted them not to allow the two to see these six new arrivals. He and Crystal needed time to deal with them.

Already they were being medically handled by Jake and Misty. The original four women that Tom had rescued from Po were brought back from where they were currently staying along with the two mermaids from the Easterlings. Ken joined Crystal, Jake, and Misty to see how things were fairing. He was relieved to see the two mermaids had already gotten their lips healed and the pipe corsets removed. He was in time to see them hopping after their two mermaid escorts from Madiera. They had believed them — that in Madiera there were many magical devices which would let them live almost independently. As Ken watched the four hopping down the long underground tunnel, he smiled. They would get great care and in time be able to live reasonable lives.

He moved up to the side of his wife and listened in as Annetta and Bianca were telling Gabriella and Celia about their new lives and how they were learning to used their feet as hands. "Yes, really, Celia, I am able to feed myself now. You've just got to come and stay with us, please. You won't regret it." Convinced at last, the two agreed to have their lips and feet healed and their pipe corsets removed. While that was occurring, Crystal headed off to find some heels that would fit them.

Antonia and Daniela were still caught up in the sheer magnitude of their physical condition and the attendant grief. "But how, Domenica? We are completely and totally helpless now. We can't do anything at all, nothing. We can't live like this? How could we ever think we were the sexiest women in the world? I wish we had never seen you two. Then, we wouldn't be in this awful mess." She began sobbing again.

"Please let us heal your lips," Misty pleaded with her.

"We are not noblewomen, even if we have them. Get rid of them and everything," Antonia wailed. "While you're at it, please put me out of my misery. I can't live like this. I'm begging you." Misty ignored her pleadings and deftly proceeded to heal the two women.

Meanwhile, Annetta and Bianca led Gabriella and Celia off down the tunnels, their heels clicking in unison. Venerada Maricela took the two, promising them they'd be well trained by her many katalyein women. Ken promised her someone would come by soon to deliver the needed therapy to the two new women.

Now they had to handle the two remaining women. It wasn't going to be easy. At the moment, Diamante and Domenica were staying with Annie and Sam. While their therapy was finished and they were cheerful and full of life, they couldn't do much for themselves except a little walking. Annie had yet to convince either to cut their long hair. Easterlings men and women never, ever cut their hair. That was a taboo going back centuries — something about losing their life energy. At least, the two allowed Annie to pin their thick brown hair up, instead of having two feet of it dragging the floor behind them as they waddled along awkwardly on their stumps.

At last, Misty and Janice decided the only thing to do

was to get these two women into a therapy session pronto. Over their protests and sobbing, they helped the two women waddle along after Domenica and Diamante. "Look, Daniela, we can at least walk," Diamante tried to be positive for the two following them.

"Take us to a cliff so we can fall over," Antonia begged between sobs.

Crystal, Ken, Jake, and Tom watched them go and silence fell finally in their small medical room. "We are stretched pretty thin," Crystal whispered, afraid to break the welcome silence. "Hope nothing else happens for a while."

"Still, Ken, what are we going to do with those four? Diamante and Domenica have been waiting for quite a few weeks now," Tom asked.

Ken finally told them his long range plans for the four, "If I can get Rafaela back here, I am going to have her work on feeding them the proper dose of psi-crystal dust and see if they can't get the *mentales* gifts. Mom and Rafaela were able to channel the mermaids' gifts into telekinesis. We need to do the same with those four at the very least."

"So we need to get Rafaela back here in a week or so," Crystal said determinedly.

"True, but where are we going to put the two aliens when they finish their therapy?" Tom asked. "We can't just leave them down here. It would be stupid of us to just move them into a house in Brom. Do you suppose you could convince Maricela to take them in too? Or would that jeopardize her?"

"I just don't know right now, Tom. Let's think about it some. At least they like wearing our fancy clothes," Ken answered.

"While you are thinking about things, what about Nadja's request to come here and study her 'telepathic society' and languages? Also, Konrad wanted to come and see a tower and castle," Crystal reminded him. "If they find out Rafaela is returning, you can bet Nadja is going to plead to come with her."

"True. True. How many more problems are coming our way?" Ken lamented. "Oh, it's mom!"

Ken, come and see me right now, please, Benjamina sent.

"Got to run. Keep me posted. Crystal, you are in charge for a while." Ken dashed off down the corridors heading to his mother's large suite of underground rooms.

"Good. Glad to see that you haven't forgotten how to run," she teased her out of breath son. "I have been following the events. Rather like a blizzard, but you've been up to the task."

"Thanks for the vote of confidence. I've got my plate overflowing at the moment."

"Ken, if I am not mistaken, far more is coming, and the impact could well be quite far reaching. I want you to go visit Rafaela and Andres. Have them arrange a meeting with this Konrad and Nadja. I have some very specific questions I want you to ask them. Yes, monitor their minds as you ask them. You must know if they are being truthful or not. Make it soon, son. Time is running out for us all on Tierra. And also bring Isabella to see me, please."

"Mom, what's going to happen?" Ken pleaded. *What the hell have I missed?* He thought frantically, but could come up with nothing specific.

"Many things, my young son. Tell me, what have you done with the two half-armed women that you rescued?" Benjamina said softly.

"I've got them with the two who lost all of their arms. They are staying under the watchful eyes of Venerada Maricela. Why?"

"You didn't recognize them, did you? Well, I suppose not. You didn't know them before. Bring them to me in the morning. I have cleared my schedule and will give them their therapy sessions myself, both at the same time," Benjamina replied.

"Mom! I've seen you do some pretty remarkable things, but two at once? Why? Who are they? What have I missed? They are just two young Easterlings women. Pretty, yes, but pretty out of it right now. I can understand that. The grief they must be feeling is pretty overwhelming," Ken asked somewhat annoyed. Not so much with his mother. He was used to her semi-cryptic utterances, especially these past ten years. No, he had failed to spot something. This was her subtle way of reminding him that he had failed to observe properly.

"One is your grandmother, my mother, and the other, her wife, Tim's mother. Jan and Amy. That's who they are."

"What! Empress Amy Blackwater? Empress Jan Bellweather?" he exclaimed, his eyes popping open.

"Yes, I am afraid what they had resisted for so long, they managed to pull in on themselves this lifetime. I wish I had invented my therapy sooner, but that can't be helped. Send Rafaela to me too when she gets back. Now write these questions down son and don't deviate from them when you are asking Konrad." She dictated her questions.

Later, Ken told the other eleven what he'd learned. "Our grandmothers?" many exclaimed. "Emperor Amy and Empress Jan?" Luisa exclaimed.

"None other. Mom said they managed to pull in the same aberrations they had lived with for so long and hated," Ken answered. He told them the rest of his conversation.

"We'd better go see Rafaela tomorrow, dear," Crystal suggested.

Chapter 19 The Measure of the Man

"I know, your mom wants me back there," Rafaela answered Ken, who had just told her about Benjamina's request. He and Crystal had teleported to Exchange City and were having tea with Inez, Andres, Isabella, and Rafaela.

"Oh yes, Isabella, mom also would like you to come and meet her. I have no idea why, just that she does," Ken said.

"She's the one who invented the mental therapy, right?" she asked. Ken nodded. "Sure, I would really like to meet this woman. I've been out there among the stars amid almost unimaginable technology and wealth, but none has any such thing to help people, not really. Sure, when?"

"Today, I suppose, though probably after supper. She's doing some therapies right now."

Inez spoke up, "Here come Nadja and Konrad." They saw the image of the two entering her elevator. She added, "Spy cameras. Useful little things. I hate surprises." Everyone chuckled.

Shortly, Rafaela did the introductions. "This is Ken and Crystal Blackwater from Brom. They are here in response to your request, Nadja, to spend some time studying our language and our telepathic society, as you put it."

"Perfect. I do hope this can be arranged. I know it's a closed world, but we should not let that stop us from learning your languages to the best we can," Nadja replied.

Following the list of questions, Ken asked, "Governor Konrad, what do you feel is the basis of personal relationships between your people and us?"

Konrad sensed he was being tested by this young man, who sounded quite serious. "That is an easy question. It is something Nadja and I worked out years ago. It forms the basis of our entire modus operandi. It is understanding. You see, first you have to find something you like about the other person. In our case, we usually adopt the local dress and physical appearances. That shows we like the others, and, by appearing as they do, we share a reality. Then, we can begin to communicate, once Nadja here has helped me master their language. Only through communication can we bring about a mutual understanding between each of us." There, he thought, that about sums it up. *I wonder why he asked that question?*

"Very good observations. There is a lot of truth in that for sure," Ken replied, sensing no deviation between what he said and what he was thinking. "Next question. If a friend shared with you something he wanted to be kept secret from everyone else and so asked you, under what circumstances would you divulge that secret to others? Assume the secret is not a harmful one or a destructive one," Ken added, almost forgetting that part.

"Hum, you say the secret is not harmful or destructive? Do you mean that if I learned something your people wanted to keep from, shall we say, the Imperium, would I keep that secret? Well, of course I would keep it, just as long as that secret did not harm the Imperium or others. Mr. Blackwater, if one blabs another's secret, he is betraying his friend and, that is, by definition, treason. A betrayal after someone trusts you. Nasty business. Always ends in disaster and loss of friends, for sure."

"Nadja, do you agree with him?" Ken asked.

"Of course. In my studies of other people's languages, I must ask very intimate things of them. Most cultures keep their sexual lives to themselves. If I don't win their confidence and get them to discuss those areas, I'll never uncover their language for such things. If I were to betray what they tell me, I'd never be able to talk with them again. They would not have me around. Konrad's right on this one. Now if that secret is a harmful one, like the person shares with me he is about to blow up our spaceport, then I am obligated to relay that secret."

"Of course. Any person would and should, in that case," Ken replied. Once more, he detected no deviance between what they were thinking and saying. "Last question, governor, what is it you and the Imperium really want from us, the people of Tierra, right now? You are here with a purpose. Can you tell me that purpose?"

Konrad flushed. *Damn, this guy hits the nail on the*

head. He is far more intelligent than I ever assumed! Well, it is no big secret what I came here to do, and, hell, I only have a month in which to achieve it. "Son, I came here in part because Sector ID Minister Emeryk is out there in space fighting a war and has no time to govern this planet. However, he gave me a very explicit assignment. I am to try to convince your people to send someone off to be your senator and representative in the Imperial Senate. While the senator would have no voting rights, he can speak on behalf of your world on any issue before this, our main legislative body. Honestly, son, it is in the best interests of your world to finally have a representative to the Senate." Only later on did he remember his own personal reasons for so wanting to come to Ashford-5.

"Thank you for telling me that. Okay then. First, let me say you are both welcome to come and spend time in Brom. Venerada Maricela Wait of Brom Tower will be your host as well as Lord Emilio Bolivar, who is the ruler of the kingdom of Brom. We here are all very close friends and aides, you might say, to both of them. However, since your visits will be in direct violation of the lease agreement, we must keep this between us. The other lords and towers may well be very angry with us and with you for this overt breaking of the lease. However, as you probably know, if you have studied your predecessors, they openly violated this agreement and had extensive relations with Valen Tower and Lord Valen in the Westerlings. So there is a precedent here for such close relations, but let's not broadcast this to the world, please."

"This is indeed excellent news! You have our word. We will keep this between us. How soon can we make visits? I hate to admit this, but I would like to present this senator thing to the assembled lords at their next meeting, which as I understand it, is on the first of July, less than a month away," Konrad asked, growing rather excited. *I finally have my big break!*

"Today, if you like," Ken replied. "The tower will provide transportation from here to Brom and back again. That way, no one will see your shuttles flying back and forth."

"But how can you do this? Isn't Brom in the far north?" Konrad asked.

"Teleportation."

"Oh!" Konrad's eyes opened wide.

"Excuse me, but will I be allowed to bring along my many field recording devices? They are so essential for my work, but I have to take these prosthetic hands off in order to use them. Isabella can vouch for that. I've broken too many monitors. No sense of touch any longer. She can tell you they are used to record my notes, do comparisons, and record speech patterns and such. Perfectly harmless," Nadja asked, almost pleadingly, knowing taking alien technology out into the field was in direct violation of the lease.

"Of course you may. There is no electricity there," Ken replied.

"No problem. I expected that; they are battery powered. Oh, I'm sorry. You probably don't know what I mean," she apologized.

"Sure I know all about batteries and solar cells," Ken admitted, then wished he'd kept his mouth shut.

Both her eyebrows and Konrad's rose. "Thank you. If Isabella can help me, I can be ready to go in an hour. How long can I stay?"

"As long as you desire, Nadja," Ken answered.

"Oh! Konrad, dear, I ought to plan to stay quite a while. I will be back for the lord's council meeting of course. I can keep you up to date on the language issues," Nadja declared.

"Perfect. I can spend a day or so, but I do need to be here some of the time, dear. I'll get my geologist to fill in for me while I am gone," Konrad decided.

"I'll come help you pack, Nadja," Isabella said. Cheerfully, the three headed for the elevator. Both finally got the very "break" they had so greatly desired!

Meanwhile, Venerada Maricela personally brought Gabriella and Celia to Benjamina's suite. Out of deference to the two women, who now had no choice but to wear the six-inch heels, she too wore hers. As a katalyein, she had no trace of arms, which the two women did note, believing she was even worse off than they were. Maricela used that to her advantage with the women, getting them to follow her without her having to resort to using her mental powers to force them to come with her. Of course, she hated having to go down the stone stairs into the basement in her heels. It was challenging and hard on her knees. The two found themselves back in the tunnels they had walked yesterday.

"Here they are, right on time. This is Gabriella and this is Celia," Maricela nodded towards each with her head. "Ladies, this is Benjamina Blackwater. I will leave you in her able care. Call me if you need anything, Benjamina."

"Thanks. I will. It is good to meet you at last. You are both very lovely young women. Please, have a seat. I hope you find my chairs comfortable," she began.

The two tossed their long brown hair off to one side and sat down. The chairs were plush and very comfortable. "So why are we here?" asked Gabriella.

"I want you to close your eyes. Good. Now let's see if you can recall when you had your arms removed, lips, waist, and feet done," Benjamina said in a normal conversational tone, but with full intention. The session began. An hour later, their screams of re-experienced pain from the massive operations echoed in the stone chambers. An hour later, that trauma had fully alleviated, but they were not cheerful. Benjamina asked them for something both similar and earlier.

As the noon hour approached, both women were laughing enthusiastically. "My god, Amy, we ended up just like we were because we were both resisting that so damn hard! We are idiots. Sorry, Gabriella, I mean."

"Jan, I remember everything! All of it. Oh shit, Jan! We don't have any of our *mentales* powers this time. We are doomed for sure now. We had best learn to use our feet like Maricela says. Wait! Benjamina? I feel I know you somehow."

The old woman smiled, "You should. I am your son, only I had a run in with the Goddess Lysandra, and I am now Benjamina. You both have quite a few grandchildren running the operation. Tim, however, is not doing so well. We don't expect him to be with us much longer, Jan, er Celia. Would you like to see him?"

"Yes, yes of course. Can't you use the rejuvenation machines we left here on him and yourself?" Jan or Celia rather asked.

"We could, but he and I figure we've lived long enough. It is time the kids take over," she explained, hoping they would understand. Not everyone wanted to live forever in the same body.

"I can see we have a whole lot of catching up to do, Amy, er Gabriella," Celia exclaimed. "Come on; let's go see Tim, and then let's get something to eat. I'm starving."

Benjamina led them to the next suite, where Petrona and Elana sat beside Tim's sick bed. They rose as the three entered. Quietly, they stepped outside, joining Benjamina, allowing Amy and Jan some very private time with Jan's son, Tim. When they finally rejoined the three, their eyes were red, and they were using their short arms to wipe their tears. Celia said, "Petrona, thank you for taking such good care of my Tim. He thinks the world of you."

Petrona gave her a warm hug. She whispered, "Tim wants me to fill you in on all that he's done, but that's years of stuff. Get yourselves adjusted first; there's plenty of time."

As the three walked back to Benjamina's room, she said, "The next step is to get you your *mentales* powers back."

"That's not possible. We don't have any trace of them this time," Gabriella explained.

"I know how everyone got them in the first place. We've already given hundreds their *mentales* gifts. I'm too old to deal with the details. Rafaela will be back soon and she will do it for me. Hang in there for a few more weeks, and you'll have *mentales* powers again, though I don't know what form they'll take this time. Can't predict that so well yet. We need further studies. It appears that to some extent, the gifts one gets can be learned and controlled. Rafaela will tell you more; she's the expert. Ah, here comes Maricela. It is done, Maricela, this is Amy and this is Jan. They have fully recovered their memories. It would be prudent to bring them up on history since the days of their stint as Emperor and Empress. I must sleep now. I'm quite exhausted myself." Maricela led the two very excited women back through the tunnels, up the stairs, and into the tower complex.

After dropping off the two women, she headed off to the tower proper to greet the new arrivals. Lord Emilio was already there waiting for her. "Do you think this is wise? Hosting the new governor and his wife?" he asked.

"I trust Ken and Crystal. This is Benjamina's doing. We are to swear them to secrecy about everything they see here. The Underground is off limits, naturally. As long as we don't reveal anything they could see as threatening their spaceport, they ought to keep our secrets. It is long past time we built up some trust between our worlds, My Lord."

"I couldn't agree more with you. However, I'm still in complete mystery on how Damiano and his army were destroyed. Everyone's taking about it, you know. It's sure to be a hot topic at the lord's council in a few weeks," Emilio pointed out.

"I agree. It's an incredible mystery. Perhaps a god or goddess had a hand in it. I can see no other explanation, really, though I can imagine some. We know that Wystan and Calder have been absent for years now. Perhaps Lysandra just had too much from Damiano and took action herself? Ah, here they come now."

Her day circle worked their magic. The group arrived on the teleport pad, a slightly raised stone area in the main chamber on the first floor. Ken stepped off and introduced Nadja, Konrad, and Isabella to Maricela and Emilio, using their full titles. After shaking hands with Emilio, all three were hesitant about how to greet Maricela. "Oh just give me a hug. Everyone does," she disarmed their awkwardness. "I am a katalyein, and those of us with this very rare *mentales* gift never have arms."

"What is a katalyein?" asked Nadja. "I've not heard that word before."

"Basically we are a catalyst telepath, someone who can bring a person's latent but undeveloped or mentally blocked talent to the forefront. Let's chat about that over lunch. I am playing hostess today. Lord Emilio will host our supper."

"Oh by the way, everything we tell you or that you see while you are here must be kept secret. Both Lord Emilio and I could get into very deep trouble with the rest of the lords and towers for so blatantly breaking the lease agreement. Lord knows several Lord Valens broke it in far worse ways, but they have paid dearly for that." Both swore and they headed off to lunch.

While eating, Nadja said, "I am so surprised to see everyone looking — well extremely well dressed. Heels, gowns, men in really fine suits. I didn't expect this. We were told this is a primitive culture. Yet, your clothing is on par with the finest nobility on wealthy worlds in the Imperium."

"We are dressing up for your state visit. I assure you I don't wear heels any more often than I have to," Maricela explained. "We use our feet as hands, though some of us also can use our gifts. Don't worry' you'll see me in my everyday clothing soon enough." Both women chuckled.

After dining, Venerada Maricela gave them a guided tour of her towers and adjoining huge manor houses. She outlined in some detail what went on in a tower. Both were impressed messages could be relayed all over Tierra in seconds. After that tour, Lord Emilio took them across the street into Brom Castle proper. When they had made the rounds there, he and his men took them on a brief tour of the city of Brom, where their notions of a more primitive culture finally bore fruit. Now they began to understand the world better.

Late afternoon, Lord Emilio and Governor Konrad sat down to discuss the senator issue, while Nadja was taken back over to the tower and assigned her own room and a helper. "This is Francisca. She's also a katalyein and my niece. She is eighteen and will be your constant companion and helper while you are with us. She can take you where you want to go and help setup interviews, language sessions, and such. She speaks fluent Westerlings and Midlands. When you are ready for a fluent Easterlings person, she can let me know. There are not that many here in Brom who speak that language well. Francisca can fill you in on many other details; just ask. Oh, and don't be hesitant because she lacks arms. She has quite a lot of powers in her young body. I've got to run; business never ceases." She bowed and left the two women.

"I see that you lost your hands, Nadja. Was it painful? Have you gotten therapy for that trauma?" she asked innocently.

"Why yes I did. Amazing. Beyond description, priceless. I had them removed so I could better relate to the people of another world, one whose women were born without hands or feet. I don't regret it. I have done a definitive study of their language and gotten it published. Now anyone who goes there can learn to speak their language well. That's the basis of true understanding between peoples."

"Sure is."

"So do you miss not having arms? Or is that too personal a question?"

Francesca giggled. "I've never had them to miss them. I do just fine without them really I do. Only sometimes, I wish I had them so I could get the really sexy toe shoes. Men really notice women who wear them, you know."

Nadja smiled. "I take it you don't have a boyfriend yet?"

She giggled again. "Not yet. Mom says that I should give it time, but I have such a hard time waiting. So can I help you set all this stuff up?"

"I don't see how you can. I was hoping Isabella would join us. I can just barely do some of these things. No feeling in these hands. Awful. I usually take them off when I am operating the machines. They are controlled by touching the screen. I'll show you."

"Oh, I can do some of it for you." She focused and several of the pieces of equipment levitated, opened up, and then lowered gently to the floor. "Where do you want this one?"

"My god! That's incredible! Oh, over here. I usually arrange them in a semi-circle around me so I can get to any of them, while not taking my attention off of the person that I'm talking to, you see. Can I ask, how heavy a thing can you lift?"

"I don't know. I've been able to lift whatever needed lifting. I could lift you, if you needed it." Thus began a very long series of surprises for Nadja.

Meanwhile, Rafaela and Isabella headed to see Benjamina, who was lying in her bed, covered up. First, she asked to speak to Rafaela alone. "I want you to see to it that these helpless new women arrivals and the two new mermaids gain *mentales* powers to help them live a better life. Control it

370

some so that they can use telekinesis, please."

Rafaela chuckled, "I already figured that one."

"And I want you to check on the two new aliens that Ken rescued. Something is not right with them, but I don't want to bias your observations with my own. Let me know what you find out. Make darn sure Amy and Jan, rather Gabriella and Celia, get goodly doses."

"I will. Darn good observation on your part to spot them," Rafaela replied.

"I am good at some things, bad at others, like we all are. Send in Isabella now, will you? And stand by."

Rafaela introduced her, "Isabella Valen, this is Benjamina Blackwater. I will be just outside if you need me."

The two women looked at each other — one was very old and looked it; the other was even older but looked twenty-five. "Please sit dear. I need to ask you some questions. I hope you will be honest with me. I know you are a Valen. Do you have any desires to return to Valen and seek power there?"

"My, you are blunt and to the point," Isabella replied. She sensed this was going to be a test of wills. Rarely had she ever encountered such a strong *mentales* gifted person. "The short answer is no. I am over a hundred years old. Everyone I knew is long dead. So much history has passed me by that I am a stranger in my own country. I would rather not return to Valen. I was hoping to find a place here in the Midlands. Perhaps helping Nadja or now maybe even helping out here in Brom. Why?"

"Good. You have lived a hundred years, and yet you do not have a husband nor any children."

"True. I survived my captivity and avoided being raped by convincing my fat employer I'd lose my 'gifts' if I lost my virginity. That worked extremely well all these years."

"Did you take women lovers?" she asked directly.

Isabella flushed. This was terribly personal, but she said, "Yes, safe sex. Safe pleasure. But none lasted for longer than twenty or so years. Why?"

"Thank you for telling me. If you had a chance to contribute something of immense value for all of Tierra, would you be willing to do it?"

"Sure, probably. I spent a century trying to get back here to my home world. I'm not sure what you're asking exactly. I would like to make a positive contribution in the name of Valen. I'm still catching up on history, but it seems the name Valen is synonymous with the devil or something like that around here. Rightly so, if what I've heard is true."

"Oh it is true enough. Good, Isabella. Something of immense importance is about to happen to Tierra, and I want you to have a hand in making it work to our advantage. It will help alter the opinions people hold against Valen."

"Okay, I am game. What is it?" Benjamina very carefully explained what was soon to happen and what she wanted of Isabella.

Isabella stared at the old woman. "You are a shrewd old woman. I can handle the marriage bit, if they can. Are you sure about this? The possibilities are incalculable."

"I am very certain. This new governor is the first one we can trust. I don't know how long an honest man can last as our governor, but when such an opportunity arises, we must take advantage of it. I've not yet spoken of this to the two women. They will need time for Rafaela to give them the *mentales* gifts. I expect they'll be most powerful when they get it shortly."

"Okay. You get it through the lords, and I will do this thing. I want the name of Valen to mean something other than treasonous treachery," Isabella replied. "I'll go and meet these two women now. I've not forgotten how to flirt." Benjamina smiled. She hadn't either, but she was too old for such things to matter now. She had all she needed with Elana.

Back in their private meeting, Konrad finished his lengthy explanation of his proposal for Tierra to send a senator off to the Imperium's Senate to represent Tierra's interests there. He used a couple of wrong words and regretted Nadja had not yet fully finished her study of the Midlands tongue. Lord Emilio was quite understanding of his failings, though. As far as Konrad was concerned, the man was most receptive to him speaking to him in his own language.

"Well, Governor Konrad, I too agree it is long past time that Tierra had an official representative to speak out on our behalf. You give your speech at the High Council of Lords. You'll attend as my guest; that'll allow you entry. After your speech, I'll do all I can to convince the other lords to go along with your proposal of our sending a senator off to represent us. I believe we can make a strong case for this. If so, we should have the personnel ready to go within a few months," Lord Emilio replied. The two shook hands, and he didn't need magic gifts to know just how relieved and pleased the governor actually was. It was plainly evident on his face.

As he left, he added, "I am most impressed with everything I've seen here, Lord Bolivar. In my opinion, Tierra ought to have had a senator when the Imperium first came here. It should have been part of the lease agreement. Every people should have a representative in the Senate. I think it was criminal of those who first came here not to have set that up for you. Well, I guess that's hindsight. Still, I intend to get Tierra its representative in the Senate, if I don't do anything else. I hope to talk more at length with you in July. Thank you for having me here."

Lord Bolivar smiled graciously. He had not detected a single deflection or hint of a lie in anything the governor had said. On the contrary, the man seemed sincere and quite intelligent. They chatted a bit as Emilio walked him back to the teleport pad in the tower. Venerada Maricela was there to greet him and to say farewell. "Anytime you wish to visit, just let Inez know. She'll contact me right away, and I'll arrange the teleport," she explained. "Hug please," she added, sensing Konrad wanted to shake her hand.

He did so. "Oh, might I ask how long that would take? I mean from the time I let her know. How long do I need allow for before you are ready here?"

"It will take her a minute at most to let me know. I have to get the Circle ready. If they are not currently tied up on other matters, give them a couple of minutes to ensure the connection before the teleport executes. If there will be any substantial delay, I will let Inez know and she will relay it to you. Acceptable?"

"Incredible. Simply incredible! Thank you again," Konrad replied, truly impressed with the way these towers operated. He began to have the notion these towers and their personnel were more skilled than his own people in some ways. They were anything but "primitives" and should not be treated as such. He vowed to make that very clear in his reports.

For her part, Nadja found herself in linguistic heaven. Francisca brought her several men and women, who were willing to help her with Midlands and Westerlings languages, including their written forms. However, Francisca had to send Nadja some calming emotions on several occasions, when she became frustrated with her lack of hands, particularly so when she discovered they had written forms of their languages. "Hey, there isn't any rush. You are welcome here as long as you wish to be here," she explained.

As far as therapy sessions went, Josh and Meg experienced benefits from their first sessions and were eager for more. Meg had erased the pain and trauma of her wound, and Josh had actually gotten back to his birth. Both were very cheerful at suppertime, as were the others receiving therapy sessions. All seemed to be on track. Lord Emilio and Venerada Maricela asked Ken to join them after dinner to discuss the proposed senator. With things finally running smoothly, Ken agreed.

"We sense this new governor means well by us and we ought to finally have a senator, Ken," Lord Emilio explained what he and Maricela had already agreed upon. "Of course, just who do we send is going to be the major hurdle. Whoever we send is going to be off-world for quite some time, as I understand it."

Maricela added, "Right. Whom do we send? If we pick someone from the Midlands, the Westerlings and Easterlings lords will protest. Perhaps even the City-States Alliance will object if we don't send one of their people. This is going to be tricky."

"I think mom is already way beyond us. I have a hunch she is working on this behind the scenes. If you want my guess, she's going to have us propose sending representatives from all three sectors, but I will speak to her about the City-States Alliance as well," Ken replied. "Whoever we actually send is going to have to be very carefully chosen, with the knowledge and ability to operate off-world, that's for darn sure. It isn't going to be me!" They all chuckled.

"Can you see if she will tell us her pick soon?" Emilio asked. "We need time to prepare good justifications to present to the lords."

"Okay, I'll go check now." A few minutes later, Ken stepped into his mother's bedroom.

"You want to know my picks for senators do you?" she asked, before he said anything.

"Mom. How do you do this? You always know what I want before I even get a chance to say anything," Ken teased her a little.

"I am your mother," she teased him back. "What else could you want at bedtime after the governor's visit? I have made three choices, one to represent each sector. Two of them don't know about it yet. Let me speak to them tomorrow, before I let you know names. They might not agree."

"How about the City-States Alliance, mom. Won't they demand a representative too?" Ken asked.

She sighed. "Right now, they really don't have any viable candidates. You must try to convince them the most important thing for them to do now is to rebuild the Easterlings cities. Promise them a voice in the next senator when these retire. I hope that'll be enough, son. Now give me a kiss. I need to sleep."

The next morning, Ken was summoned to the bedrooms of Josh and Meg. "They were just fine last night," Ken lamented. Both were deadly ill. "Was it something that they ate?"

Misty exclaimed, "Medical machines suggest they ought to be perfectly fine, but they aren't. They are burning up! Just feel their heads. What are we going to do?" Half of Ken's crew now stood looking at the two very ill guests. Just then, Misty heard Benjamina's voice in her head, well a telepathic thought would be more correct. *Check their eyes.* "Oh. Your mom just said to check their eyes." Carefully she lifted Meg's eyelids. She let out an exclamation.

From the adjacent room, Sally called out, "Come look at

Josh's eyes!" Both were turning slightly yellow.

"Go find Rafaela immediately! They have Verge Sickness! How on Tierra did they get this?" Misty exclaimed.

"My god," Jake exclaimed. "That dust that was in their noses and lungs — it must have been psi-dust from the refinery! Get Rafaela fast!"

A few minutes later, the mellow voice of Rafaela called out, "You boys rang?" Her heels clicked on the stone floor. She'd come as quickly as her feet would permit. After a quick check of Josh and Meg, she declared, "Bad cases of Verge Sickness. Okay, I will get my supplies. Back soon. Who would have figured this one? Now I again have my hands full."

Up in Nadja's room, Francesca suddenly looked "not there" and a little worried. "Is something wrong, Francesca?" Nadja asked a little concerned.

The teen blinked. "Oh, two people have gotten very bad cases of Verge Sickness. That is rather unusual, but Rafaela is now on it."

"Verge Sickness? Is it catching?" Nadja asked. "What is it? I've never heard of it before."

Francesca giggled. "No, it is something those of us who are born or somehow get the *mentales* gifts sometimes gets. Usually, it is when a child reaches puberty and often before their gifts fully materialize. They get very ill, high fevers, nausea, rather like a bad flu. Sometimes it happens because the person has a mental blockage that will not permit their *mentales* gifts to activate. If left untreated, it usually results in death. Rafaela is the leading expert on treatment of Verge Sickness, per se. But if it is a mental block that is causing it, that's where we katalyein come in. Our gift is to free up those blockages and bring out latent, but unrealized *mentales* gifts in others. I've done it twice now. Rather cool to be able save someone's life that way."

"How interesting. I wish I knew more about this whole thing. Well, that's why I am here, in part anyway. So you are either born with this gift or not, is that right?" she asked.

"Mostly, but not always. I'm not completely sure about that. Sometimes it is dormant, and we have to activate it. Really, Nadja, I am a novice at this. You ought to talk to

Rafaela about it sometime. She is the expert on it. No one but Benjamina knows more about it than she does." Nadja filed this one away to research further. Francesca didn't know whether or not to mention the mermaids and Rafaela's experiments on them that gave them back their lives. So she rightly said nothing.

As Ken watched Rafaela pouring the liquid *bacal* tea into the two patients, he whispered, "When it snows, it blizzards! What next?"

"Oh don't fret so. They will be all right, I hope. I haven't seen such bad cases of the Verge Sickness in thirty years, not since I was a young girl. How much psi-dust did you give them anyway, Ken?"

"None. Don't blame this one on us. We figure they must have inhaled a bunch of psi-dust up there on the moon at the refinery. Jake is finally getting around to chemically analyzing the dust he took out of their noses when they first got here. We've been kind of busy, if you hadn't known."

"Okay. Let me know what Jake discovers. I have to see to several more patients just now. Back in an hour. Message me if there is any change for the worst," Rafaela replied.

"Hold on a second. Other patients?" Ken probed, curiously. Instead of verbally replying because the spoken language was slower, she sent him the images of the women — the ones that he and Tom had rescued.

"Ken, be a good fellow and help everyone move those women down here into the medical suite. I will need to be watching them all very carefully," Rafaela asked. Ken knew he'd been hoodwinked into helping her again. He grinned; she always managed to get his curiosity up, and then when he bit, she got him to lend her a hand.

One by one, Ken helped move them all down. At her request, he and the others put Antonia, Daniela, Diamante, and Domenica into the same room next door to Josh's. The four fit well into one bed because of their small lengths. Celia and Gabriella doubled up in the next small room. Annetta and Bianca were put in the next room. Finally, Elnora and Gianna came hopping up and shared the bed next to those two. Rafaela now had a dozen patients to attend, two in very critical condition.

During this hurried move of the women, Misty stayed at the side of Meg, occasionally cooling her head with a soft, wet rag. Jake watched over Josh, but the four curious women next door came waddling in to see how he was doing. "Burning up," Jake whispered.

"Will he be okay?" Domenica asked, worriedly.

"Don't know, but Rafaela's on it," Jake answered. "Verge Sickness. I've seen it a couple times, and it's never good. Don't worry, ladies, you are not likely to get it, just the *mentales* gifted. You've already had your therapy completed. He and Meg haven't. They were just getting started."

"Can we help?" she asked. Jake found four chairs, positioning them around the head of the bed. He lifted each one up and gave them each a rag and a water pan. "Keep his head cool. I'm going to check on Meg. Thanks."

When Jake joined Misty, he didn't like what he saw. Meg was not responding properly. Misty said, "I've already sent for Rafaela." Shortly, the heard the telltale clicking of her heels on the stone floor. She looked a little haggard.

Rafaela took one look at Meg and then sighed. "Bad." She focused for a moment and her crystal activated briefly. "Checking on Josh," she mumbled and went next door. Seeing the four women doing their best with the rags between their arms and rubbing them across his head and face brought a smile to her face. She checked him over and told them to continue, returning to Meg.

Within minutes, Maricela came running into the room. She was wearing her everyday clothes, including her soft flats that allowed her to run and use her feet easily. "Is it really this bad — oh god, yes! Him too?" she gushed, after taking one look at Meg. Rafaela nodded. She didn't need to say anything.

"Okay, I will get the Circles on alert and get two of them active now. Give me a few minutes to wake the second shift," Maricela said hurriedly. She turned and raced back down the hall.

"Maybe it's our fault. We ought to have analyzed that dust we cleaned out of their noses when they first arrived," Jake lamented, partially blaming himself.

"Would not have mattered in the slightest, Jake. Don't be harsh on yourself. She did this to herself and to Josh. Being around that refinery with its high concentration of psi-dust without proper protections is what did it. Whatever she did there, I hope it was worth it," Rafaela replied.

Francesca was helping Nadja run her equipment while discussing the history of Brom Tower with one of their Circle technicians named John, an older man. Suddenly both stopped everything. Nadja noticed their eyes seemed far away. She had seen that look once on Francesca's face and guessed they were sharing some telepathic message. A wave of envy swept over her, but she quickly stifled it. Not professional, she told herself.

Quickly, they opened their eyes. John said, "I'm sorry, Rafaela. We'll have to continue this later. An emergency had arisen. I am needed in my Circle immediately."

"I have to go too," Francesca added.

"Can I come too? I'd like to help, if I can." Nadja asked without even thinking. How the devil can I do anything useful? These are telepaths, after all, she chided herself.

"Sure, don't see why not. We've got two really bad cases of Verge Sickness — really bad ones. And Hector has just brought his sick son here from Hilliard Heights. He has a mild case of Verge Sickness. I am supposed to help him. Come on; you can watch me," she said rather excitedly.

She led Nadja down to the first floor and into the entrance room, where guests were often met. Hector was a horse trainer and smelled like it, Nadja could not help but notice. Another man was also there, tending to his son, who was perhaps twelve or thirteen. Nadja couldn't say with any accuracy. The man had the tall, thin lad lying comfortably on a couch, covered in a blanket. He looked up and smiled when he saw Francesca. She said quickly, "Amo Bill, this is Nadja. Nadja, Bill. How is he?"

Amo Bill nodded briefly to Nadja and turned his attention onto Francesca. "Stable. Definitely blocked. I'd rather not go with *bacal*, unless you think it is necessary."

"Let me check first," Francesca replied. She leaned over the lad and Nadja saw her crystal glow in a pale blue light for a brief moment. "Yes, blocked. I will have to undo it. Don't worry. Hector, you got him to us in time. He'll be all right in a few minutes. I have to help him remove that mental block that is causing the Verge Sickness."

"Can I help? I'd sure like to see what it is that you do," Nadja whispered.

Francesca smiled, looked at Amo Bill. He gave her a quizzical look. "Okay Nadja. I will Mink Link you to me and you can see everything. Bill will monitor me and the boy and you too, just in case you have difficulties. Whatever you do though, do not distract me in any way. I'll Mind Link to you first and then to the boy. You will only barely feel Bill's monitoring touch."

Nadja saw her crystal glow once more and then she felt what she later tried to describe as an intense sexual stimulus, most pleasureful. That sensation was but very brief, replaced by the most intimate experience she'd ever felt. Francesca had merged with her, she and Francesca were closer than two lovers in the height of their shared sexual experience. For Nadja, nothing ever compared to this first joining. Vaguely, she sensed Bill's presence too, but it was only just there at the lowest level of her perceptions. Now she sensed Francesca peering into the boy's mind, and she saw what the katalyein saw, a black-grey mass around the boy's head. She knew this was the mental block that was interfering and making the boy sick, but was that recognition instinctive or was it sent from Francesca? As she watched, she saw the boy appear too, joining them. Together, they probed the black-grey mass which dissolved into mental images right before their focused attention.

Now she could see what was happening. A small boy was being accosted by a man with yellow eyes. A *mentales* gifted man. She felt the overwhelming power and control coming from the man, who was dominating the small boy. She cringed. The man forced the boy to perform sexual acts on him against his will, and then reversed the flow, raping the boy, before releasing control of the boy's mind and body. At the end, the boy was sobbing and crying, all alone in some darkened room. Slowly the black-grey mass dissipated and was gone. Francesca broke her connection to the boy and then Nadja.

When that most intimate connection with Francesca ended, Nadja slumped. She didn't want that feeling to ever end! Such a letdown she'd never before felt! But Francesca was now checking on the boy. "Ah. See, his fever is gone and he is waking, Hector. He will be just fine now."

"Thank you, Ama, thank you for saving the life of my only boy. I will sing your praises to everyone in Hilliard Heights! Thank you, thank you," Hector was beside himself. His boy lived. Soon the lad opened his eyes and stared into Francesca's, recognizing her. He smiled. She did too.

"You've had a close call, but you are perfectly fine now. The others at Hilliard Heights will be able to train you and soon you will have your own psi-crystal," she said, bringing a big smile to the boy's face. After more thank you's, Francesca and Nadja left, while Amo Bill helped them out to Hector's wagon.

"That was incredible, Francesca! Indescribable! He was raped wasn't he?" Nadja asked, finally able to form a question.

"Yes, probably a lifetime or two past. Some nasty man with the gift used his powers to control the boy and rape him. After that, the boy didn't want anything to do with *mentales* gifts and was thus fighting it in himself. I was able to get him to see it and it erased. Actually, in some ways, this is how Benjamina's therapy works; only we don't need to use our katalyein *mentales* powers to erase the traumas. Oh! I am being summoned to my Circle now. Come on. Something's up."

"What Circle?" Nadja asked.

"Normally we katalyein don't join the working Circles here at the tower. Our gifts are too specialized, but in emergencies, I am part of a forth Circle, and we're needed on one of these really bad Verge Sickness cases. Follow me; it is in the basement." Nadja followed after her, but in her high heels, trying to keep up with the scampering teen was almost more than she could do.

They arrived outside a suite of several rooms. She didn't recognize nine of the men and women, who were now sitting down in one corner, though she saw another katalyein already sitting, and Francesca hastily joined them. Ken came walking out, leading two women. Nadja blinked and rubbed her eyes with her prosthetic hands, then gasped.

The two women were sort of waddling along on leather tube-like boots. They had no lower legs and no lower arms! Crystal was right behind him, leading another two nearly identical, mutilated women. Ken looked up at her and said, "Come with us, please. They need peace and quiet in there." Mechanically, Nadja did as asked, falling in behind Crystal and her two women, whose upper arms she was holding, helping them waddle faster.

They entered the bedroom next door. Quickly, the four women were lifted up and sat on the bed. Crystal arranged their hair for them, while Ken dragged up three chairs. "Well, I hope you are not too shocked by them. I wanted to spare you such sights, but with the wild emergencies today, it couldn't be helped." Ken sighed.

"What awful thing has happened to them?" Nadja finally found her voice. It seemed like such a lame thing to ask. She chided herself for being so direct.

"This is a prime example of what can happen when alien technology falls into the wrong hands, Nadja. Okay, long story. It seems one of the Easterlings doctors, who performs surgery on men who've been badly wounded in sword fights or who have gangrene — somehow he got a hold of one of the Imperium medical machines. Yes, those." Ken said, seeing the image of her own machines in her mind.

"But they are for healing," she protested slightly.

"You and I know that. This doctor, who doesn't know anything about machines or Imperium Standard, somehow figured out how to operate the machine. Whatever we may be, we are not stupid, Nadja," Ken grumbled and decided to make his point. "He then discovered how fabulous the machine is on amputations. For some years, he used it in his practice, humanely treating his patients. Then an unscrupulous friend of his came along. The man operated an escort service, hiring beautiful women out for evenings. I won't go into details of that. Anyway, he asked the doctor to perform some modifications on his women to 'make them more exotic.' We have retrieved the machine and rescued ten of the women that were 'modified.' Lord knows how many others are still out there. These four were the worst. Nadja, this is Antonia, Daniela, Diamante, and Domenica. Ladies, this is the governor's wife, Nadja."

"I'm so sorry for you," Nadja tried to think of something to say, but this was all that she could utter. She was shocked.

"Don't be. We wanted it done; we were convinced that like we are now, we were the sexiest women in the world. Indeed, many noblemen paid a fortune to take us out evenings. We did make a lot of money at it. But we've had our therapy now and know better," Domenica explained. "Now we have to live with what we've done. At least we can walk some."

"Come on, Nadja. I want you to meet the others. Gang, I'll be back shortly," he said to the four. He led her next door and introduced her to Celia and Gabriella. Then, he moved down to the next room, introduced her to Annetta and Bianca, and pointed out that they were not katalyein. Finally, he took her to the two mermaids, who were accompanied by their sponsors from Madiera. Four mermaids were in the room. Their appearance shocked Nadja even more.

Elnora said, "Hey, join us for tea? We were about to have some." Nadja noticed they were using straws to sip their tea. Ken pulled up two more chairs and poured themselves two cups, handing one to Nadja, but making sure she had a good grasp of it in her prosthetic hands before releasing it. Nadja sensed what Ken was doing and smiled.

"You see, this is what can happen when alien technology falls into the wrong hands. This is why we want Tierra to remain a closed world for now. Yes, your technology is marvelous, fantastic, terrific, and even lifesaving at times, but without the proper education, knowledge, and training in their use, things like this can happen. You can imagine what might happen if your blasters fell into our hands," Ken philosophized.

"Ken, this is mind-blowing. I never dreamed something like this could happen. I understand, truly I do. I will tell Konrad about this and get him to understand too. How can they possibly live like this?"

"Long story, Nadja, good thing we have some tea," Ken replied. He wanted to keep Nadja away from the Circles, who were dealing with a real emergency a few doors down. He said, "You now know you are an immortal spiritual being who inhabits physical bodies, lifetime after lifetime. However, there are even more powerful spiritual beings, who do not have to have physical forms in order to operate and do the things that we do. Most call them gods or goddesses, for want of true understanding. Tierra has had five such beings." He began to tell her about Calder and the mermaids, figuring this story would last long enough.

"My god, the dust has permeated her entire body!" the healer of the First Circle exclaimed. Rafaela grimaced. She had suspected this was the case. "How could she possibly have gotten this much dust into her system?"

"I believe she inhaled quite a lot of it while around their fuel depots," she answered, avoiding a totally correct answer. "Can she be saved?"

"We are going to have to try to remove those tiny particles from her entire body. I simply do not know if we have enough time or not. We will try." The Circle focused and joined together, funneling their entire mental energies into the healer. Now he probed into Meg's body and began to remove the psi-dust particles. As Rafaela watched, a small pile of the dust began building up on the table, as if by magic. Quietly, she moved into the next room to check on Josh. She saw another Circle doing the same thing with him. She went back and sat down in a corner, watching Meg.

An hour passed by slowly. Ken finally finished his story. "So my mother helped them regain some of their former *mentales* gifts, specifically telekinesis. With that, they are able to live fairly independently now." One of the mermaids whole heartedly agreed with him.

Elnora added, "And now we are going to get the gift too. Then we can live much better. About all that we can do now is hop about well. At least that's more than poor Antoinia and Daniela can do."

"Could I meet your mother sometime? She must be an

amazing woman to have invented the mental therapy and helped all these women get *mentales* gifts," Nadja asked. Just then, a large group of men and women came down the hall.

As the two watched, the original eighteen, who had been working on the two patients, left. Nadja saw Francesca. The teen looked utterly drained, exceedingly tired, and she didn't even look up at her. One of the other men had his arm around her, steadying her as they walked back down the hall. Ken explained, "The Circle members used up an extraordinary amount of their energies. They must eat and sleep to recover. Meanwhile, another pair of Circles has come to continue their work. I hope they can save the two. Come on; mom wants to meet you too. Remember, she's old and fragile now."

Benjamina was sitting in her soft sofa chair when the two arrived. After introductions, Nadja said, "This is a real honor for me to meet you. I have heard so many marvelous things about you. Your mental therapy is — well just lifesaving. I've been to quite a few planets in the Imperium and none has anything like it." She chatted for a time, praising the work that Benjamina had done and just how fascinated she was about this entire *mentales* culture.

Benjamina finally said, "Yes, we *mentales* gifted do have enormous powers, Nadja. With those powers comes a very heavy responsibility towards all those who do not have it. Only perhaps a tenth of our population now has the gift, though in the distant past it was more like one in five. We must use our gifts to help all of our people on Tierra. Admittedly, there are bad beans in any pile. Some have greatly abused their gifts, just as you have probably seen others in your world abusing the powers entrusted into them."

"Quite right. I've seen that."

"Now then, I'd like to ask you some questions."

"Sure go ahead."

"I've heard you have said our three languages are similar to another language family. What was it? Oh, I believe that you called it Indo-European. Pray, what is that? Who speaks that language?" Benjamina asked.

"Oh, well, do you know something about linguistics?"

"Not really, but I speak and write many languages."

"I see. Well, there are a whole lot of spoken languages among all the peoples of all the inhabited planets in the galaxy. Well, at least the ones that we know of, that is. I've studied quite a few of those that are spoken within Imperium-controlled space. Plus, I have access to older records of language studies done of peoples who reside in that section of the galaxy controlled by our enemies, the Federation of Planets. Now that group of planets is terribly distant from here. Tierra, or Ashford-5 as we call this world, is on the far outer rim of the galaxy, zillions of miles from the heart of the Imperium or that of the Federation. I'm sorry by I am not up on the exact units of measurement. I was never very good in physics and astronomy. Long way by spaceships, let's put it that way."

"Where was I? Oh, so within the Federation of Planets, there is a whole family of languages that are related. I won't go into details about them, but just assume that they are related. I just came from a world where they have a variety of clicking sounds that play a critical role in their spoken language. For example, I became good friends with ^gar and his wife, ^achk. See how strange their language is? It is wholly unlike the languages spoken here on Tierra and would not be placed in that language group. Anyway, all three — Midlands, Easterlings, and Westerlings — all three languages are closely related. If you can speak one of these, it is relatively easy to learn to speak any of the other two, but it would be very hard to learn to speak that click language I mentioned."

"I see. This makes sense," Benjamina said softly. "Do continue."

"Anyway, as a linguist, I am very skilled at languages and determining into which larger family any given language fits. All three here fit into that one I mentioned, Indo-European. I have no idea where it is spoken, other than within some planets of the Federation of Planets. Obviously, I can't go there; they are our enemies, you see."

"So what conclusions can you draw from this?" Benjamina asked what she wanted to know and why she'd wanted to meet Nadja in the first place.

"Well, languages don't spontaneously create

themselves. The chances of someone inventing the Midlands to be exactly like the Indo-European English language are astronomically against that happening. Obviously, in your distant past, the original settlers of Tierra must have come from another world on which English was spoken. True, languages change over time, and there are subtle and some not so subtle differences between Midlands and English. But the important point is they are very closely related, implying your distant ancestors spoke this English," Nadja finished up.

"Very interesting indeed. And you don't know on what planets this English is spoken?"

"Nope, not a clue. As I said, they are somewhere in the Federation of Planets, extremely distant from this world. That's all I know," Nadja explained. She added, "See, isn't language just fascinating? But, now I've seen your telepathy and the *mentales* gifts are even more interesting. I sure wish I could get such a gift. It would be invaluable in my linguistic studies. Already I've seen ideas are communicated as thoughts, not as a series of words. The words we speak are used as a substitute for the original idea or thought. I can't imagine how fantastic it would be to be able to communicate by thoughts without having to translate them into words. When I make first contact with a new people whose language is foreign, such a skill would be incredibly valuable in helping to pick up that new language."

Benjamina cautioned her, "And such powers can just as easily be used to spy on others, as well as controlling and dominating others who do not have such powers."

Nadja sighed. "Yes, I've just seen that. Francesca helped unblock a young boy who was violated in just such a way. I have heard telepaths are sometimes used within the Imperium for spying, just as you said. Perhaps any power that can be used for good can be perverted and used for ill."

"Yes, you are quite right about that, Nadja," Benjamina replied with a smile. "During the centuries the Imperium has been here, quite a number of our telepaths have been kidnaped and taken off-world."

Nadja sighed. "I know. Konrad discovered this, but he says that too many years have passed for him to find the guilty men and arrest them."

"That is most honorable of him. So you wish you had the *mentales* gifts yourself?" Benjamina probed a little. She sensed what was about to happen and took a gamble.

"Oh yes indeed! I know apparently you have to be born with such a potential. Francesca allowed me to watch as she removed the mental block that sick boy had," Nadja replied.

"Who knows, Nadja? One day you might just get your wish. But I am afraid I am tired out now. It has been good to meet you." After thanking her, the two left.

"Ken, what did she mean by one day I might get my wish?"

"Darn if I know what mom meant by that. Sometimes, she is really cryptic." Both smiled. He added, "It's way past lunchtime. I best get you back to the tower so you can eat. Probably you will find few tower people about now, most are sleeping and recovering." He dropped her off at the tower's dining room.

He ran back to the two ill guests to check on them. Misty shook her head. "They're not holding out much hope for Meg. Just look at the volume of pure germanium psi-dust they've removed from her body so far!" She showed him a quart bag of the powder. He shook his head in dismay. "The capos keep telling us that even if they had started work on her the moment we got her here, they would still have been unable to get it all out of her. Josh is in better shape now. They say he has a fifty-fifty chance of making it. I can't recall all four Circles having been used at one time before. They are going all out to save them, Ken."

Just then, Bianca came walking out of Meg's room. She had been watching over the ill woman, giving all the others a much needed lunch break. Tears trickled down her cheeks. "She just passed away, Misty."

"Damn!" Misty exclaimed and threw her arms around Bianca, comforting her. Ken focused and relayed the sad news to many others.

To his utter surprise, his mother sent, *Ken, bring Nadja to see me after she's eaten. Then be prepared to teleport Konrad here. Do not dispose of Meg's body yet.*

You are not going to tell me what you have in mind, are you.

No. Ken growled, but promised to do as she asked. "Misty, what the hell have I missed here? Mom is on to something, and I haven't a clue!" Misty giggled. He headed off to find Nadja.

"You wanted to see me again?" Nadja asked. Ken had brought her back down to see Benjamina.

"Yes, Nadja. I have been consulting with the many katalyein. We believe that we may be able to unlock telepathy and the *mentales* gifts within you." While surprised by this revelation, Ken knew it was an outright fib. She could feed her psi-powder and her body would develop the gifts on its own. Rafaela was expert at doing just that. What game was his mother playing? *How can she be so far ahead of me,* he wondered?

"However, you are an alien. Many here do not yet trust you fully. As we have spoken, with great powers come also a great responsibility to resist all temptations to misuse and abuse your powers."

"I swear to you I would never, ever do such a thing," Nadja exclaimed, interrupting her.

"Good. There is one thing we would like to ask of your husband, the governor, in return. Would you mind if we asked him here to see if he would do this for us?"

"Sure. I know he wants to help all that he can, as long as it doesn't involve harming the Imperium and such," she replied.

Benjamina had Ken make the arrangements, while she continued to chat with Nadja, who was effervescent over this news.

Konrad was very startled to hear Nadja and the others in Brom wanted him there immediately. He was even more impressed, when they teleported him directly from his twentieth floor office! Bart had used their teleport machine, since all the circle members were asleep, recovering from their intense efforts to save the two guests. He landed the governor on the tower's teleport pad instead of his pad here in the Underground. Maricela had lowered their tower's protection screens prohibiting such unscheduled teleports.

Ken was there and met him, leading him into the basement. Nadja met them out in the hallway. Benjamina wanted her to explain what was being offered to her first, before talking to Konrad. While Nadja excitedly explained the news to Konrad, Ken sat beside his mother waiting for Konrad to come in. Shortly he did and he introduced his mother to the new governor.

"What is it that you wish me to do so you will be free to help Nadja gain what can only be a godlike gift?" Konrad asked, coming right to the point.

"I know you know that over these centuries, some of your people have been systematically kidnaping some of our young telepaths, taking them off-world and selling them into slavery or serving as Imperium spies. I also know you find this criminal and want to stop it."

"Absolutely! It must cease, but I don't know who is doing it. I suspect those orders come from authorities far above the governor's position," Konrad admitted.

"I know a way you can put a stop to it. Listen carefully, Konrad," Benjamina said sternly. Ken's eyes nearly fell out of his head. He'd missed this connection completely.

"My god, Benjamina! Yes, yes, I will do as you ask. I do believe this will indeed work and end the kidnaping of your young men and women! Let's do this at once, shall we?" Konrad exclaimed, very much excited about this plot.

Ken led him back to the teleport pad, where Misty and Jake were already waiting for them along with the body of Meg. "So this is she," Konrad muttered. He nodded, but before Konrad could see too much, Bart teleported Konrad and the body back into his twentieth floor office, again quite shocking him. Konrad took a deep breath and then entered the codes into his comm system, opening up a secure channel to Sector ID Minister Emeryk.

"Yes, I have some good news, boss. Yes, letting all the towers know about the two missing commandos has paid off handsomely. I have recovered them. No, both are dead. However, one lived long enough to be questioned. Yes. It seems some local men did come across the crash. They were fleeing that big army coming their way. They found this woman who was still alive and her companion. He was dead, burned badly in the fire and crash. They buried him, but brought the injured woman to one of the towers. They questioned her some but were unable to save her life. Knowing that I wanted news of the commandos, they contacted me."

"So what news? Okay listen to this, boss. Hold on to your seat! I know that all during the centuries we've been on Tierra, there has been routine kidnaping of some of their young telepathic gifted men and women, taken off-world."

Emeryk growled, justifying, "So what of it? Telepaths are a high demand, high profit commodity."

"That woman was one such victim. She swore to get revenge on the Imperium for having kidnaped her and forcing her into a life of slavery. The sabotage plan was hers, and she claims there are others like her out there within the Imperium who are planning similar revenge attacks on us! For god's sake, use whatever influence you have to put an end to these kidnappings! Every one of these kidnaped victims will be out to get revenge on us!"

"Crap! I never thought of that. You are quite right. Such people would likely do anything they could to destroy us! Send her body up on the next shuttle flight. I will pull some Imperium strings and get the kidnaping ended. Governor Konrad, brilliant work! Positively brilliant! I just knew you would be the best governor in the Imperium. Now if you can only get them to send a senator. . ."

"Hey, I am on it. I expect to close that deal in July, just a few weeks, boss."

"Amazing, Governor Konrad, absolutely amazing. I put you on this post, and in just a couple of months, you have everything sewn up that couldn't be done in three centuries. Amazing. Well, back to work here. Send the body on the next shuttle."

Konrad ended the connection and headed over to Elegant Fashions Inc to have Inez send word to Ken and Benjamina. The plan appeared to have worked to perfection. In her room, Benjamina merely smiled. She knew it would work. The guilty always fear what they've done will come back to haunt them. She'd played Emeryk like a harp, but more importantly, the kidnaping would stop. Konrad could use that to help sway the lords. Tierra had to have a Senate representative.

Ken then met with Nadja. "Mom says the katalyein will work on you after the council of lords is over. She thinks you ought to spend these last days of June helping Konrad speak Midlands better so he will sound more natural when he addresses them."

"You got it. Already, I have a mountain of data at hand. I will do so yet today. This is incredible, Ken. I never dreamed I might have such potentials locked away in my mind."

"Of course, once you get your gifts unlocked, you will need to be trained here at the tower in their use so you don't get yourself into trouble. You have to know how to block the thoughts of others. Otherwise, being in a crowd of people with their zillions of thoughts will drive you mad," Ken pointed out.

"Oh! I had not thought of that. You are right. That would occur and would drive one simply crazy! Thanks for the tip. I best get packing. I am slow with these darn hands."

During the last weeks of June, Nadja worked with Konrad, improving his mastery of Midlands. She also spent time with Inez, who had become a very good friend of hers and Konrad's. Towards the end of June, the two women were discussing what she ought to wear to the High Council of Lords.

Inez explained, "Well, I took your advice and tabulated the many women's styles — at least those I know for sure will be attending. The results are quite mixed as you can see." She showed her the breakdowns. Inez had broken them into four categories: Easterlings, Midlands, Westerlings, and City-States Alliance. Plus, she had grand totals of each category. The results were pretty well divided evenly.

Half of the women wore toe shoes; half wore the usual six-inch heels. Half of the women wore lip plates, and half did not. All but a handful of women wore pipe corsets. Half of the women sported huge, dangling earrings, while half wore more modest earrings. A third of the women wore the arm-fetter-gowns; a third wore the simpler fetter-gowns; the remainder wore tight fitting gowns with walking slits.

"Gosh, this is so hard to analyze," Nadja declared.

"It's worse, actually. It seems someone has taken pictures of what you both looked like when you arrived. You know with your huge lip plates and toe shoes. They've been circulating around the towers and castles. Already, I've had three dozen inquiries from women seeking to have their lip plates enlarged to match the ones that you wore. As yet, I haven't responded to them," Inez explained. "Plus, styles change. Some of these women may well wear some variation to the meeting, but I don't anticipate any big change in the raw totals."

"So what am I to wear? Konrad is all set with his suits. He looks fit and trim in his pipe corset," Nadja asked, growing rather worried about this. "I need to make a very good impression on the wives of the lords for Konrad's sake and for mine too. Wait! You said other women with lip plates want theirs enlarged like the ones I wore? Oh no."

Inez smiled. "Oh yes. The wife of the governor of Tierra, whether you like it or not, is bound to set a fashion example other women will emulate if they can."

"Inez, I know enough to know I will definitely upset those who were anticipating seeing me with those huge lip plates, won't I?"

Inez smiled. "I hate to tell you, but yes. If you show up without them and even worse without any lip plates, they will take that as a sure sign that you don't approve of the plates and more importantly of them. Same holds true with the toe shoes, for that matter."

"Inez, I just had not thought this all through. I'm in a pickle aren't I?"

Inez chuckled. "Aye that you are. One way out would be to show up in a whole new fashion line, but alas, unless you have some bright ideas, we don't have time for that angle."

"Well, I don't mind wearing the pipe corset on occasion, and I really do love these earrings, even if they continually threaten to pull my ears off. Whatever am I going to do, Inez? You are right; there is so little time to invent a whole new look. Besides, I wouldn't know where to start. I emulate what is in fashion on whatever world I'm on — only the finest and best fashions, mind you. I am not used to setting trends," Nadja admitted. "I guess I really have been doing just that. We've been sent to other planets where I adjusted my looks to match the local people. Here, I changed my looks after I arrived and everyone saw me. I should have considered that before I made my decision to undo so much of it."

"I don't know what to tell you," Inez replied.

"This meeting is so vitally important for Konrad. He just must get his senator idea approved. And we all know how critical those first impressions actually are. Well, as his wife, it is my obligation to help him achieve his goal. If he fails, then it affects my stay here too. Okay, Inez, can you contact Ken or Crystal for me? I need to ask them, if I redo my lips and feet, if that will harm my chances of getting the gift. I know I'd need more therapy afterwards. While the medical machines make it all seem utterly painless, my god, Inez, it is terribly painful; it's just hidden from our conscious minds."

"Sure thing, dear. I know. I'll ask them to make a Mind Link with you. That way you can chat about it, and I don't have to be your go-between. I feel like I am eavesdropping on you," Inez answered. Once more, Nadja felt that oh so intimate touch of another person joining with her innermost self, as if she and Crystal, in this case, were united as one person somehow.

Nadja explained her dilemma and asked for advice. Crystal was on the spot. Still she did her best. *In my marriage, Ken and I are equals. He supports me with my own goals and I support his. While often they're the same goal, they aren't always. Does this help? Whatever you decide, it will not affect the possibilities of your getting the mentales gifts. So you don't have to worry about that.*

Nadja sighed. *That is good to hear. I simply must do my very best to support Konrad. I know that afterwards I'll have to spend quite some time with everyone in Brom, so he will have to support me then. Thanks Crystal.*

After the connection broke, Nadja felt like something extraordinarily precious had been severed from her. Inez quietly gave her a moment to recover. She knew well what

Nadja had just experienced. "Well, Inez, it looks like I need to get my lips redone and my feet as well. I don't want to upset the women who have been looking forward to seeing me as I was. Minimize the upsets. I still have my old toe shoes and plates. I best head to our medical center now. I will be back to get some appropriate gowns, the kind with the walking slit. If I am to wear those toe shoes, I want to be able to take a reasonable stride. They are not so bad if you can do that. It must be awful to wear them with those fetter-gowns. Maybe others who wear toe shoes will emulate me and dump those style gowns."

Back at the admin building, Nadja explained what she'd learned and told Konrad that she was going back to wearing the large lip plates and toe shoes. After hearing her out, Konrad agreed. "You are right. We don't want a number of the lord's wives all upset over you. That could well negatively impact the lords and their decisions. Thanks dear for being so observant about such details. I'd be lost without you. Besides, I loved seeing you dolled up that way. Terribly sexy." She smiled and left. After picking up her old toe shoes and lip plates, she headed for the medical machines.

Later, she returned to Elegant Fashions Inc. While Inez set about getting her several new and gorgeous outfits to wear, she also had one of her engineers take photos and measurements of her special lip plates. Plus, she had Nadja explain in detail how she manipulated the medical machines to both make her lip loops large enough to handle the plates as well as thicken them. Nadja had to explain verbally the procedure. With her prosthetic hands, she simply couldn't work the machine's touch screen without damaging it.

Finally, Inez got Nadja's agreement to help her design some new fashions later on. Inez knew well Nadja would soon be setting fashion trends among some of the noblewomen of Tierra. Nadja, for her part, wanted the women to forgo those fetter style gowns.

Meanwhile, Josh was battling for his life, though he wasn't aware of it in those terms. Physically, his body was unconscious with a high fever, dehydrating, even as the Circles continued to create more fluids in his system. Then he thought he awoke. Josh saw nothingness around him. A small image of what must be the universe lay below him. A ghostly shape moved over to him, and he recognized Princess Meg. He tried to speak, but he had no body. Nevertheless, they exchanged thoughts.

She said, *Josh, I want to thank you for everything you have done for me. I screwed up this time. We inhaled too much of their fuel. Our air recyclers could not filter out all that tiny, microscopic dust. I am returning to my home now. I am so sorry I got you into all this trouble. You deserve so much more. Goodbye Josh, my good friend.*

Goodbye Princess Meg. I am sorry for you too. He watched as she floated down into that image of the universe somehow below him. *What do I do now? Where am I? Am I lost? Of course, you are lost, silly. I must be dead too. Wait, I can't be dead. I am thinking and aware as always. Maybe my body is dead and I am in heaven. No, I don't see any angels or anything at all. Boy, Josh, you sure got yourself lost this time. At least I am not surrounded by potatoes. That's something anyway. What do I do now? Where do I go? What am I supposed to do?*

The Circle members finished their current round of healing on Josh's body and had just left, exhausted and starving. One by one, Antonia, Daniela, Diamante, and Domenica waddled in to take up their positions watching over him. For days, they had done this, relieving the very tired others. Again sitting on their chairs, they used their short arms to rub wet, cool rags over his face and forehead. "He isn't doing much better is he?" Antonia whispered.

"Not really," Domenica replied in a whisper.

"It is like he has gone somewhere else," Daniela whispered. All four agreed with her observation.

"Maybe we should talk to him and try to bring him back," Daniela suggested. Again, the four agreed and began talking to Josh.

"Josh, we are here. We won't leave you. Wherever you are, this is a much better place to be — where we are. Please come back to us," Daniela spoke to him. The other three chimed in, saying much the same things.

Josh began to hear voices. Four voices. Coming from where? He strained to hear them. He tried to pull them into himself so he could hear them more distinctly. Suddenly, the four women joined him! Like Meg, they appeared more as ghostly forms, but quite real.

Who are you?

I am Daniela. This is Antonia, Diamante, and Domenica. We are here with you, and we want you to come back to us. Please, Josh. Where are we anyway? What is this place? Oh, this is so intimate, Josh. Suddenly the four women realized just how intimate they felt, almost as if they had merged themselves with each other and with Josh, becoming almost a single entity! It took them all by surprise.

This is so much better than sex, Antonia pointed out. The others agreed, but wondered what this was.

You are all so beautiful, Josh sent. He was overwhelmed with their radiance, the beauty of the four spiritual beings. The four appeared to laugh and he didn't know why.

We should try to get Josh back, Daniela thought.

But I don't want these feelings to ever end, Josh protested. The four giggled, or it seemed so to Josh, and they added that they didn't want it to end either.

But we really should try to get Josh back, Daniela again thought.

She's right. We should try, Domenica added. *Come on, Josh. Hold on to us and follow us. Do we know where we are going?*

Oops, I think that we are lost now too, Antonia thought, a little fearfully. *Well that's okay; this is the greatest thing ever!*

Misty dropped by to check on the four women and Josh. "Oh dear god! What's going on?" She saw the four women were sitting lifelessly with totally vacant stares on their faces. At once, she telepathically messaged Rafaela. She had no idea what was happening, but it couldn't be good.

Rafaela came as fast as her heels permitted her. "I found them like this," Misty whispered, unable to mask the trace of fear in her voice.

"Well, this is interesting. I best see what is going on," Rafaela replied. She sat down, focused, and her crystal began to glow bright blue.

Now another radiant form joined the five, listening in on their conversation. Once she understood what had happened, she sent to Daniela, *Follow me, and you four can bring Josh back with you.*

Hey, this is the way back. Come on, Josh. Follow us. We want you back with us, Daniela sent.

But I don't want to leave you. I don't want to give up these feelings for you, Josh protested.

Ever so gently, Rafaela sent, *You don't have to give it up. It can be yours anytime that you desire it.*

Oh! Okay. I love these four. Wait for me. I'm coming. I'm coming.

Shortly, the four women stirred and opened their eyes. Rafaela was there, quite surprising them. Josh stirred and opened his eyes. The first thing he saw was the four women sitting around his head. "Was that you four?" he whispered. "You are so beautiful."

Daniela giggled. "Yes, we came to call you back here to us."

"Welcome to the land of the living, Josh," Rafaela said softly. "You had a very narrow escape with death there, son. We call it the Verge Sickness. I am so sorry to have to tell you this, but Princess Meg has passed away from it."

"I know. I saw her. We said goodbye. Then these angels here came for me. I was lost until these angels came and found me and led me back," Josh whispered. His mouth was very dry. "What happened to me? Where were we? I heard a voice saying that I could be that close to them again. How?"

"All in good time, Josh. You are just now getting your own *mentales* gifts, as are these four women. Trust me; relax, get your strength back. You have a lot of training ahead of you, but yes, if you want to get into that intimate rapport with these women, you'll soon be able to do that anytime you and they desire. Now then, perhaps one of you ladies can get some moisture into his mouth. I think he's overly dry." The four giggled and awkwardly did so.

"I can't get over just how beautiful you four really are," Josh exclaimed a bit later. His saliva production had begun again, much to his relief.

"We are not so pretty anymore. Look at us," Daniela pointed out, wiggling her stubby arms and short legs.

Josh looked very confused. Then, he realized what he'd seen. "I mean you are really beautiful, not your bodies. Well, they are pretty too but in a different way." Now the four understood. Already on their way to having their own *mentales* gifts, they picked up his actual thought, which was so hard for him to express in words. He didn't have the knowledge yet or the training to phrase what he knew to be true.

During the ensuing days, the four were almost inseparable from Josh, even demanding their beds be moved into his room so that they could better take care of him. For a time, they were worried about Josh leaving them again. They hovered over him like honeybees to a flower. Slowly, his strength returned. As Rafaela suspected might happen, the five quickly became hopelessly in love. The bonds that the five had shared with each other had been intensely powerful.

"But how can I marry all four of you?" Josh asked them one day. He was brushing out their hair for them.

They giggled and Daniela explained, "We are Easterlings women. In our land, it is customary for a man to have as many wives as he desires. We four do not want to ever be parted from each other or you, so you must have us as your harem."

Antonia added, "But you must choose which of us will be your Number One wife and so on. That way we know who comes first always."

"But you are all equal. I can't put one of you ahead of the others. Where I come from, we don't have harems, only one wife. But I can't possibly choose one of you over the others."

"You are not where you come from anymore. You are here with us," Daniela pointed out.

Domenica added, "So you must adopt our ways and have all of us."

"Okay, I will marry all four of you, but I insist that you also compromise. You will all be Number One. You are all equal in my eyes."

"But we don't know how to do that," Daniela protested a little.

"And I don't know how to have a harem," Josh explained. "We both have to learn new ways." That pleased them and they agreed.

Not long after that, their *mentales* powers began to blossom. Rather than leaving their gifts to chance as was normally the case, Rafaela began to work with them to bring out what gifts she wanted them to have, namely telekinesis. Above all else, the women had to have this skill.

What was not apparent to these patients of Rafaela's was just how closely she monitored the intake of psi-powder and the rate of maturation of their *mentales* gifts. From much experience, she had this down very precisely and knew just when a person reached their full potential. At that point, she ceased giving them the dust in their food. Additional amounts did nothing. Well, unless they inhaled the dust as Meg and Josh had.

However, with Amy and Jan, she became somewhat surprised. All the others had been weaned from the dust and were now beginning their training, but no so for these two. Their powers just continued to escalate for an additional two weeks before leveling off. Now Rafaela had a very good idea just how much power these two women possessed. It exceeded any other *mentales* gifted that she had yet met, which explained much to her.

Chapter 20 The High Council of the Lords, July 1272

Early morning of the first, Konrad and Nadja dressed for their most important meeting yet, with the combined rulers and their wives, venerados, veneradas, and advisors. Both knew just how critical this first meeting was. "My whole career has led us up to this point, my dear. Frankly, I am a little nervous," he admitted.

"Please tighten my corset then. I simply can't with these hands. It will calm you some," she replied, suppressing her annoyance with her hands. *Will I ever get over their loss,* she wondered, but quickly suppressed that thought as well.

A while later, she asked him, "Well, how do I look?" She wore a pale blue pod-silk gown that fell below her knees and yet revealed some of her black nylons before her matching pale blue toe shoes. Her huge dangling earrings were a contrast of gold and red rubies, just a bit daring on their colors. Of course, her tiny waistline pointed out her curves extremely well. Yet it was her huge, foot in diameter lip plates that really caught one's attention. Her long hair was brushed and fell down her back.

"Darling, you've never looked finer," he complimented her, and she finally relaxed a little.

"Now how to I look?" he asked. She adjusted his tie; it was a little crooked. He wore his favorite light brown camel hair suit coat with matching pants. His black leather shoes were freshly polished, his moustache nicely trimmed.

"You look perfect, dear," she replied. "Shall we?" She offered him her arm, and they headed for the elevator and their electric car on the ground floor. Within a few minutes, they arrived outside the imposing stone walls of the old Imperial Castle with its tall, central tower surrounded by a huge manor house with its giant emerald-colored throne room and multitudes of smaller rooms. As arranged beforehand, Lord Emilio Bolivar was there waiting for him. He was dressed much the same as Konrad, including a pipe corset, but his suit was a dark brown suede.

His katalyein wife, Anita, looked radiant in her red satin gown. She too wore the usual black nylons and the tall heels. Nadja knew immediately what this meant. Anita was helpless and needed others to help her with such simple things as eating or drinking. So too did Venerada Maricela, who wore a light blue satin gown, very similar to Nadja's. Her nylons were plainly visible as were her matching heels. Nadja now knew what these two women were giving up to look gorgeous and presentably formal at this meeting. Her husband, Theo, kept his arm securely around her waist, as if she was a bird that might at any moment fall from the sky. His Squad Leader, Domineo Bolivar-Brom, and his wife Sally, had already gone inside to reserve their places.

"My Nadja, I do like your new look! Most impressive!" Lord Bolivar said as he welcomed the two. "Shall we go inside? Amo Domingo has reserved our places. When it is time for you to speak, I will lead you to the throne platform. Nadja will accompany you, but she should stand on your right side."

Arm in arm, the couples entered, along with others who were just arriving. Nadja could not help noticing the many women who were noticing her. Inside, the main throne room was rapidly filling up, but Amo Domingo reserved a spot for them on the far left side not too far from the throne. A vast array of chairs had been arranged, and the small group took their seats, thankful for Amo Domingo's action. Seats together were becoming a premium, as more men and women continued to enter. Nadja noticed a low hum of conversation and realized in all likelihood, most were chatting via telepathy. Soon, she told herself, soon I will be too.

Just then, they spotted Lord Gervasi Quito Malaca, his wife, Rosita, and party entering. She was the only woman who was hopping, quite distinctive in the crowd. Evidently, Lord Bolivar was telepathically talking to him. Nadja saw them heading their way, Rosita hopping alongside of him. They took several seats near them. Nadja's felt an instant sympathy for Rosita, who probably felt very ill at ease among so many "normal" people. She vowed to chat with her when she could.

Lord Bolivar whispered to Konrad, "This session is being hosted by Lord Wye. He will say a few opening words and then call roll. After that, we are up first."

Shortly, Lord Wye rose and held his hand out, assisting his wife to rise to her feet. She wore a fetter-gown in red satin. However, she did not have lip plates or toe shoes. Together, they made their way to the raised stone platform. The thrones behind them were never used, had not been for a very long time.

"Lords, Ladies, Venerados, Veneradas, Amos, Amas, gentlemen, gentlewomen," he began. Instantly, Konrad and Nadja knew the formal pecking order of the attendees. "I am pleased to even be here to welcome you all to the High Council of the Lords of Tierra. We have had a blessed holy miracle last month. The barbarian horde and their un-killable leader are gone. We will hold a special meeting to discuss this singular event this afternoon. Lady Wye wants me to tell you the musicians will be playing here in the throne room from six until nine tonight. Come and dance. Help us celebrate being alive. Honestly, I didn't expect to even be here because of the barbarians."

"That said, as you all know by now, Tierra has a new alien governor. Can't say we miss the old one, however." Konrad detected just how Lord Wye felt about Emeryk; he filed that tidbit for later use. "I call upon Lord Emilio Bolivar, who will introduce our newest governor who wishes to address us at this time." He waved to Emilio, put his arm around his wife and led her back down to their seats close to the raised platform.

Emilio rose, as did Konrad, who helped Nadja rise gracefully. Holding her tightly, they followed Emilio up to the platform. He carefully helped Nadja manage the six-inch step. They moved behind Lord Bolivar. He cleared his throat and began, "Due to unusual circumstances or quirks of fate, I have had the pleasure of meeting our new governor and his charming wife some months ago. Unlike our previous governors, both he and his wife will address us in the Midlands tongue, though they both also speak fairly good Westerlings and Easterlings. This is due in part to his wife who is a linguist. They both feel it is important for a governor to be able to speak to their constituents in their own language. At this time, I would like to introduce our new Governor Konrad Burkhardt and his charming wife Nadja, who sports the most impressive lip plates I've ever seen. Please notice they are not tall, skinny, and grey." Several laughs echoed around the room. "Governor," he said motioning to him with his hand. He quickly stepped down and returned to his seat. Konrad stepped forward, while Nadja moved slightly to his right.

She had this golden opportunity to see the entire assemblage at one time. Of course, at the same time hundreds of women were staring at her. Inez was right. About half wore lip plates. About half wore toe shoes, and she spotted some men wearing toe boots, usually polished black. Most all the women had noticeably tiny waists, clearly visible by their curvaceous lines. The styles of dresses and their colors varied widely, but most were pod-silk satin or silk. Then, she spotted Inez sitting at the very back of the room, taking notes.

"Lords, Ladies, Venerados, Veneradas, Amos, Amas, gentlemen, gentlewomen," Konrad began emulating Lord Wye's introduction, "I am extremely pleased to be here today to speak with all of you. And no, we are not tall, thin, or grey like those from Rigel-3. In fact, we look much as you do. When we arrived here on Tierra, I too wore lip plates similar to those I see being worn here today. I had my lips healed so I could speak distinctly and clearly to all of you today. What I have to say is very important to you and to all of your people. Nadja and I believe it is absolutely vital we be able to speak to you in your own language and properly so, though you must forgive me if I stumble a bit. I've only been here a short while."

"That said, I'll get right to the main points I wish to communicate to all of you. There has been a significant change in governorship. While I have been here only a few weeks, already I have been able to make some fundamental changes to your great benefit. I have an open door policy. Anyone can bring anything to me at any time. I promise you I will listen and do my best to follow up."

"Now for the first change. As some of you well know, during the past centuries, some Rigel-3 criminals kidnaped some of your young telepaths, took them to other worlds, and sold them into slavery or used them as spies. I cannot pretend to be able to hunt down criminals from a century ago; they are probably long dead. However, I have already gotten this practice *ended*. From now on, I will be arresting any alien, as you would say, who kidnaps anyone here on Tierra, and I will see they are prosecuted to the fullest extent. I have gotten the backing of the Sector ID Minister on this one. No more kidnaping, period."

Lord Bolivar began clapping and shortly the room burst into a hearty round of applause. Konrad graciously accepted it, but presented a humble look on his face. When the applause died down, he then continued.

"I have come here today for a far more important reason. All the previous governors and those who ran the post from above, such as the Sector ID Ministers, have all done you people a most grave *disservice*! You see, in the Imperium, we have a legislative body called the Imperial Senate. It is they who make the laws that affect the many worlds within the vast Imperium. Every regular world has one or more senators in that body to represent their world's interests. Each senator has one vote."

"However, Tierra is a closed world. However, every other closed world in the Imperium has a senator at the Senate to represent their interests as well. While senators from a closed world do not actually have a vote, they can and usually do speak to the combined group on issues that affect their worlds. From the very beginning nearly three centuries ago, Tierra *should* have had a senator there to represent your interests, to bring up such crimes as the kidnaping of your young telepaths, and many other things. Yet, all of my predecessors have failed utterly to even mention this *vital*, critical detail to you, the ruling lords. That must *end*. I come before you today to do everything in my power to convince you that having a senator on Proxima Prime, where the Senate is located, is absolutely *critical* for your planet's well-being. Your senator and his or her aides and wives will be granted dual citizenship. That means, that they will be able to travel freely anywhere within the vast Imperium, as well as returning here to Tierra, which otherwise is closed to all visitors, except in extremely rare situations."

"If you like, I can outline what this senator will be able to do, what his or her duties are, how he or she will be able to communicate back to this council of lords, and anything related to the position. When I came here, that was the first thing I asked about? Who is your senator? I was *appalled* that not only did you not have one, but you were not even *told* you could and *should* have one! Well, I will do my very best to get this horrible wrong rectified here today. You have my sworn word on this one."

Lord Wye spoke up, "Excuse me Governor Burkhardt, but just what can a senator do for us if he has no vote? It seems pointless to me." Several hushed voices agreed with him.

"Please, just Konrad. At first glance, that would seem to be the case. Let me assure you that is far, far from the truth." Konrad talked for nearly twenty minutes outlining various things their senator could do for Tierra. "Let me summarize by giving you one recent development in which Nadja and I played a role. Prior to being assigned here, we were assigned to a newly discovered world. When we arrived there, we discovered that the women of that world had no hands or feet. At first, we thought this must be the most barbaric world ever. Soon, in conversations with their leaders, we learned every female baby ever born on this world was born without hands and feet. I assigned my doctor to investigate this phenomenon that very day. He soon discovered through the marvels of Imperial medicine that the women had a defective gene which was responsible. The male gene was the dominant gene. In simple terms, when males were born, their dominant gene gave them hands and feet. When a female was born, she did not have the male contribution, and thus her recessive genes caused her body not to develop hands and feet. More importantly, my doctor developed a cure for this. Sadly, the women did not wish to change at this time, calling us 'sky people.' However, they did send off a senator to represent their world. At such time as they change their minds, their senator can immediately request a medical team go to their world and use the cure on every woman."

His anecdote caused quite a stir, and he had to pause briefly. Lord Wye then asked, "How are these senators chosen? Do we get to pick them?"

"Of course you get to pick your own senator and his or her aides. In many worlds, this is done by holding elections. Here on your world, I would anticipate this High Council would choose your senator. How long is a senator's term of office? As long as you lords wish. It could even be a posting for life, but I would suggest changing senators more often than that. Fresh points of view and all that," Konrad explained.

Konrad continued to field other questions from other lords. Time flew by and Nadja's toes were throbbing. She'd been standing in one place far too long. Finally, Konrad appeared finished. Lord Wye rose. "Thank you, Governor Konrad. This has indeed been a most interesting meeting. On behalf of us lords, I hope we can meet again in the future as matters come up. In the meantime, on behalf of we lords, I would like to invite you and your wife to return for our Royal Ball that begins at six tonight. I look forward to seeing you here."

"Why thank you, Lord Wye. Nadja and I would be delighted to attend. I do hope some of you would be so kind as to show us how to dance your dances. I'm afraid she and I are wholly ignorant of them." He then took Nadja's arm and felt her heavy reliance on him.

She whispered, "My feet are giving out! Don't let me fall, please." They got to their seats, giving her a much needed breather. One by one, the crowd began moving for the doors that led to the huge dining hall. While Nadja recovered, Konrad chatted briefly with Lord Bolivar.

"I hope this went well," he said, looking for some feedback.

"Indeed it has. Perfectly setup with the kidnaping ruling. Never has a governor been formally asked to join our Royal Ball. I believe much progress has been made. Now comes the hard part, finding a senator and aides on which everyone can agree," Emilio replied.

Konrad chuckled, "That is always the case on every

world. Best of luck to you. We will be here at six." Enough had filed out so they had a clear shot for the door. Konrad helped Nadja to her feet and they took their leave.

On their way home, Konrad said, "Well, it's too soon to tell for certain, but I do believe we are going to get them their senator."

"I think so too, dear. We ought to know far more by tonight," she agreed with him, but wondered how she could possibly dance in her toe shoes. Then, she thought of the other women and men who wore them and relaxed.

"We were not asked about the transport ship that crashed in the Midlands yet. What are we going to tell them about?" she asked. "We ought to have our stories straight."

"True we should. Be careful only to tell the truth. According to that listing of *mentales* gifts, some are able to detect when someone is lying. We can swear we know the object was not any Imperium ship. We do not know where it came from. We suppose it came from the Federation, but it may well have originated elsewhere within the Imperium. So we say it wasn't ours. But we did detect it crashing and exploding. I did send out ships to investigate and recover anything salvageable so alien technology did not fall into their hands, as I am obliged to do to honor their lease. We leave it at that. Lord knows, we have no idea how that army got swallowed up by those earth fissures." Both agreed on their stories. This was prudent because later they were asked about it several times during the evening.

Rested and recovered, Nadja and Konrad again entered the Imperial Castle and made for the throne room. This time, the chairs had been removed, allowing a huge open space for dancing or friendly chatting. The musicians were now on the raised platform before the thrones. Against the back wall, tables with refreshments beckoned. Once more, the place was packed. The two did very little dancing, however. Almost at once, various lords came up to chat privately with Konrad. Many women commandeered Nadja pulling her away from Konrad, who she didn't see for the rest of the evening.

"Such incredible lip plates!" Lady Ross, the wife of the Lord of Villa del Rey began. She too wore lip plates and asked her many questions, speaking in the Westerlings language. Nadja fielded them with aplomb. By the end of the evening, three dozen women with lip plates expressed their admiration for hers and begged her to convince Inez to have Elegant Fashions Inc copy hers. Other women, who also wore toe shoes, chatted about how freely she was able to walk in them. She pointed out her walking slit made taking reasonable sized steps possible. Many women, who also had no hands, asked her about her difficulties with them, and she discovered that she was not alone. All who wore them complained of having similar problems caused by no sense of touch. Other women asked about how she lost her hands. Others wanted her to have Inez replicate her fantastic earrings; they only hinted about their cost or worth.

Still other Easterlings women suggested she ought to begin wearing arm-fetter-gowns as they did. "We Easterlings have always been bound, so we are used to taking very tiny steps," one older woman explained. She went on to give Nadja, who was a good listener, a goodly history of Easterlings culture, with emphasis on women's issues. At least the music was not loud enough to interfere with the many conversations.

By the end of the evening, Nadja was trying hard to keep from laughing as Inez came up to her. Every aspect of her physical appearance, apparel, accessories, and shoes had been commented upon. The women were nearly equally divided on praising an aspect or discounting it. She told this to Inez, who laughed. "I might as well stand here naked," Nadja exclaimed, which only caused Inez to laugh harder.

"I told you that you would find yourself center stage in women's fashions. You look like one of us, and you are the governor's wife. Speaking of which, I haven't seen much of him all night. I think the lords have absconded with him," Inez replied. "Say, have the women been asking you to ask me to copy your lip plates?"

"Yes and my earrings. Ah well. I wonder how Konrad is faring?"

Just then, Lady Wye came up to her again. "Excuse me Nadja. We women are holding our own luncheon tomorrow at noon. Ladies only. Let the men fend for themselves. We would all just love to have you attend, if you can."

"Why, I would be delighted. Thank you for asking, Lady Wye."

"Oh just Sally, please. Good. Noon, I will have someone watching for you, and they will show you the way. It is very easy to get lost in this huge castle. Til then," she said gaily and moved off to connect with another woman.

"I'll come with you, if you don't mind. I think you might want someone to watch your back," Inez half-teased.

When the music finally ended, again the group began filing out. At long last, a tired looking Konrad walked over to them. As they headed home, Konrad said, "I am exhausted. I've had my arm twisted in every conceivable direction tonight. But I do believe we have gained their confidence. How did it go with you?" She laughed and chatted about her evening.

The next day, Inez and another woman were there waiting for Nadja to arrive. This time, she braved the trip herself. After all, she told herself, she had chosen to wear toe shoes again, and she must make the best of it. "Right on time," Inez complimented her punctuality. Quietly, Inez slipped her arm around Nadja's waist, giving her some support.

The dining room was filled with the women she'd met the night before. Today, Nadja wore a red satin gown, matching the rubies in her earrings, with red toe shoes to match. She soon discovered many women, who had lip plates, wanted to see if she could even eat with them in place. She did so, showing them how to bring the food into her mouth from the sides. She also noticed several women, who did not have them, watching her as well. Nadja imagined what they were likely pondering.

Later, she found herself talking with an Easterlings woman from Southbend. Nadja remember the word that she had heard. "Say, I came across an Easterlings word that I don't know what it means. It was *sesso disposto*." The woman chuckled. She also wore lip plates and earlier had tried to get her to begin wearing arm-fetter-gowns, as a proper woman should, according to her.

"In the Easterlings, a man may have as many wives as he can support. If he should die in a battle with another, his wives may then demand *sesso disposto* of the victorious man. That is a holy ceremony for the late widows. They go to the victor's bed and prove to him they can fully satisfy the victor and his needs. If they do satisfy him, then he is obligated to accept them into his own harem and fully support them. Easterlings women are traditionally bound to their husbands for survival, you see. The loss of a husband is about the worst thing that can happen to her. This way, if she can please the victor, he must then accept her and support her, for he took the life of her husband. See how perfect this is for we women?" she asked. Nadja agreed to its merits.

Again, she was besieged with questions like these. Isn't it way too hard to walk in those toe shoes? Those toe shoes look so good on you, is it hard to learn to walk in them? Those lip plates look extremely attractive. Don't those lip plates of yours interfere with nearly everything? Again, she was bombarded from both sides of all issues, but always it was friendly, and she realized these ladies accepted her into their society as one of them. One went so far as to ask her why the governor never held any balls and invited all the lords, ladies, and nobles to attend. She promised to see if Konrad would do just that. Many women overheard that one and added their agreement to the suggestion.

In stark contrast to the women, the men were bickering and verbally fighting among themselves. They had all agreed to the idea of having a senator to represent them. That part had been easy. Ten minutes of discussion and that motion passed. Now into their second day of discussing just who should go off-world to represent them was still being hashed out.

Lord Bolivar was quite shred. He knew what Benjamina wanted and just who she had already picked to be their senator and aides. Timing, he knew, was everything. Every time a lord nominated a man for the post, his suggestion was shot down. All four groups wanted their person to be the senator. Emilio waited patiently. Mid-afternoon of the second day of deliberations, at long last, Lord Wye realized Lord Emilio had not yet said a single word, either for or against any of the proposed men.

Vic Broquard

"We are at an impasse, but Lord Bolivar there has not said a darn thing all this time. Surely, you have something to contribute, speak up man. I assure you we are all listening." Now was the proper time.

"My Lords, I have a workable solution I would like to propose. First and foremost, our senator *must* and I do mean *must* be highly experienced at living off-world and dealing with the wild things that are out there. Do you not agree?"

"Yes, yes, it would be a disaster to send someone off-world who has never been off-world. But who here has been? None of us. Your point?" Lord Wye countered.

"I know someone who has been off-world for almost a century and has only recently returned here. The person is *mentales* gifted, very highly educated, knows well how to spy on others, which would be most useful for our senator to be able to do, is independently wealthy in Imperium credits, knows their way around the Imperium bureaucracy, and how to drive a very hard bargain," Emilio said, rather slowly allowing each aspect a chance to soak in to their minds.

"Who is this miracle person? He is obviously the ideal senator for us! Out with it, man," Lord Wye nearly screamed in impatience. Many others echoed his sentiments, calling out, "he is perfect!"

"It is not a he, but a she." The men sat back stunned for a moment. "You all just agreed the attributes are perfect, just what we need. So why the back off just because she is a woman?"

Lord Wye grumbled a little and said, "Well, you have a point. No man here can remotely meet those requirements that she has. Just who is this mystery woman?"

"Hear me out. There is more than this involved in my selection," Emilio needed to prepare them for more than just a name, which he knew would raise tempers. "Her name is Isabella Valen." As anticipated, the fireworks began. It took them a half hour to calm down.

"Let me tell you about her. She was kidnaped by the Rigel-3 men when she was just fourteen. She was taken to another world and forced to use her telepathic skills to help a fat man make better business deals. Eventually, she extricated

412

herself from that and has spent over a half century trying to find a way back here. We are a closed world, and she was only recently able to find a clever way here. All the people she knew are long dead. She has no aspirations to attempt a coop in Castle Valen. In fact, she isn't interested in returning there and now is making Brom her new home. She has agreed to be your senator representing the views of the Westerlings. However, there is more, gentlemen. What about the rest of us?"

"Yes, what about the rest of us," Lord Valen of the Renegade Tower exclaimed. He had been fighting bitterly for a City-State Alliance representative.

"I have all of us covered, at least in part. Isabella has never married a man in her long life and for good reasons. She wanted to return home somehow. I have convinced her to wed two other young women; one will act as her wife; the other as her aide, and thus meeting the governor's requirements. One of these women comes from the Easterlings and specifically from the City-State Alliance. She is willing to represent both interests since, in her case, they are so closely allied." Someone called out what city. "Po, Arad, my lord. Now the other young woman has agreed to represent the Midlands. Both of these young women are also *mentales* gifted. Thus, all of our sectors are covered. We have the undecided advantage of having three telepaths working for us. That ought to be a powerful advantage, since as you know, they can also subtly bend other's minds to agree with them. My Lords, to my way of thinking, having a highly experienced off-world senator, along with three telepaths, three *mentales* gifted, gives us a huge advantage in this Senate."

As he had hoped, the discussion now focused on just what might be accomplished by having three *mentales* gifted representatives there. A half hour later, Lord Wye called for a vote. The lords were in complete agreement with Lord Bolivar's suggestion. They then wanted to set up meetings with their sector's new representatives, and they all wanted to meet Isabella.

"I will see if Venerada Maricela can arrange for the three women to be teleported here, say this evening. Will that be satisfactory?" It was and he sent word to Maricela, who was chatting with other the few other veneradas. Most towers were now again controlled by men.

Isabella, Celia, and Gabriella, dressed in identical red satin gowns, with pipe corsets, black nylons, and the requisite six-inch heels, arrived just after supper. At once, they were escorted into the private meeting room, where all the lords, their advisors, and tower representatives were seated. Isabella was prepared to be grilled. The new Lord Valen and those from Valen were instantly on her side, but she expected this.

As the lords began attacking her, primarily because she was a Valen and the treachery of the Valens was still in everyone's mind, she finally got angry. "Damn all of you anyway! Where the hell were you when the Rigel-3 men broke into my bedroom and took me away? I was only fourteen! Who of you came after me? Who tried to rescue me? Who even alerted the governor I had been kidnaped? Who insisted and demanded I be located and returned home? A defenseless fourteen year old girl you let be tossed to the wolves! There isn't a man here I would bed. You are pathetic! In my century of living out there among vast technology, many worlds, I have learned much! I had to survive and survive I did! I've amassed a fortune by Tierra standards. It took me nearly a century to find a way back to this closed world, but I did it and without the most minuscule assistance from anyone on Tierra."

"Excuse me, Ama Isabella," Lord Wye broke in on her diatribe, "Might we inquire how it was you were able to return home?"

Isabella mellowed a little. She smiled. "I am devious, if nothing else. I tried every way imaginable to sneak back to Tierra, but was stopped every time. Closed world. No outside admittance read the signs, rigidly enforced. So I made a way back here. I found the ideal people. One, I sensed would become stellar governor. I cleverly joined up with him and his wife. Yes, Konrad and Nadja. For quite some time now, I have been their 'computer technician.' But really, I was subtly assisting them in their work — Nadja with her language studies, Konrad with his assigned objectives. Together, we have made him the star of the Imperium governors. All along, I knew their goal was to get to this planet. Both were intensely curious about a telepathic society. General knowledge of us is a closely guarded secret, but they found clues, and I provided some as well. Both were driven to be the best governor around and so get assigned to Tierra. I made myself indispensable to the both of them, and they brought me back home here, when Konrad finally was appointed governor of Tierra. Could any of you have pulled something like this off? I doubt that very much."

"But can you be fair and represent all of us, not just Valen's interests?" Lord Rusden asked.

"Hell, I don't give a rat's ass about any specific kingdom or sector by themselves. All I have ever cared about is our whole world, all of us. I will represent all Tierra and never just one kingdom or tower, not ever. When did one tower do anything to rescue me?"

After that, they accepted her as their senator. Now they turned their attention to the two women, whose lower arms were missing. Celia and Gabriella played their roles well. Gabriella responded to one question, "We figure out there, Isabella ought to have a wife. That will keep all men at bay. We three have not yet decided if we both should be married to her. Not all cultures accept harems as do Easterlings. It may be best if one of us acts as her advisor, while the other is her wife." That went over well, though the Easterlings men would have preferred a harem.

After that, all discussions centered on just how the three women would represent them and what their desires would be. All three agreed the best way to handle this would be to come and visit each lord and discuss their needs personally. Isabella asked that Lord Brom and Venerada Maricela coordinate these visits.

So it was that on the morning of the third of July, Lord Wye met with Governor Burkhardt to tell him they had agreed to send a senator off to join the Senate. Konrad was a little surprised to learn his own computer technician would be their senator, but he was also pleased she was chosen. He also was pleased the two "crippled" women would be joining her. Minutes after Lord Wye left him, he dialed up Sector ID Minister Emeryk.

"It is done, boss. They have agreed to send a senator to the Senate to represent Ashford-5. They have chosen their personnel, but they want a month or so for the senator and her aides to visit with each lord to find out what the lords might desire from them. I will schedule their flight as soon as they are ready."

"My god, Konrad! Unbelievable! I don't know how you do it! Well done, well done. You are definitely the best governor in the entire Imperium! As such, I am not about to let you go! I hope that you don't mind, but I want you stationed there on Ashford-5 permanently."

"That is fine with me. We like it here, and there is so much to do and accomplish yet. Perfect boss. Thank you."

"No, thank you, Konrad. If you ever need anything, don't hesitate to let me know." Konrad smiled. He now had the ID minister in his hands.

Chapter 21 Changes

"Okay, let me make sure I have the names right," Konrad suggested. "Gabriella Valen will be listed as your official wife, but Celia is your Number Two and will go by Celia Dominic? Have I got it right?"

"Precisely, governor," Isabella replied. They reported to him late that afternoon to make it official. He punched in the Execute button, and the machine spat out their ID cards with their pictures and retinal scans on them. The three cards were marked dual citizenship, and they carried the official senate diplomatic stripes. Isabella knew those stripes were crucial, for many, many doors would now be open to her and her two new friends.

"Thank you. We have to meet with the lords yet. Shall we set up a departure date for the 15th of August?" she suggested, giving them plenty of time.

"Excellent, excellent. One nice feature, you may bring along as many personal bags as you need. Diplomatic wavers on cargo weight," he explained. "I believe that Nadja is to return with you to Brom?"

"Yes, she is going to meet us at Elegant Fashions Inc. We ought to pick up a few outfits before we go. We must look our best for the Senate," Isabella replied. They took their leave and headed back into Exchange City. Isabella already had sufficient clothing, but Celia and Gabriella didn't, so this shopping spree was for the two. "Hey, it's my dime, but buy what all you think you might need. It is cheaper here than out there, especially the nylons and heels." By the time Nadja arrived with her two large bags, they had filled a small crate.

"Had a devil of a time with these bags!" Nadja complained. "They weigh just over five pounds and keep pulling the darn hands off. I am ready. Honestly, I am so excited my knees are shaking. I can't believe this is happening to me."

"Slower Nadja, remember you have your lip plates again," Isabella reminded her, and Nadja flushed, but repeated it more slowly and as clearly as she could.

"I know," she added, "but I needed to get them and the toe shoes back to make sure that Konrad succeeded in getting you three as Tierra's senator and aides. Now, it seems that I am starting a new fashion trend. I hope the women who want theirs as large as mine don't regret it. Things are far more awkward and challenging with disks this big."

"Well, you are certainly getting quite noticed," Isabella replied with a hint of sarcasm in her voice. "I'll get your bags for you."

A few minutes later, they were back in Brom Tower, where Misty was waiting to take Nadja with her to see Rafaela. "Okay, are you ready for this gift?"

"Oh yes, very much so," she replied, remembering to speak slowly and carefully this time.

"Very well. In your case, the process will take a week or so of preparations. I know you will be bored, but I insist you stay here, where I can keep constant watch over you. Can't afford any mistakes. I've taken the liberty to bring your equipment down here. I figured you probably have a lot of work to do with all the data you've collected so far."

"Thanks. Right, I am way behind. It's these hands. I go so darn slow since I lost mine. But I do manage and that's what is important. While I can't actually speak properly now, I do have sound bites I've recorded that I can use in place of my own voice speaking the words. I won't be a bother to you will I?" she asked.

Rafaela smiled, "No dear. It is my pleasure to help you. I know how much you have helped others and will continue to do so. I've brought you some tea and biscuits. Enjoy. Holler if you need anything." She left, but later checked to make sure she'd consumed her first dosage of the psi-power she'd put in the biscuits. She had. The process had begun.

She made her nightly check on the others and found all was going well. Ken caught up with her. "Yes, it's begun for Nadja. I hope we are doing the right thing," she answered his unspoken question.

"I'm just glad things have quieted down some. Josh is making good progress, but he seems to have a rather heavy endowment of raw *mentales* power."

"Yes that's to be expected. He inhaled enough almost to kill him. Still, time will tell. In a way, it is working out well for the four women. They really do need him, and, from what little I know and sense from Josh, he needs them," she hinted. Ken didn't follow her but decided to see if he could work it out for himself. Just now, he felt inadequate. His mother was way ahead of him again, and now Rafaela was too. This bothered him more than he would admit.

The next day, Benjamina sent a telepathic message for Rafaela to come to her room. When she arrived, she found Isabella sitting on a chair beside Benjamina's bed. Mechanically, she pulled up another chair. Benjamina said, "Isabella here believes we are withholding key information from her. She insists on being fully informed before she actually leaves Tierra."

"And what did you say?" Rafaela asked. With the powerful Valen telepath sitting this close to her, it was pointless to attempt to use telepathy to hide anything from her.

"I told her we both would be up front with her, but that she could not share what we say here with anyone other than Amy and Jan. Sorry, I keep forgetting their new names."

"Very good, Benjamina."

"I'll begin at the beginning, but I am too old to waste time on the many details, Isabella. Grant me that much. Rafaela here can provide more details, if you truly need them. You see, it began when I realized just what the katalyein were actually doing when they removed a mental block a person had that prevented their *mentales* gifts from activating. It is the same mental trauma that we all have, only theirs specifically blocks their gifts. With the help of others, I worked out our therapy. Indeed, Isabella, one could use it on those, who have a mental block on their gifts. Since it does take time and since often they don't have time or are ill, the katalyein approach is the best way."

"Now most people believe a person is born with their gifts, that they are fixed, and whatever they have initially is all that they will ever have. We've proven that is not true. Once a person has the initial *mentales* gift, he or she can learn nearly any other gift in the old Marisol's listing."

Isabella looked shocked. "You are kidding? You can learn to do any of those?"

"Yes, it takes coaching, patience, and practice. Next, we discovered the true source of all *mentales* gifts lay in the psi-dust, particularly the germanium crystal dust, the very same dust the Imperium converts into their precious fuel. In this matter, Rafaela is the expert. She has the dosages down to a fine art. In two weeks, Nadja, for example, will blossom into a new *mentales* gifted woman. We took it further. During this formation period, we are able partially to control what gift finally materializes in the person. We had to do this with the hundreds of mermaids. They cannot live without telekinetic ability. We saw to it this was each of the mermaid's primary gift. We've been rewarded for our efforts. They have been living fairly independent lives since then."

"Absolutely amazing. Who all knows of this?" Isabella asked.

"Very few outside the Underground. The verandas of Brom Tower only. There is more, Isabella, far more. Rafaela. will you tell her the story of the Madiera women please? I need to rest a little."

Rafaela took up the tale, spending a half hour telling her about the mysterious appearance of the spaceship with its artificial city and hundreds of refugee women. She described their elemental powers in detail. "So you see where our line of thinking has gone, Isabella. These women also had mental powers, not unlike our own, but highly specialized into one of the four elemental forces. Let me tell you, these women are incredibly powerful. Petrona has fire-elemental powers. They exceed anything anyone here in Brom could ever do. The same is true of the other three elemental groups."

"Now this is highly secret information, Isabella, but it was Elana and eleven of her earth-elemental friends who wiped out Damiano's army."

"Good god! This is unbelievable, except I've seen the results with my own eyes! The earth literally swallowed up his army!"

"Yes, we have had to use their special powers before many years ago to similarly safeguard the fragile peace and prevent more wars," Rafaela added. "So for the last twenty years, we have been working out how these women get their powers. They were all born with them while they were aboard their spaceship. It has taken us some years, but we now know that their pituitary glands are greatly enlarged just as ours are. The mental psi powers are generated via that gland's secretions, but we don't know how just yet," Rafaela explained.

"Just incredible," Isabella declared.

"There is more. Mating a Madiera woman with a normal man produces children who only have a slight tendency to master the elemental powers their mother had. Mating a Madiera woman with a *mentales* gifted man produces children who have the same gift as their mother. The same elemental powers. If their mother is fire-based, their children are also fire-based. They never switch elemental forces."

"So you have been breeding *mentales* gifted men to produce more of those like the Madiera mothers?" Isabella asked.

"Not specifically breeding. We encourage the women to marry a *mentales* gifted men, nothing more. Rather, we have worked out just how in effect to create a Madiera gift from scratch — take a normal person and wind up with someone with the powers and abilities of Elana or Petrona. Isabella, it does *not* involve psi-dust. Just a massive amount of Benjamina's *therapy*! We have finally discovered the true native *powers* of spiritual beings!"

"What? More therapy and the person can become godlike?" Isabella gasped in disbelief.

"Precisely so. Some of the mermaids now have rather immense powers," Rafaela explained.

Benjamina now spoke again. "So you see the dilemma we are facing at this moment. We have the powers of a god in our hands. We can take any person and turn them into someone with almost unheard of powers. Yet, we have been hesitant to announce this to the world. It is not ready for such things. That is one major reason why I will not use the rejuvenation machine. I too am not ready to make such decisions as to who gets these godlike powers and who does not. I refuse to play god. Yet, Rafaela and I do not know how to proceed with this."

She sighed and went on. "We all know just how awful our own Dark Ages were, where the *mentales* gifted wielded enormous powers, had massive instruments of death, and very nearly destroyed our whole world. If we release this now, we are both terrified we'll simply be unleashing such vast powers, and this time there will be no preventing the total destruction of Tierra. Lord knows we don't need another hundred Wystans running rampant across Tierra. One Damiano has caused more than enough damage. You see what we are facing here? The sheer magnitude of my discoveries?"

"Yes, mind blowing, Benjamina, utterly mind blowing." Isabella could think of no other words to describe it.

"Yet there is more. The Goddess Lysandra has told us we are on the track to free all of our people on Tierra. By that, we believe now perhaps all of us were once as she is, a being who can operate fully without the need of a body, which is basically a via on the person's power lines. We believe it is her wish that we continue to chart the path to such a renewal of freedom for all people on Tierra. Yet, we are at a crossroads, and I fear that I may take the wrong path and lead us all into oblivion instead of to freedom. I do not want to do that."

Rafaela added, "Legends say in the ancient days, some of our tower lords could, by using their powers, bring down any number of the Rigel-3's spaceships, and that they even did so or threatened the Rigel-3 people with it. Isabella, we are talking about that kind of power and much, much more. Right now, we are at an impasse. We don't know which way to turn."

Isabella thought for a moment, reflecting upon these unimaginable revelations. She had expected to hear of all manner of devious spying missions. This was wholly unexpected. "Well, I have been on many Imperium worlds, the so-called civilized ones. There are many unscrupulous men and women out there as well, probably more than are here on Tierra, percentage-wise. If they got a hold of this, the murderous campaigns would make our Dark Ages seem trivial.

So it would seem to me what you need to do next is figure out how to eliminate all the evil tendencies and propensities in man and woman so they can be trusted with such powers."

Rafaela raised her eyebrows. "Benjamina, she has a very good point. Perhaps that is the direction we should look into next."

Benjamina chuckled faintly. "Isabella came here to find out vital information, and she ends up giving it to us, Rafaela. Ironic how things happen. Yes, Rafaela, she is right. We need to map out a new line of therapy, one that focuses on the elimination of evil intentions, evil purposes and goals, evil tendencies and proclivities in man and woman. That should keep us busy for a very long time. Isabella, your primary job as Tierra's senator is to keep Tierra a closed world, to keep others from coming here and by accident or chance stumbling on our discoveries, and then exploiting them to the destruction of the universe. That is your primary mission, all else is secondary. Appease the lords as best you can, but safeguard Tierra for as long as you can. The Underground will continue to research all this. It is my fondest desire that we find the solution."

"I promise you I will do so or die trying," Isabella swore. *This changes everything!* She thought.

"One final thing, don't worry about me. This body is old and not long for the world. I don't want to use the rejuvenation machine for other reasons as well. Depending on how many years I try to take off of my body, I could end up without hands once more, or further back in years in more trouble physically, or further back even as the man as I was born. All those possibilities will be a barrier to the research. I already have new baby bodies arranged for Tim and for me. We will be able to retain all our memories and skills with these new bodies, except we'll need a few years to grow them into adulthood again. Tim and I would prefer this route. Until we rejoin you, Rafaela and Andres will continue our research. Heck by that time, those two bright ones might have the whole problem solved," Benjamina suggested.

"You must tell all this to Amy and Jan, but only when you cannot be overheard. I know Jan will want to say goodbye to her son, Tim, if he can hold on that long," she added.

"Isabella, on the backs of a very few of us lies the salvation not only of all Tierra, but very likely the whole universe out there, all peoples everywhere. I am sorry to have placed this weight on you, who have born so much already, but you are the only one who has been off-world besides the surprise appearance of Amy and Jan."

Isabella chuckled. "When you put it that way, how can I possibly refuse? I spent most of my life trying to get back home. Now that I am finally here, I must leave once again. Yet, now I can return freely anytime I want. That's something."

After a moment, she asked, "Say, one small question. This Nadja. Is it wise to turn her into a telepath? I mean she is alien and the wife of the governor. Can you trust her?"

"She knows too much already. Yet, she has provided us with some key information that may one day be valuable," Benjamina answered her. "She has proven trustworthy so far. Once she has the gift, then we can exercise more control over her, if we have to. Still, I believe she has a role to play in all this, only I am not sure what it is just yet."

"Well, she's becoming the fashion model for women," Isabella joked. Both women grinned in response. "Okay I best go talk to my wives. How strange this is going to be." Again, the women chuckled.

Note, it was mid-July before Celia and Gabriella were taken off their daily doses of psi-powders. They had finally reached their peaks. That last day, Tim finally passed away. For the Underground, his passing was a great loss, and he was mourned, which pleased Celia. Her son had made valuable contributions to Tierra and would be always remembered, if only by the Underground. After the funeral, the three began their visits to the various lords, listening to what they wished their senator to do for them. Mostly such things were trivial. The men had no real conception of the Imperial Senate and its workings.

By that same time, the two armless women, Annetta and Bianca had fully realized their *mentales* gifts, carefully nurtured by Rafaela. They had telekinesis as a primary skill, beyond telepathy. Venerada Maricela sent then off to receive their tower training. Once done, she planned to assign them to the handling the vital comm networks, thus freeing up two others, who could now be used in more critical areas.

Rafaela then began spending time with Nadja. The question that she had to answer in the near future was: what form should Nadja's *mentales* gifts take? She would have telepathy for sure, but what else? She could do nothing and thus allow her to get whatever would naturally appear or she could override that and push her skills development down one or more channels, as she did with the other women. A few skills were off-limits, such as Dominate Another. Nadja was primarily interested in languages and making sure Konrad was being successful in his career as a governor. She enjoyed shopping and wearing only the finest clothing and heels available. Plus she was independently wealthy — Nadja's words. Finally, she decided to let nature take its course with Nadja.

Being cooped up in a small room for days didn't bother Nadja. Already she'd collected quite lot of recordings and data that still waited her analysis and organization. She began to work through the volume in a systematic way, beginning with the Midlands language, both spoken and written. Rafaela soon found Nadja was eager to explain her findings as she went along.

"You see a spoken language often changes over time. For example, when the Rigel-3 people arrived here, one result could have been a gradual alteration of Midlands into Imperium Standard, which is the common language that has been adopted to permit cross-planet communication between all peoples in the vast Imperium. If they had, for example, begun to rule over you or setup education centers or brought their culture widely throughout the Midlands, one would expect Midlands to sound an awful lot like Imperium Standard. It's been nearly three centuries. Yet, I am seeing nothing more than the introduction of a relatively few technical words that were not in your language before, such as spaceship and shuttle craft. Further, Midlands seems to prefer joining two existing words to form the new word as in spaceship, as opposed to the IS word, a-ce-ih."

"Is this important?" Rafaela asked.

"You have to take into consideration many such aspects of a language. For example, your language uses the subject-verb-object order for its sentences. Yet other languages arrange the three key parts differently. How one changes a statement into a question is another example. One can say: the boy throws the ball. To make a question out of it, there are many ways. For example, many languages would do it this way. Throws the boy the ball? Midlands has further modifies this. Does the boy throw the ball? You make use of the word do or how or what to help form questions."

"Is it important? Well, yes. It helps someone to learn to speak your language better. But what I am fascinated with is how closely your languages here resemble the languages in the Indo-European family."

"Where are those languages spoken? Other planets, I assume," Rafaela asked. This might be more interesting to me, she thought.

"That's what is so very strange and disturbing to me, Rafaela. Those languages are found on some of the planets in our enemy, the Federation of Planets. Yet, those planets are far beyond this sector of space. The nearest planet to Tierra on which some people speak one of the languages in this family is way beyond the outer boundary of the Imperium empire of planets. There are no planets in the Imperium whose languages are technically classifiable in that family."

"So what does this mean?" Rafaela asked, growing a bit curious.

"An isolated planet that has had no outside contact with another world develops its own sets of languages which are distinctly unique to that world and their culture. Across a large number of such worlds, we can again group those independently created languages into related families for study. On the other hand, if the planet is, shall we say, settled or originally populated by colonists from a nearby world, then the language spoken will be a derivative of the original language, usually no more complex than a dialect of the original. Naturally, there are all manner of intermediate cases between these two extremes."

"Taking Tierra in specific, if there was not this Indo-

European family of languages, then one could conclude that your people developed here in isolation from the rest of the universe. If I could find an existing language family that was somehow similar to yours, then that would suggest your ancestors came from those worlds. Yet, your language is very closely tied to this existing family. All three — Midlands, Westerlings, and Easterlings — are basically dialects of three languages within the Indo-European family. That is highly suggestive that Tierra was in fact colonized by people who spoke those original languages. That implies the colonists got here in spaceships. Yet the conundrum is: the nearest planet from which they could have come is one third of the entire galaxy away from here. One would expect to see many other worlds with these dialects between here and there. We do not see even one such world."

"So one of my goals is to collect enough linguistic data to prove your three languages are in fact true dialects of English, Spanish, and Italian, which are part of the Indo-European set, found widely on planets within the Federation. Then, let the archaeologists see if they can find any artifacts that would back up the theory that Tierra was settled from a planet within the Federation of Planets," Nadja concluded. "Isn't this stuff just absolutely fascinating?"

Rafaela smiled. "I wish we could be of more help, but our written records go back about three centuries. While there was probably stuff written down before then, none has survived as far as I know."

Just then, Nadja became embarrassed. Drool trickled down her enormous lower plate and onto her bosom. Hastily, she found a handkerchief and began wiping. "Sorry. I had my head lowered too much there. I got too excited. ^achk and the women there solved this problem by wearing bronze neck rings that held their necks rigidly in place so their saliva remained in their mouths. I wore them for a time while I was there, but that was terribly awkward and I hated them. Still, I can see their purpose now. Sorry about drooling, Rafaela."

"No need to apologize. I'm not offended. I will see if any of the other towers have any more ancient records for you."

"Would you? Oh, that would be just super great. Oh,

sorry, that was an Imperium Standard colloquialism." They chatted a bit longer before Rafaela had to leave.

When she checked up on the four women and Josh, both they and Rafaela were very happy the process was finished. Josh was fully stable and healthy once more. All five's eyes were quite yellow now with brown speckles, their *mentales* gifts full of potential. At last, she could turn these five over to Venerada Maricela, who would oversee their training and give them their germanium crystals that would amplify their powers greatly.

"Well, congratulations. You are all done here. Now it's time that Venerada Maricela Wait gets you trained so that you can best use your powers. She will be giving you a crystal just like mine and attuning it to you. It will amplify your powers perhaps a hundredfold. I'll see to the arrangements now."

"Wait a second, Rafaela," Josh spoke up. "Before we get moved elsewhere, can you marry all of us? We five don't ever want to be parted, not even for an hour. These are my guardian angels. I can't live without them or rather I should say I don't want to. Please, that way they can't separate us for very long."

Rafaela tried to convince them they really wouldn't be separated unless they wished it, but none of the five believed her. She headed off to find Venerada Maricela who, among others, had the power to marry couples. "Don't they want a formal wedding?" Maricela asked, somewhat surprised by this strange request. She was already making preparations for the five to stay in her tower, but in adjacent rooms. She amended her orders and headed off with Rafaela, messaging Tom and Ken to join them and bear official witness to the marriage.

As they entered the bedroom off the underground medical suite, she picked up why they were so insistent. None of the five had yet learned the slightest control over their telepathy. Josh desperately wanted to consummate his deep love for them, but his profound respect for them kept him from doing so until they were officially married — something to do with the morals of his world. In turn, they wanted this as well, but as exotic escorts, they were used to such things taking place far outside the sanctions of marriage or even love, it being a physical thing. Because they deeply admired and respected him, they were insisting on it too.

After marrying them in a short ceremony, the five were moved from the underground rooms over into one of her tower's great manor houses, but on the first floor. The dining room was on this floor in this house, enabling the women to walk there instead of having to be carried up and down the steps.

"But why do we need to be trained?" asked Josh.

"You need to be able to block your thoughts. Right now you are sending them out in all directions. Everyone in the building is hearing you five, as if you were screaming your thoughts as loudly as you can." All five flushed crimson, ending their slight protests. "You need to be able to protect yourselves from others who might want to eavesdrop on your thoughts. Then, you need to master your new *mentales* gifts. Practice makes perfect."

"But I don't know what mine are?" Josh admitted.

"That is part of what we do. We help you discover them and make effective use of them. So let's get started, shall we?" Maricela suggested.

Soon, she had to assign an entire Circle to their training! True, the four women now had sizeable telekinetic powers that would enable them to deal with ordinary life actions, such as feed themselves, but they also were able to levitate objects, including themselves. Rafaela had done her "tinkering" superbly. These women's unique gifts would greatly enable them to live an independent life instead of the wholly dependent one that they had been facing.

Yet that was not why an entire Circle was needed. No, it was the immense power Josh now could generate! Even without his crystal's amplification, his raw power was as great as any complete Circle. His gifts didn't seem to follow any known track or any of the specific skills on the old Marisol's List. He was more like an energy production unit of great magnitude. The problem was he wasn't stable. After a frustrating week, finally the Circle figured out what Josh's problem was. Again, they had never seen this before.

The five formed a rapport pyramid; the women

provided the solid base, the rock upon which Josh stood, figuratively. He formed the top of the pyramid. The five were interdependent upon one another, especially Josh. When they went into a light rapport, he was able to operate with stability, generating enormous quantities of raw energies. Quickly, the Circle experimented with this new facet of *mentales* gifts. Their capo "plugged" the penta-group into his own Circle, adding them much as a giant battery. Suddenly, his Circle wielded nearly double the power that they had been able to generate when each of the Circle members were at their peak output!

That very day, Venerada Maricela hired the five to work in at Brom Tower, giving the five full benefits of any other technicians. Of course, all five were extremely happy to have a source of income and actively to contribute, especially the women. Soon, the five were given the nickname penta-power by all of Brom Tower's personnel.

Still Maricela kept a watchful eye on the five. It seemed the five were almost always in a light rapport with each other, but in deep rapport when they were alone in their new quarters or actively supplying energy for one of the circles as they went about their work. Quite often, their work consisted of cutting granite stone blocks for new constructions, moving the heavy rectangular stones to the site of the new building, and then laying them in place. The penta-power team allowed the construction to double its previous pace.

Yet there was a secondary aspect to Josh's unique gifts. It indirectly involved "luck." All his life, he had managed to have lucky breaks at the right times. Months later, Maricela finally worked out the exact nature of his luck. While he could not foresee the future, if you presented him with a possible situation, using his gift, he could quickly "see" the right course of action to follow. In the future, Maricela believed this would be of immense value to Brom and perhaps to all Tierra.

By August, Nadja's full *mentales* gifts developed as did her eyes. Rafaela was pleased to discover that Nadja also had levitation and telekinetic powers. She realized that perhaps subconsciously, Nadja's physical condition helped nature develop *mentales* gifts to compensate for her disabilities. She wrote down that theory, fully intending to explore this notion in greater depth. Until now, she had not been leaving such choices to chance.

Nadja was jubilant; she felt light as a feather. To her, it seemed everything in her life had led up to this, the ultimate culmination. She was a telepath! A whole new form of communication had opened up for her. True, this skill would be of immense value in future first contact type situations, but that was relatively minor. Now she could explore a world of communication previously denied her.

Upon returning to her home on the base at Plateau Grado, she rediscovered even more. She would never forget that first night in bed with Konrad. True, he was overjoyed and bubbling with enthusiasm that she was now a telepath. He envisioned all sorts of ways she would be able to assist him in the future. But after that first night, intercourse took on a whole new meaning for both of them. She slipped into rapport with him. Between the stimulation of her large lip loops and his strong arms around her, she felt an ecstasy neither new was even possible. Getting out of bed in the morning became the most hated part of their daily routine.

After settling in, Nadja paid Inez a visit at Elegant Fashions Inc. Partly, she wanted to tell Inez about her new *mentales* gifts. Partly, she wanted to thank Inez for everything she'd done for her that helped get her to this incredible new state. Partly, she wanted to check up on the fashion scene. Such still interested her.

"I know! I heard! News about our governor and his beautiful wife travels fast," Inez replied, her face — a giant smile. The two hugged. "I am so glad for you. Now you are truly one of us. We can share so much now, but come, I want to show you something. You have already become a trendsetter."

"This many?" Nadja said, a bit astounded. Inez kept very accurate records of all transactions. Each week, each one of her many store managers scattered over the towns and cities of Tierra sent her their detailed reports. Inez had written a computer script that merged these into a single listing, broken down by types. She had two categories of lip plates now. Two dozen women had already gotten their lips enlarged and now wore twelve inch in diameter lip plates. Inez had added an extra touch. Because of the large surface available, she'd added etching personal designs to the pair of plates. Each woman who purchased a set was allowed to personalize her own pair.

"More are coming in each week. Look at this too. Toe shoes are coming back in style again as well. We've fixed up eighteen more women with them. I've been asked repeatedly what new styles of gowns you will be wearing at the fall council meeting, which will be in about three weeks," Inez pointed out.

"I never looked at myself this way. I was always trying to wear what was the latest in fashions myself. Is it permitted to wear the same gowns I wore this summer?" Nadja asked.

Inez gave her a frown and both women laughed. "No, I don't suppose I ought to do that, not this soon." At last, Nadja accepted the fact that she was setting fashions. "Okay. I need a pair of new gowns. Help me out. I promise that I will get on the stick and research what is the latest fashions on some of the worlds where elegant fashions are popular," Nadja said.

"What do you prefer?"

"I like my legs free. It is lots easier to walk in these toe shoes that way. As uncomfortable as this corset is, I should not hide my figure though."

"How about letting me design something for you?" Inez asked.

Nadja agreed. "Make them red to match the rubies in my earrings," she suggested.

Chapter 22 Countermoves

The warm sun broke through the clouds around Valen and its castle and tower, revealing the lush green hills to the west and the stark Goza Mountains to the east, just behind the outer walls. It was midsummer and the city was a hive of activities. Tradesmen were busily at work; merchants shouted in the streets, hawking their wares. Prosperity had begun to return full force after the Great Decline under their previous ruler, who many now swore was mad. Well, he was dead and their new Lord Valen, Alano, had turned things around considerably.

Barely thirty, Alano had proven himself a capable leader of men. Spearheading the rebellion against the Mad Lord, Alano had personally killed the crazy man. After a total reorganization of the castle elite, replacing the older men with his own younger friends and relatives, he'd shown he had the economic acumen to lead Valen out of the recessive pit the previous lords dug for them all. He was good with the bastard sword; he was good with the pen; he had a powerful *mentales* endowment, and he was handsome.

That last fact was not lost on his twenty-nine year old wife, the raven haired Lady Concepcion. She was a beauty herself, thick pouting-like lips, high cheekbones, dark bushy eyebrows, and deep, all-seeing eyes. *Mentales* gifted, she prided herself on always getting what she desired. If you focus on it, spent all your energy working towards it, then you will have it. That was her often spoken advice to others. Subtle — yes. Deadly — yes. It was widely rumored she'd poisoned another woman, who was also trying to catch Alano's eyes some ten years ago. No one had proven it, though. Some said there wasn't anything that she wouldn't do to achieve her goals. Yet, she was a fierce supporter of her husband and had fought at his side during the overthrow battle in the courtyard of the castle.

That she could and did handle a short sword well did not mean the Lady Concepcion was an amazon. Not at all. She prided herself on her appearance, setting new standards for proper court attire. She was every bit woman and had already bore Alano his heir and herself a daughter to dote upon. Dorita was ten and quite precocious. Pino was seven and just being a boy who enjoyed getting into minor mischief around the castle.

Lord Alano had also shaken up Valen Tower. During the long years of stagnation and decay under the Mad Lord, the tower had likewise become rotten or so Alano claimed. He replaced its top leaders. His older brother became Venerado Arturo Valen. He was thirty-one and lacked Alano's skill with the sword and his far-vision. Arturo was also an effective leader to which he owed his new position, a most powerful position second only to Lord Alano. His wife Alicia was a year younger and the circle's capa or leader. They already had two children as well. Elena was eleven and Emilio was eight. Naturally, Alano and Arturo's children were almost inseparable.

While the orange-red sunshine brightened up the dull day outside, it did little to lighten up the planning meeting between these four and Alano's older advisor, the oldest man from the older days. Benito Berenguer was now forty-five. He'd seen it all and had fought hard against the maddening decisions of the previous lord of Valen, often at great personal risk of bodily harm. That was why Alano kept him on as his advisor, when he sacked all the others. Benito's views echoed those of the common men of Valen and Alano respected that. He needed to keep the people happy, at least for now.

These five formed the Holy Pentagram of Valen, a new concept Lord Alano established. It was based upon their ancient gods, who formed a pentagram of power over Tierra. Of course, no one worshiped these long forgotten gods and goddesses of antiquity. In all likelihood, they had been but a myth created by superstitious people, just as they invented the peasant myths of "good" witches some three centuries ago. "People need living, real people to believe in. That's us, the Holy Pentagram of Valen," Lord Alano declared, shortly after his coup had given him the throne. It had worked and now some seven years later, Valen was once more thriving.

It cost him some pride. Lord Alano had no choice but to visit the neighboring kingdoms and the rebellious port towns and cities, which had jumped ship, joining the City-States Alliance. His keen intellect and sense of knowing just what the other person wanted to hear from him had worked to perfection. He now had a treaty with Lord Gervasi Quito Malaca that ensured his northern borders. With some concessions on his part in terms of trading deals, the City-State Alliance had also signed a treaty with him. More importantly, they relinquished their claims for all lands further than a hundred miles inland from the long coast that surrounded western Westerlings. It had taken the Holy Pentagram of Valen six long years to bring back the confidence of the people of the huge country and to reestablish a thriving economy. Yet the five considered their re-admittance into the High Council of the Lords to be their greatest achievement to date.

Now they finally could put the Treason of Valen behind them and move forward once more. Peer acceptance meant much to Lord Alano and Lady Concepcion. Lord Alano opened the meeting. "Well, after all these centuries, finally progress is being made! This senator business is going to give us the opening Valen has long sought. For three hundred years, it has been us, the only foresighted people on Tierra, that has seen the incredible opportunities and advantages a close alliance with this Imperium can give us."

Lady Concepcion agreed, "But I want electric lights and uniform heating like they have in their buildings."

"To say nothing of their great machines," Amo Benito added. "Think what labor-saving devices they have! Why, we could build a ring of castles around the perimeter of Valen and guarantee the safety of our whole kingdom."

"Think of the exotic technology they have," Venerado Arturo put in. "Blasters for our fighters, medical devices for healing, communications devices which we could sorely use to keep in touch with our far-flung towns and cities. All this and so much more."

Lady Concepcion flicked her lips. "Stop dreaming, all of you. This isn't going to happen just because we have a senator on some far distant world and you know it! She isn't even going to have a vote. Listen all of you; we have to *make* things happen, if we are ever going to get anything for Valen. Now is the time to make our moves."

"She's right," Lord Alano supported her acid remarks. "Always, Valen has taken the lead. For good or ill, Valen has always had an inside track with the many governors." He recalled the marriage of a Valen ama to one of the governors. "We can't marry one of our women to this governor. Alas, that easy door is closed. He's married."

"So what does that leave us with? How do we get close to this new governor?" asked Benito. "We should somehow have him on our side at the very least."

"Aye, right now, old Lord Bolivar of Brom has the inside track," Venerado Arturo pointed out. "They seem like old buddies, if you hadn't noticed. He even introduced him to the lords at the meeting. Somehow, Brom has gotten miles ahead of us. We simply cannot allow that to continue, can we?"

"This Nadja could meet with an 'accident,'" Lady Concepcion hinted.

"Last resort, dear. We need a way to react immediately. I will see to it Isabella comes here to meet with us before she goes off-world, but we need to begin to wrestle control and influence of the governor away from Brom right now. Ideas? Benito?" Lord Alano asked.

The older man rubbed his chin thoughtfully. "My Lord, it seems to me at the council, none of the lords mentioned anything about obtaining any of the valuable Imperium trade goods, electricity, shuttles, communications gear. All talk centered on the senator item. Perhaps, we should begin a concerted effort to convince this new governor that Valen is highly interested in obtaining some of the many benefits the Imperium could offer us. See if we can punch a hole in their damnable closed world barrier."

"He's got a point. We need him to see Valen as a very close ally," Venerado Arturo added.

"Yes, but not so openly," Capa Alicia cautioned. "Remember, the other lords are dead set against ever bringing any alien technology to Tierra. If they again see us as openly pushing for that, they could rescind our welcome at the High Council. Considering this new governor seems to be using them as a way to reach all the lords at one time, we dare not antagonize the lords. We must be careful and work behind the scenes this time."

"We should go meet with Governor Burkhardt soon. I will make the arrangements," Lord Alano decided. "Concepcion, you should personally invite Nadja here. Use language studies as an enticement, but get her here somehow. Perhaps, we can work on him through her; perhaps not, but we must explore all avenues. I will also insist Isabella visit too before she leaves."

"What I don't understand and what I think we all need to study is this rise of Brom Tower into political prominence as well as power," Venerado Arturo changed the topic. Alano didn't object and he continued, "By our reckoning, Brom Tower now has an unprecedented four complete *Círculo de mentes*! We barely have one now. Adelmira, one and a half at last count. Malaca Tower has two, but they are aging. Most all have between one and two circles in operation. How is it Brom Tower has four? We simply must find out."

Capa Alicia added, "Is the birthrate of new *mentales* gifted significantly higher there? Are they rounding up all such gifted people in their kingdom and forcing them into the tower? Something is going on up there that we do not understand. If push comes to shove, Brom Tower can squash us. Four to one odds are not pleasant to consider."

"Is it that bad? My god, four to one! Okay, let's make some inquiries. Try Malaca Tower and the Renegade Tower first. See what they know about this and if they are as deeply concerned about this horrific imbalance of power as we are," Lord Alano suggested. After some minor discussions on trades with the alliance, they broke up to work on their individual assignments.

A day later, Lord Alano met privately with Governor Konrad in his twentieth floor office. "My, you can almost see Valen Castle and tower from here, Konrad," Alano pointed in the general direction. The two men were admiring the ruddy view out of the broad windows.

Konrad chuckled, "Hardly. As I understand it, Valen is many hundreds of miles from here, but I see your point. The view is rather spectacular isn't it? The mountains are quite pretty to look at, but then I would not want to be out in them. Climbing has never been my strong suit. Come, sit, and let's discuss what has brought you to see me." He motioned the lord to a plush leather chair.

"I'll get right to the point. I know you must be a busy man, and I am very grateful you have taken time out to meet with me. Historically, Valen has always been a close ally with the various governors here. In the past, one even married one of our lovely princesses. Carmen was her name. Valen has always been looking to the future, whereas most of the other lords have not. We alone have always seen the tremendous benefits a close alliance, a close bond with the Imperium, could offer us. Why just having this marvelous electricity and central heating would be a godsend for us."

Konrad chuckled, "I can well imagine that. Those stone castles must get pretty cold in the winters, which I am told are very long and harsh on this world. I will be finding out all too soon, I am afraid."

"Quite true. Do you realize the magnitude of the communications difficulties I face each day trying to administer my kingdom? Valen stretches some three thousand miles to the west and nearly five thousand to the north and south. My kingdom dwarfs every other kingdom on Tierra. What I would give to have an Imperium communications system in every one of my towns. It takes months to get a message delivered from Valen to our most distant towns."

"My, that is a barrier to effective rulership. That's quite plain. Distance is definitely a barrier in all societies that lack electricity," Konrad agreed with him. "Yet, the close world policy prohibits all such things from being imported here. Perhaps you could discuss this with your senator. She may be able to lobby the Senate to make some modifications to the policy."

"I certainly will do that. We all owe so much to you, Konrad, for getting us that senator!" He changed tactics and began to praise the man for what he had done, adding, "And none of us will ever forget how you managed to end the kidnaping of our younger telepathically gifted children. You have only been here a few months and already you are the best governor that Tierra has ever had." He watched Konrad's reactions carefully. The man felt pride. That was just what Alano desired.

"I do my best to serve you," Konrad replied.

"That is plainly obvious. One good turn deserves another. I want you to know Valen stands ready to support you in any way we can. If you need or desire something, why just let me know. It will be yours or done. If your records are accurate, you probably already know that always Valen has been a very close ally of the governor, whoever it was. As you probably saw at the council meeting, the other lords want nothing to do with the Imperium and usually try to counter any positive moves the previous governors have made. But not Valen. We see the future and the future simply must have a close, shared relationship with the Imperium. You have so much to offer us that I cannot begin to put it into words. And yet, the other lords have never seen a darn thing."

"Now you mentioned this, that agrees pretty much with what I observed," Konrad admitted. "Could I bounce some ideas I have had off of you to get a feel about how they will play out at the next meeting, which I believe is in September?"

"Absolutely. Go right ahead."

"Orphanage. As you know, Exchange City is the lone meeting ground between the two cultures. Besides the expected traders and merchants, men and women have always sought sexual favors. It is especially hard on spacers, who spend long months in space. When they get planet-side, they yearn for such things. Good or bad, it exists in any spaceport town on any world. Yet here, there are far too many orphans begging in the streets as their only method of survival. While I don't personally have any children, such things do bother me. I would like to propose the Imperium build and finance an orphanage for all such children, staffed of course by local personnel. Do you think that the lords would back me if I made such an offer?"

"Oh they will bicker about it, but since they have not

come forward and built one already, they will probably back it. Emphasize you will build it and finance its operation, but use local personnel. That will be the big selling point. Money always is."

Konrad laughed. "It is in every culture I've seen." He exaggerated a little. "Another thing I have noticed, Lord Alano, there doesn't seem to be any schools on Tierra. Education is the single most vital aspect of culture. Through education, a people can learn to do new things, learn how to make and use electricity, for example."

"Yes, I can see that. Here on Tierra, it is we parents who teach our children what they must know. But how can we, who know nothing of such things as electricity, teach such things to our children? True, those who are blessed with the *mentales* gifts are usually highly trained in its use by the towers. Still, how can we ever learn such things? It would seem to me we need to have Imperium schools and teachers here, if we are ever to move forward. Is that not so?"

"Why yes it is. Very much so, Lord Alano. I compliment you on your foresight. Often, I have had to argue such points to other rulers on other planets. If this were not a closed world, the Imperium would have already established schools around the world, where the young would be taught the true scientific marvels of the universe. Why, within a few generations, these educated young would revolutionize a world."

"But that can't happen because we are a closed world. Right?" Lord Alano asked cleverly.

"You are precisely correct. Again, perhaps your senator could ask for an exception in this case, but it is doubtful she could win enough support for such a thing to be passed by the Senate."

"I see. Suppose you and I set up just such a school in Valen on the quiet. Let no one know such a thing existed. In time, my people would be able to begin to utilize such marvels as electricity. At that point in time, the others on Tierra would come to see the truly great benefits the Imperium has to offer us. It might allow you to open up our world," Lord Alano put the seeds of an idea in Konrad's mind.

"Interesting idea, Lord Alano. We could get into terribly hot waters over this overt breakage of the lease and closed world policies. I could even get fired. Still, it is something to consider. I assure you I will give your idea a good deal of thought."

"I cannot ask for more. Yet, we must in turn give back something you consider valuable, vital or important. Handouts never work; they return to bite the hand that gave it to them. While you are considering my idea, consider also what we may provide you in return. It would not be right for Valen to give you nothing in return. Imperium education is most valuable, and we must give back something that is wanted and needed either by you personally or by the Imperium. It would not be right if we did not. Let me also assure you that we would keep such things a total secret from the rest of Tierra. We have ways and means of ensuring that."

Konrad knew Alano was making a power play. He knew, if Valen did somehow get an Imperium based school, massive technological changes would not be far behind when the children reached adulthood. He also knew Lord Alano was defying all the other lords in even approaching such a thing on his own. If he went along with this, in time, it would vault Lord Alano to possibly rulership of the entire world. His power would become immense, dwarfing the other lords as he moved into the modern world. He also knew that his ass would be cooked, if word of his direct violation of the closed world policies was discovered. Not even the Sector ID Minister could save him from prosecution and jail.

Rather, his mind sought out what Valen, this primitive culture, had to offer him. He knew precisely what Lord Alano meant by the hand biting the hand that fed it. His own history lessons at the Academy were rife with such horror stories. Yet, at the moment, he could think of nothing this primitive world could really offer in return. "I will have to think about this seriously, Lord Alano. Many aspects need to be well thought out in advance. Allow me time to give this the careful thought that it deserves."

"But of course, of course. Take all the time you need, Governor Konrad. In the meantime, always remember that

Valen will be on your side. Let us know what you need or want, and we will do our best to help you obtain it. I thank you for your time today and look forward to seeing you and your beautiful wife at the September meeting." They shook hands and he left. Both men had a good deal to think over.

Konrad spent a day pondering it, but in the end, he could not think of a single thing this world could give back to the Imperium. The only valuable commodity was the fuel being refined on one of their moons. The lease already took care of that aspect. Well, there were telepaths.

Lord Alano reported back to his Holy Pentagram. "Konrad is a stickler for abiding by the rules of a closed world. However, he is considering the possibility of creating a secret education school here in Valen. We both agreed education is the best route to move into, as he put it, the modern world. Time will tell on this one. We might have better luck with his wife."

That fell through with a resounding crash. Nadja was spending the late summer in Brom! Their next chance to see her and meet with her would be at the September council meeting. They fared better with Isabella, who honored their request for a day's meeting before she left. Lord Alano got her agreement to look into the possibility of having the Imperium setup one or more schools, where they could receive a modern education. She agreed to lobby for having the Imperium share some key technologies with Tierra, namely electricity and central heating. Lord Valen found Isabella quite receptive of his suggestions and was pleased with her, bidding her never to hesitate to ask him for anything she might need.

The September High Council of the Lords turned out to be mostly a social gathering this time. While the lords did spend some time on mutual economic issues focused on helping the devastated areas of the Easterlings begin a critical recovery, mostly it was a social gathering. Konrad did present his formal request to build and fund an orphanage in Exchange City, and, as Lord Valen promised, Alano argued strongly in its favor. The request was agreed to, once more pleasing Konrad.

On the social side, Lady Edda Turda and Sultaness

Sonia Ferro attended, teleported there by Adelmira Tower. Both women found they blended well with the other rulers and ladies. Both were pleasantly surprised to find so many of these "Great Ladies" also wore lip plates and toe shoes. That had been both of their biggest worries about attending the meeting. Both were able to secure the economic assistance their country and city so desperately needed. They were unable to secure men, however. Both had lost an entire generation of young men. Lack of able-bodied men was hindering their recovery at this time.

No, rather what caused a big stir was the fact that both brought along Sisterhood women as their advisors! Communications Minister Angelica Freda e Alessandra and Donatella Alba e Falda came with Edda, while the fighter Gianna came with Sultaness Sonia. Dirty looks and snide comments flew towards the three women from the "ladies," while the men openly complained, but could do nothing about it. The rules clearly stated that the ruler could bring any advisor of his or her own choosing. Again, this marked the very first time in Tierra history that the Sisterhood had played a direct role in a High Council meeting. All three took their harassment in stride. They'd suffered far worse at the hands of men in the past. "They dress more like men than real women!" was an often-heard comment.

They wore comfortable clothing, though Gianna did wear pants and not a dress as the other two did. She was a fighter and refused to dress differently than she always had. However, gowns and fashion took center stage at this meeting. All eyes sought out Nadja!

She wore her new gown, red satin as ordered. Her left shoulder was bare. A two-inch band over her right shoulder held her dress up, though her large bosom would also have done much the same. Inez didn't think going strapless would be accepted just yet. "Take small steps," she advised. The gown fit her shapely curves well, but it opened up wide just below her knees, allowing her to walk easily and gracefully in her matching toe shoes. Inez anticipated receiving a rather large number of orders for similar dresses which would keep her many seamstresses busy during the winter.

The many ladies and men also took note of just how many other women now wore new lip plates similar to Nadja's monsters. Nearly two dozen women sported the foot in diameter lip plates with their unique artistic designs clearly visible on the top surfaces. No two were identical. Edda asked Lady Rusden, "I have a hard time seeing were my feet are at now with these smaller plates. Don't these big ones block your view completely?"

"Yes they most certainly do that. Quite challenging to get used to them. I have to be far more careful when I walk now. If I lower my head to see where I am stepping, well you know what we all face if we do that." She didn't want to mention the embarrassing drooling that inevitably followed. "On the other hand, everyone notices me now. After all, if Nadja manages them, so can we." She lowered her voice to a whisper, "Plus, the much larger lip loops are really good in bed too!" She then added, "Plus, Lady Edda, these new designs with their clip on plates are *so* much easier to manage putting in and taking out. You really should get yours upgraded, dear. You will look so much more attractive if you do."

Similar conversations abounded. Then there were others, who also wore toe shoes and one of the variations of the fetter-gowns. Constrained to take their tiny two inch strides as they had always done before as bound Easterlings women, they began to notice the far more graceful strides that Nadja made. Some began to consider getting new and similar gowns themselves.

Virtually all the women paid close attention to Nadja's massive earrings this time. Their weight did elongate her lobes rather significantly. They looked particularly good draped across her bare left shoulder, where their red rubies shone brightly in sharp relief as opposed to the right side earrings, which mostly blended in with the red shoulder satin sash that held up her gown.

As always, Inez stood in the rear of the giant throne room, both listening to the women's conversations and taking direct orders. She also began to have other women coming up to her and asking about the challenges and difficulties of wearing lip plates, especially these new huge ones that Nadja and twenty-four other ladies were wearing. As always, she did her best to convince them that such a decision to have them was not to be taken lightly. "Look, they really do obstruct your vision rather badly. Eating is quite a challenge and you must be careful. Then, there is the drooling problem they all face. If they lower their heads much to see where they are going or eating, saliva drips down. Most embarrassing. Plus, you cannot drink from cups or mugs any longer. Have you noticed they all have to use a long handled spoon to drink now?"

Often the woman would go away somewhat disappointed. Yet just as often the woman would say, "Yes, but they look fabulously gorgeous!"

What took Inez by surprise were some of the lords and noblemen, mostly from the City-State Alliance, who came by to ask her about these new large lip plates. To her surprise, they were also interested in them.

Konrad, pleased his orphanage project had so easily won approval, mingled with the various lords and their advisors and tower leaders. Several from the City-State Alliance cornered him in the middle of the afternoon. Lord Gilberto Rosa, who like most of the men from Villa del Rey and the Renegade Tower representatives wore the smaller lip plates, acted as their spokesman.

"I say, we've all heard rumors that you too wore lip plates like ours when you first arrived here on Tierra. Are those rumors true?"

Konrad was taken by surprise. "Why, yes, as a matter of fact I did. I had my lips repaired though shortly after arriving."

"May I be so bold as to ask you why? Certainly, these are the height of fashion even among we men," Gilberto probed.

Konrad chuckled. "Simple. I wanted to be able to speak your language as perfectly as I could when I first addressed you all back in July. As you know, sounds made by the lips cannot be made when you are wearing them. I didn't dare take the chance that some of you lords would not be able to understand me when I spoke to all of you. That would have been a major blunder on my part. So I had my lips repaired. I do so want to earn you lords' respect."

"Ah, yes, I can understand your decision then. You are quite right. Those lords who do not choose to wear these do have a hard time understanding us, but as you can plainly see, we all do manage to communicate well," Gilberto pointed out.

"Yes, I am quite used to the unusual speech of my charming Nadja now," he admitted.

"So Governor Konrad, some of us were wondering. Since you now have earned our trust and respect, why is it that you are not going back to wearing them again? Certainly Nadja's are incredibly impressive, to say the very least."

Konrad flushed. "Well, I don't rightly know. I have been so busy, I suppose."

"Just as some of us thought. It is always a challenge to step into a new post and try to fill the shoes of those who have come before you. Now that things have settled down some, you might reconsider. In fact, that's just what some of us are doing. Our wives with their new plates are really attracting a lot of attention back home. To be honest, we find they are outdoing us!"

Konrad chuckled. "I can see why. I don't recall ever having seen so many beautiful women in one place before," he said intending to appease the men. A little praise and admiration would go a long way, he knew. "I don't see why you cannot have larger ones yourselves. I was considering doing that myself. I just don't know if my speech would be so impaired that I would not be understood here at the council."

"Oh, you needn't fear that, governor. In nearly every court, there are women or men who wear these. While that may have been true many decades ago, nowadays, even those who don't wear them understand us who do," Gilberto countered.

"I see. I suppose I should check with some of the other lords to make sure they don't really have a problem understanding men and women who wear them. If they don't as you claim, then I can see no reason not to join you men. After all, at least half of the men here are wearing them, maybe more. I admit I have not actually counted. Been too preoccupied with other matters. But now things seem so quiet, I suppose that I ought to."

"Aye, governor. Please do so. Don't take my word for it, check with the others, like Lord Bolivar for example. Well, we've taken up too much of your time, governor. Hope to see you sporting a fine pair come spring," Gilberto replied. His group wandered off as another group moved in to chat with Konrad.

That evening, the lords and ladies participated in dancing. Having socialized most of the day, when the musicians began playing, dancing arose. "Well, this looks pretty easy," Konrad whispered to Nadja. "Think you can manage in your toe shoes?"

"Probably, as long as you hold me securely," she whispered back. In her shoes, she stood taller than he did. She was able to put her chin on his shoulder as they joined closely. Both began to emulate the way the other couples were moving. The slow dances were simple and doable by those wearing toe shoes or toe boots, as long as they had a partner.

Konrad, alone with Nadja for the first time this day, said, "You know a bunch of the lords have been asking me why I don't get lip plates again. Apparently, they somehow heard I had some like theirs when we first arrived. I guess news travels even from within our base. They seem to think I ought to have some like yours, dear."

"Oh, you would look good in them, and I would feel better if you also wore them, especially around the base, dear. Still, they are an awful lot of trouble. I don't believe how many women have gotten theirs enlarged just since July."

"Well, you have become their fashion queen, my dear. We are setting an example as we should be doing," Konrad replied. "I suppose they are right. Over half of the men are wearing them so I should too."

"That might be a wise move, dear. Bet you will get a lot of ribbing from the Rigel-3's on the base," she pointed out. "Look, there's Lady Rosita Malaca. She sure is having a miserable time trying to dance by hopping on her foot. Her life must be one of misery. I can't imagine how she manages it." Both stole peaks at Lord Gervasi and Lady Rosita.

A bit later, the musicians ended their suite of slow moving pavane pieces. Now they began a lively northern

Westerlings fandango. All eyes now turned to Gervasi and Rosita. This was a jumping dance and she excelled at this one. The women in their tall heels were unable to match her moves while those who wore toe shoes or boots stood this one out, watching the energetic couple. Both Konrad and Nadja were amazed. "Don't ask me to do that!" Nadja teased him.

When the slower dances began once more, Konrad and Nadja were interrupted. Other lords and ladies wished to dance with them, and they took this as a very good sign indeed. Lord Rusden took Nadja in his arms, while handing his wife off to Konrad. He said, "That Lady Rosita puts us all to shame. I can't possibly do that dance, not in this pipe corset." Both laughed. A bit later, he asked, "Don't you find those big lip plates of yours rather awkward?"

"Oh yes. That's true," Nadja admitted. No sense in pretending otherwise.

"Impressive though. I would like to invite you to come to Rusden Castle when you are able. Bring Konrad along, if he can get away. I know the governor is probably terribly busy, but surely you can grace our halls with your presence."

"I will do just that, My Lord. Only be prepared to answer lots of questions about your Midlands language," she teased him. As the evening progressed, she had many similar conversations.

On the other hand, Konrad had somewhat different conversations with the many ladies who chose to dance with him. Ama Natalia Valen, Venerado Roberto's wife from Villa del Rey, who wore the new large lip plates like Nadja's, danced with him. She whispered, "I am so glad that Nadja has given us her new style lip plates. These are just fabulous. We heard that you too used to wear the smaller ones. Why don't you get some to match Nadja's? I know my husband is going to get them just as soon as we get back home. You would look so handsome in them. Nadja had better be careful or one of us will sweep you away with us." Both chuckled.

Another lady asked him, "You are so widely traveled; you've seen so much. Are there other worlds where men and women boast such elegant lip adornments? I've been considering having them myself. Word is going around that you used to have the smaller ones. Any truth to that rumor?"

"Well yes, I did have them when I first arrived, but I wanted to be able to speak very clearly to all of you when we first met. I couldn't take any chances on being misunderstood, you see."

"Oh I certainly do understand. It takes a good deal of listening for me to understand them, but I guess now I do get all that they are saying. So I suppose that isn't a good reason anymore."

"Probably not, My Lady. To answer your other question, yes, we have seen some worlds where these are considered the height of fashion," he whispered into her ear. So went his evening dances.

When the council ended, Inez found herself busier than normal. However, she dropped everything when Konrad came by to get his new foot in diameter lip plates. He chose to have a pair of horses etched into his top plate as a reminder that he could learn new things, recalling his mixed experiences learning to ride them.

His first comment when she finished up and he looked at his new appearance in one of her full length mirrors was, "Oh, these do obstruct my vision significantly."

"Takes getting used to, governor," she replied. "Watch your step."

The next day, Konrad really didn't want to get out of bed nor did Nadja, but both had to. She was expected at Valen Castle, planning to stay there for four days working on the Westerlings language and visiting with them. Only with a great effort could the two tear themselves apart and actually get out of bed. She had packed the night before and had her crate sitting on a rolling cart. By now she'd learned the easy way to move her clothing and recording equipment around. She could not really push it or pull it, not in her toe shoes, but she could put her new gift of telekinesis to good use now.

After breakfast, the Imperial Circle teleported her from her bedroom to the pad in Valen Tower, where the Holy Pentagram of Valen was there to meet her. Benito handled her crate for her as Lord Alano and Venerado Arturo gave her a royal welcome. "I do hope my Westerlings is not truly awful," she hinted.

"You are doing well enough, but as you say, one can always learn to speak better. I am sure that by the time you leave you will have improved quite a lot," Alano said diplomatically. "I will let Concepcion here help you get settled in, but I would like to chat with you sometime, if I may."

Later that day, he got his chance to speak with Nadja alone. "I wanted to take this opportunity to tell you a bit of history. You see, we here in Valen have for three centuries now tried our best to help move Tierra into an open world. We fully recognize the tremendous benefits the Imperium has to offer us here. Electricity, central heating — the list is almost endless as you can well imagine. Always, the governors of Tierra could count on Valen's support. Nadja, if there is ever anything at all you need or want, please do not hesitate to let us know and it shall be yours. Do you realize that one governor once married one of our princesses?" She hadn't and he saw the surprise on her face.

"Oh yes. Carmen was her name. Quite some time ago. So you see, we are here, and you may count on our support."

"Why thank you, Lord Alano. That is most kind of you."

He changed the topic. "I would like to congratulate you on becoming one of us, a *mentales* gifted. You are not the first, pardon my expression, not the first alien to come to Tierra only to develop the *mentales* gifts." Again, he saw surprise on her face. "Oh no. Several have. Of course, the usual thing you will hear about women coming to Tierra is that after residing here for a time, their breasts greatly enlarge, but then women are supposed to have them, aren't they?" She grinned, but it wasn't visible.

"I do regret you've been held prisoner at Brom Tower for so many months. You deserve to get out and visit all the tower and lords. How else can you learn our languages well, eh?"

"Well, I wasn't a prisoner there. They were most helpful when we arrived, and they did train me when I developed this *mentales* gift. I certainly was not expecting it, but this is absolutely the greatest thing that has ever happened to me," she admitted. She sensed he had some grudge or beef with

Brom Tower, but had no idea what that might be.

He sensed her unspoken protest and changed the topic. "I find it most interesting that you alone are able to seemingly go against this closed world policy."

"What do you mean, Lord Alano?"

"You are being allowed to travel widely around Tierra and to bring all of your 'alien' recording equipment with you. That has not happened before. Surely this means we are entering a new era of cooperation between our peoples."

She chose here words carefully. "Well, I am not so sure about that. As a linguist, I am allowed to bring my recording equipment with me, and it is vital I visit with as many people that I can. You know, to learn the idiosyncrasies of the three languages. I will be able to update our language learning tapes — well they really are not tapes, but computer files. Others who come after us will be able to speak your languages far better than ever before. That's my job and passion, you see."

"And that is a most worthy one indeed. Yet, perhaps we can both use this to our advantage. Three centuries of utter isolation from all the incredible technologies that your people can offer us is just plain wrong. Wouldn't you agree?"

"Yes and no. I've seen what awful things can happen when our technologies fall into uneducated hands. Brutal."

"Ah, that is precisely the point. Uneducated hands. We need to get some schools established here on Tierra where we can learn about these things so we can improve our lives and those of our peoples. Indeed, it is readily apparent to us in Valen that our society, our people, are only barely surviving. We are forced to be a primitive people compared to your world. That is not right, don't you agree?"

"Yes, education is always the right road to travel, Lord Alano. I surely do wish the closed world policy didn't prohibit schools and proper education; yet my hands are tied, just as Konrad's are. Oops, I've seem to have lost my hands." She made a light jest bringing a smile to his face.

"Well, if you can ever figure out a way to help us with education, let me know. It could even be done in secret. As you travel Tierra, you cannot help but notice that Valen stands alone in its desire to embrace new ways, new technology. The others are satisfied with doing everything the way their ancient ancestors did it, but we Valens believe that salvation and prosperity for our people lies in learning new things, the many things that the Imperium could offer us. Never forget that. Valen wants these things. We are ready and willing to do whatever needs to be done to obtain such things for our people, beginning with education. If you have any bright ideas in the future, please let me know. You will find my ears most receptive."

"Oh yes. Concepcion wanted me to ask you if you would like a personal servant who will travel Tierra with you and assist you with your needs? Some things must be difficult for you with those hands."

"Well, there is no saying otherwise. I have no sense of touch any longer. I can't feel anything with them and that causes no end of awkwardness. But with my new gifts, I am better able to cope. Thank you for the kind offer, though," she turned him down diplomatically.

During her four days at Valen, she did learn many new details of the Westerlings language. Those in Brom had terrible accents for the most part. She left armed with many hours of recording of spoken language to analyze in detail later on, some with lip plates and some without. Further, she began to realize that in fact there were six languages spoken, not three. Those with lip plates spoke wildly differently than those without them. She wondered if the local people could actually understand what these lords and ladies who wore the lip plates said. She intended to find out for herself.

After she left, the Holy Pentagram of Valen met to compare notes. "Well, she is not going to cooperate either. She's hung up in her language studies. Rather a maniac with it," Lord Alano declared.

"And she wouldn't hear of having a servant," Concepcion added. "That would have been a good way to keep tabs on her."

Benito commented, "Well, we are just going to have to find another way to approach this. Is it feasible to 'replace' Nadja in Konrad's bed?"

Lord Alano reflected for a moment, before commenting.

"From what I have observed and sensed, there is no deep love between Nadja and Konrad. Rather, it seems to be a marriage of convenience, one that allows the other best to achieve their own goals. No children is a tip off. Better ask if it is possible for Konrad to really love a woman?"

Venerado Arturo suggested, "We could manipulate his mind."

"True," Lord Alano answered, "but not with Nadja in the picture. She would be on to that in a flash. She's *mentales* now. Don't forget that detail."

"But she did mention something that I found most curious," Capa Alicia spoke up, waiting for the proper moment to unleash her idea. "She said that it almost seemed like Brom Tower was making *mentales* gifted women. Her words — seems like and making. Consider this, suppose somehow those at Brom Tower have figured out how to make new *mentales* gifted out of normal people. That would explain why they are able to field four Circles while all the other towers can now only muster one or two at most. Can they have found a way to make *mentales* gifted out of normal people? If so, somehow, someway, we must learn to do the same thing or we are all doomed utterly."

"She has a point," Venerado Arturo replied, giving his wife a big smile. "That alone would explain how it is they always seem to have an abundance of *mentales* gifted. I say if they can do it, we ought to be able to do it as well. They are not any smarter than we are."

He went on, "What they have said is that inbreeding is responsible for the gradual loss of *mentales* gifted children — that we should branch out and couple with the other isolated villagers who happen to have a mostly untrained gift. That is the official line. From what we can tell, most of the other towers are following that advice, as are we to some extent. But I don't believe that alone accounts for Brom's incredible explosion of *mentales* gifted."

"Okay then here are our immediate plans. Benito, Concepcion, and I will work on ways and means of becoming invaluable to Konrad, perhaps even so far as to the elimination of Nadja, replacing her with one of our women. Put the entire tower onto the problem of how to make new *mentales* gifted out of normal people. That will be your highest priority project. Make it happen. If all fails, then I will consider sending a spy into Brom, but we all know just how risky that is at this point in time. That will have to be a last resort," Lord Alano ordered.

Chapter 23 Changes During the Winter of 1272

Inez looked over the massive mound of requested modifications and changes after the fall council ended. She was not in this business to make money, for she already had more than she or her husband could ever spend. Rather her passion was for designing new clothes. Moreover, she took great pride in helping others look their best, including the right color matches. With all of these new giant lip plates being requested, she began to worry about the real difficulties that Nadja was having with them. Primarily it was one vision blockage. The others who had also recently gotten theirs enlarged also voiced similar troubles. She decided to solve this problem before tacking the mounting pile of requests of others to be similarly enlarged.

Nadja, please come by my office. I have something that I want to try on you, Inez sent telepathically to her friend. She came walking into her fifth floor office an hour later.

"It is getting cold out there. Will is snow soon?" Nadja asked. "It is only late September."

"Yes, by October the snows will be here. Nadja, I believe Peter has a solution for your lip plates. He's a clever fellow. He's taken your clip-on design and improved it. Here, I'll show you on this model here. Right now, the plates look normal, perpendicular to the plane of your face. Press these latches here — oh, do the bottom one first, and presto. See, they fold downward and hang loosely, freeing up your vision. Plus, in this position, the fancy embossed designs are very visible. What do you think? Raise the top one up first, and it automatically clicks back into a secure locked position. Then raise the bottom one." She demonstrated it and Nadja was sold on them.

Inez laughed. "I just knew you would be. Here, I made this new set just for you. I took the liberty of having two women who appear to be talking to each other, but one is also writing. That's you, the linguist. What do you think?"

"Revolutionary and just perfect! Peter is an absolute genius! I'll take them and you can have these old ones back," Nadja exclaimed. Inez made the simple swap of the two plates. Nothing had to be done to the mouthpieces. With her new ones in place, Nadja experimented a little. "This is so much better that I can't begin to describe it. I was always having such a hard time seeing while walking without lowering my head, which of course promotes drooling rather rapidly. Everyone is going just love these. You and Peter have outdone yourselves this time!"

Inez smiled. "With these, I am now willing to wear them again myself. Here, these are replacements for Konrad. I kept his same design — the horses — though I just cannot imagine Konrad riding a horse," she giggled. "Now then, Nadja, it is getting cold, and it is time for you to switch from toe shoes to the soft, fleece lines toe boots. They keep your feet warm in the cold wintertime. I have set aside five pairs, different colors. They all lace up to your knees."

Inez helped her try on the black pair. "My goodness. These are so soft and warm! I'll take them all! Inez, whatever would I do without you?"

Inez smiled. "I am so happy you like them." She packaged the boots and slung the bag over Nadja's shoulders. The women hugged, and Nadja headed back to the spaceport and the admin building.

When she demonstrated her new plates to Konrad, he also became highly enthused. "These were beginning to be a real pain. Trying to work at the computer with your vision of your hands blocked is a royal pain in the you-know-what. I'll have to see her to get mine exchanged too."

"No you don't, dear. Here they are. Inez took the liberty of making you a new pair too." She helped him get his switched. Once he pressed the levers and had the plates hanging loosely downwards, all of his problems were solved. He was ecstatic over the relief that they gave him.

"We should do something special for Inez and Peter, dear. Any ideas?" Konrad asked.

"I know. Let's import some of that incredibly soft velvet

made from pacas. That should please her immensely," Nadja replied.

"I'll order some today!" He did just that.

With the acceptance of her modifications by the governor and Nadja, Inez sent a whole new set to all of those who had already had gotten modified to wear the foot in diameter plates. With each set, she retained the original designs the women had requested be etched onto their original plates. Brief instructions on how to use them accompanied each pair. Peter made several trips to the Imperial Castle and paid the small fees the Imperial Circle charged to teleport the small packages to the designated person. That done, she began to gear up for the rather lengthy list of new requests for the new sized adornments.

All during October, she handled woman after woman, including ten who had never worn these lip adornments. She saw at least one per day, sometimes two. The Imperial Circle was kept busy; they were making needed funds. With over forty women handled, she then carefully went through her records, composing a list of women who still had the smaller plates. There were only five. She then composed a message for each of them, complete with a sketch of how the new ones worked. Her last lines read: Of all the women with these lip ornaments, only five of you will still be wearing the smaller five-inch ones. You might give these new ones serious consideration.

In November, the men who wore them began making inquiries. Having seen the great benefits their wives now had, to say nothing of the impressive artwork, which was now very visible when the plates were lowered, plus having learned that Governor Konrad now wore these new ones too, they too wanted to get their own enlarged. How soon could she do them was their most frequent question. When she replied to each, she asked them to send her a sketch of what they wanted for their unique artwork. She asked them to get the drawings to her a week before the date she made for their appointments.

As the men came and got their lips thickened and enlarged, uniformly they were all very much impressed with the newfound convenience and the stellar artwork that was now visible when the plates were dangling down. She received compliment after compliment from these lords and noblemen. Repeatedly, she heard variations on: "You've made wearing these tremendously easier, Inez. Thank you."

When December came, she again made a listing of those men who had the smaller plates and who had yet to get their enlarged. There were ten. Again, she sent a message to these lords and nobles. By the end of December, all ten now wore the new larger plates.

During January, she then sent messages to all the lords and those who usually attended the High Councils with them. She outlined the new design and its benefits, pointing out that the governor himself now wore them. She suggested that if they now wanted them too, then they should get them from her during the winter before the spring council.

Lord Emilio Bolivar received one such message, as did Amo Domingo and Venerada Maricela. He summoned the three to his office, the order of which Maricela found annoying, because that meant she had to get dressed up and wear her heels over there. Nevertheless, she came dressed appropriately. "Look at this." He waved the message in the air.

"I got one too," Maricela said quietly. "So what are you going to do about it?"

"I damn well don't want those darn lip things!" Emilio growled. "What's Inez trying to do, drum up business?"

"No, she's just trying to save us from being embarrassed at the next High Council meeting. Now that the governor is also wearing them and all the other lords have had theirs enlarged too, she wants to make sure you won't be embarrassed to walk into the meeting and be in the minority without knowing it in advance. I think all she is doing is giving us a heads up warning. Kind of her, really," Maricela replied, calming Emilio's temper down.

"You think we should really consider having this done?" Emilio said with a sigh, finally relaxing somewhat.

"With the older, smaller designs, they would be just too difficult for me to manage. Your wife, too. We can ill afford to have our vision partially obscured and a fall would smash up our entire mouths. However, with this new design where they flop down, the risk of taking a fall and jamming them through our mouths is reduced dramatically. I guess the question is can Anita and I manage to operate the release levers with either our toes or with our *mentales* powers," Maricela answered both for herself and for his katalyein wife.

"Well, lowered like that, they won't interfere much with fighting, I suppose," Amo Domingo suggested. "Besides, if we find we simply cannot deal with them, we can have our lips healed. It is not like these modifications cannot be undone like they were so many years ago."

"Point taken. If so many of the other lords are having it done, I'll look like a fool or an old foggie if I don't," Emilio admitted. "Why did the governor have to get them?"

"He had them before he arrived on Tierra, I've heard," Maricela answered. "He must have had his lips healed so he could speak clearly to us all during that first meeting."

"I think we should all take the same action. Either have them or not have them. Either way, to others, it will look like we are in agreement on this issue," Lord Emilio finally took charge. "Okay, let's get this done soon so that, if we don't like them, there is time to get our lips healed back up. I'll arrange a date. Anita and your wife, Sally, will get them too, since they are with us at the meetings. Which reminds me, Maricela, what about your husband? I know that he only goes to these meetings to help you, but he ought to be seen as in agreement with us too."

"I'll talk to him tonight when he gets back. He's out with his eagles at the moment," she answered. She knew what he thought of the courtly finery, and it was not good. She knew she was going to have a hard time selling him on this idea. She added a warning, "Just realize you are making Anita's life and my life much more difficult for us."

In mid-January, these six headed to Elegant Fashions Inc in Exchange City to get their lips modified. Similar discussions were held in many other locations as well. By March, there were only a few holdouts as Inez put it. Again, she sent them a message to that effect. When the spring High Council came, everyone in attendance now wore these new collapsible, giant lip plates. One of the first actions everyone did was to have a look at the myriad, unique designs they had embossed on their top plates. In less than one year, Konrad and Nadja had created a whole new fashion for the key nobles of Tierra. Yet, it didn't stop there. During the summer, other nobles in the various kingdoms, men and women, began sending her requests also to get these new ornaments for themselves. Of course, most of these came to her via her many outlying Elegant Fashion Inc stores.

On a sadder note, Benjamina passed away shortly after that. Tierra seemed stable and at peace. She decided it was time for her to move on. Ken and Crystal now found themselves wholly in charge of the Underground. He still did not feel up to the immense challenges, though.

Early February at Valen Castle, the response of Lord Alano and his group was one of anger. They had no choice but to follow the lead of all the others. Although they held out as long as they dared, they knew they could not show up at the next meeting as the lone holdouts. Now sporting their new massive plates, all had them in the drooping position, displaying their chosen designs. Lord Alano's top plate showed a small image of his castle, while Venerado Arturo's held a sketch of his tower.

"These people have to be stopped. It is all Nadja's doing," Lord Alano fumed. "If she had not worn hers to the meeting, none of this would have happened. What is she up to anyway?"

Benito replied, "I've been keeping tabs on her, Alano. During the winter months, she has been visiting the other towers and lords, spending at least a week there. She's been reputedly recording their speech, but from my spies, she is getting an earful of Tierra's history as well. Down in Turda, for example, Lady Edda and those bitches, those Sisterhood women, have been telling her all about the Sisterhood. Probably her mind's now full of made-up atrocities men have done to those pathetic women."

"She's not been doing anything else? Making deals with other towers?" he asked. "I can't believe that is all that she is doing. She has to be spying on every damn tower on Tierra, learning their secrets and then reporting them back to Konrad. I swear this governor knows more about our private workings than any governor has any right to know!"

"No proof. But I agree completely. This woman knows far too much. We need to get rid of her soon, Alano," Benito advised.

"Just how the devil are we going to pull that off?" Alano asked angrily. No one had an answer just yet.

Venerado Arturo decided now was the proper time to relay their latest discovery. Quietly, he announced, "On another matter entirely, Alano. We've just made our first *mentales* gifted man out of a normal man."

"What?" Alano looked up shocked and very surprised. "Last I heard things were not going very well at all."

"Yes, we had a breakthrough. You see, as you know, we began by researching just how this whole *mentales* thing began. Our ancient scrolls told us they began appearing some months after the big alien explosion destroyed their original refinery on Plateau Grado. While everyone back then just chalked their sudden appearance as a chance thing, we began to see it as cause and effect. You push on a person and they back up. That being our theory, then we asked the key question. What was so unique about that explosion that hasn't happened before?"

"Mind you, answering that question took us many weeks. Capa Alicia first came up with the answer. They were crushing up psi-crystals and somehow making their fuel out of it. When the explosion occurred, there must have been a large volume of that dust there being turned into fuel. The explosion scattered the dust into the air. She figured with the winds blowing often towards the east, more of the dust would have been scattered in the Midlands. Probably all the dust settled before it reached the Easterlings."

"That starts to jive with the distribution of those who have the *mentales* gifts. We are all aware that the Midlands have always had way more of them than we have here in the Westerlings. There are almost none to be found on our far western coasts, just as there are almost none in the Easterlings lands of Domei and the Arad. So Capa Alicia's conclusion is that this psi-dust must be playing a dominate role in the creation of *mentales* gifted people."

He went on, and Lord Alano listened fascinated. So did Benito and Concepcion. "We spent a week traveling around and gathering up psi-crystals from the Goza Mountains. Admittedly, this was tricky with all the snow. It wasn't hard to grind them into a fine dust. The question then was do people inhale the dust or eat it? We reasoned perhaps initially people inhaled the dust. But after a week at most, the dust would have settled. That makes the consumption idea vastly more plausible. For the last couple of months, we've been feeding test subjects psi-dust mixed in with their food."

"At first, nothing seemed to be happening. Naturally, we have no idea how much dust needs to be consumed or over what time period. However, today we've had a breakthrough. One of our test subject's eyes have turned yellow! He has the gift, but it is still forming. It's too soon to tell how strong it will be or what form his gifts will take," Venerado Arturo finished up.

Lord Alano got up and hugged both Arturo and Alicia. His excitement overwhelmed him. "My god! You have done it! Really done it! Now we can make all the *mentales* gifted we need! This is huge, positively huge. Oh! Who all knows about this? We dare not let Brom know this or any of the other towers!"

"Just we two and now you three," Arturo replied. "Of course, we are not that dumb. Not even her Circle members know what it is we are really doing with these experiments."

"Whew! Let's keep it this way! This is a tremendously important discovery, but I don't have to tell you that, do I? Keep me posted on how this new *mentales* man works out. How long does it take to make one?" Alano asked.

Arturo shrugged his shoulders. "Who knows? The change just happened this morning. We will keep you fully informed."

Concepcion took the lull in the conversation to speak up. She hated Nadja, now that she was more or less forced to have to have her lips slit and to wear the huge lip plates, even though they were very attractive, or so Inez kept telling her.

She knew better. She looked like some freak of nature now. "So how are we going to get rid of Nadja? We could use one of our contacts in Exchange City to smuggle us a blaster and then have it discovered among Nadja's things. That would get her discredited. Even Konrad would have to acknowledge that gross violation of the lease agreement."

Alano reached for his chin, but bumped into his own new lip plates, annoying him. "Well, that is doable, but it isn't going to do more than get her a reprimand. Somehow, we need to separate permanently Konrad from Nadja. While we could have her assassinated, Konrad would be sure to launch a thorough investigation, to say nothing of the other towers getting involved since she is now *mentales* gifted."

Concepcion smiled, but suddenly realized her disarming smile was no longer ever going to be visible again. Her ire grew. "Every man has his weakness. We must find Konrad's and exploit it. Women, money, gambling, drink, lust, avarice, vanity — there must be some weakness in the man. I've never met a man yet who didn't have one."

"What are you insinuating, woman?" Alano's ire rose.

"Not you, dear, or any of us," Concepcion replied coyly, again inwardly cursing because her disarming smile was permanently gone now. He calmed down. She knew his was vanity. "Alano, it is up to you to find his weakness so we may exploit it. Visit him; test him out. Hell, I don't know, but find his weakness."

Alano grumbled but saw no other avenue. He made some arrangements and sent a message to Konrad. It read:

Not much goes on during these long winters. We've heard Nadja is often gone for days visiting other lords. Some of us are planning a friendly evening of drinks and games. Would you care to join us and have some fun this Friday at six in the Imperial Castle?

Lord Alano Valen.

He and six other men were there and worked out all manner of arrangements. They brought along some of the finest ale and wines available on Tierra. They brought along a small stash of gems and gold coins for betting purposes. He found a buxom young woman and dressed her up rather provocatively. She would serve them at their gaming table.

They decided against fancy foods, because he was an alien and probably wouldn't like their strange food anyway.

Right on time, the rather bored Konrad arrived. "So glad that you thought of me, Lord Alano. You are right, Nadja is off to Malaca, I think. The weekend is here, and frankly, I am rather bored. I don't know if I will be able to play any of your games, but I'll give it a try. Say, I do like your new plates. Is that your castle?"

"Alano. No formalities on a men's night out. Yes, that's Valen Castle. Come on in; everyone is now here." He introduced the other men, who were obviously noblemen of some wealth judging by their fine quality suits. "We've some of the finest wines and ales ever brewed on Tierra. Help yourself. There's a pile of spoons." Alano inwardly cursed. He could no longer drink his ale but had to spoon it into his mouth, taking care not to drool some of it.

"Don't mind if I do." Konrad helped himself to some ale and sat down. First, they played cards, and Konrad soon recognized it as a variation of a universal game called poker. He admitted he never was very good at it. Alano noticed he didn't mind losing some funds. Further, he only sipped his ale, though he had nothing but praise for its taste. He even asked where he could purchase it in Exchange City.

Finally, their supply of ale lowered and the buxom woman made her appearance, cleaning up the dirty mugs, replacing them with clean ones as well as spoons. As she picked up Konrad's, her nearly exposed breast brushed against the side of his cheek. Alano finally picked up a rise in Konrad. *So, it is women that interests him.* He now changed the game. "This game we call ajedrez. This piece is the king. When you lose him, you lose the game. This one is your queen; she is the most powerful piece on the board."

"Say, this looks an awful lot like the Imperium game of kings," Konrad pointed out. "Sorry, I was never very good at kings. Not my thing. May I watch?"

"Sure, fellows, you two battle it out, while Konrad here and I watch and learn," Alano suggested. He began chatting with Konrad, feeling him out, making little suggestions here and there. Then, he finally figured it out. "Konrad, may I ask a really personal question? Of course, you certainly don't have to answer it."

"Sure ask. If it is too personal, I won't answer, of course."

"I can't help but notice your marriage with Nadja lacks real passion. We Westerlings always marry for pure *passion*. Do all the people on your world lack real passion in their marriages? Perhaps yours was an arranged marriage?"

"Well, I don't know what you mean exactly. Nadja and I get along well. We help each other out always. I find it hard to get out of bed in the mornings, especially since she's miraculously gotten this *mentales* gifts of yours. I must say, I sure wish I had gotten it. A man in my position would find the ability to know what others are thinking utterly invaluable."

"Ah, yes, I can see that it would be just that. Heck, if you had that gift, why you would no longer really need Nadja. You could just automatically know what the other person is thinking, even if you had no idea of his language," Alano suggested.

"Is that so? Even if I did not know their language? My! This is most interesting. Tell me more," Konrad said, growing animated.

Alano began to elaborate in detail. Then, he cleverly altered it slightly. "You know, if you were to have this *mentales* gift and were to sleep with one of our passionate *mentales* gifted Westerlings women, you would never be the same again. It gives a whole new meaning to sex! There is nothing finer in this world than a romp in the bed with one of our passionate women. The Easterlings women are all into bondage stuff. The Midlands women are simply boring. No, our women are very hot blooded, but those with the gift will just blow you away utterly. Let me assure you that you will *not* be able to get out of bed the next morning!" Alano knew that he had found Konrad's weakness. He was very jealous of Nadja's having miraculously gotten the gift and not him, plus he had no true passion in his marriage. They were compatible and complimented each other perfectly, but their marriage lacked true passion, which Konrad had never really experienced before.

He returned very late that night. When he slipped into bed beside her, Concepcion was already asleep. The next morning while still in bed, she demanded to know what he'd found. "You are right. He is envious of Nadja and wishes he had gotten the gift instead of her. I've convinced him, if he had the *mentales* gift, he would have no need of Nadja any longer. Plus, his marriage lacks any real passion between them. I've convinced him Westerlings women are the most passionate women in the universe. He was practically drooling in my hand."

"Probably it was his ale drool, dear," she teased him. "No, good work. Now we need to exploit this. The key will be if Arturo can somehow turn on *mentales* powers in Konrad. If so, we also have to find him just the right woman. Let me work on the woman; you work on the rest." She thought, now we can get rid of Nadja once and for all!

Alano added, "If we do manage to somehow get him the *mentales* gifts, then we must act totally surprised by its sudden appearance and *beg* Brom Tower to train him as they did Nadja. Throw all suspicion off us. Once he's trained, we move in with our special woman."

Chapter 24 Betrayals

In early July, Konrad's geologist detected a large cloud of dust from the sabotage and explosion at their refinery on the moon. He thought little of it, though he continued to make observations of it. By September, he saw the cloud was slowly heading for the planet, but it was only dust and would likely burn up in the atmosphere. By November, he was able to predict the slow moving cloud would encircle Asford-5 by January at the latest.

"Boss, there is a cloud of dust and debris from the summer's explosion on the moon's refinery that is going to hit us come January," he finally reported.

"No danger, right? Just dust? Won't tiny stuff burn up like meteors?" he asked, wishing he knew a bit more about such things. "No real danger to us or the inhabitants?"

"None that I can see, boss. Right, dust will burn up."

"Good. Then there is no need for me to alert the people of Ashford-5 and cause widespread panic," Konrad replied. "Keep me posted."

Late January, Ken was awakened by a telepathic message from Venerada Maricela. *Ken wake up! Look at the sky! Something strange is happening. We are getting messages now from all over Tierra. The towers are reporting seeing the same thing.*

Just then, Sam Hays, who was running the night shift, monitoring the tower comm networks and the very quiet spaceport communications systems, came running up to his room. "Ken, something wild is happening in the sky!"

"I know. I know. Wake the others. Let's go topside." Quickly dressing and donning a fur-lined coat, he headed up the steps to the small house in Brom proper that had been owned by Amy and Jan. Outside, he saw tiny streaks of light. There were so many of them that it looked more like the whole sky was aflame! Soon everyone else came out to look, standing shivering in the winter cold.

"What is it?" a sleepy-eyed Crystal asked. Ken shrugged.

Bart suggested, "A meteor swarm or something. I'll look into it in the morning." He did so the next day, but found nothing. That evening as the ruddy sun set, the spectacular display continued. The Underground presumed it had been continuing all throughout the day, but it had not been visible. Ken grew worried. Something was causing this display, and he had an uneasy feeling about it.

Just as he was about to turn in, Maricela again contacted him and asked him to meet with her and Lord Bolivar. Now even more worried, he dashed off through the tunnels to the tower. Where he found the two lip plated people waiting for him. "Ken, we just got an answer back from the governor. Several towers sent him a message via the Imperial Tower. It is dust from the explosion at their refinery on the moon this past summer. We're being bombarded with psi-dust."

Ken's face showed the alarm his stomach felt! Even Emilio looked grim. She went on, "He assures us all the dust will burn up in the atmosphere. That's causing the incredible display. He says there is no danger or he would have alerted us months ago. Ken, I am not so sure about this."

"She's right!" Emilio interrupted. "What if some of it does reach the ground?" He didn't need to further elaborate. These three knew well what could happen later on, a completely new batch of people suddenly developing the *mentales* gifts! "He should have warned us about this, Ken."

Ken sighed. "If he had, what could we have done about it? We should keep our eyes open. I'll speak to Rafaela about the ramifications of this in the morning and get back to you." They thanked him and the brief meeting broke up. As he walked back through the tunnels, he thought, *they sure look different with their drooping, huge lip plates.* He was glad he was more or less invisible.

When he found Rafaela, she pointed out, "It will take from weeks to months for any *mentales* effects to appear, depending upon just how much dust gets onto the ground. Maybe a year, if it gets into the food we eat. But then perhaps it is all being burned up in the air above us." With little else they could do, they stopped worrying about it and continued to watch the nightly show. Two weeks later, the display finally ended.

Later, the beautiful night display was one of the topics of conversation at the spring 1273 High Council meeting, along with all the new large, embossed lip plates. Inez received an ovation for her and her husband's new design. Lady Edda and Sultaness Sofia, who also wore these new lip plates, asked all the lords to disseminate word to their people that young men were in high demand for all types of employment in Turda and the coastal areas of the Arad. In this way, they hoped to encourage immigration of badly needed work force. During the summer of 1273, there was a small migration into the Easterlings of younger men in search of their fortunes.

From late February through the spring High Council, Lord Alano continued to host his Friday night "parties" for Konrad. At each session, a high dose of psi-powder was mixed into his ale. The presence wasn't detectable as the powder was fine and dissolved readily and had no taste. While Venerado Arturo would have preferred daily doses, Alano could not induce Konrad even to try the local foods. The idea being to have him drop by an inn in Exchange City each day to get some more which would be laced with the powders. Still, both men were hopeful that this plot would work.

The other half of their plot involved finding just the right voluptuous young woman, *mentales* gifted, who would be willing to play the needed role. She needed to be intelligent, ambitious, cunning, willing to follow Lord Alano's orders, extremely attractive, in no way associated with Valen Castle or Valen Tower, highly skilled in the bedroom, and willing to do whatever she had to do to ensure that Konrad became so highly emotionally attached to her that he would divorce Nadja. They soon found this to be a very tall order indeed!

Venerado Arturo had a relatively limited area of the countryside that he could search. Over the centuries, very few *mentales* gifted had ever been found much beyond a thousand miles from Valen. The original blast dust had not fallen much beyond that distance.

After a fruitless two weeks, he turned his attention further north to the vicinity of the old ruins of the Portillo

Tower. There had been a small concentration of the *mentales* gifted there. He had Capa Anita teleport two spies to that area to conduct the search. The area was deep in snow and travel was exceedingly difficult. Like all such northern towns, the villagers spent the long, harsh winters drinking in their local pubs, passing the time tossing darts, singing bawdy songs, and playing cards, while waiting the spring thaw.

Neva de la Nieve, the eighteen year old buxom barmaid, was aptly named for this region, Snow of the Snow. Her long curly black hair draped down her back, uncut in flowing waves, much like the drifts that lined the sides of inn, whipped up by the fierce, cold winds. Unlike the zephyrs outside, hers was "blown" by the many men who frequented the pub area. She would whip around the many tables, clearing and refilling their many ale mugs. Years ago, she'd learned how to "play" men, which yielded substantially greater sales and thus profit. Neva had the art of playful flirting down to a fine art, from the deliberate tossing of her long hair across a man's face, to the "openness" of her top that revealed far too much "paleness" to these often-hungry eyes.

She could receive it as well as give it. Playful, spunky, seductively sexy — she was all these and more. Yet, when one pinned her down, she'd always reply, "One of these days I will be a great lady!" Though if asked just what she meant or if you tried to pin her down as to what a great lady actually was, she would reply in different ways on different days, depending upon her mood. "I should have a tiny waist to make you see just how big my boobs really are," she replied to one old man, who was missing his front teeth. "Great ladies have big lip ornaments and soft, sensuous gowns," she replied as she whisked away from the claws of another man who was playfully running his hands down her back and butt. "Great ladies are refined and walk on their toes, not clod-hopping in here with your muddy boots," she said to a man, who had just made more work for her to clean up. Yet more often than not, she would say, "I shall marry a powerful man and be his great lady." Of course, there were no such men for hundreds of miles around the small village.

True, she had the distinctive yellow eyes and that was

just enough to keep the men from actually getting too rowdy with her or pressing her too far. At twelve, she'd had been taken to Valen Tower to be trained in the use of her *mentales* gifts. Her upbringing and disposition did not endear her to the refined men and women of the tower. As a result, she received only the most basic of training that all *mentales* gifted had to receive by law. She had her germanium crystal dangling from her neck that also told men to keep their distance.

One of Venerado Arturo's spies sat in one corner of the inn's pub, watching carefully her antics, sizing her up. Finally satisfied, he contacted Venerado Arturo. *I think I have found what you are looking for. How do you want me to proceed?*

After telling him to stick around that village, he called the Holy Pentagram together once again. "Okay, we've found a likely candidate. We must be careful with her handling. She must not know it is us who are behind this, or sooner or later the other towers and lords will find out, and we'll be ostracized yet again," Arturo stated the obvious. All five wanted to avoid any possible link in this plot ever to come back to Valen, castle or tower.

"We can have her transformation into a noblewoman done at Elegant Fashions Inc in Arabella. We don't dare use Inez for this one. She will need a period of adjustment, that's for sure," Concepcion suggested. "Perhaps Lord Arabella could be somehow convinced to take her under his wing and bring her to the High Council of Lords this spring. She could then take a room in Exchange City, where she would be available for Konrad."

Arturo added, "She'll have to be set up with a substantial dowry too. We can't have her backing off due to a lack of funds."

"And she'll need a stable person with whom she can contact, when she needs advice or wants help or has news for us," Alano interjected. "We'll make up a fictitious person, call him Mario. He will be her unseen benefactor that is making all this possible. I'll be Mario. Yes, Mario of Modesto." Modesto was a town far from Valen, known mostly for its horses.

That night, Alano focused his mind and made contact first with the spy. Via him, he located Neva. He smiled and made telepathic contact with the young woman.

Neva de la Nieve. I am Mario of Modesto. How badly do you want to become a great lady? I have the power to make that desire come true.

Mario? I don't know any Mario. Great lady? Really? Badly, that's for sure! Anything to get out of this stinking pub with all these lecherous men!

Good. I will be your benefactor, Neva, and make it come true for you. You will have all the funds you need. First, though, you must become the image of a great lady, with all the trimmings that define our noblewomen. Then, you must learn to adapt to those new constraints. If you do precisely as I say, you will find that you will be the greatest lady on Tierra. All will look up to you as their model of beauty and excellence, but you must always do precisely what I say.

And what's that? Take you into my sack? She taunted him, figuring this was just some ploy to get her in bed. She glanced around the room to see if this person was actually here in the pub.

No, you will never see me, not ever. No, a great lady must have a great man and yours will be the greatest on Tierra, one who will give you the power and influence you seek. But to succeed, you must do as I ask. Will you promise always to do so?

Well, okay. It can't hurt then.

Good. Remember always, what your benefactor gives unto you, he can also take away. Do not fail me, and the riches you so desire will all be yours. Now then, tomorrow, you will be teleported to a place where you will be physically made into the image of all the great noblewomen of Tierra.

What time?

Let us say at nine in the morning. Be prepared. By tomorrow night, you will look like a great lady. I will contact you then. Now that you have sensed me, you can contact me telepathically whenever you have questions or need help. Until then. He broke the connection.

At the same time and acting as Mario, Arturo made arrangements with the branch office of Elegant Fashions Inc in Arabella. They would be expecting Neva at nine tomorrow.

She would be given the works, but allowed to make her own selection of gowns. The design embossed on her giant lip plates would be a field of stars, sure to catch Konrad's interest.

The following night, Lord Alano again made telepathic contact with Neva. *I can't breathe! I can't talk! My lips and ears hurt. I can't walk!* A flow of her panic swept over him. Quickly, he sent out soothing, calming waves, and she began to relax. *But I am very beautiful now. I am a great lady!*

Yes, those are to be expected. Now you must learn to adapt to these new constraints as all great ladies must do. Tomorrow, Lord Arabella will come for you. He will accept you as his ward for me. The ladies of his court will help you learn. Pay attention and learn rapidly. Lord Arabella will take you to the High Council of the Lords in late March. There you will be introduced to all the other great ladies of Tierra. You will be called Lady Neva de la Nieve. I will contact you again at the council to tell you what your next step must be. She thanked him repeatedly.

Now Lord Alano and his pentagram waited. Everything hinged upon the *mentales* gift appearing in Konrad. At the high council that spring, Neva was introduced to Konrad. As instructed, she made very sure he took good notice of her by implanting some positive suggestions into his mind as Mario asked. She didn't understand why; he was already married. Then, she took a room at the best inn in Exchange City to await Mario's next order. Lord Alano kept his distance from her, but did notice she had adapted well to the many physical changes, and she was loving all the attention thrown her way.

At their Friday gaming meeting, Alano noticed that Konrad's eyes were starting to lighten, a sure harbinger of the massive change to come shortly. Now that spring had finally come, Lord Alano made a suggestion to Lord Welsham and he took it. He invited Nadja to come to Welsham for an extended visit to study their dialect variations. She readily agreed to it and left on Friday morning, planning to spend two weeks there. She was eager to learn why they called their tower Bettingham and not Welsham. Nadja was learning history as much as she was language.

Lord Alano seized his golden opportunity. He could

sense Konrad's *mentales* gifts budding. There would be no Verge Sickness with him; that was excellent. He made sure Konrad drunk a very healthy dose of psi-powder, and that he got rather drunk. The combination of the ale and his confused mental state was all that it took totally to disorient Konrad. Into this mix, Lady Neva came. Her orders were simple. Seduce him and make sure she made such an impression on him that he would never be able to get her out of his mind.

Well that's easy, she sent Mario and headed to the Imperial Castle to do as asked. When she finished with him several hours later, Konrad was almost incoherent. His mind, out of control. He couldn't stand or speak clearly at all. Now Lord Alano stepped in to play his role.

"Konrad! What's happening to you? Oh my! Konrad, you are getting the *mentales* gifts too!"

"Is, is that what this is? I can't think. I hear voices — can't see people. What's happening to me? Help me," Konrad tried to vocalize his plea, but the words that came out sounded very strange to him.

Lord Alano focused and made contact with Lord Rusden. *Yes, this is Lord Alano Valen. I am with our governor. Yes, Konrad. He is in a bad way. He's just developed the mentales gifts. Tonight while we were playing cards, his eyes have turned yellow. He needs tower help. Would Rusden Tower take the responsibility of helping him and training him? If not, I suppose that I could ask my tower to do it, but I don't want the other lords blaming me for usurping them. You are close to Exchange City.* He fibbed a little. Actually, Wyth was a third of the distance.

What? Him too? Incredible! Why yes. You are right. If you handle his training, everyone will be most suspicious. Rightly so. I'll see that it is done. Stand by for a teleport. Contact you in a bit. Has he got Verge Sickness?

Not that I can tell. He's in a bad way though. Came on him while we were playing cards. Standing by in the Imperial Castle.

A half hour later, Governor Konrad was gone and Lord Alano cleaned up the room, returning home. Now all he had to do was to wait a few weeks. By the next morning, all the towers and lords knew of Konrad's situation. While Nadja wanted to rush to Rusden to be with Konrad, Lord Welsham wisely advised against it. "Give him time to get trained. Right now, he is one very confused man. Let the tower people do their work. How do you find our dialect?" he wisely changed the topic.

Konrad began to respond to treatment at Rusden Tower. Two ideas had been heavily implanted into his mind, and they simply didn't go away as he hoped. One, he could not get the image of Neva banished. Every time he closed his eyes, he saw her. For a time, he even thought that he was smelling her, until it was pointed out to him that he was smelling one of the women's lavender hair. Two, he didn't need Nadja anymore. He could telepathically know what another was saying, independent of the spoken language, and he could send his thoughts to that person as well.

Lord Alano now began work on the next phase, confident when Konrad finally returned to his office, he would likely divorce Nadja and swoon over Neva. This phase was even riskier. Nadja had to go. She was too closely connected to Brom Tower and would likely raise far too many questions about this whole thing. He didn't want any such questions ever asked. He needed to arrange an accident, one that would be totally accepted by everyone, including Konrad, the lords, and all the tower people.

The third week of April, Konrad finally returned home. He felt ecstatic, elated, on top of the world! He was a real telepath now! Class V in the Imperial classification scheme! He could send and receive thoughts at will. Proudly, he wore his own germanium crystal around his neck beneath his shirt where it warmly touched his skin. He did not know that his gift was one of the poorest, limited solely to telepathy. That mattered not to him.

As he sat down behind his office desk for the first time since he was stricken, he began to realize not only did he not love Nadja, he didn't really need her any longer. All his thoughts drifted to Neva. *I'm here! Are you all right? I have so missed you, my darling Konrad.* He'd accidentally reached out and made contact with her!

He focused and sent back, *Yes, I am fine. I am back*

from the tower. Now I too am like you, mentales gifted! I missed you more than I can possibly say, dear Neva. I will come to you as soon as I can. I miss you. He broke the connection, someone had come into his office.

Around noon, Nadja came walking in, having rushed back as soon as she got the word that he was back. "Konrad! This is just the greatest thing! Now you and I are alike. I know how much this must mean to you."

She felt a distinct distaste for her coming from him. "Thank you, Nadja," he said rather coldly. "Yes, now I do not need a linguist with me anymore. I can easily communicate without using language. You and I — well, we've always been together out of convenience. We each needed the other, didn't we? Well, now that we both have what we want, there is no need for us to remain together as a couple. I don't want to be a hindrance to your work, and I no longer need your help either. I think that it is best for us to go our separate ways. I've already decided that we both must now have dual citizenship — Imperium and Ashford-5. Here is your new ID card so stating it. I would like to remain friends. No hard feelings, eh, Nadja? We both have what we wanted when we joined up back at the Academy."

Nadja felt crushed. A heavy weight seemed to pull her into the floor. "What are you saying? Divorce?" Her words seemed to be coming from ten miles away.

"Yes. Don't you think that is for the best? You are free to go anywhere on Ashford-5 that you desire to do your linguistic studies, unhindered by me or obligations to me. Don't you think that is best, rather than staying together, since neither of us needs the other any longer?"

Stunned, shocked, and speechless, Nadja just stood motionless for a moment. Her voice seemed to speak on its own, "Yes."

"Good. I will have the papers for you to sign later today. I suppose you need some help moving your things. I think Inez will put you up for a while, until you decide where you want to go next in your language studies. If you will excuse me, I am wanted in a briefing." Mechanically, she turned and walked out of his office and returned to their quarters where she fell onto a couch. She was numb.

After a time, she focused and made contact. *Inez. Help! Konrad is divorcing me. He says that we no longer need each other. Can I stay with you for a while? I have all my things over here.*

Dear god! Okay. Hang in there. Peter and I will be over as soon as we can. My ID card will let us in. Are you in your apartment?

Two hours later back at Elegant Fashions Inc, Nadja finally began crying, releasing her shock and grief. "How could he do this to me?" she wailed. Inez just sat and listened.

Finally, she straightened up. "Well, he is right. There never really was any love between us. It was a marriage of convenience. He needed my skills, and I needed his ability to get to unusual planets, so I could study their languages. Konrad is right; now he doesn't really need me. Besides, I have been gone longer than I've been there with him. I suppose that he is right about this. Still, it hurts."

"I know. I know. Men can be such beasts," Inez whispered and held her tight, sensing this was what Nadja really needed — the warmth of another holding her. "You are welcome to stay here as long as you want."

The next day, Nadja took stock of her situation. With her dual citizenship card, she was free to go anywhere on Tierra or even leave the planet, which she had no intention of doing. There was far too much work for her to do now. She was the first linguist ever to study a telepathic society, and she was determined to accomplish that goal in full. She had all her own money, a huge fortune. She had all of her equipment. She had all of her own possessions and many crates of clothing. "Well, I seem to have everything I really need, Inez. I should get back to work. It is what I love to do and what I live to do, after all."

"I suppose that is a good thing to do right now, take your mind off of this," Inez attempted to comfort her and to back her decision.

"Oh, I nearly forgot, Inez. While I was down at the coastal towns, I think that I have a solution for the women who wear toe shoes down there. You see, they have a great difficulty walking on the sandy beaches. What they need are toe wedges instead of toe shoes. Let me show you," she said. Shortly, she brought up some images of what they looked like. Instead of a tiny toe sole and a tall, tiny metallic spiked heel, these had a wedge, whose surface contact was many times greater. "These ought to support them on softer ground far better. Why don't you order some and have them tested out? Use my account to pay for them, since they are terribly expensive. If they work out, you can have them locally made for a fraction of their cost."

"Thanks. I will be sure to tell them that these toe wedges are your idea, Nadja. There is no escaping the simple fact that you are still the fashion leader for Tierra."

Nadja grinned and set about working out where she would go next. Late afternoon, Inez brought an older Westerlings man up to see her. "This is Mateo. He claims that he has come across something that might interest you." Inez gave Nadja a frown, indicating she didn't think too much of the man. He wore rather ragged clothing and was in need of a bath.

"Great Lady Nadja. You are the language studier, right?" he said softly. She nodded. "Well, I was poking around a cave in the northern Goza Mountains last fall, and I came across a cache of ancient scrolls. The writing on them is strange. I can't read them. It's not Westerlings for sure. Then, this spring, I heard you are studying all our languages, and I figured, if anyone can read them, it would be you."

"Sure, this sounds very interesting. How do we get to this cave?" she asked. A cache of ancient scrolls in a foreign language? This could be the find of the century, casting light on who first settled Tierra. This was an opportunity not to be missed.

"I can take you there. It is far north of that big city of Valen, some five hundred miles or so. I have a wagon and supplies, so I can take you there if you wish, Great Lady. It's just me and my daughter, Gilberta. She's ten now. She can help you with things." He nodded towards her prosthetic hands. "She's down below with our wagon. We come into

478

Exchange City each year about this time to pick up supplies. I trade my furs for the things we need."

"Okay. Let me get things ready on this end. Can you find somewhere to stay until morning? Here, this should cover your inn expenses." He thanked her profusely and left.

"Are you sure that this is the right thing to do? He is an old man, after all," Inez cautioned her.

"Sure. I have my *mentales* gifts to protect me. Once I get there, I can let you and perhaps Ken know where I am it. At least, a Circle or Ken can home in on me when I find this cave. It could well be the find of the century, Inez. I have to go, but I ought to take something other than this gown." Inez smiled and soon had her outfitted in warm leather pants and a cotton blouse over which she wore a leather jacket. Both were oiled to repel the rain, and she also had a heavy cloak for the chilly nights. After hugging Inez and thanking her, Nadja headed for the basement. On the 28th of April, she began her first overland journey. Her anticipation was quite high; these scrolls might be the answer that she was seeking: the origin of the original settlers of Tierra.

Gilberta was invaluable for Nadja. The terrain was rough and rocky, not easily negotiable in her toe boots. The stapling young girl was always at her side, supporting her and helping her keep her balance. Before long, they became good friends. Nadja had no idea where they were going, except nearly northwards. She also had no good idea of the distance they traveled. Every other day, she made contact with Inez, letting her know that she was okay and that all was well.

Nights were chilly. Here in the high country, small drifts of snow still had not melted. Each day it seemed to rain upon them. For the first time, Nadja was being exposed to the actual climate of Tierra. Until now, she'd always been inside the stone castles and towers. Now she was out in the real world. The fresh air felt good and refreshing to her, just what she needed to get over the shock Konrad had delivered to her.

Around noon on the 14th of May, 1273, they heard the low growling of what Nadja thought was a cat or cats. Gilberta screamed, "Montaña beasts! Montaña beasts!" She had heard some talk of these creatures. The closest word she had been able to translate the phrase into was cats. The old man whipped his team, but too late. Three giant cats, nearly ten feet tall, leapt from a jagged ledge above them, descending upon the horses and the people. Nadja had an image of the old man's head inside one of these cats with enormous canines. Then he was headless.

A cat jumped for her. She raised her arms to fight it off. Pain. Excruciating pain in her left arm. Still she swung her arms wildly, hitting fur frequently. Then darkness came over her. She passed out. She didn't feel an invisible arm lifting her head up, pouring some ill tasting liquid down her throat. All was pain and darkness.

The invisible Arturo returned immediately to Valen before the three Montaña beasts caught his scent. They were busily fighting over and devouring the horses. "It is done, My Lord. Success on all fronts." Lord Alano smiled.

Chapter 25 Minstrel in the Road

Residing atop the rapport pyramid pillared by his four wives, Josh saw something that alarmed him. He pulled it in closer to himself and knew that he didn't like it, but he also saw two paths. One of those he also didn't like. He looked down the other and liked what he saw. Josh acted, forcing the second path into existence.

Los Cuatro Santos had been a legend in the central lands of Trujillo. Two men and two women traveled from small village to village, healing the sick and curing the injured with their special *mentales* gifts. While the far distant tower of Valen with its Circles was supposed to be doing such things, it never did. Bonded together just after Valen's destruction of the tower at Portillo, these four felt it was their life's duty to share their special gifts with the common man. Now long gone, still the legend of their acts of supreme kindness and humanity still lived on in the remote heartlands of rolling grasslands and forests.

Another tradition had more recent origins in Malaca. Musicians were summoned to Lord Malaca's court. Dance tunes flourished as never before. Not much is known about his early life, before 1273 other than his claim to have once been at the Royal Court of Malaca. He was Diego del Baldomero, though no one had discovered just where his town of origin was located, Baldomero. What is known is he was then twenty-six, a competent musician on the guitar and flute; his singing voice was soft but sweet. His *mentales* gifts dealt with healing. Handsome, Diego had rich black hair that he kept trimmed just above his shoulders. His yellow eyes contrasted with his black moustache and he always wore black. His leather pants were black as was his leather jacket. He did wear a white undershirt. Those didn't come in black.

Diego del Baldomero fancied himself a modern-day Los Cuatro Santos, traveling the lands. Upon entering a village, he healed the sick and injured first and then shared a night of song and dance with them, before moving on to the next village or hamlet. One thing that was known at the start, Diego was indeed well-traveled. According to him, he had visited the ruins of Portillo, where a new village had been established some fifty years ago. Now he was heading south, in search of the next village.

Without warning, his horse suddenly decided to have a mind of its own, veering sharply to his left, heading east into the rugged foothills of the Goza Mountains. Twice he tried to steer it back on his southerly course to no avail. "All right, my fine beast of burden, I will follow you, as if I have a choice," he teased his horse.

Before long, he saw a grizzly sight. Three Montaña beasts were finishing a meal of horseflesh. "I hope those were not your friends, trusty steed," he said to his horse, while leaning back to retrieve his flute. Montaña beasts were common in the high foothills, and he had figured out a way of handling these fierce-some cats. He put the flute to his lips and began to blow a high, somewhat shrill and out of tune note. The instant the sound began, the three cats raised their heads. Two rubbed their ears with their enormous front paws. Fifteen seconds later, the three cats abandoned the carcasses, leaping away on up the steep sides of the ridge and out of sight. Diego rode on in to inspect the carnage. They had been pulling a wagon, which was obvious to him from the first. He also knew these giant cats would tend to dine upon the larger prey before eating humans. Perhaps, whoever suffered this misfortune would still be alive.

He reined in and dismounted. At once, he spotted the headless man. He fought to keep from vomiting. Moving closer to the broken wagon, he spotted what was probably once a child, a girl perhaps, now barely recognizable. Then he spotted a woman. Both of her arms had been likely bitten off, but she was still breathing. From her ornate lip plates, he concluded that she must be a noblewoman, for who else would wear such things?

Diego quickly sized up the situation. She was bleeding to death. He had to act swiftly, but the cats would soon be back for the rest of their meal. He tore some strips of leather from the man's pants and hastily made a pair of tourniquets, fastening them on what remained of her arms. With the immediate threat lowered, he made a few hasty repairs to the wagon and tied his own horse to it. "I know, you are not a cart horse, but we have to get away from here, unless you want to join those two," he spoke to his horse. Apparently, the horse got the message and began to pull the wagon, while he led his horse. A mile to the west, he halted by a small bubbling spring. Here pines grew in a thicket, and there was grass for his horse. Quickly, he made a camp, spreading a blanket on the grass. He carried the woman and placed her on it.

Now Diego could use his gifts for their intended purposes. With his hands just above her flesh and body, his crystal glowed blue. He began his first round of examinations. "Horse, she's been phenomenally lucky. Only her arms have been injured." Now he set to work on them, focusing first on one and then the other. An hour later, his crystal dimmed, and he tentatively loosened first one and then the other tourniquet. His repairs held and he breathed a sigh of relief. While he still had a long way to go to get her healed sufficiently to be moved, at least she wasn't at death's door any longer. She'd lost a lot of blood, and he knew that she needed fluids and light nourishment soon. He stuck up a fire and prepared a broth using part of his planned evening stew.

When he leaned close to her mouth to try to figure how to get the broth into her, he smelled the acrid odor. "*Bacal*? What the hell?" He gently opened her eyelids and saw her yellow eyes. "Someone has purposely drugged her! What is going on here? Well, best get fluids into her somehow." Holding the top plate up with one hand, he slipped the spoon into her mouth. She partially swallowed it and regained consciousness.

Nadja awoke to throbbing arms. She was sitting up, leaning against a tree. She raised her hands up, but saw nothing. Her eyes looked down and she screamed wildly. "There, there, you are alive. That's something, miss." His voice had a melodious ring to it, soothing somehow. Nadja began to calm down a little. Her mind was black, silent, strange. She was confused.

The ghastly images returned, and she choked on the

rest of the broth in her mouth. "Gilberta?" she managed to say.

"The man and the girl didn't make it," Diego said softly. "I got to you in time. I will do more healing on you once I get this soup in you. You've lost a lot of blood. How do you eat with these things in the way?"

Nadja attempted to use her telekinetic skills to lift them up and lock them into place. Nothing happened. Diego saw her frustration and said, "Someone had drugged you with *bacal*. You have temporarily lost all of your *mentales* gifts. Tell me what to do and I will do it for you."

"Lift them up. They will lock into place," she said. "I don't understand. No one drugged me. What is *bacal*? What is this awful taste in my mouth? Your soup?"

He gently lifted them up and they locked automatically. "That awful taste is the *bacal* drug. It is used to kill telepathic powers, particularly when someone has the Verge Sickness. Here, take some soup; it will wash that taste away."

She did so, but between spoons, said, "But I never took such a thing. I was in the wagon when those cat things attacked. I fought one with my hands, but the pain knocked me out, I think. I saw them get killed." She began to sob and once more, Diego spoke softly to her. Something in his voice sent calming waves over her body. She stopped crying, and Diego continued to spoon feed her.

"I've got to work on what's left of your arms some more. Please just sit still. It won't hurt, I promise you." She trusted him, she had no choice.

"I feel like I am blind," she whispered, interrupting him as he was just getting started again.

He paused and replied, "Yes, that is a very good way to describe it. Drugging a *mentales* gifted person is about the worst possible thing anyone can do to one of us. Now please just relax and let me work." She did so. For an hour he continued healing her arms, one small area at a time. She watched fascinated. She'd never seen this aspect of *mentales* gifts in operation before, though she'd been told of it during her training. Further, while he was not actually touching her skin, she felt electrified. His non-touch was so intimate, almost sensuous.

"There, I've done all I can do for now. I need to eat and rest up some before I work on them again. Feeling more like eating now?" Diego asked. She did, saying she was famished. "Yes, that is a very good sign. Talk to me while I am fixing my stew. I am called Diego del Baldomero. And you?"

"Nadja."

"Now that is a strange name. Easterlings perhaps? I've never been there. It doesn't sound like that gruff Midlands language."

Do I dare tell him? What will he think if I tell him that I am an alien here? Well, it can't hurt. "Nadja Burkhardt, the ex-wife of the alien governor Konrad Burkhardt. I guess now I am Nadja Meike. I am from a planet called Otto-4. My name is Ottoan."

"Well, pleased to meet you Nadja Meike of Otto-4. Hope you like rabbit stew. It was all the villagers could spare me."

"I'll eat anything right now. What do you mean the villagers could spare? You have a melodic voice."

"I am a traveling musician. Guitar, flute, voice. I am also a traveling healer, following in the ancient tradition established by Los Cuatro Santos a long time ago. I go to the small villages here in Trujillo. First, I heal the sick and injured with my gift and, then, give them a night of songs and dances. They give me food for the trail so I can get to the next village." He then had to explain about the legend of Los Cuatro Santos. At this point, the stew was ready, and he sat beside her, alternating spoon fulls between them. When they finished, Nadja felt tired and soon fell asleep.

She awoke to a crackling fire and the smell of tea and something frying that she'd never smelled before. The air was crisp and clean, but chilly. Clouds were already beginning to gather in the southwest. She watched Diego as he hummed a tune, while dealing with the morning chores. His tethered horse was nearby grazing on the nearly three foot tall grass. The sky had a ruddy look to it. She felt calm but blind. "Smells good," she ventured to interrupt him.

"Ah, my princess is awake at last. You slept well, Nadja. Today, you will recover more, but we should not travel just yet. It's going to rain in an hour, so we'll stay under a tarp until the afternoon. Then we can get going. Hope you like deer strips and flat cakes with berries. The old woman gave me the berries. She handpicked them herself. I think she must be sixty-five at least. I always take what they can give, you see."

After they ate, she felt very embarrassed. "I have to go," she whispered.

Diego laughed, "Well I knew that one was coming sooner or later, princess. Come on. I sure hope that you are not bashful. I doubt that you can walk in those boots by yourself on this ground, and I know you can't get those pants down now. I'll try not to stare," he paused and then said teasingly, "too much." That brought a smile to her face, but it was only visible in her eyes.

He was gentle and soon what could have been very embarrassing for her just wasn't. He then got them both under a tarp just as the first sprinkles fell. "It seems to rain every day around here," she stated. For a time they chatted about what the weather was like, and she found that he was a wealth of information. She teased him, "Isn't there anything that you don't know?" Both laughed.

"I travel a lot. Actually, I travel all the time. New places to see, new people to meet, people to heal. Plus, I make them into my audience," he replied. They continued to chat while the rain turned into a torrent for a time, before easing off.

At last, she asked, "Can you contact someone for me? Maybe they can teleport me to safety."

"Sure, but if I don't know them, I can't. I do know some people up in Malaca, but I don't think you want to go there, do you?" he replied.

"No, I wanted to get in touch with Inez Franks in Exchange City."

"Sorry, I've never been there. Don't fret so; you're gifts will be returning in a few days. Until then, you are the guest of Diego del Baldomero. And the world out there is my kingdom." He gesture to the vast rolling plains.

Ken, Inez here. I think that Nadja may be in bad trouble. She has been checking in with me every two days since she left. I haven't heard from her for four days now. I tried to reach her but got nothing at all. Can you help?

He had her slow down and tell him all she knew about where Nadja had gone. *We will get on it now. I'll let you know, Inez.* He headed off to find Bart.

"Here you are. Nadja may be in trouble. She was heading up north along the Goza from Exchange City, something about some ancient scrolls that an old man and his ten year old granddaughter had found."

"On it. Bringing up the geo-sat system now. When did she leave? I'll back track and see if I can pick them up. That will make it a lot easier to find them," Bart replied, flipping dials and setting various controls. It took him a couple of hours of scanning through images to find them out on the open trail. After that, another couple of hours went by as he progressed through the days.

"Oh my god! Look at this one!" Bart exclaimed. He zoomed it in as much as he dared before pixel resolution dissolved. "Looks like they were attacked by Montaña beasts!" Several others had heard of Nadja's disappearance, and they crowded around Bart and Ken, staring at the grizzly images. Slowly, Bart moved forward in time, frame by frame until he spotted a man riding up on a horse. Soon, they could tell that he was rescuing Nadja.

We're going to have to go get her, but it's getting dark now. Have to wait until morning. Keep them in sight," Ken asked.

"They can't get too far from here by morning. On it boss," Bart replied.

"Well, we aren't going to get to them just yet. Heavy rain right now," Bart pointed out the obvious the next morning. Impatiently, they waited for the torrent to die down. "You know, Montaña beasts don't run in packs. It is even rare to see two in the same place. Strange. Must be phenomenally bad luck."

The rains ceased and Bart activated their teleport pad. Wearing their rain cloaks, Ken and Crystal appeared not far from where Diego and Nadja were sitting against some pine trees still under his rain tarp. "Oh. Hello, visitors!" Diego said rising quickly and placing his body between the two and

Nadja.

"Hello. Nadja, is that you? Are you all right?" Ken asked.

Crystal interjected, "Of course she's not all right, Ken."

"It's okay, these are friends of mine from Brom," Nadja called out. "I can't seem to get up on my own. Montaña beasts! Horrible. I can't do anything now, please help me."

"She's the luckiest person that I've ever heard tell of — beasts got her two companions. I got to her just in the nick of time," Diego began to explain.

She interrupted him, "He's saved me, but maybe I ought to have just died, Crystal. I can't live like this. I am blind. You tell them, Diego."

"Aye, I told her it would only last a couple of days, but — well, you know how hard it can be — especially so just now," Diego again began to explain.

"Whoa, she can't see?" Ken asked, not yet grasping what either was saying. He had been staring at the pink skin of what remained of her arms, noticing that a *mentales* healing gift had been used on her.

"*Bacal*. When I got to her, she'd been heavily drugged," Diego explained.

"What? That's criminal. Nadja, who gave you that poison?" Crystal demanded to know immediately in no uncertain terms. She had her hands on her hips.

"No one. I was fine. Then these monstrous cats jumped down on us. Horrid. The old man — his head — gone — I saw it. Gilberta — she was only ten — got her. Attacked me — remember fighting them off with my arms — and pain — terrible pain. That's all. Diego feeding me and I was choking on the soup. No one."

Ken scratched his head. She was obviously reliving the hideous trauma, but where did the *bacal* come in? "Don't know about that, but it seems right," Diego said softly. "My horse decided to go west instead of south, and I came across them. Three beasts were devouring what was left of the horses. They do that — going after the larger game first. I scared them off and found the man. Grim. Saw what was left of the child — could tell it was a girl though. Found her bleeding massively.

My gifts are healing, so I got the bleeding to subside and got her out of there — horse sort of dragging the broken wagon down here — cats would be back. Then, I worked on healing her up. But when I tried to get some liquids into her mouth, which is under there somewhere," he jested a little over the large lip plates, "I smelled *bacal*. When she came to, she verified it, awful taste in her mouth. *Bacal* for sure."

"Damn. And you saw no one else there but the two dead and Nadja?" Ken asked for confirmation.

"Yep and what was left of the two horses. I can't figure this one out. How did Nadja get *bacal* in her mouth?" Diego answered and then asked. "Besides, I've never known the cats to operate together, let alone three of them."

"That's what we thought too, Diego. Montaña beasts are solitary predators at the top of the food chain. Once in a while, you might see two, but three acting together? How very strange!" Ken mused. "Add the drugging of her into the mix and this is sounding more and more like an assassination attempt not a freak accident!"

"But who would want to harm the princess here? She's a great lady, is she not?" Diego asked politely. "No one harms great ladies. She says she is one of those aliens, but I think that is just her shock talking. Everyone knows the aliens are really tall, thin, and grey, which she isn't."

Crystal stifled a giggle. Ken smiled. "Ah now there you are wrong. She does come from another world than our grey aliens. Her ex-husband is the new governor of the aliens on Plateau Grado. Nadja, could Konrad have wanted you dead?"

Nadja gasped. "No, he still wants us to be friends. He went out of his way to give me dual citizenship and a permit to travel anywhere on Tierra that I want and to bring all my equipment with me. He still wants me to conduct my linguistic studies. It surely couldn't be him. He doesn't know anything about these monster beasts."

"So who wants you dead?" Ken asked.

"No one," Nadja replied automatically.

"Someone does, Nadja. Okay, how do we handle this?" Ken asked, thinking out loud. "Is Diego taking good care of you?"

"Yes, he is very kind. Why?"

"Diego, what are your plans? Where were you going when you found her?" Ken asked.

He got the long story about the wandering minstrel and healer, emulating the ways of Los Cuatro Santos. "Just heading west towards the next village where I will heal and sing again. I was taking her with me, if that's what you want to know."

"Good. You have healed her up pretty well. Later on, Nadja, we can finish the process and handle that awful trauma. Right now, let's let everyone one believe that you are dead, that you met a tragic accident. Perhaps we will get a clue about who is behind this when they react to the news. I am really afraid, if we take you back right now, whoever is behind this will only try again. Let us do our job and see if we can find out who is trying to kill you. Diego, I am charging you with her safety for now. We'll stay in constant contact with you, checking in every so often until the drug wears off. When it is safe, we'll come get her. For now, stay away from all the towers."

"I don't go near them anyway. You don't have to worry about that. Nothing but hypocrites in them. They say they are here for the people, but they never are. That's why I am out here. The Los Cuatro Santos had it right," Diego replied with a wry grin.

"Good. We'll see that the wagon is put back where it was. If we leave it here or you take it, the assassins might get the idea that she somehow escaped. Can she ride your horse? Toe boots are no good out here," Ken asked.

"Of course. We should get started now. Rain's stopped and there are sick and injured out there that need me," Diego replied. The three helped him break camp and scavenge some useful items from the wagon. Nadja sat bravely on his horse, as he began walking out across the grasslands, following the bubbling stream. Once they were out of sight, Bart teleported the wagon remains back to the grizzly sight. Ken and Crystal did their best to cover up the campsite before Bart brought them back to the Underground.

"So who would want Nadja dead?" Rafaela asked. Their

whole group was by the teleport pad, waiting their return.

"That's the key question isn't it?" Ken replied. "Ex-husband is always a good guess, but I can't see Konrad doing this. He's certainly mistreated her — surprise divorce and all that, but he hasn't the knowledge or skill to have done this. I suppose that he could have hired someone to do it for him."

"We need to find out fast!" Crystal added.

"We need to get her to the medical machine and fully healed too. My god, the trauma that she is carrying around now — well I can't imagine how awful she must feel," Misty put in her notions. "Why don't we bring her back here, put her into the machines for a few minutes, and then take her back out there? Luisa could go back with her and run therapy on her, maybe in the evenings or something."

Luisa spoke up, "She's right. Nadja really needs help right now, while it's fresh. God, Ken, she's lost most of her arms! Add to that the absolutely ghastly sights she saw — it's amazing she hasn't broken down completely!"

"Ken, Luisa is right. Nadja is teetering on the edge. We have to do something now to help her," Rafaela added. "I will let Inez know, and she and I will get the word out and see where the dung falls."

Luisa sighed. "He has a point; it is best that we wait until the *bacal* wears off."

Ken smiled, feeling his decision vindicated. "Right, after it does, Bart, bring her back here. Misty, get her healed up properly. Luisa, you go back with her and deal with her needed therapy. Rafaela, go to Exchange City, and let's get this thing going. For now, no one beyond Inez is to know that Nadja is all right, well mostly all right. Someone is out to kill her, and we must not take any chances. Lord knows, there could be a spy here in Brom Castle or tower."

Rafaela said, "Excellent. Andres, you stay with Maricela and keep me posted on the reactions here. Bart, teleport me to Inez now. No, I don't need to pack. I can get new clothes there if I need them. Come on gang, time is a'wasting."

A few minutes later, Inez breathed a huge sigh of relief. "I tried to talk her out of going off with that old man. He seemed honest enough and his granddaughter was cute. But still, she should not have gone off by herself like that. Maybe it is my fault. She was so shocked by Konrad's sudden abandoning her."

"It's not your fault, Inez. Sometimes jumping back into the work that you love is the best therapy. Come on; we have work to do. First, you contact Konrad and tell him that Nadja has gone missing. Let's see what happens next."

Inez and Rafaela met Konrad at the Imperial Castle and Tower an hour later. Inez carefully explained to him what Nadja had done and that she was now way overdue on making contact with her. "I still can't reach her and neither can Rafaela. I just know something awful has happened to her. Can you help?"

"Damn! I thought it was safe for her to travel about. We should send out a search party at once. Darn, I will have to get the various lords' permission to send out some of our shuttlecraft. Perhaps the towers have other ways of looking for her. You say that she was going up along the Goza Mountains on the western side?" Inez nodded. "Let's see, isn't Lord Valen's tower over there somewhere? Then again, they might have tried to cross the mountains. Help me a little. What towers are on the eastern sides?"

Rafaela said, "Wyth Tower and Brom Tower."

"Good. Venerado, please send an emergency message to Lord Valen, Lord Bolivar, and Lord Wyth. Ask them to have their towers do what they can to locate Nadja and the old man and girl. Also, ask them if they will grant me the right to send out shuttlecraft to help in the search. I'll need their permission. I think my shuttles have the best chance of finding them. I do hope that she's all right. Her language studies are really immensely valuable, you know," Konrad requested. "I'll wait right here until I hear back. Meanwhile, I am going to assume that they will grant me the flyover permission. Excuse me while I order up the flights," Konrad declared. He stepped away and pulled out a small device and began talking into it, issuing orders to unseen personnel at the spaceport.

Within minutes, Lord Emilio appeared on the Imperial Tower's teleport pad. Not far behind him, Lord Wyth appeared and then Lord Valen. All three looked very worried, offering

Konrad sympathy and all the help that they could provide. They gave him the permission he needed to launch his shuttlecraft. "I'm sure that she is all right. Probably just got all caught up in her research. Nadja gets so involved in her work," Lord Valen consoled Konrad.

"Still, it is alarming we cannot make contact with her," Lord Bolivar pointed out. "I will be honest with you, Konrad, now that you are one of us. Being unable to make telepathic contact is not a good sign at all."

"He's right," Lord Wyth added. "My people haven't been able to make a contact with her either."

Konrad looked grim. "What does this mean? She has telepathy like I do now, we all do. I don't understand how we can't reach her." He looked from face to face, searching for a better answer.

Lord Bolivar finally said, "I know of only three reasons why we can't reach a known *mentales* gifted person. None are good." He was hesitant to say more.

Lord Valen sighed. "Best tell him, Lord Bolivar. He ought to know."

Emilio let out a deep breath. "It happens when the person is dead. It happens when the person is too far away from us, but that means they have gone off-world. It can also happen if they are given the drug, *bacal*. It is a poison which nullifies all *mentales* effects for some time. It is usually used to help someone get over Verge Sickness."

Lord Valen added, "But it has also been used by nefarious men, when they kidnap someone who has the gift. Surely she hasn't left Tierra, has she?"

"Well, she was terribly upset when I told her we ought to go our own ways, now that I have the gift too," Konrad admitted. "I will have my people check all outgoing ships within the last two weeks." He again barked orders to that effect into his hand-held communications device.

Konrad sighed. "So you think that she is, is dead?" His voice faltered. Neither of the three lords chose to answer him. Their silence was answer enough for Konrad. He sat down on the floor. "This is all my fault. I should not have rushed so quickly on divorcing her."

"You can't blame yourself for what Nadja did or did not do," Lord Valen consoled him. "She is an adult and a powerful woman."

"Was I wrong to allow her to go where she desired on Tierra?" he asked.

"No, of course not. She is a linguist and travel is part of her work," Lord Bolivar answered. "Besides, you probably could not keep Nadja from traveling anyway. She's a strong-headed woman."

"You are right. Okay, thank you all for coming. I appreciate the support. I best get back to my office and stay in close contact with the searching parties. I will relay any news of Nadja to you through the Imperial Tower here. Thanks. I do appreciate your deeply felt concern. I am sure we will find her," Konrad said, but he didn't display the confidence of his own words. "Dead" kept echoing in his mind.

After he left, the three lords did so as well. Inez and Rafaela headed over to her nearby office building. Once safely in her office, Inez asked, "Well?"

Rafaela sat down before answering. "I am certain Konrad knows nothing about it. He was truly quite shook up about it. He isn't involved. That rules out the most likely suspect."

"So what now?"

"Don't know. The three lords seemed genuine as well. I just don't know. We have a mystery on our hands, a deadly one," Rafaela said grimly. "Now we wait."

A day later, messages again flew back and forth. One of the Imperium shuttles had located what appeared to be a damaged wagon. At once, the three lords came to the Imperial Castle, where Konrad waited on them. His face was grim. He'd seen the photos the crew had taken of the sight. Grizzly remains. After showing the three men and the two women the photos, Inez swooned a little. "That's — that's the wagon. That's the granddaughter's dress."

Her identification cast a very serious mood over all four men. "Look, we ought to go there and take a good look," Lord Valen suggested. "Lord Bolivar, Lord Wyth, fetch your best trackers and scouts. Then, let's have the Imperial Circle teleport us all there and study the site. We need to make sure — one way or the other."

At the site of the carnage, Lord Valen held on to Konrad, supporting him. Many others scurried about, while two buried the remains. "Well, it is inconclusive, governor. There is no trace of a third body," Lord Bolivar summarized the results.

"So what does that mean? She was eaten whole?" Konrad said, his voice shaking a little.

"Possibly, but that is unlikely. As grim as this is to say, we would have expected to find parts of her body here, as with the other two dead," Emilio said as gently as he could. "We haven't so there is a possibility that she somehow survived."

"But how? We are in the middle of nowhere," Konrad asked, pitifully. His eyes roamed from the stark, jagged foothills on out over the rolling grasslands spotted with groves of pine — all totally devoid of civilization — that is to say, his kind of civilization.

"There are traces of another horse coming up to the scene. Perhaps she was rescued by this unknown person. I would not give up all hope just yet, governor," Lord Bolivar declared.

"But how do we find her? Maybe she is badly wounded," Konrad suggested.

"I can't explain that," Lord Wyth pointed out. "If she were injured, I am sure she would have contacted us if she could. Perhaps she is unconscious and being cared for by that rider. If so, give her time to recover some. Beyond this, I'm at a loss. These are Lord Valen's lands. Perhaps he could organize a search party or something."

"Yes, of course. I'll get on it immediately," Lord Valen replied. "I'll have my tower teleport me back to Valen and make the arrangements immediately. Don't worry, Konrad, if she is alive, we *will* find her." Konrad thanked him and he vanished. Shortly after that, the others were brought back to the Imperial Tower.

Back in his castle, Lord Alano swore. "Venerado Arturo, you told us she was dead! Now it seems that she isn't, not unless one of the cats swallowed her whole! I've got to send out a search party now!"

"But I don't understand how she could be. Her arms were chewed off, she was bleeding profusely," Arturo complained.

"Apparently, someone came along in time to save her. You fool," Lord Alano cursed him.

"There, there, unforeseen chance," Concepcion spoke up, soothing tempers. "Nothing more than unforeseen chance. Now we must be seen as her rescuers."

Inez and Rafaela reported back to Ken. Rafaela then sent, *As soon as the drug wears off, you are going to have to get her back here and deal with the others finding out that she is alive. Best get your stories straight on this one.*

When Ken checked with Diego, he learned the drug was wearing off. He then acted swiftly, bringing Nadja back to the Underground. After exchanging welcomes, Misty took her into their medical room and used the medical machine to alter her short stumps. An hour later, she declared, "There, now they are identical and there are no ugly scars. That's something at least." Misty attempted to provide what little comfort she could. Nadja fought back tears, though.

Ken then worked with her to get her story straight. Finally, Nadja made contact with Konrad and the venerado at the Imperial Tower. She explained three beasts had attacked them, and she'd fought the cat off with her arms, but that the cat bit most of them off. She'd passed out only to wake up days later. A kindly man had come across her and both rescued her and healed her. She also pointed out she believed that this had been an attempt on her life, because someone had deliberately given her *bacal* after she had passed out and before she was rescued. When she recovered enough, she'd made contact with Venerada Maricela in Brom, and she'd rescued her. She was fine now. She also declared she was going to continue her fieldwork.

Many words were exchanged, some quite poignant, particularly so about the notion this had been an assassination attempt. Konrad swore to her that he would leave no stone unturned in an attempt to find who had done this awful deed. Once they had finished their telepathic communication, Ken then had Bart teleport Nadja and Luisa back to the waiting Diego, so that Luisa could give Nadja her desperately needed therapy. The plan was, when she finished that, Nadja would accompany Diego for a while. Everyone wanted Nadja more or less to disappear for a time. They needed time to uncover who had tried to kill her, and they didn't want the guilty to know where she now was. All feared that they could try again. Nadja agreed to lay low for a while, though she could not think of anyone who wanted to harm her.

In the next village, Luisa helped them purchase a wagon and team. Bart then teleported some of her equipment to her. She wanted to be able to record the local dialects she encountered. Luisa then decided to tag along for a few weeks, helping as needed.

Chapter 26 Rebirth

Early May 1273, Venerada Maricela made an unusual trip down into the underground, seeking Ken's advice. "I have been giving two matters a good deal of thought. I want your opinion on them. First, there is this seemingly amazing development of the *mentales* gifts in Governor Konrad. Totally unexpected. We both know the true origins of such gifts, such abilities — the massive growth of pituitary glands caused by the body's assimilation of psi-powder. We 'made' Nadja — that was fortuitous indeed. So what I want to know is just how did Konrad ingest enough psi-powder to cause the observed change? Notice it didn't happen to the last governor who had been here for a very long time."

"Are you saying someone purposely fed him psi-powder?" Ken asked.

"It would seem he either somehow ate local foods laced with it quite by accident or someone has deliberately put it in his food. I cannot see anyone at the spaceport doing such a thing. They are ignorant of such things, believing it is basically a raw material for their fuel. I want to rule accidental ingestion out. Inez says he really never eats out at Exchange City inns. I am confident in ruling out someone on the base slipping it to him. As far as anyone knows, he is wholly ignorant of the dust's effects on us. To whit, he didn't think the psi-dust cloud from the moon to be of any importance."

She continued, "So that leaves me with only one plausible theory. Someone has deliberately been putting it into his food or drink with the objective of giving him the gift. This then raises two fundamental questions. One, why would someone want Governor Konrad to have low order *mentales* gifts? Two, who is behind it? The really serious aspect is that whoever is behind it now knows our secret of how to make normal people into *mentales* gifted people. That scares me as much as it did your mother."

Ken replied, "Same here. I'm puzzled by it and very worried about its implications too. Any ideas who would want our governor to have telepathy?"

"No. I cannot think of any ruler who would want the alien governor able to pry into the minds of our people. It is counterproductive and could well put Tierra at great risk. Already many of the lords, who are not gifted, are quite afraid Konrad will be able to read their thoughts and minds. Some have asked their aides to concoct protections over themselves so that their minds can't be read. Yet, who else but one of our own could have done this to him? It has to be some *mentales* gifted person, who is behind Konrad's mysterious acquisition of telepathy."

Ken nodded his agreement. Her thoughts had pretty well been his own, when he first heard of Konrad's surprise acquisition of the gifts. "Any idea who is responsible for feeding him the psi-powder? Frankly here, we are all at a loss on this point."

She explained, "Well, we've been trying to gather data about his recent activities. About the only thing that we've been able to discover is that for many weeks, he's been playing cards and games with Lord Alano Valen and several other men at the Imperial Castle. Could they be dosing him up once a week and would that infrequent a dosage bring about the change?" Maricela asked and then answered her own question. "I highly doubt it, because Rafaela doses her patients several times a day."

"Don't know. Let me get Rafaela in on this," Ken suggested. They paused briefly until she joined them. Ken outlined what they had been discussing before he asked, "So could they be dosing him up once a week and would that infrequent a dosage bring about the change?"

Rafaela ran her fingers through her hair, twisting strands around her fingers, deep in thought. "Well, I suppose so. Given a large enough dose once a week and over a great many weeks, the change might occur. We've never explored such an approach. Didn't make sense to try. We know the original explosion cast psi-dust over the land, and, over time, it was on or in the food everyone ate. I suppose it could be done that way. If so, it might account for Konrad only developing the minimum amount, mere telepathy and nothing more."

"Good. I think we should credit Lord Alano Valen as the culprit. If so, once more Valen is up to no good! But why would he want our governor to have telepathy?" Maricela asked.

"Good question. I don't see any reason just now. It did cause a breakup in their marriage. Perhaps he is trying to get one of his women into the alien's headquarters like Carmen did long ago. We'll have to see if Konrad starts taking up with a local Westerlings woman," Ken suggested. "If so, we need to watch her carefully and see if she is tied to Lord Alano Valen somehow. But if he is behind it, why does he want Nadja dead?"

"I've no idea about that one. Guess all is just speculation at the moment. Thanks for hearing me out," she said. They chatted a bit more and she left.

Late May, every tower on Tierra knew they had a major problem developing. The Midlands was the first to discover it, primarily because here the various towers were continuing to send out their Circles or members of a Circle to visit the towns and villages within their respective kingdoms. Normally, they handled the sick and injured, but sometimes assisted with stone construction works. They also kept alert for new *mentales* gifted young children. As they were found, a Circle representative contacted their parents to inform and caution them. If their child became ill, that is, got the Verge Sickness, they were to send word to the tower. When the child reached fourteen, they would be sent to the tower for training and receive their crystal of power. This was routine operation in the Midlands, but far less so within the huge territory controlled by Valen Tower. Within a few hundred miles of the coastline, the City-States Alliance routinely also kept on the lookout for these new youngsters.

Without any warning, some adults were now undergoing the transformation. One by one, these unexpectedly changed men and women were sent to their respective towers to be trained. While they had the distinctive yellow eyes as the *mentales* gifted, the shade of yellow was quite dim. Soon, it was realized that these individuals only possessed basic telepathic abilities, not the more far-reaching full *mentales* gifts. My late May, within the Midlands, the numbers had grown to nearly one in twenty! The sheer numbers of these new telepaths who had to be trained began to overwhelm any given tower's staff. Only Brom Tower, where Venerada Maricela had over four full Circles, was able to keep up with the sudden appearance of so many new telepaths.

By June, Valen Tower and Adelmira Tower finally acknowledged the situation in their areas. Adelmira Tower had always been small, having been so distant from the explosion on Plateau Grado. They quickly asked the other towers for help, and Brom Tower was the only one who had the capability to assist them.

At Valen Tower, they soon discovered that these many new people were only going to be telepaths and without any substantial *mentales* gifts. Hence, Venerado Arturo decided not to waste too much time on them. He chose to ignore the ancient rules that an untrained telepath was a danger to himself and to others. Diego, Luisa, and Nadja soon began to discover older men and women within these relatively isolated villages far from Valen Castle, who now had this basic gift and thus needed help and training. When Valen Tower refused to deal with them, Brom Tower stepped in to help. Now their Circles too became overloaded and overworked. Even the members of the Underground stepped in to help train the many men and women who were being brought to Brom Tower on a daily basis.

The only positive aspect was that these new telepaths did not need a germanium crystal and only needed to learn how to block their thoughts from being broadcasted in all directions, and how to dampen out the multitude of thoughts coming from the other people who were in their vicinity. Hence, each person needed only several days' worth of training. Still, during June, all the tower members and every other *mentales* gifted, who could be pressed into service, were kept very busy from dawn until dark. Even keeping accurate records of these new telepaths was troublesome. Many names fell through the cracks, as they would later learn.

As a result of all this, the July High Council Meeting

was canceled. Only a few showed up in Exchange City to receive the annual lease payments of iron ore and gold. Finally, by the end of July, the numbers of new telepaths dropped off completely. All that remained were the children, who had been already identified and were being watched for the future. In August, the tower leaders tried to make sense of all this. The only conclusion possible was that this sudden birth of so many low-level telepaths must have been the result of the psi-dust shower last winter, the one that had produced the spectacular night fireworks.

As far as Venerada Maricela and the Underground were concerned, this bode ill for Tierra. Now every tower had a good idea how to "make" a mentales gifted person. While none of the venerados and veneradas admitted it, most were beginning to make their own experiments along these lines. All the Underground and Maricela could hope for was that they would not succeed and give it up. If not, within a few years, the sheer numbers of powerful *mentales* gifted would threaten the stability of the existing order on Tierra.

As Ken put it, "What do we do when Valen Tower has a hundred or a thousand *mentales* gifted? They could easily take over the world." Just now, Ken wished Benjamina had used the rejuvenation machine! He knew a crisis of some magnitude was brewing and that he had no idea how to deal with it.

During the spring and summer months, Konrad was oblivious to the crisis the towers were facing and struggling to handle. Rather, he was infatuated with Neva. At first, he only saw her in the evenings after he finished work. Ever so slowly, his "quitting time" crept into the middle of the afternoon. Then, his morning starting hours edged later and later, until he was arriving in his office sometime after ten in the morning. She was good in bed and their combined telepathic rapport and intercourse was addicting. In late July, Konrad finally begged Neva to marry him, which she was only too eager to do. Now she would be the greatest lady on Tierra! She began making plans for her introduction to all the lords and ladies at the fall council meeting. On Konrad's behalf, he was experiencing passionate love for the first time in his life and had no idea he was being used.

During these months of wandering seemingly aimlessly around the tall grasslands of Trujillo, Nadja and Diego found much to like and admire in each other. Before long, true love blossomed between the two. Finally, as the first hints of winter's approach came in mid-September, the two were married in a small village. Then, they were transported back to Brom Tower and from there to Exchange City, staying for a few weeks with Inez and Peter. Both were going to go to the fall High Council of the Lords.

During the long winters, Diego usually held up in some village making music for a living until the spring thaw came. Nadja suggested that instead, they take their act to the warmer southern lands. She was having a ball recording the minor dialect variations of the Westerlings spoken languages. Hence, at the council, Nadja planned to get permission from the City-States Alliance lords to travel their coastal lands.

Of course, she also had to face all these lords and ladies. They all continued to inquire about her life since the horrid accident that cost her most of her arms. She knew they would all be staring at her as well as dumping sympathy on her. Still, she had to face it. Do it now and be done with it, Diego had suggested.

As always, Inez wanted Nadja to model the new fashions. Her suggestion about the toe wedges had been wholly accepted. Now women could negotiate the softer terrain far better, even walking along the beaches. Inez and Peter had created new models, specifically fleece lines toe boot wedges that Nadja agreed to model for her. Plus, Inez took what Nadja had suggested last year to heart. Baring one shoulder had allowed the rubies of her left earring to stand out. This year, Inez became far bolder. She wanted to introduce a strapless gown and see if that would catch on with the other women. Again, Nadja agreed to model it as well. In return, Inez created an office and living quarters for Nadja and Diego to stay when they were here. Now Nadja had a permanent base for her ever-growing linguistic recordings and work. Diego found a very receptive audience for his music in the rather large Exchange City. He didn't mind spending time here either.

At the September High Council of the Lords, Nadja made her grand entrance with Diego holding her securely around her waist. It was just before ten in the morning and the many lords, ladies, and others had finally assembled in the old throne room. A dull noise came from the hundreds of voices greeting each other and light chatting. A small crowd hovered around Governor Konrad and his new bride, Neva. She looked radiant and extremely pleased and proud. Neva was the center of attention. Konrad stood at her side, much like a proud peacock. She wore a bright red, pencil gown, form fitting but with a walking slit. He wore a new brown suede suit, much like all the other lords, who had also taken the time to obtain the latest design from Elegant Fashions Inc.

When Nadja entered, all eyes turned to look. Many gasps indicated the shock of seeing her without her arms. That's not entirely true, they were about six inches long now, but there were no ugly scars. The medical machine had aesthetically shaped them into tapered stumps, ready to be fitted with prosthetic arms. Others gasped at her new strapless gown. The rubies of her huge earrings were now quite prominent and matched the red satin of her gown. She'd opted for a more of a flair from her waist down, plus it was short, falling to just below her knees.

The crowd surged away from Konrad and Neva, flowing automatically over to Nadja and Diego. As she had expected, Nadja was instantly bombarded with mountains of sympathy for her tragic loss of her arms and at the same time praise for her new gown and toe boot wedges. From across the room, Nadja felt as if Neva was about to blast her with a bolt of lightning! The governor's wife didn't try to hide her rising jealousy from anyone. "How dare she usurp my grand entrance? Konrad, do something!"

Lord Wye was running this meeting. Although he had been about to officially open the meeting, he delayed, allowing the swarm to welcome Nadja back. It would have been pointless to try to start it just now. She was quite a distraction. When the overall noise subsided, Lord Wye finally stepped onto the raised platform.

"Lords, ladies, venerados, veneradas, amos, amas, an others, it is my pleasure to open this fall session of the High Council of the Lords." He talked loudly, knowing his massive lip plates tended to dampen his voice. "First, let me welcome Governor Konrad Burkhardt, who wants to say a few opening words." He motioned to Konrad, who escorted his gorgeous bride up onto the platform. Neva's ire vanished, as she became once again the focus of everyone's attention.

"My lord, ladies, I stand here before you today a changed man. For the first time in my life, I have found true love! Yes, this is my wife, the lovely and brilliant Neva de la Nieve Burkhardt. As some of you know, she was the ward of Lord Arabella, who introduced us some months ago. I have never been happier in my whole life. Thank you all." A round of applause acknowledged them and they stepped down. Lord Wye stepped back up.

"Nadja, will you and your new husband step up here for a moment. I know that everyone here wants to wish you all the very best. We are all so terribly sorry about your narrow escape from the vicious beasts of the mountains. I am sure that I speak for all of us, our hearts go out to you. If we can ever do anything for you, don't hesitate to ask."

While he was speaking, Nadja and Diego made their slow way to the platform. A huge round of applause greeted them, drowning out Lord Wye, who stepped back. When she had the chance to speak, she said, "Thank you all. I do appreciate it. Don't worry, the loss of these," she waived her short stumps, "will not stop me from making my rounds to learn your language better." Again, more applause drowned her out, and they bowed and stepped down. As she did so, she again caught a stare from Neva, one that could kill. Many others also saw it, including Inez, who relayed it to Ken.

Soon, the lords began their discussions, primarily centered on the outbreak of new, weak telepaths and how they should be handled. What role or roles, if any, they should play became a hot topic of discussion. Meanwhile, the women gathered around Nadja, begging for the full details of her ordeal. Nadja hated this, but knew she had to endure it. The well-meaning women would be horribly affronted if she didn't.

That evening, Diego became a smash hit. He joined the musicians, who played for the dance. Soon, however, his skill and artistry shone above them. At last, the musicians ceased playing, allowing him perform his one-man show for nearly an hour. He also played two fandangos especially for Lady Rosita Malaca, who could and did dance to these hopping style dances. Neva had expected to be asked to dance by the many lords and gentlemen, and some did out of politeness and respect to Konrad. However, they swarmed Nadja, who constantly had to sit every other dance out, for she was totally out of breath. Pipe corsets and vigorous dancing didn't mix. By the end of the evening, Neva's jealousy reached new heights, but she was powerless to do anything about it. Later, she contacted Mario and complained bitterly to him.

When Venerada Maricela returned home to Brom Tower, she met with Ken. Her objective was to compare Konrad's weak *mentales* gifts to those of the hundreds of new telepaths who had been trained during the late summer. Their idea now being perhaps someone had not "made" Konrad, but he'd just ingested the psi-dust that had fallen from the moon as these others had.

"No, his eyes are definitely quite yellow with the usual brown speckles, quite unlike the pale yellow of all these new telepaths, Ken. I am sure that someone dosed him up. We are back at square one. Someone deliberately turned him into a *mentales* gifted. That means someone really knows how to do it," she declared. "Plus, there was way too much discussion about how the moon's dust must be the cause of all these weak new telepaths. I am afraid the mouse is out of the barrel now. Maybe no one will act upon this knowledge, do you suppose?"

"Let's hope so. Maybe all these new telepaths will satisfy the other towers for now," Ken suggested hopefully. He didn't feel so hopeful though, worried was more like it. They were no closer to knowing who had altered Konrad and who had tried to assassinate Nadja now than they were months ago.

Late September 1273, Josh again rose up from his power base, forming the rapport pyramid. As he looked out across Tierra, he saw another image that disturbed him. As he followed down the path of that image, it branched as he expected. Futures were not un-mutable. Events altered the flow of time. He followed each one, liking even less what he saw down them, until he backed out to where he'd started. Josh began looking for an alternate image from the original one that had caught his attention. Love flowed into him from his base, and he saw another image. This one was more to his liking. Its branches all seemed so much better. He backed out and began to tweak that point in time, ever so slightly, just enough to nudge the second path into becoming the present-time reality.

Just as he did this, a golden light appeared before him, taking the shape of a glowing, translucent woman. *Who are you?* he asked.

You may call me Lysandra. At last, I have someone who is helping me. I approve of what you've done. Allow me to both reward your good deed and support your change of the future.

Sure, as long as it doesn't force us down that other path. That one is too terrible to behold. I don't want my women to have to face that one.

Thanks to you, neither they nor the others will. There, it is done. She faded from his view, but Josh remained in his loving rapport for some time, the five basking in their shared love. In the morning when the four wives awoke, they found that their arms and legs had been restored. Lysandra had worked another miracle, but then Josh and the four already knew that.

Lysandra also appeared to Nadja. I am the Goddess Lysandra. *I give you back your arms. In return, continue your linguistic studies of Tierra until they are complete and published.* Nadja was shocked and speechless. When she found her voice to respond, the yellow ghostly image was gone. Her arms were back as if they had never been lost.

A third of the way across the galaxy in a deep space

transport ship, Lysandra appeared to Amy and Jan, rather Gabriella and Celia. *I forgive your foolishness. I give you back your hands but ask that you continue on your path. You will need them.* Again both women were speechless and Lysandra vanished before they could thank her in person. Both thanked her anyway.

A shocked Diego and an amazed Nadja contacted Ken and Crystal the next morning. Inez was ecstatic, when she discovered that Nadja's arms had been restored by the Goddess of Life and of Death. She'd insisted that Nadja discuss this immediately with the Underground. Bart hastily teleported the two to their pad, still wiping the sleep from his eyes. One look at Nadja, however, and he was wide awake! He summoned everyone else, rather surprising Nadja.

"It is a miracle, a holy miracle!" exclaimed Crystal, as she hugged Nadja. Misty quickly checked Nadja's arms and hands to make sure that they were both real and in good shape.

"Okay, Nadja. Tell us exactly what Lysandra said to you. This is very important. What sacrifice did she ask of you so that you could get them back?" Ken asked.

"I don't know what you mean. She said only, 'I give you back your arms. In return, continue your linguistic studies of Tierra until they are complete and published.' That's all. What is going on? I don't understand how this is possible. Who is Lysandra?"

Ken explained, "In very ancient times, there was a pantheon of gods and goddesses worshiped on Tierra. Lysandra is the Goddess of Life and Death. She looks after the welfare of women, though for her aid, she always extracts a sacrifice from those women she helps. Then there is Calder, the God of Waters. He used to be worshiped by those who make use of the oceans and rivers. Wystan is the God of Battles and Warriors. He is the men's god, and he loves to create conflict and strife, so that men fight and he can watch and enjoy. Ariana, the Goddess of Fertility, but no one has really seen her. Alleric is at the top of their pentagram, all powerful, but he appears to seldom mix in our affairs."

"These ancient ones have not been formally worshiped

on Tierra for centuries. But that does not mean that they don't exist. Calder was active some years ago but we think he has gone to sleep. Through his intervention, the City-States Alliance came into being. I'll have to tell you about the mermaids later. Wystan has fomented quite a number of wars, but he too seems to be sleeping now. Lysandra, on the other hand, keeps appearing, usually helping women in dire need, but not, as I said, without extracting a heavy price. She helped my dad once, but the price that she demanded was for him to become a woman."

"Benjamina? She was a he?" Nadja asked in disbelief.

"Yes, not many know that. That's why I asked you what price you had to pay. It seems nothing was asked of you, except to continue your linguistic studies. I really don't know what is going on, but I will try to find out for you," Ken finished up.

Just then, Maricela came running down the hallway and into their communications room where everyone was at, talking with Diego and Nadja. "Oh! You too! Oh my!" Maricela exclaimed. "The four wives of Josh — they have their arms and legs back. Lysandra. Oh my, Ken. What is going on now?"

Ken laughed nervously. "Something very *big*, if five have been touched by Lysandra and have not asked to make a personal sacrifice! What the heck is going on? I wish mom were here!"

Part II The Imperial Senate and War Efforts

Chapter 27 Arrival

Proxima Prime! Home of the Imperium Senate. Meeting ground for three hundred six cultures. Four hundred ten spoken and written languages. Imperium Cultural Center. Imperium Arts and Museum. The vast Imperium Library. The Central Hub of Imperium Administration. Melting pot of men's and women's fashions. Grossly overpopulated. Meeting place for two thousand six hundred ten senators plus one new arrival from Ashford-5, Senator Isabella Valen.

As their deep space transport drifted down for a landing at the Imperial Spaceport, the surface of Proxima Prime shone like a brilliant blue-white orb, reflecting the sunlight of the distant sun, Proxima-B. Centuries ago, the last square foot of the planet's surface had been covered over with metal, concrete, and granite stone, forming the Imperium Museum's new and larger exhibit hall. Further expansion had been forced to go vertically. Older buildings were taken down and new, far taller ones erected to accommodate the ever-increasing population that continued to swell this, the center of the vast Imperium. If there were any of the planet's original inhabitants left, few could honestly say.

None was also the status of indigenous plant and animal life on Proxima Prime. Those were long gone, though one could still see what they looked like in the Imperium Museum with its stuffed animals and pressed flowers. Beneath the "floor" of metal and concrete covered ground lay a vast layer of climate control, air purification and water filtration systems. Garbage and other waste products were also recycled in great underground machines as well.

Besides the many senators and their spouses and aides, here were found the millions of high bureaucrats, who ran the Imperium, a substantial police force, thousands of ambassadors with their staffs, and the very wealthy from all the planets of the Imperium. This ignores the countless millions, who did the actual work servicing all of these. Proxima Prime boasted the largest spaceport of any world, covering five hundred square miles. Every minute of every day, dozens of ships of all sizes and types were landing or taking off. The fuel repository alone was gigantic, and some speculated that, if it were to explode, it would disintegrate the entire planet. Perhaps that was an exaggeration, though.

Getting around Proxima Prime required the use of a highly sophisticated shuttle craft. It was not uncommon for a person to have to travel some ten thousand miles to get from their home to a meeting. These small, two or four person vehicles were highly automated. One punched in your destination and the massive navigation computer would then take over, flying the shuttle safely to its destination. Long ago, human piloting of these crafts had been replaced. There were just too darn many of these shuttles flying at any one given location. With this computer controlled system, accidental crashes and other mishaps had been eliminated, for the most part. One poet likened the daily scene around Proxima Prime to that of a swarm of bees around blossoming flowers. Unfortunately, most who lived here did not appreciate his poem. They'd never seen real flowers, let alone bees.

True, the very wealthy could afford a single story luxury estate in the far north. Inside their domed structures, dirt had been imported from other worlds, covering a space of the concrete or metal floor. Thus, these few had their own artificial grass lawns, flowers, or even gardens. There were only a thousand such dwellings with a waiting list a mile long for others who wanted to purchase one of these estates.

Most people lived in one of the hundred-floor condominiums. Each "home" had its own balcony on which their shuttle craft was parked. The lower floors, usually the bottom two, contained supporting stores and shops. Such daily needs as groceries could be purchased here. These square, needle looking, metal and glass structures were standardized, all identical. However, at the south pole in Low Town, one could see many older condos still in use by the lowest classes of servants. Although scheduled to be replaced with newer condominiums, a century had passed and nothing yet had been actually done. With the coming war with the Federation of Planets, few believed that anything would be done this century.

The three women already had been given their indispensable ULAT devices that they wore on a thin belt around their waists. The ULAT or Universal Language Translators were an absolute necessity here on Proxima Prime, where four hundred and ten languages were spoken. Now add three more from Ashford-5. If anyone wanted to communicate to another who did not speak your language, the ULATs were indispensable. As you spoke, it converted your tongue into Imperium Standard. When others spoke, a switch on your device allowed you to have your ULAT convert their spoken words into either Imperium Standard or your own tongue. The drawback of using your own tongue was the sometimes poor quality of the translations. Back on Tierra, Nadja had already updated the main ULAT database for spoken Westerlings, knowing that the three might really need the language assist. Of course, Gabriella and Celia spoke Easterlings primarily, but they also had been working on their Westerlings and Midlands speech during the months before the long voyage. Isabella was a good coach.

Their ship touched down gently amid the largest spaceport they had ever seen. A crewman spoke to them, "We have landed. You are to report to the customs station. Have your ID cards ready. They will be expecting you, and they have your home here already assigned to you. Your baggage will be delivered there automatically. This way," he said via his ULAT. The three rose and followed him.

Wearing their heels and latest Tierra fashions, the three women walked across the metal decking, following a path marked in yellow and black stripes — indicating senators and ambassadors. The air smelled a bit like oil and metal, distinctly unpleasant. As they entered the building, a short man with a big wart on his face met them. "Any contraband to declare? Any blasters?" All three shook their heads. "Good, pass through the detectors please, one at a time. At the box, hold out your ID cards please." He was bored; Isabella could not imagine a more boring job than his. She led the way.

Blasters were against the law to bring to Proxima Prime on your person or in your baggage. That does not mean there was none on the world. Rather one needed to "acquire" them by other means. Their security clearances and identities were confirmed. At the end of the line, the short man handed Isabella a paper, which listed her new home number, comm number, the address of the condominium, and the keys to her new shuttle craft, along with a booklet on the safe operation of said vehicle. He motioned them to move along, which the three did. After walking past a half mile of confusing side rooms, they finally entered a huge open arena, where arriving passengers were being greeted, and others were standing in lines to board their flights. Thousands were here.

Amid this chaotic scene, all three women began to worry. Where was this vehicle? They were lost in a sea of humanity. Just then, they saw a man waving a large sign that read Ashford-5. Isabella smiled and headed for the man. A woman was at his side. As they neared, he looked from woman to woman and his ULAT box questioned, "Senator?"

"Hello. That would be me. Senator Isabella Valen from Ashford-5." Her ULAT box translated her words into Imperium Standard or IS as it was called here.

Both smiled and held out their hands. "I am Carl Kalgon of the closed world of Agon-3. My wife, Jane." Nadja would have been most intrigued with their language, however. It was another one of the rare click languages. Phonetically, his name sounded more like ^kaarel ^kaul^ghon. Hers sounded like ^jhAine. Their world sounded like ^ah^ghoon. Quite intriguing and all three immediately thought of Nadja.

Isabella introduced the others. "My wives. Gabriella Amy Valen, my aide. Celia Jan Valen, our ambassador. I am afraid we are quite lost here. Supposedly, there is a shuttle craft for us."

"Yes, unless the bureaucrats fouled up, all should be arranged for you. We know what you must be going through right now. We were in your shoes not so long ago. We took it upon ourselves to be your welcoming committee. The condominium that we senators and ambassadors have is about ten miles from the Senate building. Have you ever driven one of these strange machines before?" Carl asked.

"No, thank you for being here. I am afraid we have

never even see such technologies and are a bit awed by the total strangeness of everything," Isabella lied convincingly. All three were more than familiar with everything they'd seen, just not quite on this scale though.

"The shuttle can hold four. If you wish, I can drive and show you how it is done. Pretty simple once you do it a few times. As long as you have your address, it's nearly automatic. This way." He was wearing a soft, light brown camel hair jacket with matching pants and similar colored buck leather shoes. She on the other hand looked quite unusual to these three. While she had the same red hair as her husband, hers must be very long. Some kind of tall wire frame sat upon her head and her tresses were woven into the mesh, making her seem two feet taller than he. She wore a light brown matching silk gown, with sleeves to her elbows. Obviously, she wore a pipe corset. Either that or Agon-3 women had very tiny waists. Rather what caught the women's attention was the giant hoop skirt below her top. Like a bell, it opened up to nearly twelve feet across at her feet. Her shoes were the latest style of oxfords, also light brown. However, they had platforms nearly four inches tall. Her metal spiked heel tapered down to the usual tiny point, indicative of all Imperium-made stilettos, but the heel looked enormous, some ten inches tall. She had to walk very carefully, the three women noted and inwardly groaned. She also sported very long nails, painted to match her dress.

Jane saw them watching her measured steps. "Yes, these shoes take a good deal of getting used to. Have to be very careful. Already, I've broken my ankle and leg twice. Good thing the medical machines can heal you up in minutes though. This is the current fashion for women, I'm afraid. At first, I didn't want even to try to wear such things, but I was terribly embarrassed at the various events we attend. Plus, it reflected badly on Carl here. Don't worry; you can get outfitted at a store on the first floor of our condo. There are hair and nail salons there too. Groceries and cleaning services are on the second floor. You are in the same condo as we and the other closed and partially closed worlds' representatives."

She chatted on, "Of course, your new home is on the

fourth floor. We are on the fifth floor, just above you. The most important of the three hundred-some senators in our condo live on the top floors. Naturally. The view is supposed to be quite dramatic from there, we're told. What I simply can't get over is that there are no grasslands, no water, just metal and concrete — it's everywhere, we're told. Perhaps this isn't a real planet after all. I do wonder that sometimes. Carl says it is, but well, you can't even see a trace of it anywhere."

Carl interrupted her. "Ah, here is your shuttle. Let me help Jane into ours, and I'll sit in the driver's seat of yours and show you what to do." He assisted Jane into theirs, a tall order considering her dress and platforms. By the time that Jane was inside, the three women had gotten into theirs. Carl joined them. "Okay, first, push the Enter button there. Type in your address. I'll watch over your shoulder." Isabella did as asked.

"There, that was the hardest part. Now push the Destination button. See, it already has the Senate in it and now also your condo's address. Later, I can help you enter some of the other sights you might wish to visit. All you do is scroll to the one you want and touch it. Yes, like that. Now you press the Confirm message. That's it." A metallic voice repeated the address, saying that takeoff would be in thirty seconds. An Abort message appeared on the screen, allowing them a half-minute to cancel the proposed flight. Shortly, the shuttle lifted gently off and joined the thousands of other shuttles, zipping through the skies filled with hundred story buildings.

"Now we relax. It takes a good half hour to get to our condo from the port at five hundred miles per hour," Carl explained. "See, we are automatically rising higher now and picking up speed. If you are traveling much further, then the shuttle will gain even more altitude and speed. I am always fascinated by such travel. On Agon-3, we ride horses and have nothing like this. Which reminds me, after you three get settled, Jane wants to have you over to our place for supper. Senator Isabella, you and I should have a very long talk before you go to the next Senate meeting on Monday. There are some things you ought to know about close worlds and what you can expect here. Very important."

"Of course, we'd be honored to dine with you. I suppose

that we might impose upon Jane to help us get properly attired as well. I don't suppose that I ought to dress in a fine suit such as yours," Isabella replied.

Carl chuckled, "No, now *that* would raise a stir in the Senate! Might be good for them to get their feathers ruffled though."

"Will being a female impact my acceptance as our Senator, Carl?" Isabella asked, growing slightly concerned that it might.

"Not officially. Unofficially, very likely. We'll have to see. We can talk more later. For now, enjoy the view. It is, well, most different from my home, Agon-3."

Isabella smiled, "Vastly different from our world too."

A half hour later, the shuttle descended, and came to a gentle landing on a fourth floor balcony. "Here we are. Your ID cards should open your outside door as well as the main one. Each of you should check that your cards are working on both doors. Jane has landed just above us." They heard the faint drone of its electromagnetic engine as it shut down.

Their fourth floor suite was large by Tierra standards. There were three master bedrooms, a huge living room filled with the latest in electronics. There was a study, dining room, kitchen, and pantry as well. However, the place was pretty sterile and bare looking. "This place is typical," Isabella grumbled. "We should keep our eyes open for things to make this place more habitable. Come on; best test our cards." Following Carl's advice, each tested her own ID card on both doors. As they finished testing their front door, Jane stepped carefully off the elevator.

Jane said, "Your baggage ought to be here fairly soon. Then, you can get settled in. If you like, after that, I can take you downstairs and show you the various shops." They thanked her, and the two left to go up to their home. An hour later, their baggage arrived. Three men made quick work of carrying their many crates and bags into their living room.

That done, Jane reappeared, and led them down to the first floor, where the giant boutique Imperium Fashions beckoned them. Without asking, Isabella slipped her hand into Jane's to help steady her walk. "Thanks," Jane whispered. As they walked slowly into the huge boutique, their visio and olfactory senses were swamped by the vast displays of colored gowns and fragrances. A saleswoman dressed much as Jane, came just as slowly up to the four, recognizing Jane at once, displaying a wide smile and bright eyes.

"Ah, Jane, so good to see you once again. These must be our new arrivals. Jane told me to expect a new group from a closed world. Please, step this way. All these fashions and styles must appear pretty daunting to you three. I am called Elga."

After the four took seats at a large desk with a projection screen just behind Elga, Isabella introduced herself and her two wives. Elga smiled kindly and said, "I do need to ask you a few rather personal questions right here at the start so I can get everything just right for the three of you. Isabella, is your physical body female or male?"

"What?" Isabella flushed. No one had ever asked her that question, not in a hundred years.

Hastily, Elga explained, "You see, here on Proxima Prime, some men dress as we women do, and some women dress as men. It can be very confusing at times, especially among the senators. It is just a little unusual to have a female as the head of the household, or perhaps you don't call them that."

"I am as female as my two wives are. So if we see someone in a suit, he's not necessarily a he? And a woman in a ball gown isn't always a woman?" Isabella asked, a little confused. This would make her work a bit more difficult.

"Precisely so. If there is a need," she lowered her voice and spoke rather coyly, "it is not impolite to make a discrete inquiry." Raising her voice, she said, "Now then, there are fashion customs that are nearly always observed, particularly so among the senators, ambassadors, and their wives and husbands. Let's begin with you, Senator Isabella. When you are out in public and especially so when at the Senate, you should always be wearing a ball gown similar to Jane's here, that is, unless you wish to cut your hair and appear masculine."

Isabella laughed. "No way."

Elga smiled coyly and continued. "I suppose that Jane has already shown you her stylish platforms. All the gowns are designed to be worn with these tall platforms. If you wore one with the heels you are wearing, the gown would rub along the floor, rather heavily. One alternative, that many women choose, is to wear the toe shoes instead. Either style will raise your height sufficiently for the gowns." Isabella fought hard from asking why they just didn't raise the hems higher instead!

"Your wives have just perfect earrings. You should have something akin to theirs, perhaps longer or fuller as befitting their husband. Also, all senators wear a thin golden crown, which I can provide for you as well. As far as your hairstyles go, in this, you have freedom of choice. Many wives are opting for the hive look, just as Jane is wearing."

"Will we be acceptable with ours as we have ours now, draped down our backs?" Isabella asked. No way was she going to get a hive look!

"Yes, and you also can have your hair colored or curled as you might desire. You will see all colors of the rainbow here. Styles come and go, you see," Elga went on. "Now the only real difficulty is that all female-dressed senators must have their nails at least twelve inches long, while most all wives keep theirs half of that, as Jane's are. Naturally, they should be painted to match your gown." Isabella wanted to groan, but thought better of it. For now, she thought, we ought to go with her advice and see how we blend in here.

Elga chatted on, "Of course, everyone needs to have a personal assistant to help them dress and undress. There is a corps of such women, and we call them domestiques. They also cook and clean, handling most household duties for you. I assume that you will each wish to have one assigned for you. A domestique is usually a teen, who is doing this extra work to help pay for her Academy training, you see."

"I suppose with such claws and these impossible gowns, we don't have much choice," Isabella grumbled, unable to withhold her disgust any longer. Gabriella and Celia fought to keep from giggling. Both had wondered how Isabella had avoided letting her feelings out before now.

Whether or not Elga was bothered by Isabella's obvious

annoyance, she continued chatting away. "I've taken the liberty of selecting three such teens for you. If they are not to your liking, then let me know. I can find many other teens, who desperately need such work. Academy is not cheap, you know. But then, perhaps you don't know, do you? I mean, you are from a primitive world, closed as I'm told. Ah, here they are now. This is Amala, Bruna, and Elfi. This is Senator Isabella and her two wives, Gabriella and Celia."

The three looked to be perhaps eighteen. All wore the typical unisex, recyclable cat suit uniforms that Isabella had seen everywhere on Plateau Grado. They bowed respectively. Amala said, "I do hope that you will find us acceptable. We are experienced in dressing fine ladies."

Bruna added, "And I am a good cook. We will keep your home spotless."

"Okay, we do need you," Isabella replied. "So how does this work? We only have three bedrooms."

"Oh, we don't sleep in your home," Amala spoke up hastily. "We are students. We will be there first thing in the morning to help get you dressed. Once we've fixed your breakfast, we will be off. We'll come back at lunchtime and do the cleaning and what's needed. Bruna has time to drop by late afternoons to fix your suppers. We'll all be by in the evening to get you undressed. We just need to set up a schedule that meets your needs, Senator Isabella."

"We can help you get into your new gowns now, if you like, once you pick them out," Elfi added. Her tone indicted to Isabella that she was very anxious to please them. She picked up Elfi's surface thoughts. The teen was desperate for the extra income.

"Thanks. Let's get on with it, shall we, Elga?" Isabella said, "You three are hired."

An hour later, the three had purchased six complete outfits each and many more undergarments. Already they had decided to "lounge around their home" in their dresses they'd brought from Tierra. The biggest decision had been their heels. All three found that walking in the tall platforms was exceedingly treacherous. One misstep and they could easily break an ankle or leg, just as Jane had done. The three chose to wear toe shoes instead. At least with these, they could sense the ground and had little chance of an accidental fracture. Besides, Gabriella and Celia already had years of experience wearing them when they were escorts. Isabella went along with their telepathically sent advice.

Isabella dismissed the three teens, asking them to return around seven the next morning. After that, Jane took them over to the nails boutique, where they had their nails pampered, the long extensions applied, and painted to match their current new gowns. Celia wore a scarlet satin gown; Gabriella wore a canary yellow gown, while Isabella wore a sky blue gown. An hour later, the four women headed up to Jane's home, where her domestique had dinner waiting on them. Besides, Isabella remembered that Carl had really wanted to talk with her.

The dinner was cordial and quite pleasant. Of course, the three watched how Jane managed with her long nails. Isabella had the most trouble with her extra-long ones, but continued to smile in spite of her awkwardness. Jane kept saying, "Give it time. You'll soon get the hang of it. It took me a couple of weeks to adjust to all these foreign things." Isabella again picked up her surface thoughts; Jane was trying hard to keep smiling. Isabella now knew that Jane was herself still trying to adjust as well.

After dinner, Carl took Isabella into his study. Gabriella and Celia tagged along. Jane wanted to get changed into her evening clothes and was grateful that the two joined her husband and Isabella. "Ah, please, have a seat. I know Jane is always so uncomfortable standing. She is doing her very best to blend in with the other Senators' wives. Now then, I do need to educate you some before you go to your first Senate meeting. Gar did it for me, and I promised him that I would pass it along to the next new Senator."

"Where to best begin? I don't know what you three know, so I will do my best to explain everything. If you already know some of these things, why just interrupt me. The Imperium is vastly overpopulated, and they are always looking for new habitable planets. They are always expanding their empire, as far as I know anyway. New planets that they find fall into several categories. Some are uninhabitable, such as giant gas planets, though some of these are mined, but for what I do not know. Others are uninhabited planets that could support life. These, the Imperium settle at once, moving large populations there. Of course, by uninhabited, I mean by the human species. If the new planet is inhabited by a humanoid race, then they have to take stock of its current level of civilization."

He went on, "If the inhabitants are making and using stone tools — made from flint and easily worked stone, they are usually living by hunting, fishing, and gathering what bounty the land provides them. They classify such civilizations as Old Stone Age. If the inhabitants are not even up to this point in their evolution, then the Imperium merely takes over and settles there, ignoring the primitives, who they claim are basically animals. On the other hand, if the civilization uses stone tools and has developed a crude level of agriculture, has perhaps begun domestication of local animals, and has developed pottery, then they classify that civilization as being in the New Stone Age. Any world in the Old Stone age or the New Stone Age is automatically classified as a Closed World until they develop further."

"Here's where our own world of Agon-3 fits into their scheme. The next step, according to the Imperium, is the development of bronze, a tin and copper mixture. We make and use all manner of tools made from bronze, you see. Cups, bowls, silverware, pots, knives, swords, spear tips — all manner of things. Metal workers, we are. They call our stage the Bronze Age. We were given the opportunity to be either an Open or Closed World. Our leaders are widely scattered — tribal leaders as we now see from here. Honestly, Isabella, Jane and I have learned an awful lot so far. We hope our participation in their Senate will help our world move rapidly into the modern world of planets."

"Anyway, the next step is the discovery and use of iron. Forging steel into plow hoes, swords, you name it, brings a civilization far closer to the modern worlds. They call such civilizations as being in the Iron Age. Again, Iron Age worlds are given the choice to be closed or open as well, as I understand it. Next, there are worlds that have moved into the so called Manufacturing Age. These worlds are usually opened and welcome the incredibly technological advances that the Imperium can offer them. Finally, there are the rarely found worlds, whose civilization has progressed into the Space Age. Here, the Imperium usually invades and conquers them, adding them to their collection of planets, if they don't accept the Imperium's initial offers."

Isabella took his pause to reply, "Ashford-5 is partially in between the Bronze Age and Iron Age. Our world has almost no iron or any heavier elements on it. We've been importing iron ore as partial lease payments from the Imperium for three centuries now."

"Ah, I see. You are ahead of us then. I take it that your world is not filled with thousands of more or less isolated tribes?" Carl asked.

"Nope. We have a number of large kingdoms and stone castles and such," Isabella replied honestly. She then explained what a castle was. Carl was impressed and asked if she would not mind sharing castle designs and their construction with him. Isabella agreed, seeing no reason not to help them along a little. Certainly, the Imperium wasn't going to do that or they would already have done so.

Carl continued, "You see, when we arrived here, we saw so many unexplainable things — magic. That was our first notions. How else could we explain flying in the skies like a bird? Taking into these strange devices and hearing others far away, as if they were standing beside you? Magic. Now Jane and I know better. While just how they work is still a complete mystery to us, we know such things are just mechanical inventions. Our people have so much more to learn! The best advice that I can give you three is that nothing is really magical. There is always some kind of reason, some kind of mechanical way a thing works. Our own ignorance prevents us from understanding how and why things work as they do. It isn't magic, and we should not and must not worship these Imperium people and all the others. They are not gods or divine beings. They just have more knowledge of the way things work than we do. I know you will soon be seeing so many, many things that you have never seen before and that appear to be magic. Just remember always, it isn't magic. Rather, you just don't know how they work."

Isabella was rather surprised at Carl's wisdom and willingness to share it with her. Here was a man and woman taken from a tribal home in the Bronze Age and brought into the vast, sophisticated, and highly advanced civilization. That he had such an opinion, she thought, was rather profound. "Thank you, Carl. This is very vital information. Indeed, so much seems magical compared to our world."

His face brightened up, "Yes, yes, this is what I mean. So much is so very new and unexplainable, and yet, it must just be how ignorant that we are."

"No not ignorant, Carl. Uneducated. You just don't have the knowledge that they do. You are extremely wise, impressively so. We will not be fooled," Isabella countered.

"Yes, yes, that is precisely what others like us, our fellow senators, are saying. I must also warn you, the Imperium will be trying to get all manner of concessions from you — probably soon. They will try to seduce you with their magical equipment. Some of us are holding out. We want the education instead. Teach us the ways of the world. Then, our people can progress and make these magical things for ourselves. It is slavery, if we merely accept all the magical devices that they offer us. We will not know how to make them and must depend on them for everything. Slavery. No, tomorrow, I will introduce you to several of us senators who are holding out for education."

Carl was very excited to have Isabella on his side. "We don't have any vote in the Senate, but they cannot do anything to your world without your signed agreement to whatever that may be. Don't sign anything just yet, unless it is education. If enough of us can hold out for that, maybe they will back down and give it to us all. I do hope so. There are so many magical things that we could use, like the medical machine that Jane has had to use on her legs and ankles. But I've kept you up too late. I will come by tomorrow, say around ten. I will arrange a meeting with the others who think as we do." Isabella thanked him, and Jane finally entered the study.

Now she wore her comfortable soft leather dress that she'd brought from her home world. "I do hope that I am not shocking you. This is our normal dress. It is so much more comfortable to wear," Jane said rather apologetically. "I needed to get out of that gown while my domestique was still here. She can't stay this late. She is in the Academy learning many new things. I tell her learning is the most important thing she can do."

"We agree completely, Jane. We are going to get changed into our own clothes too," Isabella replied. "See you at ten, Carl. Thank you very much." He smiled and put his arm around Jane, watching the three take their slow, careful steps out of their home to the elevator.

The next morning the trio appreciated the efficient efforts of Amala, Bruna, and Elfi. They were quickly dressed, had their new makeup applied, and had their breakfast awaiting them — all before eight. Each of their new domestique staff had an eight o'clock class and had to be gone before then. Isabella promised them this would be more than fine with her and sensed relief in the trio's minds. "Just leave the dishes in the kitchen. I'll get them around noon," Amala explained, as she and her two teen companions left the trio to their breakfast.

"How am I supposed to eat or do anything for that matter with these claws?" Isabella complained.

"Ours aren't much easier," Celia countered. "I aim to see how the computer and communications systems have changed. After the meeting with Carl," she added quickly, having forgotten about it already. Celia Jan's memories of her former vast experience and superior skills in these two arenas had returned fully. She could not hide her enthusiasm for exploring the changes that had evolved during the last century. Gabriella Amy merely smiled, all her memories had also returned, rather vividly. Isabella smiled also, recalling her nearly a century's worth of recent experiences, not all pleasant ones.

At ten, the trio stood outside Carl's front door. Isabella knocked and Carl opened the door. His tanned face revealed his gracious welcome. "Come in, come in. The others are already here and are so anxious to meet you." Of course, the many ULAT boxes were doing the translation, quite necessary with Carl and Jane, whose native language involved many clicking sounds. He led them into his living room, where four other couples had just risen to greet the new arrivals, along with Jane.

"Everyone, this is the new senator from Ashford-5 and her two wives, Isabella Valen and Gabriella Amy and Celia Jan. First, this is our senior Senator Jenkins Walkins and his wife, Aberlarde of Zelos-3, an Early Modern World. He's been here for eight years now. Both had canary yellow hair. His was short, hers was long and wavy falling to her waist. They wore the typical clothing. His suit looked much like Carl's, while her billowing gown was a royal purple. Her huge earrings sported blood rubies. Like all the other women, her nails were as long as Gabriella's and Celia's, painted purple as well.

"So very pleased to meet you, Senator Isabella," he said in a strange language, nicely translated by the many ULAT boxes in the room.

"This is Rajo ^onah ^caah and Raja ^eeha of Alzone-3. I do hope that I've pronounced your names properly," Carl said rather apologetically. Isabella sensed his discomfort and picked up just how hard Carl found their language. "Alzone-3 is Bronze Age, like our own world."

"Rajo Onah will be acceptable," the tall man replied, eliminating the click sound. He looked very embarrassed, though at first, Isabella could not sense why. He wore a suit similar to Carl's. He also sported huge earrings, quite unlike the other men here.

"I understand, Senator Rajo Onah. We are not accustomed to these customs either," Isabella replied courteously, flowing a relaxing, counter-emotion over the pair. Their language made heavy use of eight types of clicks. Isabella now realized why as she looked at his wife.

Raja Eeha looked rather uncomfortable. Like all women on Alzone-3, she also had dual lip plates that were about a foot across with matching enormously long earrings. All three suddenly realized where Nadja had gotten her enormous lip plates from! Isabella said, "Incredible, Raja Eeha. You look fabulous. Your lip plates are most impressive. On our world, the governor's wife, Nadja, has introduced lip plates much like yours. Now all of our noblewomen are wearing them too, much like yours, only they've had various designs etched into their plates. No two look exactly the same."

"Nadja? Nadja Burkhardt?" Raja Eeha exclaimed growing excited. "We know her. She was on our world not long ago, and she was responsible for our getting into this Senate and Imperium! If it wasn't for her, no one would be able to understand us or we them. She still wears these? All your women are now wearing them too? We are so proud of her. Here, I feel very awkward. No, not right word. Anyway, we are so very pleased to hear this, senator!"

"Yes, Nadja is doing a superb job with our languages too," Isabella replied.

"Amazing. Nadja was on their worlds too," Raja Eeha exclaimed, motioning to the other two couples. "We all owe her everything."

Carl took control once more. "This is Senator Helm Baath and his wife Rutha. They are from Styx-4, an Early Modern World." He shook Isabella's hand. He wore a similar suit but looked terribly uncomfortable in it. Rutha looked even stranger. She had enormous breasts the size of basketballs!

Senator Helm said, "Pleased to meet you, Senator Isabella. Forgive us for looking — well so strange. You see, on our world, we men wear skirts akin to yours, while our women wear gowns that fit their beautiful silhouettes. I feel rather naked still, and Rutha here is most embarrassed to be seen wearing a man's skirt. But we must adapt to foreign customs, as Senator Jenkins keeps telling us."

Rutha spoke up with a smile, "So pleased to meet you and your wives. I feel more comfortable now. Yes, it is humiliating to be seen wearing Helm's clothing, but I am so glad to see other women who have larger breasts too. I have been feeling like some freak for months. Mine are so big compared to everyone else's." Hers were many times larger than the trio from Ashford-5, but then the trio's were triple the size of most of the other women here.

"Yes, you should be proud of them, as we are ours,"

Isabella replied diplomatically. She could not imagine how the poor woman could manage to support such heavy weights. "Yes, we all have to adapt and learn new ways."

Carl introduced the final couple. "This is Rax Evon Wysh and his wife Evan. They are from Gallim-3, an Iron Age world." He had gold disks covering his eyes and had a golden spike through his nose. While she too had gold disks covering her eyes with a tiny hole that enabled her to see, her whole face was hidden behind a golden mask that was somehow screwed into her skull at the sides of her face. Still, her domestique had painted her lips a bright red, the only makeup she could wear. Her earrings looked an awful lot like those that Nadja always wore. Isabella made that connection at once.

The introductions finished, Carl bade them all to sit. Jenkins opened the discussion. "Carl has told us he gave you the introduction to the way that the Imperium has classified our worlds and why we are considered closed worlds, for the most part. We have no vote, as you know. However, as a unified block, we do seem to have some say, some weight."

"Let me give you a crash course on what we've learned has happened to other open worlds within the Imperium," Jenkins continued. "On those worlds, they often relocate vast populations from other worlds within the Imperium. Overcrowding is the usual reason given for this. The Imperium also extracts what they consider vital from these worlds, usually physical resources, rare earths, titanium, and such things. They essentially denude these other worlds of these valuable commodities. In return, the Imperium gives them technology."

"Tell them the rest of it," Carl interjected.

"Just getting to it, Carl," Jenkins replied. "What they frequently do not give them is the knowledge on how to create such things. On Dox-4, for example, another Early Modern World, they provided numerous nuclear power plants to provide electricity for the many cities there. They did not provide them with the knowledge of how they work or how they are built or maintained. Thus, Dox-4 is totally dependent upon Imperium technicians for the upkeep and construction of these power plants. I can give you dozens of similar stories from many other worlds."

"They provide massive machines that can level a mountain in days, but they do not provide the knowledge to make the fuel these machines need, nor how they are to be maintained. Thus, they are still totally dependent upon the Imperium technicians for such things. We reason thusly. What good is such marvelous, magical technology, if we do not know how they work, how they are built, how they are to be maintained, and so on? No, we here all agree on one thing. The Imperium must give our worlds the education and training necessary to understand these things that they wish to trade with our worlds. Otherwise, our worlds remain ignorant and dependent upon the Imperium."

Isabella spoke up, "I am astounded at the vast wisdom you are all displaying. Indeed, this is precisely why I was sent here as Ashford-5's senator. We do not want their technology. We want their knowledge. We need their medical machines, but we must also understand those machines and how they work. We do not want ever to be dependent upon the Imperium. This could very easily happen, as you have pointed out. So I am truly amazed with all of you. You can count on the full support of Ashford-5. We must lobby for schools and education, not their fancy technology."

"I am so happy you also see the wisdom in this!" Jenkins replied animatedly. "We had assumed we'd need to persuade you. Indeed, their technology and devices are so magical to us. I liken it to a child who enters his first candy store on Zelos-3. It is so tempting for us each to want to bring such incredible things back to our worlds! As you say, these medical machines would be of incalculable value on our worlds. We burn coal to produce electricity, but the filth our plants produce makes living near them a nightmare. Clean power plants would be invaluable for us. To say nothing of these amazing flying machines!"

"Yah, we'd love to have them on Agon-3!" Carl interjected. "To be able to move across our world in minutes — just unimaginable, truly magical! So tempting, but the price is too steep. If millions of foreigners land and take over, what will happen to our people? Unthinkable, truly unthinkable."

"We'd lose our identities," Rajo Onah added.

"We might be forced to give up our pride and joy, our lip plates," Raja Eeha added in her heavily click language, translated nicely by the ULATs thanks to Nadja's work on her world. "Our culture would be dissolved into theirs. Our people would vanish in a sea of these smelly, recyclable, paper-thin things they all wear here in the Imperium." She was referring to the unisex cat suits worn by nearly everyone in the Imperium, except the wealthy.

After allowing the others an opportunity to express similar feelings and attitudes, Jenkins continued. "There is one other new development, and we don't yet know what it all means. But the Imperium is going to war with another space civilization somewhere. They seem to be called the Federation of Planets, but we have no idea where they are or the true significance of all this. We can say it is taking on more and more prominence in the Senate meetings. Do you know anything about it?"

Isabella made a snap decision. "Yes, we know a little. The Imperium is mining fuel for their spaceships on one of our moons. Some time ago, the Federation of Planets tried to sabotage their refineries there and did cause some damage, we think. That's about all we know. Governor Konrad told us we have nothing to worry about. The Imperium has increased their protections for their refinery, whatever that means."

"Interesting. Now we understand why after three centuries, Ashford-5 finally has been allowed to have a senator here!" Jenkins declared. "We wondered why it took you so long to have a representative here. Your world must be very valuable to the Imperium."

"Don't know about that, but we'll stick to demanding education," Isabella replied, putting the fears at ease that she began sensing from the other senators. Although Jenkins didn't say it, Isabella picked up his thought. *Maybe Asford-5 will be able to push through education for all the rest of our worlds, since fuel is so valuable to the Imperium.* They chatted for a while longer and then ended close to lunchtime.

Chapter 28 Senate Meetings

On Monday, Isabella took their shuttle to her first Senate meeting. Meanwhile, Jane took Gabriella and Celia out for a tour of the city, at least the area around their zone. Essentially, all of Proxima Prime was one giant, planet-wide city, divided into rectangular zones. Of course, the Military Zone, the Police Zone, and the Planet Maintenance Zone were off limits to nearly everyone who did not have proper clearance.

As they walked into the enormous Imperium Senate Building, Carl was kind enough to provide a supporting hand for Isabella. The two joined the others of their group in a booth on the top layer of the giant amphitheater. Below them, thousands of senators filed in, taking their places on some dozen tiers. Laid out like a giant amphitheater, the stage looked tiny from where Isabella sat. The most important senators, those from Proxima Prime, sat on the first layer opposite the central platform. Still, the many ULAT boxes carried all the conversations being spoken anywhere within the theater, creating a uniform background of sounds.

From where she was sitting, Isabella could see all the senators. She spotted around two dozen women senators. Most wore gowns like the one she as wearing, but three had their hair rather short and wore suits like the men. She noticed that hair colors varied widely, far more so than the hues of their suits. Black, brown, blonde, and red predominated in a vast spectrum of shades. At last, a man rose and took the stage. Carl whispered, "That's the current Senate President Carlos Amandos."

Her ULAT box translated nicely for her. "Welcome senators. First, let us welcome a new senator to our midst. Senator Isabella Valen from Ashford-5. Senator, will you rise please." Isabella had little choice but to do so. Many hushed whispers echoed through the chamber, and all heads turned around to see her. She picked up many covert intentions. Somehow, her presence was deemed important by a number of these leaders, though she could not tell more. There were just too many minds present to get an accurate telepathic reading beyond the strong feeling that many here considered her appearance important somehow.

"Now then, I have been asked to relay this to you," Carlos continued, now reading from a paper in his hand. "As of this time, the Imperium has unilaterally declared war on the group known as the Federation of Planets. As the Imperium shifts to a war status, some emergency accommodations must be made for our troops. Specifically, Alliford-3, Josquin-4, and Abilard-5 will soon be seeing a significant military buildup. The Supreme Council hereby requests the Senate relocate two million from each of these three worlds as soon as possible." He lowered his hand.

"Okay, so there you have it. Our immediate task is to produce the groundwork for the migration of the required six million to be relocated to other planets. Naturally, these Imperium citizens are highly civilized and cultured. In fulfilling our Imperium obligations, we must take extreme and judicious care to see that they are relocated either in such a manner so as not to lower their standards of living or as befitting their extremely high social standings. Our prime consideration must be to choose equally advanced planets within the Imperium, as those three on which they currently dwell. Naturally, their senators will continue to represent them here in the Senate. As such, they will not impact or reduce the existing senators from the selected worlds. That said, the floor is open to initial discussion. I am told we must have our decision to the Supreme Council by the close of business today. I caution you all, if we fail in this vital mission, the Supreme Council will unilaterally make this decision for us. I don't need to tell all of you that it is in our best interests to come to a consensus today." He took his seat.

Another senator rose. "But what about the six population transfers that we already have on our agenda? It has been four months now, and we still have not worked those out. Are we just to ignore the horrific burden facing those six worlds — their severe over-population? I say no. We cannot shirk our sworn duties. I say we ought to consider these six world's requests as well. As long as we are handling population resettlements, let's finish these requests as well."

Another man rose, "With all due respect, senator, we have until the close of today to make our decision in this matter. Surely, those six planets can deal with their situation another day."

Another spoke up, "Since one of these three is my home world, Alliford-3, I can speak with some authority in this matter. The requisite two million that the military has requested be relocated from Alliford-3 are indeed quite wealthy. We are not talking of primitives or even mere technicians here. Need I tell you it is these people on whom we have relied for financial backing in the past? We simply must handle this population movement properly and in a timely manner."

"With all good and due respect for the esteemed senator from Alliford-3, Hurang-3 has already reached its maximum sustainable population. While I sympathize with his cause, we simply cannot be asked to accept any additional population increases," another senator countered.

The discussion began in earnest. Some suggested planets to be considered. Others rejected those on various grounds, often on population density or cultural grounds. One pointed out the long-standing hostilities between Alliford-3 and Graxton-4, thereby eliminating that planet from further consideration. Thus the long morning dragged out for Isabella, who quickly became utterly bored with all this talk that seemed to go nowhere at all. When they broke for lunch, Carl pointed out, "Most major decisions like this one will get sorted out over lunch or dinner, when the senators involved can discuss this privately. They make all manner of hidden deals, you see."

Carl escorted Isabella to the vast dining room facilities beneath the amphitheater. Still struggling to master eating with her long nails, Isabella was continually interrupted by other senators who came by to introduce themselves. Repeatedly, she was asked if the rumors were true that there were many telepaths on Ashford-5. Always, her reply was a guarded one, "Well, there are a few, just like on all worlds, I suppose." Usually, she followed that with, "No, I am sure none are interested in finding employment off-world." Isabella began to see that many knew of the secret of Ashford-5, and why it had remained in isolation for three centuries. Carl and Jenkins, though, took careful notice of all this attention being bestowed on Senator Isabella, as well as the constant inquiries about telepathy. In addition, many tried to schedule private meetings with her in the evenings. Isabella had little choice but to make such appointments.

When they returned for the afternoon session, Carl's observations had been correct. Three planets had stepped forward to accept these six million people. Carl whispered, "By tomorrow, we ought to hear the rumors about what these three planets were offered to take on two million more people. I bet they made some really good bargains."

"I find the whole notion of transplanting millions of people to another world utterly repulsive," Isabella declared. She got no disagreement from her allies, who smiled and nodded their agreement with her. The rest of the week's meetings were taken up with more of the over-population issues but nothing was resolved.

That evening after dinner, Senate President Carlos Amandos paid Isabella a short visit. "Come on in, President Carlos, if I remember correctly," Isabella replied as she opened her door. She had been expecting him since he insisted on dropping by when he met her at lunch. "Please, have a seat. Sorry, I walk a bit slowly."

"But of course, you look absolutely stunning, senator. You do Ashford-5 much credit. If all our senators looked half as attractive as you, why, we would reach far more agreements far sooner, I assure you," he replied rather thickly as far as Isabella was concerned. After sitting rather formally, he continued, "I would like to extend you my personal services. Whenever you need anything, please do not hesitate to call on me. I am at your service."

"Why thank you, President Carlos," Isabella replied, wishing that he would get down to business.

"As Senate President, I have a very high clearance," he began, but Isabella already sensed where he was heading, picking up his surface thoughts. "I know Ashford-5 has an alarmingly high number of telepaths per unit of population, far greater than any other planet in the entire Imperium. I also know the Imperium Science Division has been studying this for several centuries now, but have reached no conclusion as to why this is. Nevertheless, as you probably know, telepaths are in extremely high demand all throughout the Imperium. As your planet's senator, you are obligated to spread the word on Ashford-5 that any telepath can literally make a fortune working off-world. Employment possibilities for your telepaths are, how shall I put this, absolutely outstanding, far above any other occupation. The monetary gains are likely sufficient to allow one to work perhaps five years on another world and then retire on Ashford-5 a wealthy man. Please relay this to your world. I am sure many would jump at a chance to become a millionaire with just a few years of work."

"I will deliver your message, President Carlos. I wouldn't hold your breath though. Compared to all I've seen here on Proxima Prime, our people are basically primitives and would have a hard time fitting into the society here," she replied graciously.

"You would be surprise what people will do to make a million credits in so few years. I've heard rumors there has also been an inexplicable huge increase in the sheer number of telepaths on Ashford-5. If this is so, there is much to be gained with such endeavors. Many will certainly offer you most significant 'finder's fees,' that I can guarantee you." He gave her a not so subtle hint.

"I will keep that in mind as well, sir," she replied.

"Well, I must be going. I have to see five other senators yet tonight. Remember, Isabella, if you need anything — have any questions — want any advice, please do not hesitate to call upon me. Or even if you should desire male company for an evening," he hinted as he rose. "We do have perhaps the best theaters, opera houses, and music halls in the galaxy. I'd love to escort you and perhaps your wives to some of these many events."

"Why thank you, President Carlos. That would be quite nice. I am sure we would like to see such wondrous things," Isabella played her role well.

"I'll be in touch later on. I'll see myself out. I know how difficult it must be for you to adjust to all of your magnificent apparel." He rose, kissed her hand, and left. She picked up his momentary loss of words. He really didn't have any idea of how women had to adjust at all.

During the weeknights, other senators dropped by. Each made somewhat similar offers and requests. Carl kept track of their names for her, pointing out that the top five most influential senators had just paid her a personal visit, vastly different than they had for the other closed world senators.

On Saturday, Isabella finally got a breather. Lounging around in their relatively simple gowns from home, Isabella asked, "Well, Gabriella, Celia, what have you been up to all week?"

Gabriella Amy replied, "Well, I found out the latest medical machines now are programmed for couples such as us. It seems the machine can take one of our eggs and separate out one of the X chromosomes and use it to fertilize another's egg. Women couples are now able to have children without resorting to men. Interesting development."

Celia Jan laughed. "You see where her mind is at, not enough sex for her, Isabella." Both women laughed and Gabriella flushed. Jan went on, "I've been exploring the latest advances in computers and communications devices. Honestly, not much has changed. I've made some orders for us. Should be here next week. Which reminds me, you should send a coded message to Ken in the Underground."

"Right, I should. Have you verified no one is snooping on my computer? I will type up the report and let you encrypt it," Isabella answered.

"Yes, did that the first day. No snoop programs yet. I guarantee you soon many will be trying to do just that, as well as bug our home. I am on top of it. I've put a thin mesh over all the windows, supposedly to keep the harsh sunlight we are not used to seeing from 'burning' our skins. In fact, it is a scramble system. No one can listen in on our conversations nor see us when the windows are closed. I've got monitoring cams everywhere. I'll be alerted whenever any kind of spyware gets inside our home," Celia Jan replied reassuringly. "I'll encode your message with the Blackwater Ultimatum when you have it done. If the message is intercepted, it will take their super computers a century to decode it."

That night, Celia Jan sent off the first official report from Senator Isabella to Ken. In turn, he passed what was appropriate on to Venerada Maricela, who relayed it to the other towers and to the various lords.

On Sunday, the closed worlds' senators met briefly. Naturally, the topic of discussion was telepathy, Ashford-5, and the extreme interest being shown to Senator Isabella. "Okay, I will accept President Carlos' offer to take us out to cultural events. I will feel him out about exchanges for such things as proper schools and education for all of our closed worlds. I promise you it will be all of us getting these or none of us. United we stand," she declared, knowing well this was precisely what the various senators greatly wanted to hear from her. Right now, she felt the wisest course was to maintain a tightly knit group of her peers.

Slowly the days turned into weeks. Then near the end of September, Senator Carlos again asked for a private meeting with Isabella. As he entered, she knew he was extremely worried and overly serious. After taking a seat, he said sternly, "I am here under orders from the Supreme Council in charge of fighting this war with the Federation. What I am about to say to you, I would never say, if I had any choice whatsoever." Isabella didn't like the sound of this, but she listened.

He went on, "The Supreme Council has told me in no uncertain terms to reach an agreement with you and Ashford-5. They need one thousand of your telepaths within a month, two at the very latest. Each person will be highly remunerated for their work. At least I got that much for them. They must have these telepaths. I hate to put this so bluntly, but they will get them one way or the other, Isabella. First, I convinced them to let me see, if you and I can work out a fair exchange. I know full well this totally violates the lease agreement and the closed world policy that the Imperium has with your planet. Surely, you and I can come to some kind of workable arrangement. If not, they will just go ahead and take them anyway, Isabella. War gives them the authority to execute such actions that would ordinarily be totally against all Imperium Laws."

Isabella flinched for a moment. This was the Imperium she knew all too well. Still, that he was here asking for some kind of agreement was an opening. He went on, "We can give your world earthmoving equipment so you can build proper roads. We can give your world some power plants and set up electrical grids. Surely such things would be of immense value to all of your people."

"I see," Isabella replied coyly. "And where would we get the fuel to run these machines, to power the plants? Where would we get the personnel to run them and operate the plants? No, thanks, Senator Carlos. Ashford-5 is not interested in becoming totally dependent upon the Imperium. If we let them get their foot in our door like this, there would never be any way ever to close it again. We both know once our people get used to such things as electricity and such things, they would never want to give them up. This would turn our world into a massive drug addict, willing to do whatever was necessary to keep the fuel coming."

Senator Carlos smiled, "Damn, you are a shrewd one."

She smiled, "There is something we would likely consider though."

He laughed, "Okay, I give up. What could that possibly be?"

"Education. Build us say ten schools and provide teachers to educate our people. We both know that knowledge is the true source of power. Educate our people. Of course, we could also use medical machines as well. However, this is what you ought to be providing to *all* of we closed worlds. So here's my counter-offer. You provide schools and education and a few medical machines for *all* we closed worlds, and I'll do my best to get Ashford-5 to agree to send a thousand telepaths off-world for you," Isabella laid out her counterproposal.

"Damn, you are the wisest, shrewdest senator I've met in my career. Okay, come by my office in the morning, say at nine. I'll hook up a conference call between your Governor Konrad Burkhardt and us. We can work out the details. I will leave it to you to work out how you will let your people know of this deal."

"Agreed. Nine it is."

At nine, Isabella entered Senator Carlos' office. Neat, tidy, everything in its place — she rightly concluded the man was overly concerned with compulsive orderliness. He had his communications system set up for the conference. He had a second chair for her beside his large, plush swivel chair — the cost of which probably would have fed Isabella for a month. She took her seat. A video camera faced them as well as a large monitor. "Good. All set here," Senator Carlos pronounced. "Of course, there is going to be a huge delay between responses — something about the tremendous distances between us and Ashford-5 — don't know more, I'm not a physicist. The trick is to say a good deal — ask several questions — put forth several ideas — then wait several minutes for the reply. Your Governor Konrad will be doing the same thing. So expect him to toss out several different ideas at the same time. If you get too confused, let me know. I can replay what was sent. Okay, here we go." He made the connection and then spoke, "Hello Governor Konrad. Senate President Carlos here. By now, you've had the opportunity to go over the proposal and needs of the Imperium concerning Ashford-5. I have your Senator Isabella here with me. She will be making a proposal concerning how we may best handle this situation with dispatch and equality. Senator Isabella." He indicated that she was to speak.

Isabella spoke clearly. "Hello. Hope all is well on Ashford-5. In this matter concerning the Imperium's great need for a thousand of our telepaths, I have reached an agreement with the Senate and Imperium. I have proposed that we give them the desired telepaths in exchange for ten new medical machines and their establishment of ten schools, in which they will begin the education of our people so that, in time, we will have the knowledge to bring ourselves into the modern era. Over." She didn't think he needed to know about the other five worlds that would also be getting the same deal as Ashford-5. Senator Carlos flipped the switch to receive.

"Now we wait on his return message. Have you any idea how the thousand telepaths can be found?" Isabella sensed this was the key question that Senator Carlos just had to know.

"Why yes sir. I've been pondering this detail all night. Hardly slept. I believe I have it worked out, but I will need to contact the various ruling lords," she replied.

"But how? I suppose Governor Konrad could relay your messages to your lords for you," Senator Carlos suggested. Isabella picked up his surface thoughts again. He was very curious about her — whether or not she was a telepath herself — whether she had some other, perhaps devious means of contacting her people. She knew that in many ways, Senator Carlos was in fact testing her right now.

She had no idea what the man might do to her, if he discovered she was a telepath, though if he'd been in touch with Governor Konrad, he probably already suspected she was just that. Her yellow eyes with brown speckles gave that away. Why did Konrad have to become a *mentales* gifted? All this was becoming far too tricky to contain much longer. If the Imperium were this desperate for telepaths, what would prevent them from kidnaping her and her wives? Well, she was a senator, but Gabriella and Celia were not so protected. They could be kidnaped and used to force her to do what the Imperium desired! A small bead of sweat formed on her forehead, but she dare not wipe it. What to do? What to do?

"We senators have our own communication lines back to our constituents, as I am sure you must have as well," she replied. She sensed he didn't buy her explanation. She probed his mind a little deeper. *She can't have such electronic communication equipment, let alone know how to operate it. Besides, Ashford-5 is a primitive world. Hell, they don't even have electricity to power a receiver set. She's lying.*

"Hello President Carlos, Senator Isabella. Good to see you again. Yes, I've gone over the Imperium's request for a thousand telepaths. We are at war, and they will be of immense value to our winning the war against the barbarian Federation of Planets. I concur with the Imperium. The telepaths are needed one way or the other. Senator Isabella, your proposal warrants great merit. Indeed, educating your people will be a giant step towards bringing them into the modern world and into full membership within the Imperium.

You have my backing on this agreement. Several questions arise immediately. First, how will this be presented to the various lords? Obviously, they must agree to this proposal. Second, I can work with them on establishing the locations of the ten new schools and medical treatment centers across Ashford-5. Third, how will we obtain the requisite thousand telepaths? I know time is critical for the Imperium to acquire them. Over."

Isabella thought swiftly. "President Carlos, I assume I may use your communications thing here to talk to my lords to explain the situation in full and get their agreement?"

She sensed his letdown. "Of course, my facilities here are top of the line. As vital as this is, certainly you may. Will two hours be sufficient for all the lords to get to Konrad's location?" he replied, again probing for more details on her people. *How could they possibly get there that fast?*

She thanked him and spoke clearly again. "Konrad, contact the Imperial Circle. Have them relay to all the other towers this message. Senator Isabella Valen will be contacting the lords in two hours to present this situation in full. Have the towers bring the lords to your office, and I will make a connection like this to them. Hope you don't mind, Senator Carlos is letting me use his machine here to do it. Now after the lords agree on this, you may work with them in setting up the schools and medical centers as you've so generously volunteered. The lords will very likely be contacting you about the telepaths, who will be arriving at your base. Will you be able to handle that many coming to Plateau Grado? If not, do you have suggestions concerning where they should go? I guess I don't need to know this. Just be ready to answer their questions about that detail. Over."

Unable to contain his curiosity, President Carlos asked, "Will two hours be sufficient to get all of your lords there?"

"Oh sure. The towers can teleport them," she replied, as if he should already know this detail. Again, she touched his surface thoughts and knew that was true.

A bit later, Konrad replied he would take care of it, and they ended this video link. "I will be back in two hours. Thank you President Carlos. I am sure this will greatly expedite this situation." He thanked her and she left.

"He's going to have all manner of spying devices on that video conference — you know that, don't you?" Celia Jan countered. Isabella had just explained what had happened and what she was planning.

"Of course. But I can't think of any other way to do this quickly. I need to send an encrypted message to Ken right away and let him relay it to the towers and to the lords," Isabella replied. Cursing the interference of her long nails, she typed out a lengthy message outlining what was going on and what was needed, along with the proposed deal. She pointed out, if they did not take this deal, the Imperium was simply going to kidnap the telepaths. One way or another, the Imperium was getting their desired telepaths. She also suggested they use the newly created telepaths, who did not have any *mentales* gifts, per se. She underlined that point. Celia Jan encrypted the message using the Blackwater Ultimatum as the key and sent it off to Ken. Now Isabella waited nervously. Would the lords accept the deal that was being forced upon them?

Right on time, she arrived back at Senator Carlos' office. He was waiting for her, and they took their seats as before. He had freshly oiled his hair and moustache. He wore a fresh suit. It was obvious to her that he wanted to be seen in the very best of light. On schedule, Konrad opened the video conference. She saw the many lords gathered together in Konrad's office. Their backs were to the glass windows. The orange-red sunlight highlighted them amid the stark yellow Imperium standard office lighting. Konrad spoke, "Hello again Senator Isabella. The lords are here with me. I will turn the meeting over to you. Over." Konrad looked a bit frazzled. She guessed he'd been rather harried making all these arrangements for the last two hours. Senator Carlos stared at the men with their huge, drooping lip plates, quite shocked.

"My lords. Here is the situation in brief. The Imperium has gone to war with something called the Federation of Planets. They are in desperate need of a thousand telepaths. They know that Tierra has them, and the Imperium has told me they will get their desired telepaths one way or another.

Yes, this is a direct threat from the Imperium. I've come to what I believe is a mutually satisfactory solution. In return for our telepaths, they will be immediately setting up ten schools on Tierra, where we may send our people to gain the knowledge that we lack. They will also set up ten medical centers around Tierra as well. The telepaths should come from those who recently became telepaths. Discussion? Over." Isabella sat back. Would they go along with this? She highly doubted it, but this was her job now.

After a few minutes lag, the monitor again activated. Lord Rusden spoke first, "So the Imperium cannot be trusted! We should not give them a damned thing. We should run them off of Tierra now!"

Lord Bolivar interrupted him. "Some of us are quite angry over this unexpected twist, Senator Isabella. I believe your deal is perhaps the best that we can hope for. I back you in this, even if you are a Valen." Isabella smiled, she picked up his true intention. By that reference, he was recalling to the other lord's minds just how much the Midlands hated and distrusted the ancient Valen lineage. Cleverly, he had also thrown his support behind her anyway. She saw Lord Rusden's demeanor relax somewhat.

Lord Roberto Valen of the Renegade Tower spoke up, "While none of us like to be threatened and none of us are desirous of this *severe* lease agreement breakage, I believe this is for the best. I would like to negotiate with Governor Konrad for a few additional, small items that have been hither to fore banned from Tierra. Silverware, pressure cookers, small things."

"Aye," Lord Alano Valen broke in, "we too would like to negotiate for a few small things as well. No blasters — nothing like that. Konrad has already agreed to meet individually with those of us who wish."

Lord Wye spoke up, "We should tightly control what these Valen's are going to get. We don't trust them in the slightest." Several others voiced their disgust, protests, but all ultimately agreed with the deal.

Isabella then replied, "I understand your concerns, I really do. I will leave the working out of the many details to you lords. As always, protect our world. Thank you. Senator Isabella out." She sat back. "There, that's done. Turned out easier than I had anticipated. As you could see, we have a good deal of animosity towards three centuries of lease breakages with our world, to say nothing of the Directive #5. Still, you have your telepaths, President Carlos. Now the ball is in your court. That's a new expression I've picked up here on Proxima Prime. I think it means you get to fulfill your part of the bargain with the other five closed worlds."

"Indeed. I will get on it at once. Again, on behalf of the Imperium, I thank you for making this come about so easily. I am amazed at how easily you have been able to influence your lords. I would have expected a very lengthy debate, putting it politely," Senator Carlos commented.

Isabella laughed. "I wish it was always this easy to get them to agree! No, as you know only too well, they had no real choice in this matter. If they had refused, the Imperium would have just kidnaped the telepaths anyway. At least we are getting a little something in return. I best get back to work. You have so many proposed bills before the Senate now, and I surely don't understand them all yet." She made her excuses and left.

"My god! Your world has a thousand telepaths?" Carl exclaimed. That evening, Isabella asked her five fellow Closed World senators to her home to brief them on the coming deal that she'd made.

"Yes, we do have them. More importantly, I want each of you to make darn sure the Imperium lives up to its agreement with me and puts schools with proper education on your worlds. And also that they give you ten medical machines and set up medical centers for you," Isabella insisted.

"How can we ever thank you for what you have done for our worlds?" gushed Roja Onah, visibly impressed.

"We can't ever thank you enough!" Senator Jenkins added. The others added their tremendous appreciation as well. From this point in time onward, Isabella gain a newfound trust and respect from these other five senators and their worlds.

After they left, Isabella, Gabriella, and Celia mused over

what had just been done. "Honestly, a thousand of our people are just being sacrificed, tossed to the whims of the Imperium. I never thought we'd ever stoop this low," Gabriella Amy declared, rather upset by the whole affair. "Can't they fight their own wars and leave us out of it?"

"I hate this job! Why did I ever let myself get talked into it?" Isabella grumbled. "It is a no win situation for all of us. I've condemned a thousand of our people to utter hell." She'd been a slave telepath for nearly a century!

Celia Jan twisted her lips. "Well, you managed to get something useful for our whole world out of it. Honestly, we all know the Imperium would have just gone ahead and kidnaped the telepaths, perhaps taking the real *mentales* gifted as well. You've managed to contain this god-awful mess, Isabella. That counts in my book. We all know the Imperium has always been kidnaping some of us, ever since they landed on Tierra three centuries ago. Now at least we may be getting education for our people. While I think that is particularly valuable, the lords probably don't."

"I don't like the way the Imperium keeps on transplanting excess populations from one world to another," Gabriella Amy pointed out, changing the topic. "I can't imagine how those poor people feel about suddenly being uprooted from their homes and world, taken to a new, strange world and having to start over. Despicable."

"Yes, but what other choice to they have?" Isabella countered, thankful for the change in topic. "The overcrowding must be making life utterly unbearable. Still, think of the culture destruction on the receiving planet. Then, there is this incredible mess of a world whose entire surface is nothing but steel and concrete. All plant and animal life is gone. Artificial weather control has it a constant seventy-five degrees everywhere, all the time. No seasons. They've made this a totally sterile world. Do we want to see this on Tierra one day? Hell no."

"The critical thing, Isabella, is to never allow them to alter our world's status to Open," Gabriella Amy broke in. "Once Tierra becomes an Open World, you can bet they'll want to ship millions to our world too. That would soon wipe us all out. Tierra cannot ever become an open world, not ever."

"You'll get no argument from me on that point!" Isabella declared flatly.

"Meantime, gang, we keep our eyes open and learn. Acquire things that might be useful in the future for us. We are now the guardians of Tierra," Celia Jan pointed out. In many ways, the trio was just that.

Chapter 29 Uprisings Begin

During the long winter of 1273, Nadja and Diego stayed in Brom Tower. Venerada Maricela was kind enough to donate a suite for their use. Nadja now had quite an accumulation of recordings to study. She and Diego had spent a good deal of the summer and fall in the rural villages of the central Midlands as well as old Trujillo, Westerlings and the coastal cities. At last, she could relax and begin to work out the subtleties of the two languages and their relatively minor dialects. While she buried herself in her valuable work, Diego spent his time visiting with the tower folks and entertaining them with his music.

Before long, Diego found that Maricela was quite intelligent, and the two began to spend hours in conversation. "So you have traveled extensively in rural Trujillo. How do they take to Lord Valen's rule over them?" she asked, curious and hopeful of gaining an insider's point of view.

"Well, not so good, really. For at least as far back as the locals can remember, Valen Castle and Tower have been taxing them and absconding with their gifted individuals," Diego pointed out. "There is a world of difference between the castle and tower folks and the villagers. You see, Maricela, the life of a simple villager is one of almost eternal hardship. They have to deal with the wild, nearly unpredictable weather and the constant struggle somehow to make ends meet. That's why I've been so welcomed by them all. I heal those who need it and then give them perhaps the only real music they've heard. Well, that's not entirely true. Some have their local musicians. Still, Maricela, there's a whole world of difference between the common man and woman and those in power. You all are fabulously wealthy and want for nothing. The local men and women are in the opposite situation. I am no politician, but even I can see that sooner or later this huge disparity between those of you who have and the vast majority who have not is going to come to a head, probably a nasty one."

"Is it really that bad? I am so isolated here in Brom

Tower," Maricela replied. "But then, traveling is so hard for me, obviously. Still, did you find it as bad here in the Midlands as over in the Westerlings?"

"Yes, but in different ways. In the Westerlings, they tend to focus their hatred at Valen. Honestly, they can't blame Valen for all their woes, but they do. Here in the Midlands, Nadja and I have found the locals really are bothered by the huge gap between themselves and the lords and tower folks. You all think nothing of buying the latest new fashionable gowns. Yet in the villages, a woman is very lucky if she can get a new dress every few years," Diego pointed out.

"Is it that bad? I had no idea. I ought to discuss this with Lord Bolivar," Maricela said, more for her own benefit. "One spark and we could have a nasty situation on our hands. I wonder if the other lords are aware of this?"

Diego laughed. "They are not aware of their own butts."

She smiled, but her smile was no longer visible because of her lip plates. Maricela added, "No Diego, we can't see our feet." He roared.

An hour later, Venerada Maricela sat down across from Lord Bolivar. Both wore their formal clothing, and their lip plates were fixed in their horizontal position as demanded from such a meeting. She had endured the long, difficult walk over to his office, using the time to think this through. Both spoke slowly, making sure the other understood them completely. "A matter has come to my attention that bears on us all, I truly fear, My Lord." She used his formal address, and he cocked his head slightly, recognizing that she had.

"I believe our people, the ordinary citizens of our kingdom are perhaps dissatisfied with us."

"How so?" he probed.

"We live a life of luxury, compared to them. We wear the latest fashions, jewelry, eat well, and so on. Yet, I fear the ordinary person in our rural villages do not fare anywhere near as well as we do. I know, My Lord, you are providing them with protection from invaders, bandits, and the like. Yet, how often have we seen those, in say the last couple of decades? Few and far between. Perhaps feelings of discontent are not so severe here in Brom as they are elsewhere. I've been talking with Diego. And as you know, My Lord, he and Nadja have spent many, many months traveling around both the Midlands and the Westerlings, visiting small villages and hamlets. He dispensed healing to those who need it. His observations suggest to me there is a growing discontent between we who seem to have everything and those local folks who are barely making ends meet."

"I see. If this were true — mind you, I am not saying that it is, then what do you think will happen? A rebellion? Against we lords and the towers? Against our armies?" Lord Bolivar asked.

"Yes, that's just what I think could happen. Look, anytime a kingdom begins to kill its own citizens — no matter the reason — that kingdom is doomed. It's just a matter of time before it crumbles," she pointed out.

"But we haven't been killing our people," Lord Bolivar protested.

"No, but what will you do if some villagers take up arms against us?" she countered.

"Point taken. So what are you suggesting that we do? Give them all some of Ken's therapy?" he replied growing annoyed. This was something he ought to have seen and handled himself, not this armless woman from the tower.

"Are you asking me for my opinion? I don't want to step on your toes. You are our ruler," she replied cleverly manipulating him.

"Well, yes, of course. Your opinion please," he stated slightly testily.

"It's winter now. Why not send out small observational teams to each village and hamlet in the kingdom. Have them ask what the citizens need there? Then, see it's provided as best as is possible. Stem any discontent before it has a chance to fester all winter long," she suggested.

"Hum, it would give the men something to do besides sit around all winter and play cards and drink up our ale," he admitted. "Still, travel's quite nasty during our winters. Guess it wouldn't hurt, just this once, but if we find they really don't need anything, I may send you the bill for their services." He got his final dig into her rather well, he thought. If they found nothing amiss, then he did fully intend to make the tower cover the expenses.

"I'll cover the expenses. I would further suggest your men take stock of each village's overall well-being. I hope this leads to nothing, and, if it doesn't show up anything, send me the bill for my foolishness," Venerada Maricela stated dryly. "May I ask how the telepaths for the Imperium project is faring?" she changed the topic.

"Better than expected. Brom has sent off our portion. I can't see why so many young men and women volunteered to go off-world, unless it was the promised wealth and goods. I'm satisfied with what I have," he replied. "At least half of these newly made telepaths are now gone. Many say good riddance though. Guess my soldiers can inquire about that too. Say, any word on what private deals the two Lord Valens made with the governor?"

"None. That too has me worried. Still, I can't imagine Governor Konrad allowing them to acquire some of their hideous weapons like they did centuries ago." The memory of the Nuclear unleashed upon Bettingham was still too real for everyone in Brom Kingdom. The annihilated site remained uninhabitable. While no one knew why, any living creature who entered the well-marked perimeter around the site either never came back out or if they did, they died soon after. Ken had said the victims suffered radiation burns, but even Maricela had no idea what he meant by that.

Thousands of miles to the south and west of Brom, Lord Roberto Valen had just received the first batch of his secret request from Governor Konrad. For quite some time now, he had been making periodic visits to Exchange City, meeting with Neva, Konrad's new wife from the Westerlings. Via her connections, he was introduced to the Imperium computer system, specifically the Goods and Services catalogues. Already his far-flung empire of the City-States Alliance was flourishing beyond anything he'd originally imagined. He knew well what had contributed to their smashing success. Provide the merchants with what goods they really needed and in a timely, inexpensive manner. While the Easterlings port towns and cities were still struggling mightily to recover from the barbarian sacking, all the others across the coast of Tierra were doing very well indeed.

As he looked over the various "goods" of the vast Imperium, he paid no attention to weapons and machinery. Rather, he looked for the next "great invention" that would take Tierra by storm, economically that is. He found two. Stainless steel, elegant silverware caught his eye right away. The silverware in common use on Tierra was made from bronze and was anything but attractive or durable. While he had no idea what stainless steel was, he knew from casual conversations with others from the Imperium, who frequented Exchange City, that they were highly durable. Pressure cookers also caught his eye. Cooking rice in mere minutes seemed impossible, let alone the other incredibly short cooking times for various other foods, most of which he didn't recognize. Still, what woman on Tierra would not desire a cooking pot that would cut the time for her to prepare a meal in half or more?

Of course, he also realized this trade would likely be a onetime affair. Hence, when he met privately with Konrad, he promised to deliver more than his share of new telepaths in exchange for silverware and pressure cookers. Konrad, amazed at the simple request, agreed and ordered a thousand sets of silverware. Each set served eight. He also ordered two hundred pressure cookers. They had finally come and now Capo Roberto and Venerado Pino Valen began examining them.

"We have to figure out how to make these ourselves," Capo Roberto declared, making sure that he was fully understood. *These lip plates are certainly annoying when you need to be clear in what you are saying,* he thought rather annoyed once again.

"I will let your Circle work out the construction of the cookers," Pino decided, also speaking as clearly as he could. "I'll see to the silverware. Are you sure that we can sell these?"

"Absolutely, but we must be able to make more of them and in quantity. If I am right, these will become tremendous sellers, but only if we can produce them in large enough numbers to meet the demand," he replied.

Many miles north of Villa del Rey, Lord Alano Valen and his group examined their latest acquisition. He had known that there would be no way for him to get his hands on Imperium blasters, ignoring the salient fact the Imperium was at war and would be needing them for their own use. Rather, via Neva, he had learned of ancient sporting guns that shot lead or copper projectiles from a barrel. Some kind of explosion caused these pointed projectiles to come out of the barrels at a terrific speed. They were deadly, or so the advertisement proclaimed. Hence, he doubled the number of new telepaths he was supposed to deliver in return for fifty of these long barreled items called rifles and a large quantity of "hunting" ammunition for them. At least they had come with detailed instructions on their use. In the Imperium, these were considered antique hunting weapons, used mostly for sport among the very wealthy or elite.

They each took one outside, where some of their servants had set up some dummies whose bodies were straw and whose heads were pumpkins. At least the men had the good sense to have everyone stand back as they tried out their new weapons. Blam. Blam. Their shots echoed loudly in the castle courtyard, drawing the attention of absolutely everyone. Heads poked out of various windows and doors to see what was going on. Both men were elated, the pumpkin heads were shattered masses, but the projectiles had continued on through them, ricocheting off the castle walls, narrowly missing an array of pots and several bystanders. "Holy crap! Did you see that!" Lord Alano exclaimed, wildly excited.

"These are incredible! I wonder how far back we can be and still hit it?" Venerado Arturo exclaimed. Both men moved to the very entrance of the castle and fired a second time. The ricochet actually struck one woman who was watching. The Circle tended to her wound immediately as the two men began talking rapidly. Plans came faster than either could clearly enunciate them. Of course, the real problem lay in being able to make more of them here in Valen, as well as making more of the strange looking ammunition. Both men now had a wintertime project!

That was also what was taking place in Exchange City, despite the heavy winter snows. Construction crews from Plateau Grado brought their heavy equipment to the southern edge of the sprawling city at the very edge of the Goza Mountains. Already they had stripped the land down flat, removing a considerable amount of the bedrock. The foundations for the new school were laid by December. With the coming of the heavy snows, the crews erected a portable dome over the entire construction site. Naturally, the sight of this enormous white dome attracted a good deal of local attention. However, only the work crews were allowed inside, and the onlookers had to be content to watch the coming and going of the heavy machinery. Governor Konrad assured the Imperial Circle the school would be ready to open for classes in the spring. Further, he swore that the "appearance" of the school would fit in nicely with the surrounding buildings of Exchange City.

Even Inez was unable to get him to tell her more about it. However, clever Inez twisted Neva's arm when she was visiting her store. In exchange for allowing Neva to wear her latest fashion gown at the spring High Council meeting, Neva told her that the school would be a stone building, two stories tall resembling the Imperial Castle. Its name would be the Imperial School. Naturally, Inez relayed this to Ken who relayed it to others.

In mid-January, cases of schoolbooks arrived ahead of schedule. Konrad and Neva then paid a visit to Elegant Fashions Inc. "Welcome Governor, Neva. What brings you out in this weather?" Inez greeted them as they made their slow, careful way into her office on the top floor. He was escorting Neva, who greatly appreciated his steadying arm. Toe boots and the snow just didn't mix. Both had their lip plates dangling before their faces to keep their lips warm. Outside, the winds had picked up the recently fallen snow, forming a near whiteout. Only the guidance system on their electric car had gotten them safely to her store.

"Good news. The many school textbooks have arrived

ahead of schedule. I could store them at our office, but I thought to show good faith, I ought to bring them to Exchange City," he explained.

Inez grinned. "Ah, you need a place to store them, I take it?"

He grinned, but it wasn't visible. "Ah, yes. While they could be stored in one of the warehouses, I'd rather they be stored somewhere that is safer."

"Ah, and what is safer than Elegant Fashions Inc?" Inez replied coyly. She sensed both were grinning. "Sure. How much space are we talking about?"

"One room will do. They are still in their shipping crates and can be easily stacked. If it is acceptable to you, I can have some of my groundsmen bring them by and stack them for you," Konrad replied.

"Fine, let's store them on the third floor, Room 10," she decided.

"Good. I'll let them know now," he replied and used his cell phone to make the arrangements.

While he was tied up, Neva asked, "Say, Inez. I have been meaning to ask you how come you don't wear these fancy lip plates like all the rest of us nobles?"

"I need to be easily understood in three different languages," she replied, masking her real reason she disliked the whole concept. Memories of her youth returned and she quickly banished them. "Always I must deal with those just getting into the new fashions. As you know, the lip plates make it hard for someone unused to being around those with them to understand what is being said. It is bad for business if they can't understand me well."

"Oh, I see. Yes, that makes sense. Say, any idea what my new gown will look like for spring?" Neva asked curiously.

"It will be scarlet red, if that's what you are interested in," Inez teased her a little. "I'm sure that you will like it, dear. Konrad might not be able to keep his hands off you, though. I'm making a warmer gown this time. Velvet."

"Oh! Sounds positively sensuous! When can I try it on?"

"Due time, dear. If you wear it too soon, others will see you and demand one like yours long before the High Council.

You don't want to spoil your grand entrance, do you?"

"Well, no. Okay, I'll wait. Dear, she has a fabulous new gown for me to wear this spring. She says that you will love it too," Neva gushed as Konrad returned to the two women.

"Sounds delightful dearest. Inez, the groundsmen are on their way."

"In this blizzard?" she asked, having guessed they would bring them by when the winds died down.

"Yes, geo-navigation allows us to move about even in this whiteout." Konrad then slipped his arm around Neva, giving her a gentle squeeze. The three headed down to get the room opened up. An hour later, the last of the crates had been stacked into the room, very nearly filling it.

"What do they look like?" Inez asked, unable to contain her growing curiosity. That her people were soon to begin the adventure of a lifetime was not lost on her.

Konrad opened one crate. "Here is a beginning math book." He handed it to her.

"It's in Imperium Standard," Inez commented upon opening it.

"Of course, all textbooks throughout the vast Imperium are written in the only standardized language known throughout the many worlds," Konrad justified. "Everyone knows it."

"Well, I do, but then I've had too. I suppose those who are going to learn will first have to learn to read and write Imperium Standard," Inez suggested.

"Certainly. We've some language learning portable players in one of these crates. As I recall, some are in each of the three languages spoken here on Tierra, compliments of Nadja's good work. Well, we must get going. Thanks for storing them," Konrad explained. Inez picked up the real reason Konrad was in a hurry to leave: Neva. She got a flash of the two heading to bed way early today. She smiled as the two made their slow way to the elevator. Later, she relayed this bit of news about the textbooks to Ken.

Scattered around the villages of the Midlands and

particularly so in Trujillo, Westerlings, others were making their own plans. In Rancho Duerro in the central part of Trujillo, Don Alasandro complained bitterly to a large group of the other ranchers, who had come into the village for midwinter festivities. With the snows piling up on the vast rolling grasslands, there was little else to do until spring. "I don't give a pig's ass for Valen or all the damned lords and ladies there. Do they care about us? Not in the slightest. They took away our new telepaths; they take away our stock and conscript our young men into their army. What the devil do we get in return? I ask you all that?"

"Aye, but then there's that Diego fellow and the woman with him, who is always listening to our speech," another older man replied. "He's cured my arthritis. Some's got good in'em."

"Si, but not the rulers. Diego isn't ruling anything, save his guitar," Don Alasandro countered. "I say it is high time we put our feet down. No more giving without receiving. They have everything and we have nothing. I say it is time that we have and they have not."

A chorus of "si's" echoed around the smoke filled pub. Another said, "I say send them packing or kill 'em, when they come to steal our horse, hay, grain, and men." That brought another round of general agreement. "Let 'em grow their own crops and raise their own horses and men for their army," another yelled.

Thus, open rebellion greeted Lord Valen's men, when they began their spring rounds to collect taxes, food, supplies, men for the army, and checking on potential new *mentales* gifted. There was little Lord Alano Valen could do about it. His army of a thousand was spread out in small groups of five riders, who were making the spring rounds, often with a tax collector. Some two hundred of these groups had already left Valen Castle, fanning out across the vast lands of Trujillo.

"It's a bloody mutiny! That's what it is, a mutiny! I'll not stand for it. Venerado Arturo, what can we do about this? Burn down some villages? Make them see reason!"

"My Lord," Venerado Arturo replied using his formal title, thereby distancing himself from the leader of the Holy Pentagram, "if we burn the village, there will be nothing to harvest come fall. Remember what happened to the insane previous lord of Valen, who tried to use force against them. We lost all of our port cities and towns, every damn last one of them. Perhaps it would be wiser to let it go for now and raid the villages in force come fall and take what is rightfully ours."

"Dear, maybe you could bring this up at the Spring High Council. See if the other lords have similar problems. Perhaps they have more workable solutions," Concepcion suggested, trying her best to calm her husband down some. She hated it when he got angry. In the end, there was little that could effectively be done, save attempt to back their strongest local allies. Not all villages had rebelled, and many whose lands lay close to Valen had not yet rebelled. Nevertheless, belts tightened significantly during the spring of 1274.

Likewise, rebellions in Matruk, Easterlings, arose during the winter, exacerbated by the barbarian raids of Damiano and his horde. Southbend had done nothing to stop their devastating march across the heart of that prime farming country. Arad and the greater Turda areas were spared rebellions. There, all attention was focused on staying alive and rebuilding. Besides, the Sisterhood was there in force. Up in Domei, with the loss of the sultan in Teraspoli, remaining younger men also began to carve out their own small domains. These men thanked their lucky moons for having not joined up with Damiano and his men.

Most all the Midlands also had varying levels of open rebellions as well. The lands around the coastal cities and towns fared well, as did the Kingdom of Brom in the far north. Especially hard hit by local rebellions were the central lands and the northeastern Walsham area.

Lord Bolivar's prompt actions during the winter and countermeasures taken in the early spring blunted all potential upheavals in the greater Brom kingdom. Maricela was right, he discovered. He took preventative measures, promising each village leader that come spring, their biggest concerns would be addressed. In the end, that promise gave him time to work out ways and means to at least show them good faith.

To that end, he summoned Venerada Maricela, Nadja, Diego, Ken, and Crystal to join Domingo and himself in a conference. "Look, the venerada was right. All is not well in our kingdom, but it is vastly better than down south. I hear there are actual uprisings in the heartland of the Westerlings. So what are we supposed to do about all these complaints?"

"The fundamental flaw is you have a three class system going here," Nadja decided to speak her mind. Until now, she'd kept her own personal opinions to herself concerning the governing of Tierra, focusing instead on her love, the linguistics and the telepathic society.

"What do you mean? We don't have any classes here," Lord Emilio replied, a little confused, though he was pleased that Nadja spoke up.

"Not formally defined classes, Lord Emilio. Rather they are unofficial classes. First, you have the ruling lords, your Elite Guards, and the tower personnel. The real power lies in this group, as you well know; *mentales* gifts abound here. Second, you have the many nobles, the *Jefe*, who own vast tracts of land or businesses, and they lease out their holdings for others to work, while raking in the profits, leaving little for those who actually do the work. Third, you have those folk who actually do the real work, from farming, to gathering of the snow pod silk, to the milling of your grains, to the blacksmith work, to the pottery making, weaving, on and on."

"Well, it has always been that way," Lord Emilio countered.

"Yes, I suppose so," Nadja admitted. "These classes of people are then ruled by monarchies, kings or lords, if you prefer. Now there is nothing wrong with a benevolent monarch, such as yourself, Lord Emilio, but there is everything wrong with other monarchs, such as Lord Alano Valen. At this time, I believe it is his vast lands that are rebelling the most, though I have no firsthand knowledge, since we were last there some six months or more ago — just what I've been told and heard. The problem with monarchies is rather one of succession."

"Oh that's simple. It goes to my eldest son. That's the way it has always been. It beats trying to divide up kingdoms between all my sons," Lord Emilio replied.

"Yes, that is quite true. But herein lies the problem.

There is absolutely no guarantee that the son will be as good and effective a monarch as his father has been. A kingdom can go from a truly benevolent ruler to a bastard overnight. Sometimes, the younger sons assassinate the older sons so that they can inherit the kingdom instead. That's the real problem with monarchies," Nadja pointed out.

"Well, I can see that. We all try to educate our sons appropriately so that they can fill our shoes," Lord Emilio countered, justifying a little. "Are there alternatives?"

"Yes, as a matter of fact, there are many other forms of government found among the many worlds. Mind you, some are vastly worse than what Tierra has! Let's not even discuss those. I will mention one that you might consider, democracy. In this form, the people themselves vote on who they wish to govern them. These elected leaders all have finite terms and often are limited to just how many terms they can rule, such as two or three. This gives the people a true say in who governs them. If they elect a bad ruler, they know in just a few years they can get rid of him or her and elect another person."

"Seems like the governments would be running into continual chaos from one ruler to the next," Lord Emilio speculated. He obviously didn't like this idea, but then he had a vested interest in remaining the monarch.

"There are ways to deal with that to minimize the changes. They also have three branches of government, all separate. One branch makes the laws. The second branch enforces the laws. The third branch handles all judicial matters, including vetoing bad laws and bringing to justice those rulers who break the laws themselves. Checks and balances keep all three branches in line with each other," Nadja explained.

"So how does this work in the *great* Imperium?" Amo Domingo spoke up. The word "great" was said sarcastically.

"Well, there is the Senate, whose members are elected by the people they represent. The Senate makes the laws of the Imperium. The Imperium President carries out those laws. Right now, I believe he is involved in fighting some war with another space empire called the Federation of Planets. Then, there are the Imperium Courts that handle all justice matters.

They are appointed by the Imperial President, but the Senate must confirm or reject his appointees before they can take office. Every twenty years, the senators meet to elect a new Imperium President. Each planet handles the elections of their own senators, of course, and their periods of office vary widely from a few years to life, sometimes. I'm not saying this is the best form of government, Amo Domingo. It is just the way the Imperium works," Nadja explained, backing off from throwing her support behind this system over all others.

"So in this system, the average people elect the leaders?" Lord Emilio asked. Nadja nodded. "They must get idiots elected then. After all, how can you expect a poor farmer to know how to vote intelligently?"

Nadja grinned, but no one saw it. They sensed it with their "gifts." "Therein lies the biggest problem with this system. It only works well, if you have enlightened voters. People can be hoodwinked by sweet-talking speakers, who promise the masses great handouts, and yet become tyrants when they take office. However, they can just as easily be voted out of office in a few years or even arrested by the courts, if they actually break the kingdom's laws. So there are checks and balances on the power they wield. The key is to get enlightened voters, Lord Emilio."

"So you think that could help us here on Tierra?" Amo Domingo asked the key question.

"Perhaps, Amo Domingo. Right now, the average person out there — the very ones I have been listening to and the ones who Diego has been healing — the average person feels utterly powerless when it comes to his rulers and the laws that he must obey. In my humble opinion, this feeling underlies the unrest in the many kingdoms of Tierra right now. People feel helpless to alter their own futures, other than their own small farms and businesses. It leads to frustration and that can lead to further irrational forms of unrest — even open rebellion," Nadja replied.

"But I make the laws of the land," Lord Emilio protested.

Amo Domingo pointed out, "Aye, that you do, but what about the miller, who has no say whatsoever in the making of the laws? I see what Nadja is driving at. No say equals resistance at best, rebellion at worst."

Lord Emilio grumbled. "Ken, you've been totally quiet. What do you think?"

Ken cleared his throat, wishing his mother were here, not himself. "Well, Nadja and Domingo have hit the nail squarely, in my opinion. Perhaps, you could have each town, village, and hamlet select a person to meet and have that group write up a document stating the basic human rights that a citizen of Brom ought to have. You could then look it over and see if they are reasonable or totally irrational. It would give you an idea of whether or not your people are capable of such things. If they produce a good document, then perhaps the next step is to setup a group of them to suggest perhaps what the laws of the kingdom ought to be. I think you should take it one small step at a time and see whether it would even work here. If it worked out and these people made the laws that you then enforce, the average person would no longer be blaming you for everything they don't like, since you are then distant from the laws, merely the one who is seeing they are applied to all."

Lord Emilio grinned, but again, his grin was sensed, not seen. "I like that, Ken. You remind me of your mother. Yes, test them and see if they can even state intelligently what rights a citizen of Brom ought to have. I like that. It will give them something to do and take the pressure off the situation here. Of course, the towns will complain that they are vastly larger than a hamlet."

Ken countered, "Well, let there be a representative per every hundred people. You could easily divide a town into rectangles that had about a hundred living in that zone. Considering how large our kingdom is area-wise, I'd guess we'd have about five hundred representatives attending."

"Excellent idea, Ken. Okay, then let's see about getting this first step implemented. Mark my words, I believe they will fail utterly to produce any kind of reasonable document of rights, but we will see," Lord Emilio declared. Then, they tackled the details of how to proceed in a timely fashion, which would help defuse the growing unrest in the kingdom.

Mid-April, four hundred seventy-six men and women, including a dozen Sisterhood women from Hilliard Heights in the far north, assembled in the Great Hall of Brom Castle. Lord Emilio gave them their opening address and their charge. "This is an historic occasion for all of Brom. I have heard your complaints, and I am looking to make major changes in the way we run our kingdom. You represent your hundred or so citizens of Brom. Put your heads together and write up a document that states in no uncertain terms what the human rights of a citizen of Brom ought to be. When you are done, present it to me for review. If this works out, then we can move on to the next phase in which the people of our fair kingdom get to make the laws of the land, which I will enforce. But first, one step at a time. Let's see what the rights of our people should be." He discussed further details and then left them to work out just how they were going to proceed.

Meanwhile, he had a new crisis to handle. Venerada Maricela just notified him of it, and he headed to her tower just as soon as he gave the assembled people their charge. "Okay, tell me that this isn't true," Lord Emilio declared, slightly out of breath. "I don't know how much more of these changes we can handle! When it snows, it blizzards!"

Venerada Maricela sighed, "Lord how I wish I could say it isn't true, My Lord. But it is. Confirmations are still coming in. It's far worse; it is happening all over Tierra. All of those new telepaths have been losing their telepathic abilities. Their eyes have returned to their normal colors, I'm told. I have four Circles out now scouring the villages checking on them, but there can be no doubt about it. They are losing their ability."

"Well, what has Rafaela to say about this? Isn't she our expert in such matters?" Lord Emilio rubbed his hands through his hair, frustrated.

"I've sent for her. She should be here momentarily," Venerada Maricela replied, wishing she had better news. The loss of such an intimate ability was more than a little upsetting to those affected by it. Surely, their heavy loss would require therapy sessions to handle that loss.

"Sorry. I'm a bit late. This crisis is giving me fits," Rafaela exclaimed, as she made her careful way into the room, her heels clicking on the stone floor. After sitting down, she explained further, "As far as I can tell, all those who suddenly obtained telepathic abilities last year are now losing them, one by one. Already half have lost it. I don't know why, just yet."

"Well, I suppose those who have lost it ought to get a therapy session soon," Venerada Maricela proposed.

"Absolutely. I already have Henry, Sally, Luisa, and Jamie on it. They are going to coordinate the sessions," Rafaela replied. "We must do it, because we have well-established the fact that after a person suffers a significant loss, they tend to get ill or have an accident. We must avoid this. What troubles me even more are the thousand we sent off-world — to the Imperium. Is this going to affect them too? If so, what will happen to them? Frankly, I'm very frightened about this sudden reversal and its implications."

Just then, someone knocked on her door. "It's Josh," Maricela interrupted. "Come on in, Josh."

He stepped into the room. "Excuse me, but I know I am needed here. This loss of telepathic abilities. Yes, we foresaw this happening. We saw two paths opening up at this point in time. One path led to the total destruction of Tierra. The other led to the loss of telepathic abilities of these new ones and the ultimate deaths of the thousand that left Tierra to spy for the Imperium. It was my choice to sacrifice the thousand so that Tierra would survive. Balance will return to Tierra now. There was no other choice."

By now, everyone here was well aware of Josh and his four wives' unique *mentales* gifts. Though none fully understood this unique gift, they knew they could somehow see the potential futures and even tweak one of the possible paths, bringing it about. "My god, a thousand!" Maricela gushed.

"Their sacrifice should be honored across all Tierra, somehow," Lord Emilio suggested. "Perhaps we should set aside one day each year as a memorial to their sacrifice." In later years, as the other lords of Tierra finally understood the result of this new event, April 20th was declared the World Remembrance Day for those lost men and women.

Of note, due to the many upheavals and the sudden,

inexplicable loss of telepathic abilities, the Spring High Council meeting wasn't held. Instead, the lords agreed to meet on July 1st when the annual lease payments were made. That gave the lords more time to deal with their own varying situations within their kingdoms.

Additionally, the first school in Exchange City did not open as scheduled, though the construction was finished. The teachers had not yet arrived. Things were not going well at all, but they were about to get far worse.

Chapter 30 Consequences

"What?" exclaimed Isabella. Senator Carlos had just called her to his office and told her that he had just received word the thousand or so telepaths from Ashford-5 had somehow lost their telepathic abilities. On behalf of the Imperium High Command, he demanded an explanation from Ashford-5's senator. "I have no idea. Can you let me contact my people back home? I don't understand this. This has never happened before. The only remote thing I can even think of is that they lost it because they are no longer on Tierra, Ashford-5, I mean." She was visibly shaken, Senator Carlos duly noted. He concluded she was just as surprised by this catastrophic event as was everyone else involved. Now he relaxed visibly; they were not trying to hoodwink the Imperium, as he had feared.

"Okay, I give you twenty-four hours to get this resolved. You realized, if their telepathic abilities are not restored, the Imperium agreement with Ashford-5 will be voided by the Imperium," he strongly cautioned her, though she took it more as a threat.

An hour later, Isabella explained the terrible news to Gabriella Amy and Celia Jan. "Okay, I am on it. I'll have Ken online shortly," Celia Jan declared, heading to her room where she had her brand new comm network in full operation. After enabling all her anti-spying protocols and devices, she made the connection to the Underground's network. Of course, there was no way getting around the long time delay caused by the extreme distances the signals had to travel, including through hyperspace.

"Isabella, Ken reports this is happening all over Tierra too. Just with all those new telepaths. So far, no *mentales* gifted has been affected. Rafaela has no idea why it is happening. What else should I tell him?" Celia Jan called out.

"Looks like the Imperium will be cancelling our schools. Let him know that, please, and have him send us more when he knows it," she replied. "I had best think of something to report to President Carlos tomorrow. First, I ought to alert our allies." She was thinking of the five other closed world Senators.

A short while later, she did just that. "How could they suddenly not have this telepathy thing?" asked Senator Carl. "Ah well, I surely don't understand such things."

Senator Jenkins sighed, "You are right. They will certainly cancel our schools. At least they have already gotten one built on Zelos-3. That's something anyway." The others concurred; one school had been finished on each of the other five worlds. Isabella relaxed a little, believing some good may still result, if only from a single school.

The next day, she reported back to President Carlos. "We have no idea why this is happening. But I am told it has also happened to all of our telepaths as well. It is a disaster on our world, just as it must be wherever you have employed our thousand telepaths. I don't know what else I can possibly say. We are sorry this happened, truly sorry, but no one on Ashford-5 knows why it is happening. Such a thing has never happened before, at least in our recorded history."

"I see. I take it there isn't any chance of getting another batch of telepaths from Ashford-5, is there?" he asked. At least he is calmer today, she noticed.

"No, until recently, there were very few telepaths, contrary to all the rumors that seem to be attached to our world," she replied honestly. Isabella knew these days there were perhaps two hundred *mentales* gifted left on Tierra. That is, ignoring all the mermaids, who could hardly be used as spies. From Rafaela, she had already learned their numbers had been steadily dropping during the last couple of centuries.

"I see. Well, you may report back officially the Imperium is canceling its contract over these telepaths. Governor Konrad has already been informed," he replied mildly, for which Isabella was grateful. She'd expected him to be angry or hostile towards her today.

"Yes, of course. But what about the thousand men and women now in Imperium service? Can they be returned home?" she asked what she needed to know.

"I don't know. We will have to see how that plays out. They are in the service of the Imperium now and we're at war.

Who knows? I've nothing to guide myself in this matter. We've never been truly at war, not like this one," he replied. Isabella sensed he was telling her the truth, and she left it at that.

A week later, President Carlos dropped by her home on a Saturday night. "Why hello, President Carlos, do come in. What do I owe this visit? More disasters? I hope not," Isabella said as she opened their front door.

"I am afraid I may have been too harsh with you last week. I come bearing a peace offering. I've tickets for the Grand Ballet tomorrow evening. It is my wish you and your wives would accompany me and my wife to see the performance," he explained, donning a gracious smile.

"Oh. Well, sure, we'd be delighted to go," Isabella replied, uncertain whether or not she ought to accept this potential bribe for her good will.

"Excellent. We will pick you up at say six tomorrow. Oh yes, dress as you would for the Senate meetings. Until tomorrow evening then," he bowed and left.

"What's that all about?" asked Celia Jan. After Isabella explained, she added, "Well, I don't trust that man at all. Still, we've not been to the Grand Ballet yet. Could be interesting."

It turned out to be a very gala affair, but they had a good deal of walking to do to get from the parking lot to their seats. The Senate President held onto his charming wife, as she took her carefully measured steps. She wore the stylish four inch tall platforms and merrily explained how she'd managed to break both her legs and ankles five times now. Of course, she praised their medical machines. Isabella, Gabriella, and Celia clunk to each other as they walked along on their toe boots. Yes, already they had opted for the boot version since that gave them more support. Still, their feet were aching by the time they finally reached their seats, which were good ones. President Carlos certainly had political pull; Isabella granted him that point.

The evening went well, and both he and his wife invited the trio to join them next Sunday at an opera performance. Seeing no easy way to decline their offer, Isabella agreed. Before long, Senator Carlos and his wife insisted on taking them to some performance or other nearly every weekend.

Slowly, Isabella's curiosity began to rise. Why were they treating them with obviously preferential treatment? Still, she refused to probe his mind. That would be a sure giveaway she too was a telepath. Until now, she hoped the yellow eyes with brown speckles was not a known trait here on Proxima Prime.

During the long week meetings of the Senate, more and more war news was reported. By late summer, the Senate was making requests of some of the Closed Worlds to provide more iron and rarer elements. Jenkins agreed in principle, asking for the schools program to resume. He received his wish. Ashford-5 received no such request, since there were no heavier elements on the planet.

Late summer, President Carlos announced to the full Senate, "Next week, we are going to be honored by a visit of one of the queens from the Ataro Empire of the Twelve Sacred Planets of the Wasp! This is a very formal state visit by Her Majesty. Make sure you are all looking your best. She will give a short speech to the full Senate on Monday morning, if all goes as planned."

"Well, you will certainly get something to look at!" Gabriella Amy declared in no uncertain terms when Isabella returned that evening and told them about the state visit.

"Sorry, I don't know anything about this Ataro Empire," Isabella explained.

Amy and Jan sure did! Celia Jan quickly brought up the old web page she and Amy had viewed so long ago, complete with images. Isabella started in disbelief and read.

> The emperor and empress of the wasp cult have kept the peace in the Ataro System for nearly two millennia. Chosen to fill these posts at birth, their bodies are modified shortly after birth. Internal organs are moved and the characteristic waist binding is done at that time. In the adults, waists are extremely tiny, giving rise to the illusion of wasps, which these worlds hold sacred and worship. Additionally, the chosen one's feet are also modified at birth so that their feet end up with super high arches, the front of their heels aligning with the rear

of their toes. Wearing their special shoes, they appear to have wasp-like feet. Additionally, the arms of the chosen ones are also removed at birth.

The reason for these drastic body modifications, seen as barbaric on some worlds, lies in the absolute power the emperor and empress wield over their system of planets. Their word is law and binding. To offset that immense power, the high priests of the Holy Wasps remove their rulers' arms and hobble their feet so the emperor and empress cannot abuse the mighty powers entrusted to them.

Their children are similarly handled at birth and when they reach adulthood, they are sent off as their representatives to various planets within the Ataro System. Called kings and queens, they have total power and adjudicate disputes, subject only to the emperor and empress.

While seen as brutal treatment on many other worlds, within the Ataro System, this practice has produced over two millennia of peace. There has not been an open conflict for over two thousand years, quite unlike the Imperium, in this reporter's opinion.

"Incredible," Isabella murmured. "Now we know where these pipe corsets probably originated and the toe boots too. Honestly, how can they possibly survive living like that? We need to hold onto each other just to walk. So their queen will look much like this. Thanks for the heads up." Neither Gabriella Amy nor Celia Jan wanted to talk about this. They'd spent far too many years in similar straits. Isabella added, "Well, they do have a point about constraining those in power. Novel, I suppose."

Come Monday morning, Isabella was not surprised with the appearance of Queen Altha. President Carlos announced her formally, "We are highly honored this morning with the appearance of Queen Altha of the Ataro Empire of the Twelve Sacred Planets of the Wasp. Please, let's give her a very warm welcome." The woman had very long blonde hair that fell in curls to nearly her ankles, draped like a cloak over her back. She had very full breasts, though nowhere as large as Isabella's were. Her waist appeared to be even smaller than hers was, and Isabella guessed it might not even be a foot around. Her yellow satin gown fit her form tightly, giving her a very waspish look indeed, accentuated by her shiny, black toe shoes. She had, of course, no arms. However, she did have a servant, who looked almost same as she did, except the woman did have arms with which to assist her queen.

Taking small, measured steps, Queen Altha walked to the center of the central platform, and then faced the many rising rows of Senators. Isabella sensed extreme confidence coming from this young woman, who she guessed must have been in her late twenties at most.

"It gives me great pleasure to be allowed to address the full Senate of the great Imperium. I bring you all a warm welcome from the emperor himself and from the Ataro Empire." She said a few more similar remarks and then launched into her main speech. "I have come today to address you because of this war you are fighting against the Federation of Planets. As you know or in case you don't know, wars have been eliminated among the thirty-six planets of the Ataro Empire. We have not had a war for over two millennia now." A loud round of applause greeted this declaration.

"Now you may be wondering how it is we have achieved such a remarkable feat. I've been asked to share our wisdom with you today in hopes my small speech may help you with your current war efforts. Our basic philosophy is ultimate power must be tempered with ultimate restrictions. On one of the planets in our empire, I rule absolutely. My word is utter law. Yet, as you can see, I cannot physically abuse that immense power placed upon me. Eons ago, our philosophers realized that power corrupts. The greater the power that is wielded, the greater is the probability it will lead ultimately to great corruption. Personally, I might add, this is particularly so among men and not so much among women. But then, that is my own observation."

"Here in the heart of the Imperium, you believe in an alternative system of power checks. You, the illustrious Senators, you make the laws that govern our mighty, far-flung empire. Your Justice Halls try those who break them, while your Supreme High Council and President carries out those laws. However, I ask you all to consider this. Could it be your system has somehow broken down? You are embroiled in a huge war spanning many, many planets. The Ataro Empire, while we are naturally doing our best to assist in this war — we ourselves do not have such a breakdown. Our system of physical restraints upon ultimate powers has worked flawlessly for over two millennia and is continuing to work. I've come here today to suggest to you that you might wish to consider modifying your organization and base it on that of the Ataro Empire. Wars can be prevented."

"As a queen, I know how wars and conflicts start, and they are *not* the causes your leaders have put forth as the reasons. We have long ago discovered the underlying truth of all conflicts. I will share this with you today. In order for two parties to join in open conflict, there *must* have been a *third* person, known to both and yet *hidden* from view. That third person has been spreading lies and untruths to each of the two main parties. For example, suppose that Senator Isabella Valen from Ashford-5 comes up to me and tells me Senator Carlos is an evil man. She tells me all the terrible things that he has done. Then, she goes to Senator Carlos and tells him what an awful woman I am. She tells him may lies about the wicked things I've caused. How long do you think it would take before Senator Carlos and I to come to blows?" She added in a jest, "Assuming that I had arms with which to strike him." Many Senators chuckled at her tease. "Sorry Senator Carlos and Senator Isabella. I chose you two at random. But do you all see how this can work? Pass this along to your High Command. Perhaps it is not too late to perform an investigation and ferret out the truly guilty third person, who has in fact caused this war in the first place."

"If you wish to learn more, I will be here through the weekend. Please come and visit me. Further, if you wish to adopt the ways of placing physical restraints on those with physical powers, our emperor has told me that he is willing to come to Proxima Prime to help you work out the many details. Thank you all for giving me the time to address you today. I look forward to visiting with you and to see the marvelous sights of this beautiful world." She bowed slightly and accepted a loud round of applause before making her slow, careful way off the platform.

Her talk became the center of many discussions on Monday. Later that night, Isabella told Gabriella Amy and Celia Jan what the queen had said. Her words were all too familiar to both women. At last, Amy and Jan decided to tell Isabella about their past lifetime as Tierra's first emperor and empress. Isabella was shocked and listened spellbound to their long story. "I had no idea! From what I know from others, at least you brought many years of peace to Tierra, before the lords managed to regain control from the emperor and empress."

Gabriella Amy sighed, "It was futile. I made mistakes. The biggest one was in who would become the next emperor when the older one died. I failed to set up the administration that would have been needed to ensure the lords could not have done what they did to circumvent my wishes. Ah well, it's past history now."

Celia Jan put in, "But the queen is right about the source of all conflicts, her third person. We've seen that in operation so many times it isn't funny. All you have to do is look — observe. It seems the Imperium can't look." All three laughed.

That Sunday, Senator Carlos invited the trio to join them. They were taking Queen Altha to the Royal Ballet. As they rode in the shuttle, Queen Altha said, "I hope you don't mind my picking on you, Senator Isabella. I asked for the names of the leader of the Senate and the most junior Senator."

"Not at all. I found your talk very illuminating," Isabella replied. "I can see you have a hard road to walk. Life must be rather difficult for you, restrained as you are, physically, I mean."

Queen Altha laughed. "Yes, I can just barely walk. It is so hard to keep my balance without my assistant helping me. I was frightened I might take a tumble there on the platform in front of all of you senators. Truly, I am most restrained. I need my assistant for nearly everything, but that ensures I will not be able to abuse the awesome powers placed on my shoulders, you see. Even if I wanted to take a bribe, what good would it do me? I can't even touch a coin or a gem. I certainly cannot overeat, like yourselves. No, physically, I can do so very little that it balances out the immense power I alone wield on my world."

"Might I ask you a question about your government?" Gabriella Amy asked.

"Sure, I'm honored you wish to know more," she replied with a sweet smile.

"How does your world keep other lords from overthrowing your throne and your emperor? I mean there are power hungry men and women in all civilizations who want to grab power for themselves. How is your empire able to keep those from undoing all that you have achieved?" she asked.

She answered, "With our absolute power comes a heavy responsibility to always pick the best replacements. When the emperor gets too old, he picks his successor based on the very best man in the empire to fill his shoes. Likewise with all we queens. We are handpicked to be the best, most qualified for the position. Only a couple of times has a queen died unexpectedly, but always then, the emperor personally intervenes until the new queen is ready to take her office back. If we did not do it this way, then you are right, we could get a weak leader, which might give the power hungry a foothold. I assure you that we all take this enormous responsibility very seriously."

That's where you went wrong, dear, Celia Jan sent Gabriella Amy, who smiled.

The trio held hands supporting each other in their giant gowns, while Senator Carlos did the same with his wife and Queen Altha's assistant did for her. As they prepared to take their seats, the assistant carefully adjusted the queen's hair so that she would not sit on it. It was apparent the assistant was unable to speak. Celia Jan just remembered that detail and inwardly sympathized with the woman.

About this same time, back on Ashford-5, a fleet of Federation battle cruisers dropped out of hyperspace high above the planet. Almost simultaneously, a fleet of Imperium battle cruisers also appeared. As Ken later told Isabella, the sky lit up like some kind of dizzying array of streaking fires. Governor Konrad and thousands of others on Tierra witnessed the intense battle. The governor knew what the enemy's target was: the fuel refineries on the pale blue moon Palidez. As the stunned surface dwellers watched, massive explosions destroyed battle cruisers right and left.

Then the unthinkable happened. One enemy cruiser got through the Imperium lines and attacked the refinery directly! A massive explosion followed shortly. A brilliant yellow light dwarfed the dim light from the orange-red sun for all of a minute! Konrad's geologist later reported the explosion had shattered the moon, fracturing it into billions of pieces. However, somehow the pieces defied all know science and reformed back into a solid moon, wholly inexplicably.

After that, the remaining Federation of Planets battle cruisers jumped back into hyperspace ending the battle. Governor Konrad knew at once the Imperium had just lost that battle. Their precious refinery was destroyed. He began to worry now.

Deep within the molten core of Ashford-5, the Goddess Lysandra roused Alleric. *Do something before all is destroyed!*

Damn! Who are these interlopers? Relax, I am on it, Alleric sent back, sweeping up out of the core of the planet into the near absolute zero of space. As the pale blue moon began to disintegrate into thousands of shards, he expanded around them and compacted the pieces back together, reforming Palidez once more, as he had done millennia ago. *There you are, my pretty moon.* A giant cloud of dust and pieces of debris floated ever so slowly away from the restored moon. In time, the mixture would descend upon Tierra below.

A week later, Sector ID Minister Emeryk contacted Governor Konrad. "It's gone. We've lost the entire refinery.

High Command has issued a full-scale retreat from the Rim Sector 15. You are hereby ordered to pack up everything and prepare to evacuate Ashford-5. Protocol 103. Follow it exactly. You are to be on the last shuttle flight at nine in the morning on the first of September, Konrad. If you miss that flight, you will be stranded on Ashford-5, perhaps for the rest of your life. So for god's sake, man, don't miss it! You will rendezvous with my battle cruiser. We're heading to Base 43 for major repairs from the damage we sustained in that attack. Protocol 103. Follow it exactly. Over and out."

"But, but," Konrad muttered too late. The connection was severed and he dare not call his boss back. Protocol 103. Where the devil was it at, he wondered. An hour later, he read through the protocol for abandoning the base and the world. Dutifully, he began issuing the many orders to his people. Then, he headed over to the Imperial Tower to have them send a message to all the other towers and thus to the many lords of Ashford-5.

> This is Governor Konrad. The war with the Federation of Planets has taken a turn for the worse. As you suspect, they have destroyed our fuel refinery on the moon. As a result, fuel supplies here in the Rim Sector 15 are too limited for the Imperium to continue normal operations. We have no choice but to leave Tierra for now. The base will be closed in six days. It is my fondest wish we will return in a few months, but that depends upon the outcome of the war. In parting, I must say I have loved every minute I've spent here on Tierra and especially all of you wonderful people. Goodbye, but hopefully for just a short while.

"But I don't want to leave Tierra," Neva complained when Konrad told her what was happening.

"My lovely Neva, I don't either, but I have orders I must obey. I have no choice but to leave. Surely, in time we will be able to return. I hope this is just for a few weeks or months," Konrad explained gently. She whined and complained but to no avail, but it was clear to her Konrad was going to leave

Tierra.

That night, she focused and sought out her unknown benefactor, Mario of Modesto. Hastily, she explained what was happening, that the spaceport was shutting down. *Konrad is leaving and he wants me to go with him. I don't want to leave Tierra. Help me. What am I to do?*

Lord Alano thought for a moment. His mind was dizzy with all the confusions in the world that seemed to him to be happening at the same time. Rebellions ran rampant in his lands. *He is your husband. You should go with him and learn all you can about the Imperium and other worlds. Bring that knowledge back to Tierra when you do return. You can then be the Greatest Lady that Tierra has ever had.* He punched her reactive button.

Greatest Lady? Okay then, Mario, I will do it, she sent.

At the same time, Konrad contacted Nadja. *I've received orders to abandon Ashford-5. The fuel refinery is destroyed. There is too little fuel to continue any operations in this rim sector. The Imperium is pulling out of here. If you want to evacuate too, you are welcome to join me. I'm on the last shuttle out of here, at nine in the morning, six days from now. Bring all of your equipment, of course. You can certainly finish up and get all your analyses published later on.*

My god! Abandoning this world? All the rim worlds?

Yes, all of them. The orders come from the highest level. I think the war is going badly, but of course, no one will openly admit to that. Will you need help getting your things here on time?

No. Konrad, I'm staying. I like it here and I want to continue my linguistic studies. I'll be all right for a few months until you all return to Plateau Grado. I appreciate your most generous offer. Is Neva going with you?

I hope so, yes. I know it will be hard for her, but we'll manage somehow. Are you sure you want to stay behind? Lord knows how long you will be abandoned here.

Yes, I'm sure. I've more than enough linguistic work to keep me occupied for years.

Okay then. I will make contact with you as soon as we

return to Ashford-5. Thanks for all your help these many years. He broke the connection with a heavy heart. It seemed to him that she was being abandoned here, thrown to the wolves so to speak.

He was overjoyed to hear Neva say, "Okay, I will leave with you. Do we pack everything?"

"Yes, we pack everything. I am so glad you are coming with me. I don't know how I could live without you," Konrad gushed. His elation was quite real, she sensed, and that pleased her. "We will need to heal our lips too, dear. Those on other worlds do not wear lip plates like we do here. Trust me, you will see soon. I want you to always have others see you as I do, a Great Lady."

At first, she looked at him with a shocked look. All the great ladies here wore the lip plates. Her expression changed as the second sentence arrived. "Oh! They don't? Well, okay. I do trust you, and I do so want to have everyone see I am your Great Lady. Do we have to hurry?"

"One more night as we are — just to remember always — I do so love you, my Neva," Konrad replied, somewhat unwilling to lose the wonderful times they both shared in bed without their lip plates in.

The base was a whirlwind of activities during the ensuing six days. Shuttles came, were loaded, and left almost on an hourly basis. This was quite unusual though. Normally, a giant ship would have descended and taken everyone and all the cargo onboard, before taking off. This wasn't happening. Governor Konrad had little time to ponder the huge significance of this. Everyone seemed to need his direct orders. Chaos reigned. After the fifth day, the spaceport was down to a skeletal crew, just the Governor, Neva, and four others. Following the protocol, Konrad led the four on a complete tour of the empty complex, searching for anything that might have been missed or overlooked. They found only a few small items, which were also crated up.

The next morning, the six ate the last of the food. While Neva and the four waited outside for the shuttle to land, Konrad entered the new base codes into the protection unit. Once set, the base was literally locked down until someone returned and re-entered those codes. By the time he finished, the small shuttle landed. As he joined Neva, the four had loaded the last of the crates. He and Neva stood for a moment looking out over the Goza Mountains to the north, fixing the scene in their minds. Inwardly, Konrad wondered if he would ever see these again. Then, he helped her get aboard. Her toe boots made it a bit of a challenge, and she appreciated his helping hand. As the engines slowly energized, the two watched from the windows. Soon, Neva saw a sight few on Tierra ever had. Slowly, the world began to shrink before their eyes. Before long, a giant spaceship began to grow outside their viewing panes until it dwarfed everything. Thus began a whole new life for the ex-bar maid, Neva de la Nieve Burkhardt.

"Oh my god! They've closed and abandoned the spaceport!" Celia Jan exclaimed loudly, early in the morning. They had slept in, having spent a long night with Senator Carlos and Queen Altha. She'd gotten up to retrieve the encoded message sent the previous day by Ken, well really sent by Bart, his communications expert.

"What?" Isabella yelled back.

"Yes, the Imperium has abandoned all outlying worlds in the Rim Sector 15. Come here; read it for yourself!" Celia Jan exclaimed, pointing to the translated document on her monitor. "Came in yesterday, but we were tied up with the queen."

Isabella and Gabriella Amy hastily slipped on their mule toe shoes and walked carefully over to the monitor. "My god, they really have done it. How will we ever get home?" Isabella asked. "I'd best see what Senator Carlos has to say about this. Yikes, I had best hurry up or I'll be late for the Senate meeting."

Rushing as much as she could, which actually says very little as one cannot truly rush anywhere while wearing toe boots, Isabella just made it to her seat in the Senate, when President Carlos walked to the front of the platform.

"I have terrible news this morning. Our major fuel refinery at Ashford-5 has been destroyed during a massive

Federation attack. Supreme Command has ordered the total evacuation of all our spaceports and bases in the outer Rim Sector 15. There is simply no fuel to conduct any operations there. The effected rim planets that are impacted are Ashford-5, naturally, Agon-3, Gallim-3, Strx-4, Alzone-3, and Zelos-3." He listed several more. "As of this moment, all Imperium forces and personnel have left those systems and are being routed elsewhere."

After a pause allowing many to gasp, he continued, "Unfortunately for the esteemed senators from those six worlds, this means you will be unable to return to your planets anytime in the foreseeable future. Until such time as these world can be reopened once more, I am afraid those senators will have to remain here on Proxima Prime. The senators from the affected Open Worlds will continue to have their vote here in the Senate. For you senators of Closed Worlds, since you do not actually have a vote, I am inclined to allow you to continue to participate in the Senate, representing your worlds. This way continuity can be maintained, should the Imperium be able to reopen the spaceports and bases on those worlds at a later date. Nothing like this has ever happened before, and there are no protocols I am aware of covering this. So I've made this an official Senate President Declaration."

Sensing he was done, another senator called out, "So how badly did we lose that battle there at Ashford-5? Rumors are running rampant."

"I am not at liberty to say," Senator Carlos replied. Still reeling from his words, Isabella touched his mind and got the answer he was purposely withholding. They'd lost five battle cruisers and had four more heavily damaged. Apparently, they'd also destroyed six enemy battle cruisers, but one had done the dirty work.

Other senators barked out other questions, but Isabella was no longer really listening. She could not get home. Until this moment, she'd never doubted that when she was tired of this job, she only had to hop the next flight to Ashford-5. Returning home was dashed! Naturally, this re-stimulated her nearly ninety years of trying to get back home after she had been kidnaped and taken off-world to serve as a wealthy man's telepath. It had taken her eight-six years to get back home, to be precise, including many uses of the rejuvenation machine just to have lived long enough to get back home to a world that had so totally changed while she was gone that she hardly knew the place. Now she was stranded again.

She finally regained control of her upheaval of emotions and focused. She relayed the terrible news to her two wives. After that, she merely sat in her chair, unable to focus or to think clearly. At lunchtime, Senator Jenkins spoke to her, waking her up slightly. "Senator Isabella, this is a disaster. Please, we must all meet tonight. My place, say at six."

"Huh? Yes, yes of course we must. I'll be there," she said, accepting his helping hand to her toes. The group of six ate a very subdued lunch. None had much to say at all. What could they say? They were all stranded here. It seemed it might well be forever!

When she arrived home, supper was waiting. Celia Jan wanted to tell her something, but she was in no mood to listen. Besides, their domestique staff was still present. Then, she had to hustle to make her meeting with the others. She found Senator Helm was quite drunk. He couldn't handle the news at all.

Senator Jenkins was terribly subdued. "I chatted a bit with Senator Carlos after the meeting ended. I think we are likely going to be stranded here for years. He gave me his honest assessment. Until this war is over and they can rebuild that refinery, there is simply insufficient fuel to support any flights to the outer Rim Sector 15. He was hinting at it taking several years or more. What are we to do? Sit here and do nothing? We have no vote and now there is nothing even to lobby the other senators for. I am at a loss. Helm's solution is to remain drunk."

Isabella looked at one blank face after the other. She felt their raw emotions quite keenly, even though she did her best to block them out. They were extremely strong. She recalled her own emotions when she discovered she was now on another world as a young fourteen year old girl. It had taken her an entire year finally to rise above her wildly varying emotions. Then, she recalled what had gotten her out of the depths of misery.

"Learn. Senators, my advice to you all and to your wives as well is to spend all your time learning everything you can learn. Take all the education courses you can find. Learn math, science, engineering, anything. One day, you will all be able to return to your home worlds. When you do, take back with you all that learning and teach your people what you know. That is a goal truly worthy of all your best efforts."

Her words struck a chord in the senators, even the inebriated Senator Helm. Greatly relieved, Senator Jenkins exclaimed, "Brilliant, Isabella! Positively brilliant. Yes, that is precisely what we should do. Learn everything we possibly can. One day, we can bring this vital knowledge back to our worlds. That is a goal far more noble than being a senator here. Gang, we can do this, I know it. We should all meet and see what avenues we can find to learn." Their sense of utter hopelessness slipped behind them, and they began discussing various ways and means to do just that. After a time, Isabella left them, returning to her home several floors below.

As she approached her front door, Senator Carlos came walking up. "Incredibly good timing, Senator Isabella. I was just coming by to see you. The Senate will be taking its usual three-week fall break on Monday. We use this time to return to our home planets, report to our worlds, and to learn what is needed and wanted of us for the winter session. Of course, it is never really winter here; it's always seventy-five degrees, day and night. But you know what I mean. Anyway, Senator Isabella, my wife and I have talked about this, and she is most insistent. Since you and your wives cannot return home and since you have no place to go, we would love to have you accompany us to our home world. Spend the three weeks relaxing on our vast estate; enjoy the sunshine. It is summer on our world now. Please say you'll come. My wife'll kill me if you don't," he jested.

Isabella was too worn out to protest or even to think if this was such a good idea. She only wanted to get out of the uncomfortable dress and relax in bed. "Sure. Okay. When do we leave? What do we bring with us?"

"I'll send a shuttle to pick you three up around nine

tomorrow morning. Pack perhaps one dress. My wife says she'll take you all shopping first thing and don't worry about the cost. It will be our treat. See you tomorrow at the spaceport just after nine. Thank you. She will be very pleased to hear you are coming to visit. I am usually quite busy, and she so enjoys your company. Good night then." He bowed and left. She entered her apartment, but only after struggling with her enormously long nails to get her ID card into the slot to open it.

"Hi all. I'm exhausted. I have the other senators off on a big learning project. Hopefully, this will give them all something beneficial to do until they can return home. Plus, I've agreed to go with Senator Carlos and his wife to their estate during the fall Senate break. We leave at nine tomorrow. We'll be their guests for three weeks."

"Cool on the other senators," Gabriella Amy replied, "but what's this about visiting his estate?"

"I'm too drained to deal with this tonight. We bring one dress; pack light. Leave at nine tomorrow. Can you please help me out of this outfit before I collapse? Never have I felt so utterly drained!" Isabella sighed.

Back on Ashford-5, Josh and his four wives had already seen this bit of future. Again, the future paths diverged at this point. One led to the utter annihilation of all the *mentales* gifted on Tierra; they were being hunted down like wild horses and shipped off-world. Josh did not like what they were seeing down the second path either, but the harming of three would be far better than the destruction of them all. Supported by the solid base of his wives, he pushed an energy drain onto Isabella that night, which shifted the future down the second path, though he still didn't like what he saw would be happening. It was the better of the two alternatives.

Chapter 31 Into Slavery

"There's our beloved Beltzar-4 below us. Isn't it just beautiful — blue, greenish — those are white-grey clouds, but the dark grey ones are thunderstorms," Imelda, the Senator's wife of some twenty-three years chatted happily. Isabella sensed her immense relief at returning to her home world. Even this momentary flicker caused heartache in Isabella, who only nodded, afraid her voice might give away her deeply felt feelings. "And there's our continent — that one there," she pointed with her long nails, accidentally bumping the view windows. "Darn these nails anyway. I can't wait to get them off me. I bet you would like to have yours removed too, if only for three weeks. Honestly, what we women have to put up with," she chatted on, more or less oblivious to Isabella, who was sitting beside her.

"Look there. That's Caltran — our city — there's our local spaceport. We'll land there and take a shuttle to our Amandos Estate. It's about a hundred miles south of the city. Ten million live in Caltran, but that's way too many for us. Thank goodness Carlos bought this estate twenty-one years ago. I can't wait for you to see it. It's just beautiful. Formal gardens — swimming pool — beautiful lawn — there is even a hedge maze. But don't worry, you can't really get lost in it, just always take the turn to the right. Oh, and the statues — they are white marble and so evocative."

"You will just love the ranch style house. It's all on one sprawling floor, so no elevators to deal with. You three will be staying in the west guest wing and will have two personal assistants to help you with your needs. We've a staff of fifty here. Of course, it takes that many just to keep it all running smoothly. Carlos often holds his business meetings here too. So you will probably not see too much of him while we are here. He can't do much business while we are on Proxima Prime, though some of his assistants do continue his work here while we're away, naturally," she continued to chat. Isabella still had not been able to say more than an "uh hu."

She didn't try though, content to just feel the woman's happiness at returning to her home. Isabella realized Imelda hated being cooped up on Proxima Prime. Probably the other senator's wives felt much the same way, she mused.

Soon they landed and several ground crewmen in their unisex, recyclable cat suits lifted the four women in their enormous skirts safely down and out of the transport ship. While Senator Carlos held on to Imelda, Gabriella Amy and Celia Jan held onto either side of Isabella, steadying the three as they followed slowly after their hosts. Behind them, a number of ground crewmen began busily unloading the transport ship. The spaceport was positively huge. Ships were departing and landing, even as they walked some hundred feet to the doorway of the central hub where small electric trains awaited them. Soon they were zipping down long corridors towards the private shuttle craft section on the far south side of the station. Imelda explained that Carlos kept their private shuttle here.

An hour later, the giant city of towering skyscrapers of steel and glass was left behind. Unlike Proxima Prime, Beltzar-4 still had much of its surface untouched by the giant cities. "There it is! Amandos Estates," Imelda gaily exclaimed. Ahead, they passed over an enormous arch from which hung a sign with foreign looking letters on it. Skimming along a hundred feet above the landscape, they got a good view of the low rolling grasslands and park. The manor house was squarely in the center of the estate. The hedge maze was clearly visible as was the swimming pool and formal gardens. The house was shaped like an enormous U with the beginnings of the formal gardens at the center of the U just beyond the tiled area surrounding the blue waters of their pool. The only detrimental aspect from the trio's point of view was the intense brightness of the yellow sun. If only it were a dull orange-red, they would have felt more at home here.

As they entered the U from the backside, the hallway gave way to the spacious living room, where tall glass windows allowed a picture-perfect view of the patio, pool, and beginnings of the formal gardens. To the right of the living room was the master dining room with attached kitchen. On down the long west hallway was a suite of guest rooms. Isabella and her two wives were given the master suite, large enough to hold all three of them. Imelda said, "Let's get changed out of these monster gowns into something simpler. I can't wait to get these tall platforms off my feet. I'll take us all shopping tomorrow and get you some relaxation clothes. These two will help you change," she indicated her two middle aged women, dressed in some kind of simple uniforms. At least they were not the awful cat suits that most all wore.

Their single bag had already been brought to their room. Isabella was surprised to see it there, but then realized they moved so slowly in their toe boots that the workers had simply passed them up. She was still rather hazy in her mind. Graciously, the two older women helped the trio out of the rather complex ball gowns and into their own satin gowns from Tierra. At last, they felt far more comfortable. "The Misses would like you to join her by the pool for some refreshments," one woman finally spoke, translated nicely by her ULAT box and then by each of the trio's boxes. Isabella realized even here these ULAT boxes were a necessity for communication among the vast number of languages spoken throughout the Imperium. Isabella suddenly had a far higher respect for the work Nadja was doing, work which allowed all of these people to be able to communicate with each other, no small feat indeed.

The trio made their way down the low pile, carpeted hallway to the bottom of the U where they saw open doors. Just beyond them, they spotted Imelda. She too had changed and was wearing a light cotton dress and flats. She was lying back on a lawn chair with a small table nearby. Glasses and a pitcher of fruit juice sat invitingly upon it. "Ah, there you are. Please, come and relax. Have some fruit punch. It is simply delicious, the best. Ah, I do so enjoy just relaxing after all those weeks confined on that metallic planet. Sit, sit. Here, have some punch. Take a load off your feet, er toes I guess. Now me," she continued chatting while pouring each a tall glass of the fruit punch.

"I decided to accept the many broken ankles and legs and wear those awful tall platforms rather than have my feet modified like yours. I know, you three can walk so much better than I can and without the constant danger of a misstep and fracture, but at times like these, I can once again wear flats. Sit, sit, lie back, and breathe deeply. Well, as deeply as we women can in these pipe corsets. I do so hate that metal smell of Proxima Prime. Can you smell the grass?"

"Thank you, Imelda. It is truly beautiful here. I can see why you so love this estate from the little we have seen of it. It is perfect," Isabella complimented her hostess. "Ah, the punch is quite delicious. Thanks. I admit. It is very refreshing not to have to smell Proxima Prime. So sterile." The women continued to chat, and Isabella felt she could really come to love an estate such as this one. True, she had lived on many that were somewhat similar during her early years off-world as a telepathic slave. This place felt somehow different though.

Time slipped by the four. Overhead, the clouds moved gently by. Time seemed to move so slowly. Then, the clouds seemed to darken. Isabella knew she should be alarmed. Perhaps a storm was coming. But then her hostess would surely have them move indoors if it came. Her glass felt so heavy in her hand. Oops. Her grip loosened, and she saw the glass falling, as if in slow motion. So pretty. The shattering pieces moved in many directions, but at the speed of a horned snail. Something was wrong! Her mind sensed danger. She tried to sit up. She couldn't. Slowly darkness descended over her. Beside her, Gabriella Amy and Celia Jan had already blacked out. Isabella's last vision was of them before she saw and felt no more.

She didn't consciously hear Carlos and some others speaking. "Sorry Imelda. I had to do it. You will understand tomorrow. Okay, men, carry them into my workroom in the east wing." Strong hands lifted the three women. Heavy footsteps marked the long walk from the patio to the far east end.

Isabella finally came too. She was in an unfamiliar room. Some hideous smell woke her sharply up. She felt dull pains from her waist, breasts, lips, neck, feet, and arms. Something was terribly wrong. Senator Carlos stood out in front of her. She blinked and raised her hands to her face.

They weren't there. Two nicely conical stumps came upwards. Her lower arms and hands were missing. Now she saw the foot in diameter lip plates that all the lords and ladies were wearing back on Tierra. But she couldn't move her neck or head. Her breasts felt terribly heavy, and she could scarcely breathe. *Focus! Focus! What's happening?*

"Ah awake at last, Isabella. Good. Now we can talk some. You and your two wives are Ashford-5 telepaths. No need to bother even denying it. Your yellow eyes gave that away when I first met you. You see, I have been carefully planning this for many months. The convenience of the loss of the refinery on Ashford-5 only makes this easier for me. You three are now going to be working for me, using your telepathic skills to assist me in making highly advantageous business deals."

He sneered and continued. "You see, don't bother to try talking. Konrad told me how widespread these monstrous lip plates are among your wealthier class on Ashford-5. I had him send me three sets, along with the medical machine's script used to install them properly. Of course, now your ULAT box will be wholly unable to translate your speech. It is unrecognizable to the translator box. To communicate with me, you have no choice but to use your telepathic powers." He laughed heartily. "If I do say so myself, this was a brilliant piece of work. Now then, I've removed your lower arms and hands and those of your wives. This way, you can't escape. I saw how much you enjoyed the Royal Ballet, so I took the liberty of modifying your feet as well. I have fused your feet into the ballet en pointe position. Now you must wear these marvelous ballet boots. You see, now you are all my ballerinas, though I am told walking will be exceedingly difficult, most precarious. Ah, but then as the years progress, you will adapt and be my gorgeous telepathic ballerinas. So you see, you cannot even attempt to just walk away from here."

He went on. "I was so inspired by the visit of Queen Altha that I went ahead and further modified your waists down to the twelve inch waistline the queen has. Now you three match hers. Impressive. However, in order to get them so reduced, I took the liberty of taking some years off your bodies. The rejuvenation machine lowered your bodies' ages to eighteen so that the medical machine could further reduce your waists to twelve inches. I hope you don't mind being eighteen again." He laughed heartily, like this was some kind of joke to him.

"I also had a brilliant idea to help disguise your planet of origin. Rutha Baath of Strx-4 gave me the inspiration. Now you three have basketball boobs, just like hers. Don't worry. I've made the proper measurements for your new gowns. Twenty inches larger than just under your boobs — Imelda told me how to measure properly your new sizes. Anyone who is curious will automatically believe you are from Strx-4, particularly so since you will not be able to speak and be understood by anyone. Sometimes, I even amaze myself."

"Yes, I had access to all of your Governor Konrad's files on his previous assignments. I took the further liberty of making you three a fancy set of neck rings similar to those that the handless women of Karlson-3 wear. His report stated those women have just perfect posture. Nothing is too fine for my new telepaths. Indeed, no one will recognize you or your planet of origin now, and you cannot speak and tell them otherwise. I know, Isabella, I am truly brilliant. I didn't get all my wealth by playing fair. Only fools play fair."

"Don't worry. I've assigned some of my servants to attend to your many needs. However, in return, you will use your telepathic skills to assist me in my business dealings, starting tomorrow. I was going to say nod your head if you agree to assist me, but now I see that will be impossible for you to do. I guess you can just bend forward a little to indicate you are willing now to work for me. So, Isabella, do you and your wives agree to be my telepaths and help me secure lucrative deals? Bend forward a little if you consent," he said sharply.

Panic had been slowly creeping into her mind, like an insidious ravenous beast. Her stomach knotted. She tried to move her head to the left or right, but her neck was immobilized. "Oh, you need to see how your wives look?" he sneered. "Okay, I think you must pivot in your chair to see them. They are behind you, but they are only just now coming around."

Isabella strained every muscle in her body, gasping for breath, but she manage to pivot enough to see them from the corner of her eyes. They both looked just as he had been describing how she appeared. Panic flooded over her like a bursting dam. Trembling, she did her best to shake her head "no!"

"No? Are you saying that you will not help me now? Oh Isabella, you so disappoint me. I am not a man to be toyed with!" He grew angry, and Isabella thought that, if he would just kill her now, she would be put out of her misery. She waited for the blow that was sure to come. She'd seen many angry fits in her nearly century of abuse. It didn't come, though.

"Okay then, you need more persuasion!" He forced her body back into the medical machine.

"What are you doing to me now? Just kill me!" she gushed, but heard her ULAT box speaking, "Error. Unknown language. Error. Unknown language." Over and over until she shut up.

As if guessing what she wanted to say, he stated, "What am I doing now? Removing what's left of your arms. Now you will be just like Queen Altha. Won't that be just grand?" She screamed to no avail. A few minutes later, he lifted her out of the machine and sat her back stiffly in her chair. Isabella tried to raise what was left of her arms, but saw nothing at all this time. From the very corners of her eyes, she saw her now empty shoulders and let out a terrified scream before passing out from lack of breath.

The next thing she knew, there was that hideous smell in her nose, but try as she might, she couldn't move her head and nose away from that stench. She roused. "Ah, back again, Isabella. Now you do look precisely like Queen Altha, well except for the boobs. Now you are even more helpless, Isabella. I ask you once again, will you and your wives use your telepathic skills to help me with my business dealings? If you continue to refuse, I will remove your feet and then your legs. I don't care if you end up as a head and torso. I've special wheel chairs to move you around if need be. Or perhaps I should also remove what's left of your wives' arms?"

589

That struck a nerve in Isabella. It was one thing to mutilate her and quite another to do it to those two who were blameless in this mess. *Stop! Stop it! I agree!* She placed into his mind, as if shouting.

His hands involuntarily covered his ears, as if that could somehow dampen her mental shout. "Not so damned loud. Okay. Accepted. Now then, your new servants will come and get you dressed in some new form fitting gowns. I had them specially made for your new body shapes a month ago. I do hope you like them. The servants will then help you to get to your suite, your new home for the rest of your lives. Tomorrow, I have an important business meeting which you three will attend and use your telepathic skills to make sure they are not cheating me. Now I had best wake up Imelda. She was knocked out by the punch too. I will have to explain about you telepaths to her, but I'm sure she will understand. We'll see you at suppertime. Imelda will still want to be seen as the gracious hostess that she is. Until supper then," he rose and left the room. Three silent older servant women entered carrying some new satin dresses.

Isabella fought against her rising panic once more. The servants slipped her new blue satin gown on her and zipped it up. Now the woman urged her to stand up. As she attempted to do so, her utter immobility and lack of arms turned her stomach into a solid knot. She wobbled wildly, unable to find any way to keep her balance. She did see her two wives wildly waving their short upper arms around, helping them, but only a little. These knee-high ballet style boots made standing beyond difficult.

As Isabella stood there immobile, terrified of taking the first step, she suddenly felt an overwhelming calm descending upon her. Finally, her body relaxed. *That's better. We should be able to walk now. We've been walking without seeing our feet beneath those twelve-foot skirts for months now. This isn't much different,* Gabriella Amy sent her.

You? Thanks! I lost it all there. Okay, you are right, I hope, Isabella sent back. Tentatively she began walking. Soon, she found it little different from before, except that she had no easy way to counter the occasional wobble. Plus, her massive bosom continually kept her off balance. Each time her panic rose up, she attempted to fight it back down. Never was she so thankful to sit down on a soft chair in her bedroom. She was panting for breath. and she heard the others doing likewise.

I'll kill him the next time I see him! I swear I will, Isabella sent.

Not yet, Isabella. Give me time to see about making an escape, Celica Jan sent back. *It is so damned hard to breath, but if I remember right, in time we will adjust. Isn't that right, Gabriella?*

Yes, it will just take a good deal of getting used to this immense pressure. Isabella, don't do anything rash just yet. Give Celia Jan some time to work this out, Gabriella Amy sent. Their three helper servants proceeded to brush out their hair, which had become rather tangled up during the lengthy procedures Carlos had performed on them. The three sat like the marble statues on some lawn. Finally satisfied, the three servants left them alone.

"I'm going to try talking, can you understand me?" Celia Jan ventured. At least Carlos had switched their ULAT boxes to receive only. She didn't hear any more of those silly error messages she'd heard coming from the box around Isabella's waist.

"Sort of. We must sound like the lords and ladies now," Isabella answered. "I can hardly understand what I am saying. Can you understand me at all?"

"Barely. Take it slow. Okay, gang. I had a hunch something wasn't right. So I took some precautions before we left. If I don't get to a computer network and send a message to mine back in our home within a week, then my safety net will activate," Celia Jan explained.

"What safety net? How can anyone help us now? We are doomed. I can't live like this," Isabella almost whined, suppressing her grief and misery. "It's all my fault. I don't know what came over me last night. I should have been more alert. It's my fault; it's all my fault."

"Isabella, I don't think so. You were under some kind of strange spell or something when you got back. I could sense something was operating upon you, but what I didn't know. So

I made sure to activate my safety net," Celia Jan replied.

"Someone was making me so dopey?" Isabella asked. "That would make more sense. I seemed so utterly exhausted that I just went along with Carlos to get him out of the way."

"Someone was doing something to you, but it wasn't Carlos. He is a dead-head. Anyway, in a week, it will activate," Celia Jan said.

"What will active, love?" Gabriella asked.

"My system will send a message to Carl telling him that we are in bad trouble. It will tell him to expect a new ID card in the post on Monday. It will tell him to use it to sneak into our home and to pack up all our things, putting them into shipping crates. It will tell him how to ship them. Once he does that, the rest will occur automatically. Bogus shipping orders will eventually get our things to safety where no one can find them. But before we escape from here, Carlos must pay dearly for this treachery, and I need about two hours on a computer system to make that happen. I will launch my Credit Dispersal Program," Celia Jan declared.

"What are you talking about?" Isabella asked. Gabriella Amy grinned, but suddenly realized that her grin was no longer visible because of the huge lip plates.

Celia Jan explained, "Once I have found his accounts, my program will remove all the credits but one from each of his accounts. The credits all go into a single account on Proxima Prime, which, if he is any good at all, he can discover for himself. However, once there, that sum is subsequently broken down into small credit transfers to thousands of accounts all over the galaxy, giving the appearance of one's money simply evaporating into thin air. From those small accounts, a timed transfer goes to other accounts. Eventually, it all ends up back here in my Tierra account that we setup years ago. It will be untraceable. Once I've launched my Credit Bomb Program, then we can escape. Never mess with Sly Fox and Eager Beaver. Dear, are we still going to use those pseudonyms?"

"Sure," Gabriella Amy replied, wishing she could see her grin. But then they would have to use their feet to pivot their bodies just to see each other. The neck rings were extremely debilitating.

"I don't understand all this. But what good will it do us to have all his credits?" Isabella asked. "I'm completely helpless now."

"I need to recoup my er — recent expenses," Celia Jan answered. "I sort of got all carried away back there on Proxima Prime. So many new goodies to play with and acquire. I rather spent most of our fortune, Gabriella Amy. Now I will just get some of it back from Carlos."

"Celia Jan!" Gabriella Amy said with a distinct annoyance in her tone, indicating in no uncertain terms that she was quite concerned. "We had billions. What could you have spent it all on?"

"Our own deep space transport ship. I outfitted it with all the latest goodies, among other things. I'm sorry, Amy, I felt like a child in a toy store. I'll get it back for us from Carlos. He must be loaded."

"A ship? You mean we could use it to get home?" Gabriella Amy asked incredulously.

"Yes. Well, at least I think so. Not sure on its range. Might have to refuel somewhere along the line. Don't worry; it's well hidden on Proxima Prime. All we have to do is get there somehow," Celia Jan answered.

"You devil you! Well done, love, well done indeed! Sly Fox strikes yet again!" Gabriella Amy exclaimed.

"I don't believe what I'm hearing," Isabella whispered, suddenly very excited. "You got us a ship that could take us to Tierra?"

"Yep. And lots of other goodies too. So please, Isabella, let's play along with this bastard a while until I can get my Credit Bomb Program going and find us a way to get back to Proxima Prime," Celia Jan replied.

"I could kiss you, but I can't move!" Isabella replied. "Don't worry. I can handle anyone who tries to stop us. I am quite skilled in all manner of attacks. Why did Carlos have to mutilate our bodies so badly?"

Gabriella took the initiative to answer this one. "He needed to make sure that we are unable to communicate to others via the ULAT boxes. Hence the lip plates. We are now going to be unable to talk to anyone, except via telepathy, which we dare not do broadly. Others might get the bright idea to kidnap us from Carlos. He needed to make us completely dependent on others so we don't just get up and walk away, that's why the loss of our hands and your arms. He needed to make sure we are not easily recognized as being from Ashford-5, hence the monster boobs and the tiny waists, which are like the Ataro System and that other world. The neck rings are just his being sadistic, I think."

Celia Jan interjected, "But he has no idea with whom he is dealing. Us. Say, Isabella, how good are you with telekinesis?"

"Not very good at all. I've been able to move a piece of paper, that's about all. Pathetic. My gifts lie in other areas," she replied.

"Well, we need to delay some, while we get your telekinesis skills greatly enhanced," Gabriella Amy declared with a note of determination.

"But you can't change what gifts you were born with," Isabella protested.

"Little known fact, Isabella. Any *mentales* gifted can learn to do anything on that old Marisol's list of gifts. It just takes a lot of practice and patience. So the first thing that we have to do here is to get your telekinetic skills up to par. You will need them to get by on your own," she replied. "Time's a wasting. Let's get started. See if you can lift up a bit of your hair. Conveniently, they have left it draped across your front so you can more or less see some of it."

Thus began weeks of training for Isabella. For most of the time, the trio was left alone, sitting in their bedroom suite. At these times, Gabriella Amy continued to drill and drill Isabella. After a few days, she slowly began to make progress. Amy knew in time this would work. Before they made their great escape, she needed Isabella to be able to be somewhat independent. She had no hands with which to help her.

Late that first afternoon, the servants came again to escort them to the plush dining room. Again, the trio fought the panic that threatened to overwhelm them, as they precariously tried to get to their feet without falling over. Then came the long walk to the room, leaving all three gasping for breath.

"Oh there you are. I am so sorry for all this," Imelda chatted to them, as if nothing terrible had been done to them. "I never had the slightest clue you three had strong telepathic abilities. But then, I suppose I ought to have had, since you are from Ashford-5. Everyone knows they all have telepathy there. It is so good of you to help dear Carlos with his business deals. I am so glad you will be staying here at the estate. I am sure you will find it so utterly lovely, especially the formal gardens. I will have to take you all on that tour of them, you know. I haven't forgotten I promised you that. Well, perhaps tomorrow, as it is getting late. Oh, yes, please sit beside them, and I suppose you will have to feed them too. Isn't it nice to have such willing and able servants around. Of course, they do cost us a fortune, but they do such a nice job of everything. I just know you will get only the best care from them." She finally stopped chatting, having just filled her mouth with a bite of the roasted bird.

Carlos, who had been silent, now spoke up, "Ladies, this is my original telepath, Hernando Gervasi. Yes, he is blind. He's been with me for quite a long time. Rejuvenation, naturally. Telepaths are so damn hard to come by, you see. Anyway, you four will attend my business meeting tomorrow and use your telepathic skills. You see, I don't yet trust you three, so Hernando here will be able to let me know if you are lying to me. Clever, don't you think? Oh, you can't talk, can you? How sad. No one can hear your tale. But then no one would believe you anyway. I am the President of the Imperium Senate." He could not help but boast and brag. The three mostly ignored him, biding their time. At least in three weeks, he would he back on Proxima Prime and out of their hair for a time.

Time was just what these three needed most right now. At least after dinner, the servants unlatched their lip plates, allowing them to drape down to their chins. Now their massive bosoms blocked their vision, which they found just as annoying, as they made their treacherous way back to their suite. Later, the servants undressed them and prepared them for bed. Thankfully, they removed their lip plates before helping them get into bed. At least Imelda had the good sense to have their toe mules placed beside their beds in case they needed to get up to use the bathroom during the night. Their feet were rigidly frozen pointing downwards, and they simply could not walk without the slip-on toe mules. The three spent a very miserable night.

After breakfast, their servants led them into a room in the East Wing, sitting them on chairs at the back wall, beside the blind man, Hernando. Shortly, Senator Carlos and three other men dressed in fine business suits entered. An hour later, they left, and Carlos was satisfied with their telepathic work. They dared not tweak it because of Hernando's presence. They were left alone in their room for most of the day, during which they worked on Isabella's telekinetic skills.

The next morning, Carlos again used them for another business meeting. However, after lunch, Imelda insisted on taking them on a tour of her formal gardens. She seemed utterly oblivious to the panic the three women felt as she insisted on leading them around the gardens. They would have fallen many times, if their servants had not been there to catch them. Worse, all three were soon gasping for air, but again Imelda seemed not to notice their extreme discomfort.

Slowly the days passed until at last, Senator Carlos announced over supper, "Well, tomorrow it is back to the Senate meetings once more. The servants will look after you, until we return in about three months. At that time, I will have far more business to conduct. Oh, you might also look after Hernando. He can't see and does need some help getting around too, you know."

"Oh yes," Imelda spoke up. "You are free to wander through the gardens and out on the lawn. The perimeter guards will make sure you are safe and that no one can get inside the walls of the estate. You can even use the pool, if you desire, though I am not sure how that will work. Anyway, our house is your house, as we Beltzars always say. Besides, this is your new home now. Enjoy. I surely do."

After breakfast the next day, the trio found themselves alone at last. Isabella's point of view was her tormentors had gone at last. Many of the fifty estate workers also left. Only a token crew remained. Their servants began talking more as one might expect. The masters were away. "You'd best get to your rooms now," one spoke up. For a moment, Isabella panicked. *Does she think that I can do this by myself? Are they going to make us fend for ourselves now that Carlos is gone? Oh god no!* "Up you go. Come on, you can't be as lazy as the master claims."

Squelching her rising panic as much as she could, Isabella lunged upwards to get to her feet, jarring the table and spilling some juice. "Okay, don't get your titties in a sweat, dearie," the servant said jokingly. She put her arm around Isabella's waist, steadying her. Before long, they were safely in their rooms sitting on their sofa chairs once more.

"Well, I sort of figured we would get far worse care once they left. Looks like I guessed right," Gabriella Amy declared. "We best continue working on your telekinesis, Isabella. You have to be able to use it to maintain your balance, if possible. You know, push and pull on your body."

"I'm never going to be able to do this," Isabella broke down, crying again. "I'm hopeless and I've drug you down with me."

"No you haven't. We're all in this together," Celia Jan countered. "We aren't abandoning you either. So get with the program." She talked sternly. That was enough to get Isabella to stop sobbing and at least to continue trying. She added, "Look, already we are adapting to the overly tight corset now. We're not gasping for breath after just walking to and from the dining room. That's a start." She didn't add that they would need to be able to walk long distances, if they were to make good on their escape plans.

While Isabella definitely had a terrible time, Gabriella Amy and Celia Jan were not in good shape either. Constrained as they were, in order to turn their vision beyond straight ahead, they had to take some small steps in place, turning their whole bodies to face a different direction. While they still had their upper arms, they were pretty much useless except for helping them with their balance a very little bit or to steady themselves by pressing against a door jam, for example. Both knew somehow they had to get the awful neck rings off their necks. Otherwise, escape might not be possible.

Ideally, Celia Jan thought, *we should get our lips healed and boobs back to a reasonable size, lose the corset, and while we're at it, get our feet partially healed at least. That means I need to find his medical machine, besides his computer.* The next morning after they returned to their suite from breakfast, she announced, "Okay, Gabriella Amy, you work with Isabella. It is time I start exploring this place. I've got to find a couple things."

"Okay, love, but what things? Oh, I get it," Gabriella Amy replied, picking up her lover's intention.

"Wish me luck. I am sure glad the servants are now lowering our lip plates after eating. If I take a fall, at least I won't kill myself by jamming them into my skull," she replied. Carefully she got to her feet, waving her stumps about until she was steady. She headed out of the room taking slow, measured, but unseen steps in her sturdy toe boots. She had no idea where either of the two things would be located; the estate home was huge. She also knew the servants must have rooms in the building as well, and she certainly didn't want to run into them. If she did, they might just decide they didn't need any more help walking, and Isabella certainly did. She decided to explore the West Wing first, since their suite was here, the very first set of rooms.

She walked down the carpeted hall to the next door. Here, she paused and listened for sounds. Hearing none, she carefully took several small steps in place, turning her body around to make sure that no one was watching her. Seeing none, she took several more steps and again faced the door. She focused on the door and her crystal activated. The door opened and she peered inside. One glance told her that this was a servant's quarters. She focused. Again, her crystal activated and the door closed. She moved on down the hallway. An hour later, she'd finished the West Wing. Here were the servant's quarters and the other blind telepath's room. Rather exhausted by her exertion, she returned to her own suite to sit down a while.

While shallow panting, Celia Jan began to think about

the rest of the huge building. It was highly likely the many servants would be in the main U area where the kitchen was located along with the main living room and such. Carlos would not leave such equipment there. She needed to examine the East Wing, but how to get by the many servants remained unknown. Celia Jan considered her options, too few for her liking. If she just walked past the servants, she had no doubt they would react in one of two ways. They might just stop her from going on — Carlos might have told them the East Wing was off limits or they just might not allow her to go walking around on her own. After all, they were under the servants' care. On the other hand, the servants might just decide, since she was getting around well enough on her own, they would no longer assist the three women while walking. *I can handle that, but Isabella can't, not just yet. My hands are tied.* She laughed sarcastically; she didn't have them any longer.

Before long, the three servants came to lead them down to lunch. While they were being fed, the head woman said, "This afternoon, you ladies are going outside near the pool. You need some sunshine. You're looking too pale. Hernando, you go with them and keep them out of mischief."

"Yes, ma'am," he replied politely. An hour later, they were carefully escorted outside and helped to sit down. The servants then left them alone. The sun was shining, perhaps too brightly for the three, but it was warm. The air felt fresh. There was a detectable fragrance coming from the formal gardens, which began not far from where they were sitting. They could not easily lie back on the lawn chairs as they had done that first day. Now they sat perfectly erect on three chairs the servants brought out for them. Hernando, with his tapping cane, had followed them outside, and another servant brought a chair for him, saying, "Okay, Hernando. You are sitting in front of the three young women. Keep an eye on them."

He laughed, "But I don't have any eyes. Remember? They are glass marbles I think."

"Silly man," she said teasingly and left them.

"Hello. I am Hernando Gervasi. Can you understand me? I can't see you so I don't know what your situation is, but from what I've been hearing, it can't be good."

He looked to be about twenty, Isabella thought. She tried to speak, "I am Isabella Valen and these are my wives, Gabriella Amy and Celia Jan. Can you understand me?" She need not have asked, his ULAT box kept saying "Error. Unknown language."

"We have a slight problem. My ULAT isn't working properly. But what is really strange, is that I can sort of make out what you are saying. Can you repeat it slowly? Wait, let me figure out how to turn this darn thing off." From the corner of her eyes, she saw him fiddling with it. "There. Please try it again, slowly." She did so, speaking as clearly as possible, given the massive size of her lip plates and their mutilation of her speech.

"Are you saying that your name is Isabella Valen and you have two wives? Are you a woman, Isabella? I must be misunderstanding you."

"No, I am most definitely a woman, but I have two women as wives. Here, come feel my body. You can get a better sense of our horrible situation, Hernando," Isabella suggested. She'd never been around a blind person before. What with the difficulty in her speech, she thought this might help him.

He felt his way over to her. "Oh, is this your head? No, you have two heads?"

"No, Carlos gave us mammoth breasts. Move your hands up a little. Careful, he split our lips and stretched them, putting in these foot across lip plates. They are dangling from my mouth right now." She felt a strange tingling sensation as his gentle finger tips probed her body, feeling along the outlines of her lips, then moving across her face. His fingers came on down the sides of her face, touching her long earrings, felt the gold neck rings, and then rested on her shoulders. A shocked look came over his face.

"Where are your arms?" he asked. His face and voice reflected the shock that his fingers had felt.

"Carlos cut them off me to make me work for him. He cut off the lower arms and hands of my wives too," she explained. "He put these neck rings around us and we cannot move our heads at all, not even a tiny bit."

"My god! Carlos is a bad man!" His hands continued down her sides and stopped at her waist. "Have you no waist at all? No, it is so small. Are you a child?"

Isabella laughed. "No, certainly not. He's shrunk our waists terribly so, we can just barely breathe. He's got us laced into an almost unmoving pipe corset that makes us have a tiny waistline."

His fingers traced out her bulging hips. "Ah yes, you have adult hips. I feel them now." her legs tingled as he continued going on down to her feet. "What kind of feet are these?" He felt her toe boots for quite some time, and she explained what had been done to them.

"So your feet are frozen pointing downwards?" he asked a little confused.

"Yes, we have to walk on our toes. It's rather hard to keep your balance," she answered. Finally, he tapped his way back to his seat, felt it carefully, and sat down.

"Carlos did all this to you three? He is a very bad man indeed," he said again.

Isabella suddenly realized he had not been repeating her words for some time now. "Say, are you understanding me better now? How is it that you can understand me without your ULAT box?"

"Yes, I am picking it up mostly. Please keep going slowly. It is hard, but I am getting it. Mom. She taught me when I was very young. No one speaks this language."

"You mother? Where is she?" Isabella asked, thinking that perhaps she might be able to lend them a hand.

"She has passed away many years ago, many. I can't really say how many it has been. I have a hard time keeping track of the years. Maybe fifty or so."

"But you don't look like you are fifty, Hernando. You are very young still."

"Carlos keeps putting me into a machine. He says it makes me younger. I must be a hundred now more or less, I just cannot tell for sure. Mom used to know, but that was a long time ago."

"Where did your mother come from? It is very strange; you are speaking my language, Hernando," she asked, still mystified about him and his mother.

"I don't know. She said strange men brought her here when she was very young. She was his telepath for many years. She told me to be always on the lookout for someone with yellow eyes, but alas, I cannot see. I don't know why she wanted me to do that, only that she said they might help us. She taught me to speak this way. It was our secret language. Carlos didn't know it back then, but now the ULAT does know it, so I never speak it when he is here. He is a bad man."

"I see. We will remember that," Isabella said. "We don't want Carlos to understand what we are saying either. So were you always blind? It must be hard for you."

"Oh no. I had yellow eyes like my mother when I was little. Then I got very sick. Mom cared for me. I remember that. But when I recovered, I had no eyes any more, but I had telepathy like mom did. She told me that Carlos took out my eyes and gave me these black glass marbles for eyes so I would not run away from him. He is an idiot. I would never leave my mother, but then maybe he wasn't so dumb. After she died, I would have run away."

"He has to be stopped! We aim to do just that! Say, did your mother ever tell you the name of the world on which she was born?" Isabella asked.

"No. If she did, I've forgotten. Maybe it started with a 'T' but I can't be sure. It has been so very long ago."

"It must have been our world, Tierra, Hernando."

His face brightened up, "Yes! That was it. Tierra," he said slowly and with some pride. "I will not forget it now. Thank you."

"Yes, in the past, the aliens kidnaped many of our young telepaths and took them off-world, selling them into slavery. Your mother must have come from my part of Tierra, called the Westerlings. That's the language we are speaking — well that you are speaking. Mine hardly sounds like it at all — these accursed lip plates!"

"Keep talking slowly, Isabella. You went a little too fast there. It is hard to understand you." She slowed down, repeating what she'd said.

He then asked, "Are you able to walk on your own? I

keep hearing the servants talking and hear them close to you."

"I can't yet, not without someone holding on to me. I've nothing left to use to keep my balance while walking on my toes. My wives still have their upper arms to help them a bit. No, we are most helpless in all things now. Carlos made sure of that, damn him!"

"Celia Jan here, Hernando. Are we allowed to walk all around the house or will the servants stop us?"

"Oh no, you can walk anywhere you want. You can't leave the estate, I'm told. I've no idea where that is at. There are guards there with guns, whatever those are. Beyond leaving, you can walk anywhere. I sometimes like to walk in the gardens. The smells are so exotic there, but I have to be very careful not to get lost. Count my steps and all that. That's how I get around — by counting the steps that I take. Perhaps, Miss Isabella, I can help you walk and you can guide me," he suggested. "I'd like to do much more walking and smell and touch the world, but I lose count after too many steps and turns. Maybe we can help each other out."

"Thanks. It would help me. I don't trust the servants very much," she replied honestly.

He chuckled. "You are right there. While they will not say so, they feel very much, how should I say this, put out, bothered, annoyed — with all the care and attention they are forced to give you. Some are saying Carlos is not paying them enough credits to do all this extra work. I would not be surprised if sooner or later they will stop helping you three all that much. I suppose they will have to keep on feeding you, though. If not, I can try to help with that too."

"We have been getting that feeling too, Hernando. We can use all the help you can provide us. We'll help you in return," Celia Jan replied. "Another thing. Do you know where Carlos keeps his computer system or his medical machines?"

"Alas, I do not know of such things. I know he keeps some rooms in the East Wing locked. Not even the servants go in those rooms. Perhaps he keeps them there. They are the last two doors on your right as far as you can do down the hall before the back doors. That's all that I know. If there are not there, then I don't know. If you want me to help you with those, I don't think that I can. I know nothing about either of them."

"Thanks. That's a good place for me to start looking, Hernando. We're going to escape and put Carlos out of business. When we do, we'll take you with us, if you want to go," Celia Jan offered.

"I don't know how you can escape him. Carlos is a very powerful man. Many connections. Many business partners. Still, if you can get free from him, I would like to come with you. I will help as I can," he replied with a smile and the tiniest glimmer of hope on his face.

Gabriella Amy spoke up, "Well, first things first. Hernando, Isabella, you two should start working together to figure out how you can help each other. Why don't you both get started now? Let's see if we can do some walking around this giant patio area. Hernando, it is very difficult for us to walk on the grass. It was tough enough before Carlos mutilated our bodies. But if we are going to escape, we're going to have to do just that, so we need to get in a lot of practice, especially so for Isabella. At least Celia and I have some arms left. They aren't good for much, but it's better than none at all. She feels so helpless right now."

"I cannot imagine, Miss Isabella. You must be a very brave young woman. I will come to you, and you help me get you up. There is a lot to smell and sense around here and in the gardens, though we must be careful because it is mostly grass and gravel paths in there," Hernando suggested.

"Mostly, it is just terrifying, Hernando. I keep wanting to use my arms, and they are not there," Isabella admitted. "If you can, put your arm around my waist. Keep me from falling." As those two began working out how to move around, Celia Jan and Gabriella Amy also put their steadying arms on each other's shoulders so that they also could practice.

A bit later, Celia Jan whispered to Gabriella Amy, "We're simply going to have to get these neck rings off of us first. We can't possibly escape wearing them."

"I know. This is a nightmare. I'll work on them tonight after they leave us alone in bed," she suggested.

As the days passed, the four continued to do as much

walking as they could tolerate. Celia Jan continued to push them gently to do more and more. She knew just how much walking they would have to do, if her escape plan was to be executed. They had to be prepared, especially since they moved at a snail's pace. After some experimenting, Gabriella Amy believed she could get their neck rings off when the time was right. Finally as anticipated, the servants began paying the four almost no attention at all, save at meal times and getting them dressed and undressed, plus helping them go to the bathroom. Now Celia Jan took a big gamble. She had to find the computer system and the medical machines, if her plan had any chance at success.

She'd found the two locked rooms yesterday and noticed the servants rarely were down this hallway and never as far as these two rooms. She was highly annoyed at the extreme problems caused by her inability to turn or move her head. Having to take tiny steps to turn her whole body around just to make sure no one was watching her was a tricky action at best. Satisfied that no one was in the hallway, she focused on the lock and then the door. After it opened, she carefully stepped inside and again focused. The door closed.

Celia Jan paused, her eyes taking in as much of the room as she could, before moving her feet and thus her body a little. Here was his enormous computer system. It occupied most of the far half of the room. What protections did he have installed? Again, she focused and began her search. She sensed a video spy camera. Her crystal activated further. The unit short-circuited and went dead. She continued and disabled two more. Finally satisfied those were handled, she sat down at the console, wishing that she still had her hands.

Ah well. I used to do it without them so I guess I can do it again. I have to, she thought. She focused and again her crystal activated. Buttons pressed as if by magic, but actually, she was just using her telekinetic skills to press them. Soon the system powered up. The basic system was not protected, but he had installed password protection on his business side. She made use of the available system for now, bringing up his calendar. She took note of the current date and when he was scheduled to return. Good, she thought, they had seven more weeks to prepare themselves. Next, she visited a secret Underground site and downloaded the right software. This she activated at once. It would take time, but it would crack his password-protected system. Now she downloaded a special worm program. Then, she entered some very specific codes into it and sent it on its merry way. This one would travel through hyperspace, piggybacking on standard Imperium Network signals, until it reached her new computer on board her new transport ship. Once there, it would load up several of her "special programs" and return them back to this machine. Again, that would take some days to complete. Satisfied, she put the system back into hibernate mode and headed to the door. Again she focused and activated her crystal. No one was in the hallway. She carefully unlocked and opened the door, stepping outside. After turning around, she used her *mentales* gifts to relock the door.

With no one still in the hallway, she moved on down to the last door and repeated her actions. Soon she was inside and spotted the medical machine and the rejuvenation machine. Immediately, she recognized this as the room in which she had awakened and watched as Carlos removed Isabella's upper arms. Everything was just as it had been that awful day. Perfect, she thought. She slowly surveyed the equipment. She found a few extra sets of lip plates, tiny waist corsets, and even toe boots and neck rings. The medical machine was one of the newest models, and she knew just what this one was capable of doing. She also spotted another machine that she had not seen before. A minute of study passed before she realized this was the machine that had installed the awful neck rings. *I have to come back and study this one.*

As she prepared to leave, she sensed someone in the hallway, and she waited breathlessly for what seemed an eternity. Finally, they were gone, and she quietly exited the room, re-locking the door. All this took an enormous amount of concentration on her part and more than once, she nearly fell over in the process. She knew they would have to be free of the neck rings before she could really do what needed to be done with the medical machine. She thought, *Carlos is diabolical! Physically, nothing is easy to do now, but our minds are intact, as he wants. He is going to get more than he bargained for, if I have anything to say about it.*

Chapter 32 Escape from Slavery

During the mornings after the servants finished dressing them and feeding them, Isabella and Gabriella Amy worked on getting Isabella's powers increased. Constant drilling and for variety, more drilling. Then in the afternoons, Isabella and Hernando headed off to the patio, while Celia Jan snuck into the computer room to continue her work. Meantime, Gabriella Amy kept an eye on the servants and acted as look out.

One afternoon, as the two moved very slowly and carefully around the huge patio, Isabella sighed. "I am so sorry that I am such a terrible burden to you and everyone else. I have never been this helpless in my long life."

"But you are not a burden. Look, I am able to walk without counting and tapping. You are helping me become freer that I have ever been. You are not a burden but a beautiful flower," he countered.

"Oh no I am not, not now. I look like an utter freak," she declared with passion.

He laughed. "I do not see a freak, but a beautiful flower."

She laughed, "Ah, then you must be a blind man."

Hernando laughed at her tease. "Indeed, that I am. I will put it another way. I feel the beautiful flower that is you. Though I cannot see it, I can touch it, hear it, feel it, sense it, smell it, and taste it. How's that? Tell me about your long life, if you like. I can listen well."

Isabella decided why not? She began by telling him about her having been kidnaped at taken off-world to become a slave telepath, just as his own mother had been. She outlined all the shady actions she had been forced to do for her "owner." She told him about how she'd managed eventually to slip away from there when the owner died. She described the eternal loneliness of the long, long years of fending on her own on many worlds, but always trying to find a way to get home. "It took me eighty-six years to do it, but I finally got back home. Of course, it was not what I expected. Everyone I knew was dead. All the social orders had changed many times over. I was a total stranger in a new and strange world, yet some things were so familiar." She went on to tell him about having been drafted to become Tierra's senator. "There really wasn't any other person who had the off-world experience I had or that would have been acceptable to all the ruling lords. Gabriella Amy and Celia Jan were wholly unacceptable, since they were born as Easterlings women. So it was me."

She went on, "So you see, Hernando, I am not a beautiful flower. I have killed men, stolen many things that were not mine, lied, and deceived so many men and a few women that I can hardly count them. I am more like the evil, wicked witch of Tierra. And now I do look like an utter freak and a completely helpless one at that."

"But you did like being their senator?" he asked, sensing she had.

"Well, yes, now that you mention it, Hernando, I really did enjoy that. Particularly because I was helping all of those other Closed World senators. They respected me for what I am or was. They did not treat me less because I am a woman, like so many lords do on Tierra."

"That is good. So tell me, what would you have done had you not been kidnaped?" he asked.

She laughed. "I had wanted to join one of the towers so I could put my special gifts to good use helping other people. I do admire Maricela. She was born without arms, and yet she has more power and wisdom than most men."

"See, you are not an evil, wicked witch after all. You did what you had to do to survive, just as I and my mother before me had to do." He began to outline his own long life of telepathic slavery.

When he finished, she said, "See, you are not evil either. Looks like we both have had to do many repulsing things just to survive. And yet, here we are now."

"Yes, here we are now. You cannot know how much I am treasuring these hours with you," he admitted. She smiled, but realized it wasn't visible anymore, plus he couldn't see it. "Not since I was a little boy have I been able to just forget that damned cane and all the counting and just walk, smell, listen, and enjoy life. Words cannot express how thankful I really am, Isabella."

"I'm glad, Hernando. At least I am able to do a little something. I had such plans to do so much good. You know, kind of like starting over with a rejuvenated young body. Now that is all dashed beyond all hope. Hell, I am completely helpless now. It's all that I can do to walk as long as you hold onto me."

"Oh, I don't know if that is all that you can do, Miss Isabella. You are helping me. You have your mind and your gifts. Perhaps you and I — perhaps we can find a way to help others in spite of everything. We are not our bodies, you know. My mother taught me that when I was a boy. I will not give up hope if you will not give up."

"Hernando, you are one amazing man. Okay, I won't give up hope unless you let go of me."

He laughed, "No, that you can count upon, for if I let go of you, then I am also lost as well. I do not wish to be so lost ever again. It is a shame we could not have met before you married your wives."

She laughed. "Oh that. Silly. We did it so we would be both acceptable to the many lords and to the Senate, which expects women to be married. It is only a marriage of convenience for us three. On the other hand, Hernando, as you can tell, I have a strong — no, make that an overpowering hatred of men. I was able to keep from being raped for eighty-six years and against all odds."

"So in all those years, you never felt love?" he asked. He couldn't tell if she would answer that one, and he continued, "Neither have I. Carlos never allowed me to meet women. I have often wondered how much of life I was missing. But I did have the unconditional love of mom, and I loved her too. That must count for something."

She sighed, "I should be honest with you, Hernando. Yes, you are right. I've never felt love, not real love. For eighty-six years, love was a luxury t I could not afford, not if I ever wanted to find a way home. I do care about Gabriella and Celia some, but it's not passionate love, but more of a deep respect and admiration. Actually, Hernando, I am a little jealous of those two. They are madly in love with each other. Sometimes when I am not looking, they share such an intimate relationship. Okay, I am more than a little envious of those two," she chuckled, feeling light as a feather for having admitted all of this to another person. "You know, I've never shared this much of my life with anyone, not even those two."

"Ah, then I am both special and honored you have, Miss Isabella," he replied. "Might I ask something of you?"

"Sure, what?" she replied, growing curious.

"In the gardens, there is a flower that smells so lovely. I know it must be hard for you to walk on the grass, but if I take you to it, could you tell me what it looks like? It was my mother's favorite flower here, but I never took the time to see it when I was a boy. Now I would like to 'see' it, if I could."

"Okay. Gabriella Amy says we have to be able to walk across grass, so why not. Direct me, but for heaven's sake, don't let go of me!" she replied, growing slightly nervous. She found the walking a bit challenging, mostly because she had no way to keep her balance. Finally, they arrived at the flower. Now she had to try to describe this orchid. Frustrated at her inability actually to give him a good description of it, she focused and placed the images she was seeing directly into his mind. "Oh! Oh! This is so beautiful. How did you do that? Am I seeing it as you see it?"

"Yes, it is a very lovely orchid, I think. Your mother had very good taste in flowers, Hernando. I wish I could have met her," she answered. As she stood there almost facing him, she could actually see his black, marble eyes very well for the first time. They looked strange indeed. Yet something was not quite right about them. She decided to have Gabriella Amy have a look at them later on.

Meanwhile, Celia Jan was hard at work. She had to get them new ID cards and make any number of sneaky arrangements, if they were going to be able to get off this world and back to Proxima Prime. She also was able to hack into Senator Carlos' many accounts. What she discovered shocked her, though in hindsight, she realized she ought to have predicted it.

That evening when they were in bed, she relayed some

of what she found. "Carlos has been doing some very nasty things. Besides dealing heavily in the telepathic slave trade, he's been running blasters to all sorts of illegal areas. One of his companies even sold some to Lord Valen way back when. Some of his companies market prostitution and various illegal drugs. He has no scruples at all."

Isabella sighed. "I suppose I ought to just kill him, but after talking with Hernando today, somehow I wonder if I have the right to fry his brains? Is revenge really justified? Stopping him certainly is, but to do it out of revenge? If you had asked me this last week, I'd have said absolutely. Yet now, I wonder if doing something just for revenge is right. He needs to be brought to justice, but then there isn't any real justice now. According to Imperium laws, all is fair in times of war. If you ask me to, I will fry his brains, though. We have to escape. Say, will you both take a close look at Hernando's eyes? There is something not quite right about them. I've no real medical knowledge, and I know that you both are more knowledgeable about such things than I."

"Sure, I'll look at them tomorrow," Gabriella Amy agreed.

The next day, everything got put on hold. Carlos' son paid them a surprised visit at breakfast time. "Hello. Dad asked me to check in on you three, his new telepaths. Got to make sure you are doing okay. You are doing okay, right? The servants are treating you well?" he asked with a sneer. Then, he added, "Oh, I see, you can't talk any more. Too bad. Great boobs though." He turned to the head servant and chatted with her about the three. To their great annoyance, he stuck around for several days, watching them closely.

After he left, Celia Jan did study Hernando's eyes, but decided this mystery would have to wait a while. The Senator was due to arrive home in just a few more days, the middle of December 1273. Now she had far too much to do. Ordinarily, she could have done it all in less than a day. Hobbled as she was, it took her nearly a week to get everything ready. Timing would be critical, and she drilled the others on what they needed to do.

Celia Jan took charge the next morning. Via Hernando,

she learned the servants were preparing for their arrival during the late afternoon. Meanwhile, the servants bustled around the large home, tidying everything up, making it difficult for her to sneak into the computer room. She finally managed it, but with little time to spare. Once more cursing her terrible restrictive movements, she got the computer up and running. Again, using her strong telekinetic powers, she launched several programs. The last two had to wait for just the proper moment. At last, she could hear the private shuttle craft setting down. She fired off the first of the two programs. Now she depended on the others, particularly Isabella.

As Hernando and Isabella made their way to the main entrance, he held tightly onto her, stopping at the wide doorway where the living room met the entrance hallway. Meanwhile, a number of servants bustled about, several heading outside to retrieve their bags. Soon they saw the two just entering the wide double doors, held open by two servants. As before, Senator Carlos held onto his wife in her billowing gown and tall platforms. Both brightened up as they spotted Isabella standing at the opposite end of the hallway. Senator Carlos' smile was more of a self-satisfied sneer, but Imelda's was genuine. "See, she's doing well. Even come out to greet us, dear," she chatted away.

Isabella focused and took control of both their bodies, via their minds. She was using her highly honed skill of Dominate Others, to use the ancient Marisol's List's descriptive tag. Imelda repeated the words Isabella planted. "Dear. I am very tired. I am going to retire to my room for a nap." She then let go of his arm and headed to her room to obey Isabella's command.

Senator Carlos spoke what she intended, "Fine dear. I am just going to check on my computer network." He passed by Isabella and Hernando, heading to the east wing, but moving very slowly, most unusual for him. When he got to the proper door, he stopped and waited expressionless. Now Gabriella Amy moved up from where she was standing beside the door he was facing. She took over control of his body, forcing it to open the door. She followed behind him into the room, where Celia Jan was waiting, everything prepared.

Carlos saw something was very wrong, but he was powerless to make his mind control his own body. Fear began to take hold of him. Once the door shut, Gabriella Amy focused a bit more, sending a Mind Stun into him, knocking him unconscious. He would have fallen, except that she also wrapped him with her telekinetic grasp, holding him up. Celia Jan added her telekinetic powers to hers. Together, they lifted him up and into the medical machine. Gabriella Amy then waist nodded to Celia Jan, turned slowly, and left to help Isabella.

That done, Celia Jan, using her telekinetic powers, pressed the last of the buttons and prepared to work on Carlos. Outside, Isabella had been stunning each of the servants as they entered. Now Gabriella Amy focused. Her germanium crystal glowing bright blue, she began moving them into various bedrooms, shoving the bags they had just carried from the shuttle out of the way. An hour later, she expanded her awareness outward, sensing for the presence of other servants she might have missed. She found none. "Okay, you two know what to do. I am going to check on the shuttle and get it ready." She didn't say she hoped she didn't fall while walking alone across the grass to the shuttle, some three hundred feet from the front doors.

Using extreme care and an occasional telekinetic lift, she made it to the shuttle and proceeded to open its cargo bay doors. She knew she could not climb in, not as immobile as her body currently was. Instead, she focused and her crystal activated once more. Her body appeared to rise up and float into the cargo hold. Once stable, she moved up to the driver's seat, where Carlos always sat. After sitting down, she used her telekinetic powers to activate the controls and brought up the flight path he'd just used to get here from the spaceport. She entered the reverse course into the flight controls. Finally, she went through the pre-flight checkout, leaving the shuttle on standby. This took her nearly an hour to complete, again because of the extreme difficulty she had, due mostly from the damnable neck rings that made her head immobile. Then, she carefully headed back into the house.

Hernando and Isabella were just about done with the packing. She could not do any of it, of course, but she patiently directed Hernando. He had already packed everything he owned into one small bag. Now he had packed the three women's few things and most importantly, their old gowns from Tierra. All three hoped they would soon be rid of the massive breasts and all else. If so, they would need properly fitting dresses. Gabriella Amy watched the two working relatively efficiently together and smiled. She thought, *this is really good for both of them. They are working together as a team. I could not have planned it any better.*

"What now?" Isabella asked. "We are done here."

"Bring them with you, Hernando. We are to wait in the living room for word from Celia Jan," she replied. A few minutes later, the three sat carefully down — he, feeling for the seat, while the two women moving slightly on their toes to position themselves properly so they could mostly fall down into the chairs. Now they waited, though Gabriella Amy found herself gasping for air once more. She'd done far more than she was used to doing on her own. Time passed.

"What's keeping her?" Isabella began to fret. Was something going horribly wrong?

"It's fine. She'd have let me know if she had difficulties. No, she isn't turning his mind into mush. Her plan is as diabolical as Carlos' was. Be patient a little longer," Gabriella Amy explained.

Okay, it is done. I am going to float him out to the living room now. Need some help moving the equipment to the shuttle craft though. I'm pooped, and we've a long way to go yet tonight, Celia Jan sent her.

Both women gasped. They saw Senator Carlos floating towards them, his body floating parallel to the floor. Isabella quickly focused and placed images of what she was seeing in Hernando's mind, sharing her surprise and awe. "Is — is — is that Carlos?" Hernando exclaimed, just as shocked as she was.

"Yes, it is him or rather her now. Celia Jan, what have you done?" Isabella gushed, seeing the concentrating face of Celia Jan moving carefully behind the floating body. After setting her down carefully on the couch, Celia Jan broke her contact and answered them.

"I am teaching Carlos a lesson. Let him experience what

he has done to us," she replied. She had done an amazing amount of body modifications on him. First, she'd changed his sex, compliments of this newest medical machine which now made gender modifications very easy to accomplish. She then turned her into a duplicate of Isabella. That is, tiny waist pipe corset, toe shoes, neck rings, monster breasts, and lip plates, and she had removed her arms as well. She'd also grown the body's hair a couple of feet to add some spice to Carlos' new appearance. "He'll sleep until morning. Okay, Hernando, Isabella, you are up. Get to the shuttle and into the cargo bay doors and seated. We are bringing some stuff along with us. Be following you shortly. I can't let all this marvelous equipment go to waste."

Hernando and Isabella talked of nothing else but what had happened to Carlos, as they made their extremely careful way out of the house and across the lawn to the shuttle. By the time they reached it, Gabriella Amy and Celia Jan had caught up to them. Both had several large shipping crates floating along just ahead of them. As the two reached the ship, Isabella knew she could not physically get into it. Again, she focused and used her vastly improved telekinesis skills to left herself up and into the bay. Hernando felt his way up and in, and she directed them to the rear seats. After sliding the two crates into the hold, the two women duplicated what Isabella had done to get themselves inside.

"Okay, I am utterly drained! It's all yours now, love. I'll get the doors," Celia Jan said. Gabriella Amy headed to the driver's seat. After Celia Jan sat down, she promptly fell asleep. She had considerably overdone it. Soon the shuttle craft lifted off. Thank god for automatic pilots, Gabriella thought to herself. She watched the instruments for some time, until the shuttle began to land at the giant spaceport. At this point, she carefully made her way to a rear seat ready to play her next role.

It was full dark when the shuttle landed somewhere in the vast spaceport of Caltran there on Beltzar-4. After sitting down, she made sure all four had their ID cards visible; the three had theirs hanging around their necks. "Okay, Hernando, you are up. Don't worry, if you forget, I'll be sending you what to say," she whispered, while rousing Celia Jan with her short arm. "Remember gang, look confused."

Just then, a crewman opened the shuttle's door. He looked at his clipboard and muttered, "Senator Carlos' cargo manifest 1452634. Two crates, four crippled people. Okay, up and out of there. Need to see your ID cards. Oh crap! He spotted the four and spoke into his shoulder-held comm device. Need four wheel chairs and help at Bay 409 now. Tight schedule." Looking at the four, he added, "Just be a minute."

The three women made pathetic noises, indicating that they were totally confused. Hernando spoke up, "Please sir. I'm blind. Where are we? What are we supposed to do now? Where are we going?" He waved his hands out in front of his body, as if feeling for the door.

"Relax sir. I have transportation and assistants coming for you now. Sit tight," the crewman replied. "Oh, I'm moving the crates out now. Sit still." Before long, three other men joined him and strong hands lifted the four out of the shuttle, sitting them in four wheel chairs. From there, they were pushed across the concrete pad into a building.

Down one corridor and up another, they were pushed through a seemingly endless maze of halls until they arrived at staging area. "Okay, wait here. Someone will soon come to put you on your next flight." Celia Jan pushed her feet onto the floor and slowly moved her body around until she saw the area number. Then, she relaxed, so far so good. They were where she had arranged. Shortly, a sleepy transport pilot walked up to the desk.

After picking up a clipboard and scanning it, he spoke up, "Two crates, four handicapped passengers. Ah, you must be the ones. Let me check your ID tags." He used a handheld scanner on each of the tags and those on the crates. "Yep, all present and accounted for. Unusual trip, but then he's the senator. Crew will be here shortly to load you up. Take off is in five minutes. Can you even understand me?"

"I can sir," Hernando called out, purposely looking towards him but at a weird angle. He was playing his role well, thought Isabella. "They can't speak. Senator Carlos didn't tell me where he was taking us. Can you sir? Are we in a spaceport somewhere?"

The pilot laughed. "Sorry, that's not my position to say. The flight to Proxima Prime will take four hours, so just relax sir." Soon, four men arrived, pushed them out onto the concrete tarmac, and then lifted them into the transport, while still in their chairs. Conveniently, they also strapped the chairs down for the flight, instead of lifting them into the soft, more comfortable seats of the transport. Their two crates and two small bags followed. Celia Jan held her breath, anxiously awaiting liftoff.

Finally, she relaxed as the transport ship began ascending vertically. From the side windows, the three watched the rapidly shrinking lights of the port and huge city. Then, they felt a lurch, as the transport shifted into hyperdrive. Now Celia Jan relaxed. She had gotten them off Baltzar-4. In four hours, they would be back on Proxima Prime. There, her advanced planning would be fully tested. She anticipated by that time, the Senator's household would have discovered the treachery; she imagined all of their wild reactions and frantic searching for the four of them. Would all of her countermeasures actually work?

Four hours seemed like an eternity for the four. On their way here months ago, Imelda had been chatting gaily all the way, telling them about the marvels of her estate. This time, worry and fretting replaced that frivolity. More than once, Celia Jan took as deep a breath as she could muster against the unrelenting twelve inch, metal re-enforced pipe corset. She found herself wringing her non-existent hands and laughed at her silliness. Gabriella Amy calmed her, "Don't worry dear. I am confident that you have worked it all out superbly as you always have, Sly Fox." Celia Jan flashed her a smile, before realizing it wasn't visible, but her partner picked it up anyway.

At long last, the transport pilot announced they were about to land at the huge spaceport on Proxima Prime. Would they make sure they were securely fastened? All four laughed at that for two different reasons. Hernando muttered, "How am I supposed to even see if I am fastened?" He laughed again.

Once they were on the ground, the ground crew arrived

and unloaded the four who were still in their wheel chairs. The three women sat perfectly erect and unmoving, like three marble statues. None had any real mobility above their hips. Celia Jan took careful note of the arrival location's number. She focused and made contact with the small laptop computer buried inside one of the crates. Using her telekinetic skills, she pressed the keys, entering that number and hit the Enter key, before she broke her concentration. Somewhere in the giant computer network that controlled this huge base, the entries were switched. Anyone tracking this transport ship would be directed to the opposite side of the port. This ship apparently had just come from the far side of the Imperium!

Once inside, their handlers swiped their cards and put the four and their crates onto one of the conveyor systems. They made sure that their ID cards and the crate's tags were visible to the remote scanners. Then, one man said, "Okay. You are all set. Just keep the tags where they are now and the conveyors will take you to your destination." The conveyor system began moving them along, though at a fairly slow pace. Every so often, they passed by scanners that read their tags and continued their automated delivery. Marvels of a totally computer-controlled system.

"Okay, tricky part. Switch ID tags now," Celia Jan ordered. The three women focused. Their crystals glowed pale blue for an instant, and their tags flipped over to the other side. Isabella handled Hernando's for him. Just in time, they passed by another scanner. Before long, the conveyors shuttled them off onto an entirely different path. "Now, Hernando. Take out the new ID cards and hold them up. We'll grab them with our telekinetic powers. Yes, that's the way. Just hold them." Again, their three germanium crystals glowed briefly. The new ID cards moved over to the old ones. However, there was some confusion now since neither woman could look down to replace her own. Celia Jan went from person to person, handling the swap, while Gabriella Amy switched Celia Jan's for her. The next thing Hernando felt was the four old ones being laid in his open palm. "Okay, put those in your right pocket. Here comes the next scanner." She held her breath.

Once more, the scanners picked up their tag numbers and soon shuttled them on down yet a different path. After a half hour, Celia Jan had them flip the ID cards over displaying yet another new set of numbers for the scanners. Now she relaxed. If all went well, they would arrive in a little used warehouse, where she hoped everything was all setup for them. A long half hour passed before they finally did enter a dimly illuminated warehouse. Here the conveyor system halted. It was obvious to her at this location, workers used to load cargo and crates onto the automated conveyor system, from which they would be transported to their proper destination flight.

"Where are we? What now? Is anyone around us?" Hernando whispered nervously.

"All clear. We are in a warehouse, I think," Isabella whispered. "Celia Jan, now what?"

"We made it this far. I had my doubts. Hernando, you were great. Okay gang. Now we have some time before the next move. We have to find the collapsible large shipping crate and get our small crates, bags, and us inside it. Then close it up. Come on; let's see if we can find it. Hernando, help me out of this chair and onto my feet, please. I've used up way too much energy today."

Soon, she was pivoting in place so she could scan the warehouse. At last she found what she was looking for far over in one corner, just as she had ordered. She directed the others to follow her to it. "Okay everyone, get inside to a seat. Isabella, guide Hernando. Have him get us all strapped down in case the crate gets turned upside down during shipping. Gabriella Amy and I will move the crates and our two bags over here while you are doing that."

A half hour later, the four and their two crates were firmly strapped down. Isabella made contact with Hernando's mind, relaying what she was seeing. The sides of the giant crate rose up and formed a tight box around them. All heard a clicking sound as it latched shut and the low hiss of oxygen being released so that they didn't suffocate. "What's happening?" Hernando whispered, more than a little nervous.

Celia Jan answered, "We are inside a shipping crate.

Hopefully, it won't be too long before some machinery comes to move us onto the conveyor system and automatically begins the next phase in deception. We can't go directly to where I have our new fancy transport ship waiting. It's another shell game with baggage numbers so our path cannot be easily traced. Sit back and snooze if you can. I'm not entirely certain how long this will take. That's why I erred on the side of caution with the oxygen tank."

Inside the crate, it was pitch black, and the three lost track of time, drifting in and out of a light sleep. Their adrenaline rush had long subsided, to say nothing of being way past their usual bedtimes. Their biological clocks suggested outside it was probably morning. They were also tired, thirsty, and hungry, but there was nothing they could do about these just yet. All were roused when the crate shook. Outside, a giant forklift machine latched onto the crate, lifting it up, depositing it on the conveyor system. Again, the automated computer-controlled machinery of which the Imperium was so proud was being exploited by Celia Jan, who was a master of such things.

She whispered, "There should be four more number switches before we arrive. That should confuse anyone who is trying to track us. Until we actually leave Proxima Prime, we can still be found. All the equipment and our ID cards have built-in RFI tags that identify the object. The security forces can scan the planet for these tags, which will respond when hit with the energy beams, revealing its location. So we are not going to be totally safe until we actually lift off and get into hyperspace. A lot depends on whether or not they think of trying to find us using those tags."

"Is that likely?" Isabella asked.

"Not really. Carlos would have to have jotted down the RFI tags of his equipment and such. He would have to have a way to communicate those numbers to the security forces, which I don't think he, or rather she, can do at the moment. We are pretty safe, I think," she answered. "They could more readily backtrack his shuttle and find that we stole his private transport ship. That's highly likely, in fact. They ought to be able to track it quickly and us back here to Proxima Prime.

However, our devious re-routings of that ship and our devious route here to this crate should delay them for days trying to sort out that mess of dead ends. Still, there is always a chance they could accidentally figure it out. Let's hope not."

"You are a genius, Celia Jan!" Isabella commented. "But where are we going now?"

"To our new fancy deep space transport, now fully paid for by Senator Carlos and his various businesses which now only have a single credit in their many accounts. Never mess with Sly Fox!"

"But how? How could you do all this? When?" Isabella asked still in awe and still a little confused.

"I set up much of this while you were playing Senator. I always have a backup plan in place. I never trust the powers that be. Call me paranoid if you like. I arranged the first actions we took from his computer system at his estate, while you and Hernando were walking. I cracked his security codes and got access to his bank accounts and those of his satellite companies. Long ago, I wrote a worm program that will drain any account, leaving one credit remaining. Of course, the program has to be very sophisticated so they cannot trace where the credits actually end up. It has worked perfectly many times. After the initial withdrawal of the credits into one account, they are then split up into small credit transfers to millions of other innocent accounts. No one pays any attention to a small credit transfers and withdrawals, you see. Those zillions of individual transfers bounce around through ten more accounts before they are slowly regrouped and eventually sent to my account. So Gabriella Amy, I've replaced all the funds of ours I spent on these many new things, including the transport ship."

"Well done, dear, as usual," Gabriella Amy replied with a grin.

"So now we wait," she replied. "I'm going to try to doze some."

Several hours passed. Only the occasional jostling of the crate, as it was shifted from one conveyor system onto another, jarred them awake. Celia Jan knew when they arrived, though. Everyone again felt and heard a crane lifting the large crate into the air and off the conveyor system. She waited patiently for the slight jar that accompanied the crate being sat upon the metal floor. She strained her ears but heard nothing.

"Okay, time to open up. If you are a praying person, now is the time for that. I hope we are where we are supposed to be," she whispered.

"Where's that?" asked Isabella. "I don't sense the presence of any people in our vicinity."

"About two miles below the usual surface of Proxima Prime — that is, the surface you are all familiar with. You see, the actual so called ground level is many levels below that. They've all manner of subsystems on the lower levels I would have dearly loved to explore. Okay, let me get this crate opened." She focused and her crystal activated. Slowly the sides of the crate unfolded. Dim illumination showed them they were inside some giant metal area. Dripping noises and a metallic odor greeted their senses, especially those of Hernando.

Moving in a small circle on her toes, Isabella looked all around. "I don't see anything. It's totally empty!" Panic began to sweep into her compressed belly.

"It's cloaked. That's the newest feature that's been invented. Hang on while I deactivate it," Celia Jan replied. Again, she focused and her crystal activated briefly. Suddenly, the sleek, shiny, brand-new, deep space transport appeared some hundred feet from them. Its side door slowly opened accompanied by a low hissing sound of its mechanical machinery.

"It's beautiful, Celia Jan!" Isabella exclaimed. Her brief panic evaporated. She placed images of it into Hernando's mind. He too was impressed.

"Okay, Hernando, Isabella, get yourselves on board. Gabriella Amy and I will get our crates onboard and see if we can't get this ship airborne," Celia Jan ordered. Again, Hernando put his arm securely around Isabella's waist. He supported her, while she guided him. His cane was pretty useless. The metal floor was actually a grate and far from solid, leaving them both wondering what lay below them.

A half hour later, the four were onboard and the door shut. "Okay, why don't you two take this room here? Make yourselves comfortable. We'll be up front trying to get us going and into hyper-drive. As soon as we get into hyper-drive, we'll then figure out what to do next. This is as far ahead as I have been able to plan," Celia Jan advised them.

A bit later, the two erect statues sat across from each other, the many controls laid out in panels before them. "Hands would have made this a thousand times easier," Celia Jan complained. "Plus, I can hardly see what I'm doing."

"I know dear. We can do this, but what do we do now? I'm not familiar with these systems. They are really new aren't they?"

"True. I've read the manuals. Hope they are accurate. Pre-flight checkouts come first. On that monitor, press that symbol. It should be nearly automatic," Celia Jan told her.

A few minutes later, the pre-flight checkouts were finished. Now the main power came on. "If we are so far underground, so to speak, how do we get up there?" Gabriella Amy asked.

"Elevator. The floor is really the elevator's floor in this warehouse. It is used to service old transports. Okay, I've sent the signal. Up we go. When we get topside, we should be invisible. I have the cloaking machine going now. Of course, when we actually lift off, that is going to register with the computer systems. We'll be challenged, of course. What we need to do is to jump into hyperspace as soon as we get clear of the ground. That's the control for it there. When I tell you, notice the coordinates on that screen," she pointed with her arm. "Then enter those into the automated controls, but add a hundred to the Y-axis coordinate. Okay, get ready. I can see the dome opening over us."

Slowly the transport entered the bright yellow daylight of Proxima Prime. All around them, they could see hundreds of ships coming and going. At least they were in a more remote section of the huge port. Up they rose until the elevator stopped. Now Celia Jan pulled on the control stick slightly. The transport ship began slowly rising. Both women tried to see if there were other ships nearby, but they simply could not move their bodies enough for a clear view. "Guess we'll have to take a gamble here. I can't see. These damned neck rings. Okay, get ready. Now. Punch in the coordinates. Add a hundred to the Y coordinate. Shit! The control tower is on us, demanding id and flight confirmation codes. Hurry up. Get us out of here!"

"Done!" Gabriella Amy called out, though she need not have. The ship lurched and the brightly lit world around them vanished, replaced by the total darkness of hyperspace.

"Now we can relax at last. They cannot get to us here. Of course, now we have to figure out what the devil we are going to do. I've got the ship on minimal fuel consumption. Let's go to the charting room and figure out what to do next," Celia Jan suggested. Carefully, the two near statues rose and made their cautious way down one room to the charting and navigation room. After sitting down, Celia Jan brought up the three dimensional display of the galaxy. A red dot indicated their current location in a globular cluster somewhat close to the central hub of the galaxy. She punched in her previously recorded coordinates of Ashford-5. A green dot appeared far out on the rim of the galaxy, their destination.

"Here is where I was at in my planning, dear. The orange sphere there shows our maximum range. We are fully loaded with fuel. Ironically enough, the fuel came from our own moon. Anyway, as you can see, we can't make it home without refueling one or more times. That's what I have yet to be able to solve," Celia Jan stated factually. "Ideas?"

The two studied the three dimensional display, rotating it some, zooming in here and there. As they did so, the names of the worlds appeared, though most, neither woman recognized. "It looks like if we choose the right planet, we might be able to do it with only one stop for fuel. What're the odds that we could land on one of the planets and get refueled?" Gabriella Amy asked.

"I have no idea, honestly. It all depends on whether or not the hue and cry has gone out for us by the time we get there. I just don't know. Perhaps we should bring Isabella and Hernando in here too. They ought to have a say in where we go from here."

"I'll get them. You keep looking. Probably we want to refuel as close as we dare go to our fuel's limits, don't you think?" Gabriella Amy asked.

"Right. I'll take a look while you bring them," she replied. From the corners of her eyes, she looked at the touch screen controls and used her upper arm to manipulate the holographic display before her eyes. At least the designers of this system had the breathtaking image at her eye level. Still manipulating it was quite challenging for her.

A short while later, the three made their way into the now cramped navigation display room. Isabella made a semi-permanent connection to Hernando's mind so that he could see what she was seeing. "It is amazing and so beautiful. So this is our galaxy," Isabella exclaimed. "I've never seen a display quite like this one."

"It is the latest feature," Celia Jan explained. She launched into her explanation of their situation. "So we need to attempt to refuel somewhere along this orange sphere's edge. I've added a purple sphere centered on Tierra. From anywhere from within the intersection of the two spheres, we ought to have enough fuel to get to Ashford-5, assuming we can be completely refueled that is. The question is where do we try this? It might not work. They could be on war rationing of fuel or they could be on the lookout for us too. A thousand things could await us once we drop out of hyper-drive and try to land. Ideas?"

"What are those greyish dots there?" Isabella asked. "Shit, I can't even point anymore. Can you see what I mean?"

"Those or those?" Celia Jan asked, pointing with her arm.

"The first bunch."

"Let's see." Celia Jan twisted as much as she could, perhaps a quarter of an inch. From the corner of her eyes, she could see the console below her and used her arm to manipulate that zone, magnifying it. "I'll be damned. That's the Ataro Empire of the Twelve Sacred Planets of the Wasp! They are in a prime spot for us to refuel."

"Cool. I had a good relationship built up with a Queen Altha from there. Perhaps we could go there and make contact with her. She might be willing to help us out," Isabella suggested. "Maybe I can put all my senator experience to some real value."

"Okay, then we should probably try to contact her before we commit to the use of all our fuel. If she won't help, we have all these other possibilities we can try," Celia Jan suggested. "It might work, Isabella, since now you look so much like her."

"Tell me about that! Say, perhaps I can say that I am returning to Ashford-5 and want to see if I can implement the type of peace she and the others have there in the Ataro Empire," Isabella suggested.

"Hey, it is worth a try. Okay. Let's get you to the comm center. That's the room across the hall. It will be too crowded with us all in there. Isabella, you and I will go. I'll set up a video chat with this queen, if they will allow us to talk directly to her. I will leave the discussion to you. Just make sure that she is willing to refuel us," Celia Jan suggested. "Easy does it. You are on your own mostly. My arms are about useless." Very carefully, the two statues moved out of this room and across to the comm center. "Okay. You stand there. You can see the images that'll be sent to her on that screen in front of you. I'll sit here and run the controls. Good luck, Isabella."

She tossed her hair back and sat down. Again, she had to use her *mentales* gifts to operate the controls. "I am going to try to translate what you say into Imperium Standard, overlaying your actual speech, since the ULATs cannot handle it any more. Okay, here goes nothing." She entered the coordinates and pressed the Talk button, enforcing Imperium Standard words to be sent.

> This is Senator Isabella Valen of Ashford-5 calling
> Queen Altha. I am requesting a direct delayed video
> communication with Queen Altha. Senatorial
> business. Please respond.

After a five-minute delay in hyperspace transmission, a control voice responded. "This is Central Communications for Winno-3, home world of Queen Altha. Your senatorial request has been sent to Queen Altha. Please stand by for identification. Send image of yourself."

As quick as she could, Celia Jan captured a still image of Isabella and sent it. "Now we wait. Keep your fingers crossed," Celia Jan said without thinking.

Isabella felt rather amused. "But I don't have any fingers. Are you as blind as Hernando?" Both women laughed, breaking their nervous tension. So much rode on this delayed communications link. Minutes passed.

Suddenly, the image of Queen Altha appeared on their monitor. "Senator Isabella! So good to see you again! What have you done to your body? You look years younger. You look like I do! Over."

Celia Jan translated what Isabella said into Imperium Standard. "Queen Altha. You look as gorgeous as I remembered. Yes, you have inspired us. I have taken what you and your empire have done to heart. I am trying to bring your system of government to my home world of Ashford-5. There, our nobles have taken to wearing these fancy lip plates, so I am trying to make a good first impression on them. Unfortunately, the ULAT boxes can't understand my speech any longer. It is being translated into Imperium Standard. I was hoping we could stop on your world and get refueled. I would love to spend some time with you and learn all that I can about your governing system so I can implement it back on Ashford-5 when I return. If I can prevent wars and conflicts among my people, then I will have the only reward I could possibly desire. Yes, I had to remove a few years so I too could get the twelve-inch waistline that is needed. Over." Celia Jan smiled, Isabella played Queen Altha perfectly!

After another long wait during which both women fidgeted nervously, the reply came, but everything hung on Queen Altha's reply! "Senator Isabella! This is the greatest news I've had in a very long time. For centuries, our emperor has been trying his best to get other worlds to adopt our incredible form of government to no avail. Yes, yes, please come to Winno-3. I will see to your proper training myself! You are doing me and the entire Ataro Empire the greatest of all possible honors! Of course, you can refuel here. How else could you return to Ashford-5 and begin your life's incredible works? Please, come as soon as you can. Are your wives with you? As I recall, you had two beautiful wives. Over."

"Yes, they are with me and look nearly as I do, though they still have their upper arms left. Will that be a problem? Over."

After the long delay, Queen Altha replied, "What an unusual variation with your wives. No, I don't believe that will be any problem at all. They will be just as physically helpless as we are. I will put you up with me in my palace so we can get right onto your training. If you have any men with you, I'll have to make some other arrangements for them. Men are not allowed in my personal quarters. I am so very pleased you are doing this, Isabella. I can't tell you how happy you have made me. When will you be arriving? Over."

"Oh no. What about Hernando?" Isabella asked Celia Jan. "I don't what him to have a very hard time there. How long will it take? What should I tell her?"

"Two days travel time. This new ship is more efficient than the older transports. Tell her to anticipate us arriving in forty-eight hours or so. We can talk about what to do with Hernando when we're done here," she replied, thinking fast.

"Queen Altha, it is we who are so very privileged to learn from you. I'm told we should be there in about forty-eight hours or so. We look forward to learning all that we can. Thank you ever so much. Over."

Once more, they waited on the comm delay. "Terrific. I will have all the arrangements made for your arrival. I'm sending the landing coordinates to your system now. Well, I'm not actually doing that. How could I? Rather, the technicians are doing it. I will be counting the hours. See you then. Over and out."

"Well what a fortuitous stroke of good luck," Isabella said as the two struggled to get safely to their feet without falling. "For once, being a senator has done something positive for me and for us. But what about Hernando?"

A few minutes later, they relayed all that was said. "So what about Hernando? We can't just toss him to wherever they put their men. He needs assistance too, only different than we do," Isabella asked, pleadingly.

"Well, there is one thing we could do," Celia Jan

suggested coyly. "You see, the queens always have personal attendants who help them with things, such as eating. They are always women, but they too are altered considerably, but worse, they are unable to speak. However, we could use the medical machine on Hernando to change his gender or mostly so. I can make it so that he would pass as a she or nearly so. Then, Queen Altha might allow him or her to assist you with some things like eating."

"But I don't want him to lose his manhood," Isabella protested.

"I can leave that part untouched, but make the rest of his body look like that of a woman. If he's careful, no one would be the wiser," Jan suggested. "Otherwise, he'll just have to somehow fend for himself while we play our roles."

Hernando spoke up, "I don't want to be a burden for you. Already you have enough of those to last a lifetime. No matter what you do with me, I will always be a burden for you."

"No you are not a burden. You've helped me immensely. I don't know how I could have gotten by without you. I am not going to throw you to the wolves. Are you willing to play along with these changes for a while — as long as she leaves your manhood in tact and restores everything as soon as we leave there?"

"Sure. I can't see it anyway. I would like to continue to help you, Isabella. You know that. I owe you everything," he replied.

"Okay then, Isabella, take him back to the room numbered six. I've got my new medical machine setup there. Meanwhile, we best get this transport on its way there," Celia Jan replied.

An hour later, Celia Jan joined Isabella and Hernando. "Okay, Isabella, you can leave us now and I'll work my magic on Hernando. I guess we need to start calling you Hernanda," she teased a little. Isabella touched the front of her lips to his cheek and left the two, making her slow, careful walk back to her room. Already, she missed him. She had to swivel at her hips to get her long tresses to slide to her front side so she could sit down. *I hope he doesn't hate us for doing this to him, but it should only be temporary,* she justified.

"What will you do to me?" he asked once he sensed Isabella had gone.

"Well, I'll be growing your hair a good deal. Any desired length that you'd like? I'll be forming Ashford-5 type breasts. We've got gowns that will fit them. To make this realistic, I'll need to shrink your waist. Hope you don't mind wearing a tight corset like the rest of us. Don't worry. I won't touch your privates, unless you want me to go all the way. I might not be able to put your privates back, but I can restore the rest of your body once we are on our way to Ashford-5," she explained.

"If we don't need to touch my privates, then let's don't. Make my hair whatever is most believable. I just want to be there to help Miss Isabella, who needs my help always. How will you and Gabriella get by? I can feed you both too. I know I am very clumsy at it, but I want to help as I can. You can't imagine what it is to spend a century being unable to help others much at all and yet depending on the help of others. It has driven me nearly nuts," he admitted.

"I think you've done a remarkable job of keeping your sanity, and I know how much Isabella has come to depend upon you. That's why I am doing this. I have a feeling she is really going to need your help while we are there. Okay, this is going to take some time. Don't worry; you won't feel any pain, just a few pin pricks."

First, she altered his waist, removing a pair of ribs. Gabriella Amy found a spare corset that would work. Together using their *mentales* gifts, the two managed to get it on Hernando. That took them nearly an hour. To his credit, he didn't complain. Next, she set to work on using the stem cells of the machine to enlarge his breasts to the proper size for a Tierra woman. Isabella found one of her red satin gowns from Tierra that would fit him. Another hour passed by as the two worked hard to get him properly dressed, complete with a white slip, hose, and a pair of heels. At last, she began to work on her hair, deciding to lengthen it to about two feet. No sense in making it longer just yet. She'd have enough trouble adapting to the changes. Celia Jan was more concerned about how he's be able to manage walking in the heels, since he couldn't see.

That reminded her Isabella had wanted her to check out his eyes. While the machine was working on her hair, she adjusted the machine slightly, bringing up the menus that dealt with a person's eyes. Before long, she examined the readout. Something was definitely not adding up here. According to the machine, his eyes were not glass marbles as he had said. Rather, the readings suggested he had human eyes, but she could only see the black spheres. What was going on here?

She did some more tests. Again, they indicated he had human eyes somewhere. At last, she began to wonder if somehow the black she was seeing was some kind of covering placed over the entire front surface. She began to browse through all the eye menu options. At the very bottom, she discovered a pair labeled "Coverings" and "Un-coverings." I wonder, she thought to herself. She activated the anesthetic option. Shortly, Hernanda was sleeping quietly. It can't hurt, she thought. He's already blind. She activated the Un-coverings button and waited as the machine did its work.

When the arms retracted, she looked down into his yellow eyes with brown speckles! "Well, I'll be! Carlos, you are truly a number one bastard! Best check on their health. They don't look so good. Infections, I'll bet." Again, she activated the machine. Indeed, she was right. Both of his eyes had massive infections, and his or her vision would be almost not worth restoring as they were now. Again, she utilized the eye menus and activated the healing sequence. A half hour later, the two arms retracted. She now saw normal looking eyes and she smiled. Did she ever have a surprise for Hernando and for Isabella!

An hour later, she smelled food. Gabriella Amy had somehow gotten a long overdue meal prepared and Hernanda began to waken. She moaned a little. Her abdomen felt compressed. She opened her eyes and nearly fainted. "I can see? I can see! Celia, I can see! I really can see you! How is this possible? A miracle? I can see!"

"Carlos lied to you and your mother. He didn't remove your eyes, but rather put a black covering over them. Your eyes were pretty bad off. Massive infections. But I cured that and have your eyes restored back to perfect vision now. Congratulations, Hernanda. You can see. This is really going to help us all!"

"How can I ever thank you, Celia Jan? This is a miracle to beat all miracles! Now I can see my flower, Miss Isabella. I smell food. She needs me."

"Come on; up you go. Careful walking in the heels. Take small steps. Come on, let's surprise Isabella, shall we? Oh yes, you do look most presentable, like a real woman from Tierra." The two headed back up towards the cramped galley, which just had room for four people to sit down at the small table. Gabriella had merely heated up a can of stew, keeping it simple.

"Wow! Hernanda, you look really good!" Isabella exclaimed from her seat facing the door. "Your eyes? They are yellow now."

"I can see! I can really see! She worked a miracle on me. Now I can see you all so perfectly! Miss Isabella, you are prettier than I ever imagined! I'm coming." She sat down beside her and began to feed her. "Now I can really take proper care of you, Miss Isabella. Now I can truly help all of you! I am so happy I think that I'm floating. No, fainting. I can't breathe!"

"Take shallow breaths, Hernanda; don't fight it. Relax, there. Celia! Thank you, thank you, thank you!" Isabella gushed.

"You were right. There was something strange about his or her eyes. The latest medical machines can place a colored disk over one's eyes. That's what Carlos did to him, er her. I think there is a medical need to do such things in emergencies, but I'm not a doctor," Celia Jan replied. "I'm starving. Hope you don't mind if I help myself this once."

"Sure I am too. After this, though, we had all best get used to having Hernanda help us. We don't dare display our powers around Queen Altha and her court," Gabriella Amy replied. "So Hernanda, we will be depending upon you for many things once we get there. I think we are about halfway there."

633

"You can count on me! I will be here for all three of you," Hernanda replied eagerly.

Isabella laughed, "Well, now Hernanda, you can see just how freakish that they and I look."

"But Miss Isabella, you do not look like a freak. You are as beautiful as the orchid is. Please stop saying otherwise. I know your breasts are way too big, and the neck rings look so strange as do the lip plates, but that is because I have never seen them before. Like with my orchid, I see below all these surface things and see the most beautiful woman ever. Perhaps Miss Celia Jan can fix you all up before we arrive wherever it is."

She flushed but remained silent. Gabriella Amy spoke up, "Gang, I've been thinking about this very thing. Queen Altha has seen just how Isabella now looks. If we go ahead and try to remove the rings and fix ourselves up, she may well become far too curious about how we did it. After all, Hernanda here doesn't know anything about the medical machine and its procedures. She won't believe Celia here could possibly operate the machine. No, if she sees us any differently than she first saw Isabella, we could blow this whole thing. I believe we best endure this a little longer until we leave Winno-3."

Isabella spoke up. "I had not thought about that. I am certain you are right about Queen Altha. She's not going to believe Celia Jan could have done it. I would have broken her trust and faith in me. Since my Hernanda can now see to help us far better, I am willing somehow to endure this a little longer. What has me worried — and I talked with Gabriella Amy about this while you were both back there — what has me worried is how will we be able to talk to them when we get there? I had thought we could use Hernanda to speak for us, since we don't dare get our lips fixed just yet."

"I will do it, Miss Isabella. Don't worry," she replied, still noticing how her voice had changed so drastically.

"Okay, we'll just use telepathy, Hernanda, to let you know what needs to be said," Gabriella Amy replied. "After we eat, we ought to catch up on our sleep. Tomorrow, Hernanda needs to practice dressing us and practice her walking. Those heels take a good time to get accustomed to wearing."

Chapter 33 Ataro Training

Right on schedule, the blue-green world of Winno-3 appeared through their view panes. At this point, the automatic landing pilot took control, obeying the coordinates that Queen Altha had had relayed to them. They watched, as the globe grew larger and larger. Landmasses appeared, and then they slowly began to descend upon the major city of Winiana, in which Queen Altha's Royal Palace and Court were located.

Soon they landed and the door opened. Their sun was bright yellow and warm. The air was clean and fresh, quite the opposite of the stale, recycled air of the transport, which was also filled with that "newness" odor. A well-dressed man wearing a business suit with twin tails met them as they disembarked. "Are you Senator Isabella Valen and party?"

"Yes, I'm Isabella. These are my wives and our assistant." Hernanda quickly interpreted as soon as she heard the error message coming from the man's ULAT box.

"Ah, excellent. If you will follow me, I will take you to Queen Altha. She is most excited about your visit. I myself am most amazed to see off-worlders looking like our esteemed and revered Queen Altha." They followed him, walking across the concrete base to a waiting air car. As always, Hernanda had her arm around Isabella, making sure she had all the support she needed.

As they drove through the huge city, they noticed many life-sized statues of the emperor and empress. Several were obviously of their beloved Queen Altha. Even more interesting, they spotted many buildings designed to look like wasps as well. Their ground floor looked more like a giant sphere or bulb with a tiny cylindrical connecting section that joined the second floor, also shaped like a bulb. Some were three stories tall and resembled wasps, remarkably so. "Oh, those are our Holy Temples," the man explained. Memories flooded back to Gabriella Amy and Celia Jan, not so pleasant ones however.

Shortly, he stopped at an enormous complex, where dozens of wasp shaped buildings rose from the ground. Green grass actually grew in the intervening spaces between the buildings. "We cherish nature and the gardens are just lovely, attracting many wasps that come for the pollen. If you will follow me, the queen awaits you. Your bags will be brought here shortly and taken to your quarters."

They followed him inside, past several security men. It felt strange walking into the bottom of a bulb shaped room, but once inside, it was even more curious. Well decorated, it felt comfortable and homey, somehow. Having curved walls with curved windows seemed weird at first glance, but all the usual things were inside: reception desk, chairs, a picture gallery. For Gabriella Amy and Celia Jan, many memories returned to them. They'd seen similar buildings these before. They walked to the center where the elevator was located. Now Isabella realized the elevator was housed within the small cylinders that connected the bulb shaped portions. They went up to the third floor.

When the doors opened, they smelled the unmistakable fragrance of fresh flowers and discovered the huge room was filled with them. A red carpet led up to two thrones. A number of smaller thrones lay on either side but were unoccupied. They were for the queens or children, all of whom were now on other planets. Ahead, a well-dressed man stood on one side of the queen and a woman wearing an elegant satin gown stood on the other side. Queen Altha looked just as she had when she visited the Senate.

As in any court, there were a fair number of courtiers present standing off to the far right and left. Many of the women also had been modified into wasps as well as some of the men. Each of those also had a servant at their sides.

Queen Altha carefully rose from her throne, though the man paid close attention to her, making sure she didn't lose her balance on her tiny feet. His waist was so tiny that Hernanda felt she could put her hands around it. His white satin shirt was tailored to fit his unique shape. His white satin pants also were fitted to his form, with a contrasting black belt around his tiny waist, adding to the tiny wasp waist illusion. She noted the ULAT box attached to it. Her eyes turned to the queen, who wore a form fitting white satin dress that accentuated her form greatly adding to the wasp illusion. She too wore a black belt with attached ULAT box. All three of their feet were incredibly tiny, making standing still as challenging for them as it was for Isabella and her two wives.

"It is so very good to see you, Senator Isabella. I am so proud of the new way you look! You have outdone me, and that is saying something. Oh, yes, I have updated our ULAT boxes. We can now understand your speech. I tried to contact Nadja Burkhardt back on Tierra. I didn't know she had divorced Konrad. Actually, I forgot the Imperium has abandoned your sector of space. That makes what you are trying to do for your world so incredibly more important! Anyway, I finally got through to her and she was kind enough to send us a ULAT box update so we can now understand your speech. I imagine others find it hard to understand you — what with those enormous lip ornaments. Nadja says all the lords and ladies are wearing them, so I can see why you need to wear them too. Those will be the major ones you'll need to work with when you return. Oh dear, I seem to be just rattling on! Forgive me; I am so very excited about your visit. You must be tired from your long trip. Please, follow me. I'll take you to your new quarters while you are here with us. Oh, this is my personal assistant Evon, she is unable to speak, as is our custom. This is my top advisor, Herbon; he does speak, but mostly about important matters. Evon, shall we lead them?"

"It is we who are blessed and honored by your allowing us to learn your ways and to attempt to take them to Ashford-5. Is it permissible for my assistant to help me walk?" Isabella asked.

"Certainly. Evon helps me too. It would be very unseemly if we should take a tumble in public." She lowered her voice slightly, "I must admit I've taken several tumbles, but not in public. I can't tell you how scared I was walking alone onto your Senate platform. Still, I had to do it as our queen." She chatted as if no time had passed since her visit to Proxima Prime.

"These are my private chambers. We can spend evenings in here. I've arranged for you to have my guest quarters here, right next to mine. Of course, Herbon was against it. He thinks you wish me harm. How silly of him. What are you going to do? Hit me with your lip plates? Silly man. We are so completely helpless, which is the way it should and must be, since my word is law, subordinate to the emperor and empress, naturally. Ultimate power must be counterbalanced. The temptation for abuse of power is far too great otherwise, as you well know by now."

"Oh that we very much know with absolute certainty!" Isabella replied, thinking of President Carlos.

"I am so glad you have such certainty, Senator Isabella. So very few actually do, you know. Here we are. I do hope you and your wives will be comfortable here. Will you be needing some additional assistants for your wives? I can have a couple of women here to help you out at the critical times, mornings and nights."

"Would you? I am sure they would really appreciate the assistance. Hernanda has all she can do to assist me, as I'm sure Evon has with you," Isabella replied graciously.

"Absolutely. We are a handful, aren't we? But then, that's as it should and must be. I will see that two are assigned to you yet today. I see your few bags have been brought up already. Do you have sufficient personal things with you? If not, I can see if we can somehow provide what you might lack."

"Oh that would be wonderful, Queen Altha. Please, your kindness is most overwhelming. Yes, we left with almost no personal items. These are the only dresses we have that will fit our new dimensions. Of course, I insist we pay you for them."

"Nonsense, Senator Isabella. You are my guests and the ultimate honor you are showing me more than pays for such minor, physical things. You and I, we have our whole worlds to watch over and safeguard. I insist. I will send a dressmaker at once along with two assistants. Of course, the assistants will not be able to speak, but they can show you around and such things. I will leave you to get settled in. We can talk more at suppertime. Until then," she bowed. Isabella tried to bow in turn, but all she could manage was to bend slightly at her hips. The rest of her body was held nearly immobile, as were those of her two wives.

Their room was filled with the most enticing, marvelous fragrances from six bouquets of freshly picked flowers resting in beautifully made ceramic vases. Two very large beds occupied the middle of the room, with two dressing bureaus on either side, each with a tall mirror. They blended admirably with the curved walls and windows that offered a magnificent view of the adjacent buildings and the grounds, filled with far too many flowerbeds to count. An elegantly carved wardrobe stood against another central wall, where its height could be easily reached by the women. Their fully equipped bathroom lay snugly against the curved outer wall. Of course, electric lights were present.

Just then, two young teens, barely a year older than the trio, made their silent way into the room. Both had just as tiny a waistline as the trio's and wore similar toe shoes as the queen. Their skin had a yellowish hue to it. Their rich, black hair hung down to the middle of their backs, and they wore two wasp-like clasps in it, holding their hair behind them. Their gowns were quite form fitting and were a brilliant yellow satin. They bowed to Gabriella and Celia, each one pointing to a woman and to themselves, getting across the idea that they would be their personal assistants.

Then another woman arrived, the dressmaker. She was all business, taking the women's measurements very efficiently. She asked what colors the women liked, explaining they would soon have six new gowns. Isabella asked for various shades of red and asked if Hernanda could also have some new gowns. The dressmaker smiled and said she would have some as well, but Isabella insisted that Hernanda's gowns match each of hers. Gabriella asked for various shades of yellow, while Celia wanted hues of green. After she left, the two new helpers indicated the two should sit on the bed and they would brush out their hair before dinner. Hernanda took the hint and worked on Isabella's very long black hair as well, trying hard to emulate how the two helpers did this.

Then, the two helpers made eating signs and assisted the two to rise, an action they found rather pleasant in that they didn't have to make Herculean lunges to get to their feet. Hernanda followed suit; this she had down very well. While the two helpers tried to get Isabella to go first, they quickly realized she didn't know where to go and that her mobility was too restricted. They then took the lead, heading out towards the central hub. There they took an elevator down one floor, where the large dining room, which doubled as a meeting hall for special events, was located. Again, fresh flowers dotted its perimeter. Queen Altha and Evon were already there, seated at one end of the nicely decorated table. Wasp figurines dotted the table and a few held burning candles that gave off an additional pleasant scent to the room.

Evon indicated Isabella should sit directly opposite from Queen Altha, and Hernanda escorted her there, pulling her long hair around to her front, and helping her sit down as gracefully as possible. Her wives and their two helpers were positioned on either side of the table. "First, we must pray and give thanks for all those who have lent us a hand in the creation and preparation of this fine dinner lying before us. Many hands have gone into this meal, from the farmers, to the butchers, to the millers, to the chefs. To all of these, we express our deep gratitude for their physical labors on our behalf. Amen. There, now Evon may begin to serve me, as your assistants may do for you. We can talk over tea when we've finished. Do try the chicken; it is always extremely delicious. Of course, we don't eat very large amounts, as you well know."

A while later over tea, Isabella asked, "Do your people worship the wasps? I am afraid that I really know so very little about your people." She thought this would be a light after dinner conversation. Little did she know, and even less, how much of an impact this discussion would later play.

"Actually we do, but not as you might think, though long ago this was truer than it is today. You see, over three millennia ago, our great sages recognized a fundamental truth about all life. Each of us is a unique spiritual being; we are not made of physical matter. Some suggest we are immortal, but that has yet to be proven. All life contains a spiritual being as well, though they are lesser in abilities than we are. All life is a composite of the physical matter plus the spiritual being, which is not made of physical matter. It is a union of the two. They remain an inseparable whole until the physical body dies.

Only then are the two separated. The physical material dissolves and eventually its particles are reused to form new physical bodies. We have yet to ascertain with any certainty what happens to the spiritual beings when the union ends, though. There is some speculation that just as the dead physical form dissolves and later reforms into a new physical form, so the spiritual beings re-enter these new forms, forming a new union. Of course, that has yet to be proven. So you see, these discoveries all came from their studies of the many wasps that are in abundance on our worlds."

"The wasps here in our systems live in harmony with themselves and all nature. Yet, if they are threatened, they act as a whole, defending their queen and nests with their lives. From them, our warring leaders finally learned their long overdue lessons. Life is meant to be lived in peace and prosperity and harmony, not in conflicts and wars. Yet, if that peace is threatened, then all shall unite as one to combat the threat, you see."

"The great sages also learned something else from the wasps. And that is ultimate power almost always tends to corrupt the wielder. When they have such powers, only a strong willed person can resist the many temptations that come their way. Often such corruption has led to conflicts and even wars — the presence of the third person actively fomenting it aside. Yet, when our leaders looked to the wasps, they saw no such thing. Here, our wasps have queens who are immobile, much as you and I are. They can barely move on their own, and yet from them comes all the new generations. I'm told this is much like the bees found on many other worlds, but of that, I cannot say from firsthand knowledge. It was from these observations the great sages and ancient leaders of our past realized we humans would do well to emulate the wasps. That is why we hold these wasps in such reverence here. They are nature's model for us to follow."

"Since that time, we leaders of the Ataro System have been molded into physical forms such that we are very nearly physically helpless, dependent upon all others, just as the wasp queens are. Onto us has been bestowed the ultimate power to rule our people with the full knowledge we cannot abuse our immense powers for personal gain. After all, what could I possibly want? I can't hold anything, touch anything, or do much of anything. About the only thing we have to be alert for is someone playing to our own egos. So in a way, our people worship the wasps, but not like a religion, but as the true way of nature, which we see as a form of perfection in this universe."

"We see wisdom and spirituality as closely interrelated and possibly interconnected. Out there among the many worlds of the vast Imperium, we have seen and studied many forms of government. For short periods of time, there have been some excellent monarchies, whose reigns have been quite exalted. Always, those benevolent monarchs have been extremely strong willed individuals. Yet, they suffer from the destructive problem of succession. Almost never is the benevolent ruler succeeded by one of equal caliber."

"We've seen other forms, such as that of the Imperium itself, base their rule upon a theoretical system of checks and balances. The Senate makes the laws, the Supreme Council enforces those laws, and the Imperial Courts handles all jurisprudence. In theory, they each could act as a check on the other two. In practice, however, men and women in those top most positions become corrupted, and the system breaks down, as witnessed by the current situation. The Supreme Council with its president has overruled both the Senate and the Courts, claiming wartime emergencies give them the ultimate powers to set aside all checks and balances. Ha. Someone is getting wealthy because of the war."

"We here believe, if those Senators, those on the Supreme Council, and those in the high courts were physically restrained as we rulers in the Ataro System are, there would be vastly less chance for the corruption and abuse of their powers. We've tried to convince them of this for nearly two millennia now, but without success. Can you see why I am so excited about your willingness to give it a try on your world?"

Isabella finally got a chance to speak up. "Now I can see why. Indeed, we four know precisely what you are talking about when you say those in high power positions have become corrupted by their ultimate power. I am really looking forward to learning more from you. Your discussion of your rule of always needing a third person to foment a conflict or war rings very true to me. I am dying to learn more."

Queen Altha laughed, "It is not a rule, Senator Isabella, it is a *natural law* at work. You see, this is one feature that separates humans from nature's wasps. As far as we know, wasps do not communicate as effectively and readily as humans do. True, they have some form of communication. When danger comes, the whole nest is alerted, as is their queen. But little more. It is with humans and our incredible mastery of language and the spoken word that enables us to bring about conflicts between two people. A third person is able to run down another person, to make less of the other person, and to invalidate, enturbulate, and upset others. That is the basis for that natural law, you see. Thus, it is our ability as leaders, untouchable by the corruption of power, that allows us to see through the fog the third person had spread over the relationship between two people."

"With great power over others comes a great responsibility towards the others. We leaders take our immense responsibilities very seriously indeed. For if we fail, then we are in fact failing all of our people, who are dependent upon us for peace and prosperity. In many ways, Senator Isabella, the weight we carry on our shoulders is immense. We can never be free of it nor would we ever want to be free of it, for that would also be a betrayal of the confidence and trust that our people have placed in us. That would be treason, by definition — in short, a betrayal after trust."

Isabella replied thoughtfully, "I see that and I agree with you; treason is just that, a betrayal after trust. I've endured. So does this mean you here have a strong moral code that you follow? I mean do your people see me being married to two other women as somehow wrong?"

She laughed. "Oh dear me. Two things at once. First, you are confusing morals and ethics. Don't feel bad; most all people have them totally confused. You see, morals are merely an agreed upon set of rules of conduct that enables the group which subscribes to them to survive better. I've read about one of those more underdeveloped worlds that Nadja studied a few years back, where the women have no hands, wear nearly identical lip plates as you do, have enormous necks of golden rings similar to yours, and wear toe shoes because they have no feet either. In that culture, the men follow a moral code of constant protection of their women. Anything that threatens a woman, harms them, or even upsets them, is totally taboo. As Nadja reported, the women suffer from a genetic defect that has formed the basis of their society."

"On many other worlds, they have a moral code that it is taboo for anyone to engage in sexual relations with either member of a marriage. Why? Because they have seen when that is done, the marriage often is destroyed. Yet a marriage is the fundamental building block of any society. So for the survival of the society, moral codes are adopted."

"Now ethics is an entirely different matter. To be ethical, one must base one's decisions upon those actions which benefit the most while harming the least. By this, I mean one must consider the action's impact not only on oneself, but also on one's family, on the various groups one is a part of, on perhaps all mankind, on all plants and animals, and on the physical universe itself. While a president of a company stealing money from his company may help his own self out nicely, it certainly harms his company and could well harm other arenas as well. So that theft would be unethical, as it harms more than it helps."

"Moral codes and ethics can sometimes be at odds with each other, you see. Moral codes usually condemn all actions that break up a marriage. Yet, what if that marriage is a very abusive one for the man or woman? Is it not more beneficial to all concerned and more areas than just those two to break up that marriage?"

She concluded, "So you see, we in the Ataro System do our very best to utilize ethics and not moral codes. Certainly, this is an absolute must for us rulers, as you will soon see once we get you going on your training. However, we also admit that many who are not so well educated do need to have simpler moral codes to follow."

"As far as your own personal marriage goes, that is your own personal matter and decision. None of us would even consider discussing your choices. How are we to know what has led you to these marriages? On the other hand, women bear children who become the future generation. Without children, there can be no future for a people. Yet, we also recognize with today's marvelous medical machines, it is easy for marriages as yours to bring forth children of your own. Of course, those children are always going to be girls," Queen Altha replied to her second question at last.

She then went on, "Quite naturally, this brings up the roles that men and women play in society. We have studied nearly all the worlds within the Imperium we can. In all cases, women bear the children. We have yet to find a human species in which men bear the children. While not always true, women are usually physically weaker than men, who are usually the physically stronger sex. Women tend to be nurturing in nature, probably because we bear and raise the children, though on some worlds, men do the raising of their children and are nearly as nurturing as us women are. Most physical conflicts and battles occur among men, though sometime women do so as well. Women can sometimes use words, bitching, and nagging to control men instead of using physical force, though not always. Both men and women sometimes use sex to gain control or to dominate their partners or others. There are no absolutes anywhere, but one can make some strong generalities about the differences between men and women. We recognized these as fundamental physical differences, and we accept them as Nature has given them to us."

Isabella wanted to nod, but couldn't. Instead, she asked, "So is this nurturing nature of women the main reason you have mostly women in the top most positions of power? I mean there is only one emperor, but there is an empress and many, many queens."

She smiled, "Observant. Yes, that is correct. Millennia ago, this simple fact was recognized by everyone. It was reasoned if we truly wanted eternal peace, then that peace would have to be nurtured; hence, we women stepped up to assume the immense mantle of responsibility. The many kings were slowly retired. Still, in times of crisis, we need the strength of men, and men need to see there is someone strong in charge as well, hence the emperor, who has authority over all us women rulers. Again, that has proven most successful in our system of planets."

Isabella frowned. "On our world, men are frequently causing strife and conflicts. They are always scheming and conniving for more power, wealth, and material goods. Does that go on here too?"

Gabriella Amy suddenly paid close attention to what Queen Altha's answer. This had been precisely what she had faced as Tierra's first emperor.

Queen Altha laughed. "We have to be far more observant of men than we do of women on our worlds. Men are quick to rile. Again, you will learn more of this in the days to come. Essentially, you are quite correct. Men, by their very nature, are often prone to such things. But I must also say women have been known to be very vicious as well. Still, you are correct. While women are behind some troubles, more often than not, it is a man who is the guilty party. Women are more often found as the third person who is actively promoting a conflict between two unsuspecting men. Isn't that interesting? But then, that too is part of the nature of the differences between men and women. In general, a woman cannot hope to better the strength of a man, so she uses different tactics in her misguided attempts at controlling others. Again, you will soon be learning about such things."

Isabella smiled, even though she knew it wasn't visible. "I can see I have a whole lot to learn. How can we ever thank you for teaching us?"

Queen Altha smiled, "By taking what we can teach you and using it to make your world a better world for all men and women. But golly, we've talked half the night away. You must be exhausted from your trip. Let's get you to bed. Tomorrow begins the first day of your education, Isabella."

With that, Evon rose and assisted Queen Altha to rise gracefully. Likewise, the two new assistants did the same with Gabriella Amy and Celia Jan. Hernanda hastily emulated the three assistants, much to the pleasure of Isabella, who was able to stand fairly gracefully as well. Soon, they were back in their bedroom. Efficiently, the two assistants undressed their two, while Hernanda dealt with Isabella's needs. Then, she removed Isabella's lip plates. The two assistants watched her carefully, and they emulated her, removing Celia and Gabriella's lip plates.

At this point, the two assistants began making gestures and signs. After watching their motions, Celia Jan caught on to what they were asking. Who was to sleep in which bed? They were pointing to the two wives and the second bed. "Yes, why don't you both sleep in that bed? Hernanda can sleep with me tonight and help me first thing in the morning," Isabella suggested. The two assistants nodded and helped their charges get into bed without more or less falling into it, since they lacked nearly all mobility from their hips upwards. Hernanda emulated their actions, lowering Isabella gently into her bed. Only after the two assistants left did Hernanda turn out the lights and slip into bed beside Isabella. She whispered, "Hold me, please, Hernanda." On the other bed, the two women grinned to themselves.

Over breakfast the next morning, Queen Altha made a suggestion. "I have been chatting with Evon. She and I believe, Senator Isabella, that walking and many other things would be easier if you had your feet altered to be like ours are. Your feet are fused so they don't bend, forcing you to walk only on the tips of your toes. You cannot even stand without wearing your toe boots. The way we have our feet fixed, our toes rest flat on the floor. We can stand without wearing shoes and get into and out of the bathtub and bed. Of course, we can't stand on just our toes in a stable way for any real length of time without our shoes, but we manage much better than you and your wives. It is something to consider, though perhaps you might not be able to purchase new shoes like these on your world."

Isabella smiled instinctively. "Oh please, could we? I was wearing shoes like yours when I was a senator. We all would dearly love to wear them instead of these ballet en pointe boots! I could walk so much better and be less reliant upon poor Hernanda. Would we be able to purchase a supply of your style heels to take back with us?"

"Yes, I insist you take many back with you. I know you'll

have a much easier time walking and standing," Queen Altha replied, encouragingly. Isabella picked up her surface thoughts: I do hope they do this. I can't imagine even how they can stand, let alone walk in those ballerina-like boots.

Isabella pivoted and looked at Gabriella Amy. She and Celia Jan had many memories of wearing shoes of this type from their experiences here long ago. She said decisively, "Thank you, Queen Altha. Wearing your style toe shoes would be most welcome indeed." She hoped the queen would not ask why they all chose to get their feet fused and wear these ballerina style boots. She didn't dare tell her the truth, that Senator Carlos had done this to them.

"I am honored to assist all of you. Then, it's settled. We'll get your feet fixed up in proper Ataro fashion right now. Will Hernanda wish to have this done as well?" She looked over at Isabella's assistant.

Hernanda felt like she was suddenly on the spot. Clearly, Evon wore them and was the queen's assistant. Since she was now Isabella's assistant, she said, "I would be honored, if my mistress desires it." She sent, *Her assistant Evon has them. It might be wise if your assistant did so as well. What do you think? Shouldn't we play along with their culture?*

"Correct me if I am wrong, Queen Altha, but isn't it customary for your assistant to also wear the same type of shoes as you do? If so, then I think Hernanda should also wear them as I will."

"Yes, that is the custom established over two millennia ago. Then, it is all settled. Come with us; we'll get you all properly done. I will personally assist you in learning to walk as gracefully as a queen does. That will be your first lesson," Queen Altha said cheerfully and somewhat relieved.

An hour later, the four looked at their newly modified feet. Their previously inflexible feet no longer pointed straight downwards. They could flex and wiggle their toes as they had always been able to do prior to having them fixed for toe shoes and boots. Indeed, all could stand up. Their toes, at least, were flat on the floor. However, their arches were enormous. The bottom of their heels now aligned with the back of their toes.

Isabella allowed Hernanda to comment, "Oh, this is more difficult, isn't it!" Since she had been wearing them since becoming a senator, she was finally relatively comfortable in the once more. Hernanda wasn't. Celia Jan and Gabriella Amy had worn them in their previous lifetimes and said memories returned to them. Still, both struggled to relearn to walk in them, though Hernanda had the most trouble, naturally.

"Now, we must practice your walking. Take small steps like Evon and me," Queen Altha said proudly. For several hours, the small group walked around the Royal Palace. Then, she took them outside for a long tour of her grounds and gardens, where flowers grew in hundreds of well-tended arrangements.

After lunch, Isabella's formal training began in earnest. All four of them participated, though the emphasis was on training Isabella. For two weeks, Isabella worked on all aspects of handling conflicts by finding the real third person who was in fact behind the conflicts. She was amazed at how the training was done. While at first, she was given lectures on it, soon she was thrown into practice sessions were she actually had to apply what she'd learned. Queen Altha explained these first sessions would be easy, but gradually they would become more difficult to resolve. She was right.

After two full weeks of drilling, Queen Altha then had Isabella do it for real, helping her settle some actual conflicts. At the end of the third week, Queen Altha assigned her a particularly challenging conflict for her to resolve. The court announcer introduced the two parties, a pair of company presidents. "This is Mr. Atonis Bursi, President of Bursi Manufacturing. This is Mr. Gordi Zona, President of Zona Bearings. Case Number 35932, now being heard in Queen Altha's Court. Senator Isabella Valen presiding, assisted by Queen Altha. The ruling of this court is final. Both parties have agreed to abide by the judgment of this court. Mr. Bursi, step forward and present your case." The man stepped back and proceeded to make the official records of the hearing. Hernanda sat beside Isabella, writing pad at hand, fulfilling her duties as her assistant, just as Evon had been doing for Queen Altha.

A man in a finely tailored grey suit stepped forward. "Your Majesties. For the past three years, Zona Bearings has been undermining Bursi Manufacturing's ball bearing contracts with the government. Specifically, our bearings are the finest available in the Ataro System, always has been. They have to be the finest, since they are being used in deep space spaceships. Specifically, I know that Zona has stolen our designs. Now they are manufacturing them, but with structurally deficient outer rings, which leads to a rapid failure of the bearings. These faulty bearings are imprinted with Bursi's logo and sold to the government at half of our price per bearing. At this time, this practice has undermined the viability of my company and has ruined our reputation with the government purchasing officials. In short, this highly illegal practice of Zona's is putting me out of business. I insist and demand not only Zona be ordered to cease and desist in these illegal actions, but also recompense Bursi twenty-five million credits to compensate us for our losses and also to notify the government purchasing officials of what they have been doing so our reputation is restored. Corporate espionage is illegal and cannot be tolerated."

Isabella asked, "Is the only defect the outer rings?"

"Well, no Your Majesty. The government technicians have also found faulty inner rings and even faulty ball bearings as well. This has placed many new spaceships at a high risk of damage while in flight! Surely, you cannot allow this to continue. It will destroy our entire space fleet in time," he replied highly animated. "Besides, the Imperium is at war, which makes this sabotage even more damaging, if not treasonous! He should be executed for high treason, in my opinion, that is," he hastily added, realizing it was not his position to suggest such punishment.

"Yes, of course we must not allow this to happen. That goes without saying." Isabella used her feet to shift her position slightly so that she could see Hernanda a little from the corners of her eyes. "Do you have all that down?" Hernanda nodded. "Thank you. Now let's hear from the other side, Mr. Zona."

He stepped forward. He too wore an equally fine

business suit, a light navy tweed. "Your Majesty. Everything that Mr. Bursi has just told you is an outright lie! Well, not everything. His company has been making the defective bearings for the last three years, that part is true. Never in the long history of Zona Bearings have we ever participated directly or indirectly in any corporate espionage! We have our own contract with the government, but we make completely different bearings that are used in the hyper-drive systems. His are used in the impulse drive systems. Completely different bearings. Further, his company is also manufacturing faulty bearings of the type that we make, selling them to the government using our company logo! It is he who has stolen our plans; it is he who is making the faulty bearings; it is he who is underselling our products; it is he who is trying to bankrupt and destroy the reputation of my company; it is he who is the guilty party here, not me nor my esteemed company! He is the treasonous culprit not me!"

Isabella replied, "I see. About these faulty bearings, are they faulty in the same way? Inner rings, outer rings, and ball bearings?"

"As a matter of fact, yes, they are faulty in the same way. He is using wholly inferior materials, not remotely up to the specifications as listed on the government contract."

"Okay. Let me see if I have understood this. Both of your companies manufacture different types of bearings that are being sold to the government. Correct." Both men nodded. "And the government has discovered some of both bearings are defective in inner rings, outer rings, and also the ball bearings themselves?" Once more, both men agreed with her.

"Good. We agree on this much then. Is it fair to summarize each of you claim the other is also manufacturing each other's products only defectively so?" Once again, they agreed with her completely.

"Good. You both believe the other has somehow stolen your company's design for said bearings?" Both men nodded vigorously.

"All right. Indeed, we have quite a situation here. No wonder there is quite a conflict. Let's get to the bottom of this, shall we?"

"Okay, Mr. Bursi, do you have direct evidence to present that shows someone somehow connected to Mr. Zona's company has stolen your bearing designs?"

"Well, not exactly. But how else could they have possibly gotten our design? Everyone knows these defective bearings are of our design. He even has the gall to put our logo on them!"

"So where do you keep these designs?" she asked, thinking perhaps there would be some security breach to be uncovered.

"I keep all of our company designs locked in my personal safe. Only I have the combination. I check them out and watch over the engineers, as they use them, and put them back in the safe when they are done. My security is not under question. His henchmen obviously cracked my safe and copied them!"

"So you never allow your designs out of your sight, not even while you grab lunch?"

"No! That is an invitation for disaster. No way." He seemed quite sincere about this point.

"Okay, has your company been broken into? Are you therefore suggesting you've had a break in and theft? Did you report it to the proper authorities? When did this break in occur," she asked.

Mr. Bursi became very flustered. "Er, well, not that we know about. Our company's premises are secure. We've had no robberies."

"Oh, no robberies, no break ins. Hum, so how do you know Mr. Zona has stolen your designs?" she asked pointedly.

"Well, he must have. How else could they be making the faulty parts using our designs?"

"That's what we are going to figure out, Mr. Bursi. So you have no actual evidence that Mr. Zona or anyone has actually broken in and stolen your designs?"

"Well, no, but he must have! How else could he be making the same parts as we are? Answer me that one," he countered defensively.

"Okay, now then, Mr. Zona, do you have direct evidence Mr. Bursi or his agents have broken into your company and stolen your designs?"

"Well, not exactly. His company is selling bearings that are duplicates of my secret design, only faulty ones. So he or someone he hired must have broken in and stolen them. Stands to reason. Common sense. Anyone can see that," he justified.

"I see. Well, I am not anyone. I take it someone suggested that this was the only reasonable explanation for Mr. Bursi to have gotten a hold of your secret designs. Correct?"

"Well, I suppose so. Mr. Ferris mentioned it, as I recall."

"I'm sorry. Who is Mr. Ferris?" Isabella asked.

"He runs a very small bearing plant that makes bearings for earth moving equipment. Small time business."

"I see. And what exactly did he say to you and when?" she asked.

"Let me see. I think it was about two years ago. We were having a beer, and I mentioned how the government was jumping on my company for producing faulty bearings. I think he said if I wasn't guilt of doing it, which I most certainly am not, then it was obvious. Plain as the nose on my face. One of my competitors must be behind it. I've only got one competitor, Mr. Bursi, so it's obviously him."

"I see. Now then, Mr. Bursi," Isabella reversed her attention to the other man.

"Wait, Mr. Ferris suggested the same thing to me about twenty-five months ago. I was telling him how someone must be sabotaging my bearings because the government was after me about them. He suggested someone must have stolen my designs. Of course, that could only have been Mr. Zona. Just last month, he suggested I bring Mr. Zona to the Queen's Court and sue him for everything he's got. I'm doing just that now."

"I see. Interesting. Might I ask if Mr. Ferris has ever purchased any of your bearings, Mr. Bursi?"

"Of course, he uses them in some of heavy equipment. Why?" he replied.

"How about you, Mr. Zona. Has Mr. Ferris ever bought any of your bearings?"

"Well, sure he has. I sell bearings to many other companies besides the government," Mr. Zona replied. "What of it? He is a reputable dealer."

"I find it interesting Mr. Ferris knows both of you and has purchased some of the bearings in question from each of you. Queen Altha, could we find out if the government purchasing officer has been purchasing some of these same bearings from Mr. Ferris' company? I believe the answer might be illustrative."

"Of course, the court will take a short recess. Herbon, please make that inquiry immediately and report back to Senator Isabella, please," Queen Altha replied solemnly.

A half hour later, she resumed the proceedings. Isabella stated the findings. "Mr. Zona, Mr. Bursi. I have some interesting news for you both. It seems since the discovery of so many faulty bearings from each of your companies, the purchasing officer is in the process of working out a new deal with Mr. Ferris and his company to supply them with both types of bearings. It seems Mr. Ferris submitted a dozen samples last year for their analysis. They were identical to your designs and met all the requisite standards of quality construction."

"Why that dirty weasel!" roared Mr. Bursi. "He got the originals from me and then simply copied them, putting his own logo on them."

"You have a point there, Mr. Bursi," Mr. Zona spoke up, "He's copied our designs from those he purchased from us. Look, what if he was the one who made the faulty bearings? If he ruins both of our companies, then he is free and clear to take over the lucrative business of both our companies! He should be on trial here, not us!"

"Good point. I'll bet he dreamed up this whole scheme to both put us out of business and make himself the sole supplier of both bearings, doubling the profits that either of us get!" Mr. Bursi exclaimed.

"You are right! We won't take this without a fight, Mr. Bursi," Mr. Zona declared.

"Precisely Mr. Zona. We've worked all our lives to build up reputable companies. We're not about to let a scoundrel like Ferris bring us down! Senator Isabella, I hereby withdraw my suit against Mr. Zona here. We both would like you to investigate Mr. Ferris for these crimes, right, Mr. Zona?"

"Absolutely! Stop the purchasing officer from making a huge mistake," Mr. Zona added, enthusiastically.

"It is so ordered. Suit is withdrawn, gentlemen," Isabella declared.

Queen Altha now spoke up, "Herbon, see that Mr. Ferris is fully investigated by the authorities, and let the purchasing officer know these findings. Gentlemen, we will let you know the outcome of the investigation, but I believe we all know what will be uncovered." Both men bowed and left, talking rapidly to each other about the treachery of Mr. Ferris.

"Well done, Isabella. That was a tough one, but you got to the heart of the matter very rapidly. Perfect," Queen Altha praised her work. "Now it is time to advance to other subjects."

Isabella laughed. "I don't even know what a ball bearing actually is!" Everyone laughed.

Sound financial planning training came next. A week after that, she was immersed in statistics, specifically identifying trends based upon actual production statistics. First, she had to be able to identify if the production statistics were properly graphed — that is, scaled right. She discovered if the quantity a factory produced over a three week period was 10, 20, and 30 units respectively, by graphing them incorrectly, a wrong picture emerged. One such graph had the Y-axis scaled in units of 1000, and the resulting picture was a flat, horizontal line. Another one had the top of the Y-axis at 30 units and the resulting picture was a steeply rising line, also a false reading. Once properly scaled, she learned to identify an optimum result being a sharply rising line over several weeks; a good result being a rising line; a so-so result being one that was almost flat but still perhaps rising a little; an emergency line being one that was going slightly down indicating troubles; a dangerous line being one that was going sharply down, and a disaster line being one that had virtually no production. Hernanda got a work out drawing up all the graphs.

After she had these graphs down, she then learned why

she was spending so much time on them. Queen Altha pointed out, "So when you are managing a production unit, you want to manage it by using these statistical graphs and act accordingly. Let's go over just what a manager should do for his or her workers in each of these line types. For example, you don't give raises when the line is so-so or worse. That is foolishness." Isabella spent another week learning how to manage production workers by using their weekly statistics and thereby making the proper decisions on what needed to be done as their manager to get production up. She found this line of study to be highly valuable.

Her studies then examined actions, situations, and results from the standpoint of which were positive indicators and of which were negative indicators. Often these were based upon actions that benefitted the most while harming the least. From here, she began to learn how to find the correct reason for some failure, error, or bad situation. She had to use direct, personal observations, combined with an analysis of the two types of indicators and the proper actions to take based upon the production line graphs. In short, she had to conduct her own investigation into the root cause of a situation, finding the correct reason for the failure or problems. Like magic, when the actual, real reason was isolated, the handling of it, so as to put the project back on track, was usually very simple indeed. However, this subject was not so easy to actually do and do well. She spent three weeks getting this one down to Queen Altha's satisfaction.

It was at this point in time that both Gabriella Amy and Celia Jan realized that their former training from the emperor and empress over a century ago had been very rushed so that the rulers could leave on their planned trip to Ashford-5. "If we had only known some of these things," Gabriella Amy lamented when she was alone with Celia Jan.

"I know. Isn't hindsight just perfect?" Celia Jan countered humorously.

It wasn't until June 1275 by Tierra's calendar, that Queen Altha finally finished Isabella's training. "Tomorrow," the queen proclaimed, "will be a day of celebration on Winno-3. Never before have we made a queen for another world. We both will be highly honored! The emperor and empress are coming here to congratulate us both and to wish you well! There will be the official ceremony first, followed by a royal feast and dance in your honor. Of course, we don't actually eat that much, but we will be expected to dance a little. I should teach you the basic steps. It is really, really hard for us to actually dance, so don't worry. You'll only be asked to dance one or two times — probably the emperor will dance with you first. But all the others in the court will feast away and dance til they drop, or so I've seen."

A bit later, she assembled some musicians and began teaching the four their basic wasp dance. "I'll be the emperor. I step forward with my left foot and you step back with your right — very small steps or you'll fall down. Then, bring your left foot back and then bring them together. They you step forward with your right foot, then bring your left foot forwards, and then together. Six beats. We'll start with this much of it first." Their assistants acted as partners for Hernanda, Gabriella Amy, and Celia Jan. After they group got the hang of it, Queen Altha explained the next part of it.

"Now we have been mostly forming a simple square, but actually, you need to be turning clockwise as you are doing these steps so as to make a turnabout after one set of six motions, so that you are where I started and I am at your position. With two sets, you are back to where you started. The turning part is really tricky for us and the emperor too. Ideally, we need to do this dance fairly briskly so that our long hair flairs out behind us some. You'll see as you get better at it," she explained.

They practiced the dance for nearly an hour before stopping. All were gasping for breath from the exertion; their feet were aching some. All four of them, including Queen Altha nearly lost their balance several times, though none actually took a nasty tumble. "Hernanda, if I should actually fall, you've got to help me up. I can't possibly get myself up," Isabella whispered to her. Well, she could get herself up, but that would involve using her *mentales* gifts, blowing their cover. Thus far, they had given no one here any clue they were telepaths or had other powerful abilities. Isabella intended it to stay that way.

The next day, the four plus their two assistants were met by Queen Altha and Evon in their room. She was very animated, her face was flushed. "He is here, the emperor. It is time. Follow me. This is so exciting," Queen Altha gushed, making no attempt to hide her emotions. They headed into her throne room, where Isabella had held court resolving real conflicts. The emperor was sitting on her throne. The empress sat on a smaller throne at his right side. To either side of them, their own assistants stood watching.

He wore a light green tweed suit with a white satin shirt. His toe shoes were highly polished and black, reflecting the sunlight that illuminated the room. He also had a nicely trimmed moustache that matched his black hair. She wore an emerald satin gown with matching heels. What struck Isabella the most was that both had tiny waistlines, similar to hers, barely a foot around, and that they too were as armless as she and Queen Altha. While she anticipated they would look this way, seeing them in the flesh took her a bit by surprise. Their assistants were similarly attired. While they had their arms intact, she knew that neither could speak and thus unduly influence their charges.

Another throne was to his left and Queen Altha walked slowly towards it. To Isabella's eyes, it seemed as if she were flowing to the throne, not walking. She also spotted another temporary throne just to the left of Queen Altha's. As instructed, Isabella then walked up to the emperor and stood before him, accompanied by a musical fanfare. She tried to flow as gracefully as Altha had and hoped she did. Behind her, the throne room was utterly packed with guests. Later she got to look at them. All wore elegant gowns and suits. Many had tiny waists and toe shoes as well, but not all did. However, none were missing their arms.

When she stood before him, the emperor rose and a hush fell on the room. "Today, we are gathered here to welcome the graduation of a new queen. But she is not an Ataro Empire of the Twelve Sacred Planets of the Wasp queen! No, she is the first queen of Ashford-5! This is an historic day for the Ataro Empire, for at long last, another world beyond our system has requested a fully trained queen so she can return to her world and rule her world as we rule ours. Some of you know we emperors, empresses, and queens have been trying for over two millennia and then some to get other worlds out there in the vast galaxy to emulate and duplicate the fantastic success that we have had here. Today, Queen Altha has made this a reality for the first time in our history! To commemorate your stellar achievement, I wish to present you with this emerald necklace engraved with your name and your achievement."

Queen Altha rose, while Evon placed the small engraved emerald on a gold chain around her neck. She received a loud round of applause. He then spoke again, moving closer to Isabella. "Be it known throughout the empire that as of this day, I hereby proclaim from this point in time forward that this woman you see before me shall be known as Queen Isabella Valen, deserving of all the rights and respect of any queen of the Ataro Empire. Yes, I have examined her training and do hereby certify she is as capable as any of our queens! Indeed, she has been perhaps pushed even harder than we push our future queens in training. That is because she is not from the Ataro Empire, and we wished to make very sure she was more than capable. Ladies, gentlemen, it is with immense pride I present to you Queen Isabella Valen." Hernanda slipped the small emerald on a gold necklace around her neck, adjusting her very long black tresses. Again, the room erupted into a loud round of applause. As instructed, she then took her seat beside Queen Altha. Hernanda moved to her side, emulating Evon.

While the musicians played background music, many of the guests moved up to greet the emperor, empress, and Queen Altha. More importantly, they all greatly desired to introduce themselves to Queen Isabella. Quickly, she lost complete track of who was who, but she did realize these men and women were some of the most important and powerful people in the entire Ataro Empire of the Twelve Sacred Planets of the Wasp. While she didn't realize it now, she and they were forming connections that would become quite beneficial in later years. The ties and bonds they felt for her would last for a very long time.

Finally, they took their lunch break or rather indulged in the Royal Feast. I say feast, but only about half of those here actually ate any significant amounts. Those with the pipe corsets could only eat relatively small amounts, naturally. Around one, they again headed back to the throne room for the Royal Dance. As anticipated, the emperor requested the first dance with Queen Isabella. She nervously took her place before him. How strange, she thought, we are facing each other, but neither of us can actually touch or hold the other.

Then, the music began and Isabella focused all her attention on duplicating the dance steps, trying hard to follow his lead on the turning. At least, he was forced to be as careful as she to avoid taking a tumble. She sensed he was as nervous about doing this dance as she was and that gave her some comfort. Shared misery.

Fortunately, the dance was not very long, just a couple of minutes, out of respect for the extreme difficulty the two had in dancing. He then took another turn with the empress and then one more with Queen Altha. Isabella guessed that this was protocol.

However, Queen Isabella didn't get to sit down. Rather many other men came up to her asking her to dance with them as well! She dare not turn them down, though she desperately wanted to do just that. The first young man put his arms securely on her thin waist line, whispering, "I have you securely. We can go faster and you can whip your hair around some. I won't let you fall. Might I inquire about your incredible lip ornaments?"

"Yes, the lords and ladies of our world wear them. Quite the fashion statement," she replied before the music began again. She was more than a little surprised by just how fast he twirled her around and her hair did flair out some behind her. After the two additional short dances on the emperor's behalf, the musicians then play longer sets for the benefit of the guests.

Poor Isabella, man after man requested to dance with her, dance after dance. Before long, she was gasping for breath, but she persevered in spite of her growing discomfort.

In a way, she felt elated, being almost swung around by the men, her hair flying out behind her. Finally, Queen Altha intervened, "Gentlemen, let's give our exhausted queen a chance to catch her breath." Hernanda put her arms around her and made sure that she got safely to her throne, still panting rapidly.

Others now came up to her to chat. Most wanted to know about her lip plates, neck rings, and long earrings. She did her best to explain about her world's customs with two of the three, saying nothing about the neck rings. Isabella was never so glad for the end of a party. She was exhausted and fell into a deep sleep as soon as Hernanda helped her lay gracefully down on their bed.

The next morning at breakfast, Queen Altha explained, "Your ship has been fully refueled for your trip home. I have taken the liberty of having a dozen new gowns made for each of you, with all the necessary accessories. Plus, I've included two dozen of our style toe shoes for each of you as well, since you might not be able to get replacements in a timely fashion — what with this infernal war going on. After the war is over, I do wish you could take some time off to visit me and let me know how you are doing on Ashford-5. I know the emperor would also like to know how it goes as well. It would prove invaluable feedback so we can all do an even better job with the next foreign queen. I do hope you are but the first of many, many future queens. Together, we can help make this universe of worlds a safe place for all peoples to thrive and prosper."

They thanked her repeatedly, and Queen Isabella promised to return when she could. Finally, their assistants gathered up their things, filling another shipping crate, which was swiftly taken to their ship. After saying farewell to Queen Altha, Evon, and many others whom they had gotten to know well, they were taken back to their transport ship and helped onboard. Celia Jan then shut the large door, closing officially this lengthy chapter on their long voyage home. A half hour later, Celia Jan nudged the ship airborne and swiftly engaged their hyper-drive once more.

Shortly, Gabriella Amy announced to everyone, "I'm stretching the fuel supply so we have a week's travel ahead of us. We should be landing on Tierra around June 15, 1275, landing on fumes, I might add." The four headed for the galley to make some tea and to discuss their next moves.

"We've endured this torture for nineteen months now. I never thought I could live like this for a week," Isabella pointed out. "I admit it was an incredible challenge not being able to use our gifts, but Hernanda, you were absolutely brilliant. I could not have done this without you. You are the most amazing person I've ever met. I can't imagine how hard all this has been for you. I guess we all have a lot to discuss about the future. Somehow, I feel both obligated and challenged to try to implement what I have learned here on Tierra."

"I think we are all in agreement, Queen Isabella," Gabriella Amy spoke up, "we should make use of what we've learned. Some of it is absolutely mind blowing, incredibly valuable, as far as I am concerned. We'll have to see just how we can implement these things when we get home. Does everyone agree with me — that we should do our best to bring these things to Tierra and somehow get them implemented across our world?" All quickly agreed wholeheartedly.

"I guess the next question is now that we have some free time, what of all this stuff," she wiggled her arms towards her neck and lips, "do we try to undo and get rid of?"

"Well, I don't know about all of you, but I am actually rather used to all of it now, especially since we can stand on our toes. I would kind of like the various lords to see just what Senator Carlos did to us. Make it real to them," Isabella suggested. "I know we are going to continue to need lots of help from Hernanda, but why don't we wait until the lords get a good look at us before we undo some of these modifications?"

Celia Jan agreed, "I like her idea, Gabriella Amy. Let the lords see just what treachery the so-called great Imperium has done to their senator and wives. That might go along way to changing some of their opinions about the exalted Imperium. As she says, we are used to everything now. I can't believe it has been nineteen months, though, but she's right. It has been that long. Besides, now we can use our telekinesis and not be such a burden for Hernanda."

"Okay, are we agreed on this, you two?" Gabriella Amy asked. They were.

"But what about Hernanda? Ought I undo the gender changes we more or less forced on him or her?" Celia Jan asked. All eyes turned to her, after pivoting their bodies with their feet that is.

She blushed. "If it is all the same to you, I like the way that I am now. I can best help my beloved Isabella this way. Few questions are ever asked this way, unless Queen Isabella wishes me to be turned back the way that I was."

"I'm happy either way, Hernanda, but I think we all see exactly what you mean," Isabella replied. She flushed beet red, and then decided with everyone being a telepath, she could not hide her true feelings any longer. "I don't know how to say this properly, but Hernanda and I are madly in love with each other. I've never met a man like him before. Will you two be upset with me if we dissolve our marriages when we return, so that Hernanda and I can be wed?"

Gabriella Amy laughed. "We thought so! No, not at all. This was a contrived marriage to meet the needs of your becoming Tierra's senator, and the three of us satisfying the desires of the different lords to have a representative there. Besides, then Celia Jan and I can get married. We want to make use of the new feature of the medical machines and have each other's children."

Celia Jan sighed, "Perfect. May I suggest we two couples spend some quality private time with each other during the coming week? We might not get much chance once we land on Tierra. We've been out of touch with what's happening there. Lord knows what a mess we will find when we arrive."

"Thank you. Hernanda and I will do just that!" Isabella replied, her face still rather hot. "I just can't believe it though. Hernanda is just the best man in the universe! Come on, dear. We can now flirt in public and not have to hide our feelings any more. I feel like a sixteen year old girl on her first date."

Hernanda replied, "Well, your body is that of a twenty year old girl." Everyone laughed. For seven days, the two couples had truly enjoyable private times with their lovers.

Note: the special rapport that is only possible between two *mentales* gifted takes on a completely new meaning when two lovers join in this way. Spiritually, the two are almost as one. The distance separating the two beings becomes almost negligible, not only heightening their love, but also adding a new dimension — the sharing of their physical bodies. Each just knew what the other desired at any given instant, dramatically increasing their satisfaction and physical pleasure.

On the second day, like a tardy schoolchild walking into her class, Hernanda visited Celia Jan in their room. She fidgeted a little before Celia Jan asked her what she wanted. "Well, I was wondering if you could fix me up with lip plates like you three have. You see, if all the lords and ladies are wearing them, I would like to not draw undo attention to me about why I am not. Isabella would also like them on me too."

"They are a royal pain, but sure, I see your point. We're about to return to Tierra where these things are the norm. Makes sense. Anything else?" Celia Jan asked.

"Is it true that most women on Tierra do not cut their hair?"

"For the most part yes, though some do. I see your point; the noblewomen never do such a thing. Certainly not in the Easterlings were we were born. Okay, I can lengthen yours some so it will look like it hasn't been cut. Anything else?" Celia Jan asked.

"Well, could these also be made like yours? I am going to look totally different from you three when we land and meet all these powerful people. They are going to see me as being different than you three. Isabella has promised me she won't tell others about the partial gender switch, so how will we explain I look so much smaller? I am worried about that."

"Good point. The less attention you attract to yourself from us as a group the better. Come on. I'll get you fixed up quickly. Of course, we may well be undoing some of these fairly soon, but we'll see," she replied. Two hours later, Hernanda modeled her new physical appearance to Queen Isabella, who complimented her and pushed her body into Hernanda's, the best she could do for a hug.

Chapter 34 The Brom Document of Human Rights

With the continuing rebellions within many kingdoms demanding the full attention of the many lords and with the sudden loss of the spaceport and the aliens, the July 1273 High Council of the Lords was again postponed until fall. Many doubted the situations would be under sufficient control to allow even that meeting to occur. Further complications arose, since several key lords were now scrambling to find new sources of iron ore, having become totally dependent on the yearly lease payments from the Rigel-3 aliens. The old mines of Brom, Malaca, and Domei suddenly regained the former prominence they once enjoyed some three hundred years ago. Lord Emilio Bolivar scrambled to meet some of the voluminous requests for iron ore that other lords were begging from his kingdom.

Early September 1273, the special assembly Lord Brom had formed and charged with preparing a document of Brom citizen's rights finally finished their work. Their elected chairman, Thomas Blackbell, formally made the presentation before Lord Emilio, Amo Domingo, Venerada Maricela, Ken, Crystal, Rafaela, Andres, and many other lesser court personnel of Brom. Thomas was obviously quite nervous speaking before these powerful lords and rulers of Brom, but he'd guided the five hundred men and women for nearly six months now, preparing their document.

At first, the general dissatisfaction with the way things were being run led to attempts to turn the whole meeting into one grievance session. Once they had gotten their beefs off their chests, Thomas was able to get them to focus on the real issue: what should the basic rights of a citizen of the Kingdom of Brom actually be? His hand was shaking slightly as he stood before Lord Bolivar, waiting for his lord to make his formal presentation. He sensed the tensions in the throne room. That only added to his overall nervousness. For his part, Lord

Bolivar had thus far avoided all the nasty open rebellion that was plaguing many other kingdoms by focusing everyone's attention onto this proposed document. He truly hoped whatever they came up with would prevent the anarchy from entering Brom.

He gave a few introductory words and then said, "Since they began their work last spring, Thomas Blackwell has been serving as the chairman of the vital rights project. He is here with us today to make the formal presentation of their lengthy work. I give you Thomas Blackwell. Go ahead, Thomas." He sat down on his throne to listen.

"My Lord. I've been instructed to simply read our carefully worded document and not say anything further. I will abide by the committee's request," Thomas said nervously. He cleared his throat and began to read.

The Declaration of Brom Human Rights
Composed This Fifth of September 1273

All human beings are born both free and with basic rights. They are entitled to these rights as long as they use reason and treat others with both dignity and respect.

These basic rights make no distinction on the person's race, country of origin, language, culture, ownership of property, or any other status. Such things shall not be used for discrimination of these rights.

All citizens have the right to their own lives, their freedom, and security.

No citizen shall be subject to torture, slavery, or to degrading punishments.

All citizens are equal before the law and the ruling lords. That is, Lords, Ladies, Jefe, noblemen, noblewomen, *mentales* gifted, and farmers, for example, are all equal before the law and subject to it.

All citizens have the right to move freely about the kingdom and to leave or freely visit other lands.

Any citizen who is charged with an offense against the law must be presumed innocent and has the right to a speedy and fair trial or hearing, during which both they and their accusers present evidence. The citizen has the right to face his or her accuser, face to face. To be found guilty of the offense, the citizen must be found guilty beyond any reasonable doubt.

The family unit is hereby recognized as the fundamental building block of the kingdom. As such, marriages are to be valued and protected from all those who seek to destroy the union by whatever means.

Each citizen upon reaching the adult age of fourteen has the right to choose their own marital partner.

Every citizen has the right to own property or land.

Every citizen has the right to the freedom of thought and to speak freely their own opinions to others, as long as their speech does not baselessly slander another. No one has the right to harm another's good name without just cause.

Every citizen of our kingdom has the right to elect their own leaders and those who make the laws of the kingdom that they have to obey, as do all citizens of the kingdom.

Every citizen has the right for equal payment for equal work or products.

Every citizen has the freedom of choice of employment.

Every citizen has the right to a standard of living that maintains their health and that of their family, especially so for mothers and children.

Every citizen has the right to worship their own gods in the manner of their choosing, subject to the rights of others stated above.

Every citizen has the right to the best medical care available in a timely manner and has the right to choose the method of their treatment.

Every citizen has the right to have a day of rest from work to worship or relax as they so choose.

Every citizen has the right to demand their rulers provide a safe and secure kingdom in which to live and prosper.

Every citizen has the obligation to protect these rights of other citizens as well as their own.

The law of the kingdom must protect these rights.

When he finished, he anticipated Lord Bolivar to vent his outrage against him. That was the source of his nervousness, but he had accepted this fate, when he agreed to be their chairman and thus spokesperson. A profound silence followed, while he sifted his weight from foot to foot, waiting for the explosion of anger that was sure to follow. After all, they had insisted upon electing their leaders!

Lord Bolivar rose slowly, still absorbing what he'd just heard. He was not a fool, whatever else he might be. The populations of many kingdoms were in various states of rebellion throughout the Midlands, the Westerlings, and Matruk, Easterlings. Only Brom here in the Midlands, Turda, and the Arad had relative calm these past six months. Brom's relative quiet was due in no small measure to his rule and having set up this very committee. The five hundred or so members were pressed together at the very back of the room, waiting to hear his response. Lord Bolivar knew whatever he said would soon be spread throughout every town and hamlet in his kingdom. He chose his words carefully.

"Amazing, Thomas. Simply amazing. What an incredible forthright document you and your fellow committee members have produced. Indeed, anyone can see these are truly basic, fundamental rights we all share in common. Of course, a few of these are radical concepts, and I and the others must now study how those could possibly be implemented. At this point, I would only like to make one suggestion for an additional line in regards to the idea that the citizens are to elect their own rulers and makers of the laws of the kingdom. That is, every citizen has the obligation to become as fully informed as they can as regards to the issues and candidates for which they are voting. And another one — well perhaps it belongs in a subsequent document, but these elections should be free and open with no intimidation or threats to those who are voting. I could see a bully might try intimidating the voters in his town to vote for him threatening them with dire consequences."

Thomas didn't quite know how to respond. Lord Bolivar was apparently not angry in the least — wholly unexpected! "Then, then, you are going to accept this document? I will discuss the additional ones with the committee at once. I think the additions are reasonable ones."

"Of course I am going to accept it. The radical new idea of elected rulers and lawmakers is going to take some time for us all to figure out how to do it. When you meet with the committee members, ask them if they would be willing to return next spring to assist in the formulation of just how we are going to implement these radical changes here in Brom," he replied.

Unexpectedly, from the back of the room, the hundreds of committee members began slowly clapping, bringing a smile to Lord Bolivar's face. Quickly, the other lords and nobles began to also smile and clap, whether or not they agreed with this whole situation. After that, the committee members left with Thomas. At this point, everyone began talking with those around them. That their leaders should be elected and that others should make the actual laws became a very hot topic. Why? Many of their positions at court were being threatened, if new rulers were elected at periodic intervals. They could well lose their lifelong positions if a different lord was chosen.

Lord Brom broke in on the many conversations. "Look, we have already met many of their needs. Venerada Maricela and her tower folk have a good medical program in operation, getting one of their healers to the injured fairly rapidly. We owe it to our people to look seriously into the possibility of elected leaders and lawmakers. Just look to the kingdoms to the south and west of us to see what will happen here, if we do not address the needs of our people. We have all winter to see what kind of new establishments we can work out that will meet the letter of this declaration of citizen rights. If we do nothing, by spring the rebellions may spill over into Brom." That was a sobering thought and made an impression on the group.

Not long after that, Thomas returned with the revised document, complete with over five hundred signatures. Now it was official, and the many volunteers returned to their respective towns and villages, promising to spread the word about the acceptance of their document and radical changes. Lord Bolivar hoped this would squelch thoughts of rebellious behavior throughout the kingdom. His hopes panned out. Now came the hard work of trying to figure out just how to implement the sweeping changes. Well, he had all winter.

Ken, Bart here. You have to come see what I've just discovered. It's bad. How's the meeting going?

It's done and went very well actually. I am impressed. On my way, Ken sent back. He, Crystal, Andres, and Rafaela made their excuses and headed back down the steps into the maze of underground tunnels. Fifteen minutes later, they joined Bart at his comm center. Everyone else was already there, staring at the images on his large monitor.

"Ah, you're back. As you know, the Imperium shut down their entire operation here as well as their geo-sat systems. Well, I've finally hacked into them and gotten them back online and downloaded all their stored images. Look what I've found. The moon, the refinery. Watch."

The four stared at the monitor, as the pale blue moon seemed to explode into a million pieces. As if by magic, somehow it reformed back into a solid moon once more. "Impressive. How did it reform?" Ken asked.

Bart shrugged his shoulders. "Physically, that could not have happened, but it did. Call it magic, if you like. I sure am. But that's not why I called you back. Keep watching." Now a very distinct cloud of fine dust and larger particles floated away from the moon, moving very slowly.

"Is that another psi-dust cloud coming our way?" Ken asked.

"Yes, it is moving far slower than the other one. Not sure why. As soon as I spotted this, I began tracking it. I've done a simulation." He switched to a different computer generated model of the cloud and Tierra. "It is going to envelop the whole planet in about two weeks. Further, from the model, you can see we will be bombarded twenty-four-seven for a period of three weeks before the cloud goes beyond Tierra. This is going to make the last one look like nothing at all!"

"With this much psi-dust coming down everywhere, many people are going to be affected. We could well get hundreds or thousands of new *mentales* gifted out of this one," Rafaela speculated. "Bart, figure out the total quantity of psi-dust we can expect to receive all total. This is really important. The last time, we only got just enough to change a thousand more or less but only temporary. We need to know the full magnitude of this one. From the looks of it, this could be a really big one."

They then were asked about the big meeting, and Ken outlined what had transpired. It took Bart another day of feverish work on his many computers to find the answer that Rafaela wanted. At last, he summoned her with his results. He had worked out a three-week accumulation model. As she examined the overall amounts week by week and then factored in the certainty that the dust would also contaminate all food products for at least the next growing season, she realized the sheer magnitude of this encounter.

"My god. It is going to be widespread. Gang, the total dosage any person could get between then and say next fall is more than enough to create permanent *mentales* gifts in relatively large numbers. I am going to have to let Marisela know about this one. She needs to get prepared well in advance. Any word from Senator Isabella? She ought to be informed about this event."

He promised to alert Isabella, while Rafaela headed off to consult and advise Venerada Maricela. A bit later, she added, "Yes, I estimate one in ten people will be affected. We could have thousands of new *mentales* gifted appearing as early as springtime. We best be prepared to handle them."

The October sky display was phenomenal and taken as an evil omen by many rural folks. As Bart had computed, the psi-dust spread fairly evenly over all of Tierra. Larger meteoroids descended everywhere. Some smashed through roofs and even caused a few fires. The biggest fires were in the resinous pine forests of the northern lands. That heavy snow now blanketed these regions prevented a disaster from occurring. Only one person was killed during the three-week display and most wisely chose to spend as much time indoors as possible. Considering that winter had already come to the northern regions, this wasn't a problem, though further south, farmers gambled with the falling stones as they worked their harvest season. That many larger crystalline germanium chucks landed and were buried would become a future problem. Most everyone soon blamed this display on the Imperium, and some lords began to talk of asking the Imperium for recompense whenever they might return.

Needless to say, the overall opinion of the Rigel-3 aliens dropped considerably.

Lord Bolivar had asked repeatedly, if somehow their Senator Isabella could be contacted. He was desperate to get her input on the proposed changes and how best to do them. He saw her as the most knowledgeable on Tierra, although she wasn't actually on Tierra just now when he really needed her. Bart was very frustrated and concerned. November had come and still he could not make contact with Isabella on Proxima Prime. He'd checked his equipment a dozen times, even hacked into some of the Imperium's comm systems on that world, just to prove to himself his equipment and protocols were not faulty. He'd already ruled out any interference from the closing of the spaceport on Plateau Grado. His system was wholly independent of theirs.

"What can possibly be going wrong?" he complained. He'd just gotten another plea from Lord Bolivar and had to report he still was unable to reach her.

Ken said, "Okay, let's take this from the top. When was the last time that you actually was able to reach Celia Jan's system?"

Bart ran his hands upwards through his hair and leaned back. "Well, that would be late September. I got a very brief message from her that they were spending the three week Senate break at the Senate President's estate. I have not heard a damn thing since then. Plus, I haven't been able to reach her comm system. It's as if it's turned off, but we both know Celia Jan. She'd never turn her system off. She's like us; run it twenty-four-seven. I don't get it. Could something terrible have happened to her, to them? Could her system have crashed perhaps? Still, it would not take her this long to replace the blown components."

Just as Ken was about to say something, Bart nearly fell out of his chair reacting to an incoming message from Celia Jan! "My god, she's contacting us. Wait, look at the weird routing! She must be using someone else's system. She's good at disguising her point of origin. I doubt I can trace it. Well, let's see what she has to say." He opened the text message and the two read it together.

CJ here. Captured. Now held as telepathic slaves by President Carlos Amandos. At his place. Caltran, Beltzar-4. G and I have no lower arms. No hands. I has no arms at all. Have large lip plates. Not able to be understood now. Neck rings immobilizes heads. Overly tiny waists. Can't move anything above hips. Using my t to type on his computer. Planning escape soon. Alive and well. More when can.

"My god! They are in big trouble! The Senate's President? Where the hell is Beltzar-4 anyway?" Bart asked. Both shook their heads in dismay.

"Well, I'll relay this to Maricela and Emilio. She can relay it to all the other towers and they, to the lords," Ken said grimly.

"Well, she does say they are planning an escape soon. That's hopeful. What does she mean they can't move anything above their hips?" Bart asked. Neither knew that either.

"Treachery! Damn those aliens anyway!" Lord Bolivar fumed when he got the news. "Now what the hell do I do? I've got to figure out how to implement the changes and with no way to talk this over with Isabella."

Damn was the thought echoed at nearly the same moment in time, but this one came from high atop a desolate peak beyond Hilliard Heights, some five hundred miles north of Brom. Ariana, the Goddess of Fertility, swore and shot a bolt of energy into the sky, disintegrating another falling chuck of germanium crystal. Its particles now rained down on her. *Damn Alleric. Now look what you have done to the humans! I know, you just had to fix the pretty blue moon, but did you think of the smaller debris? Hardly. We both know what that stuff does to their pituitary glands.* She got no reply. Alleric was sleeping soundly amongst the warmth of the core of Tierra. Furious, she summoned Lysandra, the Goddess of Life and of Death.

Oh. Here you are. I rather lost track of where you were, Ariana. Why are you so angry? Wystan and Calder are now stuck being humans. For once, I wholeheartedly agree with what has happened to Wystan and Calder too, for that matter. *They are learning their lessons the hard way.*

I'm so angry because of the shortsightedness of Alleric, that's why.

I don't understand, Ariana. He saved Tierra from being annihilated by the moon's explosion. What are you doing up here anyway?

I like it up here. I think this was once a dwelling made by the humans centuries ago. It makes a good place for me to monitor Hilliard Heights down there. I use them as my yardstick of fertility. And yes, he did do that, she softened her anger. *Our whole game would have been destroyed if he had not acted so swiftly. But he ought to have handled all the rest of the debris that is now falling onto Terra. Look at the stuff. Zillions of dust particles. It will contaminate everything. We both know what that stuff does to some of the humans.*

Yes we do. The last time, it took all of my efforts to undo it. We learned a whole lot three centuries ago when it first happened when the alien port blew up, Lysandra pointed out.

I think that you pissed a whole lot of the humans off when you undid their pituitary growth. This time, just look at the amount that is falling. No way can you undo all this, not if you spend a century at it. We're stuck this time, Lysandra. It is going to change a good many of them, and we both know it.

Yes, but I have been nurturing some in Brom along nicely. You've seen how so many there now are aware they too are spiritual beings?

Aye, that has not escaped me. Well done on that. It's the best progress that we've ever made. But Lysandra, with so many getting such huge powers and lacking the knowledge and wisdom for its use, are we not heading into yet another Dark Age? Have you seen all the strife and conflict within the many kingdoms? I've been protecting Hilliard Heights personally. The women rulers here are doing quite well. But now with this stuff falling, all bets are off.

I see your point. There are now so few of them left they may not be able to get to all of those who suddenly develop the incredible powers. Perhaps you are right; we are watching a new Dark Age descending. Isn't there anything that we can do to circumvent it? Lysandra asked.

Not that I can think of. At least the savagery will be less than if Wystan were still around. With rampant wars and killings, how can a woman successfully bring new babies into the world and yet be able to feed them? Remember the last time? The food they must eat was in such short supply; many young died before they even had a chance at a new life. I can't stand that! Well, I have an idea that is worth exploring. I think that I have been idle too long. This time, if the world enters another Dark Age, I will see that the young have more of a fighting chance. You best work on your projects too. We may not have too much time left, Ariana declared. Lysandra agreed and left. This snow covered land was just too cold for her liking. She never could figure out why Ariana liked the colder temperatures.

Not long after Lysandra departed, Ariana sensed the presence of another being close to her location. She angrily sent, *Who the hell are you? What are you doing here?*

I am called Josh. A confluence of paths meet here. I want the people of Tierra to survive. You are contemplating an action. There are two future paths ahead of us. If you do not do what you are thinking of doing, that path runs into a great darkness. The other path leads towards the light. I want to encourage you to lead us towards the light.

Well, I am just ornery enough to do just that! Look where men have gotten this world and are yet again about to take us! I don't need you to tell me what to do! Be gone! She sensed the presence vanish. *The nerve. Who the hell is this Josh? Well, forget him. I have work to do. Men have to learn their lessons and by god, I am sure going to teach them!* Later on, when her work was finished, she began to ponder this brief encounter. Had he affected her decision in any way?

The next day, Lord Bolivar summoned everyone he could think of to his throne room, including the Underground and the tower members, who were not sleeping or on duty that is. "Look, we have a big problem. Our people have demanded our leader be elected somehow and that some others, who are also elected, are to make the laws of the kingdom. I wanted to talk with Senator Isabella Valen about this, since she's had a century of off-world experience. But she's apparently been kidnaped, becoming another telepathic slave, just like before. So it is up to us to try to make some sense of what the people of our kingdom actually desire. I hope some of you have some good ideas, because I sure as hell don't." He opened the meeting.

The discussion was lively, but wholly unproductive, save to enumerate the many related problems such a drastic change entailed. Who would issue the silvers and coppers, their coinage? What would happen with the army? Lord Bolivar was responsible for it entirely. When the leadership changed, would the old army be disbanded and a new one formed? How could there ever be any stability in the kingdom with everything changing every few years? The list of potential difficulties seemed insurmountable.

Venerada Maricela finally had a suggestion that was heartily adopted at once. "Look, we are not getting anywhere. Come spring, why don't you reassemble the five hundred folks and get them to work with you on this. Get what they had in mind when they wrote it. At least then we'd have some idea what the people really desired."

Lord Bolivar bellowed, "Adopted! Everyone, think about all this over the winter. We'll all meet come spring. Surely, they had some more concrete ideas in mind. If not, perhaps when we go over all these potential pitfalls, they might change their mind on this." Everyone breathed a huge sigh of relief. While putting it off until spring was perhaps only delaying the inevitable, maybe she was right. The committee might just have some notion about how they envisioned this all working out and not creating a horrible mess.

As the hundreds began filing out, Lord Bolivar began rubbing his chest. He noticed several other men doing the same thing, but thought nothing of it. Winter had come and skins tended to dry out.

That evening as Maricela was getting ready for bed, she said, "Phil, can you please rub my breasts a little? They are rather aching a bit, almost like I was pregnant or something." She noticed he was rubbing his chest a little too.

He chuckled. "I always like to do that, my princess." Both laughed. After he removed their pairs of lip plates, he crawled in beside her and gave her a good massage, which as a katalyein she could not do for herself.

In the morning, following their usual routine, he helped her get into her day dress. As he put on his own shirt, he commented, "Hum, something's a bit strange, princess. It won't close all the way. I swear I must be getting fat or something."

She looked down at his shirt and saw that his top two buttons would not close. He moved the two sides together as much as they would go a couple of times, showing her. "How strange. I guess I best call the tailor. Just sort of tie the front shut for now." He did so. She didn't tell him that men didn't get fat there, but around their waists.

As he did so, he picked up her unspoken thought, and he exclaimed, "What the devil is going on? I swear that I'm developing breasts!" Now they both took a good look at his bare chest.

She giggled, "You do look like a very young girl."

"Stop that! It isn't funny, well not exactly. I'll tie it shut for now," he grumbled.

By the time they joined many others in the dining hall, that other men were beginning to experience similar effects became readily apparent. "Something strange is going on," Venerada Marisela spoke up loudly. "Healers, front and center. I want everyone examined, men in particular."

By suppertime, everyone was aware something was most definitely happening to every male who was past puberty. None of the women's breasts had grown any; they were still the large melons. Records traced their previously massive bosoms back some centuries. Now, it seemed the men were somehow undergoing a strange and similar growth. Shockingly, the men were beginning to show definite signs of developing mammary glands themselves, which should never happen.

Lord Bolivar had already summoned her, but she was overwhelmed with all the commotion in the towers. He'd come over personally, but he left almost as quickly. Everyone was experiencing the same phenomenon. By nightfall, the tower's comm network was nearly bombarded with messages coming in from all the other towers, all reporting the same phenomenon and asking for cures or help.

In the Underground, Rafaela became the focal point of frantic research and analysis. Their men too were being impacted by the sudden changes. Upon further checking, she found the five hundred or so mermaids were not being impacted just as the women of Tierra were not. It seemed isolated only to the men. There in Madiera she met with Alpha. "Ideas?" she asked after explaining the situation above ground.

In his mechanical voice, Alpha attempted to sound sympathetic. "Beta is taking air samples now. It cannot be the result of something you have ingested since you say this is occurring planet-wide. Something in the air is more likely the source. Patience. Beta is analyzing it now."

After a few more minutes, Beta spoke in his metallic, inhuman voice. "Rafaela, the air contains substantial quantities of minute germanium dust, likely from the explosion on the moon. By the way, has anyone figured out how the moon was reformed yet? We have found no physical forces that could have done that. It remains a mystery to us."

"No, it is a mystery to us as well. We know about the dust. Could it be behind these physical changes? It is the root cause of the explosive growth of our pituitary glands," Rafaela asked, curious about his theories.

"I cannot state that is the cause. Nevertheless, since we know it does cause explosive growth in human pituitary glands, perhaps it also affects mammary glands as well. However, why is it not affecting your women, only your men?" Beta both suggested and asked. "We are working on ways to filter it out of the air for those in Madiera, but the particles are so tiny, we might not be entirely successful."

"Good idea, Beta. The mermaids have enough difficulties without adding more to them. Okay, I best get back. Everyone's asking to see me," she replied.

The next day, the comm networks of the towers were swamped with messages. Every lord was asking every tower what was happening. At last, Rafaela sighed and visited Maricela. "Well, any answers?" Maricela ask her as she walked into the venerada's office.

"We know for certain the air is filled with minute germanium dust. We know for certain in the right dosage, the dust caused explosive growths of pituitary glands. That is, it creates the *mentales* gifts in men and women. The only theory I can come up with at this point in time is that it is also causing the growth of all men's mammary glands. However, why it is not doing the same to us women's is a complete mystery," she stated factually.

"Dear god! Our boobs are already way too huge. Now the men too? Well, I concur. Phil already has the breasts of an eighteen year old girl. So have most all men here in the tower. Okay, I will get the word out to the other towers and thus to the lords with that explanation. Any idea how much they will grow or how long they will continue to grow? The men are becoming very annoyed and quite upset," Maricela asked.

"Just like a man," Rafaela laughed. "No, I've no idea. I just hope nothing else starts growing. Mine had enough milk in them to feed an army of babies when I had my children. I can't imagine why we would ever need them even bigger than the monsters they are now, unless we are going to start having quadruplets or more — like dogs."

"We aren't? Are we?" Maricela asked growing worried Rafaela was being serious. Without arms, she knew she had enough trouble dealing with one child at a time.

Rafaela laughed. "No, don't be silly. I was just teasing, that's all. I will continue to monitor this and study it. Keep you posted." She returned to her quarters in the Underground, wondering what, if anything, she could realistically do. She then went to their medical machines and had them run some diagnostic tests on her own breasts.

After examining her results, she ordered all the other women in the Underground to report to the medical room. "What's the urgency?" Misty asked, the last to join the ten other women there.

"I am running a diagnostic test on our mammary glands. Get in line, Misty. This should not take more than an hour of our time." Rafaela patiently tested each woman in turn. Crystal, Luisa, Anita, Janice, Sally, Sally Humberhills, Annie, and Misty. She even tested the two sixty year old women, Elana and Petrona. Rafaela refused to comment on any results until she finished the last one, Misty. Now she turned to face them all, smiling relief on her face.

"Well, we've been patient enough," Crystal said. "What's going on? Why the tests? Are we sick or something?"

"No, the medical machine has the capability of analyzing growth. It has analyzed all eleven of us and the results are remarkably similar. At least, if the machine is at all accurate, I can tell you our mammary glands are definitely not going to grow during this strange time."

"Well, that is a relief. But what about the men?" Crystal declared slightly annoyed about the whole thing.

"I am using us women as a base line of calibration on the medical machine. Besides, all this has me a little worried. Now we all can relax. Whatever is going on, this time, we women are not being impacted. Only the men. When you get back, send all the men to me, please. Someone take over for Bart too. I want to see if the machine here will be able to give us a clue about the fellows. They are all taking this rather badly. Kind of ironic though, they want us to be buxom." Several laughed, but most giggled.

Two hours later, the men simply stared at Rafaela and the medical machine in complete disbelief! She had withheld all results until the last man was checked. She had just explained what the end product would be. "When the growth stops, you will all have perfectly functioning mammary glands. They will be the size we women now have. Yes, you too will have melons likes these," she jiggled hers a little. "Yes, that big, Bart. The size of yours will be the same monster melons you guys like to see on us."

"But, but men don't have them, not ever!" Bart burst out.

"You do now, kiddo," she could not help but tease them.

"How, how soon?" Ken found his voice and asked the key question.

"As far as the medical machine's analysis goes, it is

showing this explosive growth in all you men will be finished within two weeks, three at the outside, but more like two."

"What will we wear?" Bart asked in complete frustration.

"Good question, Bart. There simply will not be enough time to make new properly fitting shirts for all the men on Tierra in two weeks. Since it is predicting yours will end up the size that ours are, a temporary solution might be for you guys to wear some of our gowns or perhaps blouses. I am going to let Maricela know these results and then talk with Inez Franks. See if Elegant Fashions Inc can somehow help."

"Wait a second. You said fully functioning. Are you saying we can feed babies?" asked an incredulous Jake.

"It would seem so. Guess you fathers can now help us mothers out." She left them with that sobering thought.

Jake asked, "So what are we to do about it? Can't we use these machines to reduce them in size after they get done growing?"

"Yes, we could, Jake. Point taken. However, as you know, this is affecting every man on Tierra. If we did that, you would look vastly different from all the other men," Rafaela replied. "Besides, we haven't enough machines to reduce them on every man on Tierra. Not possible."

"So what are we to do?" Jake whined.

"Right now, I have no idea. I will continue researching and studying this," she answered honestly. The men left extremely sober!

Maricela sank back in her chair, when Rafaela told her all the results. "I can't believe this is happening. That big? All men too?" Rafaela nodded solemnly. "Okay," she sighed, "I'll get the word out now. Why is this happening to them? Has the whole world gone completely insane?"

"Germanium dust from the moon. Perhaps, that's the culprit. I'll keep on working on it. Maybe there is some way to halt it before it gets out of hand," Rafaela replied, knowing that was about as likely as the dust suddenly vanishing.

Later, she had Bart teleport her to Elegant Fashions Inc in Exchange City. After spending an hour explaining everything to a very worried Inez and an even more worried

Peter, she asked for their help. "You have most men's sizes stored on your computer, at least those who have purchased a suit from you. If you just add an additional sixteen inches over bust, the shirts may well fit enough to get by for now. I sure as hell don't know what to tell you to do about men's jackets and suit coats. For now, I've told the Underground men to start wearing women's gowns or blouses, because it looks like they will fit them more or less when they stop growing."

"Okay, we will get on this right away," Inez promised. "I guess I need to think outside the normal lines for the men. Gosh, as big as we are? Working too? Incredible. There is no way even to disguise them! They are melons."

Peter moaned. "I can't believe this is happening. Men don't have them."

"Well, you do now, so men are going to have to adapt. Just think of how we women have had to manage with our melon breasts all these years!" Rafaela replied curtly.

During the next two weeks, Rafaela could do little except to monitor the daily growth. By and large, the final results were much as the medical machines had predicted. The explosive growth ended by the end of the third week. As she had suggested, the men had already begun to wear their wives' gowns or blouses over their normal pants, as nothing else remotely fit them. A few men found drastically larger shirts that would button over their impressive breasts, but the amount of extra material below their busts looked absolutely awful.

Inez worked her design magic. Since it was winter, she opted for a heavier flannel type long sleeved shirt, based on a man now having breasts similar to her own. Then, putting to work every available dressmaker and tailor that she had ever used and all others she could find, she ordered up thousands upon thousands of these new shirts in various men's sizes. Within a few more weeks, each man who had ever ordered a shirt or suit from Elegant Fashions Inc received one. Then, she began sending quantities to every city and town in which she had a storefront. Still, this only would be able to reach perhaps a half of the men of Tierra, but it was a start.

Meanwhile, on the twentieth day after the start of this

phenomenon, Venerada Maricela summoned Rafaela to her office once more. "Thanks for coming in a hurry. Follow me. We've got a new problem!" She didn't elaborate, and Rafaela followed along after her.

She entered the suite of Sally and Henry Smythe. Sally had just given birth to a fine son and was quietly nursing him with her enlarged melon breasts. All was normal here, Rafaela quickly noted. The problem lay with Henry. He was lying on a make shift cot near the bed, moaning in pain. Rafaela crouched down and began examining him. One of Maricela's healers named Lynn was also beside him. She gently made contact with her. *Look at his breasts. See, they are lactating heavily. If Henry were a woman, I would say that his body was demanding that he nurse his son. Can this be? I've seen this happen to a dozen women shortly after giving birth, especially when the baby dies shortly after birth. But he's a man. This should not be happening.*

Rafaela didn't need to be a doctor to see the situation. She'd seen her own breasts swell up with milk after the birth of her own children. *I concur. It sure seems like this is what is happening to him. Why not let him try to nurse his son? It can't hurt, can it?*

Lynn then spoke. "Henry, we are going to try something. Bear with us." She took his son from his mother. The baby was greedily nursing and began crying at being pulled away. She placed him on Henry and oriented the small mouth. He began nursing at once.

"Oh, god, this feels so weird," Henry whispered. "Oh, god! Relief! It's helping, it's helping!"

Rafaela stood up. "Well, it seems that is the proper action to take. How *very* interesting." She and Maricela left quietly, returning to her office.

"So are men now supposed to share the nursing of their children?" Maricela asked. "If so, we women are going to *love* this one!"

"It would appear so. Best get the word out to everyone. I ought to have anticipated this strange twist, Maricela. After all the medical machines did tell me they would be fully functional breasts. How strange."

"I thought so, but I wanted to check with you first. I'll get the word out now. Thanks. Any more surprises?"

"Good lord, I hope not!"

But there was. Over the next few weeks, reports slowly trickled into the tower. It seems this strange phenomenon had all but ended the rebellions. Men now had a whole new situation to deal with. Besides dealing with their altered anatomy, men's voices rose. Those whose voices had been in the tenor range now sounded in the soprano range, while those in bass range rose upwards to altos. This only added to men's embarrassments. That their hair grew some two feet during the month and their facial hair didn't grow at all was mostly ignored. They could cut their hair. The lords, as much as they hated what had become of their own bodies, appreciated the lull in the skirmishes within their kingdoms. Everyone had something else to talk about now.

Rafaela and Andres also noticed another aspect. He was now far more readily sexually excited. Both began to suspect that behind all this would be a new baby boom. Soon others in the Underground also noticed this, as did those in the tower.

Lord Bolivar took some comfort in the simple fact the Brom Document of Human Rights now would be on the back burner. Everyone had their attention fully elsewhere.

From atop a far northern mountain, one being smiled. The coming catastrophe was being avoided.

Chapter 35 Homecoming

During the long winter of 1273-4, men across Tierra had all manner of reactions to their plight. The spectrum ran from the extreme action of taking their own lives, down to farmers, who merely took note of all this and went about their winter work. Those who were fighter-trained found all their balance and timings were significantly off, due to the heavy weight of their new melons. These men fought against the physical changes the most. However, the many rebellions had been ongoing for months ended abruptly. Fighting was temporarily out.

Late November, Tom, a miller's son in Brom, staggered into Brom Tower. "Help me!" he cried. "I can't get all these thousands of voices out of my head!" The doorman took one look at his yellow eyes with brown speckles and sent a summons to Venerada Maricela. She also took one look and knew she had the first of the new *mentales* gifted on her hands. Two weeks later, Tom returned home, having mastered his new telepathic gifts and with his own germanium crystal hung around his neck, resting between his breasts.

Rapidly, word spread to the other towers to be alert for new *mentales* gifted men and women. All during November, more and more trickled into the towers begging for help. Thankfully, the numbers were small, barely a hundred scattered from all over Tierra. During December, the bitter cold and deep snow prevented all but a handful that lived in Brom from coming there. However, in the southern kingdoms, approximately another hundred arrived for training and help. During January, only a few were able to seek help and these were in the far south.

When spring finally came in 1274, hundreds flocked into Brom Tower begging for help. The usual complaints were massive headaches and the total disorientation of hearing hundreds of voices simultaneously in their heads. Even though Brom Tower had four complete Circles, they were swamped. Training of each new person required at least two and sometimes three weeks.

The other towers faired far worse. Those had between one and two Circles, wholly insufficient to handle the large numbers arriving daily for help. The worst case of all was Adelmira Tower, the only one in all the Easterlings. Venerada Maricela had no real choice but to send one of her Circles to help them out. Frantic — that would describe most of the tower workers during the spring and summer months. By late August, however, the influx died down.

That did not mean all who had received the *mentales* gifts had been handled. Rather, only those who either had the good sense to somehow get to their nearest tower or were brought there were handled. Many more were out there. One of the cardinal rules was an untrained telepath was both a danger to others and to himself. During the fall and on into that winter, the towers began methodically visiting all towns, villages, and hamlets within their respective kingdoms, looking for those who had gotten the gift but had not yet gotten their requisite training. These were often teleported back to the tower and handled.

By late that fall, Elegant Fashions Inc had finally gotten enough shirts produced to meet the huge demand. Of course, many local tailors and dressmakers had also been extremely busy as well, filling the needs not met by Inez and her group. She had not been idle either. Using her husband as a guide, she developed several prototypes of new men's shirts. The two finally settled on the designs that fit snugly beneath the bust line. Of course, this style only emphasized the men's bosoms, but they looked the most like a man's shirt. Now she had to deal with two types. The lords and noblemen often wore pipe corsets that further slimmed their waistlines, making the busts even more prominent.

Having settled on the shirt designs, she then set to work on modifying men's suit coats and jackets. Again, she opted to have them continue to emphasize their new prominent features. By fall, the first of these new types were coming out of her overworked tailors and seamstresses. She sent the first batch to Brom. Her estimates suggested by late spring or early summer of 1275, she would finally finish up the project.

One footnote. Across Tierra, the many tailors and

seamstresses quintupled their annual income during those two years. Indeed, several hundred more men and women hastily began apprenticeships in hopes of participating in this highly lucrative business. In addition, an entirely new industry also formed: recycling materials. No longer fitting apparel was collected by these enterprising individuals and sold to their nearest Elegant Fashions Inc store. In turn, they salvaged a good deal of material and buttons, reusing them in the new shirts being constructed. This whole episode taxed the production of cloth on Tierra to the maximum. Pod silk from the northern lands had never brought them so much profit before. Even wool fetched a premium price. Teamsters also saw an increase in profits from so many extra runs. Overall, this massive re-clothing of men was a financial boon to Tierra.

The significant cost was born by both Elegant Fashions Inc and the many ruling lords and to a lesser extent by the more wealthy nobles around Tierra. Again, the lords saw this as a way to help appease those who had been rebelling. As a pacification process, it was only marginally successful.

By the early spring of 1275, the rebels had begun to regroup. Many saw this entire transformation as the gods backing their rebellions. At least the fighters by now had learned to compensate effectively for the extra mass they were now carrying around. Further, with the final tallies nearly complete, Tierra now had some three thousand newly trained *mentales* gifted men and women, divided about fifty-fifty between the sexes. Some of these had joined the various towers, forming up new Circles. The long drought of so few with these gifts had ended.

Now the rebel leaders began to find ways and means to acquire numbers of these gifted men into their growing small bands. Their idea was to use some of their special powers, such as balls of fire, to help them win their battles against the ruling lord's armies. They had lost almost all of their land gains during the last many months of the crisis. Now they were bound and determined to overthrow many of the southern kingdoms.

The lords were just as determined to put down these rebels. They too began recruiting many of the new *mentales* gifted to fight for them. During the spring and early summer, a buildup of fighting forces began in earnest. Now the miners, smelters, and weapons-makers saw a sharp increase in their products. Once again, Lord Bolivar attempted to work out a way to implement the Brom Document for Human Rights, but with little success.

The Underground continued to monitor the various uprisings, primarily located in the Midlands south of Brom, in the Westerlings, south of Malaca, and in Matruk, Easterlings. With so many minor conflicts so widely scattered, Ken was at a complete loss about how the Underground could possibly prevent so many minor battles and perhaps the overthrowing and destabilizing of a number of kingdoms. He was particularly worried about the breadbasket kingdoms. If chaos overran them, food shortages would become widespread.

Early June, Bart let out a yell of joy. As always, he monitored their large comm network and just picked up a coded text message from Celia Jan! "Ken! Come, they're on their way back here. Isabella, Gabriella Amy, and Celia Jan." Ken came running, as did several others. Looking over Bart's shoulder he read the brief message.

"My god! They have their own personal deep space transport ship!" Ken exclaimed. "How the devil did they get that? Okay, she wants us to figure out where they can land. I'm on it. We have a couple of days before she contacts us again."

"Yes, but she says they have a lot of new equipment for us. Now that is more like it!" Bart exclaimed. Already his mind was imagining all manner of new computer equipment. His were well used — very well used at this point in time. Although parts had worn out and some failed, he was able to patch it together and keep it running. Solid-state drives were worth their cost.

Others heard him yelling and came to see what was up. They too were very happy after reading the brief message from Celia Jan. Andres suggested, "Ken, talk to Alpha about a suitable landing spot. We need to hide the ship from prying eyes." He still believed that the Imperium would be returning soon.

"On it. I'll also let Maricela and Emilio know that

Senator Isabella will be here soon. He's going to need her. Heck, we all need them," Ken replied. He dashed off to deliver the message in person and to visit with the robot.

"I need to see Senator Isabella as soon as she gets here. This Human Rights thing," Lord Emilio declared, greatly relieved. "Finally, we get something going in our favor." Ken agreed and headed back down into the tunnels to find Alpha and Beta.

After explaining that Celia Jan had her own deep space transport ship and that they needed a good hiding place for it, the two robots agreed to see what arrangements could be made for it nearby. A lot depended on its size, Alpha pointed out.

Meanwhile, Rafaela and Andres prepared two of their underground guest rooms for the arrivals. Based upon what Celia Jan's original terse message has said their condition was after their kidnaping, she knew that they would need medical treatment and therapy sessions. The medical procedures, while seemingly painless at the time, were actually rather severe traumas hidden beneath the extensive anesthesia. That is, they contained both unconsciousness and great pain, though seemingly buried. The two wanted them fully back to battery as soon as possible.

"Celia Jan to Bart. Are you there? We're on our approach to Tierra now. Flying on vapors. Over," Celia Jan spoke as clearly as possible, considering the muting effect of the lip plates.

Bart gave a yell to the others and pressed Talk. "Bart here. We read you. Where are you landing? What's the plan? Good to hear your voice. Over."

"Landing at the alien spaceport. We don't have the coordinates for any place else. Besides, we are out of fuel. I am hoping and praying that we can steal some from whatever the aliens left behind. Can you pick us up? Better, can some of you meet us here and lend us a whole lot of help? Looks like touchdown in five minutes. Over."

"Okay, we'll be there ASAP. Over and out."

"It is so beautiful," Hernanda exclaimed, looking out of the viewport. She and Isabella watched Tierra growing larger and larger. Tears trickled down Hernanda's face. "I never thought I'd ever see mom's home. I wish she could be here with us now."

Isabella desperately wanted to put her arms around Hernanda and comfort her. She too felt similar emotions, recalling her own arrival home here, a few years back. The best she could do was to lean on her. "I know. It is okay to cry. I am too. It took me eighty-six years to get back here just a few years ago. I'm feeling the same thing all over again." Hernanda slipped her arm around Isabella's shoulders, pulling her solidly against her own body.

"Are we really going to make it?" whispered Gabriella Amy. The fuel gauge showed empty. After all their efforts, were they going to crash just as they reached Tierra?

"Think so. One more minute, one more minute of fuel, please, please," Celia Jan whispered back, focusing on her controls. The automated navigation system was still functioning flawlessly. She flipped off the cloaking device which had kept their entire flight hidden from detection by anyone. This was one of her more expensive additions to the ship. Ship cloaking was a relatively recent Imperium invention. With luck, no one would have been able to track their arrival. "Oops." The engines gave out and the ship landed with a significant jolt. "We're down. Hope there isn't any real damage. Come on; let's get the door open. I hope the Underground folks are here. We need help now."

They had landed at the passenger terminal portion of the giant spaceport on Plateau Grado. Not a soul was around this normally bustling port. No ships, no tall, thin, grey Rigel-3 support personnel. The place was desolate. Weeds had sprouted in some cracks in the concrete base. The giant buildings were dark and vacant. "Spooky," Celia Jan whispered, as if she might rouse some ghosts. Dust clouds floated off from their landing.

Then, she spotted a large group walking their way from the side of the Admin building. Ken, Crystal, Jake, Misty, Henry, and Janice waved to them, and they all rushed over to greet the two women, who waved back with their short stumps. Behind them, Hernanda brought Isabella out, holding her securely around her waist.

"My god!" exclaimed Ken.

"My god!" exclaimed Celia Jan. "What happened to you guys?" She saw that the four men now had bosoms that matched their wives and her own, before she'd been kidnaped and altered by Senator Carlos. Plus, his voice was now a woman's soprano! Their hair was as long as a woman's was. Well, some women, she corrected her thought. Theirs fell to their lower middle backs, fluttering some in the light breeze blowing across the flat plateau.

Ken looked down. His face flushed. "Lactating. We've had our first child, but I help Crystal nurse him now. All men on Tierra have undergone massive changes. God, you are in worse shape than we really imagined. Can you get down or should we lift you?"

"How about a lift?" she replied. Ken obliged.

Once the four were standing on the concrete, Isabella introduced, "Everyone, this is Hernando Valdez, the no longer blind son of a Trujillo *mentales* gifted woman who was kidnaped and sold as a telepathic slave about a century ago. He and I are going to get married as soon as we can. But how have all you men gotten so changed? Are you still men? I mean with — well, you know?"

Ken laughed. "Yes, still got that. Boobs, voices, and hair changed. Plus we've gotten thousands more new *mentales* gifted, and we're in the middle of a baby boom everywhere. We men have no choice but to help nurse our babies now. If we don't, it's a painful torture. Hurts like hell." Crystal laughed, as did Misty and Janice.

Hernando visibly relaxed. Somehow, this was all working out for the best, he thought. "I cannot tell you how pleased I am to come to my mother's home. She yearned for Tierra always. I only wish she could be here today. My Isabella is now Queen Isabella, too. She's worked very hard to achieve this Ataro System status."

"Well, Queen Isabella, we are under orders from Rafaela to get you to her pronto," Ken replied. "I can see we both are going to have a lot to tell each other. Bart is standing by to teleport you and Hernando to our place. She and Andres have rooms all prepared for you."

"Good. Thanks. Do we need to stay and help unload or anything?" Isabella asked.

"No, you and Hernando get teleported now. We'll help these two with the cargo and ship," Ken replied. He signaled Bart, and he teleported the two to his platform in his comm center, where Rafaela and Andres were waiting them. "Okay, what's next?" Ken asked. "You tell us, and we'll unload it."

"Come on. I want to give you a tour of this incredible machine. You are looking at a billion in credits here," Celia Jan declared rather proudly. "We've also got quite a lot of cargo with us too. Do any of you read Imperium Standard?"

"I do," Thomas replied.

"Good. Walk around this place and see if you can find where we can refuel this ship. It's completely empty, and I sure as heck don't want to just abandon it!" Celia Jan replied.

He left to do just that. The others got a quick tour of the gleaming ship that still had that new ship smell about it. Finished with the inspection, they began unloading the shipping crates. As they did so, Bart teleported them to his teleport pad. Two hours later, they had emptied the ship.

With a big grin on his face, Thomas pulled up with a fuel truck. "How about this? I'm driving a fuel truck. Probably have to make a couple of runs with it though. Where does the fuel go, Celia Jan?"

"Good question. Have to read the instruction manual. Come on Thomas. I'll let you lend me your hands," Celia Jan replied. Another hour passed before they managed to work out how to hook the fuel truck to the ship. It took them another three hours to refuel the ship.

"Okay, Celia Jan. Alpha and Beta have worked out where you can safely store your ship. They have measured it and believe it will fit in their ship's cargo bay. Beta will guide you to it. Can we come along for the ride, please? Pretty please?" he begged.

Celia Jan laughed. "Sure. All aboard the Celia Jan express." The six got their first ride in a spaceship, albeit just a short hop up to Brom. There, Beta raised their "back door," revealing their huge cargo bay. His metallic voice guided them down safely. Soon, he activated his tractor beam, and Celia Jan shut down her engines completely, allowing Beta to bring her fancy ship safely inside the cargo bay. There the imposing Alpha was waiting for them.

"Welcome Celia Jan, Gabriella Amy. Beta and I would like to study your ship, if we may."

"Sure, but don't damage anything," Celia Jan replied. Ken and Thomas put their arms around Gabriella Amy and Celia Jan, steadying them, as they made their way through the spaceship and into the tunnels. Ten minutes later, they arrived at the medical room, where Rafaela and the others were waiting to examine these two. Ken excused himself to go nurse their three month old baby boy, causing Celia Jan to smile, even though such could not be seen. Crystal's broad grin told all, though.

"Okay, let's get you two examined," Rafaela took charge. Hernando and Isabella were now sitting on chairs nearby. She looked almost as if she had been crying, Celia Jan thought.

"What's the matter, Queen Isabella?" she asked as she cautiously maneuvered to the medical table and sat down.

"We'll talk about this after I finish examining the both of you," Rafaela said quietly. "I'm going to lay you back now." Celia Jan appreciated the helping arms so she didn't have to use her telekinetic gift. Rafaela did a thorough examination.

"I've brought along some of the newest medical machines, if that will help," Celia Jan mentioned as Rafaela finished up. After helping her sit up, she asked, "So find anything?"

Once more Rafaela was tightlipped. "Let me examine Gabriella Amy first." Another half hour passed as she examined her fourth patient. At last, after helping her up and into a chair, Rafaela sighed. "Okay. All the results are in. It's not good for the three of you. I'll be blunt and honest with you. I've already explained the results to Queen Isabella. This Senator Carlos actually did something really bad to your necks. It seems that your neck rings are very much needed." Both women gave her a hard stare. She went on, "He first fused the vertebrae in your necks. The rings are a safety precaution from breaking your necks if you take a fall. If I remove the rings, you still will be completely immobile from just below your neck here to the base of your head. The only good thing is that he didn't fuse those going down your backs. But as we all know, after wearing such restrictive corsets for so long, your muscles have gown weak."

"Shit!" Celia Jan replied as she finally realized their immobility was permanent. "That beast! I should have killed him. How the hell can we live like this?" She raised her aesthetic looking upper arms into the air, frustrated. "We can't see over our boobs and now this too? Double shit!"

"I'm truly sorry, Celia Jan. I will redo these tests when I get the new medical machines up and running. At least your feet can be partially restored and I can get those mammoth breasts reduced too. That will help a little."

Queen Isabella spoke up, "But we are going to wait a bit on that. I wanted all the lords to see just what the Imperium has done to their senators first."

"Right. But we ought to get this done as soon as possible. Removing the lip plates would help too," Rafaela added.

"I know, but if it is as you say, all the lords and nobles are wearing them, I we ought not be different. Not right away," Queen Isabella replied. "Can we get something to eat now? Plus, I want to know what's been happening here while we were gone. It seems like the men have taken the brunt of it."

Rafaela laughed. "Big time. Let me tell you, they were none too pleased with all the changes. Yet, in a way, perhaps it has been a good thing. All the many active rebellions suddenly stopped. Of course, now that the men have more or less come to grips with the changes, they are back at it again. Plus, we now have a dearth of *mentales* gifted men and women. I think at last count, there are two hundred children who also have the gift. What is really wild is all the twin births that have been happening all over. One in three births this past six months has been twins. Can you believe that?"

"Incredible birth rates. But will these new ones lose their gifts in a year or two like the last batch?" Isabella asked.

"We don't know. Based on my own research in making *mentales* gifted, I would expect these will be permanent. All these have the full gift, not just basic telepathy as the others had. I know some of the men are hoping and praying their changes are not permanent. I've never seen anything remotely like what's happened to them, except by using a medical machine to make such changes. Frankly, I'm not holding my breath on that one. Besides, many women really do appreciate the help with all the nursing. Some claim their families are much closer now. At least some of the new fathers now appreciate what we women go through with the three a.m. feedings." All four women chuckled.

"So is Brom also facing rebellions too?" Queen Isabella asked.

"Not exactly." Rafaela explained about Lord Emilio's bright idea and the resulting document of human rights. "Of course, he is now desperate to see you. He thinks you can help him figure out how actually to implement some of the drastic changes the document suggests.

Over a long lunch, Queen Isabella related their many adventures, pointing out just how they had managed to escape the clutches of Senator Carlos. After that, Rafaela took the four to meet with Lord Emilio and Venerada Maricela.

"Oh my god, Isabella! This is criminal — what he's done to you three," exclaimed Lord Emilio. The group had gathered in his office, along with key members of his staff as well. All had gasped when they saw the physical appearance of the three. Now that they had heard the terrible news about their fused necks, he'd reacted angrily, though in a soprano voice, which the four found rather amusing, though they dared not show it.

She then told them about her lengthy Ataro System training with Queen Altha. "So you see, I am designated officially now as Queen Isabella Valen. I could be a ruler of one of the planets in their system. However, I wanted to try to bring their social technology here to Tierra and see if I can help make Tierra a better world."

Lord Emilio looked apologetic and said, "Well, I for one am quite desperate for your help, Queen Isabella. I've been forestalling open rebellions in Brom for several years, but I'm going to have somehow to implement what the people desire.

Frankly, we are all at a loss on how to proceed. I hate to ask anything of you, considering that you've just returned and are almost totally helpless now."

"My mind is sharp, and I want to see what I can do to help. First, I want all the other lords to see us as we now are. After that, Rafaela is going to undo what she can so we have a bit more freedom of motion, though there isn't much that she can really do for me. I am just plain screwed."

Rafaela interrupted, "Plus, they all need to get some therapy to handle all the trauma they've suffered. I intend to see that happens after we get done undoing what modifications can be repaired."

Venerada Maricela suggested, "Okay. Why don't we try to have all the lords come by tomorrow morning for a look at you three? You can also get a quick update on the situation in their kingdoms as well. Perhaps in the afternoon, Rafaela can work her medical machines and then get you four into therapy sessions in the evening."

"Okay, let's make it happen," Lord Emilio replied. "But if Isabella, I mean Queen Isabella, if she is ready to help me tomorrow, I would really appreciate it. I can't begin to tell you how desperate I am. We all are. I'll see you get a copy of this document of rights later today."

He then added, "I wish something could be done about us men. I'm not cut out to be nursing babies. Anita has just given birth to twins, a boy and a girl, who will be another valuable katalyein too. Still, I know how much Anita is depending upon me to help her." Queen Isabella found herself wondering how the armless Anita was dealing with her twins. He went on, "We've at least gotten over our humiliation and embarrassment. I kind of like my hair long like this, but I can't stand my own voice like this. The gods must have done this to us all."

"They must still be active," Venerada Maricela spoke up. "After all, the moon exploded but instead of disintegrating, it somehow reformed as if by magic. The massive cloud of dust and debris that fell all over Tierra accounts for the *mentales* gifted for sure, but it does not explain the massive changes in our men. I've gone over the ancient tower documents and found reports that it was only after the alien base on Plateau Grado blew up three centuries ago when the first *mentales* gifted appeared. That's also when Tierra had its Dark Age and so many died of starvation. That's also when women's breasts became the melons that they are today — assuming those ancient documents are at all accurate. Still, it leads me to believe the Ariana, the Goddess of Fertility, was active then. If so, my own personal speculation is she is once again behind this sudden baby boom and the alteration of our men's bodies."

"Why do you say that?" asked Queen Isabella.

"Well, the Easterlings barbarian wiped out a whole generation of young men in Domei, Arad, Alba, and much of central Matruk. Lady Edda of Turda and Sultaness Sofia of Arad have been constantly begging for men to immigrate there to help fill the tremendous loss of manpower in those lands. It is almost as if Ariana has seen that we were getting desperate and somehow created this baby boom."

Since no one interrupted her, she elaborated on her theory, "If we suddenly have a great many babies, having the fathers able to help all the mothers out with nursing is a great benefit. I know just how much Lady Anita is depending upon Lord Emilio, now that she has twins to handle and feed. To my way of thinking, this must be part of Ariana's plans."

"Yes, but that doesn't explain our high pitched voices or the incredible hair growth in just a month or so back then," Lord Emilio countered.

"Perhaps she saw that as a way to forestall the ongoing rebellions. They certainly stopped fighting for nearly two years now," Maricela countered.

"Say, venerada, if you are right about this, then may be after this baby boom, men will return to normal," Lord Emilio suggested hopefully.

She shrugged her armless shoulders. "Don't know, but I can say part of the reason for this baby boom lays with the expanded sensuality of you men. Theo's breasts are hypersensitive, and I tell you it's darn hard to get him out of our bed in the mornings. It's a bit easier now that I'm pregnant. Twins. Three months along now," she admitted.

"Congratulations!" Queen Isabella replied. Others added their words of encouragement as well.

Lord Emilio flushed. "Well, we can't help it now. All Anita has to do is to touch them, you know. When she does, I just can't help myself. All of us are like that."

"My point exactly, Lord Emilio. You men have a much-heightened sexual drive now, and that translates into more pregnancies than normal. Rebuilding our population," Maricela replied. "It is almost like Ariana is watching over us all somehow. She knew with the barbarian's sweep across the Easterlings and the loss of a thousand of our new telepaths, we desperately needed to increase our population. She is the Goddess of Fertility."

He offered a counter-suggestion, "I see. It couldn't be the one called Lysandra trying to get even with us men, could it?"

"No, Lysandra always asks for a supreme physical sacrifice for her help. I do wonder whatever happened to Wystan and Calder? He abandoned all of his mermaids. Such a tragedy," she replied.

"I like the idea of blaming this on a goddess. Still, maybe once we have enough babies, we men will get our original bodies back," Lord Emilio replied.

Venerada Maricela could not help but tease him a little, "So you really want to give up your heightened sexual drive — give up your boobs?"

His face flushed as did several other men. He muttered, "Well yes and no." He decided to leave well enough alone. He was sufficiently embarrassed.

She then said, "We've taken up enough of their time already. They need to get their things unpacked, and I need to arrange this meeting in the morning." Lord Emilio was quite ready to have the meeting adjourned.

"Wait one second, please. Lord Emilio, can you dissolve the fake marriage between myself and Gabriella Amy and Celia Jan? Then marry Hernando and me?" She looked at her two wives and added, "And marry those two? Keep is really simple, please."

He laughed. "I would be honored to do that, Queen

Isabella. That is something I can do." A half hour later, the two new couples headed back down to the Underground.

"God, going down stairs on your toes when you can't see the steps or hold onto anything is scary and frightening!" Queen Isabella gasped, as she tentatively felt for the top step of the stairs that led to the underground tunnel systems.

"I've got you, dear, but I can't see either. We go really, really slow," Hernando replied. "You two can wait up here for me, and I'll come get you when I have her safely down."

"Thanks, Hernando, but we can manage somehow," Celia Jan replied. Once Hernando and Isabella were safely down, the two simply used their gifts to lift their bodies down the stairs,. He then asked, "Why does this Venerada Maricela want to see me later tonight?"

"She is a katalyein. Her gift is to remove mental blocks that others have that keep them from being able to fully use their gifts," Queen Isabella answered. "But I don't know why she wants to see you though."

The four spent the rest of the time until supper sorting out their many crates. Bart lent Celia Jan a hand, highly excited over all the new computer equipment she'd brought back with her. She also had a dozen more solar panels to add to their existing ones. They would provide more electrical power, which the Underground definitely needed.

That evening, Misty led Hernando through the tunnels and then up the stairs into Brom Tower to Venerada Maricela's office. She then waited outside to help him find his way back. "Thanks for coming, Hernando. You must be wondering why I wanted to see you." He nodded. "It is simple really. Your mother had the gift and passed it on to you. However, she was unable to train you beyond handling telepathy. You actually have some mental blocks that are preventing most of your gifts from materializing. I suspect you had a bout of Verge Sickness when you were younger."

"That is what mom called it, Verge Sickness," he replied.

"Okay, close your eyes, and let's get you freed up. Then tomorrow, some in my tower will begin your training. No charge." She added that last, having picked up his thought that he had no money at all.

"What do I do?" he asked.

"Just relax. This is my special gift." She focused and her crystal activated. He had a large black mass over his head, and she gently touched it, revealing the traumatic images it contained. He saw himself flying a spaceship in some large battle. Suddenly, his ship exploded, bits flying off in all directions. He'd fought hard to pull it all back together. Failing that, he tried to keep himself from fracturing into bits, flying off in all directions as well. Failing yet again, he found himself flying off into the bitter cold of space. Within minutes, the black mass evaporated and he smiled. Maricela broke her contact and her crystal dimmed.

"I've lived before. That was a spaceship wasn't it?" he exclaimed.

"I think so. Now you have your true gifts available, far more than mere telepathy. I believe you will be able to have powerful telekinetic skills and more. Tomorrow, after the big meeting and after you are done with the medical machines, one of my tower folk will begin training you on how to master you skills that you inherited from your mother."

"How can I ever thank you? I feel so light headed."

"You already have, by looking after Queen Isabella. She needs you now more than ever before."

"I promise I will always be there for her. She's saved my life, and Celia Jan has given me back my sight." He returned elated and Queen Isabella gave him her best hug.

The next morning, Hernando dressed her in her best satin gown and brushed out her hair. "There you go. You look like a queen now, my love. I think it is time we go meet all these men. I hope I can just stay in the background. I've never been around lords before."

"You'll do no such thing. You stay at my side, always, just as you were trained. You don't have to say anything unless you want to, but give me a kiss first."

A half hour later, the four made their precarious walk into the crowded throne room of Lord Bolivar. Dozens of the other rulers had been teleported here for this brief meeting. As the four took their tiny steps entering the room in their fancy toe shoes, gasps echoed from all quarters. Yes, these lords were shocked at what they saw. They'd last seen the trio just before they headed off-world.

Queen Isabella then sat on Lord Emilio's throne, but only after Hernando adjusted her hair so she wouldn't sit down on it. She then launched into a lengthy description of what had happened while she was away. An hour later, she finished up by explaining she was now officially a queen of the Ataro System and highly trained in running a world.

"In the days to follow, I will be meeting with each of you to see how I can help you. Please give us a few days to get settled in," she finished up. After the lords agreed and left to return home to their own problems, Nadja walked up. She'd come along to hear as well. "Nadja! You saved us. Thank you."

"I am utterly appalled at what that senator did to you! He is a sadistic criminal! Wait, how did I save you?" Nadja asked. She too was very pregnant.

"When we got to the Ataro System and out of fuel, with these lip plates, the ULAT boxes couldn't translate our speech. However, Queen Altha got you to send her an update to the boxes so she could understand us when we arrived on her world."

"Oh that. It was nothing. She asked for it, and I already had it worked up. Really, we are terribly hard to understand with these plates," Nadja replied. The two chatted a bit longer, before Rafaela dropped by to insist they report for lunch and the medical procedures.

During the long afternoon, each had their monster breasts reduced to the normal melon-sized breasts of the women of Tierra. That alone increased their visibility a good deal, but they could still not see their feet. Each had their feet partially restored. Now they only had to always wear the usual six-inch heels making walking far easier for the four. For the time being, they kept their awkward lip plates. All the lords wore them at the meeting, and she believed it best they do so as well.

After supper, Hernando headed off to get his first training lesson, while the other three headed into Madiera, the artificial town within the huge spaceship run by Alpha and

Beta. Here the rescued mermaids lived, taking advantage of all the automation the two robots could manufacture. All three were surprised to see the many children running around outside, playing various games. Some were little mermaid girls, but not all the girls were mermaids. Some were as normal as the boys.

Thus began a long week of therapy sessions for the three. Later, Hernando received his, but he was utterly shocked to see the physical bodies of the mermaids. After seeing them, he commented to Isabella, "You are so far better off than those poor women. I don't see how they can possibly survive." His heart went out to them, more so after they finished his therapy, giving him a newfound vitality in life. Long years of blindness had taken its toll on his viewpoint. Now, he felt as if he was reborn.

However, after about two weeks on Tierra, he discovered changes in his own breasts. They became hypersensitive to touch, just as the other men's were. Isabella discovered this and she made good use of it. All she had to do was to brush her body against his breasts to get him excited. A week later, she too was pregnant with twins! She was more than convinced that some other force was at work on Tierra.

Meanwhile, Queen Isabella began studying the document of rights, focusing on just what would satisfy the requirements. It was quite clear to her the "citizens" of Brom wanted the power of choice over both their rulers and those who made the laws. Further, they wanted a clean separation of the makers of the laws from the enforcers of the law. They also wanted some way to get justice as well. Yet, she also saw Lord Emilio's problems with such a system. Who would maintain the kingdom's army? Certainly, they had to remain a constant across the time span of several rulers. Just how would their coins, their money exchange system, be maintained across various successive rulers? What would the role of the towers take in all this? Those members could not be elected. One either had the gift or they did not.

Slowly, she began to formulate a plan: a senate-type legislature and a replacement for the ruling lord or lady. She knew she needed to change the name of the ruling position.

King, queen, sultan, sultaness, lord, lady — those could not be used, since they would be a constant reminder of the past monarch systems. Then, she hit upon a little used Westerlings term and opted to use it. "Sorry to make you have to write so much, Hernando," she said as he jotted down all her ideas. "Being like this is the pits!"

"I am your arms, just as Queen Altha taught us, my love. It is I who am honored to do this little for you. So are you ready to make the presentation to Lord Emilio?" he asked.

She sighed, "Yes, if I keep on thinking about all this, I'm likely to never decide it is done. Let's have Ken arrange a meeting."

Chapter 36 Dealing with the New *Mentales* Gifted

The next day at ten, Hernando escorted Queen Isabella into Lord Emilio's throne room. This time, all of his aides, his *mentales* Squad Leader, Domingo Bolivar-Brom, Venerada Maricela, Ken, and Crystal were present, along with Gabriella Amy, Celia Jan and Rafaela. Hernando held her notes up so she could see them.

She began, "My Lord, I have worked out a system I believe will meet everyone's needs. First, at least two institutions must remain permanent, unaffected by the elections of the citizens of Brom. These are the army and the Treasury Department, which makes our coins. No matter who is elected and for how long, these two must continue through time, undisturbed. I am proposing we have three branches of government, one to make the laws, one to execute the laws and rule the kingdom, and a third to handle justice matters. In essence, it provides a system of checks and balances."

"To make the laws, I propose a Senate Legislature. These elected senators will have a term of four years and cannot serve more than four terms, whether successive or not. They should be based upon population, perhaps a senator per every thousand citizens. They will need a permanent building in which to meet and conduct their business of making the laws of the kingdom. The ruler, who then runs the kingdom and sees that these laws are enforced, would be called either rey or reina, depending on the sex of the elected ruler. Their term of office would be longer, six years, so that they can oversee a transition of senators, providing continuity during the election period. They cannot serve more than two terms, whether successive or not. This guarantees us of not having a 'bad' ruler around more than six to twelve years."

"Now both of these two branches need security. Therefore, I am proposing the establishment of the Royal Guards, whose task is to guarantee the safety of the rey and senators. Like the army, these people will have a permanent job. Initially, I would hope that you, Lord Emilio could form up the Royal Guards."

"Finally, to handle justice matters, I am proposing the establishment of a two-tiered system. First, there should be local a Kingdom Court, so that any citizen, who is accused of a crime or who wants to accuse another of a crime, can have their day in court. These justices must be trained by me and their positions will be a lifetime commitment, since they must know all the laws, especially as the laws may undergo frequent alterations as time goes on. Again, I would expect that you would setup these local Kingdom Courts initially. When one of the justices wishes to step down, the current rey or reina can appoint their replacement, but the senators must vote on their acceptance. Again, a check and balance. Further, I am going to setup a Tierra-wide Supreme Court, and run it as Queen Isabella. Any citizen, who believes that the local Kingdom Court has not given them proper treatment or has made an error in judgment, can appeal that verdict to the Supreme Court, where I will hear the case. My judgment is final."

"This way, if the rey or reina believes the senators have made a bad law, they can bring the matter before the Supreme Court for a ruling. If I find it is indeed a bad law, I can then strike it down. Also, if the senators believe the rey or reina is failing to enforce a law or trying to make up their own laws, they too can bring the matter to the Supreme Court, where again, my ruling is final. Thus, there will be a check and balance on all the elected official's powers. Note also, that the Supreme Court cannot make any laws nor replace a rey or reina. Further, if either of those two branches believes that the local Kingdom Court has run amok, either one can bring that case before the Supreme Court as well for adjudication."

"When it is time for me to step down as queen, I will fully train my own replacement in all the incredible knowledge that Queen Altha entrusted in me. As far as handling the actual elections, there should be a locally established Election Committee to oversee and run the elections, making sure that those who vote are citizens of Brom and that no one is allowed to illegally alter or modify the election results or even vote more than once in an election. To that end, the election should take place on the same day throughout all of Brom."

She went on, "Finally, where does the tower fit into all this? They should retain their own organization as they have always done. Their goal is to provide protection and assistance to the kingdom and its citizens, particularly in healing, katalyein aid, and the training of new *mentales* gifted. I still feel that those of us with this priceless gift must use it to help others and our kingdom. So there you have it. What do you think of my proposals?" Now comes the hard part, she thought. Will he accept these ideas or will he raise too many objections?

Everyone held their breath, glancing overtly or covertly at Lord Emilio. After all, at this point in time, he was the ultimate ruler in charge of everything. He ran his fingers through his now long hair thoughtfully. "Well, on the whole, I think this could well work out for the best. Checks and balances. Yes, that is absolutely the most vital point in the entire proposal. Brilliant even. I can see two potential problems. First, what happens if the elected rey or reina is assassinated? It could be at a very critical time, such as during a war, when their leadership is critical. Who runs things until a new one can be elected?"

"Ah, good point. Without needlessly complicating matters, why not have the spouse of the rey or reina take over until the election? If they have none, before the election occurs let them declare who will be that person to take over in the event of their death or disablement. That way, the citizens who believe the choice would be a bad one can vote otherwise. Would that work, My Lord?" she asked.

"Ah, yes, that would be fine. If I was assassinated, I am sure that Anita would take over for me until someone else was elected. Where was I? Oh, second, how many of these senators are we going to have? The committee I setup to come up with their document had over five hundred members and that was too unwieldy a number. Also, there should be an odd number of them so there cannot be any tie votes."

"I agree on the number. The Imperium has an impossible number of senators, and it is very hard to get any real work done. Perhaps fifty-one would be a reasonable number. It's your call. Whatever you think is more manageable," she replied.

"Let's go with the lower number. Now where will you hold your Supreme Court and how are we to deal with problems between kingdoms?" he asked.

"I'll use the Imperial Castle and the Imperial Circle, since it is only used to host the High Council meetings. I can host those meetings in the future, and the Supreme Court can also hear disputes between kingdoms as well. Another thought I had, My Lord, is since there is now an abundance of *mentales* gifted, why don't the towers create some satellite towers within the kingdom. Here, for example, you could use one up at Hilliard Heights and over at Chester at the very least."

Venerada Maricela spoke up. "My very thoughts, Queen Isabella. I think that we should do just that. I like your idea of you running the High Council meetings. Someone needs to keep them running smoothly. Besides, I think I can convince the Imperial Circle to go along with your proposal, but what about the other lords — the other kingdoms? They are in turmoil at the moment. I've been in close contact with the other towers. Open rebellion is about to begin again, only this time, the consequences are going to be disastrous. It seems a fair number of the new *mentales* gifted are siding with the rebels."

Queen Isabella frowned, "I see. So if I don't do something fast, there's going to be widespread blood baths."

Lord Emilio sighed, "Precisely. That's going to make a mess of our food supplies, since the breadbasket kingdoms are fending off rebellions. If there are all out conflicts, we're in for a belt tightening winter, I'm afraid. Perhaps this is why men are now able to nurse. With all these babies and a widespread shortage of grains and meats, survival is going to be a challenge. At least we have enough cattle and goats to provide milk here in Brom. Of course, those are always in short supply during the long winters. We're going to run way short of grains, though I've already placed larger than normal orders with Lord Rusden. Worse, we might not be able to get our dried fish deliveries from the coastal cities, unless we begin to teleport them here."

"Okay, I can see I must take unilateral action here, if only to save Tierra. Lord Emilio, how soon can you assemble that committee of yours — the five hundred or so? I want to present this to them directly, with you permission, of course."

He consulted for a minute with Maricela before replying in his now soprano voice, "We can get them here in two days. Meeting at say ten that morning."

"Good. Thank you venerada," Queen Isabella replied politely. "Now then, let's have an assembly of the High Council of Lords and representatives of the various rebellions on July 1st at the Imperial Castle. I know we ought to be able to get the lords to come. Getting the rebellious fractions also to appear is going to take some persuasion. Venerada, let's meet when we're done here, please."

"Of course," she replied.

"Might I make one additional suggestion?" Rafaela spoke up. Until now, she'd been silent, observing how incredibly well this major ruling change was occurring. "As long as we are going to be building a new Senate building, might I ask we also build a new building which is accessible by our mermaids? They would like to expand their therapy sessions by offering them free to all other peoples of Tierra. As you know, they are not really capable of either traveling to other towns or even being able to live there on their own. Perhaps this could also be used as a 'selling point' to convince others to adopt this new way of rulership."

"I don't see why not," Lord Emilio declared, glancing at his staff. "Certainly, the location ought to connect easily to their tunnel system so they could get to and from the new building. Rafaela, consult with my master architect. He's going to be busy, I can see that."

"Thank you, My Lord," Rafaela replied. At long last, she'd been able to easily implement Benjamina's plan to expand this vital therapy beyond just the city of Brom.

The meeting adjourned. Hernando put one arm around Queen Isabella and one around Venerada Maricela. Since this was a formal meeting, she had to wear her heels and gown, making it a bit of a challenge for her to navigate the halls and stairs, though nowhere near the difficulty that Isabella had. They headed out of the room. With their short arms on each other's shoulders, Celia Jan and Gabriella Amy followed the trio. Once in Maricela's private office, Hernando helped each to get seated and took out his pen and papers once more, ready to take notes.

Venerada Maricela said, "Give me a minute to get the messages sent to the comm network." She focused and sent several telepathic messages before her crystal dimmed. "Okay, the Imperial Circle will be expecting the meeting. They didn't have any objections to your moving into the castle, but they would like you to add more members to their Circle as well."

"Consider it done as soon as I can get to it. Now then, the lords will be getting word of the July meeting shortly. The real question is how are we going to convince the rebel leaders to also come?" she asked pointedly.

Gabriella Amy spoke up, "One thing is for sure, they will be very hesitant to come, believing it is some kind of trap — that their lords will be trying to kill them while they are there. We're going to have to overcome those very real fears. I would not put it past some of the lords to try to do just that — assassinate the rebel leaders."

"But we don't even know who these rebel leaders are," Celia Jan protested. "How can we invite those we don't even know? Seems impossible to me."

"I agree; we just don't know who these people are," Queen Isabella replied with a sigh. "We need a very bright plan — something that'll get their attention. Something that'll convince them to come." The small group discussed various ideas, but essentially didn't really resolve the problem.

Just then, Maricela received a telepathic communication from the capo of the daytime Circle. "Damn. Several of the lords are declining, citing they must not be away from their kingdoms right now because of the rebellions. Now what are we going to do?"

"Damn it! If our bodies were not so damnable helpless, we could do something about it," Gabriella Amy swore angrily. "I've had quite enough from these other lords. If we were not so hobbled up, we could do something about it. Jan, we're simply going to have to get ourselves some new bodies soon."

"What did you have in mind, Gabriella Amy?" Venerada Maricela asked, speaking soothingly, hoping to calm her down. She felt a twinge of pity for the three women.

"If we weren't almost helpless, we could fly the transport around Tierra and deliver Isabella's message directly and in such a way it could not be missed," she replied rather testily. "You don't know anyone besides Jan here who can fly the spaceship do you? I thought not. Damn it anyway."

Celia Jan smiled, though she knew it wasn't visible. "Can you give me a few minutes? I have an idea. Meanwhile, Queen Isabella, you work out what kind of ultimatum you'd like to say to these people personally."

Gabriella Amy looked quizzically at her lover, but Celia Jan only smiled, rose, and very cautiously made her way out of the office. Hernando jumped up to get the door for you. "Need me to come with you?" he asked.

"No, you stay with Queen Isabella. She needs your help more than I do. Thanks, Hernando." She headed carefully down the hall and then faced the treacherous steps, feeling for each one. A half hour later, she finished explaining what she wanted. The robot Alpha smiled. Beta said, "I believe that I can fly it. Naturally, we have been studying it since you parked it in our shuttle bay. If you can show me how it is to be refueled, I will see that it is topped off when we return. How soon do you wish the flight?"

"Cool, guys! Let you know. Probably later today, I think anyway. Back in a bit," she replied and left.

She found that Hernando had written down Queen Isabella's speech. Hence, she said, "Okay, I have us a competent pilot. When do you want to leave? I need about an hour to prepare everything."

If she had arms, Queen Isabella would have put them on her hips, as she asked defiantly, "Who? A pilot?"

"Beta. He's got it all worked out."

"Brilliant, love! Brilliant," Gabriella Amy replied.

"Well, Hernando has my speech written down. How are we going to deliver it?" Queen Isabella asked, still thinking about whether or not to trust the ship to a mere robot. She decided if Celia Jan trusted it, then she should too.

"Come with us and we'll show you. Thanks for helping Maricela," Celia Jan replied, effectively ending the meeting. As the four made their careful way down the steps, she kept quiet. Once on the stone floor of the tunnel, she added, "We're going to show you something that must be kept absolutely, utterly secret. These are not supposed to exist any longer."

A while later, she led them to the original section of the tunnel-room complex located just below the small house above ground there in Brom. In one storage room filled with currently unneeded items, shoes, dresses, and such, she walked to the back wall and pressed her stumps on one spot on the wall. A grating sound echoed in the room. Part of the stone wall slid open, revealing a hidden room. "What's in there?" asked Queen Isabella.

"Best that you don't know. One should do the trick," Celia Jan answered mysteriously. Shortly, she stepped out holding what appeared to be a basketball sized rock covered in a snow pod cloth bag. Gabriella pushed on the stone door, shutting it. She also noticed the thick layer of dust. No one had been in here since the two of them had stored their things here a very long time ago.

"This doesn't exist, Queen Isabella," Celia Jan said, again being quite mysterious about it. Using her gifts, she pulled back the pod silk covering a little, revealing a very large bluish germanium crystal that was at least a foot across.

"Oh dear god! Is that what I think it is?" Queen Isabella whispered.

"Yes, come on; let's get to the transport ship," Celia Jan replied. Hernando carefully took the stone from her. She didn't really have any choice, as hobbled as she was, carrying it all the way to the ship would have been far more than she could have done without using her *mentales* gifts all the way.

An hour later, Beta hovered over Walsham. Gabriella Amy and Celia Jan slipped into rapport with Queen Isabella and with the giant ancient crystal of power. Hernando held the papers up so Queen Isabella could easily read them. As she spoke, her words were both tremendously amplified and heard in nearly every mind within a fifty-mile radius of the hovering transport ship!

"This is Queen Isabella Valen, who used to be your senator. On the first of July, all current ruling lords and their advisors are to report to the Imperial Castle for a major meeting at ten in the morning with me. I am solving the entire rulership situation on Tierra, whether you like it or not. Plus, all of you who are currently rebelling against your rulers, send a representative to the meeting as well. Those of you, who do not come, will lose this opportunity to have a say in the new governing system. I give you my word no harm will come to anyone who comes to the meeting. Rebels, if you use this temporary absence of your rulers to launch an attack, I will not hesitate to wipe you out. Same goes for you lords, if you should launch an attack against the rebels, while they are at this meeting. This is not open for debate. There will be peace. My word is final. Come. Those of you, who need transportation to and from the meeting, contact Brom Tower or the Imperial Tower Circle."

The two broke their connection to the giant crystal. Queen Isabella declared, "There, that ought to be clear enough for any nincompoop!" All three laughed, and Beta moved them about another fifty miles away, where she repeated her speech once more. Hours later, the ruddy sun was setting, when they finally finished up and landed on Plateau Grado, where Beta quickly topped off their fuel supply. Full dark encompassed them by the time Beta maneuvered the transport ship into the tractor beam operated by Alpha. "Thank you two. That went far better than I had hoped. Now we'll see who shows up," she replied appreciatively, as Beta opened the transport door.

Beta's monotone voice merely said, "Glad to be of service."

Two days later, before the large crowd of the assembled committee members, all the Lord Bolivar's staff, ten of Venerada Maricela's staff, and the Underground members, Queen Isabella Valen introduced herself and made her lengthy formal presentation. She outlined in detail the various plans for how this new change in rulership would be created and operate, including the proposed new constructions of more towers, a Senate Legislature building, and the new Trauma and Spiritual Rehabilitation Center.

Finally, she explained Venerada Maricela's recent idea formed only the day before. "What with the availability of so many new *mentales* gifted men and women, Brom Tower is putting a new program in place. Shortly, every small town, village, and hamlet will have their own local Brom Tower contact. If someone there is in need of healing, have someone contact your local representative who will immediately contact the nearest tower for help. One or more healers will be sent to help as soon as possible. Yes, this is the same lifesaving program that has been quite successful in the larger cities such as Hilliard Heights and Chester for several years now."

When she finished, she received a hearty round of applause. The official meeting broke up and many wanted personally to thank her. Lord Emilio and Tom, their chairman, stepped aside to begin outlining the next step: the equitable division of the kingdom into fifty-one smaller regions of roughly the same population. Each would then begin the work of electing their own senator. Plans called for the first Senate meeting to begin on May Day, 1276.

The next day, Bart handled the lengthy teleport project. Queen Isabella's party moved all their things south into the Imperial Castle. Inez and Peter Franks along with Nadja and Diego del Baldomero joined them to help get the Imperial Castle cleaned up and ready for constant occupation. Peter and Inez also saw to the doubling of the staff. Only a skeleton staff currently worked there, handling the needs of the small Imperial Tower Circle members. Plus, they made arrangements for a large temporary staff to handle the needs of the many visitors expected on the first of July.

The night before the meeting, Gabriella Amy asked Queen Isabella to follow her into the throne room. Dim lanterns provided the only nighttime illumination, most all were asleep in anticipation of a very confusing next day. Never had the castle anticipated so many visitors at one time. "I know it is challenging for us to walk alone, but I want to share something of vital importance only Jan and I know. I'll put my arm on your shoulder. Come, let's take it slowly." The two women made their cautious walk down the halls and into the spacious throne room. She led Queen Isabella up to the former emperor's throne. Unable to bend much at all, the two used their feet to feel for the stone steps that led up to the raised platform and stone thrones.

"Okay, now sit down please." Queen Isabella did as asked, landing rather hard on the cushions on the seat.

"Isn't this just the pits?" she growled. "Hell, I can't even sit down gracefully."

"I know. I know. Now what I am about to tell you only Jan and I know about. You see, she and I rebuilt this place long ago, when she and I became the first emperor and empress. In those days, all the towers had these enormous psi-crystals that amplified *mentales* powers more than a thousandfold. With them, even the very stones of castles were easily destroyed. Jan and I outlawed all such crystals and had them confiscated and destroyed."

"Yes, but not all of them. Wasn't that one of them we used to help broadcast my speech to everyone?" Queen Isabella asked, wondering where this was going and if perhaps more of those crystals of power had not actually been destroyed.

"True, not all of them were destroyed. In fact, I want you to use your gift and pervade the stone beneath your seat. Go down about four feet," Gabriella Amy asked in a whisper.

Queen Isabella did as asked, focusing her mind, and then sending it into the stone beneath her. Suddenly she stopped. Her eyes opened wide. Gabriella Amy smiled invisibly. "Yes, one is there. If you have need of power during the meeting, simply focus on that crystal, and your powers will be enhanced about five thousand-fold. Keep this a secret between us three. Jan and I figured tomorrow you might just need its support."

"Incredible. No one else knows of this?"

"Nope. She and I put it there in those turbulent times, and we thought you might need its support tomorrow, if things get out of hand. Come on; let's get ourselves safely back now. Oh, how are your twins doing?"

Queen Isabella smiled invisibly too, as she carefully

lunged upwards to her feet, silently cursing Senator Carlos once more. After regaining her balance by wiggling, she replied, "They are doing fine. Terribly small right now, but growing. Too soon to tell their gender. It's only been a month. Are you and Celia Jan planning a family soon?"

Gabriella Amy sighed, "No, once we make sure all of this goes well and gets established, we're dropping these bodies and starting over with some new ones. Honestly, if our necks were not fused, we'd probably keep these. But like we are, she and I have decided we don't want such a life, not when there are so many new babies on the way. Besides, we've only had these for such a short time."

"I see. I wish I had the kind of certainty you both have. I hate the way I am now, utterly dependent on poor Hernando. Lord knows what I'd do without him. In a strange way, I am glad he will be able to help with the nursing and caring for our twins. I could not possibly do it myself. I don't know how I can face living another fifty or more years like this, but I have accepted the responsibility of an Ataro System queen, and I aim to see it through somehow," she replied stoically.

"We are all thankful you are doing this for all Tierra, Queen Isabella. You may well be ushering in a new era of peace and prosperity for everyone. That is a goal worth doing," she replied.

The next day, Hernando dressed Queen Isabella in her fanciest red pod-silk gown, brushed out her luxurious, long black hair, and placed her official Ataro System crown on her head, securing it. Then, he helped her into the throne room ahead of time. Once seated, he adjusted her hair so it fell across her lap and to her feet. "You look absolutely stunning, my princess," he whispered. "I will be here at your side, and I have all the papers at hand, but I am nervous."

"No kidding. I'm almost scared, Hernando. Together, we must make this work. I'd take a deep breath, but we can't do even that little thing. Well, here comes some now." Hernando deftly adjusted both of their sets of lip plates up and locked into the horizontal position. This way, the plates would not block her mouth and allow her words to carry. He did note this room's acoustics were designed to permit the voices of those on the thrones to carry well throughout the room. They watched as their friends and some tower members and guards took up positions around the outer perimeter of the room. Overhead, the stained glass windows let in the dull orange-red glow of the sun.

Slowly the room began filling up. The ruling lords, ladies, and their contingents, which included venerados, veneradas, capos, capas, amos, amas, and aides, took up their usual positions around the center of the room, standing before the throne. The various representatives of the rebel fractions were escorted into the room by Queen Isabella's new staff. Most had never been here before and came well-armed for trouble. Almost a thousand packed their way into the hall filling it up. Around the room, enforced polite conversations created a low din, but all voices sounded feminine to Queen Isabella, who still was not used to hearing men's voices in the soprano and alto range. Further, everywhere she looked, everyone sported the same melon-sized breasts, though the men wore the newly design shirts and suit jackets Inez had created. Still, massive bosoms were everywhere. This, she found very strange indeed and a little unnerving.

At last she rose, though Hernando used his arm to help her rise as gracefully as possible, under the circumstances. As she did so, an expectant, but hostile, hush fell. She began by introducing herself. "Welcome one and all. I am Queen Isabella Valen Gervasi, your ex-senator to the Imperium Senate. I and my two fellow women were appointed to be your senators and represent all of Tierra's interests in the Senate. However, as you all know, the Imperium has abandoned Tierra. Our treatment there was beyond criminal. We three stand before you today as living proof of what Senate President Carlos Amandos did to us. Yes, he took us prisoners, holding us as his telepathic slaves. He not only cut off my arms and those of Gabriella Amy and Celia Jan, but he also altered our ages to eighteen so that he could reduce our waists to barely a foot around. Yes, we can barely breathe now. He altered our feet so we had to wear the Imperium style toe shoes. He altered our breasts to an enormous size. If you think yours are big, you ought to have seen what we looked like! But

718

the worst thing of all, he fused all of our necks. Yes, none of us can move our necks in the slightest. He wisely put these neck rings on us to help prevent us breaking our necks, if we should take a fall." Many gasps echoed around the room, but mostly from those who had not heard this before.

She went on. "However, we three escaped with the help of my husband, Hernando, who Senator Carlos kept blinded since he was a child. His mother was kidnaped from Valen something like two centuries ago. Senator Carlos kept her as his telepathic slave. Yes, we escaped from his clutches. However, to return to Tierra, we had no choice but to make a refueling stop on one of the planets in the Ataro Empire of the Twelve Sacred Planets of the Wasp."

"Let me tell you a bit about their system of government. It is important for us all." She launched into an explanation of their culture and methods of ruling. "So you see, they have not had a single war or open conflict on any of their three dozen planets in over two millennia! I find that utterly remarkable." She then described her lengthy training under Queen Altha. "Their emperor personally bestowed my title as Queen Isabella. I am here today to honor them and to fulfill my commitment to helping ensure long lasting peace and prosperity on all Tierra."

"To that end, I am making good use of the major changes have been ongoing up in the Kingdom of Brom. Yes, they too had many who wished to rebel, just as so many here are currently doing. Yet, they had the good sense to listen to Lord Emilio Bolivar. He had them construct a document outlining just what they, the people, the citizens of Brom, really wanted, what they were demanding. Today, I am going to read you that final document, which I am unilaterally going to apply to all of Tierra. After you hear it, you will see what I mean. It is called:

The Declaration of Human Rights
Composed This Fifth of September 1273 in Brom

All human beings are born both free and with basic rights. They are entitled to these rights as long as they use reason and treat others with both dignity and respect.

These basic rights make no distinction on the person's race, country of origin, language, culture, ownership of property, or any other status. Such things shall not be used for discrimination of these rights.

All citizens have the right to their own lives, their freedom, and security.

No citizen shall be subject to torture, slavery, or to degrading punishments.

All citizens are equal before the law and the ruling lords. That is, Lords, Ladies, Jefe, noblemen, noblewomen, *mentales* gifted, and farmers, for example, are all equal before the law and subject to it.

All citizens have the right to move freely about the kingdom and to leave or freely visit other lands.

Any citizen who is charged with an offense against the law must be presumed innocent and has the right to a speedy and fair trial or hearing, during which both they and their accusers present evidence. The citizen has the right to face his or her accuser, face to face. To be found guilty of the offense, the citizen must be found guilty beyond any reasonable doubt.

The family unit is hereby recognized as the fundamental building block of the kingdom. As such, marriages are to be valued and protected from all those who seek to destroy the union by whatever means.

Each citizen upon reaching the adult age of fourteen has the right to choose their own marital partner.

Every citizen has the right to own property or land.

Every citizen has the right to the freedom of thought and to speak freely their own opinions to others, as long as their speech does not baselessly slander another. No one has the right to harm another's good name without just cause.

Every citizen of our kingdom has the right to elect their own leaders and those who make the laws of the kingdom that they have to obey, as do all citizens of the kingdom.

Every citizen has the obligation to become as fully informed as they can as regards to the issues and candidates for which they are voting. These elections should be free and open with no intimidation or threats to those who are voting.

Every citizen has the right for equal payment for equal work or products.

Every citizen has the freedom of choice of employment.

Every citizen has the right to a standard of living that maintains their health and that of their family, especially so for mothers and children.

Every citizen has the right to worship their own gods in the manner of their choosing, subject to the rights of others stated above.

Every citizen has the right to the best medical care available in a timely manner and has the right to choose the method of their treatment.

Every citizen has the right to have a day of rest from work to worship or relax as they so choose.

Every citizen has the right to demand their rulers provide a safe and secure kingdom in which to live and prosper.

Every citizen has the obligation to protect these rights of other citizens as well as their own.

The law of the kingdom must protect these rights.

"There you have it. I think that I have never heard such a clear, precise statement of what every person's rights ought to be. No sentient person could condemn these."

One by one, the rebel associates began applauding, as she anticipated. Soon, some of the lords' members joined in. Reluctantly, the ruling lords began clapping, though quite reservedly. They were none too happy with the way this was going. Their powers were being usurped!

"Now then, the problem arose on just how this is to actually work. Lord Bolivar asked me to lend my newfound wisdom, learning, and experience to this task. Subsequently, I have come up with a very workable method by which to implement these basic human rights we all share in common with each other," she explained.

She went on, "I have worked out a system I believe will meet everyone's needs. First, at least two institutions must remain permanent, unaffected by the elections of the citizens of any kingdom or alliance. These are the standing army and the Treasury Department, which makes the kingdom's coinage. No matter who is elected or for how long, these two must continue on through time, undisturbed."

"I propose that we have three branches of government, one to make the laws, one to execute the laws and rule the kingdom, and a third to handle justice matters. In essence, it provides a system of checks and balances — the single thing that is wholly absent in the current forms of government. Indeed, it has been lacking since the dawn of time here on Tierra."

"To make the laws, for each kingdom, I am proposing a Senate Legislature. These elected senators will have a term of four years and cannot serve more than four terms, whether successive or not. They should be based upon population, perhaps a senator per every thousand citizens. Try to limit their numbers to around fifty-one, but always an odd number to avoid tie votes. They will need a permanent building in which to meet and conduct their business of making the laws of the kingdom."

"Next, the ruler, who then runs the kingdom and sees that these laws are enforced, would be called either rey or reina, depending on the sex of the elected ruler. Their term of office would be longer, six years, so that they can oversee a transition of senators, providing continuity during the election period. They cannot serve more than two terms, whether successive or not. This guarantees us of not having a 'bad' ruler around more than six to twelve years at the very most. The citizens of a kingdom can vote a poor ruler out of office. This should make the rulers far more responsive to the actual needs of their people than ever before."

"To handle the possibility of an untimely death or disablement of the ruling rey or reina, when they are running for office, they should declare openly, who will be the person to take over in the event of their death or disablement, until new elections can be held. That way, the citizens who believe the choice would be a bad one can vote otherwise."

Again, loud clapping and cheering broke out among the rebels. Queen Isabella also anticipated this response and allowed them to vent before continuing.

"Now both of these two branches need security. So I am proposing the establishment within each kingdom a Royal Guards, whose task is to guarantee the safety of the rey and the senators. Like the army, these people will have a permanent job. Initially, I would hope the current rulers would form up the Royal Guards."

"Finally, to handle justice matters, I am proposing the establishment of a two-tiered system. First, there should be a local Kingdom Court, so that any citizen, who is accused of a crime or who wants to accuse another of a crime, can have their day in court. These justices must be trained by me, and their positions will be a lifetime commitment, since they must know all the laws, especially as the laws may undergo frequent alterations as time goes on. Again, I would expect you rulers would setup these local Kingdom Courts initially. When one of the justices wishes to step down, the current rey or reina can appoint their replacement, but the senators must vote on their acceptance. Again, a check and balance."

"Further, I am going to setup a Tierra-wide Supreme Court and run it as Queen Isabella. Any citizen, who believes the local Kingdom Court has not given them proper treatment or has made an error in judgment, can appeal that verdict to the Supreme Court, where I will hear the case. My judgment is final."

"This way, if the rey or reina believes their senators have made a bad law, they can bring the matter before the Supreme Court for a ruling. If I find it is indeed a bad law, I can then strike it down. Also, if the senators believe the rey or reina is failing to enforce a law or trying to make up their own laws, they too can bring the matter to the Supreme Court, where again, my ruling is final. Thus, there will be a check and balance on all the elected officials and their powers. Note also, that the Supreme Court, namely me for now, cannot make any laws or replace a rey or reina. Further, if either the rey or Senate believes the local Kingdom Court has run amok, either one can bring that case before the Supreme Court as well for adjudication. Checks and balances."

"When it is time for me to step down as queen, I will fully train my own replacement in all the incredible knowledge that Queen Altha entrusted in me. As far as handling the actual elections, there should be a locally established Election Committee to oversee and run the elections, making sure those who vote are truly citizens of that kingdom and that no one is allowed to illegally alter or modify the election results. To that end, the election should take place on the same day throughout all of any kingdom."

"Finally, where does your tower fit into all this? They should retain their own organization as they have always done. Their goal is to provide protection and assistance to the kingdom and its citizens, particularly in healing, katalyein aid, and the training of new *mentales* gifted. I still feel that those of us with this priceless gift must use it to help others and our kingdom."

"I will use the Imperial Castle and the Imperial Circle to house the Supreme Court. Plus, I will act as permanent host to the High Council meetings. More importantly, I can also hear disputes and adjudicate *between* kingdoms as well."

"With the new abundance of *mentales* gifted, all towers should begin to create some satellite towers within the kingdom. Up in Brom, they are putting new ones in Hilliard Heights and over at Chester. One last point, some of you have heard of the fantastic handling of trauma and spiritual needs that Brom has been offering. I am pleased to announce to everyone a new Trauma and Spiritual Rehabilitation Center is being built in Brom. Once open, anyone on Tierra can go there for help. I have just had all the trauma I suffered at the hands of Senator Carlos erased. Obviously, that was quite a lot."

"That about sums up everything. Lord Bolivar is already implementing these many changes as we speak. I am here to assist anyone in working out the pertinent details for their kingdoms. At this time, I would like to open up any discussion relating to these overall plans. Let's discuss the specifics for each kingdom separately so we don't take up everyone else's time."

Lord Rusden spoke up, cursing his soprano voice. He still was not comfortable with the many changes his body had undergone. "I protest! You are usurping the ancient traditional powers of we kings and lords! What gives you the right — let alone the damned authority to impose your will on my kingdom?" Several other lords echoed his sentiments, rather loudly. She could not reply for nearly a minute, so strong were their protests.

She allowed them to vent a little before answering Lord Rusden and several others. "Quite simply, Lord Rusden, your kingdom is in revolt. Your own people want changes; they want freedom; they want some control over the laws of your kingdom and a say in how it is run. It is obvious they have not been given such. I point out, Lord Rusden, history has long shown that any ruler, any government which harms or has its own people killed unjustly is on its way out. Rebellions come, if not assassinations of those rulers and officials. Good grief, how many times have we seen that happen? Far too many. If you and other such lords do not handle this now and handle it according to the will of your people, I wouldn't wager a copper on how long your life will be. So if you want to leave and not work with me on bringing change and prosperity to your kingdom, then go right ahead. The rest of us will merely count the days that remain until you are assassinated. For as sure as I am standing here that will happen. If you don't believe me, just look at Valen's history this past century. How many of their rulers were assassinated, eh?" Many eyes turned towards Lord Alano Valen, whose face flushed. He didn't say a word; that's how he came to power in the first place.

"Well, everyone knows the average person in our kingdoms is an idiot. They don't even know what they want," Lord Rusden bellowed as best he could, again cursing his high-pitched voice which was no longer so dominating.

"Oh, I see. Everyone on Tierra thinks the average person is an idiot do they, everyone? I see some average people here with us today. Take our new chef, who is standing in the back there; he's prepared a nice feast for us this evening. Let's ask him. Sir, do you think you are an idiot?" All eyes turned to see the chef, with many whispering, asking where? Where? He was too embarrassed to say anything, shaking his head no.

"Oh, I'm sorry, Lord Rusden, it seems not everyone here agrees with you. Might I ask you who suggested to you the average person was an idiot?" Queen Isabella countered, hitting him with her full attention. A face flashed in his mind and she saw it.

"Well," he fumbled, "my advisor told me so. He ought to know."

"I see, and this advisor of yours — he has gone out and met every average person in your kingdom? My, that must have taken him at least a year to do all that. What were his criteria for proclaiming this person is an idiot and that one isn't?"

Lord Rusden flushed red and didn't answer. She continued, "You see, this is one small technique I was taught. Whenever you hear someone speaking in broad, sweeping generalities, such as all people are idiots, you can be absolutely certain it's not true. Rather, if you investigate a bit, you will discover it is always just *one* person who is telling you that generality. Further, you can bet that person has his own motives behind doing that, and those are not the same motives you have. In this case, Lord Rusden, might I ask you about this advisor? Does he stand to gain financially, if you have to use force of arms to put down this rebellion of yours? Does he own, perhaps, a weapons making company?" She already knew the answer, having picked up both the lord's thoughts and those of the man in question.

Lord Rusden face contorted angrily. "Well, as a matter of fact, Beckhold is supplying a good deal of new swords for the army I'm raising."

"Ah point taken, My Lord," she softened her words. "One of the skills drilled into me by Queen Altha is to help others spot these kinds of subtle and often overlooked sources of great troubles for rulers. Lord Rusden, forgive me for picking on you in front of everyone else. I guarantee you if you will allow me, I will be able to help each and every one of you lords and your supposed 'rebels' sort this out. I don't ask you to take my word for this, but there simply cannot be a conflict between two people without there being a hidden third person who is actively trying to create that war, that conflict, that strife, and often doing it for his or her own personal benefit. I am an expert now in sorting these things out, thanks to weeks of patient training by Queen Altha, who does this on a daily basis."

"But you are destroying our hereditary kingship," Lord

Alano Valen pointed out, trying to gain some standing by coming to the support of the Midlands Lord Rusden.

"You are quite right, Lord Alano. While history has shown repeatedly perhaps the very best form of government is a beneficent monarchy, and I wholeheartedly agree, history has also shown us the key problem with that form is one of succession. After the wonderful and great monarch passes away, almost always his successor simply cannot fill his predecessor's shoes and chaos erupts, one way or another. But of course, Lord Alano, you know that only too well. Your kingdom had a great ruler ages ago when Valen Castle and Tower were first built. Those that followed have been, to quote Lord Rusden, idiots, including your own predecessor, right?"

He nodded in agreement. He could not do otherwise than admit her key point. After all, half of the world hated and despised the terrible treason that the previous two Lord Valens had inflicted on much of the Westerlings and all the Midlands. Some of the older rulers of the Renegade Tower were present, with their prosthetic hands, living proof of that treachery. She'd played him well. In a flash, he saw she had done just that! She was not a fool! She was not this helpless woman standing precariously before them all. He realized she was truly a force to be reckoned with and changed his viewpoint accordingly.

He changed tactics. "So what benefits will we see from these changes? Twelve years is not very long for us to rule our kingdoms."

"The benefits will be many, not the least of which will be peace and prosperity for all your people. None of us here is going to toss any 'blame' onto your plates. What has been done in the past is in the past and shall remain there. Let us focus on the present and build a magnificent future. Honestly, My Lords, think of just how much money you have had to squander on combating these open rebellions in your lands? Such a fortune could be far better spent on improvements within your kingdom, ones that will aid everyone's fortunes. Think of just how many hours each day you lords have to spend dealing with all aspects of these rebellions. That time and effort could be far better spent. Plus there is another point to all this. Power. My Lords, think of just how much more *powerful* you would feel knowing you had the *full* and *complete* support of all of your people, because they freely elected you to be their ruler!"

She continued, "Plus, each of you lords who implement these changes in your kingdom will become famous. History will remember you with great pride and honor as being the *single* person who brought *true* freedom and human rights to your own people. I dare say you will be the most famous of all your leaders in history," she played to their vanity this time. It worked; she sensed many echoing her thoughts.

"Now then, it is time to break up into smaller groups so I can work with each kingdom on resolving their own unique situations. Gabriella Amy and Celia Jan also know how to resolve conflicts. Lord Emilio Bolivar has volunteered to assist them as well. So here's what let's do now. Will the lords, ladies, sultanesses of the following please go with those three: Domei, Arad, Turda and Alba, Malaca, Matruk, and the Alliance of the City-States. The remainder stay here, and I will arrange to work with each of you in turn, beginning with Lord Rusden. After you sign up on the sheet Hernando has here, you can adjourn to the Great Hall. Our chef has some lunch and refreshments waiting you. As we finish with one of your groups, someone will let you know when it is your turn. Lord, ladies, this day will go down in history as your *finest* hour." She left them with that bit of upbeat encouragement.

In Malaca, the changes were readily accepted, and Lord Gervasi agreed to build three new *Círculo de la Torres* at Toledo, Manca, and Alba. The City-States Alliance decided to build towers in all their major port cities, as well as allowing each of the major cities to become independent kingdoms, but still maintaining their position within the alliance itself. This greatly benefitted the Renegade Tower, who had been hard pressed to counter the barbarian invasion. Now they saw this formation of new kingdoms as a way to help deal with future hostilities, should they ever break out once more. Thus, Lady Edda of Turda became Reina Edda of the newly formed Kingdom of Turda-Alba, as she chose to call it. Also, with Adelmira Tower's help, a new *Círculo de la Torres* would be built at North Umbria, about halfway between Turda and the existing tower to the north. This solidified the Sisterhood gains there. In the Arad, Sultaness Sofia agreed to build towers in her city of Tecuci and at Po.

Queen Isabella handled Lord Rusden and his kingdom first. Quickly, she saw the single-most fear he had: the many new *mentales* gifted. More than a few were siding with the rebels. Right away, she proposed they build new *Círculo de la Torres* at Leedsburough, Woodhall, Hayden's Crossing, and Oakham. Seeing these new towers would absorb so many of these new gifted men and women, he readily agreed to the changes. Matruk was happy to have their own tower built at Southbend. Similarly, towers at Wycombe and Haverhills satisfied Lord Wye. So it went.

Lord Alano Valen and the situation in the huge land of Trujillo didn't go so easily. The rebels controlled much of the central lands and bitterly complained Valen had never given back anything to them, only taxed them, took their *mentales* gifted away, and conscripted their young men into their armies. After much discussion and fact sorting out, they reached an agreement. The rebels would create their own new Kingdom of Central Trujillo, stretching from Nueve del Toro down to Salamanca that bordered the new Kingdom of Benito. Valen would rule the remainder of the western portion of Trujillo, which had always been their strong base of support down through the centuries.

Of note, several times Queen Isabella had to resort to drawing power from the hidden crystal beneath her throne to preserve the peace between the warring factions. It took two full days of negotiating to reach agreement among all the lords. One thing that helped as well was the incessant pleas from Reina Edda, Reina Sofia, and Rey Teraspoli for men to come to their lands to help the massive rebuilding projects. Thanks to Damiano, there were few able-bodied men left in those lands, though some young boys had come of age in the last two years. Promises of high wages and women aided greatly in their latest recruitment exercises.

The evening of the third of July, the last had left, and the throne room was nearly empty. "Well, I've actually done it," Queen Isabella commented, breathing a huge sigh of relief.

"Well done," Gabriella Amy exclaimed. "I never thought such dramatic change would be so easily accepted."

"Ah, the timing was right, Gabriella Amy," Queen Isabella pointed out. "It has less to do with my charm and wisdom than it has to do with all the unrest that was widespread, after the shocking march of the barbarian lord Damiano across the Easterlings and much of the Midlands. That acted as a strong wake-up call. They saw what rebellions could easily do. While they would not admit it, most of the lords were looking for a gracious way out of the mess in which they were stuck. That their bodies are so physically changed is also playing a factor."

"Still, well done, Queen Isabella."

"True, but now comes the hard part. As you can see, my daily schedule is booked solid from now until October. They all want many private meetings to hash out their own specific details. All this would be so much easier if we were not so physically disabled; damn Senator Carlos anyway."

"Look, if he had not done this to us, you would not likely have gotten trained by Queen Altha. It is her extensive training that has given you the knowledge and confidence to pull this off, Queen Isabella," Gabriella Amy pointed out.

"True, but if only my neck would work," she lamented, "the rest might be bearable."

Chapter 37 Babies

Lysandra found Ariana still observing from her mountain perch. *So how long are you breeding them?*

Until I am satisfied their numbers have grown sufficiently. Besides, I like how the men are finally caring more for their young. Kind of funny. Wish old Wystan could see what I've done to his mighty warriors. He'd be really annoyed, don't you think?

Probably come after you with a vengeance.

Yep, he would at that. Ah well, it will end soon. I am satisfied. Have you seen Calder around? I sure haven't. He's abandoned his creations. Are you going to do anything for them? They are breeding true, you know.

Not unless they ask for it. You know me. Besides, what have they got left to sacrifice to me? Damn Calder anyway. Breeding true?

Some. Not the ones the mechanical men have altered, so I guess that is something. Still, my plan worked. Peace has come again and few were killed this time.

The baby boom began officially in late 1274 but picked up steam by late 1275 and didn't end until late 1276 or perhaps 1277. Most reports suggested the boom dropped back to normal sometime in 1277, though it was difficult to say with any degree of accuracy. Birth records were simply not kept. The end was marked by most midwives, who claimed they assisted in fewer births during late 1277. Others, mostly men, argued for a later ending around 1280. Why? During that year, many men's bodies began to alter once more. Their melon sized breasts slowly vanished, and their voices deepened to what they had been before, much to their great relief. However, not all men's bodies returned to what they had been before.

Queen Isabella was due early April 1276. Gabriella Amy and Celia Jan had long ago decided to pick up a new pair of baby bodies. Both were unwilling to live so crippled up, not when they were barely twenty again. The world was at peace, and this seemed a fine time to try again. Celia Jan asked, "So should I get a male body this time for us? I'd rather not and just use the new medical machines that can allow us to fertilized each other."

"Let's do it that way. I'm just wondering who we should have as our parents this time. We were dopes to go over to the Easterlings last time," Gabriella Amy replied.

"No kidding. Say, what about our responsibilities to Tierra? You know as well as I do Queen Isabella is going to have to have a replacement down the line. If her peace continues to hold, eventually she will need to retire, and then one of us is going to have to take over, don't you think?" Celia Jan pointed out and asked, rhetorically since she already knew the answer.

Gabriella sighed, "You are right. One of us is going to have to take over from her when the time comes. We simply must not let the ball down this time!" She sighed, "I guess it's going to have to be me. Perhaps Queen Isabella will train her own daughter. Let's hope so. I'll take one of her twins. What about you?"

"I'm going to make sure I know everything about all the comm equipment and machines this time. I've my eye on one of Bart and Anita's twins. That way, I will be assured of staying on top of the Underground's needs this time. Back on the Imperium planet, I just more or less guessed what was really needed here. Next time, I aim to know precisely the state of all the equipment, especially since it can't be imported anymore, unless the Rigel-3 folks return," Celia Jan replied rather pointedly. "Say this time, let's make sure our parents name us right!" Both laughed.

1276 was baby year in the Underground. The six women each had twins. Fortunately, the babies came about three to four weeks apart, beginning with Crystal in April. She and Ken welcomed Ben and Lana into the world. Then came Anita's twins, Lilly and Jan, making Bart a very proud father. Why? Only a month before, Celia Jan told them that she would be taking one of their new little girls. Everyone was amazed, when one morning Celia Jan's body was found lifeless in the guest bedroom. Anita and Bart roared with laughter, when they were deciding names and they heard in their minds, *Hey, you better name me Jan if you know what's good for you!*

About a month apart, the other four mothers gave birth to their twins as well. The following year, Bart and Anita had a son, Tom. The six men had no choice but to share nursing duties with their wives. Laughing about this strange quirk of fate, the six men did so, much to the pleasure of their wives.

About the same time, Queen Isabella and Hernando had twins, Amy and Bernardo. The following year, she had another girl, Gabriella. Inez and Peter Franks had unexpected twins. She thought she was past her childbearing years, but in June, she gave birth to Henry and Nita. Nadja and Diego were also not immune. She gave birth to Hidalgo and Adrianna in July, much to the great pleasure of the young couple. They compromised; he gave their son a Westerlings name, while she gave her daughter the name of her grandmother.

Lord Emilio Bolivar and his katalyein wife, Anita had Drina and Antonio in August of 1276. To both their great pride, Drina carried on the katalyein line, as armless as her mother and with yellow eyes at birth. The following year, she also brought Desi into the world and was thankful for no more twins. His close friend and Squad Leader Domingo and his wife Sally were the proud parents of Ernesta and Benito. A year later, she bore him another son, Fausto, pleasing him greatly.

Not to be left out, Venerada Maricela also had twins, making Theo very proud, though he had to temporarily halt his eagle training business to help her care for them. Beltran and Casilda, also a katalyein like her mother, arrived in August. The following year, she bore him another son, Carlos.

All over Tierra, these baby boom years were rather wild. More twins were born than single births, though those huge number of multiple births died down in 1277. Everywhere, fathers had no choice but to assist their wives with the nursing of their children. Many men tried not to do so at first, but their swollen breasts soon left them no choice in the matter. More than one woman got a good laugh at her husband's expense, but they also were greatly relieved as well.

In the Easterlings, the extreme shortage of young men was quite severe. By six months after Damiano swept through the desert kingdom conscripting the able-bodied men, most realized their loved ones would not be returning soon, if ever. Instinctively, the older men, young teens, and the many women of childbearing age began to realize they were doomed unless they had many more babies and soon. Campo Oasis was quite typical. Their population had fallen to some five hundred, where women outnumbered the men by five to one. Worse, they were facing starvation, when the trio of mermaids returned. Elena, Felisa, and Adalina returned home to their father, Beppe Venuto, bringing with them three bags of gemstones worth about ten thousand gold each, to say nothing of their huge, dangling earrings.

When they arrived, they created quite a sight, and the entire oasis turned out to see them. Sporting the twelve-inch lip plates, tiny waist lines held rigidly by their pipe corsets, dangling earrings touching their melon breasts, and their elegant, form fitting satin gowns, they made quite a sight and were the topic of conversation for quite some time. Everyone wanted to know what had happened to them.

Elena tried to explain, but everyone had a very hard time understanding her drastically altered speech, frustrating all three mermaids. Within just a few days, the three were utterly depressed; their sexual behavior modifications were lost. No longer could they use their mouths and teeth as they had been able to before, they could not even bend over at the table and eat from their old plates any longer. Their lip plates and corsets prevented such things. Crying, they could not even pull their covers up with their teeth, they had become almost completely helpless mermaids, dependent upon their loving father, Beppe.

However, quickly they struck a bargain with the others in Campo Oasis. They had the one thing that was needed: seemingly unlimited funds. Beppe doled out the gems, and some of the older men and middle-aged women began making supply runs to the coastal towns, bringing back lifesaving food supplies. In return, some of the women began to care for the three's physical needs. By early 1274, Elena and her sisters were hailed as the saviors of Campo Oasis. Their funds had allowed the villagers to purchase two new supply wagons and two teams of donkeys. Now weekly supply runs were bringing goodly amounts of supplies to the oasis, while delivering the few items that they had to sell to markets in Po, such as dates, figs, and herbs.

Eventually, the village elder, Alfonso, held an oasis-wide meeting. "Look, it is plainly obvious now our young men are not going to be returning. We've heard tales of the invader's army being wiped out. Unless we rebuild our male population, we cannot survive much longer. Until now, we owe our survival to Elena, Felisa, and Adalina. If they had not returned bearing such wealth, we would all be starving to death. As I see it, we have to abandon our homes and go in search of another oasis that has more men."

"Couldn't we form up harems?" another older man asked.

"Aye, but who among us could afford one? We can barely support ourselves as it is. If not for our mermaids, we couldn't even do that," he countered. "There is one thing we can do. We simply must have all available women, who can bear children, do so. I have taken stock of the remaining funds of our mermaids. If we use their earrings as well, we can likely survive for another dozen plus years until the baby boys reach adulthood and take over."

One woman chided him, "Just like a man. They want to get us all in bed." Many laughed.

Another woman spoke up, "But Elder Alfonso is right. Unless we women have many babies and soon, we will exhaust Elena's funds. Then what will we do? We must do as he suggests, have many babies soon." After more discussion, the village agreed with the elder.

Then someone asked, "What about Elena and her sisters? Should they have babies too?"

Everyone turned to look at the trio. Elena spoke up, speaking as slowly and as clearly as she could. At least by now, the trio no longer wore their lip plates. All three were terrified of taking a fall and smashing in their mouths. Still without working lips, their speech was most difficult to understand. "Please, we want to have babies very much, please."

"Well, they want to have babies too. We cannot deny this to them," Elder Alfonso decided. After some discussion, the task fell to a young fourteen year old lad, Alfeo.

So at long last, Elena got her first real passionate kisses and sexual experiences, as did her sisters. However, when the men's bodies began to change, their urges to procreate became even stronger. "What is happening to you, Alfeo? You have breasts like ours and your voice is changing the wrong way," Elena asked, as he helped her into her bed.

"I don't know. I am scared. Maybe I can't do this," he replied bashfully. She hopped a little, brushing her melons against his. Almost at once his passions ignited again.

A while later, as he held her against his side, he whispered, "That was incredible, Elena! I guess this part of me still works."

"Better than ever, Alfeo, but now I am a little afraid too. How will I ever be able to take care of my baby by myself?" she whispered back.

"Well, I guess I will have to help you, Elena," he replied, wondering if the elders had thought this far ahead.

As the days progressed into weeks, all three became noticeably pregnant. The last months were particularly difficult for the three, who could barely hop with the extra weight. At least the body modifications had lowered their wombs below their constricted waists. Within a few days of each other, Elena, Felisa, and Adalina gave birth to Benigna, Erica, and Francesca in 1275, respectively. Their baby girls were mermaids like themselves. A year later, they gave birth to Adriano, Archangelo, and Carlo, all boys.

Trying to raise two infants themselves, all three mermaids were frantic with desperation. They themselves were quite helpless, but with the added pressure of trying also to handle the young infants, they were extremely depressed young women. Alfeo had no choice but to help them, not only with the six babies, but he found that he had to share nursing them. Between the almost constant needs of the three women, the six babies nearly drove Alfeo mad as well. While he had begun to care deeply for these three women, their constant care coupled with the babies was almost more than the young lad could handle. Around the oasis, most all the other young women had their own hands full with their young babies. Never had they seen so many twin births! Even the older men found themselves sharing nursing duties, while struggling to maintain weekly food supply runs to Po.

After Benjamina's body died, she headed for the Easterlings. Her trauma therapy, which also demonstrated a person was an immortal spiritual being, was now firmly established in Brom, Midlands. With the devastation caused by Damiano, the Easterlings needed a tremendous boost, which is why she decided to spend her next lifetime there, founding another therapy group, spreading her therapy over the Easterlings. However, as she surveyed the lands, she spotted the three mermaids. From the Underground men, she had heard they had refused to come to Brom for help, begging to be sent back to Campo Oasis and their father. She checked up on how they were doing.

For months, she monitored them and saw the depths of their despair. Yet, the villagers were helping them. When the many changes in the men occurred, she decided to take Elena's first-born baby so that she could help the women. She also used her gifts to know what their babies would be like — duplicates of their mothers, mermaids. When they became pregnant the second time, she used her gifts to ensure that all three had boys. Unfortunately, there was little that she could realistically do with a tiny infant body. She settled for using her gifts here and there to help, such as preventing Elena from taking a spill. One day as she put out a telekinetic push to keep her mother from losing her balance, while getting up from the bed, she made contact with Elena's mind. *My god! She's Calder!* Little Benigna saw what had happened to him and how he'd become trapped in the body of her mother.

With plenty of time on her little hands, Beni, as she would choose to call herself, began to see how a spiritual being could go from being a powerful god to a mere human being with no recall of his former state. Calder had committed far too many harmful acts upon others. The abandonment of his mermaids had been the straw that broke the donkey's back, as they say in the Arad. She concluded Wystan had probably met the same fate, since his atrocities against humans had been far worse than Calder's.

Now she had a moral dilemma to face. Did she really want to risk giving her mother, Elena, therapy? Elena was actually Calder. Benjamina had worked long and hard to salvage somehow all the mermaids Calder had created, missing only a few. Did he or she deserve therapy now? Worse, she guessed there might be a chance, if Elena got therapy, she might recover enough to become the god Calder once more. Did she dare let such a being loose again?

Things got a bit more confusing. All three became pregnant yet again, giving birth in 1277 to three more mermaids, Christiana, Delfina, and Floriana. Beni cursed herself for not having paid attention to her mother, who still greatly desired her physical relationship with Alfeo. The only redeeming factor was when these three were born, Alfeo was working to get Benigna, Erica, and Francesca hopping about on their own, like good two year old children. *What have I gotten myself into?* Beni began asking herself. *Do I dare use my mentales powers? I must observe them all some more.*

Another thought also bothered her. While Alpha and Beta had worked their science magic on the rescued mermaids so that their offspring had normal human bodies and thus were not begetting more of these horribly modified forms, Elena and her sisters were handing down their forms, at least to the female babies they had. Their three boys seemed normal, but now there were nine of these mermaid forms. If they continued to breed true in their female line, in just a few more generations there would be a rather large population of these mermaid women. Lacking *mentales* gifts, they would require tremendous support from those around them in the oasis.

This posed a moral dilemma for her. On one hand, these mermaids were human beings and deserved life as much as the next. On the other hand, without a powerful *mentales* gift of telekinesis, they were nearly helpless women, dependent upon others for nearly everything their lives. Even these nine were beginning to consume far too much of the precious resources of those here in Campo Oasis and at a most critical time when their very survival was in doubt. It was too late to have Alpha somehow work its science magic on Elena and her sisters. The damage was already done. Further, if she and her five sisters reached adulthood and had babies of their own, at least half would very likely breed true, creating even more mermaids. What was still unknown was whether or not Elena's son and the other two baby boys carried the mermaid genes. If those three later bred, would they too pass this deformity on down to their children? Calder had done his work far too well, Beni thought. She could see in the not too distant future these mermaids would eventually destroy the very people of the oasis, who out of kindness were caring for them now.

For several years, Damiano continued to live his life of abject misery in a small stone home on the southern edge of Exchange City. There the old woman, Agata, continued to care for his constant needs. At least she always kept his round booties tied securely to his leg stumps. This way, he would move about somewhat, just as his wife had done. Each morning, she lifted him down out of his bed, sitting him on the commode. Then, she dressed him, but made him walk into the small dining room. "Look, I can't be carrying you. You can walk, just like the others did," she scolded him.

"Please, kill me! I can't live like this," he pleaded with her, each and every morning. She only smiled and continued fixing their morning meal. One morning he asked her why she was not going to kill him.

"Silly man. How many men have you and your band killed or maimed? Untold thousands. How do you think we women are to live without our men? So I have you now and I have needs too," she winked at him.

Suddenly, he got her meaning! She wanted to bed him! "Oh god! No!" he shrieked.

"Then shut up and give me some peace and quiet in the morning," she replied, grinning to herself. That ended his daily outbursts.

Once the mightiest warrior Tierra had ever seen, Damiano was reduced to a pathetically helpless existence, which seemed to have no end. If he lived until he was sixty, he faced nearly forty more years of this hideous existence. He found it utterly unbearable, but was wholly helpless to do anything about it. It was all he could manage to do to walk on his upper legs from the bedroom to the dining room and later to the living room — a whopping twenty feet!

His unending nightmare took a drastic change for the worst. Like all other men, his breast began to grow, as did his hair. His booming voice began to rise until he talked in a high soprano voice! At least Agata kept his hair in a braid and then tied up. Eventually, his huge melons blocked his vision of his legs so much so that he could no longer see his stumps, making his wobbling attempts at walking even more precarious.

At this point, Damiano believed his life could not get any worse. Two days later, again he was proved wrong. That winter morning, Agata did not come to get him out of bed as she had always done. He yelled until his high voice gave out, to no avail. With the greatest of effort, he got himself turned over and precariously began to slide himself out of his bed. His stumps hit the floor hard, sending a jarring pain through his upper legs and spine. He shrieked, but could do nothing about it. Minutes later, he struggled to his legs and wobbled to the commode. After an enormous amount of wild struggling, he got his underpants off and finally relieved himself. Naked now, he had no way to get them back on. Instead, he made his precarious way to her bedroom. Agata had passed away during the night. Her body lay cold on the only bed that she had ever owned. Her face had a peaceful look on it. Now Damiano panicked. He was hungry and shivering. The fire had gone out. The cold of winter already had invaded the stone home.

Shivering, he struggled to the front door where he was stopped cold. Reaching up with his arm stumps, he could just barely touch the doorknob. He was trapped inside, destined to slowly starve to death or freeze, whichever came first! He slumped to his butt just back of the door, depressed beyond even crying out.

Exchange City was also home to many local women, who had sold their services to some of the Rigel-3 spaceport workers. Prostitution was found on every planet of the Imperium. Tierra was no exception. Faced with being away from their own worlds for dozens of years, these men and women sought other outlets for their sexual urges. Cross-species children were a natural outcome of such activities. Most were unwanted by either parent, though the mothers managed to keep them alive, until they reached adulthood, that is age fourteen. After that, they were on their own. The half-breed men found ways and means of survival, taking menial jobs or even moving away from Exchange City. The women had a far harder time of it. Women simply didn't travel beyond their town or city without a male escort, unless they were Sisterhood members.

While a few half-breed women did join the Sisterhood, many joined into small groups, eking out marginal communal living. Often, they took in laundry, but many became seamstresses for Elegant Fashions Inc, working out of their communal homes. Three of these women, Sally, Nellie, and Beth had a tiny hovel of a home on the southern edge of Exchange City, where they sewed clothing for Inez. They had no prospects for male companionship, let alone marriage. Yet, they wanted families of their own, just as everyone did. All three were in their late teens. This snowy morning, Sally was returning from Elegant Fashions Inc, having delivered another dozen men's shirts in return for their desperately needed funds.

As she passed by old Agata's stone home, three times better than their own, she noticed that there was no smoke coming from her chimney. "That's funny," she said to herself, but she walked on past it to her own shanty. After stepping inside, she felt the rush of warmth hitting her grey-white face, and it felt good. So did the heady aroma of fresh spices. Beth was whipping up a curry pie. Sally's mouth watered in anticipation. "Hi all. Got a good price this time. Inez wants as many shirts as we can make."

"That's a lucky break for us. Pie is about done," Beth called out. "Nellie's sewing another one. If we work at it, we might get another dozen done in three days. Did you see any men while you were out?"

Sally replied with a laugh, "Sure did. I can't believe that they have knockers as big as ours. Peter's hair is as long as a woman's now and his voice is quite high. He sounds almost like Inez." She heard both women giggling. She lowered her voice a little, as if sharing some dark secret, "I asked Inez if Peter was now a woman and not a man. She said he is more of a man where it counts. She says his sexual drive is stronger than it ever was!"

"Well that's something. I sure wish we could get some!" Beth declared. Then, she sighed and added, "But then who is going to bed three half-breeds like us? We're doomed to be old maids, unless we want to sell our bodies like our mothers have." She shuddered at that thought. Indeed, in part, this is what kept the three women together, a strong desire to make their own way in life without selling themselves to men.

No one really responded to her outburst. Instead, Sally mentioned, "Did see a funny thing. Agata's fire must be out. No smoke. I bet she is darn cold by now."

"Do you suppose that she ran out of coal?" Beth called out. "Pie is done. Food's on."

Nellie joined them. "Well, she is terribly old. Perhaps something happened to her. I suppose after we eat, we could go check on her and see if she is all right. After all, she did loan us startup money so we could get the material to make shirts for Inez."

After eating their meat pie, the three bundled up and walked through the snow-packed streets two blocks to the stone home. Last evening's snow was untouched on the short path to the front door. Again, this was taken as a sign of trouble. With the large amount of winter snow that fell on Exchange City, one had to keep up with the snow or become buried in your own home. All was silent. Sally knocked. "Agata? Agata?" She heard a woman's voice calling out. "Did she say help or something? Can't quite make it out."

Beth suggested, "We best go inside and see about getting the fire going for her." Sally opened the door and the three went inside. They found Damiano shivering and naked on the floor. "Oh, it is the half man she'd been caring for. You there, where is Agata?" Beth asked.

Since he couldn't speak well and was barely conscious, the women fanned out. Beth headed for the fireplace and soon got a fire going again. Sally found a blanket and covered Damiano, while Nellie discovered Agata's body. She yelled, "Agata has died. Probably during her sleep. Now what?" She joined the others around the fire that was quickly warming the room.

His teeth chattering, Damiano cried out pathetically, "Help me please." They ignored him for now.

"She has money. We should find it," Beth suggested.

"Hey, what about half-man here? He is a man and we could use him," Sally suggested, grinning wickedly. Beth picked up her intention, as did Nellie. She added, "We want children, right? Here is our chance!"

"Hey, we could take over Agata's house now. She doesn't need it any longer, but we best call the guards to get them to take her body out of here," Beth suggested.

A confusing hour later, three city guards hauled the corpse away, storing it until the snows melted in the spring, when it could be buried. They agreed the three could have the house as long as they took care of the half-man. None of the guards wanted anything to do with him. The trio moved their possessions over that afternoon. While Beth fixed supper, Sally and Nellie cleaned up the place, preparing their own beds, jamming all three into Agata's old room.

As they assembled to Beth's call for supper, Sally declared, "Okay, whoever feeds him gets first dibs on him in the bed." She beat the others to him, lifting him up and sitting him in a chair. "Okay, half-man, I feed you tonight. Then, you are going to earn your keep. I go first, then Beth, then Nellie tonight. Got that, stud?"

"Wait! No, you can't do this to me. You are not my wives, no. I won't," Damiano finally realized what these three women were going to do with him.

"Look half-man, we are going to have to take care of you, so you have to earn your keep. You will perform for us anytime we desire it. Period. End of discussion," Sally declared pointedly.

"No, this is rape! I won't stand for it! You can do this!" Damiano protested, waving his arms about.

She taunted him, "What are you going to do about it, half-man? Bat us with your stumps? Lot of good that'll do you!"

Nellie added, "Look half-man, you will do it. We don't give a damn whether you like it or not or even whether you want to do it or not. We're half-breeds, and there isn't a man in Exchange City that'll even look at us. So you are it, bud! We want children of our own, and you are going to perform. You can't do a damn thing about it, so shut up."

Later over his continuing protests, Sally carried him into their bedroom and stripped him. Although he wiggled trying to prevent her, his actions were fruitless. Even worse, she undid his overly long hair which was twice the length of his now short height. After plopping him in her bed, she undressed herself. He tried again to get up from his prone position, but only managed to get to a sitting position before she pushed him unceremoniously back down. "Performance time, half-man."

"I won't. You can't make me! This is rape," he wailed in his high soprano voice. She laughed and massaged his melons lovingly. She smiled, for it had the desired effect. Damiano found himself raped by each woman that evening, before Beth finally put him into his own bed.

They repeated the action in the morning, before settling down to sew more shirts for Inez. However, they made him walk to the dining room and living room, but to his discomfort, they left his hair un-braided. It dragged along the floor behind him causing him even more problems when it caught on something. His life had turned into an even worse nightmare. He never dreamed he would be forcibly raped six times each day. Only after a month did they stop. All three had gotten what they desired from him, they were pregnant.

August became baby month for the three women. Each gave birth to twins. Now Damiano discovered as he as much as he despised it, he had to help nurse the six babies. His own breasts ached and throbbed, bloated with milk. Humiliated beyond words, he had no choice in the matter. The three women worked him like a cow during the summer and fall, though they also made sure he ate well.

Late winter, their passions again took hold. Once more he was raped repeatedly and forced to nurse the six babies afterwards. He found himself praying they would soon become pregnant and cease raping him. Damiano was only too relieved when they did just that. Still his breasts ached from so much nursing. They had more or less ceased nursing their babies, leaving him to be their wet nurse. Damiano knew he had to do something drastic.

One warm spring day, Sally and Nellie had gone to visit Inez and Beth left the front door open, allowing fresh air to circulate throughout the small house. His hair dragging behind him like some bride's erotic wedding train, wobbling wildly, Damiano made his big break out. This was his first time out of doors since he led his army to its destruction. He had no idea where he was at, but headed towards the outskirts of the city. As he wobbled slowly along, people stared at him, pointed at him, and whispered. One little boy ran up and stood on his hair, causing him to lose his balance and plop down. After that, the boy teased him and ran off. After his usual awkward struggle to get back upright on his stump legs, he waddled along. Finally, he left the city behind him. Then he saw his big chance! Ahead on his left was a steep gorge, perhaps twenty feet down. He headed for it. Just as he got there, Beth came running up behind him. "Hey, where the hell do you think you are going to, half-man? Get back. You will fall down there!"

That was his intention. Hurrying as much as he could, he reached the edge and fell over. His long hair caught on a rock as he fell. Intense pain followed. His stumpy arms reached upwards, but could not touch it. Then, the ground came up fast. He felt a sharp pain in his neck and then discovered he was floating in space, free of that decrepit body at long last! He soared upwards to get his bearings and headed back to the Easterlings. He knew he needed to get a new baby body and soon. If you had asked him why he needed to do this, Damiano would not have had any rational answer, simply that he must.

As he moved along, he felt or sensed various women giving birth down below him. He did his best to ignore the reactive pull to swoop down and take one. Then, the deserts of the Arad appeared and he swooped down to get a better look and orientate himself. He wanted to return to his home village in Domei. However, as he moved swiftly long, he suddenly felt another baby being born. Try as he might, the more he resisted being pulled into it, the stronger the pull became. He came smashing into the baby's head just as it slid out of Elena's womb. The baby's head throbbed, and he went temporarily unconscious. He felt as if he were also freezing somehow. Later, he awoke and found himself craving to nurse. A young man laid him beside his new mother and he eagerly began nursing, as if he were half-starved.

Finally full, he took his bearings. His eyes opened wide! His new body was one of those mermaids! So was his mother. He saw three adult mermaids, two of which were expecting any day now and three two-year old mermaids, his sisters. He shrieked and tried to flee, but only became further stuck solidly within her little head. He fainted.

"You have a little sister, Benigna," Alfeo talked to her as he laid the newborn beside Elena. "What do you think of her?" He didn't expect the two year old to say much, though.

Benigna managed to mimic him, "Sister." She looked carefully at the new born. Then, she peered into her mind, sending soothing thoughts. *Oh my god! Damiano and Wystan! Damn! They both are here! What the hell do I do now?* She sighed. *Well, now I've located the two missing gods, but they sure as hell are not gods anymore. If I work my therapy on them, I could well release them from these bodies. Do I dare return them to godhood? Damn! Damn! Damn!* Now Beni had a serious situation facing her.

The mermaids critically needed therapy sessions. Yet if she delivered them, surely both Calder and Wystan would discover their identities and probably recover their spiritual freedom. Most likely, they would be able to depart these mermaid bodies and resume being Tierra's gods. Calder had been responsible for the mermaids, and Wystan had caused many wars and the deaths of countless men. Try as she might,

Benigna just could not bring herself to unleash those two back onto Tierra. Not just yet anyway. Still, the mermaids were in very sad shape and needed therapy. Worse, they were developing the *mentales* gifts as well!

Her own eyes were yellow from birth, but her two sisters' eyes were now turning yellow with brown speckles as well. Her three brothers' eyes remained a dark brown, at least for now. She knew if she had her way, she could develop telekinesis powers in her sisters so they could manage a little better life for themselves. Still, if she did the same to Elena and Christina, what would those ex-gods do with their new powers? *Reincarnation can be a bitch,* she thought. *Men make their own graves by virtue of their actions.*

As the days passed, Benigna experienced just how awful the lives of these desert mermaids actually were. Although only two, she was hopping around well, as were her two sisters. Yet, other than that, she couldn't actually do much else. Poor Alfeo had to do everything for her and the others. He looked utterly exhausted. She began to wonder how he could keep up with the nine mermaids' needs?

One hot summer's day, Alfeo gaily told everyone, "Today, we are going for a picnic out in the warm desert sands. That way, you won't get hurt if you take a tumble, little Benigna. Come on; hop outside all of you. I've rented the donkey wagon for us all today."

"Really, you shouldn't have," Elena protested, but she too struggled to her feet and hopped on outside, following her daughter. After lifting the three women onto the cart, he then lifted the three older girls, the three one-year old boys, and the three newborns into the cart, placing them carefully on reed mats. He then climbed up to the crude driver's seat.

Looking back, he said, "Time to get away from here, if only for a few hours. We all need a change of pace."

"But this is costing too much money, Alfeo," Elena complained, though she couldn't do anything about it.

"But you three are worth it. Relax and enjoy the beautiful sunny day," Alfeo countered and then became quiet.

Benigna began looking at the great sand dunes that soon appeared, fascinated with them. For her part, she did enjoy getting away from the oasis, if only for a little while. She relaxed and enjoyed the ride. After what she thought must have been quite some time, she said, "When stop, papa?"

"Just a bit further, Beni. There is a good dune not far from here where you can play," he replied.

She smiled, anticipating hopping about in the soft, warm sand. *This is crazy. All I can do is hop about! I can't even scratch my own head or get my hair out of my eyes without using telekinesis. Crap. I think I ought to have insisted that Elena and her two sisters were brought back to Brom when they were discovered in Po! This is just plain nuts!*

Soon, he stopped the wagon and carried a blanket out onto the hot sands. Next, he lifted the three women down and told them to hop over to the blanket. Then, he lifted Benigna and her two sisters down. "Go hop after your mothers," he ordered. Next, he carried the three infants over to their mothers, who were trying hard to sit down on the blanket without falling over. With only the single leg and no gifts to help them, all three fell and rolled over facing upwards. Alfeo laid the three infants beside their mothers. "Got to get the boys next. Enjoy the beautiful day, dears." He walked back to the wagons, noticing the three two-year olds were hopping in the deep sand, complaining it was too hot. He climbed onto the cart, turned it around, and headed back the way he'd come.

"Alfeo? Alfeo! What are you doing?" Elena cried out. Benigna looked up after the receding cart. She touched Alfeo's mind and knew what he was doing and why. "Alfeo! Please come back!" Elena screamed. Soon, Felisa and Adalina added their terrified screams to hers. Alfeo was abandoning them deep in the desert! With a Herculean effort, Elena got to her foot and began hopping after the wagon. Benigna followed after her for a while until the sands burned her foot too much. Eventually, Elena gave up the chase and hopped back to the blanket. She was sobbing as well as her two sisters. Alfeo had abandoned them in the desert. Here they would certainly die!

Benigna knew he planned to report they had an accident, but he was only able to save the three boys. Further, she knew from his parting thoughts that caring for the nine of them was beyond his ability and that he had talked this over with the village elder as well. She got an image of a flock of mermaids pictorially drowning the others in the oasis, caring for them instead of caring for their own families. *Wise move,* she thought, *and probably quite right.*

The midday sun bore down on them as sweat poured off the nine. The three women fell back onto the blanket and cried their hearts out. They knew they could not last long without water. They and their babies were doomed. Exposed to the direct searing sun, the tiny infants didn't last very long at all, though their mothers tried to shield them as best they could. Benigna watched Christina carefully. When the exhausted Damiano-Wystan finally left the body, she followed him and was amused to see him sucked almost at once into another baby girl being born in another oasis to the north of their location.

When she returned above her own body, she noticed the yellow glow forming and knew at once that Lysandra was making another appearance. *Welcome once again, Benjamina. It seems that you are ahead of me. You do know the man made a wise decision with this, don't you?* Lysandra sent her.

Yes, very wise. The whole oasis knows these mermaids breed more mermaids in their female babies. At this time, there are nine, but within a couple of generations, there would have been so many of them to care for that the village itself would have been threatened. I hope Alfeo is not further bothered by what he had to do, she replied.

If he made the right decision, he ought not have any regrets. What about these that are still alive? Calder? she asked.

They deserve a merciful death. After all, these three saved their whole oasis from starvation.

I will give them that and ensure that they have new bodies soon. What about yourself?

Well, I came here to deal with these mermaids and to get my therapy going here in the Easterlings.

Surely you don't want such a helpless body, do you?

Not really. It appears Tierra is getting another batch

of mentales gifted now. Here in the Arad, there is not much, if any, support for them. The nearest tower is thousands of miles to the south. I think I best stick around the Arad and help them if I can.

Yes, this is a very wise course for you to follow. This area is going to have its share of the newly gifted, but they do not know anything about such powers. They need guidance within a few more years at most. I hope the other towers will build similar ones here in the Arad, but I suspect they will focus on the larger cities and towns, if I know humans. These desert dwellers are going to be left on their own, more or less.

That is not good, Lysandra. We both know an untrained telepath is both a danger to others and to themselves.

Quite true. So what can we do about it?

Well, if I can, I will stay here and work on training all I come across while I am working my therapy sessions. It's a shame I am going to get delayed by having to start over with a new body.

Are you willing to continue your mission with this mermaid body?

I suppose so, if I can use my mentales gifts. I did not dare to use them around Calder and Wystan. I didn't want them getting any ideas. They've caused enough troubles for Tierra as it is. Still, the little body down there is melting. It won't last long in this heat.

Okay. I will see your two-year old body is saved, but I expect you to begin working with the new mentales gifted and on your therapy. In the end, Benjamina, if mankind has any real hopes, it will come from your therapy.

All right. I'll do it. It is only a body, after all.

Again, I must thank you. I will see the others are given a merciful death and have new healthy bodies right away.

Beni felt a cooling breeze, cooling down her overheated small body. As she watched, one by one the others passed away. Elena was the first, and she watched as Lysandra gently soothed her and got her into a new female baby being born south of their location. Within a half hour, all the mermaids were gone excepting her own two year old body. Lysandra moved her little body some distance away. A localized wind picked up, and soon the remains were covered with sand, protecting them from the circling scavenger birds. Then, the blanket appeared once more and Lysandra placed the small child on it.

Your rescuer is coming now. I will leave you now. As always, I wish you the best of luck. The yellow glow vanished, but Beni still felt rather cool. She looked around and saw a man on a horse making his way towards her. Soon, she saw him clearly. He was about fifteen with long brown hair done in a single braid. He wore a white cotton shirt and loose fitting white cotton pants with the typical desert style sandals. He reined in and dismounted, walked up to her. As he drew near, she saw he had yellow eyes. His thoughts were being broadcast to the whole world, an untrained telepath.

"Hello strange little girl. Where are your parents? How come you are out here in the desert all alone?" he asked in his alto voice. As he leaned over here, she could not help but see his melon sized breasts.

"On a picnic. They all died. Sand covers them now. I am Benjamina. Who are you?" she said in her childish voice. She decided not to shatter his already stretched reality by talking like an adult. He had never seen a mermaid before and probably knew nothing about them.

"I am called Archangelo Bulini. Would you like me to rescue you? Do you know where your village is? Its name perhaps?"

"No sir, I don't. Yes, I do need rescuing, if it is not too much trouble," she replied.

He bent over and lifted her up. "My, you are light as a feather. Have you been on a horse before?"

"No Archangelo. She is beautiful though. What's her name?"

"Just horse. My, you are one helpless little girl. It is a holy miracle that you survived out here in the desert all by yourself." *How did she know it is a mare?*

Cause I can read minds too.

"Well, isn't this something? You too? How strange it is. I left my oasis because I could not get all of their voices out of my head. It was driving me mad. Strange, I am not hearing your mind."

That's because I am not letting my thoughts out. I can teach you how to block all those other's thoughts and keep others like us from hearing yours, she sent.

"Deal, little Benjamina. What a strange name. Okay. Careful now. I am going to balance you on the saddle while I get up. Hold real still." He perched her sideways in his saddle and then slipped up himself. He kept her sitting sideways and wrapped his left arm securely around her. "Very good. I've a small camp a few miles from here. I saw the carrion birds circling and came to see what had died. Just in time for you, my strange little one."

"Thank you. Water, please?" she asked. "I can lift it." He watched as she used her gifts to lift the water skin up to her lips and drank greedily. After she put it back, he suggested she also take a little salt. Again, she lifted a small amount out of his bag, dropping them into her mouth. "My, you are talented indeed, strange little one."

"I don't have any real choice, do I?"

He laughed, "No, that's as true as the fact that we're riding my mare! I sometimes wonder what I can do, but I've no idea what that might be."

"I can help you, Archangelo," she replied. Benjamina settled back, resting on his chest. Her body fell asleep at once. She felt safe, secure, and no longer worried about displaying her awesome powers. She needed all of them to survive with this screwy body. She made a mental note to visit Brom and get her self treated before she had any children. No way was she going to pass these horrific genes on to her children.

His camp was little more than a cotton sheet propped up by some sticks, providing minimal shade. Still, she began training Archangelo on how to block out the thoughts of others. She knew this was vital, because soon they would have to return to an oasis for more water. He was a quick learner, and, three days later, he proudly rode into his old oasis with her sitting in front of him. No longer would he be driven mad by all the thoughts of those around him, though he was still broadcasting his in all directions.

Others came to greet him and to stare at the freakish child he'd discovered. He stopped at his parent's adobe home, carefully dismounting and lifting the child to the ground. "Father, mother, this is Benjamina. Her family perished in the desert, but I was able to save her. What is all the commotion over there?"

"So you have come back?" asked the village elder, who had seen him arrive and walked over to greet him and to stare at the deformed child he'd brought back.

"Aye, she has been teaching me. I no longer hear voices in my head," he replied.

"It is Mariella, she's in a bad way. They are trying to cool her off," his mother answered his question. "You should go see her; her time is near."

Archangelo cringed, and Benjamina sensed she meant something to Archangelo, but didn't probe. "Watch her will you?" His mother nodded, and he walked briskly over to the life-giving blue waters of the oasis, where a crowd of women were bathing a near-naked young teen.

One of the women whispered, "She's burning up. Very weak. No hope, really. Sorry, Archangelo." He knelt down and gently touched her forehead. She was extremely hot and barely breathing, if at all. Tears formed in his eyes.

The elder whispered, "What kind of malformed creature has he found? No arms, one leg. She's nothing but a hideous freak and a terrible liability. She ought to have not been allowed to develop this far. Dino, we should put her out of her misery quickly."

"But Archangelo found her. Is she not his responsibility?" the father asked.

"True, but now he brings her into our village, where she will eat our precious food and require constant care from our women. We can ill afford to waste our meager rations and time on such a malformed creature such as this. She cannot do anything and will always be a liability. Surely you don't want your son burdened with a liability such as this one, now do you? I will do it myself," the elder declared.

Benjamina didn't like the welcome she was getting and decided to hop on over to the others. Perhaps she could cure the ill woman, gaining favor from these people who rightly took her to be some freak of nature. She didn't get too far before she felt a sharp pain in her neck. Her little body fell to the ground. She looked down and saw that the elder had nearly severed her head from her body, which was now dead. The elder sheathed his scimitar and began wrapping up the body.

What the? Well, he did have a point. No sense in doing anything about that. Best see what's wrong with the woman. After that, I am going to have to find another baby body quickly. She floated over the woman and noticed Archangelo's grief. He had strong feelings for this young teen. Benjamina knew at once what was wrong with her: Verge Sickness. She was probably fourteen and had the distinctive yellow eyes with brown speckles. Benjamina tried to contact the being herself, but saw that she was literally embedded within a huge black mental mass. She sighed spiritually.

Had she gotten here before the teen had gotten this bad, her therapy could well have erased that black mass that was causing the sickness. Now only a katalyein could possibly disintegrate it in time, but there were none. The nearest ones were in Brom Tower, thousands of miles away. Even as Benjamina watched, the being that was the young teen floated up and away from her body. She'd given up; it was hopeless, and she went in search of a new body. The physical body exhaled once and stopped breathing. The women around her started to wail, and Archangelo cried, "No!" Then, he too began sobbing.

Benjamina acted swiftly. She moved behind the prone teen's head and energized the body. Suddenly, the teen's body gasped loudly. She felt life-giving air flooding into its lungs. Again and again, she gasped for breath and felt her blood flowing again, dissipating the high fever within a minute or so. Several women shrieked. Archangelo lifted up her head, holding her gently in his arms. "Mariella! Mariella! You live! Breathe! Breathe! It's a miracle! Her fever is gone! She lives! Oh, Maricella, I won't ever leave you again, I promise," he gushed.

Archangelo, don't be mad. Maricella died. The elder

just killed my strange little body because it was so deformed. I have revived Maricella's body. It is little me, Benjamina now. Please don't be upset with the elder. He was only doing what he thought was right.

What? He killed you? Maricella's dead too? But you are her? How? I don't understand.

Maricella had Verge Sickness. It happens sometimes when a mentales gifted reaches puberty or thereabouts. It is a huge blockage of their nerve channels. If untreated, it results in death. A katalyein might have been able to save her, but there isn't one around here. That's why I am here. I want to start helping everyone who needs it here in the Arad. Please don't be angry with me for taking Maricella's body. She really did pass away in your arms and that meant a lot to her. She has already found a new baby body to have next.

"I don't understand all this. I saw her die and I see her live again," he whispered.

"Give her air! Make way," the elder ordered, taking charge. Archangelo lifted Maricella up to a sitting position. Half of the villagers crowded around to see the miracle. Nearly everyone had long ago given up on her.

"I'm all right, really I am fine now. It is past. Archangelo somehow saved me," Maricella spoke up. "I feel lots better. Thirsty though. Hungry too."

"I don't know what you did to her, Archangelo, but take her to her parent's house and get her food and drink. I have gotten rid of that freak of nature that you brought back with you. No sense in keeping something like that alive, wasting our precious food and wholly unable to carry her load around here. Now get going, son," the elder ordered.

Archangelo helped Maricella to her feet. She leaned heavily on him. *Archangelo, I don't know who my parents are or anyone around here except you. Help me from making a total fool of myself!*

Okay. I still don't understand all this.

We have time. How many others in your village have yellow eyes?

There are six of us, counting you.

Okay, then we should help those other four very soon. I

bet they are also going mad with all the voices in their heads too. Thus, Benjamina began her new life in the desert of Arad. She had taken on an enormous task and singlehandedly at that.

The ensuing years brought peace to Tierra. Reorganization became the topic everywhere as each kingdom tried to setup the new political units, under the watchful eyes of Queen Isabella. Helping out, Nadja and Diego opened the first school which the Rigel-3 personnel had built, but never operated. Since there were no textbooks on Tierra, they made use of verbal teaching, utilizing the best of the new textbooks written in Imperium Standard which only she could read.

Although chaos seemed to lie in every corner, the more the leaders pushed towards their new political organizations, the more the chaos died down. Peace had come at last. The aliens were not missed.

The End.

Other Books by Vic Broquard

Without Warning (fantasy)

The Trident Series: (fantasy)
>Volume 1 The Trident and the Book
>Volume 3 The Trident and the Scepter
>Volume3 The Trident and the Resurrection

The Adventures of Elizabeth Stanton Series: (science fiction)
>Volume 1 The Evolution of the Path
>Volume 2 The Great Messiah
>Volume 3 Of Kings and Queens and Troubadours
>Volume 4 Chaos in the Aftermath
>Volume 5 Power Plays
>Volume 6 Age of Exploration
>Volume 7 Abducted
>Volume 8 The Emperor and Empress
>Volume 9 A Job Worth Doing
>Volume 10 Degradation
>Volume 11 The Second Crusade
>Volume 12 When Worlds Collide
>Volume 13 Dark Ages

The Lindsey Barron Series: (fantasy)
>Volume 1 The Rod of the Apocalypse
>Volume 2 The Board of Governors
>Volume 3 The Crown of Moses
>Volume 4 Dominus for President
>Volume 5 The National Health Care Program
>Volume 6 States Justice
>Volume 7 Cross and Double-cross

Zoran Chronicles Series: (fantasy)
>Volume 1 A Dragon in Our Town
>Volume 2 Dragons, Power, Courts, and War

Planet of the Orange-red Sun Series: (science fiction)

The Return of the Wizards: Twelve Companions – The Making of Wizards (fantasy)